SHODDY PRINCE

Sheelagh Kelly was born in York, though now she divides her time between there and Australia. The seeds for her first novel, *A Long Way From Heaven*, were sown when she developed an interest in genealogy, and decided to trace her ancestors. It was followed by the bestsellers *For My Brother's Sins*, *Erin's Child* and *Dickie* – the acclaimed *Feeney Saga* – as well as *My Father, My Son*.

Sheelagh Kelly is currently at work on her next novel.

SHEELAGH KELLY

Shoddy Prince

HarperCollins*Publishers*

HarperCollins*Publishers*
77–85 Fulham Palace Road,
Hammersmith, London W6 8JB

This paperback edition 1996
3 5 7 9 8 6 4

First published in Great Britain by
HarperCollins*Publishers* 1995

ISBN 0 00 649649 0

Set in Sabon at
The Spartan Press Ltd,
Lymington, Hants

Printed and bound in Great Britain by
Caledonian International Book Manufacturing Ltd, Glasgow

For my grandson, Paddy

PART ONE

I

The woman had thirty-seven knife wounds. Nat had stopped counting at twenty; not because he was squeamish, but at eight years old and a regular truant, this was the limit of his numerative power. He peeked between the stone balusters of Foss Bridge, facing downriver as the policemen hooked her nude body from the rubbish-laden water. It was very white – bloodless. Of course it would be, thought Nat, with all those punctures in her.

There were few murders in York. Nat had been born in 1881 – just in time for the last census, his mother had told him – and this was the first one he could recall. Stepping back a few paces, he took a running jump and scrambled onto the parapet of the soot-engrimed bridge for a better view. Looping an arm round the iron lamp standard which adorned it he sat, legs dangling, watching the long dark hair move with the current as the body was hauled nearer the bank. The air reverberated with the grind of carriage wheels and horseshoes on granite setts. Today being market day, the traffic was particularly heavy and the resulting noise provoked bad temper amongst the shopkeepers who had to endure it from dawn till dark; there had been several arguments to entertain Nat this morning.

It was September. The air held a chill yet there was brilliant sunshine and the grit-stone was warm to his touch. One hand came up to shove at his hair; this was very dark, looking almost black until caught by sunlight when it took on the more reddish sheen of a plum. It was quite long and straight, apart from one wave at the temple that often fell down to obscure his vision. Parting in the centre, it swept past his ears, framing a face too serious for that of an eight-year-old. The eyes had pink circles under them, the irises were blue and habitually grave, and there were lines of anxiety on the brow above — not always a reflection of his inner feelings, for Nat could feel quite happy and still present this same expression. However, it was his cheekbones which most detracted from his youth: too defined for a child, they produced an overall image of starvation. Only the nose was that of a little boy, a tiny point of upturned flesh. All in all, Nat was an inoffensive-looking child, not a boy that would immediately spring to mind when the word troublemaker was bandied; yet trouble did seem to gravitate towards him.

The woman's body had reached the bank. Her long hair emerged dripping and plastered with duckweed as she was unceremoniously slapped onto dry land like a fisherman's catch. Many of the knife wounds were deep. Nat decided they looked like mouths opening and shutting in mute objection to this treatment. The sight was horrifying yet at the same time held his fascination. She was fatter than his mother. There being only one room at home, Nat had sometimes chanced to see her without clothes if she had accidentally woken him when retiring herself. He wondered now why she lacked the strange body hair of the woman below.

The sergeant-in-charge looked down at her, one thumb tucked into the belt around his navy blue tunic, the other pulling thoughtfully at his moustache. With each move of his body the sun would catch the row of metal buttons down his front, causing an intermittent glare, like miniature heliographs. Nat squinted and used his arm to shade his eyes. The sergeant chanced to look up and caught the boy's observation. 'Be off with thee! This is no sight for a lad.'

Nat did not budge.

'I said, run along or I'll tan your backside!' The sergeant's eyes were concealed by the peak of his helmet but there was threat in his voice, and when Nat's response was to pull a face, he uttered, 'You little . . .' and wearing an expression of menace, advanced on the boy. Nat, well aware that he could not be reached from up here, stood atop the bridge and began to contort his face and body into postures of disrespect. The sergeant made firm his helmet and, hanging onto an elder bush which grew from the water's edge, tried to dislodge the parasite with the hook that had just pulled the body from the water, but Nat danced nimbly along the parapet, still offering insults.

It was unfortunate that Nat had quite a few enemies, for at this stage one of them chanced to be strolling over Foss Bridge on his way home from school for lunch, saw Nat's gyrations and, with the casual employment of one hand, sent him toppling into the water. His mouth agape, Nat sampled a good quarter-pint of the stagnant brew before gasping for air. 'I can't swim! Help!'

A cheeky face laughed down at him, then was gone. The hook that had failed to shift Nat from the bridge now grappled with his collar and hauled him towards the muddy bank, whence the policeman extracted his carcass. Sodden, Nat barked twice more, nipped the water from his nose and found himself next to the corpse. He jumped to his feet and backed away, panting.

'Aye, not so nice, is it?' mocked the sergeant and gave him a clout round the head for his cheek. 'Now clear off home!' He rejoined his associates who were wrapping the body.

'What happened to her?' Nat rubbed his smarting head.

The sergeant put his hands on his hips and flopped his

body with impatience. 'She was standing on the bridge making fun of a police officer – now will you clear off home!'

'They're watching.' Nat raised a dripping arm at the crowd that had gathered behind him. Word had reached the ears of schoolchildren emerging for their midday break. Besides those from Dorothy Wilson's school nearby, the pupils of St George's had postponed their meagre dinners to tear up Walmgate for a glimpse of the corpse, some travelling half a mile out of their way for the spectacle.

The sergeant wearied of arguing. 'Oh, suit thiself!'

Encouraged by Nat's proximity to the body, another boy edged closer and asked, 'D'you know 'er?' Nat shook his head, sprinkling the other with droplets. 'I do,' said the older boy with a leer. 'She's a prostitute. Know what one o' them is?'

'Course I do.' Nat's small hands took hold of a corner of his jacket and wrung it out. He had begun to shiver.

'Bet you a penny you don't.'

'It's the opposite of Catholic,' announced Nat and held out his hand.

The other cackled. 'What're you talking about? A prostitute is a woman what takes money for jiggering with men.'

Nat showed derision. 'That's not a prostitute, that's a whore. Gimme the penny!'

The boy stopped laughing. 'It's you who owes it to me.'

Nat weighed him up, noticing that he was big but not dangerous. 'I haven't got a penny.' Employing great pathos, he wrung out another section of his jacket.

'Cheat!' spat the other. 'You shouldn't wager if you've no money.' He moved away.

'You don't know owt,' muttered a shuddering Nat under his breath and moved his attention to his knee breeches.

While he was still trying to remove the moisture from his clothes, he felt another presence and revolved to see a girl of about his own age who would not take her eyes off him.

4

She had hair of a colour hard to define, not light enough to call blonde yet too attractive to dub brown. The image she evoked in Nat was one of a baby thrush, legs all spindly, eyes dark-brown glittering beads, and face covered in a rash of freckles. Not prickly by nature, he tolerated her attentions for as long as he could before demanding, 'What're you staring at, throssle-face?'

The whippet-thin creature did not respond but continued to stare. She wore a crumpled pinafore, black stockings with holes in them and high boots with no laces that looked comical on such skinny legs. He released his wet breeches, marched up to her and pushed her in the chest.

She tottered and fell over, looking bewildered. 'I didn't know ye were talking to me. I wasn't staring at you. I'm blind.'

Nat felt thoroughly ashamed of himself, passed grudging apology and helped her up. She smiled forgiveness, her sightless eyes directed over his shoulder. He asked how long she had borne this affliction. She replied that she had been blind from birth – then impulsively jabbed a finger, shouted, 'Look at that!' and when he turned to look she delivered a shove that almost catapulted him back into the river. Laughing her glee, she made an ungainly dash out of harm's way, whence she continued to giggle into handfuls of grimy pinafore at his undignified sprawl, the brown eyes no longer visionless but oozing mischief.

Her laughter was non-malicious, but Nat projected fury. 'You shouldn't say a thing like that! I hope you do go blind!' He tried to wipe the clarts of mud from his wet trousers, shunning her.

In the realization that she was not to be chased, the grinning creature edged her way back to him, boots slopping on and off. 'Can't ye take a joke?'

Nat turned his back in exaggerated gesture. 'I don't think it's anything to joke about!'

Her innocent glee tainted, the girl bobbed down beside him. 'Maungy.'

He sought a way to even the balance. 'See her?' He jerked his nose at the corpse. 'She's a prostitute. Know what one o' them is?'

The girl had overheard Nat's conversation with the other boy. Wanting to appease, and not knowing what a prostitute was anyway, she said, 'They go to a different church than me.'

He showed approval. 'That's what I told him there, but he's stupid. Are you a Catholic then?'

She nodded. 'Are you?'

'No, but I know all about them 'cause Sister Theresa – that's a friend o' me mam's – she's one.'

The conversation flagged then. Nat wasn't much of a talker and was really quite shy unless angered, as a moment ago. Becoming aware that his feet were squelching inside his boots, he sat down, took them off and produced a dribble of water from each.

It was left to the girl to find a new topic. She embraced her bony knees and asked, 'What's your name?'

'Nathaniel Prince.' It was actually Nathaniel Smellie, but he had suffered enough humiliation and had lately decided that his years of being called Smellie Nat were over. It was too late to re-educate those who already knew him, of course, but each new acquaintance was provided with the more regal appellation. However, there was a deeper reason for the choice of Prince than its noble ring: Nat had never known his father and though his mother always changed the subject whenever it was raised, Nat was convinced he must be someone of note. When his mother was in a good mood she would tell him stories about a poor little boy who was forced to live in poverty but was in reality a prince. Nat had the feeling that she was trying to convey some message and this reinforced his opinion that his father had been of high birth. For what other reason would she be so secretive? Obviously he couldn't go around calling himself Prince Nathaniel in these plebeian quarters, so he had turned the names about, secure in the private knowledge that he was much better than his neighbours.

He laced up his boots. The drenched neckerchief had begun to chafe. He removed it and wrung it out, damning the unfairness that condemned him to wear this lower class rag instead of the attire befitting his true rank. To Nat, a white collar and a proper necktie said everything about one's status. When he grew rich this would be the first thing he would buy.

He didn't ask the girl's name, but she told him anyway. 'Mine's Bright Maguire.'

'That's a queer name.' He crammed the wet neckerchief into his pocket.

'Tisn't.' She looked offended and inserted a finger into one of the holes in her stocking, stretching it for a while, then used the explanation that was by now familiar lore to tell him how the name had originated.

She had been baptized Bridget, but her father, unable to spell, had written it on a census form as Bright. He had asked if the official collector would scrutinize the paper for inaccuracies and in doing so the man had smiled and exclaimed, 'Bright – that's a pretty name!' And her father had looked at his golden babe and said approvingly, 'Bright – yes, it suits her.' Hereafter, this was how she had been known, and her nature had come to match her name.

Bright rattled on. 'I live just over yon side o' the river behind The Three Cups and the Pig Market. Me mam and dad're Irish.' That explained the accent which, although sprinkled with regional words, was definitely not local. 'They came from Ireland in 1880, driven from their home by rack rent – I don't know what that is exactly but it sounds awful cruel, doesn't it? An' the famine o' course. There's always famine in Ireland.' This was a quote of her

7

father's. 'I'm the only one of us to be born in York. I got six brothers and two sisters. I go to St George's School . . .' and so it went on and on. Nat merely listened. It was a pleasure just to have company.

At the end of her introduction she asked, 'How old are you?'

'Eight.'

'Same as me. Ye don't talk much, do ye?'

How would I get a word in edgeways, thought Nat, but merely shrugged. The girl smiled, extended her limbs and tilted her pert face to the noonday sun, presenting the underside of her chin. A dark-brown mole stood out, which Nat mistook for chocolate. If she had been eating chocolate she might have saved a bit for later. He was curious and greedy enough to ask, 'What's that on your neck?'

'A mole.'

'A mole?' He looked confused. 'Moles are animals.'

At the thought of having an animal stuck to her chin, she laughed, displaying a cavern of gaps where the milk teeth had been pushed out by half-emerged adult ones. Nat suddenly found himself bewitched by that cheeky little face. Her parents had been right to call her Bright for, shabby clothes apart, everything about her was: bright hair, bright eyes, bright smile.

He was not given much to grinning, but she drew one from him. His front teeth were more advanced than hers, looking huge in such a little face.

Then abruptly she announced, 'I'm off for me dinner now – tara!' and with a flash of grubby drawers, performed a clomping skip along the riverbank.

Nat's smile faded. She was only leaving in order not to share her chocolate with him – he didn't believe the tale about the mole for one minute.

He stood awhile. The cadaver was lifted onto a two-wheeled stretcher and toted away. Now added to the earthy hum of the Foss and the reek of the Pig Market, was the aroma of luncheon being cooked at a nearby restaurant. Driven by hunger, Nat turned towards home, and caught a last glimpse of the girl waving merrily as she lolloped over Foss Bridge.

Fossgate was a street of much antiquity, a melange of buildings, some of which had been in existence for centuries. Nowadays, the medieval beams were hidden beneath rude and crumbling stucco, their jettied upper floors teetering over the cobbles. Like those of neighbouring Walmgate the leprous façades belied the commerce that thrived within. Linked by the bridge, these decrepit Siamese twins formed the longest and busiest thoroughfare in York.

Nat was ignorant of their history, seeing only the goods that he could not afford. The quaint buildings were festooned in wares: tin and copper, leather, sheepskins, pheasants, hares with dripping noses and white bobtails hanging limp, slabs of wet fish, candles and clogs, books and journals, blacksmiths, whitesmiths, dead smiling pigs, their eyes squeezed shut against the blade, and pub after pub after pub . . .

A tattooed navvy approached on the other side of the road, strutting like a prince with swelled chest and head high. That's what I need, exclaimed Nat to himself, a princely walk to match the name, and his next few steps were an imitation of the workman's.

Outside the Blue Bell Inn a drayman hefted barrels from his cart. Nat hopped nimbly around the obstruction and carried on. His gait became erratic as he took up the game that all children played of avoiding the joints in the paving flags – stand on a line, marry a swine. Being perverse in nature Nat jumped on every line. Who wanted to be like the others? The idea of being married to a swine was much more amusing. He faltered. There were some boys in his path crouched over a game of marbles. Nat knew better than to ask if he could join them, having grown up with the answer: 'Me mam says I'm not allowed to play with you 'cause you haven't got a dad'. Observant of people, if not of his surroundings, he had learned to watch folk closely in case they should suddenly turn nasty on him, as folk were wont to do. Wary of attack, he tried to edge past them unnoticed, but just when he thought he had won, one of them glanced up. Nat's lips formed a defensive smile. If you smiled at people they would be less inclined to hit you . . . at least one could only hope. This time it failed, and there came the baying of hounds: 'Smellie! Gerrim!' And the instant he took flight they were after him.

They were bigger and older than himself, but if he could just reach a certain lane ahead then he knew they would not dare to pursue, for at the other end of that lane lived tougher rogues than them. Hampered by his ill-fitting jacket that slipped from his shoulders and caught the wind to drag him back, Nat moved his little arms and legs for all he was worth and pelted up Fossgate with the horde chasing him, getting nearer and nearer, reaching out for him . . . almost there! Keep running!

Just before The Old George Hotel, between a grocery and a wine merchant's, was a lane. A triumphant Nat had almost reached it when he felt an almighty thump on his back which knocked him into the sharp corner of the wall. Disregarding the pain, he cannoned off the wall and hurled himself at the passageway, down which he kept on running. Their footsteps followed him for a while, then petered out. Knowing he was safe, he drew to a breathless halt and spun to face them.

'We'll wait for you tonight, Smellie!' Their threat echoed off the passage wall. 'We'll get a hook and pull your brains out through your nose, if you've got any!'

In riposte, Nat shrugged his shoulders back into his jacket and wiggled his bottom at them before performing a leisurely swagger, as if their blows had been nothing.

The cottage in which Nat lived was at the far end of the lane and the stench of urine and rubbish would accompany him until he reached home. It was an odour to which his nose had become accustomed, just as he had become accustomed to people's loathing. To make his journey more interesting he kicked an apple core until he came to the end of the line of buildings where a grimy sign told newcomers this was Stonebow Lane. Nat's front doorstep, being sited on a junction, was convex. Above the lintel an additional streetname perched at right angles to the other – Hungate: one of the most deprived areas of York. On the opposite corner of the insalubrious lane hung a gas lamp which was hardly ever in working order thanks to the mischievous deeds of the local youth. The homeward trek in pitch blackness was a terrifying ordeal for a little boy and Nat would run down the lane as fast as he could to escape the goblins who he was sure lurked here. Giving the apple core a parting kick that splattered it over the flags, he shouted 'Goal!'

The woman who lived in the basement came to her tiny window which was level with the pavement, squinted out like a blind mole, then retreated to her underground room.

Before Nat could enter, a black and white terrier rushed barking at him. Fond of animals, he bent to pat it. 'Hello, boy!' It circled him, sniffing at his legs. Nat crouched on his heels and ruffled its fur briskly. 'What's your name? D'you want to be my dog? I'm gonna call you Toby.' A rough tongue licked his hand. Nat beamed and jumped up. 'Come on then!' He turned quickly and slapped his thigh. The dog jumped up, wagged its tail and sank its teeth into the seat of Nat's breeches. 'Aagh!' Nat leaped for cover, beat the dog off and slammed the door shut behind him. 'Savage! Traitor!'

On closing the door he slouched in malevolence, rubbing his posterior whilst his eyes became adjusted to the dinge.

Then, leaving wet bootprints on each step, he climbed the linoleumed stairway to the upstairs room that was home to himself and his mother.

Hardly was he through the inner door before his mother had seized him by the ear. 'You haven't been at school this morning!'

'Aagh! I have, Mam, I have!' Nat was dragged on tiptoe into the parlour which was basically furnished.

'Liar! I've had the kid-catcher here – again.' A furious Maria Smellie released his ear and thudded across the bare boards, arms crossed. 'He hammered on that bloody door at half past ten this morning till I had to get up.' Her work being nocturnal, it was unusual for her to rise before midday. Hoping that the people downstairs would answer the door, she had shoved her head under the blankets, but had eventually been forced to respond to the persistent knocking.

Maria rubbed a hand over her tired face, her hair hanging as a lank curtain over one eye until she tossed it back over her shoulder; it was dark like her son's. They were very much alike in feature too. It was easy to see from whom Nat inherited his starveling looks. Her white un-pressed blouse hung virtually straight at the front and once the bustle on her green skirt was removed her hips were as narrow as a boy's. 'You promised, Nat!'

'I did go – eh, Mam, a dog just bit me!'

'Good! It serves you right for not being at school. You swore you'd go – and look at you, you're dripping wet!'

'I were sat on t'bridge and somebody pushed me in.'

'You shouldn't've been sat on the bridge, you should've been at school!'

'I did go . . .'

'He's brayed you again, hasn't he?' guessed his mother.

Nat had great difficulty in reading. His teacher, an impatient man, often tried to aid his concentration with blows round the head. Then Nat's innate obstinacy would overrule his fervent desire to read and he would clamp his lips together refusing to say anything at all.

Maria was correct in her assumption. This morning the blows had been particularly savage and Nat had finally run out of the building. He had not volunteered this information to his mother, for she would charge down to school as she had done many times before and give the teacher an earful of abuse, then all afternoon the other boys would poke fun at him. In answer to her question he hung his head.

'Right! Well, I'm going down to see him.' Maria rolled up her sleeves to indicate that she meant business.

'Aw, Mam . . .'

'He's had enough warnings, Nat. He'll have to be taught.'

Anyone not knowing this delicate-looking girl would have taken her words for bravado, but Nat was well aware of her capabilities and began to panic. 'He'll have gone for his dinner!'

The reply was forceful. 'Then I'll catch him when I take you back this afternoon.'

'Aw, Ma . . .'

'Hold your tongue! I'm taking you to make sure you go. Here, get your bloody dinner.' Maria almost threw a tin plate onto the table, then sat down opposite to watch him eat its contents, apparently oblivious to the fact that he was still wet through. She had mixed feelings about her only child. Some days she loved him so fiercely she would die for him, yet at other times she could not bear to be in the same room. It was one of those latter moments now. She wanted to reach out across the table and grasp that narrow white throat and squeeze. Many a time during his eight years she had felt this emotion.

Maria had been only fourteen when she had given life to him. The bitterness was not because he had robbed her of her own childhood – Maria had been working the streets for over a year prior to his conception – no, the crux was that he had robbed her of her income during the time she had been laid up at the workhouse giving birth, and in the penniless days that followed she had been compelled to scrub floors to earn her keep until fit enough to return to her profession. Some women might have been grateful for the change, but not Maria. She detested her occupation but it was better than hard graft. This opinion was reflected in her habitat which, though it had few chattels still managed to look untidy. She had been shown little example of domesticity as a child, but had taught herself how to cook through trial and error – evident from the ingredients on Nat's plate.

Maria leaned her bony elbows on the table and used both hands to keep the hair from tumbling over her face, glaring at Nat. It was those eyes that did it: got her back up. Why did they have to be blue when her own were brown? All her family's had been brown so why in heaven's name couldn't his have been brown too? But no, they had to be blue to remind her that any one of a hundred men could have been his father. She felt like poking the blasted things out.

Her mind drifted. Everything had gone wrong that particular year. The necessity of hiring a girl to mind her bairn while she worked had meant there was little over for food and rent. In the end she had eschewed the services of the minder and left Nat alone on an evening from seven till midnight; alone, apart from the bugs which infested the entire building and made it stink of rotten apples, the bugs that nibbled and sucked on her child's body whilst some perverted human parasite did the same to her. Despite every precaution of standing the legs of the bed in jars of paraffin to stop the bugs crawling up, she would return to find the infant covered in red blotches.

When Maria was back on her feet, financially speaking, she had re-hired the minder, for by this time baby Nat was into everything. This up-turn was not to last; she had contracted a nasty infection which kept her off work yet again. However, there had been a nest-egg to fall back on that time. Maria had sworn they would never get her in the workhouse again and from every sovereign she earned a good few shillings was put by to this purpose. One day, she promised herself, she would have enough to escape from this life. Unfortunately, every time she had a little accrued there would be a hefty fine for soliciting and she was back at the foot of the mountain again. Yes, Nat had certainly brought a load of bad luck for his mother. Her only blessing was that she had never conceived again – nor would she. Maria did not realize that it was the dose of gonorrhoea and not luck which she had to thank for this.

Nat stole glances at her whilst he ate. For all his worldly talk this morning about whores, he had only become familiar with the term because of two other women who lived in the same row of buildings. He was unaware of how his mother earned her living. How would he know, when she looked nothing like them with their lewd talk, their rough manner and their common faces. The only time she ever swore was when he made her angry, whereas their conversation was peppered with expletives. With good clothes his mother could have passed for a lady – was better looking than some ladies he had seen – and she didn't seem anywhere near as old as other boys' mothers. He knew little of her background, either. He had asked but his mother was very mysterious about her kin. Nat was left to imagine what his grandparents had been like. His innocent mind could never have pictured the grim truth: her own mother had been a prostitute, and her father a bully and a drunkard who had enrolled Maria in the family profession when she was twelve. For almost a year she had endured him taking every farthing she earned before resolving to branch out on her own, sleeping rough until she had the funds to rent a room. In her naivety the haven she had found turned out to be a brothel. Not only did the madam extract high rates but there was violence too. When Maria had refused to part with her hard-earned cash she had been beaten and kept virtual prisoner until, with the aid of a client, she had managed to escape, only to find herself imprisoned a few months later by an unwanted pregnancy. Desperate though she might have been, Maria had never dreamed of having him aborted, not just through fear but because this baby was something she would have of her very own, the one who would give her the love she craved. The master and matron of the workhouse had tried to force her into placing Nat in an orphanage, but she had rebuffed their offers of help and had run away with her son, though over the following years she was often to regret this decision. Far from bringing unconditional love, all this child seemed to do was take.

Nat was in blissful ignorance of all this. All he knew of his mother's work was that it required her to put him to bed far too early, then took her away until God knew what hour. As soon as she had gone he would put his clothes back on and go out in search of company until he decided it was a suitable time for bed.

It was not simply good fortune that kept him from bumping into his mother; Maria deliberately plied her trade as far away from home as possible so as to hide it from her son. However it was certainly pure luck that no one had acquainted him with the truth. Maria worried about this often, imagining his face crumpling with shame.

Nat munched on the lump of cheese and avoided his mother's eye by concentrating on the gnarled pine table. It was older than both of them put together. He knew this because his mother had pointed out to him some carved initials and a date – J.W. 1847. There were dark cuts and gouges all over it. In moments of boredom Nat had added a few of his own; there were so many she wouldn't notice.

He felt awkward eating with his mother staring at him, and asked, 'Aren't you having any?'

She hunched over. 'I don't feel like it. I'm in such a bobbery over you I couldn't touch owt.' In its forlorn mood her face was almost identical to her son's, young and vulnerable, belying the gross debauchery it had witnessed.

He stopped eating and hung his head. 'Sorry.'

Despair rekindled anger. 'You say that every time! It means nothing. You're not bothered that I'll be sent to prison if you keep playing truant, are you?' Nat said that he was. He adored his mother and would never upset her deliberately. 'Yes well, I'm making sure you go to school this afternoon.' She jumped to her feet and began to move about the room, making as if she were tidying up but to little effect. The curtain which hung across part of the room swayed in the draught from her efforts. Behind this curtain was their 'bedroom' in which stood an iron bedstead and a table just large enough to hold a pitcher and basin for their toilet. 'I don't know what you find to do on your own. You'd be much better off with the other boys at school.'

'They don't like me.'

'You're just imagining it.' Yet Maria knew that what he said was correct — or rather she knew that the boys' mothers were behind the ostracism. It was nothing they said openly, just the way they behaved towards him, blaming him for his mother's misfortune. The injustice of it all boiled up inside her. Unconsciously she clenched her fists. She hated the world and everyone in it. How could they be so mean to such a pretty little face?

'They pulled a dead woman out of the river this morning. A Protestant.'

His mother turned sharp brown eyes on him. 'What?'

From her manner Nat felt he might have got the wrong word, so did not repeat it. 'She'd got no clothes on and she had loads of stab holes in her, and —'

'That's enough! Just get yourself ready for school!' Maria grabbed his plate then threw some dry clothes at him. At least his mother's profession ensured he had a change of clothing, which was more than could be said for most of those who behaved all high and mighty. 'I expect your boots are soaking an' all, aren't they? Aye, well you'll just have to put up with them while tonight.'

Peeling off his wet garments and dropping them at his feet, Nat remembered. 'I've brought you summat.' He bent down to rummage through his breeches pocket, afraid that the gift had been washed away. But no, here it was. 'A luckystone.' He handed it to her.

Maria jerked her thoughts away from the dead woman in the river and took possession of the ordinary looking pebble. There was a jar full of these 'luckystones' on the shelf, brought home by her son. They didn't seem to be very effective. Yet she forced a smile and tipped it into the jar. 'Let's hope it helps us to cope with that schoolteacher.'

Nat, who had hoped to disarm her with the present, dawdled over his task, but it didn't help. Chivvying him for his tardiness, Maria tied her hair up in order to look more respectable, donned a black bonnet, wrapped a shawl around herself and accompanied him to the school, which was jammed amongst crowded rows of dwelling houses in Bilton Street. He begged and pleaded for her not to take him all the way there, but she stayed with him until the bell clanged. Worse, when the boys fought and jostled through the narrow entrance into the classroom, she was amongst them.

The internal walls were much the same as those outside, composed of rough bare brickwork. Their only adornment was a portrait of the monarch, whose doleful face did nothing to aid welcome. Neither did the master, who gave Maria a look that questioned her right to be there. The slightly built young woman stood her ground. She had met his type dozens of times; the type that would probably want her to use the cane on him had they been meeting on different terms. 'I'd like a word with you, Mr Lillywhite, if you'd be so kind as to grant me a hearing.'

'Quiet!' The master quashed the shuffling of feet and the drone of voices as boyish posteriors slid along benches, deliberately ignoring Maria until every one of the pupils was located. Concealing her impatience, she used the time to take stock of his face which, with its many crags, held plenty of interest. His hair was turning grey. It was neatly combed with just the correct amount of bear's grease. He stood like a monolith in his highly polished boots, the black frock coat and trousers pressed to perfection. His winged collar would have been pristine too, but for a greenfly which had been accidentally squashed on it. His nose was patrician and his top lip was so thin as to be almost non-existent. There was about him an overall air of control. Lillywhite was a most distinguished man – and isn't he aware of it, thought Maria as, finally, with great condescension he turned to her. 'If you wish to see me, you may call at four o'clock after school is over.' Not even the courtesy of her name.

Maria abandoned all patience and dignity. 'Don't think you're talking to me like one of your victims, you tight-arsed pillock!' She stuck a finger within an inch of his left nostril. The boys gasped and sniggered. Nat wished the floor would open up and engulf him. 'You might fritten them but you don't fritten me. I've told you before about hitting my lad round the head, you'll be sending him daft! I don't mind a whack with the cane if he's done summat really wrong but when he's trying his best to – '

Lillywhite's voice incised with great emphasis, 'What goes on in this classroom is no concern of – '

'It is when it involves my son! Now, I won't give you any more warnings. If it happens again I'm off to the police.'

The schoolmaster looked down on the termagant, be-holding her as if she were something in the gutter, thought

Nat. 'Yes . . . well, I am certain you are much acquainted with the police, *Miss* Smellie.'

Maria said no more, she just hit him — a bone-crunching hook to the nose. Whilst Lillywhite rushed a handkerchief to his face, she wheeled on Nat. 'Now, you bloody well stay there and pay heed to your lessons!' Then she stormed out.

'Atkidsod,' the master, eyes brimming, spoke through blood-drenched linen, 'go ask de headbaster to sed for de police.' He himself left the classroom to tend his throbbing nose. There was a chorused, 'Whoo!' from the boys, on the premise that Smellie Nat was in for it now, as if he had not guessed.

On his return, Lillywhite was carrying the punishment book which he opened with great deliberation, and entered the victim's name and the number of strokes. Then, picking up a cane he ordered, 'Nathaniel Smellie, come to the front of the class!'

Nat supposed he should be grateful that the man did not share the melodramatics of another teacher who would lash the air a number of times before making contact with flesh, just to prolong the ordeal. At least Lillywhite waded right into the flogging, though this was hardly a comfort to the recipient. Each blow was accompanied by an instruction: 'I do not,' — whack! — 'expect' — whack! — 'a repetition,' — whack! — 'of this afternoon's' — whack! — 'performance,' — whack! — 'Do you,' — whack! — 'understand?' Then an extra whack for luck and a shove of dismissal. 'Mother's boy!' The rest of the form were permitted a chuckle as a wet-eyed Nat made ginger contact with the bench.

With imagination his only vengeance, Nat saw again the murdered woman's body and superimposed it with that of his tormentor, visualizing Lillywhite perforated with knife wounds, particularly in the bottom.

The master's voice interrupted. 'Oh, and I should not

anticipate that your mother will be at home when you get there, Smellie.' Lillywhite gloated down his crimson proboscis. 'She has been arrested.'

2

Fear preoccupied Nat for the rest of the afternoon. All he could think of was his mother cowering in a dungeon. Terrified of going home to an empty house, he dallied at his usual haunt of Foss Bridge, hoping for inspiration. Whilst here, he glimpsed Bright Maguire skipping in his direction along Walmgate and waved to her, but she failed to see him as she gambolled round the corner out of view. Disappointed, he lounged there for a moment longer before concluding that he was not going to find an answer to his problem here and so dragged his feet towards Stonebow Lane, fearing the worst.

Hence the rush of joy on finding his mother safe at home! Even the bad-tempered tirade which greeted him could not dampen it. From what he could gather she had been released pending the hearing at the Police Court next week. That would mean another early rise, hence the grumpiness, but Nat gave only half an ear to her chastisement now, for he had noticed the man seated at the table, leaning back, ankles crossed, all relaxed and smiling as if he owned the place. He was a bit older than Nat's mother, the boy guessed, with very wavy, thick dark-brown hair that fell low over his forehead. He had thick eyebrows, too. His eyes were hooded and his lips full. He had on a drab suit and a checked waistcoat which was only fastened by a top button, making his stomach appear larger than it was. The boots he wore were brown and deeply scuffed; they had not seen polish for many months.

Maria noticed that Nat was not paying full attention to the lecture and so abandoned it. 'I can see I aren't doing an aporth o' good! This is Mr Kendrew. He helped me at the police station – well go on, thank the gentleman! It was all because o' you I was there, you know.'

Nat mumbled his thanks but took an instant dislike to Kendrew; not for any particular reason, he just hated anyone who might spoil the relationship he himself shared with his mother, and by the familiarity in the man's attitude it appeared as if this was his intent.

Alas, the man shared their tea as well, remaining until it was time for Maria to go out to work and so ruining the usual hour of intimacy Nat enjoyed with his parent. Indeed, most of her chat was for Kendrew. When she ducked behind the curtain to wash for work the man tried to strike up a rapport with the boy, who remained sullen. Nat was never loquacious in adult company, but there was added reason not to like Kendrew now; he had the most unattractive dimple at the corner of his mouth that turned a grin into a sneer. Nat became increasingly irritated by the dent and perversity glued his eyes there. Kendrew put a hand to his mouth. 'What's up, have I got a crumb on my face?'

Nat shook his head.

'What d'you keep staring for then?'

Nat blushed and looked away to where his still damp clothes hung over the embers, filling the room with the odour of scorched river water. Becoming conscious of his wet boots, the boy took these off and put them on the hearth with his stockings draped over the top.

Maria returned so quietly that she was unnoticed at first and had time to appraise Kendrew more closely. She guessed he was about twenty-five. In profile he was rather more good-looking than when viewed full face. From the front his lower cheeks were too round, like a hamster that has crammed food into both pouches, but from this angle his Grecian nose was very striking. With his eyes cast downwards she could see, too, that he had very long lashes, dark like his hair. In repose, his lower lip tended to bulge sensuously; ignored by the boy he had begun to tweak it, until from the corner of his eye he felt her observation and turned towards her, grinning.

Maria enjoyed a tingle of unaccustomed pleasure at this male attention, feeling none of the contempt she felt for those who hired her body. Maybe it was the dimple; she came up to screw a gentle finger into it.

The familiarity of this act sent a jolt through Nat's entire body. His heart thumped as he watched Kendrew's reaction. There was nothing, absolutely nothing, that could promote outrage, Kendrew did not even touch her, but that laugh, that hated dimple . . . Nat experienced such jealousy, such fury, that he felt his head might blow off.

Maria was apologizing. 'I'm sorry, we'll have to part company now Sep, I've work to go to.'

What was that she had called him? Shep? Sounds like a dog, thought Nat. Go on, dog, leave us alone and don't come again.

Kendrew shoved back the wooden chair, picked up his hat and stood facing her. 'Might I call on you again?'

No! Say no, Nat urged his mother.

'If it takes your fancy.'

Nat cringed at the embarrassing coyness portrayed by his mother, and willed the man to leave. With a wink and a jaunty pat of his bowler, Kendrew left. Still happy, Maria told Nat to go to bed. At his downcast expression she realized how upset he was that she had had so little time for him that evening, and in a burst of good spirit said, 'All right, then, you can brush my hair out for me – but it'll have to be quick.' She planted herself on the chair that Kendrew had vacated, whilst Nat ran the brush through her long dark tresses. 'Did you get into trouble at school after I left?' He nodded, though did not elaborate on how severe the trouble had been; his buttocks hurt even now.

She gave an angry murmur of futility. 'Damned teachers . . . how's your reading coming along, then?'

'All right.' He picked up a bunch of hair and used the brush to stroke the ends.

'I haven't got time to hear you tonight, but tomorrow before I go out you can read me a few pages from the book.'

This wasn't such an ordeal as it might sound for someone who could barely read. There was only one book in the house, a puny volume of children's tales, which his mother's friend Sister Theresa had read to him so often that he knew it off by heart and what he didn't know he could guess from the illustrations. His mother wouldn't notice if he missed a word, for she was hardly literate herself.

'Who's that man?'

'I told you, he's Mr Kendrew.' Maria had closed her eyes, enjoying the light caress of the brush strokes.

'You called him Shep.'

'No, Sep. Septimus Kendrew.'

'You didn't tell me he was coming.'

She uttered a laugh. 'I didn't know, did I?'

'Well, who is he?'

Maria opened her eyes. 'Are you daft or summat? I've just told you.'

'I don't like him.'

'Nobody says you have to. Right that'll have to do, Nat!' She snatched the brush, rose and delivered a brusque kiss. 'Off to bed with you now.'

Head bowed, Nat shuffled away. After he had gone, she ignited a paraffin lamp. It was barely necessary yet, but Maria hated coming home to a darkened house. She then put the finishing touches to her appearance, replacing her ankle-length skirts with a shorter dress and a pinafore, as worn by a child. There was a mirror on the wall; much of its silver had flaked off but it served its purpose. Posing before it, she tied a ribbon round her head and into a bow, schoolgirl fashion. This was where the emaciated body had its advantages. There were men who preferred young girls. Notwithstanding the look of knowledge in her eye, dressed like this Maria looked little more than fifteen, which guaranteed her a good few years of income.

Whilst getting ready, her mind relived the events of the day: battling once again with the supercilious Lillywhite — as if once hadn't been bad enough — then moving on quickly to her meeting with Sep Kendrew. She had told Nat that the man had 'helped' her at the police station; helped was a bit of an exaggeration. He had merely been sitting opposite her in the corridor whilst she waited to be charged and they had started chatting about the recent murder. Even if she had wanted to answer Nat's question she couldn't have, for she knew nothing about the man. When she had asked what he was doing at the police station he had replied that it was all a misunderstanding, which meant that he could have been anything from a debtor to a rapist. But no, she knew the male species well enough to be sure he wasn't the latter. There was no evil in him. He was probably a petty thief, which was of no consequence to Maria as long as he didn't steal from her. When she had told Nat that Kendrew had helped her what she actually meant was that he had defended her vocally when the police sergeant had called her all kinds of filthy names, but of course she couldn't say that to her innocent son.

After the contretemps she had asked, 'What're you being so nice to me for?' Kendrew was aware of her line of work because of the manner in which she had been treated by the police sergeant. 'Are you just after a free ride? If so you can think again.'

Sep had been genuinely aggrieved. 'I defended you 'cause I think you're very attractive! Fair enough, I don't like seeing you in such a low line of business, but I know that circumstances must have driven you to it and you shouldn't be treated in such a disrespectful fashion – and if you'll allow me to, I'll make sure you never have to endure this sort of thing again.'

Accustomed to such flannel she had scoffed, but by and by as he hastened to emphasize the innocence behind his motives she had come to believe that he actually meant it and found herself attracted to his rough charm. She had remained wary of inviting him in after he had walked her home, but he hadn't so much as touched her hand. On the contrary, she had been the familiar one, tickling his dimple like that. The memory caused a smile. She hoped he would call again. A quick rub of her cheeks and she was ready to go.

Nat listened for the door to click, waited a few minutes, then relaced his boots and wandered out into the street for a nightly perambulation of his kingdom.

Nat did not attend school the next day, either. When he came in at four Kendrew was there again. He had apparently brought a gift with him, a pair of red stockings embroidered with swallows. Maria was trying them on in the bedroom.

'There's a bit of a hole in the knee,' Sep forewarned her, 'but somebody as clever as you will be able to mend it.'

Maria came out from behind the curtain to display her gift, parading up and down with her skirts above her knees and wearing a smile that made Nat feel ill.

'Like 'em, Nat?' queried Sep.

The little boy shrugged.

'I would've brought you a present too, but I didn't know what you'd like.' Kendrew dipped into his pocket. 'Here, go and buy yourself some sherbet.'

Nat stared at the halfpenny in Sep's grubby palm.

'By, he's never been so backward in coming forward!' grinned Maria. 'Go on, take it – but you'll have to wait while after tea to spend it.'

Loath to accept but equally loath to refuse, Nat put the halfpenny in his pocket. After tea, when Maria gave him leave to visit the shop, Nat did not budge from the table. 'I don't feel like any sweets.'

A look passed between Sep and Maria, one of amused frustration. Maria shepherded her son to the door. 'I don't care what you spend it on, just go! And take your time.'

Nat looked up at her, then at the smirking Kendrew, understanding now that the halfpenny was an enticement to get rid of him. Feeling unwanted, he left them and wandered round the streets, though resisted their instruction to buy himself confectionery. He would rather starve than be grateful to that man. The halfpenny was still in his pocket when he returned. Thankfully, Kendrew was in the act of leaving; Nat passed him on the stairs. Maria was preparing for work. 'Bedtime, Nat!'

Her son lingered, wringing his hands. 'Why does he keep coming here?'

'*He* being Mr Kendrew, I presume.' Maria bustled about. 'He's only been twice. You make it sound like he's living here. He's lost his job and he's just making use of his spare time until he finds a new one, that's all. Come on now – bed!'

Nat obeyed, reassured that Kendrew's visits would be curtailed as soon as he gained new employment.

Unfortunately, it became clear that Kendrew was making little effort in this field, for he turned up on Saturday too. Saturdays were precious to Nat, when he and his mother would go shopping and she would treat him to an iced bun, but this afternoon she packed him off on his own with a list while she entertained her caller. Even the Sabbath was not inviolate. Normally he would rise at the clamour of churchbells, make the fire, hang the kettle over it, fetch his mother a cup of tea then climb back under the patchwork quilt beside her and they would snuggle up lazily until late morning. This particular Sunday, however, she was up before him and when he finally woke it was to the aroma of roast beef. It turned out that Kendrew was to be a guest at dinner. Nothing, swore the little boy to himself, nothing could possibly surpass this violation. Alas, it could, for on Monday Sep arrived at a quarter to nine in the morning to accompany Maria to the Police Court, and the pair of them escorted Nat to school before going on their way.

Once inside the school, Nat hid behind some coats in the cloakroom until he was sure his mother had gone, then he sidled off. He maundered around the river for a while, poking half-heartedly at the water with a branch, then finding a piece of string he made it into a fishing rod and sat for half an hour dangling it over the water.

A passing workman loitered behind him. Nat turned and squinted at the intruder. 'You need a hook and a worm on the end if you want to catch owt. Doubt there'll be owt living in that scum anyroad.' Nat had never liked people telling him what to do and remained hunched in his futile position until the man laughed and moved on. 'You'll still be sitting here when I'm on me way home!'

'Shitty bum,' muttered Nat, then hurled the branch into the river, wondering what to do next.

The wind carried distant cries of children at play in the schoolyard where he himself should have been, bringing an idea to mind: he would go and visit his new – his only – friend, Bright Maguire. She would be on her morning break too. Out of eagerness he ran most of the way down Walmgate and arrived breathless at the girls' playground. His eyes did not have to scan the hubbub for long before falling on her laughing face. That lovely face. It took Bright a moment longer to spot him. He waved both arms frantically, drawing unwanted attention from the other girls who giggled and jeered when Bright finally saw him and came over, rather reluctantly in his opinion.

'What're you doing here?' she hissed through the gate. 'If Sister sees ye there'll be the devil to pay.'

Having expected a warmer greeting, he was annoyed. 'I'll go, then.'

'No!' Her twig-like arm shot out to draw him back. 'I'm glad to see ye. It's just that I didn't want ye to get into trouble.'

'Me mother says I should be called Trouble.' Nat lifted one side of his mouth. 'I'm always in it.' When asked why this was he explained, 'For not being able to do me lessons – well, I can do 'em, but I just don't like 'em.'

'What don't you like?' Holding onto the gate, she balanced herself on the very tips of her boots, an ungainly ballerina.

He shrugged and scuffed his own boot around the pavement. 'Reading, sums . . .'

'I'll help ye,' was her instantaneous reaction. 'I'm the best reader in my class.'

Nat felt resentful. 'Show-off.'

She blushed; then, after a moment's awkwardness, re-dressed the balance. 'I'm not too good at sums, though. I keep forgetting my times tables. What are you up to?'

His face showed he had no inkling as to what she meant.

'You know, two twos are four, three twos are six – I'm up to nines. Listen.' She recited parrot fashion her nine times table, faltering only once. 'I'll teach you if ye like. Say it after me . . .'

'Don't want to, it's daft.'

'It's not daft if it stops ye getting a clout.'

Nat thought about this and saw the wisdom in it, but was never one to accept good advice. 'I don't care.'

'Go on, let me,' pressed Bright, then noticed he was studying her closely. 'What's up? What're you looking at?'

Nat's eyes had been searching for the chocolate mark; there it was under her chin. Had it really been choco-late it would have melted and smudged by now so, disappointingly, he would have to believe her former explanation that the mark was permanent. 'What did you say you call that thing on your neck?'

She touched it self-consciously. 'A mole – now, will ye let me help ye with your tables or not?'

He acted nonchalant. 'If you want.'

Bright pulled back her shoulders, clasped her hands and deported herself like a teacher in class. 'Right, how far can ye count?'

Nat hesitated. 'Twenty.'

The girl's mouth fell open. She herself had been able to count to a hundred when she was seven, but seeing his look of defiance she refrained from mockery and told him that all you did was to add one, two, three and so on, and after twenty-nine, came thirty.

Nat was just getting the hang of it when a bell clanged. Bright wheeled around, heeded the motioning arm of the nun and cast a warning at Nat. 'Better go! Wait for me at dinnertime and walk home with me. We'll carry on then.' She galloped off, hair cascading, and the babble of the schoolyard died.

Nat wandered back along Walmgate deep in concentration. 'Thirty-one, thirty-two . . .' With fifty came such a burst of achievement that he was spurred on to run and tell his mother – but no, he would have to wait until dinnertime or she'd be angry again. Oh, but he must tell someone!

At once feeling peckish, he delved into his breeches and found the halfpenny that Sep Kendrew had given him. He had not wanted to spend it, had fully intended to throw the coin away, but could not bring himself to do so. Resolve weakened, he used it now to purchase a bag of lozenges. The woman in the shop looked upon him kindly as she handed over the bag. Encouraged, he wanted to boast, 'I can count to fifty!' but was far too reserved.

Instead, he drifted on to the medieval Shambles where he

perched on a cobbler's window ledge to eat his sweets. A youth came out of the shop and ordered him to move. His mind on other things, Nat paid no heed. The youth grabbed his bag of lozenges, stuck one in his mouth and the rest in his pocket. Nat leaped up to object. The youth picked him up under the armpits, carried him a few yards to a butcher's shop and hung him on a hook between the dripping joints of beef. Then, while Nat squirmed and grew red in the face, the youth crammed his mouth full of Nat's lozenges and gloated for a while before his master called him back to work.

Nat wriggled and kicked until he heard an ominous rip which stilled him. He hung there, petrified and tormented by bluebottles. The butcher, who had been enjoying the entertainment from inside the shop, now took pity and lifted him down, warning him that he would be in for it when his mother saw his ripped jacket. As Nat passed the cobbler's the youth took out his bag of lozenges and taunted him with it. Nat stuck out his tongue and then ran.

Shortly afterwards he had a stroke of unaccustomed luck: amongst the rubbish in the gutter his observant eye glimpsed a sixpence. He was about to pounce on it, but then thought it more expedient to hide it under his foot until he ascertained whether anyone was watching him. In possession of so much money, his first thought was that he would buy his mother a gift. Entering a shop he was about to purchase another bag of lozenges, intended for her, when he noticed a card displaying toy watches. A watch! He had always wanted one, but they were sixpence each. He could not afford both items.

When he emerged from the shop he was wearing the little tin watch suspended from a button on his jacket by a piece of elastic, and feeling splendidly rich. His mother would understand – the thought had been there.

The remainder of the morning was given to twisting the little knob that moved the watch hands round and round.

He had assumed that being in possession of a time-piece would automatically render him with the time, and was annoyed that this turned out to be fallacious. After the novelty wore thin, he went back to practising his counting and when he met up with Bright he was able to announce triumphantly, 'I can count to tenty!' Her confusion was answered when Nat, after reciting up to ninety-five, continued, 'Ninety-six, ninety-seven, ninety-eight, ninety-nine, tenty.'

She couldn't prevent a giggle. 'It's not tenty! It's a hundred.'

'How can it be?' Nat was forceful. 'You say eighty and ninety don't you? It must be tenty.' Bright tried to explain, but he refused to accept that he was wrong. 'You don't know everything! I'm telling you it's tenty.'

Bright gave up. Nat was a know-all, but there was something about him that invoked compassion in her – the mistiness of those blue eyes was at odds with the defiance in his voice and the belligerence of his manner. Young as she was, Bright recognized that he was deeply wounded and trying not to show it, and she felt ashamed of herself for mocking his achievement. They walked in silence the rest of the way up Walmgate. When they parted, he said out of the blue, 'Anyway, I've got a watch and you haven't!' Then he went home to canvas his mother's praise.

The room was empty. He cut a piece of bread from a loaf, which sufficed as lunch. Whilst he was eating this, Sister Theresa called to see his mother, but finding her not at home sat and talked to Nat for a while. To the boy she was just a friend of his mother's; he was not to know that Sister Theresa had made it her special mission to reform and convert prostitutes. The girls endured her interference, partly because she was nice to them but mainly because she never came empty-handed. Today she gave Nat a piece of ginger cake and, whilst he devoured it, asked how his education was coming along. He said proudly that he

could count as far as tenty now. To his mortification, the
nun laughed uproariously and told him the same as Bright.
There was no question of apologizing, but when Bright
came out of school that afternoon Nat was there with a
sheepish face, telling her she could still teach him to read
and count if she wanted to.

She flashed her warm, gummy smile, said that she would
and danced out of the yard to walk alongside him. He
showed her his watch, upon which she was still eulogizing
when a war cry went up to their rear. 'Aagh! Kill the
English bastaaard!'

Bright spun round to see three boys from her school.
'Come on run, they're gonna hit ye!' She tugged at Nat's
sleeve, but he was too slow. The Catholic boys were on
him before he could react. They rained blows upon his
crouched back, arms windmilling, boots scuffling, whilst
Bright tried desperately to wrest them away.

Then another figure waded into the affray. Robes
flowing, Sister Martha burst upon the scene, her winged
wimple like a dove taking flight. 'John Kelly, you uncivil-
ized rogue!' She took a handful of the culprit's red hair,
delivered a punch and threw him aside as if he were waste
paper before dealing each of the other participants –
including Nat – a stinging blow around the ear. They fled.
Nat, rescued from his mad Irish assailants, tried to run too,
but was seized and being the only one left at hand was
given further blows by the puce-cheeked nun.

Bright stepped in. 'Please, Sister Martha, it wasn't Nat
who started it! The others were hitting him.'

Sister Martha held Nat prisoner, hauling him this way
and that by his jacket and tearing it further. 'You'd do well
to think about the company you're keeping, Bridget
Maguire. Tis a bad end you'll come to, dallying with such
scalliwags.'

'But Sister, it wasn't Nat!'

'Don't you dare argue with me, child! Come to my room

after registration tomorrow morning.' The nun gave Nat a shove and swept off.

Nat disregarded his friend's consternation, too worried about how his mother would view the torn jacket. 'Can you sew?'

The freckled face was preoccupied, thinking of what was to happen tomorrow. Nat asked again if she could mend his jacket in order to deliver him from further wrath when he got home. Bright returned to the present. 'Why, will your dad hit ye?'

'I haven't got one,' Nat mumbled.

'What?' She wrinkled her nose.

'I haven't got a dad.'

'Oh. Have ye got a mother?'

'Course I have! She'll go mad when she sees this.'

'My mammy'll sew it for ye. Away home with me.'

'Won't she mind?'

Bright shook her head. All guests were welcome in the Maguire household.

As they walked, Nat asked in a pained voice, 'What did they hit me for? I've never even talken to 'em before.'

Bright expressed her disgust. 'They just don't like people who aren't from our school. They're eejits.'

Nat wanted to ask what an eejit was, but would not show his ignorance. Assuming it had something to do with the attacker's appearance, he muttered, 'I hate people with carroty hair.'

When they reached Bright's house Nat loitered in the courtyard, which was strung with washing lines. Bright might want him to come in, but her mother wouldn't. He had had doors slammed in his face before and was quite prepared for it to happen today. Therefore he was taken aback when a quietly spoken Irishwoman put her head round the jamb and invited in her soft brogue, 'Come in, come in, we won't be after biting ye.' And he was even more delighted to hear Bright's affirmation when

Mrs Maguire asked, 'Will your young friend be taking tea with us?'

Only two of Bright's siblings – Eugene aged eleven and Patrick aged ten – were attendant. They barely looked at the visitor, too intent on arguing between themselves. The others, the eldest of whom was twenty, Bright told him, were at work. Though Mrs Maguire was still capable of bearing children she had not produced a live one since Bright. There was an ancient looking crone in a black dress and shawl sitting in an armchair by the fire. Atop her silver hair was a tiny black bonnet tied with ribbon under her jaw. Her face was heavily wrinkled; one of the lines that ran from nose to mouth was so deep it looked like a scar from a knifewound. Her eyes were vacant until Bright's cheerful hug, when she responded with warmth and patted her granddaughter's cheek with a bony hand. It was obvious that Bright thought the world of her, although Nat could not imagine why. Somewhat repulsed by the old woman, he waited awkwardly until the girl broke free and told him, 'This is me granny. Say hello to Nat, Gran!' The old lady smiled and nodded, then reverted to her former trance. Bright kissed the furrowed cheek and came away. 'She's lovely, me gran. It's just sometimes she goes away to a place in her head. So long as we keep her pipe filled with baccy she's happy. I tell her all my troubles.' This was said in a whisper to Nat alone. 'She makes everything better.'

Nat wondered what troubles Bright could possibly have in a nice home like this. Smelly it might be with its neighbouring pigs, but it was a lot bigger than his own. Most of the tiled floor was covered in rugs, and the table by the window had a cloth over it and was surrounded by eight wooden chairs. Eight chairs! There was a sideboard in the room too, and in addition to the sofa on the opposite wall there were two armchairs, a footstool, plus cushions galore for the family's comfort. It was a great contrast to Nat's basic dwelling.

'And where is it you'd be living, Nat?' Mrs Maguire came from the scullery with a plate of bread and butter.

Nat was confused. Did Mrs Maguire mean where would he live if he had the choice?

'Stop that now and wash your hands!' She slammed the plate down on the table and dealt a clout to each of her boys who were still arguing. 'Aren't they the demons, Nat – sorry, I didn't catch your answer.'

Unsure, Nat looked at Bright. 'Where d'ye live?' she asked him.

'Hungate.'

'Oh, would ye be after knowing Mrs Doyle in Garden Place?'

When Nat shook his head Mrs Maguire added, 'Not to worry. Sit ye down and have a bite to eat. You boys stop arguing in there or your father will be told!'

After participating in a light meal of bread and butter, the Maguire brothers were sent out to play. Bright was ordered to fetch a pail of water from the standpipe in the yard – there was no tap in the house and the supply was shared with other cottages in the area. When she withdrew from the table Nat went with her, undesirous of being left alone with the adults. He discovered that this house was not standing back to back with another as was his own – as indeed were most of the houses round here – but had the benefit of both front and back door, if little else. The smell of pigs was appalling and followed them on their return to the house; the Maguires seemed oblivious. Whilst Bright and her mother washed the few pots Nat was left to sit with Granny Maguire, perched on the edge of his chair in anticipation of more questions, but the old lady appeared not even to know that he was there, happy to draw on her pipe. Nat began to relax, enjoying the smell of tobacco. Craning his neck, he peered through an open doorway. Apparently there was another downstairs room along a passageway.

Bright returned in time to catch his curiosity. 'I'll show ye the front parlour if ye like!'

Nat tried not to look impressed as she gave him a tour of the entire house, though it was hard not to utter exclamation on discovering there were three bedrooms!

Reseated at the table, Bright opened a book and tried to teach Nat how to read. Mrs Maguire smiled benevolently as she mended his jacket, inserting the odd question such as how old was he? Between attempts at reading, Nat snatched covert glances at the woman who seemed very old to be anyone's mother. She was waif-thin like Bright, but this was the only similarity. Her hair was dull and tendrils of it had escaped the bun at her nape. Her eyes were an insipid blue. The front of her apron was stained and the rest was none too clean either, but she smiled on Nat and did not treat him in the normal patronizing role of adults, which was good enough for him. Nat liked her. She had an aura of serenity that made one blind to her unkempt presentation. 'And when is your birthday, Nat?'

'Haven't got one.'

Mrs Maguire dropped her restive air to project astonishment. 'Holy Souls, of course ye have! Tis a celebration of the day you were born. Ye have one every year.'

'I don't,' said Nat.

'Everybody has a birthday.'

'Not me.'

Mrs Maguire rested the jacket on her lap and showed patience with the stubborn boy. 'D'ye know when ye were born?'

'Winter.' Nat remembered his mother saying he had arrived a few weeks after Christmas along with a very heavy snowfall. He knew that he was eight because his mother had recently shouted after one of his truancies, 'You're eight years old, you should've got used to school by now!' But he had never heard her mention the word birthday.

'Did herself tell ye she'll be nine in a couple o' weeks?' Mrs Maguire inclined her head at Bright, then took up her sewing again. Nat shook his own head, none too pleased at the information that the girl was older than him. 'We'll be having a little party. Would ye honour us with your presence?'

Stunned, Nat could only nod. He had never been to a party.

'That's good.' Mrs Maguire smiled, then took a look at the clock and her face turned anxious. She handed over his mended jacket. 'Well now, there's your wee coat all done and dusted. You'll want to be making tracks. Sure, your father will be home from work — where is it he'd be working, by the way?'

Nat pretended that he had not heard as he donned the jacket, without thanks for its repair. Words of gratitude did not spring easily to his tongue, so seldom did anyone do him a favour, but he smiled awkwardly to show he was pleased. Mrs Maguire was used to receiving little thanks from her own menfolk and made no comment on his lack of appreciation, merely repeating her last question as she thought he had not understood. Again, Nat played dumb though his cheeks were pink.

'Nat doesn't have a daddy,' explained Bright.

'Oh, tis terrible sorry I am.' Mrs Maguire's concern was genuine. 'Has he been dead for long?'

'He isn't dead,' mumbled Nat, and looked so uncomfortable that Mrs Maguire immediately guessed the situation and said quickly, 'Oh well, and sure your poor mother will be missing ye, and Bright's daddy will be home from his work on the railway any minute so we'll not delay ye – don't forget that party, now.' During the last fifteen minutes, her nervous glances at the clock had grown more frequent, and now she went to check the oven to ensure that her husband's meal would be ready for his homecoming, which led Nat into thinking that Mr Maguire must be some sort of ogre, hence he was not too unhappy to depart.

Bright said she would walk with him as far as the large draper's store on the bridge. 'Just let me put some more newspaper in me boots. They're rubbing and causing awful blisters.' Whipping them off, she raked the now crumbling paper from their insides and threw it on the fire. Screwing a fresh sheet into a ball she rammed it home into the toe, then put her foot in and folded another sheet round her heel, doing the same with the other foot. The boots were more snug now, though by tomorrow noon they would probably be slopping off again.

She and the boy picked their way through the malodorous Pig Market. Nat was about to take his leave at Foss Bridge when Bright saw her father come striding through the dusk and pointed him out, a man whose looks owed more to the Spaniard than the Celt. She waved. Mr Maguire checked his rolling gait to wave back, disconcerting Nat with his affability. Where was the imagined brute? Beneath the grime of sweat was a pleasant-looking fellow with a kind gleam in his eye and hardly enough meat on him to thump a flea. Bright went lolloping over the bridge to meet him. His haversack tumbled from his shoulder as he scooped her up in his arms as though he had not seen her for a month. At this point two more of the Maguire daughters appeared, they too fussing over Bright and one of them giving her a bag of broken chocolate she had pilfered from the factory where both worked. Nat, consumed by envy, said a quiet hello to them before proceeding home. A wistful backwards glance saw the jaunty Mr Maguire carrying his little girl home on his shoulders.

Nat was glad of Mrs Maguire's repair work on his jacket, for his mother was less than ecstatic when he got home. Maria sat unpicking a bustle in order to replace it with a more fashionable compact one, and as he came round the door she lunged in his direction with a pair of scissors.

'Ten shillings I got fined for sticking up for you!'

Nat turned sullen and decided to punish her by not showing her his new watch.

Kendrew, who was there too, tapped Nat on the chest, a smirk on his face. 'You should've seen her though, Nat. She gave the bluebottle a right contemptuous look and threw this half-sovereign on the counter as if it were a penny. By, his face were a picture!'

Nat ignored Sep and accused his mother, 'You weren't in when I came home for me dinner.'

Maria stopped ripping at the bustle and abandoned her frown. 'Oh . . . yes, sorry. Sep took me for some new shoes as a treat to make up for the horrible morning. Do you like 'em?' She lifted her hem to disport the Magpie shoes – black patent leather and white buckskin. They were far too small, dug into her heels and nipped her toes, but she hadn't even contemplated leaving the pawnshop without them. Such exquisite footwear was worth a little discomfort.

Sep noted the distaste with which Nat beheld his gift. It was hard not to interpret. 'He's jealous 'cause I didn't buy him a pair.'

Nat religiously ignored the man. 'I'm off to a birthday party,' he told his mother.

'Are you indeed?' Maria stopped cavorting. 'Whose party is it, might I ask?'

'Bright Maguire's. It's in a couple o' weeks.'

Kendrew responded first. 'Got yourself a ladyfriend, eh?'

Maria tittered. Nat could not condone this disloyalty and vanished behind the curtain to throw himself onto the bed.

'D'you want any tea?' called Maria.

'Had it.'

Only now did she enquire as to his previous whereabouts. 'Where?'

'Mrs Maguire's.'

'Eh, he's got himself mixed up with a married woman!' laughed Sep.

The quip was met with disdain. Lying on the bed, Nat rested his chin on his hands. A picture formed of Bright in Mr Maguire's arms. Well, much as he envied her a father he could never accept Kendrew in that special role.

Alas, in only a matter of weeks this unthinkable proposition became dangerously close to enactment. Though Kendrew had a job now as a hospital orderly, it did little to reduce the amount of time he spent in Nat's abode. Every teatime, every Saturday, every Sunday, the wretch would pop up to destroy Nat's home life. He was, it transpired, a determined man who never wearied of trying to coax a positive response from the boy. It was relatively easy for a self-possessed child like Nat to ignore these attempts at infiltration. What could not be dismissed was Maria's obvious attachment to the man, for which the only feasible explanation could be Sep's propensity for showering her with gifts. His mother had been well and truly duped by this indolent charmer. It disturbed and sickened the little boy, who began to have fantasies in which his father would burst through the door, knock Kendrew to a pulp, then take Nat and his mother off to live in a palace. But no one came.

Nat found himself having to rely more and more on Bright's company. He liked Bright, she was different from anyone he had ever known. The children of such areas were normally sullen, their pinched faces carrying all the worries of the world – as indeed did Nat's. In contrast, Bright's shone out like a beacon, always ready for laughter rather than tears. She was vivacious, impulsive perhaps, but never overbearing in manner and had the knack of making him feel warm on the coldest of days. If she had one fault it was that she told awful lies. He had noticed some red weals on her hand. When he had asked what they were she told him Sister Martha was responsible. As if a nun would do that! He never knew when to believe her. However, he enjoyed her birthday party and liked Mr Maguire enormously. Now there was a man he'd be proud to call Father. The jovial Irishman kept everyone entertained with songs, tales and jokes. He was very strong too, despite his wiry build, and was forever displaying his talents by doing balancing tricks with the furniture, the sinews bulging out on arms that looked thin enough to snap under the weight. Everything about him was so far removed from Kendrew, nothing more so than his smile which extended to eyes that were very dark and twinkly. And that smile was never more in evidence than when directed at Bright. He doted on her quite blatantly, the other children having to content themselves with the odd word of praise. However, to Nat he was immensely kind, as indeed were all the Maguires. Even in the knowledge that he had no father, circumstances which seemed to damn him in others' eyes, they did not temper that kindness. Whatever they had, be it precious little, they shared with him.

'Come whenever it takes your fancy!' they told him, and so, instead of pacing the streets when his mother went to work he began to spend the better part of his evenings by the warmth of their black-leaded range. When Bright had merrily informed him that he would become immune to the stench of pigs he had disbelieved her. Now, however, the only smells he noticed were the comforting aromas of freshly baked bread or another of Mrs Maguire's excellent recipes. Even the smell of clean linen as it hung over the fire on a rainy day was an improvement to the lonely decay of his own home. At times, though, it could be a little intimidating; with five grown men in the house there was always the danger of a brawl when one of the sons made a stand against their father's rule. Even twelve-year-old Eugene and Patrick, eleven, seemed a lot older and rougher than Nat. Fortunately these episodes were rare and were soon brought under control by the womenfolk. More of an ordeal to Nat was their insistence that he join in their conversation. If only they would allow him to sit here quietly, watching and listening, all would be perfect, but no, it was questions, questions all the time until he hardly dared catch anyone's eye lest the encounter provoked another bout of interrogation.

Tonight, though, Nat was being spared, as it was the eldest son Michael who was their target. He had acquired a sweetheart who was also crammed into their midst, having to put up with a lot of joshing from his brothers. In the end, Michael sprang up. 'Is a man not allowed any peace with his intended without having to put up with this lot o' chattering magpies! Come on, Dettie, let's be going into the front parlour.'

'Aren't ye forgetting something?' Mrs Maguire barely glanced up from her knitting. 'Didn't Bernadette's mother say she had to be chaperoned?'

Michael groaned. 'Away then, Bright.'

'Oh sure! Take the most innocent one so's she won't know when you're doing anything ye shouldn't,' laughed Martin.

'Shut that or I'll gob ye!' warned his father.

'Ye can take Mary,' instructed Mrs Maguire.

'God Almighty,' heaved Michael as his sister complied. 'Won't I be glad to be away from this blessed place – and would the person responsible for that wretched stink get shut of it by the time I'm back!'

'Christ, if he isn't right,' muttered Mr Maguire as his son shut the door. 'I've been wondering all night if something's crawled in here and died.' He leaned over and sniffed at Granny Maguire.

'Tis Nat,' returned Gabriel, the second eldest.

Mrs Maguire scolded. 'Now that's not a very nice thing to say . . . are ye sure?'

'Aren't I sitting right next to him?' Gabriel took a theatrical sniff of Nat, who was crimson by now, then reeled away.

'Away over here, son.' Mrs Maguire beckoned. Reluctantly, Nat came to stand before her chair. She took a tentative sniff and made a face. 'God love us, tis right you are, Gabe.'

'It's the bacon,' mumbled Nat, shamefaced.

'What?' Mr Maguire was confounded.

Nat opened his shirt to reveal two fatty ends of bacon sewn into either side of the garment.

'Jesus, tis almost bloody putrid!' bawled Maguire. 'D . . . d . . . d . . ,' he stuttered and made frantic scissor movements with his fingers at his wife. 'Get rid of it, woman, else we'll all expire o' something horrible! For what does the silly b – why does your mother want to be doing a foolish thing like that?'

'To stop me getting a cough.' With the onset of the cold, damp weather Nat always suffered from bronchitis. Every year his mother adopted this remedy and never once had he known it to do anything other than make him even more unpopular than ever with his classmates.

'Stop ye getting a cough?' barked Maguire. 'Why, a few weeks o' wearing that and ye'd not catch anything – ye'd be dead from the smell.'

'Don't be taking it out on the lad,' said Mrs Maguire and, performing the delicate amputation, carried the bacon in outstretched hand to the fire.

'Don't put it on the fire, woman!'

'Dad wants it for breakfast!' Gabriel fell about laughing.

Every occupant of the room lurched away with hand over mouth, covering both laughter and revulsion as Mrs Maguire followed her husband's directive to, 'Stick it on the midden pile – preferably in the next street. Ah sorry, Nat!' Maguire reached out to pat the boy, who was highly offended by the episode. 'We meant no harm. Er . . .

45

Mother, have we a spare shirt the lad can wear till he goes home? Funny how smells linger, ain't it?'

'I'm off now.' Nat went to the door.

'There's no need!' Bright tried to prevent his departure. 'Ye barely smell at all now.'

'Nevertheless, I wouldn't go home through the Pig Market,' warned Gabriel, with as straight a face as he could muster. 'The pigs might complain.'

Bright lashed out at her nineteen-year-old brother, who accepted the beating with laughter then grabbed her in a bear hug and kissed her. She was still trying to wriggle free when the front door banged.

'Nat! Nat! Oh look, you've upset him now,' she scolded the lot of them, 'he can't help it if his mother made him wear it.'

'I wonder what he'll have inside his shirt the morrow,' mused her father. 'Pig's trotters, a necklace of chitterlings?' And everybody thought it was a huge joke except Bright.

'Poltroons all! I wouldn't blame Nat if he never came again – an' if he doesn't then I'll never forgive yese.'

'Don't fret,' vouched a cynical Martin. 'Your man knows when he's onto a good thing.'

Martin was wrong. Nat refused to visit the Maguires for many weeks after this. At first his failure to do so was due to being offended by people he had thought were true friends. He avoided the places where he knew he might run into the youngest Maguire daughter, for though she had not hurt him she would bombard him with questions that he did not want to answer. By the time his injured feelings had healed he had fallen prey to the December rains and was now in the full throes of bronchitis which, if true to form, would keep him indoors for a month. Too ill to object, he allowed his mother to tuck him up in bed where he remained for the duration of his illness.

'I don't like to leave you but I have to earn the money for

46

the doctor's bill and medicine and extra stuff you need.' Maria sat on the bed and pushed the hair back from his glistening brow. She had done the right thing and taken Nat to a doctor, for she knew from experience that to treat the malady herself would only prolong it and this had once brought him close to pneumonia. She did not wish to go through that again, though caring was expensive.

'Sorry.' The effort of that one word caused a bout of painful coughing which overtook his whole body. His eyes bulged and his face turned crimson as he tried to expectorate the filth from his lungs.

Maria looked both concerned and irritated at the same time. He had been barking all day and every day for weeks. There was only so much a mother could endure. 'Don't be silly, you can't help being ill.' She waited for the tremors to cease, then attempted a joke. 'Least it keeps you off school.'

Nat swallowed and gave a sickly grin, then closed his eyes, trying to keep his breathing shallow in order to prevent the coughing he knew annoyed her. For once he willed her to leave, for then he could cough and cough to his heart's content until the woman in the room below hammered on her ceiling with a broom handle.

'Here, let's sit you up a bit.' She lifted his thin body, banged at the pillow, then gave him a sip of water before lowering him again. 'Now, I'll have to go. Will you promise to remember your medicine at ten o'clock?' She pointed at the bottle on the table. He nodded. 'Right, well you're all set up, you've got your drink of water there and you're nice and warm . . .' The bed had been pulled up to the fire where a kettle was steaming to keep the atmosphere moist. 'I'd better take this off else it'll boil dry.' She took it from the fire and left it on the hearth. 'I'll put it back on when I come home. Now, you've got your poultice . . . what else? Oh yes!' She rushed to a shelf, took down a bottle of brandy and poured out a spoonful. 'There! That'll warm your cockles. Was a boy ever coddled so much? Now, I know I've said it half a dozen times but I definitely have to go. Be a good boy and I'll see you later.' She left him with a kiss.

Being ill did have its recompenses, a mother's kisses not the least of them. Apart from not having to attend school Nat had been spared Kendrew's visits of late. The boy's coughing had become such an irritation that Sep had taken to meeting Maria outside the house. Conscious of his new power, Nat maintained the cough long after his illness was past its worst, until Maria got wise to his artifice and instead of offering sympathy delivered a cuff round the head and the opinion that once the New Year arrived he would be well enough to return to his education.

Once again, when he returned from his trials and tribulations at school Nat had to endure the detested Kendrew. There was no other option than to fall back on the Maguires. Even though they had hurt him with their laughter their youngest daughter remained in his favour. Bright had not mocked him. One January night when his mother had gone to work he braved the freezing, slithery alleys and called upon his friend. Bright was the one who answered his knock and in her delight at seeing him threw wide the door. 'Tis Nat, everybody!'

'Well, for God's sake tell him to come in or piss off!' shouted Gabriel. 'But shut that bloody door!'

Nat was ushered down the passage just in time to witness Mr Maguire's retribution. 'Go wash out your filthy mouth! I'll have no foul talk under this roof.' He dealt the young man a blow to the head before spinning congenially on the visitor. 'Ah, if it isn't G-nat! We thought ye must've been off globe-trotting, hasn't it been so long an' all since we last saw ye.'

'I've been poorly.' Nat tried to edge his way through the crowded room to the fire.

'Oh dear, nothing contagious, I hope?' Mr Maguire

pulled out a rag and covered his mouth.

'I don't know.'

'Sure and Mr Maguire is only having a bit o' fun with ye, pet,' Bright's mother donated her serene smile. 'Cup o' tea, is it?'

'Aye, wouldn't mind.' Nat wriggled in between Eilleen and Mary who were making a rug, and perched on the fender to enjoy the heat from the fire.

'We had the notion we might see y'over Christmas,' remarked Mr Maguire, settling back into his chair.

'Oh, didn't we have a lovely party!' Bright grinned and sat on her father's knee. 'There's the decorations I made.' She indicated two paperchains that were strung, criss-crossed, from corner to corner of the room.

'Aye, they should be coming down.' Her mother eyed them and passed a mug of tea to the boy.

'Aw, just a wee bit longer,' pleaded Bright. 'Don't they look so pretty, Nat?'

Face hidden in the mug, Nat was thinking about the party he had missed. Guessing that his own birthday must be imminent, he swallowed the mouthful of tea and mused, 'We could make some for my birthday party.'

Bright clapped her hands. 'Ooh, are we all invited?'

'Course.'

'When is it?'

'Er . . . I'll have to find out.' He lowered his face into the mug again.

'You'd better take this up with your mother before inviting all these hooligans round,' warned Mrs Maguire.

Nat was adamant that there would be no difficulty. If he had already invited them his mother could hardly refuse.

The next morning before school he put forward what he thought to be an academic question. 'Can I have a party?'

'A what? You cannot!'

'But isn't it my birthday soon?'

Maria paused for thought. 'Aye, it's next Saturday, but nobody said anything about a party.'

'I've invited all my friends!'

'Then you'll just have to uninvite them. Here, eat your porridge – it's no good whining and looking all forlorn! I haven't the money to waste on fripperies.'

This was hard for Nat to grasp. The Maguires were obviously not rich but they always found the means to enjoy themselves.

His look of dejection pricked both conscience and temper. Maria had only yesterday bought herself two new dresses in town – after all, it was necessary to look nice in her line of work. 'It's all very well for them friends o' yours!' Nat had told Maria everything about the Maguires. 'They probably have half a dozen wages going into that house. No, I'm sorry but I just can't afford it what with having to fork out all that money on doctor's fees – think yourself lucky you've got a mother who puts her son's health before her own enjoyment.'

Nat was doomed to carry this excuse back to the Maguires. 'Me mam spent all her money on the doctor, you see. So I can't have a birthday.'

Spontaneous in their generosity, they declared that he should celebrate his birthday with them. 'And won't we give him a right old hooley!' promised Mr Maguire. 'D'ye know what a hooley is?'

'Yes,' lied Nat, unwilling to look a fool.

'Good, well when is your birthday?'

'Saturday.'

'Then, Master G-nat, come Saturday and you put on your best togs, present yourself at this establishment and the Maguires will give ye the best party ye never had!'

Nat assumed his mother would be delighted that he was to have a party after all and was taken aback by her terse response. 'They must think you're hard done by. I never had a party in me life and it never did me no harm.'

Bewildered, Nat did not raise the subject again and neither did Maria. Saturday began like any other Saturday. He and his mother rose late, went shopping and partook of the usual iced bun. When they returned in the late afternoon Kendrew was on the doorstep with a bunch of snowdrops and a lecherous grin. Nat did not linger. 'I'm off for me party now.'

Maria divested him of the shopping basket. 'Righto.'

'Party?' Sep looked amazed. 'Can we come?'

A moment of panic. Nat backed away. 'Er, no . . .'

Sep did not appear to be too worried. He stamped his feet against the cold and winked at Maria. 'Pity. We'll just have to make our own fun and games here.' And with a roar he chased Nat's mother into the house, slamming the door behind him.

Nat wasted no further thought on Kendrew. Having past experience of a Maguire party he enjoyed a thrill of anticipation as he hurried over Foss Bridge.

'Ah, the guest of honour's finally arrived!' At Nat's entry Mr Maguire sprang up. 'I hope you know we've postponed our bath night for this.' He pulled his own chair away from the table and directed Nat into it. 'Away over here, the important man always sits at the head of the table.' He himself shoved the youngest boys from the chair they were sharing, and they in turn displaced Bright from her seat. Mr Maguire planted her on his lap. 'Well now, and how are ye today, G-nat? Bitten any good people lately?'

Nat could never understand why Mr Maguire insisted on calling him this; he himself couldn't see anything amusing in it, though the rest of the family always sniggered. Squashed between two large bodies, he shook his head.

Mr Maguire laughed then clapped his hands at his wife. 'Come on then, woman! Get those victuals in. The wee midge hasn't had any blood to drink today, he's been saving up for this feast. Michael, light the lamp so's we can see what we're eating.'

Whilst the eldest son put a taper to the paraffin lamp, Mrs Maguire and her daughters brought in plates of food, only Bright being excused. She made a sound of appreciation as the food was laid out.

'Ooh, lovely! I'm absolutely ravished.'

The adults tittered and her father gave her a cuddle. Nat examined each face. Never had he seen one jot of resentment at this favouritism. Indeed, all were equally besotted with the youngest child.

Here at the head of the table he experienced an unaccustomed rush of importance and, all previous slights forgiven, he indulged ravenously of Mrs Maguire's excellent fayre whilst the others looked on amused.

Bright's mother remained standing to provide for the others. 'Nat, dear, would it be easier if ye rested your chin on the edge of the table and I were to scoop the whole lot into your mouth?' There was laughter.

Nat blushed and kept his gaze lowered.

'Ah, tis all right, pet, tis only teasing I am!' Mrs Maguire patted him. 'But there's enough for all, it isn't a race and you'll get pains in your stomach if you bolt your food like that.'

'Doesn't your mother feed ye?' asked Mr Maguire, popping a sliver of ham into Bright's mouth.

Nat was offended. 'Yes! This is just good, that's all.'

'Well, I'm glad you're enjoying it.' Mrs Maguire gave the signal for him to continue, which he did with no lessened enthusiasm. Only when everyone else was catered for did the hostess herself sit down.

Over the meal there was plenty of laughter and conversation, though Nat was not much of a participant. His ability to sit there quite contentedly without talking at all drove the garrulous Bright mad. She sneaked a look at her friend and wondered why he was so unappreciative; he had barely cracked a laugh, was hard-pressed even to answer a question, and seemed far too busy stuffing his face. She herself blessed her luck in having this family, with Mr Maguire such a liberal father. She had been in other households where there was no talking at mealtimes, no laughter when father was around. Oh, her own dad had a quick temper it was true, and there were times when even Bright knew to keep out of his way, but these outbursts soon died. She snuggled against his chest enjoying the closeness and wished Nat would show some gratitude. This she whispered to her mother when she helped to transport the pots to the scullery. 'After all the trouble we've been to! Ye'd think he'd be a bit more lively.'

Mrs Maguire gave a sad smile and explained, 'Nat has never learned to have fun, Bright. I suppose we must take a lot of getting used to for a boy with no family. Besides, ye don't have to shout and bawl like that lot o' jackdaws in there to show you're enjoying yourself. Nat is more your quiet man, I think.'

Bright laughed in acknowledgement of the understatement. 'But he hasn't said thank you – he never says thank you.'

Her mother clattered the pots into a stack. 'Do we give our friends hospitality just to hear them shower us with gratitude?'

Bright was taken aback – if ever she herself forgot to say thank you to anyone she was quickly reminded by one of her parents. 'No but . . .'

'We invite them here because we like them,' continued Mrs Maguire. 'Or are ye saying ye don't like Nat any more because he doesn't talk the legs off the chairs like you do yourself?'

Bright was rather annoyed that her mother could not understand what she was trying to say – Nat was her friend after all, not her mother's. 'Course I do!'

'Tell me now, what was it that ye first liked about him?'

Bright responded immediately. 'His bonny face.'

Mrs Maguire finished stacking the pots and looked

down her nose at the child. 'So, ye just wanted a friend with a pretty face, did ye?'

'No! I mean . . .' Rendered uncharacteristically tongue-tied, Bright could not explain what she meant. She did like Nat's face, not just because it was bonny, but also because of the way it looked at her, because of what was in his eyes, that air of loneliness that made her feel that she was his only friend, whilst she herself being popular had dozens. Despite the fact that his callow words often wounded her to the core, it was this quality which made her value his company more than that of any other acquaintance, drew her back even in the knowledge that she would be hurt again. But for a little girl of nine this was impossible to articulate. 'I just like him. He's not like a proper lad.'

'Quiet, ye mean?' Mrs Maguire gave a cryptic nod. 'Doesn't go round shouting and banging his chest – an' that's the very thing you're standing here complaining about!' She patted her daughter kindly. 'Let Nat enjoy himself the way he wants to, darlin' – tis his birthday party after all.'

A little wiser, Bright smiled back at her mother and went to collect more pots.

'Ye should've brought your mother with yese,' Mr Maguire was telling Nat, though it was not a genuine sentiment. He would have been horrified had such a woman turned up on his doorstep. The very fact that she had no husband labelled her unfit for decent folks to mix with.

'She's at work.' Nat, feeling replete, leaned back in his chair as Bright cleared away.

'The poor wee rascal,' said Mr Maguire in a private aside to Gabriel on his right. 'Doesn't deserve a slut like that for a mother. Come on now, G-nat, let's have you singing! What? Ye don't sing? Well, who's going to start us off?'

Gabriel, nineteen, launched into a song about an Irish martyr, the others joining in after the first line, their mournful combination almost lifting the ceiling off the hovel. Countless verses followed, then more songs and games. Alcohol was brought out for the adults, increasing the volume of their voices. With the last glimmer of daylight gone the paper blinds were drawn against the cold. The Maguires sang on, a sea of jolly faces in the glow of the fire.

Towards the end of the evening, when all were exhausted and flopped in their chairs, another voice took over. Granny Maguire suddenly withdrew her pipe and wailed a Gaelic lament that had Mr and Mrs Maguire crying and singing with her. When she had finished she stuck her pipe back between her black teeth and Nat never heard another peep out of her. Before saying goodnight to Nat, Mr Maguire presented him with a surprise gift: a tin whistle. Nat accepted it without thanks. Never having been the recipient of gifts he was untutored in voicing appreciation.

Bright, used to being the centre of attention within her family, was a little jealous of her friend tonight, especially as he did not even offer gratitude for the whistle – and she knew he did like it from the splendid noise he was creating as she accompanied him to the main street.

'I'll have to go back now.' She paused, shivering, outside The Three Cups and wrapped her shawl about her little body. The stars glimmered; there was a keen frost.

Nat's fingers, tacky from buns, continued to dance over the body of the whistle, producing the most horrendous shrieks. A passing drunk called, 'Is it a cat you're murtherin? Hold your din else ye'll be playing it out o' your arse!'

Giving a few last notes of defiance, Nat lowered the whistle and said, matter-of-factly to Bright, 'I'm going to marry you when I grow up.'

'You're not, then!' Bright showed great offence and with

a twirl of her shoulders made for home, feeling secretly very flattered.

'I am, then,' muttered Nat under his breath, adding a louder, 'Tara!' to which he received her response before scampering off for home.

Tonight, the darkness of Stonebow Lane was not quite so frightening as he tooted and shrieked on his whistle. He was soon climbing the stairs, eager to show his mother the gift they had given him. The parlour was empty when he entered. Ah yes — disappointment ruined the party mood — she'd be at her work. Spirits doused, he flopped at the table and propped up his chin in his hands.

Then a small noise from behind the curtain alerted him. His mother was in after all. Grinning, he put the whistle to his lips. To dubious musical accompaniment he burst through the curtain — and saw Kendrew lying next to his mother, his greasy repugnant head on Nat's side of the pillow.

'You don't come barging in like that!' Maria sat upright, a sheet clutched to her naked bosom, face pink with anger.

The whistle had fallen silent, poised in mid-air. Nat wanted to protest that it was his room too, but he could only gape at Kendrew's hairy torso. Deep in drink, the man was slow to come round, grunting and arching his back.

'Out!' ordered Maria. 'And take that noisy bloody pipe with you!'

Shocked and embarrassed into a daze, Nat backed away and let the curtain fall on them. Heart thumping, he felt the whistle in his hand and looked down at it. He was still in this pose when his mother appeared in a dressing gown. Sorry for the shock she must have inflicted, she wore an expression of remorse but did not know how to articulate this and instead offered a lame explanation. 'I thought I'd have a night off for a change. Sep took me out for a drink. Good party was it?'

Nat didn't answer, just kept twisting the whistle through

his hands. His mother looked down at it and, pulling her dressing gown over her sparrow-like breast against the cold asked, 'Who bought you that, then, your friend?'

He nodded, unable to speak.

'Very nice, too.' Maria feigned cheerfulness. Tightening her sash, she busied herself at the mirror, primping her hair. 'I'm glad you've got a friend, Nat. We all need someone to be our pal, don't we?'

'I don't.'

'Of course you do. Everybody does.'

Nat remained stubborn. 'Not me.'

'Argumentative!' With great difficulty, Maria contained her temper and made one last effort. 'Here, look, I've made you this jelly for your birthday.' She lifted the plate down from an otherwise empty shelf. 'Come and have a bit before you go to bed.'

'Don't want none.'

Maria uttered a sound of exasperation. 'This is all 'cause of Sep being here, isn't it?'

Nat grumbled into his chest. 'Don't like him.'

'Well you'll just have to get used to him!' His angry mother slammed the quivering jelly back onto the shelf. 'Because I like him, an' from now on he'll be living here.'

Nat was startled into looking at her. 'I don't want to sleep with him!'

'Don't worry, you won't have to!' Maria threw a blanket at the hard sofa. 'That's your bed, selfish!'

3

By the autumn of that same year, 1890, Nat's truancy had become chronic. The reasons were manifold: his hatred of school; the increased intimacy of his mother's relationship with Kendrew; the way Sep had adopted the role of father and kept trying to force him into going to school – which made Nat want to do the exact opposite. Who needed school with a teacher such as Bright? That's what Mr Maguire said. Where others had failed, this ten-year-old child had succeeded in teaching him to read quite fluently. He was now able to tackle the same books that Bright was given at school. His writing was not so good – Bright said this was because he insisted on using the wrong hand – but his arithmetical progress, though not remarkable, would at least enable him to get by in life without being shortchanged.

Another contribution towards his truancy was that the sofa had now become his permanent bed. It wasn't just the discomfort of the lumpy horsehair that kept him awake during the nights and thus made him oversleep in the mornings, but the even more uncomfortable thought that his mother was cuddling up to that hated man, warming him with her body through the cold nights as had once been Nat's privilege. The sense of rejection was overwhelming.

To aggravate this, Nat was no longer at liberty to follow his fancy. Kendrew did go out occasionally, but most evenings he'd sit by the hearth with a bottle of beer and a newspaper and Nat was forced to sit with him whilst Maria was out plying her trade. 'You're too fond of going where you please,' the man informed him. 'Your mother and me never know where you are.'

'Why should you care?' This was very daring for Nat, who normally confined his opposition to sullen looks.

'I *don't* care!' retorted Sep. 'But I'm damned if I'm being held responsible if you go out and get yourself murdered while under my supervision. You can sit there and lump it.'

Encouraged by the lack of physical punishment from the man, Nat pressed his case. 'Bright's expecting me to call round.'

Kendrew flicked his newspaper. 'Have you seen what it's like out there?' Fog swirled through the narrow, dingy streets. 'Anyway, don't you see enough of her at school?'

'She doesn't go to my school.'

'No, neither do you very often. Well you can see her after school, then. You are not going out and there's an end to it.' Nat mumbled something in reply. Sep cocked his ear. 'What did you say?'

'You're not my father.'

'I will be if I marry your mother.'

'You won't 'cause I already have a father, he's a prince,' boasted Nat.

Instead of making Kendrew angry it caused loud laughter. 'A prince, eh? I'd like to meet him.'

'He'd let me go out if he was here,' persisted Nat.

'Well, I won't, and until this prince appears I'm the boss!'

So Nat was compelled to sit there until it was time to get the blanket out of the cupboard and make up his bed. This act was always performed with the gravity of some funeral rite.

'I don't know why you kick up such a fuss about sleeping on t'sofa,' an exasperated Kendrew told the child after another grumpy performance at bedtime. 'You're far too big to be sleeping with your mother anyway.'

Nat wanted to retort that if he were judged to be too big

then how come Kendrew was allowed to sleep beside Maria? But he contented himself with one of those sad, reproachful looks at which he had become adept. He had found this the most effective way of dealing with the problem.

Being a man who liked to talk, Sep was most frustrated by these tactics. He vacated the sofa in order to let Nat have his bed and reseated himself on a wooden chair to take a final puff on his cigar before retiring. The child's long face and the way he dragged his feet proved too testing this eve. As Nat slouched past, Kendrew put his foot out and tripped him. Nat fell heavily, but cushioned by the blanket in his arms did not hurt himself.

'You want to try pickin' your feet up,' advised Sep. Tossing the cigar butt at the fire, he flung aside the curtain and undressed for bed. Anger kept him awake for a time. He had not yet resorted to violence with the boy but if Nat maintained this stupid resentment he wouldn't be able to stop himself. It was only out of fondness for Maria that he kept his hands off the wilful little pup. 'The Lord knows,' he had complained to her, 'any other boy in his position would be glad to have a father.'

He was still half awake when Maria slipped into bed beside him, making him jump with her cold feet. 'Sorry, I didn't mean to wake you.' She huddled under the blankets. 'It's bloody freezin' out there.'

Sep allowed her to thaw herself on him. 'You'll be pleased to learn they've got the bloke who murdered that lass. It was in tonight's paper.' At her sound of pleasure he added, 'Mindst, there was nearly manslaughter committed here while you were out.'

Maria groaned. 'What's he done now?'

'Nowt,' mumbled Sep, eyes still closed. 'That's just the point. It wouldn't make any difference if I had murdered him, it's like talking to a corpse at the best of times. He'll never like me.'

Though Maria had begun to share his irritation at her son's behaviour, she defended Nat from habit. 'Yes he will. Just give him a chance. He's bound to be jealous after having me all to himself for nine years.'

Sep put his warm arm around her and she melted into his embrace. Sometimes, after a particularly degrading night's work, Maria felt dead inside. It was lovely to come home to a kiss and a cuddle with Sep. He was a very demonstrative man. She herself had always found it hard to express affection, not having been shown any as a child. Until Sep came along she had rarely hugged Nat or told him she loved him – though the feeling was there inside her. Now Sep had helped to release that emotion and Nat was getting the benefit too. One would think this would make him happy, but he made it quite plain that he wasn't. However, these were early days; stubborn as Nat could be he must eventually yield to Sep's charm.

Maria's hope was in vain. In October she found herself in court again, explaining her repeated failure in sending Nat to school. Waiting alone in the corridor, the boy was terrified that his mother was to be sent to prison – the magistrate had seemed very harsh in his grilling of Nat. He was vastly relieved when she emerged from the courtroom without handcuffs, accompanied only by Sep.

'I swear I'll never do it again!' He ran to her and grabbed two bunches of her skirt. 'I'll go to school every day.'

His mother opened her mouth, but Kendrew spoke first. 'You won't have to – not to that one anyway. They're sending you to Industrial School for two years to teach you a lesson.'

'You didn't have to tell him like that!' An indignant Maria rounded on him, then turned back to watch the fear envelop her child's face. She immediately bent to comfort Nat. 'It's not as long as it sounds, love.' She rubbed his head reassuringly. 'And they might let you out earlier if you're very good.'

'Let me out . . .' Nat was stricken. 'You mean I have to stay there, sleep there?'

Maria gave a sympathetic nod and brushed at his wayward lock of hair with her fingers. 'But they say I can come and visit you.'

Sep couldn't help a cruel tweak in retaliation for all the times Nat had snubbed him. 'Well, you've done nowt but complain about sleeping on the sofa. This should make you realize how lucky you are.'

Nat's drained face was still aimed at his mother, who had shot a look of reproach at her companion. 'When do I have to go?'

Maria hesitated.

'They're coming for you on Sunday,' Kendrew informed him.

Nat reared his head. 'I don't want to go – Mam, tell him! Don't send me away.'

Maria gave Sep a pleading look. Angry at the boy for causing her pain, Kendrew led him out of earshot and bent his face close. 'You're going,' he said in a tone that was hushed but promised retribution, 'and you'll damn-well stay there till your time's up. And don't even think of running away before Sunday 'cause I'm not going to let you out of my sight, d'you hear? You're not going to your blessed Maguires or anywhere. Look at the shame you've brought on your mother, dragging her through the courts. The least you can do is take your medicine like a man and not a whining, spoilt little brat.'

Though he felt like crying, Nat straightened his shoulders in defiance and made no more complaint, not even on Sunday when the policeman came for him.

'Will they let me take my whistle with me?' His eyes were nervous as he looked up at his mother. She replied that she didn't see why not. 'And will you give my watch to Bright? I'll be too old for it when I come out.'

Her face collapsed. At this wan response, Nat allowed

himself to be led away. His mother attempted a half-hearted wave and bit her lip to prevent a flow of tears.

Sep laid a protective arm around her, saying, 'Nat'll be fine. This is just what he needs to show him how fortunate he is at home.'

The Industrial School for Boys was in Marygate, a street off Bootham on the northern side of the city. At its upper end stood a limestone tower and part of the ancient wall of St Mary's Abbey. A row of tall, narrow houses lined the slope to the River Ouse. Formerly, the school had been held in the old workhouse building but fifteen years ago this had been deemed obsolete and a new school was erected on the same site. The building was quite modern and well-equipped.

Three older boys were being admitted at the same time. Nat did not care for the look of them. On entering, each was divested of his possessions, though these were of no value. Nat wished now that he had entrusted his whistle to the safekeeping of his mother until he came home. He and the others were then ordered to remove their clothes, inspected for lice and given a cold bath. No uniform as such existed, but there was little variation in dress, the inmates' shirts and trousers being composed of the rough drab and grey beloved by institutions. Afterwards, their heads were shorn and a pungent liquid rubbed into their scalps before they were given to the charge of the matron who, dressed in a black bombazine dress and a little lace cap, marched them along a corridor that stank of disinfectant and cabbage with all the tenderness of a sergeant-major.

'Left, right, left, right – get in line, boys!' Her shoes clip-clopped behind them.

Some of the lotion that had been rubbed into Nat's scalp had trickled into his eyes and was burning like acid. His back and shoulders itched from the hair clippings that had fallen inside his shirt. He put a hand up to rake the irritation and was immediately told by the matron to, 'Stop scratching, boy!'

He turned and gave the large grey-haired woman a pathetic look. All it earned him was a cuff. 'Eyes front! Keep in time. Left-right, left-right!'

At the end of the corridor the matron curled her lip with its incipient moustache, barked, 'Halt!' and, with a tug of her starched white collar and cuffs opened a door on which a plaque announced that this was the office of the superintendent, Mr Raskelf. The latter had an air of great piety about him as he welcomed the boys in and told them to stand before his desk. Like the matron, he was grey-haired; also like her he had a moustache, but his was more walrus-like, completely covering his mouth, and was joined on to a beard that divided under his chin to form two long and rather bedraggled looking tufts. His nose was not large in itself but had a lumpy growth upon it like an under-ripe blackberry that held Nat's fascinated eye. Raskelf had been in the post for only a year and had had to tackle a great deal of unrest at the beginning. Boys had absconded by the half-dozen – as was quite usual with any change of superintendent. However after the recalcitrants had been captured and made to see that such behaviour would not be tolerated he had been able to establish his own brand of discipline, though this was based on Christian doctrine and not on tyranny. Raskelf considered himself to be very sparing of the rod compared to others.

Nat's eyes left the man's nose and examined the contents of the office. It was what he considered to be a rich person's room, with lots of shiny wood and brass. Around the walls, hanging on long cords from picture rails, were a number of portraits, one of them an elderly man with a beard. This was the founder, though of course Nat could not know and did not care. There were portraits of past and present managers, and one of the Queen, which reminded Nat of the classroom at his old school and immediately turned his mind even further against this establishment. The other frames held samplers of tapestry which spelled out potent messages: *Be Ever Cheerful, Obedient and Willing* . . . *The Devil Makes Work For Idle Hands*, and more ominously, *Prepare To Meet Thy God*.

Standing and clasping his hands behind his black frockcoat, the superintendent addressed Nat and his three companions in a rather simpering voice. 'It is understandable that you will wish to know a little about the place which will be your home for the next few years . . .' By the rules of the establishment, no boy was received for a term less than two years. 'You have already met my good wife, Mrs Raskelf, who is the matron here.' He indicated the woman who had overseen their admittance. 'We also have several officers . . .' He listed their names and departments. 'It is a lot for you to digest but I am sure you will soon become acquainted with them all. Besides yourselves, there are almost one hundred and twenty boys in residence, whose conduct gives me great satisfaction. I should like this happy state of affairs to continue. If you devote yourselves to hard work, be assiduous and cooperative in your lessons, and Christian in your outlook, then your period of detention will be a happy and informative one. You will also be rewarded with a fortnight's holiday in Scarborough in the summer.' His tone conveyed great magnanimity.

Then it changed. 'If, however, you choose to persist in your intransigent ways, are disrespectful to your officers and lax in self-discipline, then you can expect to reap the consequences.' He pinned each boy with a disapproving eye. 'I trust that there are no Roman Catholics amongst you?' This was usually ascertained before the boys' admittance but it had been known for a papist to slip through.

There followed the shaking of heads. 'Good. You shall

receive religious instruction every morning and evening and on Sundays you will attend church. As for secular instruction, this will consist of reading, spelling . . .' Nat groaned inwardly, '. . . writing and ciphering, with occasional lessons in geography and history, taught by our schoolmaster and mistress Mr and Mrs Screeton. This will take place after morning worship. For the most part, the remainder of the day will be dedicated to learning a trade that will be of benefit when you leave here. You will spend a short time in each department in order that we may assess your aptitude for any particular trade. Our departments are: turnering, shoemaking, tailoring and carpentry. You may on occasions be put to work in the garden or on general duties. You will have two hours recreational activity per day, which may include football and cricket, and it is our policy to teach every boy to swim. There could also be the opportunity to join the school band, of which we are very proud. There shall be no work on Sundays which is devoted to worship and religious instruction, some of which is undertaken by our Lady Visitors.' The simpering voice became more firm. 'Let me make it very clear now so that none of you is in any doubt: I will brook no impudence to our Ladies. If I find out that there has been one word of disrespect the culprit will receive the severest punishment that the rules permit. Parental visits will occur every two months. As the last one took place only recently then the next will be . . .' he peered at a calendar, 'ah, at Christmas!'

Nat received a jolt. Two months sounded an awfully long wait to see his mother.

Raskelf looked at the ceiling. 'Now, is there anything else you should know? Ah yes . . . Matron, would you be so kind as to excuse us for one moment?' Mrs Raskelf bowed her head and left the room. After she had gone, her husband spoke again to his audience, enunciating each word. 'Should an officer find any boy abusing himself there will be retribution not only from the officer but also from God. This accursed practice will not be tolerated. Not only does it contaminate the body but it also perverts the mind and if habituated will rot the brain.' After touring the row of innocent expressions his sternness receded. 'But I can see by your demeanour that you are not yet tainted. Let it remain so, and should any older boy attempt to lure you into this malpractice then you must come straight to me. Normally I do not encourage tittle-tattle, but this is a most serious offence and must be curbed.

'Last but not least, each boy is responsible for his own appearance and I expect him to be neatly turned out at all times. I understand that this is a new experience for you and you are bound to feel unsure. If you have any worries then Matron will be as a mother to you.'

The tick of the clock's brass pendulum had been the only thing to interrupt his flow; Raskelf looked at it now. 'You will be shown to your dormitories and allowed to settle in before the midday meal. I trust that all our future exchanges will be as civilized. What is your name, boy?'

He was looking at Nat, who answered in a quiet tone, 'Nat.'

'When you address myself or any other officer you will refer to me as sir. What is your surname?'

'Prince, sir.' Self-conscious, Nat attempted to bury his hands in his trouser pockets but found them sewn up.

The superintendent wrinkled his brow, then referred to a list on his desk. 'Prince . . . I do not seem to have anyone of that name. Each of you, recite your identity.' They did: Cobbins, Larkin and Dalby. The superintendent peered at Nat over the growth on his nose. 'Then you must be Smellie.' Nat waited for the inevitable sniggers.

'You think that is amusing?' Raskelf shouted at the boy who had dared to laugh.

'Yes, sir.' The culprit showed no remorse apart from tucking his chin into his chest in an attempt to muffle his laughter. He had dealt with tougher characters than this old bible-thumper.

The superintendent's voice was quiet again. 'Repeat your name.'

'Cobbins, sir.' The boy was about fourteen with large nostrils, an insolent air and a crop of pimples on his chin.

Raskelf's sibilant tone held a warning. 'Well, let me inform you, Cobbins, that I do not like people who mock their fellows – even those who are without sin, which I doubt applies to you. You had better watch out.' He looked down at his list, reading against Nat's entry, 'Mother: Maria Smellie. Father unknown. Why did you not give your correct name?'

Nat tried to entreat sympathy with his eyes. 'I don't like it, sir.'

'Well, like it or not that is the only name you have and you cannot change it on a whim. Lies will not be tolerated, Smellie. However, your name shall be no longer a handicap to you. Pay close attention to the number I am about to assign to each of you. Smellie, you are to be known as twenty-seven . . .'

After giving the other boys a number he turned back to Nat. 'Twenty-seven, open the door and ask Matron to step in.'

Nat readmitted Matron, who then marched the boys down to their dormitory – a stark, unwelcoming room. Of the twenty or so iron bedsteads she pointed out four, on each of which was a bare mattress, a pile of neatly folded bedlinen, a grubby pillow and a grey blanket. 'Make up your beds. I shall return to inspect them in five minutes.' In military fashion she left.

One of the boys immediately mimicked her, performing a marching salute between the row of beds. 'Do we have to call her sir an' all?'

The amusement was shared by number fifty-nine, alias Tom Larkin. 'D'yer fink she's ganna tack us in ternoight?

Oy, an' wha' aba' ol' Bramble Conk givin' us ve lecture about grapplin' wi' ve ol' middle leg! I bet 'e gets loads o' practice lookin' at 'is missus.' He grinned at Nat who, not understanding one word of the Cockney dialect, did not respond.

'What're you ven?' asked the older boy with a shove. 'A bleedin' dammy?'

'Don't know,' mumbled Nat.

Larkin guffawed. ''E don't know wha' a dammy is! He mast be wan!'

'Not just a dummy,' mocked Cobbins, 'but a smelly dummy!'

'Pooh, I'm not sleepin' next to him!' Laughing, they began to toss Nat's bedding all over the dormitory. When he tried to retrieve it they pulled it off him and attempted to throw it out of the window, but that was locked. Then the fourth boy warned that the old grey mare would be returning soon and a hurried bedmaking session ensued. When Matron Raskelf returned, poor Nat was still trying to stuff his pillow into its case. 'What! Not done yet?' Matron boxed his ears, grabbed the bedding and performed the feat in a few seconds, telling him, 'That is how it is done!'

There was some consolation in that each of the other boys got his ears boxed too for not having neat enough corners. Then, lobes burning, all were marched into another corridor where after a few moments of silence the entire male population of the world seemed to converge on Nat from every direction, a horde of shaven-headed, ring-wormed thugs. Terrified, he pressed his back into the tiled wall away from the herd of pigeon chests and knock-knees, hoping not to be noticed, but Matron handed him and the others into the care of the biggest, roughest-looking boy in the school, and so began the march to the dinner hall.

Here, like everywhere else, there was great military precision, each line of boys in turn collecting their plates and moving in clockwise fashion around the hall to the appropriate table. Nat just copied the others, whilst simultaneously keeping a shifty eye on his overlooker, number eight, previously known as Bowman. The youth resembled a bulldog standing on its hind legs, broad at chest and shoulder, tapering to narrow hips and short muscular legs. He sported the same cropped hair as the rest of them. His eyes were passionless, his neck thick, his lower jaw heavy and his upper lip dark with the beginnings of a moustache. To Nat he seemed huge, but in truth he was quite short and it was only his dedication to physical exercise that had put muscle on the stocky frame. Short or no, he looked formidable. His robustness was inconsistent with the rations: four ounces of compressed beef, two slices of bread and a mug of coffee. Nat was too nervous to eat and merely nibbled on a sliver of the beef. Bowman asked if he was going to leave the rest, and Nat barely had time to answer before the meat and bread was stuffed into Bowman's mouth, thereby explaining the paradox. With nothing on his plate to occupy him, Nat looked around at the other inmates who used a variety of accents. Apparently the school took boys from every corner of England. Very few of them appeared to be his age —some of them were much older and very tough, with the sunken eye that denotes innate villainy. The oldest in fact was sixteen and the youngest eight, but the average age of the institution was thirteen years and three months. Statistics didn't matter to Nat. He wanted to go home. His hand kept roaming over the stubble on his head.

Bowman was talking to one of the other newcomers, Cobbins. 'What're you in for, then?'

'Liftin' baccy,' provided Cobbins through a mouthful of beef.

The same question was asked of each. Dalby answered, 'I got thrown out on the street and were copped for bein' a vagrant.'

Larkin, like Cobbins, was a thief. Bowman turned his thuggish face on Nat. 'What about you?'

'I wouldn't go to school.'

The other new boys roared. 'A real criminal, ain't he!' scoffed the Cockney.

To his credit, Bowman defended Nat. 'Well, let's see how hard you are, plushskull, when Matron catches you tossing yourself off on a night and puts your goolies in the crusher.'

Larkin stopped leering and gawped. By means of a nudge, Bowman encouraged Nat to share the joke, but Nat, barely understanding anything that was being said, judged Bowman as bad if not worse than the rest.

'How come I'm number forty-six and he's twenty-seven?' demanded Cobbins, jabbing a thumb at Nat.

'There's nowt important attached to your number,' replied Bowman. 'Otherwise I'd be number one. They just give you the numbers of kids who've left.' There came a roar of, 'Silence!' which set Nat trembling, and the interrogation was curtailed for the time being.

Meal over, the same military precision as before eventuated in the clearance of tables and hall. Afterwards, the Lady Visitors mentioned by Mr Raskelf came to teach them the Scriptures. This lasted all afternoon and upon its end the boys were marched to tea. This time, though still churned up inside, Nat ate his bread ration and drank his cocoa.

In the evening the boys were permitted to associate quietly. Nat found himself amongst a fresh group of inmates whose first query was, 'What are you in for?' There was again derision when he said he was only here for truancy and he discovered that a larger percentage of his fellows were in for theft, the remainder having been detained for begging, frequenting, or simply because their parents were criminals. A few of the boys were here because they were deemed uncontrollable. Due to Mr

Raskelf's Christian discipline these were now impossible to pick out. For the rest, most chatted amiably to the newcomers and the atmosphere was quite relaxed until bedtime when tension returned as the boys were marched to their dormitories. Nat lay rigid in his narrow bed, not daring to go to sleep for fear that Matron might burst in and catch him in the unspeakable act that every boy seemed to know about except himself. What was this tossing off? How could he avoid it if he didn't know what it was? Thoughts of his mother produced the urge to cry, but he would not succumb; his peers held him in low enough esteem as it was. Thrusting his face into the pillow he squeezed his eyes shut.

Then, from the bed nearby, came a muffled sob. Nat turned his head to listen – Cobbins was crying! No, not just Cobbins, there were wet sniffles emerging from all corners of the dormitory. Encouraged, he allowed his own silent tears to flow, relieving the great lump in his throat, and shortly fell asleep to nightmares of Matron descending upon him with her goolie crusher.

It was still dark and bitterly cold when he was roused from his bed by number eight's voice the next morning. 'Rise and shine, tossers!' The bulldog prowled the dormitory, throwing blankets off and shaking ankles. 'Away. Larkin!' He poked at the Cockney. 'Get them slops emptied sharp.'

Larkin groaned and turned over. Bowman lifted the edge of his mattress, tipped him to the floor and dragged him towards the pail at the end of the dormitory that had served all the boys through the night. 'Last in gets the job!'

'I weren't the only one to come in yesterday!' objected Larkin.

Bowman grabbed him by the throat. 'Don't argue with me, chum, else I'll tip the piss on your head – now move!'

Taking it for granted that he would be obeyed, Bowman swaggered from the dormitory.

'Bastard!' spat Larkin. 'He needn't think I'm doin' that.' His puffy eyes looked for a stand-in. Nat, one leg into his trousers, felt Larkin's gaze fall on him and expediently averted his own, but it was too late; the Cockney grabbed him and shoved him in the direction of the bucket. 'That's more in your line, Smellie!'

Breeches around knees, Nat stumbled. Without defence he must do Larkin's bidding. Fumble-fingered, he managed to do up his trousers and bend over the pail, wrinkling his nose at the stink. Buckling under its weight and having no idea where to empty it he padded from the dormitory, looking to right and left. After a couple of wrong turns he saw another lad with a bucket descending a flight of stairs and, slopping the urine over the sides, Nat followed. Others performed tasks too, applying matches to fires and boilers, though the effects could not yet be appreciated; Nat's bare feet were mauve with cold. Pail emptied, he made his return. There was the rumble of much activity now. Boys started to teem from the dormitories. He tried to fight his way upstairs but found the route impassable. An officer came along, saw him standing motionless and lashed out at him. 'Look sharp, boy, or you'll be late for roll-call!'

Nat held up an arm to protect himself whilst trying to struggle upstairs through the tangle of bodies. The officer hailed Bowman. 'Number eight! You'll have to organize these new boys better than this!'

Observing Nat with the pail, Bowman narrowed his eyes and began to seek out Larkin. The Cockney was at the back of the queue. He saw Bowman waiting for him and hung back.

'Smellie!' Bowman hollered at Nat who had just managed to negotiate half the crowded staircase and now had to come down again. Bowman took the pail off him and crooked a finger at Larkin. 'Did you rinse it out, Smellie?'

Nat's heart fell. He was in for a beating. 'I didn't know I was meant to.'

'Doesn't matter today,' said Bowman, eyes fixed on the approaching Larkin. When the latter was before him, Bowman upturned the pail and rammed it upon the unfortunate Larkin's head. 'When I give you an order, plushskull, you do it! If I want Smellie to do a job I tell him myself. Now take that bucket back upstairs and every morning you have the job of emptying it till I say different – got that?' He thumped on the bucket to endorse this and made Larkin grope his way back upstairs with it still on his head. 'An' if you're late for prayers I'll break your legs.'

Unable to credit his luck, Nat was ordered to go and finish dressing, make his bed and join the others for roll-call and morning worship. Larkin managed to wriggle in just before the doors closed. From then on, there was no time for boredom. Every second of the day was accounted for, from breakfast to bedtime, and the merest insubordination was quashed instantly with a cuff. After morning worship came a vigorous drilling with dumbbells followed by a breakfast of oatmeal porridge, and then there were floors to be swabbed and woodwork to be polished. Nat was given the task of picking cinders from a pile of ashes to be used again. He was content to perform any job so long as it postponed that which he dreaded most – lessons.

On entering the schoolroom with its bare wooden floor and high ceiling he searched the rows of benches for a place that was inconspicuous. Alas, Mr Screeton was wise to the ways of the sluggard and dragged him to the very front bench. Nat resigned himself to the blows that would follow when Screeton discovered he was left-handed – a sin punishable by death in Lillywhite's book. However, Screeton was imbued with more patience than Lillywhite and apart from firm insistence that Nat should use his pen with his right hand, the morning, though wearisome, passed without violence.

At lunchtime Bowman made it plain that he wanted some of Nat's food. 'I look after you, don't I?' Ah, so that was the reason for his amity. Nat weighed the consequences of a refusal, and decided it was worth going hungry to have Bowman's protection.

In the afternoon, being a little young to be taught a trade, Nat was put to sweeping up after Bowman in the carpentry department. Contrary to his rough handling of Larkin, Bowman had a friendly nature for those who did not question his superiority and those such as Nat who catered for his large appetite. Nat could have liked him had he not given so many orders.

'You'll like Old Chippy,' said Bowman. Even this emerged as an order to the little boy, who swore to himself that he wouldn't. 'He's not so hard on the new blokes.' Nat was pushed into a room where the smell of cabbage and disinfectant was masked by that of timber. 'Lovely, in't it? Got a new one for you, Mr Chipchase! Twenty-seven, Smellie.' The name was still enough of a novelty to cause hilarity amongst the other boys.

Chipchase did not laugh, indeed he barely looked up from the piece of furniture he was examining. 'Come here and take a look at this, twenty-seven.' Unlike that of the superintendent the accent was Yorkshire and the tone pleasant, though his pleasure appeared to stem more from the furniture than the newcomer.

Bowman gave Nat a shove. The boy pursed his lips and approached the officer, a man in his fifties who, without an ounce of spare fat managed to appear somehow elephantine. This was largely due to the casual but deliberate movement of his limbs and the small brown eye in the creased cheek, an eye that had seen everything.

Chipchase presented an oak chest which one of the older pupils had made. 'This is what you can achieve if you put your heart into it. Look at these lines!' He removed a drawer and showed it to an indifferent Nat. 'See those joints? Exquisite!' He ran his fingers over them. 'Just like silk – feel.'

Nat went through the motions, unable to detect anything special – it was only a lump of wood.

Heaving with pleasure, Chipchase inserted the drawer. 'See how it glides! Oh, that all you boys could achieve such excellence instead of blighting my life with furniture that looks as if it's only fit to hold apples.' Chipchase, a thoughtful, moderate man, had entered the post with a view to helping life's unfortunates by imparting his passion for crafting wood, but fifteen years' experience had displaced zeal with cynicism. There were those here who neither wanted help nor indeed were worthy of it. At first he had despaired when they had not shared his passion, nor even the vaguest interest. Nowadays he wasn't sure he even cared any more, except perhaps on the rare occasion that one boy excelled with a piece of furniture-making worthy of a craftsman. With the rest it was just a case of there being boys he liked and boys he disliked. He wondered, though without great interest, which category Nat would fall into.

'Right! Well, there won't be much for you to do until the end of the lesson, twenty-seven. Just take that brush there and whenever you see a pile of chips start to grow, sweep them up. Now then, number eight, about this table you're making . . .'

Walking across the room he came to stand by Bowman's work. 'What did I tell you about fitting the legs?'

Bowman pondered for a moment. 'You said . . . the legs should look as if they've just grown there, Mr Chipchase.'

'Correct! However when I said they should look as if they'd grown there, I didn't necessarily mean like a bunch of bananas.'

Boys doubled over. There was laughter from all but Nat.

76

'Look at this!' Chipchase lifted the end of the table and waggled a leg. 'Call that a right angle!'

'I thought it might be useful for people who live on a hillside,' quipped Bowman.

Chipchase delivered a light blow to the youth's head. 'Please rectify the matter!' He glanced at Nat, who refused to smile. Here was a deep one, but the officer could not be bothered to probe him just now.

During the lesson Chipchase wandered around the classroom offering praise, criticism and advice. Stooping, he rescued an off-cut of wood from the pile that Nat was sweeping and threw it into a box. 'Too big to waste.'

'Aye, it'll make half a pair o' clogs for a mouse,' cut in Bowman.

'Less of your insolence, number eight,' Chipchase pointed.

'You can't bear any waste, can you, sir?' Bowman spoke for Nat's benefit. 'Only owt smaller than an inch square goes in the bin. It's a wonder he doesn't have us making patchwork quilts out o' wood.'

'You've been reading my mind. Except in your case it'll be a patchwork coffin. Come on now, back to work.' He turned to Nat. 'I trust you won't use number eight as an example of how to behave towards your officers?'

Nat mumbled a, 'No, sir,' but did not take up the friendly offer of conversation.

Despite the lack of communication Chipchase decided he liked the boy's face – not that it mattered what he thought. For here was one of the villains of tomorrow. It was all very well saying that a short sharp shock and a good dollop of Christianity would put them back on the right road and that might well be true about some, but this boy was not such a case. The lad was neither cocky nor disrespectful, nor was there that quiet insolence paraded by many; he would simply not respond to anything, neither beatings nor kindness. Chipchase had had great experience of boys like this. Nat was quiet and uncommunicative, but he had spirit that would buck against everything the authorities threw at him, regardless that they were trying to assist, viewing it only as punishment. He might not voice one word of defiance but defiance was there in the cut of his shoulders and in the slant of his mouth. Whilst other officers might try and beat number twenty-seven into submission Chipchase had little confidence in the effectiveness of violence. Though not averse to punishing the out and out thug in this mode, he preferred his own method of coping with boys such as Nat; if you wanted them to turn right you said turn left. Nevertheless he could not prevent a sigh as he watched Nat's half-hearted efforts to sweep up. It was going to be a hard two years for this boy.

After a week Nat's body had become attuned to the regime but his mind still rebelled. There was much for a small child to remember and Nat found plenty to confuse him. Whilst old Chippy's name fitted his occupation, the shoemaker was called Mr Taylor and the tailor was called Mr Boot. The drillmaster was called Baker and the cook was called Turner, whilst the head of the turnery department was called Carpenter. In the end, though, names were irrelevant. All were out to subjugate him – even the female officers were not to be trifled with – and Nat loathed everyone. The only person he did not hate was Bowman, but even he could infuriate Nat with his patronizing air. When Nat had summoned enough courage to ask the older boy what this 'goolie crusher' was, Bowman had looked down at him, laughed and said, 'I don't think you need worry about that.'

Nat did worry about it. He could not sleep through fear of it. It became his obsession to discover the nature of the offence which the superintendent termed 'that repulsive and sinful practice' but which the boys called 'tossing off', for he had the dreadful suspicion that he might already be guilty of it. Out of self-preservation, Nat was a lad who watched everyone and everything and during his careful surveillance he had noted that after the lights were turned out there was a lot of movement under certain areas of the blankets; even in the darkness he knew where that area was. His mother had once caught him with his hand there and had told him he was a naughty, dirty boy and he was never to let her catch him doing that again, and he hadn't – hadn't let her catch him.

It was quite a revelation to know that other boys did it too. At least he surmised that that was what they were doing. He could not be positive, for sometimes a boy would leave his bed and climb in with another boy and there would be all sorts of noises and groans, but then they would hardly be doing that in front of each other would they? He hated being in such ignorance. If only the lights were on.

However, the revelation was to come in broad daylight. He had been granted rare permission to visit the latrine during lesson time and hurried down the corridor to relieve his distended bladder. There was an outside door on the latrine building, but the doors on the cubicles had been removed in order to prevent sinful acts. When Nat entered he heard a voice. He would have ignored it but for its pleading tone. 'Oh please, do it for me, Merry.'

The voice was coming from the end cubicle. Nat held onto his water and crept along the row of stinking closets.

Another voice said, 'No, you'll tell.'

'I won't, I promise. Oh please, go on.'

Nat paused a while to listen on the other side of the partition. One of the voices came again in a low moan of euphoria. Unable to contain himself, Nat peeped round the corner and was so shocked that he let out a gasp. Merryfield's hand left Watson's flesh as if burned, whilst a red-faced Watson scrabbled to stuff his turgid member back into his breeches. Then, noting that it was only a younger boy, their fear turned to anger and they grabbed him, pushing his head down the pan.

'Swear you won't rat!'

Nat struggled and tried to escape.

'Swear!' repeated Watson.

How can I swear when my head's down here, thought an angry and terrified Nat, at which point Watson hauled at his collar and grimaced into his red face. 'Swear you won't talk or you go back in!'

'I swear!' coughed Nat.

'I'll make sure you don't!' Watson hauled Nat's trousers to his ankles, groped a cold hand between his legs and spat, 'If you ever say one word I'll sprag you to Matron and you know what that means!' He gave the boy's genitals a vicious squeeze just to emphasize his threat.

'Ow! I promise!' squealed Nat, and half in fear, half in retribution let his bladder run free.

'You dirty swine!' Watson withdrew his contaminated hand which he used to slap Nat's face before hurrying away with his partner in crime, leaving Nat to mop up the puddle.

They watched him warily for a few days, terrified that he was going to tell. Despite the hazard this posed, it gave Nat an unaccustomed feeling of power. In fact he felt brave enough to risk Matron's wrath with a sinful act of his own. But afterwards such guilt! Would anyone be able to tell? When he entered assembly he felt that all eyes were upon him. All through the Lord's Prayer his glance flicked furtively from side to side, but retribution did not come. After prayers, Mr Raskelf made his usual morning speech. Lulled by the pious drone, Nat's mind dwelled in his loins. Lots of things now fitted into place. He had often wondered why every pair of trousers had its pockets sewn up — had imagined that it was to prevent slovenliness. It made him grin to be conversant with the true reason. Ooh, it was lovely; he couldn't wait to do it again.

'. . . And now it is my duty to perform a sad task.' The change of Raskelf's tone jerked Nat from his dream. All ears pricked up. There was going to be a punishment. 'Last evening, when all good boys were sound asleep, the most dastardly act occurred. Mr Screeton visited one of the dormitories and discovered that we have among us a most repulsive character . . .'

Nat tensed. A nerve started to twitch in his buttocks.

'In his abhorrent practice he defiles not just the body which the good Lord created in His own image, but the innocent minds around him . . .'

Nat felt sick. His thighs quivered. He badly needed to go to the closet. Glancing to his right he saw sheer terror on the faces of Watson and Merryfield.

'I would not soil my tongue further, we are all aware of his sin. So, let him come forth and receive his punishment. The most disgusting, the most vile boy in the school . . . one-one-five.'

Nat almost wet himself with relief, as did numerous others. Yet in a moment he tensed again, this time with excitement as he strained on tiptoe for a better sight of one-one-five's goolies being mangled in Matron's instrument of torture. It was almost disappointing to witness the receipt of six strokes of the birch, though encouraging to know that the goolie crusher was a mere invention by Bowman to frighten the new boys. With only a beating as a threat he felt quite happy to risk his nightly thrill.

Having tasted the birch themselves, Watson and Merryfield were not so cool and still watched Nat like hawks, fearing betrayal. Occasionally he would enjoy making them squirm by pretending to approach a master, then veering away at the last minute. Watson tried to buy him off with the loan of a special key that would open any door. It just looked like a bit of bent metal to Nat, but Watson demonstrated by gaining entry to the food store and providing him with a slice of Matron's ham.

Merryfield shared his knowledge too, as did others. Nat was to learn all about life and survival and sex. Indeed he was to learn many things during his confinement here, most of them illegal.

He was happy to suck on their knowledge but gave no friendship in return. The only one to whom he warmed was Bowman, who would always defend him when others taunted; this and the way Bowman talked quite frankly to him, doubly made up for the way the older boy ordered him around. Nat started to copy Bowman's movements, to walk like him, repeat his phrases, dream that Bowman was his father.

Today, as at every opportunity, he clung to the youth's side as he and a party of boys were led down Marygate to the swimming and shower baths on Esplanade. There was an air of excitement. Old Bramble Conk had promised that those who could not swim would be able to do so when they returned for lunch. In this expectation, Nat strode out beside his friend, bouncing off the soles of his feet in the manner of the older boy.

'Looking forward to being able to swim, Nat?' Bowman rarely used the boy's surname, knowing how offensive it was to its owner. Only when Nat annoyed him did he resort to it.

Nat responded with eagerness. 'Aye! Can I be in your group?'

Bowman had been assigned to help with tuition. 'If you like.'

They had reached the end of Marygate and entered the baths, whose doors had been closed to the public at the end of the summer but as it was not yet frosty were opened occasionally to the inmates of the Industrial School. Bowman gave instructions to his group. 'Get changed, no dirty business, and come straight out again.'

Nat and the others piled into the changing rooms and disrobed. Naked, he felt more vulnerable than ever amongst those who were his enemies and changed very quickly. Even so he had time enough to compare the other boys' genitals with his own. One of them caught him looking. 'What's up, d'you fancy some o' this, Smellie?' The boy grasped himself pointedly. Nat tried to leave but a mêlée ensued whence he was grabbed and nipped in the most indelicate manner until Bowman, hearing his squeals, bawled into the changing room, 'Come out now!'

Nat was last to emerge as the others barged and punched their way past him. Bowman sighed and shook his head. 'I don't know what you're gonna do without me to protect you. I'm off tomorrow, you know.'

Nat stood shivering and nonplussed. 'Off where?'

'Into the Navy – my time's up.' And with this he picked up Nat and threw him into the pool.

There was a splash, the water closed over his face, then silence as he plummeted to the tiles below . . . and there he remained for interminable seconds. The devastation of losing his only male friend was replaced by terror. Nothing was happening! He was going to die down here! Air seeped from the corners of his mouth and bubbled its way to the surface. Frantic, Nat pushed his heels against the tiles and by some miracle found himself rising, but the surface was miles away, he would never reach it before he drew breath! His lungs felt about to explode as he burst through the barrier to loud instruction from Bowman. 'Now move your arms like this!'

Nat panicked and lashed about wildly.

'Stop panicking.' Bowman was firm. 'Be calm. I won't let you drown. Just move your arms slowly like this and paddle with your legs. That's right! Not so fast now . . . good. There you are, you can swim – next!'

Nat realized through his terror that he was still afloat, though now he became aware of just how cold the water was too. Keeping up the arm movements he gradually made his way to the side of the pool where he clung to a rail and gasped for breath, chin juddering. 'Well done,' said Bowman, and calmly dunked another reluctant candidate.

Later, when he walked back to the school with damp clothes and chafed groin, Nat questioned Bowman. 'Are you really going in t'Navy?'

'That's right. I'm off to sail around the world, me hearty. S'pose you'll be gone by the time I get back.'

'Do you mean you get sent back in here after you've been in t'Navy?'

The pugnacious face cracked. 'No, clot! I meant I'll just come visiting from time to time, see how the officers are faring an' that.'

Nat found this incomprehensible. 'What d'you want to come and see them for?'

Bowman chuckled. 'They're not bad blokes. Well, most of 'em. Good or bad they're the only family I've got. I never learned anything till I came here.'

Number eight had never spoken of his past and Nat, though curious, had been too nervous to probe. It was too late now. 'They can't learn me owt,' he retorted.

'That's obvious,' came the sarcastic observation. 'You're too cocksure for your own good. With an attitude like that you'll just finish this stretch and get bunged up for another.'

'I won't,' declared Nat, and repeated the thought to himself the next day when, with a sense of loss, he witnessed the ceremony of Bowman's proud departure and watched his friend shaking hands with the masters whom he himself loathed. I won't ever be sent back here. I won't ever like the masters and they won't tell me what to do, never ever.

4

Life after Bowman left was dreadfully lonely for a time, not to mention dangerous. With his protector gone, Nat fell prey to Larkin who terrorized him at every opportunity during the following week. The longest week of his life. As yet, no one had filled Bowman's role as supremo – though there were many candidates – and this left the way open for Nat's oppressor to do as he liked. He leaned over the table now, inserted his fork into Nat's sausage and transferred it to his own plate. Nat glared ineffectively, then resigned himself to eating the lonely pile of mashed potato before someone could steal that too.

'Hang on!' A boy seated lower down the table espied the theft. He began to clamber over the bench and made towards Larkin.

'Sit down that boy!'

The order was ignored. Keighley, a fifteen-year-old with fluff on his chin but determination in his eye, prowled up to stand over Larkin. Without explanation he grabbed the sausage from Larkin's plate.

'Oy, that's mine!' Larkin scissored his legs over the bench and confronted the other.

'No it isn't – you just pinched it off him, and now I'm pinching it off you!' Keighley held onto his prize. Larkin tried to retrieve it.

'What is going on up there?' Mr Raskelf's walrus face peered down the hall, then called to the officer nearest to the incident. 'Mr Chipchase, please be so good as to sort out the disturbance.'

Chipchase hated these anarchistic episodes, which

always ended with injury, usually his own. He went slowly in the hope that it would have sorted itself out by the time he arrived, adopting a conciliatory air. 'Now, now, boys! Settle down.'

Keighley defended his action. 'Sir, he's got two sausages and I've only got one little un! It's not fair.' Younger boys were now in fits of laughter at the dialogue.

'How come you've got two?' asked Chipchase. Then spotted Nat's bare plate. 'Where's your sausage, twenty-seven?'

Larkin jumped in. 'He's eaten it, sir! Haven't you, Smellie?'

Nat was to be championed. 'I don't believe you,' replied the officer and turned to Keighley. 'Put it back on twenty-seven's plate.'

'But, sir, he's only little, he doesn't need a whacking great sausage like that – look at the totty one I've got!'

Keighley ran to his own plate and brandished his sausage in the air, comparing the two.

'I refuse to stand here with a tape measure whilst my own dinner goes cold,' sighed Chipchase. 'Just give him one of the sausages – and fifty-nine, I'll see you later.' Larkin glowered.

A triumphant Keighley put the inferior sausage on Nat's plate, yet once the officer's back was turned he snatched it up, grinning, and carried it to his own plate. But the episode had sparked unrest and the moment he sat down to eat, another boy grabbed the extra sausage, and just as quickly another boy tried his hand, then another and another. The battle for supremacy had begun.

'Mr Chipchase, I thought I asked you to deal with the matter,' objected Mr Raskelf as punches began to fly. 'Please attend to it straightaway!'

Chipchase had had a difficult morning and now risked sarcasm. 'Yes, Headmaster, what would you like me to do

– write a stiff letter to the butcher insisting that in future he makes all his sausages an identical length?'

Luckily, Raskelf did not hear this due to the commotion that had erupted into an out and out brawl, involving almost every boy in the school. 'Go and call for reinforcements! Fetch a weapon! I want every officer here right now!'

'Yes, sir,' muttered Chipchase. 'Every man on deck – shall I summon the cavalry too?' Ever calm, he made for the nearest exit, having no need to inform anyone for the noise of the riot had alerted officers all over the building and now they came running with cudgels, straps and whatever they could lay their hands on. 'Ah well, they won't require my humble assistance, will they?' smiled Chipchase, and taking the precaution of locking the doors of the dinner hall behind him, he retired to his carpentry room for a smoke until the distasteful episode was over.

Nat and fellow weaklings showed similar expedience and fled to the edges of the hall, where they watched with excitement as the battle for leadership ensued with plates being thrown, benches and dinner-tables being upturned, table legs being wrenched off and used as weapons, blood and mashed potato splattering the polished floor and as many sausages as the audience could eat, before an army of officers waded into the affray wielding blows to shaven heads and delivering broken bones and bleeding flesh until the wrecked hall was finally called to order.

Somehow, there emerged a victor. At the end of the day when the main perpetrators had been thrashed or carried off to the medical bay, word spread that Keighley had taken over Bowman's leadership. Nat did not know how the vote had been arrived at and cared even less. Keighley had another year to serve. With the barter of food Nat could buy protection against Larkin. For another year he would be hungry but safe from assault.

Safe maybe, but never happy. For all he abominated the

vigorous weekday regime, it did at least keep his mind occupied. Sunday was a time of depressing boredom, a time to wallow in the acute loneliness of imprisonment. No one, not even his mother, had told him they loved him, but with her he had at least felt loved. Here there was nothing. He was just number twenty-seven. A no-nowt.

The weather grew colder. Ice formed on the dormitory windows. Nat got chilblains on his toes and fingers, which drove him mad with their itching; even worse were the ones on his heels that split open and crippled him so badly that he wept when he put his feet to the floor in the mornings. Matron smeared ointment on them but ironically they only improved when Nat fell ill with bronchitis and was moved to a warm medical bay for three weeks.

During the run up to Yuletide Nat felt a new kind of tension amongst the boys, a sense of impending explosion, a feeling of being watched even more closely by the officers. Nervously expecting a riot, he was not to know that it was always this way in the weeks before visiting day – especially at Christmas with all its added pleasures. Any misdemeanour could spell a withdrawal of these benefits, no one was going to risk that, hence the air of apprehension. Informed as to its cause, Nat became infected with nervous excitement. The last few days before visiting day were almost unbearably anxious. He had not seen his mother for two months. Was she still under Kendrew's wicked spell? What if Kendrew accompanied her? What if the man prevented her from visiting Nat at all?

Christmas finally arrived. In material terms Nat had a better time of it here than at home, there being several legacies from rich old ladies of fruit, plum puddings, money and sweets. Marvellous though all of this might be it was surpassed by the appearance of his mother's tearful face at visiting time – and, most importantly, she had come alone. Nat was too overjoyed to ask why Kendrew had not accompanied her, and wriggled delightedly in his seat.

Their discourse began awkwardly at first, with her asking was he all right several times and did he get enough to eat, Nat answering both with a yes. With his last response, silence fell between them, both perched there uncomfortably, looking round at the other visitors. Then Maria said again, 'So . . . you're all right then?' At his nod she laughed. 'Listen to us. You'd think we'd have loads to say after two months wouldn't you? Still, you never were much of a talker – come on then, tell me what sort of things they have you doing.'

He shrugged. ''Part from the work it's the same as ordinary school: sums, reading . . .'

She groaned. 'Well, I hope they don't clout you too much.'

'I haven't been clouted at all. Not by the masters.'

'Oh, we can't have that,' joked his mother. 'Come here and I'll belt you one!'

Nat was forced to laugh and after this perked up enough to tell her more about the school and its inmates. She asked him to point out which boys he liked. Nat replied that he didn't like any of them. Maria's heart went out to her son, and she changed the subject. In no time at all the visiting period was over. With the call for everyone to leave, Maria tucked her scarf into her coat and made to rise. 'Well, I suppose I'd better . . .'

Nat panicked. 'Don't go!'

Maria's stoical expression collapsed. 'Aw Natty, don't make it worse . . .'

But he clawed at her arm. 'Don't leave me, Mam!'

Mr Chipchase, who governed visiting, spotted the difficulty and came over. 'Come on now, twenty-seven, your mother will be coming again soon.'

No, not soon! It would be two whole months before he was allowed another visit. He clung onto his mother's shawl as she tried to depart, begging her, 'Please, please don't leave me!'

Chipchase tried to prise Nat's fingers from the cloth but each time he uncurled one the others dug deeper.

'Twenty-seven, you'll earn yourself a punishment,' he warned.

'Eh, he has got a name you know!' objected Maria, then begged her son, 'Nat, let go! You'll only make it harder on yourself.'

At his mother's entreaties, Nat finally released her. After she had gone, the little boy was overcome by a depression that kept him awake all night and continued into the next day. Even with his hands occupied he felt it controlling him. He was in the chip shop collecting the oddments of wood when the impulse eventually took him. Quite calmly, he laid the piece of wood that he was holding in a box and asked Mr Chipchase if he might be excused to go to the closet. The officer being a lenient sort, permission was granted.

There was one cubicle with a small window. Nat balanced on the lavatory, tried to open the sash, then heard a steady tapping and looked over his shoulder. Mr Chipchase was leaning against the wall, tapping out a code with his carpenter's pencil.

'I shouldn't bother, lad – it's nailed up.'

Nat slumped. He gave up trying to force the window and jumped down from the lavatory seat.

'I've been watching your face since your mother visited,' explained Mr Chipchase, still toying with his pencil. 'If you knew how many times I've seen that expression . . .' He shook his head in a weary manner and summoned Nat out of the cubicle.

Nat met him with an air of persecution. The officer leaned forward and touched his shoulder with the pencil. 'You ought to be thanking me, lad, not hating me. I've just saved you a beating. You think it's hard now but you'll

90

make it ten times harder for yourself if you choose this path. They'll catch you and fetch you back and birch you and then you'll be singled out as a troublemaker.'

What do you know? Nat refused to look at him, sulking.

Chipchase straightened himself and replaced the pencil in the top pocket of his apron. 'I won't mention this to the superintendent but I want you to give me your word that you won't try to escape again. Do you promise?'

'Yes, sir.' Nat hung his head.

'Right, back to the workroom and we'll say no more.'

Nat went meekly, but was now even more determined to escape. However, he withheld further attempts for the time being. Although Chipchase had not publicized his break for freedom, he himself remained vigilant and Nat was left in no doubt as to his surveillance. He was not even permitted to go to the latrines alone. There was no chance of escaping by night for every door and window was locked, but Nat bided his time and pretended that he had settled down.

January brought an overnight flurry of snow. When, after breakfast, it ceased to fall, a contingent of boys was sent to clear the footpaths. Nat, having been judged after this period of time by Officer Chipchase to be no longer a risk, was amongst them. The work proceeded well at first, until the boys could no longer resist the lure and a snowball fight ensued. Nat saw his chance. When the officer in charge went to intervene, Nat dropped his wooden clearing implement and slipped away.

Familiar with most of the city's streets, he went directly home, leaving a trail of melting snow on the brown linoleum as he climbed the stairs. There was no one in the parlour. Should he pull aside the curtain and see if his mother was in bed? Would Kendrew be there? On tiptoe he picked up an edge of the curtain and peeped round it. His mother was alone and fast asleep. Relief forced his breath out. Maybe Kendrew was gone. She did not wake. He hovered at the bedside wondering whether to shake her. No, she would be angry. He remained there just looking at her. His concentrated gaze pierced Maria's slumber. Her eyelashes fluttered, lifted, then lowered again – then flew open and she screamed.

'Oh, Nat!' For a moment she could only gasp, clutching at her heart which was thudding like a sledgehammer. Then she railed at him. 'What the devil are you doing here? You nearly gave me a bloody seizure!' With a cry of frustration she pulled him to her and gave him a hug and a kiss before thrusting him away so that she could get out of bed.

'What did you run away for?' Shuddering at the cold room, she hurried to put on a dressing gown and tied the sash. 'I thought it wasn't too bad.'

'I missed you.'

He looked so forlorn that she came to hug him again and urged him towards the fire which she stoked and stabbed with a poker, gave him a cup of tea and a biscuit, and demanded to know the whole story.

With a midday meal on offer he was just beginning to think all was well, when the door opened and Kendrew came in shaking the snow off his hat. His hand paused in mid-air when he saw Nat. 'What the hell is he doing here?'

Maria approached him like a fawning dog on its belly. 'He's just run away because he missed me, Sep.'

Kendrew did not empathize. 'You damned fool!' He banged his hat against his leg. 'You'll get done for harbouring him. And it's not going to do him any good, is it? The longer he's absent the worse the punishment when he goes back – and he will have to go, love, there's no question of that. This'll be the first place they'll come.'

With a heavy heart Maria agreed and turned to Nat, 'Sep's right, son. We won't be able to hide you.'

Nat pressed himself into the chair and beseeched her

with grave eyes, while Kendrew rammed his hat back on and came towards him. 'If we take him back now it might help his case, rather than the authorities having to come for him.'

'Oh, I couldn't bear it, Sep.' Maria clutched her cheek. 'You do it.'

'See what you've done to your mother again!' demanded Kendrew, grabbing Nat's hand. 'You blasted nuisance, I suppose me dinner'll have to wait. Come on, let's have you back where you belong.'

'You must consider yourself very fortunate indeed that Mr Chipchase has spoken up for you,' the superintendent informed Nat after Kendrew had deposited him and left. 'A runaway would normally earn very stiff punishment . . . but I am ready to accept Mr Chipchase's defence that you were unsettled by your mother's visit and agree with him that she should not come again until you are more stable in your ways.'

Unmindful of Chipchase's help, Nat raged inwardly at the discipline; but this was not the full extent of it.

'Furtherto, you will be confined for two days and forfeit all privileges,' added Raskelf.

Too late for lunch, Nat was marched along to a small room in which was a bed, a table, a jug and bowl of water and a chamberpot. His sole occupation in the next forty-eight hours was to pick oakum. The only time he was let out was to empty the chamberpot. During his confinement he reached the end of his tenth year. His birthday passed unmarked.

Far from being a deterrent, the punishment only served to bolster Nat's resolve, though it was not until Good Friday that he made his move. The boys attended a church service at St Olave's. Afterwards, as the others filed out, Nat dawdled at the rear, then when the master in charge looked away he ducked to the floor behind one of the pews, escaping later when all was quiet. This time he did not go straight home but went to lean against Foss Bridge, not quite knowing what to do or where to go. With the shops closed for Good Friday the street scene was tranquil.

He felt that he had been dallying there for ages when a voice said, 'Hello! Where've you been hiding?' He looked round into Bright's smiling face – a much changed face from the one he had last seen six months ago. The gaps in her smile were in a different place now. Her front teeth were fully grown but one of her adult incisors was as yet a white stump on the gum, and her freckles had faded during the winter months. Her hair, though, was the same, an untidy bright cape hanging around her shoulders, its ribbon half undone.

'I haven't been hiding.' Looking cross, he turned back to the bridge and there rested his brow.

Bright leaned on the stone too, pressing her hands against the balusters as if trying to push it down. 'I didn't know you with your hair like that. Where've you been? I haven't seen you for a long time.'

'I've been away.'

'Where?'

'Don't be so nosey.'

'Tut! That's not very nice after we gave you a birthday party, is it?' objected Bright. 'I don't know why I bother with ye.'

'Don't then.'

'I won't then!' Offended, Bright pushed herself upright and walked backwards.

Angry at his own impulsiveness and desperate for her to stay, Nat blurted without looking at her, 'I've run away.'

She returned in fairysteps, to ask for details. He told her as briefly as he could about his incarceration at the school. 'Was it them who cut your hair off?' She didn't like his crop. 'It makes ye look . . . obstroculous. Where y'off now then?'

'I can't go home 'cause that Sep'll be there. He'll send me back again. He did it once before.'

'Isn't he horrible!' spat Bright with feeling. 'Ye can come home with me if ye like.'

Nat turned a hopeful eye on her. 'Are you off for your dinner?'

'No, I've had it – but me mam'll let ye stop in our house for a bit.'

With no meal on offer, Nat didn't really want to go with her for there would be questions – there were always questions at the Maguire house – but Bright hauled him in after her. The house stank of fish and with all the clan assembled it was difficult even for a small child to squeeze in. Nat cast a hopeful eye at the table, but all it bore was a jam jar full of daffodils.

'Why good day to you, young G-nat!' cried Mr Maguire from his place at the table. 'And where've you been hiding yourself?'

Still as shy as ever in the company of adults, Nat was not quick with his response. Bright answered for him. 'He hasn't been hiding, he's been away.' She went to sit at her grandmother's feet.

Mr Maguire had undone the top button of his trousers to accommodate his dinner. 'Away – where?'

Nat looked at Bright who provided, 'At school.'

'And what sort of a school is it where they don't let y'out to see your pals and cut your hair with a lawn-mower?'

Nat spoke for himself at last, rubbing his head self-consciously. 'I wouldn't go to ordinary school so they made me go to this special one where I have to live.'

'So they let y'out today, then?' Mr Maguire saw the change on Nat's face. 'Ah, ye've took it upon yourself to have a day off.' After a moment he gave a dismissive wave. 'Ah sure, I don't blame ye. School's rubbish, aren't I always sayin' that?'

'You are,' endorsed Mrs Maguire, drying the dinnerpots with the aid of Eilleen and Mary.

Nat was pleasantly surprised at the lack of condemnation and was encouraged to admit, 'I've run away. I ran away in winter but me mam sent me back. That's why I haven't been to see you for a while.'

'An' what sort of a woman would have her own child locked up?' demanded Mr Maguire, and stepped over Patrick and Eugene on the hearth rug to reach Granny's tobacco.

Nat was quick to defend. 'She didn't want to. It's this man she knows, he made her send me back and now they won't let her come and visit me.'

'The scoundrels!' Mr Maguire sat down again and proceeded to fill the old lady's pipe. 'Ah well, if ye can't go home then ye must stay here.'

A rather nervous Mrs Maguire pointed out, 'Tommy, we'll get into trouble with the law.'

'Bedamned the law! I'm the law in this house an' if I say our young friend stays then stay he will. He can sleep in one of the boys' beds — isn't himself getting wed soon.' He nodded at Michael who was reclined on the sofa with two of his brothers.

'Oh no, we're not having three to a bed again!' Gabriel and Martin had been looking forward to their brother's departure.

'Get yourself a wife an' ye won't have to,' replied his father, and lit the pipe for Granny.

'Sure, don't be wanting rid o' them too!' cried Mrs Maguire. ''Twill be bad enough coping without Michael's wage.'

'He's not sleeping with us!' chorused Pat and Eugene.

Mr Maguire kicked at the nearest buttock. 'Shut your gob and get the mother a cup o' tea!' He handed Granny the pipe.

The objections continued until Bright stepped in to

96

mediate. 'We've a nice rug on the floor of our room, Nat could sleep on that.'

'God love her!' Michael bent over and swung his ten-year-old sister over his shoulder, laughing. 'The things she comes out with.'

'What's wrong with that?' Bright squirmed at the rough bristles on his chin as he kissed her and set her down.

'Never you mind!' Mr Maguire wagged a finger. 'Nat can sleep on the rug in the boys' room.'

Gabriel stood and hitched up his trousers. 'I think I'll away and make a start on finding that wife.'

'Just make sure you're back in time for the Easter Vigil this afternoon,' warned his mother.

Nat was to discover that the Maguires went to church an awful lot – they must have gone half a dozen times over the weekend and he was dragged with them. Though he didn't understand one bit of the ritual he quite enjoyed watching Bright take part in the Easter procession through the mean little streets, dressed in her white frock and veil, carrying a bunch of spring flowers, a prayerbook and a rosary. He even enjoyed the enforced bath on a Saturday night, for it meant inclusion in a family ritual when the men would take their turn in the zinc bath in the kitchen, whilst Bright and the other females remained in the front parlour. Then Maguire, his sons and Nat went off to the pub leaving the women to their own mysterious toilet.

Most of all he enjoyed the company of the youngest Maguire during that Easter holiday, until one morning he woke to find that this was the day Bright and the boys must return to school.

'And aren't I glad?' exclaimed a harassed Mrs Maguire, who had been up since five because her husband was on early shift. 'Sure, the house has been like a zoo. Eugene, straighten that collar! And have you combed your hair?'

'Yes, Mammy,' replied the younger version of his father.

'It looks like it – come here!' She dragged him to her and

with a wettened comb raked his hair into a tidier style. 'That's better! Get back to the table and eat your breakfast. Bright, why are you not eating?'

Bright jumped and her spoon clattered into the porridge bowl. 'Sorry, Mammy, I was thinking.'

'Well, save thinking for school. Just eat.' Mrs Maguire frowned. 'You look a bit flushed, are ye not well? Maybe ye'd best not go today.' She was never averse to her daughter taking a day off for another pair of hands was always welcome.

'No, I feel fine!' The ten-year-old gulped down her porridge and smiled to show she was in good health.

Nat thought she was mad to throw away the chance of staying at home.

With Bright and her siblings gone the house seemed dead, but for Mrs Maguire's industry. She always seemed to be on the move. Nat wandered out into the yard and watched her pounding at her washing in the steaming tub. Face glistening she smiled and, still pummelling, asked, 'D'ye not think your mother would like to know where y'are? The school may have been on to her.'

Nat replied with a mute nod. He wanted to go but knew what lay ahead if Sep had his way.

Mrs Maguire broke off to puff at a wisp of hair that was tickling her face, eventually having to use a bright red hand and leaving suds on her brow. 'D'ye want I should go with ye?'

Nat shook his head. 'I'll go in a minute.'

The woman squeezed water from a sheet and lugged it over to the mangle, asking Nat to turn the handle. 'I'm not trying to get rid of ye, son. You know you're always welcome here an' if your mother isn't in you're to come right back.' She fed the sheet between the wooden rollers, then went around the other side to catch it. Water gushed into a bucket. ''Tis just that if I were your mother I'd want to know where ye were.'

Nat finished winding the mangle and nodded.

Mrs Maguire studied his flushed face and overly bright eyes. 'I might be wrong but sure, ye look as if you're sickening for something, too.'

'I feel all right,' muttered Nat, ready to wind the mangle again.

'You're certain? Must be the weather — it is awful muggy.' To emphasize this she tugged at the front of her blouse, then smiled a welcome as one of her neighbours wandered over to gossip. 'Well, away off to see your mother then, I'll manage these.'

Without another word Nat left. He was almost home when the policeman emerged from an alley and grabbed him.

'What's your name, lad?' Suspicious blue eyes pierced his.

Nat did not flinch. 'Prince.'

The officer studied the shorn hair. 'Hmm, you don't look much like a prince to me. I've been given the description of a boy who's decamped from the Industrial School. I've reason to believe that's you.'

'No, that's not me.' Nat fought rising panic, trying to keep his tone even. 'I've just been at church and now I'm off home.'

'Where d'you live?' The officer saw the slightest hesitation. 'Aye, I thought so — come on, let's have you back where you belong.'

Defeated, Nat allowed himself to be led, if not meekly then without resistance.

Mr Raskelf gave him a long lecture, ending with the opinion that it was now dubious if twenty-seven would be allowed to accompany the school trip to Scarborough that July. 'The lenience which you were shown at your last misdemeanour has been treated with contempt. You are obviously of a mould which requires a sterner lesson.' He opened a dark blue ledger which Nat knew to be the punishment book. 'Go with Officer Chipchase now and prepare to receive six strokes of the birch.'

Nat was taken to a cell where he was left to stew for an hour. During that time he alternated between pacing the room and sitting on the edge of the bed, dangling his legs and picking the skin from around his thumbnails. The main cause of his nerves was the knowledge that his punishment would take place before the whole school; floggings always did. He conceded that it must hurt; one-one-five had screamed and cried during his whipping, but then one-one-five did not have the experience of Lillywhite's viciousness which Nat had endured. The seconds ticked away. Come on, get it over with!

At last two officers escorted him to the dinner hall where the meal had been delayed for the occasion. Knowing what to expect, Nat looked straight ahead as he was marched between the long rows of apprehensive faces, but his bold tread faltered when confronted by the special table that had been reserved for him, and Mr Raskelf with the birch. Trembling from head to foot, he was ordered to strip to his underwear then spreadeagled on the table where his limbs were roped to its legs. The officers stepped back. Mr Raskelf, who had been waiting patiently nearby, now came forward. There was a nerve-racking pause. Nat blinked and waited. Then came a whoosh! The twig he had erstwhile despised made great impact on both flesh and mind. He gasped with the shock of it, his eyes wide and smarting. Never could he have imagined a pain like this! The second lash was even worse. He yelled in agony. The birch fell again. This time Nat was spared. Just before passing out he made a sensible decision: never would he escape again.

Bright was rather put out when she came home from school at lunchtime. 'Where's Nat? He said he'd meet me.' She flopped into a chair and looked petulant.

On her way to the scullery with a pan, Mrs Maguire glanced at the clock. 'I suggested he go visit his mother and he went, but that was hours ago. Maybe he decided to stay.'

Bright's demeanour changed. 'Or maybe she sent him back to that school! Oh, Mammy, why did ye tell him to go?'

Shrouded in steam, Mrs Maguire laid into the pan of potatoes with a masher. ''Tis no good blaming me for what his mother's done. Anyway there's no saying she has sent him back.'

'No, but that Mr Kendrew would!' argued Bright.

'Well if he has there's nothing we can do about it. Sure, tis none of our business really. Join your brothers at the table now.'

'I'm not hungry.'

'Eat!' Mrs Maguire spooned out a dollop of mashed potato.

Throughout lunch, Bright picked at her food, causing Mrs Maguire to return to this morning's observation. 'You're sure you're not going down with something? I know how keen you are to win this prize, but maybe you'd best stay off this afternoon.'

'No, I'm dandy!' Though not dandy at all, Bright forced herself to consume the meal in its entirety. Last year, due to one paltry day off she had lost the attendance prize which she so desperately coveted. She wasn't about to be robbed of it this year and her mother was well aware of this.

'You look awful hot.' Mrs Maguire reached out to touch her forehead.

Bright shied away. 'It's sunny out there! Anyway, I'd better be off. Please may I leave the table?'

''Tis customary to ask before ye get to the door,' chided Mrs Maguire. 'Patrick, Eugene, you get yourselves back to school too.'

Bright faltered. 'If Nat isn't here when I get home can we go find out where he is?'

'You'll have to ask your father. Look at you scratching! Come here and let me have a look at ye.'

Bright, who had been rubbing her body, ducked out of the door. 'I've got to go — bye, Mammy!'

She was to return in an hour's time, escorted by one of the nuns. 'Mrs Maguire.' Sister Sebastian wore a disapproving frown. 'Would you be so kind as to tell me why you sent your daughter to school with measles?'

'Measles?' Bright's mother clapped a hand over her mouth.

'Measles!' Came the disgusted echo. 'Have you not seen the rash on her?'

'Why, no, but I thought she looked a bit feverish . . .'

'Feverish indeed! She needs to be isolated at once, and to receive medical attention.'

'Yes, yes, of course!' Mrs Maguire portrayed guilt. 'Won't you forgive me, Sister, twas just that Bright kept harping on about the attendance prize . . .'

'And so you were prepared to put the whole school at risk!' The nun turned on her heel. 'Doubtless when I return I shall find the pupils falling like skittles!'

This exaggeration gave way to some truth. Within a week half of Bright's classmates were absent through the disease. Chastened, the girl languished in her darkened room, wondering what had happened to Nat — for her incapacitation had taken precedence over the search for him. Upon being deemed officially ill, Bright was a terrible patient, letting all the world know how she felt and having them all run around after her, bringing her books to read and lozenges to suck and any other treat she could elicit.

With the onset of recuperation she asked Mr Maguire, 'Dada, can we go to Nat's house and see if he's there?'

'You've asked me that an' I've told ye tis not the kind o' place my daughter should visit.'

'But ye never said why.' Bright had always been curious.

'I don't have to say why. I'm the father and I say who goes where.' However, as Bright's face crumpled Maguire relented. 'Oh, well now, maybe I could go on my own.'

Bright cheered up, but alas, her happiness was to be shortlived. Mr Maguire returned from his humiliating visit to tell her that Nat was once more incarcerated. 'And if you ask me, the boy's a lot better off in there than he is with that trollop! God, ye never heard the like of it when I asked after Nat. Her and that fancy man . . .' Red-faced, he turned to Mrs Maguire who put a finger to her lips.

'Later, Tommy, tis not fittin' for little ears.'

'You're right there!' Mr Maguire calmed his temper and addressed himself in a crisp tone to Bright. 'I'm sorry about your friend darlin', but there's nothing I can do.'

His daughter, still confused over Nat's mother's behaviour, pleaded, 'Couldn't we go and visit him?'

Mr Maguire grimaced and rubbed the back of his neck. 'Ah well . . .'

She clapped her hands and squirmed up to him in the way that had always borne results in the past. 'Please, Dada, we could go before bedtime, it wouldn't take long and I know Nat'd love to see us.'

'Before bedtime?' Maguire pretended outrage. 'Sure you cannot!'

The pleading turned to confidence. 'Then we can go tomorrow?'

'Had my arm twisted again as usual,' complained Mr Maguire to his wife. 'All right, if ye think you're up to it we'll go tomorrow when I get home from work. Now, let's hear your prayers and off to bed!'

Had Bright known there was to be further disappointment at the Industrial School she would not have skipped off to bed so happily.

'Nathaniel Smellie is here, yes,' said the officer who

answered the doorbell on consulting his register. 'But he isn't allowed visitors.'

'No, I said Nathaniel Prince,' corrected Mr Maguire politely.

'Yes, I am aware of the boy to whom you refer,' said the officer. 'I remember that he likes to assume an alias, but his correct name is in fact Smellie.'

Smellie! Bright felt herself redden in embarrassment for poor Nat. She resolved never to mention this awful handicap when in his presence.

'However, the name is of no consequence,' proceeded the officer. 'Neither he nor any of the boys are permitted to receive visitors; the entire school has been put under isolation. The majority of our inmates, number twenty-seven included, have contracted measles. One boy has in fact died from the disease.'

Bright flinched and, sensing her father's eyes upon her, reddened again. She could not look anywhere but at the floor.

Mr Maguire said lamely, 'Well, in that case, sir, I'm sorry to have bothered you. Would ye please be after giving Nat a message?' At the responding nod he added, 'Tell him the Maguires hope he's soon better. Er, before ye go . . .' The officer had been about to close the door. 'How long will this isolation last?'

'We will certainly not be accepting visitors for the next month at least.' After informing Mr Maguire on what date he expected visiting to recommence, the man closed the door, leaving Bright and her father to wander away.

'Did I do that?' Bright spoke in a little voice, not daring to look up at her father as they walked along the riverbank towards home.

'Do what?' Maguire was still annoyed at his foolishness over giving the wrong name. What other lies had Nat told them?

'Give them measles and make that boy die.'

He squeezed her hand. 'No, darlin'. Why sure, it could've been Nat who gave it to you. We don't know who got it first.'

Her eyes beseeched him like a puppy's. 'Can we go and see him when this desolation thing's over?'

Maguire sighed. 'We'll see. We'll see.'

Bright and her father were eventually allowed to visit Nat in June. Maria, too, had been granted leave to see her son. She was as apprehensive about this as Nat was, both remembering how distressing their parting had been at Christmas. This latest meeting, if anything, was even more awkward than the last. Nat was angry with his mother for allowing him to be sent back here after his escape. Of course he made no great display of emotion, it was not in his nature, but the lack of response to Maria's questions and the way he just sat there picking at his fingernails was sufficient illustration of his feelings towards her. With her topics of conversation exhausted and silence falling between them Maria decided to leave before visiting time was over.

'Well, if you're not gonna talk I'll go then,' she issued lamely.

Though consumed by anger and sadness, Nat was determined not to let her see how deeply she had hurt him, and did not make an exhibition of himself like the last time. 'All right. Tara, then.' His eyes remained downcast as his mother rose. Then as she turned to leave, he blurted, 'Will you come again?'

Maria smiled tightly and, nodding, hurried from the room.

Nat was about to return to his dormitory when Mr Chipchase informed him that more visitors had arrived to see him and he reseated himself at the table to receive Bright and her father.

Initially, the meeting with the Maguires was hostile. Whilst on the one hand Nat was glad to see them, on the other he resented them witnessing his humiliating treatment by the officers, and most irrationally of all he found himself venting the anger he felt towards his mother on them, responding towards Bright's innocent questions with sullenness. It was only when an impatient Mr Maguire pointed out, 'Look, we won't be allowed another visit for two months. Are ye determined to waste all our time by behaving like an eejit?' that the boy was jolted to his senses and became more affable.

This mood was not to spill over into everyday life and he was as incommunicative as ever to his masters, but at least he was wise enough to keep out of trouble, a fact which enabled him to be included in the school's holiday to Scarborough.

Contrary as ever he was determined not to enjoy it, but faced with the exciting prospect of a train journey he could not maintain his sullen expression for long. This was the first time Nat had been on a train. He and the others were divided into groups. Officer Chipchase had been appointed to take charge of Nat's section so there was more chance of horseplay in this compartment than in other groups – though there was little reason for this with so much to view from the carriage windows. When the train pulled into Scarborough Nat was almost disappointed that the journey was over. The boys were taken directly to their lodgings, a huge house that overlooked the sea. An excited horde swarmed to the window en masse. 'Can we go down there, sir? Can we? Can we?'

'All in good time!' Mr Chipchase tried to calm them. 'First, you can make up your beds, then put your clothes into those lockers – neatly! Then assemble downstairs for dinner.'

'Then can we go?' The persistent boys danced round him.

'If good behaviour continues, yes. Now get on with it.' Mr Chipchase left to a loud cheer and great activity.

In record time the officer's instructions were carried out and the boys pelted downstairs. Where once he might have been last due to someone ripping the blankets off his bed, Nat careered downstairs at the centre of a good-humoured throng. Since his birching he had been granted more respect from his peers. Besides, with new boys entering each month there were plenty of weaker victims for Larkin to bully.

Lunch consisted of kippers, bread and butter and a jam pudding. Eager to be on the beach the boys wolfed it down in no time but were forced to wait impatiently until Mr Raskelf had finished his, hanging on his every spoonful.

At last permission was granted to clear the tables, but even now there was infuriating delay whilst Raskelf made a speech. 'Every year the good citizens of this delightful watering hole are kind enough to accept you into their midst, as I trust they will continue to do so for many years to come. I understand that for boys who have been cooped up for many months there is a danger that you may become over-stimulated by all the fun on offer and thus commit some foolish act. I must warn you to consider your actions very carefully. Should I receive but one complaint against one boy then I shall not hesitate to cancel the holiday and take the entire school back to York.' His eyes moved up and down the ranks of boys so that all should be impressed. 'In a moment, your officers will escort you down to the sands where you will be allowed to play unsupervised for the remainder of the afternoon.' This was met by excited grins. 'I am trusting each and every one of you to uphold the fine reputation of the school and to ensure that your fellows behave in the same manner. You may now go to your dormitories, remove your boots and stockings and prepare for an afternoon's fun.'

A race to be first up the stairs and first down ensued. When all were assembled outside, each officer led their respective group to the beach. 'And behave yourselves!' Disposed of their burdens and unfettered from their wives, the officers relaxed in deckchairs on the Spa Pavilion where a band played military marches and attractive ladies sauntered for their extra delight.

Unleashed, the boys seemed unsure of what to do first. They teetered on the verge of excitement, scraping their heels at the sand and making patterns – until one broke for freedom and at once the Riviera of the North, sedate and elegant, was riven by a Mongolian horde that careered towards the sea, demolishing sandcastles and scattering toddlers with a tribal yell of delight. The sea shrank away, repelled, but the mob invaded her, plundering, splashing, yelping savages, hurling themselves about so that their clothes were drenched, gyrating in the usual madcap way of boys, leaping in the air, taking giant strides and making idiotic noises.

Nat loved the feel of the sand beneath his feet. He bunched his toes, using them to pick up the grit and squeezing it until the pads of his feet became sore. Moving to the water's edge, he stood to gaze at the vast expanse of sea and then – how inexplicable – was once again swamped by loneliness, by the whole pointless exercise of life. So great was the depression that it threatened to engulf him, until a wave rolled over his ankles, causing the sand beneath his feet to shift. He tottered and cried out in alarm, fleeing to dry land to await the fate of his companions, but soon saw that they were still enjoying the waves unharmed. In the knowledge that he was not to be sucked under and buried alive Nat returned to the water's edge, made footprints in the wet sand and stood back to watch in fascination as the eddying wavelets filled his imprints with water and carried them away – and with them the brief spell of depression.

Excited cries drew his attention and brought him running to a crowd of his companions. One boy had found a little fish, another produced a soggy paper bag in which to put it, but the water kept dribbling out and the fish faced certain death until the sea washed up a tin can. Others gathered shells, whilst more mature companions ogled the ringleted girls with their dresses tucked into their bloomers. Yet another enclave had noticed that an infant had left his spade several yards from where he now sat picnicking with his family, and moving as one, edged closer and closer, circling it in a huddle, whence one of the boys grabbed the spade and the rogues then spirited it away for their own entertainment; this involved one of their number being entombed up to the neck for the whole of the afternoon until the tide came in and they thought to resurrect him, crying and windburned. 'If you tell old Bramble Conk you're for it!'

The afternoon was over in a flash. A hostile tide drove them further back up the beach where, within calling range of their officers, they were summoned to tea. A muttered command was passed between the boys. 'Pretend you haven't heard!' They continued their capers, forcing Mr Chipchase and two fellow officers to come down onto the sands. 'Aw, can't we stay a bit longer, sir?' they whined as they were rounded up.

'You've a whole fortnight ahead of you,' replied Chipchase, one side of his face crimson where he had fallen asleep in the sun. 'Right now, it's time for tea.'

'Sir, you've got a wasp on your hat!'

Mr Chipchase ducked and brushed wildly at his head. The wasp flew up, then resumed its attack, hovering and darting into his face whilst Chipchase lashed out as if conducting an orchestra. With one lucky blow he knocked the wasp away towards Mr Screeton, who in turn lashed out and directed the furious insect back at Chipchase, back and forth, back and forth like a dangerous version of tennis, whilst the boys fell on the sand laughing hysterically until a final volley sent the wasp spinning into their midst and with one united yell they fell apart and escaped up a slope to the road, with a perspiring Mr Chipchase taking up the rear.

'Sir, I got bitten!' Larkin showed the officer a red lump on his arm.

'Thank goodness,' puffed Chipchase, mopping his brow, 'a wasp with distinction – and they don't bite, they sting. I'll put something on it, if we ever get back to the house. Come along now, fall into line. I'm sure you must all be famished.'

'I could eat one o' them donkeys.' Nat pointed up the beach.

'Aye, me too,' agreed Cobbins. 'A good day, weren't it?'

'Your enjoyment is by no means over,' divulged Mr Chipchase. 'After tea I'm going to take you on a clifftop walk so that you can appreciate the flora and fauna of the east coast.'

'Where did he say we're off?' frowned Cobbins, when later they were led back out into the evening sunshine.

Nat shrugged. 'I dunno – to see Flora or somebody.'

'This is boring,' muttered Cobbins when, half an hour into the expedition all they had done was look at flowers and moths. 'I'd rather be down there on them merry-go-rounds and things.'

Murmured agreement rippled through the half-dozen boys who lagged at the rear. 'But we've no money,' said Nat. 'Anyway, how do we get there without Chip seeing?'

As if to answer the unspoken prayer, a cry went up, 'Sir, wh – sir, sir!' Mr Chipchase was in conversation with another and only now looked up. 'Sir, what's that thing what just ran into them bushes? It were a rat thing wi' a long skinny body.'

'Oh, that would be a weasel!' Mr Chipchase hurried over in the direction of the pointed finger, hence allowing Nat and his five accomplices to sneak over the edge of the cliff where, by means of a well-trodden path, they scrambled first to the beach, then walked on to the greater lure of the penny arcades.

It turned out that it was not such a futile venture after all. Cobbins had money — a whole shilling's worth of change. 'I'm gonna be generous and give you each a penny, but if you win owt it belongs to me, right?'

At the first go, Nat succeeded in milking five new pennies from the machine. He gave a crafty look around to see if Cobbins had observed. He had. Reluctantly the five pence was handed over. There were three other winners. At the end of half an hour Cobbins' pockets were weighted down with almost half a crown's worth of pennies. Not a stingy boy, he bought each of his friends a plate of cockles and enjoyed his own so much that he embarked on a further nine until, with his last mouthful, he suddenly announced, 'I feel a bit sick.'

Nat, who felt bilious too, merely at witnessing Cobbins' gross consumption, suggested, 'We'd better be getting back. Chippy might've missed us.'

Looking up and down the seafront Galton pointed. 'Our house is just up that slope . . .'

'Ooh, listen to him — our house!' laughed Nat.

Galton continued, 'We might as well go there and hide in t'garden till the others come back.' And with this they set off, accompanied by a moaning Cobbins.

'I'm gonna be sick. Oh, God, I'm gonna puke!' Half way home, Cobbins deposited his ten plates of cockles onto a Scarborough resident's petunias. The others ran, fearing retribution, but no one saw and when they successfully regrouped with Mr Chipchase later it was obvious he had not even missed them.

The period up until bedtime was taken up by a sing-song and cocoa. When an exhausted, windburned Nat fell into bed he had time only to note that his feet were cleaner than they had ever been in his life and were covered in white blisters — then, there was happy oblivion.

The second afternoon of the holiday was spent once again on the beach. Cobbins, now recovered, suggested that he and his cronies sneak off to have a donkey ride. Thus, the man who owned the donkeys found himself besieged by a group of suspicious-looking characters, Nat amongst them.

'Can we have a ride, mister?' asked Galton, idly swinging a banner of seaweed around his head.

The man pointed with his stick to a board that advertised the price.

'We haven't got any money on us,' explained Cobbins. 'But that's our dad up there . . .' He pointed in the direction of the Spa. 'He'll pay you when we've had our ride.'

'Brothers, are you?' The donkey man looked around at the shaven-headed urchins who in feature could not have been more different.

'Yes.'

'And I'm the Duke of York.'

'Ooh, are you?' Galton cocked his head with interest. 'Where's your crown?'

The man threatened them with his stick. 'Get back down yon end with the rest of the rabble!' He turned away as a little girl was brought for a donkey ride and lifted into the saddle by her father. Other children joined her and when all saddles were filled the man took hold of the reins of an animal and led it forward. Nat and his group took up the rear behind the jingling procession.

The man looked over his shoulder. 'You can trail up and down as much as you like, you won't get a ride!'

The lead donkey reached the allotted turning point and began its journey back. The others followed suit, so did Nat and his friends. Each time a group of children were taken for a ride the posse trailed them. Their presence finally became too much for the donkeys' owner. 'What do you think you're larking at?'

'You said we could trail up and down as much as we

like,' said an innocent-looking Galton, still dragging the strand of seaweed.

The man raised his stick again, the group stopped in their tracks . . . but when he moved on, so did they.

Towards the middle of the afternoon there was a lull in business and the donkeys stood idle, heads drooping from their labours. After several nudges the group of boys edged forward again. 'You haven't got many customers now, have you, mister? You could let us have a ride . . . your donkeys look a bit fed up.' Galton offered a donkey his seaweed to eat.

'Fed up? Fed up!' The man descended on Galton with his stick. 'I'm bloody well fed up of you lot pestering me!' And he brought the stick down hard on Galton's shoulders.

'Aagh! He's broken me arm!' Galton fell but was soon up again as the man repeatedly hit him whilst his friends made a hasty retreat.

'Bastard!' he puffed on catching up with them, gripping his arm to his side. 'I'm gonna get me own back, you see if I don't!' And the rest of the afternoon was spent concocting revenge which resulted in an evening raid on the larder.

It took a lot of patience and subterfuge but it was worth the wait. The rhubarb powder that Galton managed to slip unseen into the donkey's feeding bags was most effective, polluting yards of golden sand and rendering the donkeys out of action. Overjoyed at the outcome, Galton chuckled with his partners in crime and reached triumphant arms at the bright blue sky. 'Avast, boys! The sun shines on the righteous!'

The weather remained clement for the duration of the holiday, allowing the boys access to similar clandestine fun. Nat felt sure that these sins would have to be paid for, yet in his final address Mr Raskelf was to tell the assembly that the boys' behaviour had been exemplary, and added hearty congratulations. 'I have not had one single complaint!' he beamed. 'Not one!'

'The folk round here must be bloody daft,' smirked Galton as he picked up his bag and joined the un-enthusiastic exodus to the station.

The homewards trip was subdued as each boy reflected on the lovely time behind him and the much longer term ahead. There would not be another treat until Christmas. One tiny compensation remained in the grains of sand which lingered in their clothes and bedding for weeks afterwards. Every night Nat religiously tipped the contents of his boots into a jar. 'If we all do this we might have enough for a sandpit!' The others gave up after a while but he persevered; even if he never accumulated enough for a sandpit he would keep the jar of sand as a memento of his holiday, a holiday that had been the making of him, as Mr Chipchase had observed to another officer. 'Twenty-seven's a changed boy, much more amenable, much more.'

This latter part was true. Some time during that fortnight Nat had grasped the concept that would serve to make his time here a fraction easier. Maybe it was the buffeting motion of the sea that had knocked sense into him, teaching him how useless it was to try and fight against the greater strength. Don't buck the system, give the powerful ones what they wanted to see and they might leave you alone. How long this state of affairs would last Nat could not say, but for now he felt able to portray the image that those in charge required; that of a model inmate.

Nat's mother, too, noticed an improvement in him from the last time she had seen her son. He appeared to be more settled – even happy. Maria was astonished and delighted by his excited chatter as he told her all about his lovely time in Scarborough.

'Old Bramble Conk said our behaviour was ex – exemplary. What does that mean?'

Maria looked unsure. 'Did he look mad when he said it?'

Her son shook his head. 'No, he were smiling.'

'Then I suppose it must mean you were all very good.'

'Oh . . .' Nat looked thoughtful. 'Yes, he said he hadn't had no complaints from people. They can't have seen Cobbins puking over a lady's wall. He ate ten saucers of cockles!'

'Ugh, them snail things? I can't imagine anything more horrible.' Maria grimaced.

'And you know them donkeys what take people for rides on the beach?'

'Don't know, I've never been to the seaside,' said his mother. 'God love us, I think I ought to get meself locked up in here! It's a poor show when people who are meant to be in here for punishment have more fun than we do on the outside.'

'I'll take you when I'm grown up,' promised Nat, wanting to make up for the way he had behaved on her last visit. 'Well, they have these donkeys and Galton tried to give 'em seaweed to eat and the man whipped him with his stick, so Galton put rhubarb powder in their food . . .' Indeed, the holiday provided a topic of conversation for several visits to come.

On none of these visits was Kendrew ever mentioned. Maria had no inclination to douse the new enthusiasm in her son and Nat himself still clung to the shred of hope that his mother's companion had departed.

Nat's eleventh birthday was marked by unexpected visitors. Bright and Mr Maguire turned up, bringing him some toffee. The rest of that year passed more quickly than the previous one. Outwardly, Nat was responding well to the discipline and was deemed trustworthy enough to be hired out to a local resident for cleaning boots, chopping wood and polishing cutlery. After his second holiday in Scarborough it was decided to grant him an early release date. Mr Chipchase passed on the good news to Nat, who was elated. Only one thing marred the thought of his homecoming. Would Kendrew still be there?

Nat's two-year absence had certainly helped Kendrew. Without the pressure of having to endure Maria's truculent bastard, life with her had become very cosy indeed. He was without work at the moment, having lost his job at the hospital, but Maria had voiced her willingness to look after him until he got another.

'The trouble is,' Sep's face creased in anxiety, 'there's a lot of unemployment about. I might have to try another town.'

Maria responded as he had hoped. 'That's fine by me, as long as you take me with you, mind!'

Kendrew was much amused. 'Of course! You don't think I'd move without my little sweetheart, do you? Truth be known, I'll be glad of the opportunity to take you away from this life. You deserve better.'

A matter of weeks later Sep heard that there was work on the docks at Hull and borrowed the fare from Maria to go and find out if it was true. When he arrived all the jobs had been taken, but by chance he met a man who offered something better: not only a job but also a rent free cottage to go with it. The post was one of gardener to a big house. Sep had never turned so much as a shovelful of earth in his life but managed to convince the man that he was an expert in this field.

When he went home and told Maria, she could not believe that her luck had finally changed and kept grabbing him in excitement and saying there had to be something to ruin what appeared to be a perfect situation: there was. Like her, Sep was eager for them to start this new life in Hull, but he didn't want Nat to go with them.

'Oh . . .' She ceased dancing and bit her lip. 'Maybe if I tell him this is his last chance . . .'

'Anyone can see it'll never work between the pair of us,

sweetheart.' He held her by the upper arms and spoke fondly. 'I've tried to be a father to him – you've seen how hard I've tried, haven't you? He just won't bend.'

Maria reviewed the twenty-five years of her life and had to agree with Kendrew that most of her troubles were due to Nat. Oh, she loved him, but his attitude towards Sep made her so angry. Why after all she had done for him did he deny her the one chance of happiness she'd ever had? Deep in thought, she wandered over to the fireplace. Nat's little watch sat upon the mantel; Maria had failed to carry out her son's instruction to give it to Bright. She picked it up now and rubbed the cheap face with a thumb.

Kendrew continued persuading her, speaking kindly. 'You're only a young lass, Mari. You've a right to your own life. You'll never tame that lad o' yours, he'll end up a real villain and he'll drag you down with him. You've done your best, you can't do any more – and I don't see why you should.'

'But, I can't just leave him.' She gripped the watch tightly in her palm.

'Why not? He gets fed at the Industrial School, doesn't he?'

'He won't be there for much longer.' The slight pause before she had answered encouraged Kendrew. She was weakening.

'Won't he? D'you think when he comes out of there he'll have learned his lesson and go quietly to proper school like a meek little kitten? No, he'll be back in there quick as a flash. And mixing with the type o' boy you get in them places, well, I reckon he'll be gaol fodder, a burden for the rest of your life. I've seen plenty of lads like him, with good parents like you. He'd let you give him the skin off your back and he still wouldn't appreciate it. Anyway, I doubt they'll allow him to come back here. I mean, they might not consider it a suitable home.'

'The cheeky devils!' Maria was outraged. 'Who are they

to say a thing like that after the way they treat him in there? I've given that lad everything . . .'

'I know, I know!' Kendrew shared her objection. 'That's exactly what I'm saying. Why don't you think of yourself for once in your life?'

Yet there came excuses. 'But he's only eleven.'

Sep was quietly blunt. 'You won't get another chance like this, you know. No other man'd take you as I'm doing, knowing your line of work. What's the alternative? Keep hawking your body about and become old before your time?'

'I've years in me yet,' objected Maria, looking at the mirror for confirmation.

Kendrew's hands beseeched. 'But do you want it for years?'

She shook her head, remembering last night when a client had ordered her to urinate over his face. Oh, it was not the first time, but she had never become accustomed to it and could almost vomit now at the memory.

'Then marry me – if only to get rid of that bloody awful name you've got.'

She looked at him. He was quite obviously fond of her – must be, to accept her for what she was – and she returned that fondness. Oh, but did it have to be like this: torn between the two of them? Why, oh why wouldn't Nat understand? She'd sacrificed her youth for him. Instead of getting rid of him she had grovelled and scraped to feed the two of them, for what reward?

The tin watch dug into her palm. After a great deal more agonizing, she capitulated and replaced the toy on the mantel, rubbing nervously at the imprint it had left on her palm. 'All right then, I'll go with you – but I'll have to make provision for Nat. I can't just abandon him.'

Sep put his arms round her, smiling. 'By, lass! You do have a low opinion of yourself. All the stick you've taken on his behalf . . . you're not abandoning him, for pity's sake. The authorities have made him their responsibility by taking him away from you, haven't they? Weren't they the ones who took you to court 'cause he was truanting?' Maria thought about this and gave an indecisive nod. 'Well then!' cried Sep. 'You leave it all to me. I know it'll be painful for you. I'll go down to the school and make arrangements for when he's released, try to get him put with somebody who'll look after him as well as you do.'

Maria felt a mixture of emotions: shame, guilt, remorse . . . but at the same time excitement about the new life that lay ahead of her. Here was her chance to be happy. *You must take it, you must.*

'I'd make sure he's in good hands.' Sep was very plausible. 'But of course if you want to do it . . .'

'Oh no . . . no, I'll trust your judgment.' Maria was grateful that he was willing to divest her of this responsibility; she hated dealing with officials. 'You promise he'll go to good people, though?' A shadow of guilt crossed her face – she was talking about her son as if he were a worn-out horse!

'Promise.' Kendrew cupped her cheeks in his hands, his expression grave. 'But I can also promise you that he'll be back inside as quick as you can blink. I doubt they'll be able to do any more with him than his own mother could. Stop scourging yourself, Mari. I shan't ask you again, you know. I'm not one to keep getting down on my knee just to be rebuffed.'

She found a smile then and punched him lightly. 'You've never been down on your knee!'

'Haven't I?' Kendrew feigned surprise. 'Then it's high time I did it.' He kneeled down and clutched her hand. 'My darling Maria, pray, will you marry me?'

She simpered and giggled with pleasure. 'I will!'

Nat's future was sealed.

5

'Ah, good day, Mr . . .'

'Kendrew, sir,' provided Sep, and shook hands with Superintendent Raskelf into whose office he had just been shown. 'I've come with regard to Nat Smellie.'

'Pray, be seated.' Mr Raskelf indicated a chair and himself took the one on the other side of his desk.

'Thank you, sir.' Sep felt uncomfortable here and fingered his grubby collar. 'I'm acting on behalf of Nat's mother, she's too upset to come herself. The thing is, sir . . . she's very worried about his release.'

'Ah, yes.' Mr Raskelf opened a ledger and flicked through its pages. 'I believe Smellie is due to go home very shortly . . .'

'Well, that's just it, sir,' blurted Sep. 'She doesn't want him home – I mean, she understands her responsibilities but well, you know how much of a handful he is, refusing to go to school and everything, well, the truth is, he's just too much for her to manage and she was wonderin' whether you could find him a suitable place with folk who could keep him in order.'

'I see.' Raskelf looked up from his ledger, his face thoughtful.

'She thinks it would be better for all concerned,' added Sep.

'Yes . . .' Raskelf gave a pensive nod, then looked down at his ledger again to see the exact date of twenty-seven's release. 'You know that young Smellie's behaviour has greatly improved this last year? You see normally it's only those in moral danger who are not returned to their home.'

'But he is in a way,' burbled Sep, twisting his hat. 'I don't know if you're aware of his mother's profession – I mean, I know I'm acting as her representative but I'm not exactly a friend or anything an' I don't agree with . . . well, what I mean to say is . . .' he trailed off lamely.

On consulting Nat's records Mr Raskelf saw what Kendrew meant. 'Ah yes, this has been discussed and I did have misgivings about sending him back, but the boy was only in here because of truancy, Mr Kendrew, and several of my officers have testified that he and his mother are very close. I find it somewhat contradictory that she does not want him back. It's rather short notice for us to find a home for the boy. Perhaps it would be an idea if I were to reassure Miss Smellie myself . . .'

'It wouldn't do any good, sir!' His plan in danger of going awry, Kendrew racked his mind for another tack. He contemplated doing nothing, just pretending to Maria that he had made arrangements for Nat's welfare before taking her off to Hull, but then the authorities might try to contact her and she would find out that he had lied. Better for both parties to be satisfied as to the boy's whereabouts. 'I've tried to persuade her myself but her mind's made up, and to be frank I feel that Nat needs a father and a proper family who'll repair his moral fibre before it's too late.' An idea came. 'I wonder, would it help if I were to suggest a suitable home? I know some good people who might be willing to take him. They're very Christian folk, and I know they'd do the boy a world of good.'

Mr Raskelf thought upon the matter, but not for too long. It was a satisfactory arrangement. 'Very well, if this is in accordance with Miss Smellie's wishes then I too am in agreement, but I would wish to have the mother's consent in writing.'

'I'll have her do that, sir.' Kendrew rose and took his leave. 'And I'll send my friends to see you as soon as possible.'

*   *   *

On the morning of his release in late summer, 1892, Nat was called to the superintendent's office. Besides Mr Raskelf there was another man and a woman present, both seated by the window. Nat glanced at them, but after this paid little heed.

'Now, twenty-seven,' began Mr Raskelf, without looking up from the paper in front of him. 'Shall we see you again?'

'No, sir,' replied Nat.

'I sincerely hope that we will not.' Raskelf looked up briefly. 'And I trust that you will not let Mr and Mrs Rawlinson down.'

Presumably this must be the couple by the window but Nat, itching to be away, did not waste time asking. However, Raskelf confirmed his supposition by indicating the visitors. 'Mr Rawlinson has kindly consented to accept you into his home. If you continue to behave as you have been doing lately and to work hard at school then I am advised by Mr Rawlinson that he would be willing to give you permanent employment in his household when you are of age.'

Nat was stunned. They were trying to keep him from his mother! But if he had learned anything at this establishment it was that it was futile to argue. He could soon remedy the matter once he was outside. Without the ceremony that this occasion deserved, his tin whistle was returned – only when he asked for it – and he was handed over to the couple. Even as he was being ushered from the office Nat was contemplating methods of escape.

To his amazement however, all these were totally unnecessary. Barely had they reached the top of Marygate than Rawlinson said, 'Right, sling your hook.'

Nat looked up at him, agog, but did not need telling twice. Off he ran towards home. Happy with a role well-acted, the Rawlinsons, too, went on their way. Kendrew had asked if they would foster Nat but they had refused as had everyone else he had approached. In desperation Sep had pleaded, 'Then just pretend to do it. I'll pay you two quid. I'll arrange everything with the school, all you have to do is turn up on the day, crack on you're taking him home, then do what you like with him. If anybody comes snooping you can say he's run away – he's well known for it.' Once he and Maria were in Hull the boy would be no longer a nuisance.

The clothes which Nat had worn on entry to the school were naturally too small for him now and so he was perforce discharged in the institution garb. This and his shorn head made him a marked man and there were several unpleasant incidents before he reached home. Bounding up the stairs, he hesitated outside the door. Would Kendrew still be there? Preparing two different greetings, he turned the knob, only to be met with anti-climax: the parlour was empty.

On the table was his jar of lucky stones. Taking out his tin whistle he wandered up and down trying to remember the tune that Mr Maguire had taught him, but it had been a while since he had played it and it sounded sweeter in memory than it did now. Soon bored, he flopped down onto the sofa and lay motionless for a long time, gathering his thoughts. His innards began to rumble. With no one to give the order that it was dinnertime he sat for a good while before realizing that he no longer needed permission from an officer when to eat and when to sleep. He was his own master again, until his mother got home at any rate. The bold decision to visit the larder turned out to be academic; it was completely bare. Nat paced indecisively, sat down again, counted the luckystones in the jar, then went to stare out of the window for a while, pondering over the odd behaviour of the people who were meant to have been his foster parents. There were voices below. Nat hauled up the sash and poked his head out, but when the women looked up he drew it in again quickly.

He waited a long time. Nobody came. He went to lay on the bed which had no covers – his mother must have taken them to the laundry. He fell asleep. On waking, the position of the sun and his grumbling stomach told him it was well after noon. He decided to call at Bright's where he would surely be fed, but there was no one there either to answer his call. After a moment he peeped round the door, but the parlour was empty except for Granny Maguire who, with gaping jaw, sat snoring by the fire. Disappointed but afraid to linger he decided to go down to St George's School and wait for Bright.

The playground was silent, a silence that wrapped itself around him blotting out everything else. For one moment of panic it seemed to Nat that every person he knew had vanished off the face of the earth. He slumped down on the kerb, leaned on his knees and focused on a dead bird on the road. It had been squashed to a pancake by numerous cartwheels, yet one flight feather wafted back and forth, back and forth in the breeze. Nat watched it, growing more desolate by the second, until a low rumble alerted him to the pupils' exodus. Remembering the previous attack by the Irish boys, he jumped to his feet and sought out a less conspicuous place to wait.

Even though she had seen him before with his long hair shorn to grey stubble, Bright did not recognize him at first. A brief expression of fear passed across her face as his hand pulled her into the back lane. Then alarm turned to delight. 'Nat!'

'Shush! I don't want to draw attention to meself.'

She raised her eyebrows in glee. 'Have ye run away again?'

'No, they let me out.' Nat peeped round the edge of the wall. She was quick to interpret his concern. 'Oh, don't worry about John Kelly, he's left our school.'

'I'm not worried about him!' Nat squared his shoulders. 'I can look after meself after being in there.' He glanced into the street again. The crowd of schoolchildren had thinned and those that were left were mostly girls. 'Shall we go to your house?'

'I'm not going home, I'm off to Louisa's for me tea.' Bright pointed at a dark-haired girl who sat on the kerb playing jacks. 'I'll have to go now, she's waiting – come to my house tomorrow if ye like though. Bye!'

And Nat had no opportunity to tell her that he had not eaten since breakfast. At his half-hearted nod she was gone. Annoyed, he leaned against the wall, but it was too cold to tarry for long. Surely his mother would be back from the laundry by now. Nat set off at a jog and kept up the pace for most of the way home.

His mother wasn't there. Another period of waiting ensued. After a time, he braved the dark Stonebow Lane and went out to look for her, but was soon driven in by the cold. It wasn't much warmer in the house, with powdery ashes in the grate and no coal to light a fire. He went to crouch on the top stair, ready to hurl himself at her the moment she came through the door.

The door opened. He half rose expectantly, but it was the woman who lived below and he replaced his chin in his hands. The woman did not like him and never spoke to him. This evening, however, she appeared to falter as if she wanted to engage him in conversation, but then she went into her own quarters, abandoning him to the darkness.

An age later, or so it seemed to the child, she opened her door again, casting light into the stairwell, and looked up at him. 'Here.'

Nat could not see what she was holding out to him, but in the hope that it was food he went down. After handing over the crust she said nothing more and shut the door again.

Nat's teeth ripped into the bread, but the hours of abstinence and the growing worry over his mother had shrunken his gut. When it came to swallowing, the crust became a boulder. Self-pity brought tears to his eyes. Shoving the bread into his pocket he dragged his feet up to his room and curled up on the bare mattress, praying that his mother would be there beside him when he woke.

Dawn stole into the mean alleyways and over his sill. Nat had woken constantly throughout the night to feel for his mother but cold had been his only bedfellow. Now, mercifully, his fitfulness gave way to deeper sleep and he was granted three hours of oblivion until a knock at the door forced him to rise and answer it.

The landlord looked down at the shorn head and asked if Nat's mother was in. Nat rubbed his itchy eyes and said no.

'No, she wasn't in the last time I called neither.' The landlord looked villainous. As a matter of fact he had always appeared extremely suspicious to Nat, with his shifty eyes and his hat pulled down over them even in the middle of summer. 'I thought I'd come through the week; she never seems to be in on a Friday nowadays.' He gave a disparaging sniff. 'What time will I find her in?' Nat said he didn't know, he was waiting for her too. 'How long have you been waiting then?' The landlord brushed past him and looked around.

'Since yesterday,' answered Nat.

The landlord gasped as the truth took only seconds to dawn on him. 'The bloody cow, she's done a moonlight!' Nat frowned and asked what he meant. 'She's run off without paying my rent!' His mouth was still open at the audacity of it.

'She wouldn't leave me,' protested Nat. 'Anyway, the furniture's still here.'

'I don't know about you,' said the landlord, looking him up and down, 'but the bloody furniture's only good for matchwood. The little whore . . .'

Nat overcame his natural reticence. 'Don't you say that about my mam!'

'Out!' Without further ado, the man pushed Nat outside and locked the door behind them.

It was then that Nat remembered his whistle and the jar of luckystones standing on the table, but was too afraid to call after the landlord. He slumped on the top stair, wishing that he had a key like the one Watson had shown him so that he could rescue the precious stones. His mother would be furious when she returned.

Shortly after the noise had died down, the woman who had given him the bread came out to find him sitting outside on the front step. 'It's no good waiting there, lad. Your mam's gone.'

He refused to believe her and shook his head. 'She'll be coming back for me.'

The common-looking woman folded her arms and tried to offer a solution. 'Haven't you got any aunts or uncles you could go to?'

Nat shook his head. 'I have to stay here or me mam won't know where I am.'

After a moment's silence, she muttered reluctantly, 'You'd better come in with me till we decide what to do. Come on,' she urged him to get up, 'you're not far away if your mam does come back.'

He didn't like the woman, despised her lumpy features. 'S'all right. She won't be long now.'

'She might be longer than you think . . . I wasn't privy to where she was going, but gossip has it that she went to live in Hull with that fella of hers.'

Nat pressed his lips together. That . . . bugger! Well, Kendrew hadn't bargained with his adversary's dog-gedness. He scrambled to his feet. 'Which way's Hull then?'

'Too far for you to go today. Come on in and we'll talk about it.'

Nat was still tired out and hungry. He finally accepted the woman's offer. She told him to go and have a wash whilst she made him some porridge. He did so, but eavesdropped at the door as she spoke to her companion.

'Poor little mite. I can't say I like him but you have to feel sorry for him. He doesn't realize she's cleared off and left him. What sort of woman would do that to her own bairn? And her acting all stuck up, reckoning she's better than us. Well, she needn't think she's landing me with him. We'll have to tell the authorities . . .'

Nat had only to hear the last word and he was out of the window in a trice, running for his life down Stonebow Lane and stopping only to ask the first person he saw, 'Which way's Hull?'

The postman in his fore and aft hat continued to trundle his handcart full of parcels but nodded at Fossgate. 'Down there and carry straight on.'

Nat carried on. He rushed past Bright Maguire's, not having time to dally. Anyway, she would ask questions and it was none of her business. *Mam, how could you leave without telling me where you were going?* Eventually he came to Walmgate Bar. Emerging the other side, he flopped against the barbican to catch his breath and looked around. He had not been this way before, his geographical knowledge confined to the streets inside the walls. The area was full of drovers awaiting the trains that would bring the Irish cattle to market. Still panting, Nat bent over and leaned on his knees, letting his head sag. A bell clamoured somewhere to his right. He looked up. A train carrying flour from the mill up Navigation Road was now crossing Foss Islands. Summoning courage, Nat pushed himself from the barbican and approached one of the loafers to ask, 'Is this Hull?'

The man guffawed and said something unintelligible to his companions who chuckled too. Detesting anyone who laughed at him, Nat turned on his heel and stalked away. It was some time before he had recovered enough to go and ask the man in charge of the level crossing the same question. This man laughed too. Even though it was not as unpleasant a sound as the other's, Nat was abashed. 'Where have you sprung from?'

Nat muttered in his usual stumbling manner. 'Stonebow Buildings. I'm going to Hull. Postman told me it was this way.'

'It is, but it's too far to walk.' Another train had pulled into the sidings, belching steam. Nat asked if that would take him. The man pointed out that it was a cattle truck. 'They wouldn't let you in anywhere stinking o' bullocks. Anyway it's going back west. Hull's t'other road.'

Nat felt squashed and asked how far it was. The railway man astounded him. 'About forty miles.'

'I'll go after dinner,' decided Nat, feeling hungry.

'Dinner? You've just had breakfast haven't you?'

'Haven't had none.' Nat eyed the cow-wallopers who were unloading the bellowing cargo. The sun was trying to get out but the morning was still bleak for this abandoned child. 'I haven't had owt since yesterday morning.'

'Good Heavens! Doesn't your mother feed you?'

Nat was exasperated. 'Course she does, but she's gone to Hull and I have to go and find her.'

The man rubbed his whiskered chin thoughtfully and perused Nat's shorn scalp. 'Hmm, bit of a problem that, isn't it? You sure you haven't run away?' The boy shook his head furiously and made to escape, but the railway man grabbed him. 'Hold still a minute! I'm trying to think how to get you there. Have you any money?' Another shake of head from Nat, who determined to run once the man freed his grip. 'What about your dad, you haven't mentioned him.'

Nat thought it easier to say, 'Me dad's dead.' His eyes held the man's face, ready for that expression that would indicate he was going to be handed over to the authorities. The railway man sensed his fear and tried to allay it. 'Harken to me and stop wriggling. I reckon you have run away from some boys' home or the like — I said stop wriggling! I'm not about to send you back there, I've been in one myself and I know what it's like. Believe me or not I want to help you. Now then, I'm going to let go of your arm and you can either run away or you can have a sandwich from me lunch can. You please yourself.'

Now starving, Nat decided to accept the food, but kept the railway man in his sights all the while he was eating.

A question from the man: 'Were you telling me the truth about your mother being in Hull?' Munching ravenously Nat moved his head. 'Well now, I know somebody who's going to Hull this morning. I might be able to wangle a free ride for you.'

Nat was immediately on alert, but desperation made him trust this man, and how fortunate that he had, for later that morning he was on his way to Hull on a merchant's cart.

The journey was tedious. Both the cart and the merchant stank of fish, but Nat was too immersed in thought to care much. Why, why had not his mother left word for him? It didn't make sense. During the dusty, uncomfortable ride he had much opportunity to mull over ways to find her, though this did not help. When the cart finally rumbled into the fishing port of Kingston-upon-Hull he was appalled at how busy the place was. Where on earth would he start looking?

His benefactor eased an aching back whilst continuing to steer his horse down the highly populated thoroughfare of Hessle Road. 'Well, you wanted Hull and here it is. Whereabouts d'you want dropping?'

Nat lurched with the motion of the cart and stared miserably ahead. 'Dunno.'

'Then I might as well stop here.' Several times the man had tried to involve Nat in conversation and had received such a response. He would be glad to see the back of his dull travelling companion.

The boy climbed down from the cart, looked around, then began to wander away. Peeved at the lack of gratitude, the man did not offer to buy the lad a meal as he had fully intended. Without sympathy he flicked his reins and moved off, leaving Nat to fend for himself.

Existing on the contents of dustbins, and bedding in doorways, Nat padded the streets for the next two days hoping for a sight of his mother, looking into every face, exploring every alley – even loitering around the many public houses in the area on the off-chance of seeing Kendrew – but there was no sign of either of them. Each night he changed his dossing place, moving on to a new street where he would begin his quest again in the morning.

On his fourth morning, a Monday, he was woken from his cold and uncomfortable bed of newspaper by the sound of clog-irons resounding from the pavement. Aching with cold he rubbed his eyes. It was still dark – seemed like the middle of the night. For a moment he leaned in the doorway and watched the bunches of dockworkers lope past, unable to see their faces, just dark shapes. One of them noticed his own shadowy form, took pity on him and threw him a penny. Grasping it, he rose, yawned and decided to follow the men to see where they were going.

His journey took him into an even darker subway that echoed eerily to the sound of clogs and voices. When he emerged he found himself on what was obviously the fish dock. Apart from the odour he could see the outline of half a dozen large trawlers against the early morning sky. Yawning again, he became aware that the quay was as busy as a Saturday afternoon's market in York – busier. The men who landed fish – the bobbers, who had disturbed him – now formed into gangs, each unloading their appointed vessel, some below deck, some above, some on land, working like ants. Speed was essential with this perishable cargo. On deck, swingers despatched baskets of fish to the winchman on the quay who emptied and weighed its contents, which were in turn barrowed off to the market. Meanwhile, on the trawlers men in rubber aprons scrubbed the boards to remove blood, scales and ice.

Clutching his penny, Nat wandered about the quay, occasionally slipping on the greasy ground, watching the great activity as men rushed in preparation of the seven-thirty market, sorting fish into type and size, stacking each trawler's catch into heaps ready for auction. He found a soup wagon where he spent his penny, gratefully cupping his hands to the warmth. Long after the broth was finished he continued to watch the scene. Each trawler was divested of its catch then moved away by tugs to the dry docks for repairs. By now it was light, though still early, and the fish merchants had begun to arrive. Once the warmth of the soup had lost its effect Nat began to walk again, watching, watching all the time for a familiar face. He came to the auction. St Andrew's Dock was now busier than ever. After each sale the merchant's label was slapped onto the heap of crates then transported by barrowboys to the filleters at the buyers' stand. Knives flashed, fillets were packed in ice. Gulls screamed and dived on the pile of offal that grew at the workers' feet until it was carted away to a factory and the flags hosed down.

Over the rest of the day Nat covered every inch of the fish dock, eventually coming to the conclusion that he was wasting his time here. Tired, disillusioned and hungry he wandered around seeking an exit, only finding one by shadowing a group of bobbers on their way home, tripping over ropes, jumping out of the way of gushing hoses and feeling generally miserable. Once again he followed them under the subway and out into a network of streets. Soon he would need a place to lay his head for the night, but right now he was too tired to go any further. Dropping to the paved ground he leaned his back against the wall of a school, hugged his knees and rested his brow upon them.

There was no danger; the pupils had gone home. Horse-drawn traffic clip-clopped up and down this main route to the docks. The sound of clogs clip-clopped past him too and marched on up the street . . . then paused and made their way back. 'Here!'

When Nat lifted desolate eyes to see an outstretched hand offering half a sandwich – the remnants of a docker's lunch tin – he grabbed it.

'Oy! No need to take me bloody hand an' all,' complained the Samaritan before walking on.

It was whilst Nat was gobbling up the morsel that he saw Kendrew emerging from a public house. Immediately alert, he ducked behind one of the pillars of the school gates, then peeped around the edge of the brickwork, watching Kendrew like a hawk. Kendrew, sauntering in his normal indolent manner, did not see the boy, or at least did not recognize him, and walked on past the school. Leaving a respectable distance and hugging the wall, Nat followed him up the avenue and out onto Hessle Road. All lassitude vanished. At the thought of being led to his mother Nat would have pursued Kendrew for miles. However, his enemy merely crossed the road and travelled a further fifty yards before rounding a corner and entering a dilapidated cottage. After he had closed the door, Nat came up to stand before it, unsure of what course to take. The door opened directly onto the living quarters; through it he could hear Sep's call.

'Good evening, Mrs Kendrew!' Sep threw his hat on a chair, then enthroned himself at the table to await the meal which Maria was now transporting from the kitchen.

She smiled a welcome and put his meal before him, sitting down opposite to eat her own. Even now it was hard for Maria to believe that she was married at last. These past weeks in Hull when he had kept delaying the wedding . . . well, after a lifetime of not trusting men one couldn't prevent misgivings. But she had faced him with her worry and he had been so amazed that she could think he had been offering her falsehoods that he had gone straight out that very day and arranged the wedding, and here she was a respectable married woman! Well, almost. Unfortunately, Sep's new job had not lasted long. He had a tendency to oversleep in the morning and this had resulted in him not only losing his job but the cottage that went with it. Maria had been forced to go back to her old line of work in order that they might live. Sep detested it of course, and was profusely regretful that he had forced her into this, but she said she didn't mind and anyway it wouldn't be long before he had another job if he went out every day hunting, as he had been doing.

'Any luck today, Sep?'

He sawed at his meat. Maria's cooking had not improved but it satisfied Kendrew who, never having been used to rich living could not miss it. 'Sorry, love, there's nowt. I've been all over town. My feet are killing me.'

'Aw. I'll get you a bowl of water after tea and you can soak them.'

'By, you do look after me,' he smiled warmly. 'Go fetch us the sauce will you?'

It was while Maria was in the scullery that the knock came. Normally, Sep would have waited for her to answer it, but feeling generous today he called, 'I'll get it!'

When he opened the door to reveal Nat he slammed it behind him with one hand, grabbed Nat's throat with the other and dragged him around the corner. 'What the hell are you doing here?'

Almost choking, Nat was unable to speak. Kendrew released a little of the pressure and shook an answer from him. 'I've come to see me mam!'

'Well you can sling yer hook, she doesn't want to see you.'

'She does!'

134

Kendrew rammed Nat up against the wall. 'Why d'you think she didn't let you know where she was going?'

'It's you! You what took her away!'

'No! She went because she's sick of you, sick of the trouble you've caused her. Now I'm telling you, you can get back to where you came from and keep away from here. Otherwise I'll bloody kill you. I mean it! Just you stay away.'

His face a mask of viciousness, Kendrew thrust Nat from him and, brushing back his hair, stormed off round the corner. Nat heard the door slam before shedding a brief burst of tears at Kendrew's accusation; could his mother have left him because he was a naughty boy? No, no it wasn't true! She wouldn't do that. Kendrew had tricked her into leaving, Nat was sure of it. Undeterred in his intentions of seeing her, he went round the corner, looked briefly at the closed door then moved further up the street to wait until his mother came out.

'Who was it?' Maria had resumed her meal and did not look up, giving Kendrew time to iron out the lines of anger before seating himself opposite.

He had removed his stock to wipe the perspiration from his face. 'A bloke I know. He's been looking out for a job for me. Says there might be a chance of one at the factory where he works.'

'You don't look very pleased about it,' observed Maria.

Sep tried to grin as he retied his stock. 'Oh, well . . . it's just that it's nothing special, I'm afraid. Still, it's work and I shouldn't complain.' He managed to smile more convincingly, whilst inside cursing Nat. 'Keep your fingers crossed. We'll soon have you being a housewife.'

Maria was delighted at the prospect and reached into her apron for a handkerchief with which to mop her lips. Her fingers encountered something small and hard. She did not have to examine it to know it was the little tin watch on its piece of frayed elastic. The watch she had been meant to give to Bright but could not bear to part with; it was the only link she had with her boy. Behind the handkerchief her smile turned wistful as she wondered what her son was doing now that Sep had arranged for him to live with somebody on his release from Industrial School. Not stupid, Maria knew there was a possibility of it being lies; she loved Sep, but he could be a crafty devil when he wanted anything. Despite this knowledge, she hadn't checked up on him. If it was a lie, well . . . she did not want to know.

After washing the pots Maria got ready for work, rushing to meet the high tide. With most of her customers drawn from the fishing industry her hours were dictated by the sea. As usual when Maria went out on her evening's mission, Sep would accompany her. Tonight, though, whilst she was putting on her hat, he threw a furtive glance up and down the street in case the boy was still lurking. From his hiding place behind a stationary cart Nat watched his mother walk away from him, powerless to waylay her. As the couple headed for the docks, he followed at a respectable distance.

St Andrew's Dock was as busy in the evening as throughout the day. Several more fishing smacks had landed and a host of wenches paraded on the quay, hoping to divest some lusty lad of his wage. Nat dodged in and out of the crowd as his mother and Kendrew appeared to wander aimlessly. When they stopped so did Nat, hiding behind a group of fishermen. When Kendrew left Maria's side, Nat's excitement grew – now was his chance. But no, Kendrew had gone only a few paces and was speaking to another man. Nat shrank back to watch as Kendrew's associate came over to Maria and the pair of them began to walk off together. Would Kendrew go too? No! His enemy sat upon a capstan and lit a pipe. Using the crowd as a shield, Nat took off after his mother. She and the man were walking too fast for him to catch up without running. He was going to lose her! 'Mam!'

Kendrew saw and heard him at the same instant, leaped up, grabbed him and, almost throttling him in the process, dragged him out of view of his mother behind a wall of crates.

Maria stiffened and looked round, then just as quickly turned her eyes back ahead. It couldn't be Nat! And if it were whatever would she do? Heart thumping, bile rising to her throat, she linked her arm more tightly with that of the man and hurried on.

A slap across Nat's cheek preceded Kendrew's words. 'Didn't I warn you what I'd do to you if you showed your face again? Didn't I say your mother doesn't want you?'

'She does! Let me talk to her.' Nat looked desperately at the crowd, hoping one of its members would help.

Kendrew pinned him against the stack of crates. 'Let me tell you summat and then let's decide if you still want to talk to her. All this talk about your father being a prince, I don't know if she was the one who told you that but if she did it's rubbish! You never knew him at all, did you?' Nat didn't answer. 'Well, neither did she. I think you're old enough to take a bit of plain talking. Your mother's a whore. Do you know what that is? Aye, you dirty little tyke,' he saw the look of horror on Nat's face, 'I see you know all about it. Well, that saves me having to explain. You know what your mam's gone off to do with that bloke?'

'No!' Nat tried to struggle free.

'Yes!' Kendrew shook him. 'Do you still want to talk to her?'

'Let go!' Nat kicked out at him.

'Do you want to see her?'

'No!'

Another vicious shaking. 'And will you come to my house again?'

'No! Let me go!'

Kendrew threw him aside. Nat fled blindly, pushing between lads and their wenches, bobbers and filleters, barrowboys and deckhands, tearing round corners, not knowing where he was going. Consumed by panic, he ran smack into a tower of crates. They toppled over with a crash and so did Nat, but just as quickly he jumped to his feet and danced upon one of the crates in a fury, jumping hard with both feet, slipping and sliding on the colourful mackerel that belched over the quay, mashing them into the ground, sobbing with rage and shame. When these were destroyed he jumped upon the contents of another crate and another; box after box was mashed to pulp before the owners saw what he was doing and came running to waylay the maniac. Jerked back to his senses by their shouts, Nat fled with the youths in pursuit, but he was tiring and his boots were slippery with fish scales. He skidded on the cobbles, the youths were able to get a better grip with their clogs and closed in on him. He was going to be beaten . . . then salvation! He saw a gathering of people with their backs to him and pushed his way through the bodies which closed behind him like a wall. The youths tried to battle their way through but were ordered to, 'Stop pushing in!' by a heavily built man and so had to stand cursing at the back. Wide-eyed and panting, Nat glanced over his shoulder ready to take flight again, but his pursuers were still arguing to be allowed through.

He turned his frightened gaze on the man and woman at the centre of the crowd who were providing the entertainment. Both were naked from the waist up. For that brief moment Nat forgot his pursuers and goggled at the bouncing breasts as the woman laid into her antagonist – not like a woman with slaps and scratches but like a man with fists, great blood-spurting blows. Her opponent hit back with equal vehemence, not pulling his punches at all. Nat winced as each blow connected but watched in fascination as the woman appeared to be winning! With one last smash the man went down. A united groan arose from those who had bet money on him and the crowd began to thin. Once more Nat saw his hunters and decided the best place to be was beside the woman.

'Here's your blouse, Mam!' He seized the garment from the floor and ran to her. The youths, who had been about to accost him, now had second thoughts. Nat continued the pretence. 'Let me help you, Mam.'

'What the hell . . .?' The coarse-looking creature with lopped hair shrugged off his attempts to help her on with her blouse and began to lumber away, wiping the blood from her chin with the back of her hand. Nat tagged on, casting a worried eye at the youths who were tailing him.

'Are we going home now, Mam?' he asked in a voice loud enough for them to catch, just in case they hadn't heard the other times.

'I don't know who you are but if you don't stop hanging onto my bloody skirt I'll fucking well flatten you.' The woman ignored him then, in order to count her winnings.

Nat fought his natural inhibitions to whisper, 'Can't I just walk beside you for a while? Them men are after me.'

'Suit yourself.' Coins clinked from one big hand to another. 'But stop calling me Mam.'

The ploy worked. None of the youths was yet brave enough to confront this hoyden with the news that her son owed them for a hundredweight of ruined mackerel. However, they trailed him for a while, deciding how to approach the problem. To Nat's dismay the woman did not leave the docks but began negotiations for another fist fight. Once this was underway Nat's protection was gone. His trackers pounced, determined to take vengeance on his hide. 'Aagh! Get off, pigs!' He screamed and tried to wriggle free.

A united roar of horror went up. 'Oh Christ, who said

that? Get the little bastard!' A man seized one of Nat's arms. 'Where the hell are you from, Timbuctoo?'

'I don't know what you mean!' yelled a terrified Nat.

'Don't you know it's bad luck to say – *that word* – around here? And the bad luck's yours!' He raised a fist.

Nat cowered. 'Sorry! Sorry!' He could not remember using any curse.

'Sorry? Sorry's not good enough! We won't be able to take the boats out tomorrow with that bad luck hanging over us! You soft little . . .'

Dozens of growling fishermen were about to join the retribution when a cry went up. 'Police!' In a flash everyone on the dock scattered, whether guilty or not. Nat was dropped to his feet and ran with the others, taking the same direction as the fighting woman for she was his only hope of reprieve – though he had to run fast to keep up.

Once they were out of danger, she braked to a masculine plod, never once remarking that Nat was still with her.

The threat gone, Nat relapsed into his normal shyness, and went back to brooding over his mother, asking no questions. There were none from his companion either. All that passed between them was the sound of panting. When she walked Nat merely followed her through the dark and echoing subway, taking a different route to the one he had used earlier until she came to a crumbling tenement building and entered the ground floor apartment. Dull of spirit, he waited for her to shut the door in his face but she left it open; taking this as invitation to follow, he did so.

Besides the fighting woman there was another female in the room, but there was no exchange of greeting between them. The woman, not quite so rough-looking as his unwilling benefactress, eyed Nat and made some jocular comment. The fighting woman growled a reply. Nat, fishing for sympathy, produced tears – which was not hard; all he had to do was think of his mother. Neither woman took the slightest heed, but when Nat's misery eased and he wiped his eyes there were three plates of bacon on the table. The fighting woman pointed a dirty finger at one, indicating for Nat to sit down, and shoved a plate of bread at him.

The meal was eaten in silence. At the end of it though, the two women began to converse, the fighting woman telling her friend about her evasion of the police. Nat had never heard such swearing from a woman. 'Bastards! That's the third frigging time this week. If this carries on I'll have to move somewhere else.' Unexpectedly, she turned on Nat. 'Where d'you live?'

He shrank at her fierceness. 'Nowhere.'

'You must live some-bloody-where, even if it's on a shitheap.'

He fingered the rim of his plate, not looking at her. 'I used to live in York but I had to come here to find me mam.'

Uninterested, the woman did not bother to ask if he had found Maria. It saved Nat the pain of an answer.

She narrowed her eyes, then nodded as if coming to a decision. 'York – that's where I'll bloody go! If I remember rightly there's a race meeting this month. Ought to be able to make a few quid if the bastard police are kind enough to allow it, then be back in time for the Fair.'

Nat hated this place with all his heart and if he was going to be alone in life he would be better off in a town he knew. After a nervous pause, he asked, 'Can I go with you?'

'I thought you said you came to find your mam?' The other woman broke in.

'I couldn't find her,' murmured Nat. 'I'll have to go back to York.' He asked the fighting woman again. 'Can I come with you?' *Please*, please say yes, he begged silently. I need to get away from here.

'If you want, but I'm not paying your bloody train fare.'

Nat swung his feet beneath the table and looked dejected. 'I've no money.'

'Hard luck then.' The fighting woman examined her knuckles which were grazed raw.

'Poor likkle sod.' The other woman went to fetch a bottle of iodine which she dabbed on her friend's hands to much cursing and ingratitude. 'He's lost his mam. Take him with you, Clem – stick him in the trunk if you won't pay for him.'

'Why should I be lumbered with him – ow! Is that bloody acid you're using?' Clem tugged her hand away.

'Don't be such a baby, Clem Giblet,' scolded her nurse, and tried to dab the cut lip.

'I'll give you frigging baby!' swore the harridan.

Her partner giggled. 'That'd be a miracle, wouldn't it? You'd make a lot o' money out o' that!' Ramming the cork back into the bottle with an accompanying squeak, she tried again on Nat's behalf. 'Go on, don't be mean. If you're going to York anyway it'd be no trouble to stick him in the trunk now, would it?'

Clem Giblet shrugged.

'That means she'll take you,' explained the other to Nat.

Relieved, he settled down to pass the evening with the weird couple. Neither of them bothered to ask his name until it was time to retire.

He was told to bed down on the mat by the fire, though he slept very little, his mind re-enacting the evening's scenario. Maria had heard him call to her, he was sure of it. Why, *why* hadn't she answered? He relived Kendrew's words. Why d'you think she never told you where she was going? *Because she doesn't want you!* Enraged, he threw himself onto his other side trying not to face the truth, but try as he might to evade it the truth kept lapping at his brain and eventually swamped him with its awfulness. Why, why did you leave me, Mam? The last thing he could remember thinking was, *I hate you, Mam.* I love you but I bloody hate you, and this was the thought with which he faced the following day.

* * *

142

He had lain wide awake for a good two hours before Clem Giblet and her friend came down to breakfast – bread and a cup of water. Afterwards the other woman produced a trunk. Nat still did not know her identity. 'I've cut a likkle hole in one corner so you won't suffocate. See? Put your face up yon end and you'll be all right.'

'Oh Christ, I forgot about his lordship.' Clem Giblet looked even more vinegary this morning, and made Nat drag the trunk by himself to the railway station. Being of cheap materials it was not all that heavy, though the station seemed a long way, especially with such a grumpy partner. Still, it gave Nat plenty of time to think about yesterday's episode with Kendrew and to plot his revenge.

'Get out o' the bloody way!' Clem pushed a man off the footwalk. He staggered in amazement but did not offer retaliation, having previously witnessed one of Clem's fights.

Nat tensed. But of course! Here was the answer, to one problem at least. Heaving the trunk behind him, he glanced up at Clem, swallowed, then forced out the question. 'Will you hit anybody?'

Clem was not selective. 'If the pay's right.'

Nat grew bolder. 'If I can save enough money will you hit somebody for me?'

She cast a disdainful eye at him. 'Who might that be?'

'A bloke called Sep Kendrew. He's got brown hair and a hole in his cheek and he lives near that fishy place where we were last night. When you come back to Hull will you get him for me?'

Clem uttered what passed for a laugh. Nat did not know whether this meant agreement and did not have time to enquire, for they had reached the station. Clem waited until there was no one nearby then said, 'Climb in!'

Making sure that his head was at the end where the hole was, he rolled up inside, hugging his knees. It was horrible hearing those locks snap shut. He felt a great lurch, then a series of bounces and bangs as Clem tried to lift the trunk onto a trolley. He heard her holler for a porter, then felt himself being tipped upside down with his face squashed into a corner and the blood rushing to his head. Despite it being the corner with the hole in, Nat felt sure he was going to suffocate and sucked desperately at the hole for air. After being trundled what seemed like miles down the platform, he was loaded aboard and mercifully did not have to wait long before the train jolted into movement.

The journey was terrible. Nat could hardly breathe. He started to cry but discovered that this made breathing worse and so instead tried to sleep. After what seemed like hours of hell they arrived in York. Again the trunk, with Nat contorted inside, was balanced on a trolley and wheeled down the platform.

Once outside the station his gaoler casually released him. Nat clambered out, then had to sit on the path to recover. 'Oh, oh me legs!' He rubbed them and rocked back and forth. 'They're paralysed, I can't walk!'

Totally unsympathetic, Clem put the trunk on her shoulders and moved off. Nat gave his legs a final brisk rub and got up, stamping his feet. 'Ow, it feels as if I'm walking on a bed of pins!'

'Thought you said you couldn't walk.' Clem offered a final sarcasm.

Nat ran after her. 'I almost peed meself in there.'

To his shock Clem spun and hit him around the head. It was only a tap by her standards but it knocked him to his knees. 'Don't be so vulgar!'

'What? I only said . . .'

'I heard what you said! There's a little old lady over there, she doesn't want to listen to your foul language!'

Amazed, Nat simply stared. Clem hefted the trunk and moved off. The boy hastened to his feet and followed. Not pausing, Clem turned a gimlet eye on him. 'You asked me to fetch you to York, you didn't ask me to be your mother.'

Nat faltered. 'But I won't know where to find you when I want to give you the money to hit Kendrew.'

Clem frowned. 'Kendrew?'

'You know! I said I'd save up . . .'

Clem groaned. 'All right, all right! Stop wittering, I'm too tired to listen to your rantings.' She threw down the trunk. 'If I'm still to be encumbered with you, you might as well carry that.'

Nat picked up one end of the trunk and dragged it after him.

'Don't expect me to feed you, mind!' Clem warned him. 'You'll have to earn your keep.'

Nat vouched that he would, little guessing what she had in mind. That evening, when the two were ensconced in the poky upper room of a medieval inn by the riverside, she gave him instructions; he was to go around all the taverns, drumming up custom for a fight.

How would this shy boy accost the sort of men she had described and recite her invitation? A flogging would have been kinder. Yet fearful of Clem's wrath, he made a start in the taproom downstairs. Approaching a hard-looking man he said, in quaking voice, 'Bareknuckle fight, eight o'clock St George's Field. Crippling Clem Giblet'll take on any-body. Tell your friends.' The man eyed him, then simply nodded over the rim of his tankard. Nat backed away, then went outside. Not knowing whether he had been success-ful, he visited two more hostelries and repeated the invita-tion many times. Then, deciding that if the men told their friends there would be enough spectators without him having to carry on, he went back to Clem.

Luckily for Nat a fine crowd turned up. The punters, having first believed Crippling Clem to be a man, were quick to spot easy money and large bets were placed on her opponent, a local man. Nat was given the money to hold and threatened that his throat would be cut if he moved so much as one inch. He clutched the purse and watched the fight intently, hoping to pick up some tips in self-defence and coming to the conclusion that if one wanted to win one had to fight dirty. Clem had the man annihilated in five minutes, winning almost twenty guineas. There were no further candidates. Well pleased with Nat, she treated him to supper and said that he could hang around for the races where they would find more custom.

It was a different type of custom to that which he expected. Clem didn't bet on the horses, telling Nat she only placed money on certainties. Instead she sat on the grass amongst the racegoers and spent the afternoon doing absolutely nothing – or so it appeared to Nat. In fact she had been watching her next source of income.

The yokel was the embodiment of innocence with his fresh face, his linen smock and his billycock hat. He had brought his farm products to the market that morning and had stayed for the races. It was his first time in York without his father. He felt very grown up. Clem could see that by the way he swaggered, and during the afternoon his lucky wagers on the horses made him strut all the more. After the last race of the day when the crowds went home, Clem shadowed him. A bored Nat ambled behind. The yokel made his way back to where he had left his horse and cart. Before he had time to move off, Clem approached him. 'Excuse me, squire, could I trouble you for a ride back into town? It's a long way for my son to walk and my husband's lost all our money on the nags, left us to find our own way home.'

The yokel had not actually been going back through York but, flattered at the term squire, he bade them climb up. Whilst they rode Clem chatted – Nat had never heard her talk so much without swearing. By the time they arrived outside the pub where they lodged she had persuaded the young man to join them for a noggin. The guest tarried so long that Nat fell asleep.

In the morning he woke to the sound of groans. The

yokel was laying on the floor, his face purple with bruises, and Clem was nowhere to be seen. With her victim in too befuddled a state to catch him, Nat picked up his jacket and ran, cursing bitterly that he had lost his only chance of wreaking vengeance on Kendrew.

6

Alone again, Nat was at a loss as to what to do, roving aimlessly along pavements encrusted with dried vomit, cabbage leaves and orange peel. He could of course have gone to the Maguires yesterday, but as that would mean having to explain about his mother he chose not to, though he felt a desperate need to see a familiar face, especially Bright's.

He turned the corner into Parliament Street, a broad expanse of road flanked by tall buildings, mainly banks and shops. Outside the latter hung the commodities to be purchased within: kettles, pots and pans, racks of clothes and boots, linen and lace. Today was a market day. Five rows of covered stalls ran the length of the street, with intermittent gaps to allow access for horse-drawn transport. Nat weaved his way in and out of the busy shoppers, coveting the fruit on the market stalls. He had never stolen in his life, but might have to resort to it now. The way became blocked where housewives with baskets queued at a stall that had better quality fruit than the rest. Nat ducked under the counter to escape the crush and in so doing he noticed another stall that appeared to have no one in attendance. Other market holders were too busy to notice a little thief. After crafty surveillance, he reached out for an apple . . . just as the owner who had been stooping at the front of his counter bobbed up. Hands on hips, he tilted his boater and beheld Nat with a look of mordancy. 'Don't take it from the back, son, I put all the rubbish there. Why don't you have one of these nice ones from the front.'

Misreading the sarcasm, Nat said, 'Thank you,' and reached out to take the man at his word.

'You saucy litt–!' The trader made a bid to cuff his ear.

Dodging, Nat grabbed a bunch of bananas, scrambled under another counter and was away. The man chased him. Nat snatched at a rack of linen and brought it crashing down to impede his pursuer. The man leaped over it and continued to chase him: 'Out of the way! Stop, thief!' Then Nat swerved right into Jubbergate where the trader lost sight of him and gave up with a harsh curse.

Nat ran on into Newgate where a choice of alleyways offered certain escape. Looking over his shoulder he saw that the man had abandoned the chase and, after wheeling into Patrick Pool, Nat decided it was safe to slow down. Breathing heavily, he came to rest by a medieval church surrounded by railings, laughed to himself and leaned against the iron gate belonging to what remained of the church's graveyard – when suddenly the support gave way, he was pounced on by ruffians, his bunch of bananas was wrenched from his hand and he was dragged into the churchyard and sat upon.

There were four of them. Craning his neck upwards, Nat could see three boys gloating at him whilst they devoured his fruit. The fourth was sitting on his back. All Nat could gauge of him was his weight and that he ate very noisily.

'Get down till I say you can move!' A rough hand shoved his head at the ground.

The bananas were consumed with leisure. Powerless, Nat felt his hip-bones grinding into the tombstone upon which he had been spreadeagled.

'What shall we do with him now?' The boy on his back dangled an empty banana skin over Nat's nose, then draped it on his head like a cap.

The others began to make suggestions, none of them agreeable either to Nat or the boy on his back who seemed to have authority here. He jumped to his feet, dragging Nat up with him. 'I've got a better idea —let's thump him.'

Nat flicked the banana skin from his head and struggled to confront his tormentor, but the boy had him around the throat. 'I've some friends who're bigger than you! Touch me and they'll get you!'

His captor sneered. 'I don't see them.'

Nat twisted and writhed. 'They're locked up at the moment but when they get out . . .'

This seemed to impress. The leader asked where they were locked up. 'Marygate,' supplied Nat. 'I've just done two years there meself.'

The ruffian's approach altered. Freeing Nat, he allowed him to turn. 'Ragged school? What did they stick you in there for?'

'Murder.' Nat pulled himself to his full height and tugged his clothes into order.

This was a little too implausible. The boys fell about laughing. 'They don't stick you in ragged school for murder!' scoffed their leader.

'Well . . . I *nearly* murdered somebody,' blustered Nat. 'His name was Kendrew. He pinched something what belonged to me so I waited for him in the dark and hit him over the head. Then when he fell down I jumped on his face and broke his nose and did other things to him. Then the police came and stopped it before I really killed him.'

His audience did not know whether to believe him or not. These were not street arabs but ordinary schoolboys; their kneebreeches and stockings might be darned, but they weren't pauperized and all wore boots. Nat, realizing with burgeoning confidence that he was getting the better of them, let his eyelids droop at the edges to make himself look tough as he returned their stares.

The leader jumped up onto the tombstone, looking down on his underlings. 'How old're you?'

'Eleven, nearly twelve.' Nat looked the speaker up and

down. His legs were pronouncedly bowed — obviously a result of rickets. Due to this, the leather of his boots was in a very poor state on the outer edges. He had curly brown hair and eyes that were an abnormally pale shade of blue set into what Nat considered to be the face of a wax doll, his skin sallow. The tough image he tried to present was offset by a girlish, rosebud mouth and the frailty of limb. Nevertheless, he was dangerous. There had been a boy with eyes such as this who had spent the briefest of terms at the Industrial School. He had gone there completely uncontrollable and had left the same way within days; everyone had said he was mad.

'I'm twelve and a half,' retorted the leader, and fixed Nat with his pale blue eyes. 'I'm meant to be at school but I jigged off after the first lesson. I'll be leaving soon anyway, so I do what I want.'

'What about you?' Nat enquired of the other boys.

'They jigged too,' their leader answered for them. 'They do what I tell 'em. So, d'you want to be in my gang, then?'

This was unexpected. Nat made himself appear nonchalant. 'Could do.' He joined the other three boys to sit cross-legged on the grass.

'You have to go through an initiation ceremony,' said the leader, hitching his wrinkled stockings and jumping down from the gravestone.

Nat tried not to flinch. There had been plenty of initiation ceremonies at the Industrial School, most of them unspeakable, but he couldn't lose face now.

'Right, what's your name?' the boy asked Nat.

'Nat Prince.' Nat squinted up warily.

'Mine's Denzil Kneebone, the boss of this gang.' He reached down for his cap, which had fallen to the grass in the scuffle, and put it on his head, tugging the peak. 'This is my right hand man, Roger Carter.' He kicked at a thick-set boy, of a similar age to himself, dark like a gypsy with almond shaped eyes and a felt hat pulled well down over his brow, no jacket, just a shirt, a neckerchief and a waistcoat.

'That's Spud Cato.' Nat was later to discover that Spud was so named because of the rather tenuous link with his surname. At first he had been known as Cato Potato, then somebody had called him Spud. However, for now Nat assumed the nickname to be because of the boy's likeness to a spud; he had a lumpy face and tiny eyes, a slack mouth and a slack jacket that hung off his shoulders like a bag. His waistcoat had been buttoned in the wrong holes. The overall impression was one of a dullard.

'. . . and Gunner Ray.' A bigger boy than the rest, to Nat it seemed anomalous that Gunner wasn't the leader, for he put Denzil in the shade. He had dark eyes and hair like Roger, but was less swarthy. His head was particularly large; the cap he wore looked ridiculous perched on top. For this reason alone Nat didn't like him, but was impressed by the military sounding name.

Denzil relaxed on the tombstone and commanded, 'Right, all stand!' The boys rose, leaving circles of flattened grass in their wake. 'Tell him what he has to do, Rodge.'

It transpired that the initiation consisted of robbing an item from a pawnbroker's shop and selling it to another. Fresh from the thrill of hooking the bananas, Nat considered this a tame enrolment.

However, when they arrived at the symbol of the three brass balls in Low Petergate he saw that this would require nerve. The man was behind the counter. There were a few items by the door, but Denzil ordered Nat to go right in and take something from the shop. Caution began to tickle his gut. The boys shoved him inside. Mr Merriman looked at him and said, 'Yes, what can I do for you, young man?'

Nat's mind whirred. 'Er, you've got a telescope in the window. Can I have a look at it, please?'

The man leaned on the counter. 'You just want to look or you want to buy?'

Nat hoped he sounded convincing. 'I don't want to buy it until I've had a look through it.'

'Show me your money.'

Nat looked innocent. 'Why?'

'Because I'm not taking the trouble to get it out of the window if you cannot afford it.' Obviously it was the boy's shorn head that was the giveaway.

Through the window the others watched his performance. 'I can afford it,' pleaded Nat.

'I don't believe you.' Merriman's expression was challenging. 'You'll wait until my back's turned and then you'll steal something from me. I know you boys.'

Nat was outraged. 'I don't steal!'

'Empty your pockets then.'

Nat beheld him in disgust, and turned to walk out – then saw the looks of ridicule on the other boys' faces. He must do something. In a trice, he seized the arm of a jersey, catching another with it as a bonus, and ran out of the shop. The looks of scorn turned to ones of disbelief. Even before Nat emerged with the man on his tail they had taken flight.

'Stop thief!' The pawnbroker ran a few yards, but being unable to leave his shop unattended, was compelled to stand there shaking his fist. No one else tried to accost them. Running for his life, dodging carts and hansoms, Nat followed in the trail of the others, heading back for the camp in St Sampson's churchyard.

When they caught their breath, Denzil thumped Nat in the chest. 'You daft idiot! You nearly had us all copped. If you ever do that I'll kill you.' And Nat could tell that he meant it.

The next part of the initiation went without a hitch. Nat walked into another pawnbroker's shop, this time Haythorne's in Walmgate, handed over the two jerseys to Uncle, gave a false name and received a few pence, which he was then forced to hand over to Denzil. 'Am I in the gang now?'

Though satisfied with his performance, Denzil replied, 'Not yet, you've another part of the initiation to go through.'

'I'm starving,' complained Nat.

'So am I,' agreed Denzil. 'Let's go get summat to eat first.'

There was a greengrocer's nearby with a mound of produce outside. The old lady in charge was half blind and did not see the boys loading carrots and apples down their fronts for all they were worth. Their booty was consumed as they loped through town and along the riverside to their other camping ground, which was near Lendal Bridge on the west bank of the Ouse. The earth here was unwalled and sloped down to the water. In the shadow of the bridge with its toll booths at either end they had piled branches, planks and stones from a demolished building to make a fort, though almost every day they were forced to rebuild it due to sabotage. Whilst they crouched inside, eating apples, keeping an eye on some other boys on the landing stage across the river, Nat was pumped for his life story, which he embroidered in grosspoint.

When they had taken their fill, the boys used the apple cores as missiles to bomb one another. One of them caught Denzil on the nose and Nat had a glimpse of just how unpredictable the leader could be as he fell upon Gunner and beat him until he cried.

'I'm gunner tell me dad o' you!' Gunner ran off sobbing, thereby providing Nat with an explanation of his nickname.

Totally unconcerned, Denzil shouted an insult, then calm as one pleased, announced, 'Right! It's time for the second part of the initiation. Lie down!'

Dreading violence, Nat lay on the ground. The other boys stood round him, made sure no one was about, then unbuttoned their kneebreeches and proceeded to urinate on him. Never had Nat experienced anything so ghastly.

He thrashed from side to side, trying to escape being drowned, but Denzil's aim followed his movements. When the flow stopped they used their feet to roll him in the mud and laughed uproariously at the end result. Nat hated and despised them.

'You are now a fully-fledged member of the gang!' pronounced Denzil. 'Wash yourself off in t'river.' Giving Nat little choice the leader pushed him in.

After his dousing one of them asked the leader, 'Do we teach him the special handshake?'

Denzil agreed, showing Nat what to do. 'It's so we don't get any spies from another gang trying to pinch our secrets. A spy wouldn't be able to do the handshake, see?'

Nat thought it ridiculous that with only five in the gang none of them would recognize an interloper even without the handshake, but went along with it anyway.

'Gunner'll give you a tattoo tomorrow an' all,' promised Denzil. 'He's good at that, even if he is a bit weedy. Right! Let's have a fire, Rodge.'

Roger lit a fire – it transpired from later conversation that this was his own speciality – and Spud went to hunt for more food.

Nat was still very damp when in the late afternoon they announced that they had to go home. He had forgotten that most people had homes to go to. They asked where he lived and he told them that he would live where the fancy took him. The news that he had no parents nor master to order him about elevated him even further in the eyes of Spud and Roger, though Denzil failed to be impressed, announcing that they would meet him at their headquarters in Patrick Pool tomorrow after school. Left alone, Nat felt utterly miserable and after spending a couple of hours wandering around hotel dustbins, looked for a place to sleep, gathering bits of newspaper as he went. Eventually, he curled up beneath a limestone arch. It was a very cold night.

✳   ✳   ✳

By the next morning he knew that he would have to find somewhere more civilized to live. It would have been quite easy to go to the Maguires, divulge that his mother had left him, and they would have taken him in. However, he refused to do that. Nat did not even want to think about his mother, let alone face a barrage of questions, though it would be nice to see Bright.

How was he going to eat? If he continued to steal he would eventually be caught and he was determined not to be sent back to that school. As he lounged there watching the early morning sun play over the river, he mulled over what employment he might be qualified to do. He was good at sweeping up and picking oakum, that was about all. The small amount of carpentry he had learned under Mr Chipchase might just get him taken on as an apprentice, but Nat was determined to have no master save himself.

A tramp shuffled past. Deep in quandary, Nat took little notice of him at first, but on paying more attention noticed that the tramp was collecting odd bits and pieces of what appeared to be rubbish. Why had he not thought about it before! He would be a scavenger. Jumping up, he stood there briefly tapping his chin, working out a routine. The vagrant had probably taken everything worthwhile around here, but there would be plenty of scrap metal near Foss Bridge. Wasting no time, he went there.

When Nat arrived, to his dismay there was an old man already in loco who shouted at Nat to go away. Annoyed, the boy moved a little further downstream. The man had a sack. Nat had nothing in which to put his find. With his clothes still damp from yesterday's dip it wouldn't matter if he got them wet again. He waded into the blanket of scum, feeling about with his boot. Encountering something, he crouched under the water, trying to keep his head free whilst grubbling with his hand. He took hold, revealing a piece of lead pipe. With no idea whether or not it was worth anything he threw it onto the bank and continued to grope.

Shortly after this he noticed to his alarm that the old man was approaching. He might be going to steal Nat's find; splashing to the bank he hovered over it like an eagle over its prey.

The old man grinned, much friendlier than before. 'Doing this for your dad, are you?'

Nat shook his head, loosing drops of water. 'It's mine.'

'What're you going to do with it?'

'Sell it and buy food,' answered Nat.

The old man rasped his bewhiskered chin. His nails were filthy. 'Haven't you got any mother to give you food?'

When Nat shook his head, the other nodded with empathy. 'All on your own, eh? I know how it feels.' He sighed and tapped the piece of lead with a worn-out boot. 'I don't like to say it but you won't get much for that bit there. Hardly enough to buy you a loaf of bread. Hungry, are you?'

Nat returned a dismal nod.

The man appeared to undergo deep decision, then with a magnanimous gesture he plunged into his greasy overcoat. 'Tell you what, I don't like to see a youngster in trouble. I'll exchange this gold coin for your scabby bit o' pipe.'

Nat asked to see the coin. The man held it out but refused to let go, showing that it was very valuable. Nat was not totally gullible. 'Why haven't you spent it yourself?'

'Can't spend it, it's not English money – came all the way from Egypt, but it has a lot of gold in it and the goldsmith'll give you a good price. I've been keeping it as a sort of talisman, it's brought me quite a bit of luck, but I reckon it's somebody else's turn to have a bit. Go on, take it, you look like you could do with it.'

Nat was still dubious. No one had ever done him favours and if they had then they wanted something in return. He dithered; then the lure of the bounty defeated his good sense. Once Nat had accepted it, the man was quick to drop the lead piping into his sack and hurry away.

Feeling optimistic, Nat turned the gold coin in his fingers, then sought out a goldsmith's to exchange it for money. On being shown the tiny piece of base metal, the goldsmith dealt him a swift clip around the ear and chased him from the shop. 'Take it to a scrapyard!'

The scrap dealer was a little kinder, telling Nat, 'This is really what you should be looking for.' He held up a piece of lead piping. The boy's face crumpled. 'Somebody diddled you, have they?' asked the man. Nat gave a glum nod. 'Learned your first lesson then. It's the ugly things that're worth the most – course if you find a big bit of brass I'd not complain.' He laughed. 'But anything metal'll do – screws, nuts. I'll give you a halfpenny for every pound of scrap you bring me.'

Nat returned to the river and searched all morning, collecting nails, rivets, washers, anything that might make up the weight. By tying the tails of his shirt around his waist he managed to form a bag into which he dropped his prizes. Judging by the clinking sound he had accrued a fine haul. This he took back to the scrapyard. The scales barely dipped. Nat wondered how dozens of nails could weigh so little.

Out of the goodness of his heart the man gave him a halfpenny anyway. 'But this is the last time! I'm not a charity.' He had a sudden idea. 'Tell you a better line of work for you, if you can get hold of a bucket and shovel, that is. The tannery'll pay you for every bucket of dogmuck you take them.'

Nat was angry at such blatant fraud, but the man announced that he was not trying to humiliate him. 'It's right! Heaven knows what they use it for, I'm not sure I want to know.' He studied the pathetic waif before him, the kind of waif he saw every day, but inexplicably this one touched a nerve in him. 'Look, to show I'm not stringing you along I'll do you a favour. I'll lend you a bucket and shovel until you've got enough to buy your own. I'm trusting you, now.'

Nat took the bucket and shovel, but before making a start on his new employment he used the halfpenny to buy food. Whilst eating his bread he looked up and down the street. There was plenty of excrement of all kinds but the man had specified dogmuck, so dogmuck it would be. Brushing the crumbs from his chin he braced himself, then set about his revolting task. Notwithstanding the amount of detritus about, it took a long time to fill the bucket. Anticipating mockery, he dithered outside the tannery for a long time before summoning the nerve to go in.

But no one laughed! A man just instructed him to tip the contents of his bucket into a pit, gave him a halfpenny and that was that. Pocketing his fee Nat spent the afternoon refilling his bucket. Whilst he was doing this he saw Bright and hid to avoid being caught in this humiliating position. It was for this same reason that he hid the bucket and shovel before going to meet Denzil and the gang that evening – not that he liked any of them, but they were better than no company at all.

Throughout September he continued to meet them on an evening, shovelling faeces during the day. From this insalubrious occupation and collecting bits of scrap he had almost earned enough to purchase his own bucket and shovel, but was reluctant to waste his money in this way. The scrapman had not yet asked for his implements to be returned, and until he did Nat would continue to make use of them.

Food was not a problem now, though finding a warm sleeping place was. Also, his boots had been too tight for some time and with a big hole in one of them they would have to be replaced. He was about to discard them when he noticed a smaller urchin without any footwear at all and asked if he had any money. Receiving a negative answer, he told the boy that if he could come up with tuppence the boots were his. The urchin rushed off to accost passers-by and soon returned to claim his prize. Nat added the coins to the rest in his pocket. If his feet could withstand the weather he would not be frittering his money on boots. He was saving it to buy himself a house.

Nat found other ways of earning money too – he should have done, he spent enough time thinking about it as he cleaned the city's footwalks. To save on buying food he began to wait outside factories for the men to leave and begged the scraps from their cans. If there was anything whole like a cake he would sell it for a penny. The scraps he would give to other boys in exchange for favours. He was going to be rich. No one would push him around again. It was amazing, the good ideas that came to one whilst shovelling dogmuck. On Sundays, when the bells rang out from St Saviour's and St Cuthbert's, he followed the rest of the parishioners into church. When the collection plate came round and others put money in, Nat took it out. He had become very adept at this, would hold a penny between his first and second fingers and lower his hand over the plate, then at the precise moment that the penny was released his thumb and third finger would nip a threepenny piece – or if he was lucky a sixpence – and transfer it deftly to his palm. With the services at different times he could manage to visit a number of churches; so many at the early service, one later in the morning and another two in the evening. Church provided a bed too, if he could manage to hide under a pew before the vicar locked up for the night.

One night, towards the end of September, he lurked in St Margaret's off Walmgate, only a few hundred yards from where Bright performed her worship. That was one place he had not visited for fear of encountering the Maguires, but greed was beginning to get the better of him and as he lay on his pew trying to sleep the thought kept niggling at his mind. St George's was just about the only church in the city from which he had not pilfered. It irked him, knowing the Catholics were more inclined to put a higher denomination of coin into the collection plate than anyone else. What was to say the Maguires would see him anyway? The church would be full, and a small boy like himself could easily evade their eye.

He waited until one rainy Sunday evening when the light was poor before chancing an encounter with the Irish family, hiding and watching until most of the congregation was in and the doors were about to be closed before making a dash inside.

He should not have waited: all the pews at the back were filled and he had to go further into the church to look for a gap. Someone grabbed him and hauled him into a space. With tentative eyes he looked up, but it was no one he knew. Only half relieved, he glanced around at the other worshippers, but being small did not have a very good field of vision. What matter, if he could not see them, the Maguires would not see him either.

In part he was right. Though seated only two rows behind, none of the Maguire family had noticed him, at least not for a while. However, in the brief change of position when the worshippers in front kneeled down to pray, the youngest Maguire caught a glimpse of him and, delighted, craned her face to watch him through a little gap between two elbows, praying for Mass to be over so she could be reunited with her friend.

To Nat the droning of priest and congregation seemed interminable, but he endured the tedium in the knowledge that there was to be reward at the end of it. Finally the ordeal was over, and he became alert as the collection plates began to move up and down the rows.

To his rear, Bright dropped her Sunday penny into the wooden bowl and watched it travel along the row in front.

She was always fascinated by the amount that some people put in and paid great attention to it. Eventually the bowl came to Nat. He took it with his left hand and used his right to put the coin in – no, he had taken a coin out! Bright's jaw fell open as she saw his fingers come away with a threepenny piece which was swiftly hidden in his fist and the bowl passed on. Oh, how could he?

The Maguires began to shuffle out of their stall. Nat, eager to be gone now, stepped out of his own pew, saw them and immediately jumped backwards. It was too late; Bright had seen him. Whilst her parents led the family out she lagged behind to confront him. Reluctantly he was nudged forward by those behind.

To Bright's indignance, he did not even have the decency to look ashamed. 'Hello,' was all he said.

Pursing her lips she turned and left the church, but was waiting for him outside to accuse him. 'You've stolen off Our Lord! I saw ye!'

Nat did not deny it. 'I need it to buy food.' It was raining. He began to walk.

Bright moved after him. 'What're ye talking about? Why don't you eat at home like everyone else?'

'I can't.'

Bright was still angry at this most heinous of crimes. 'Why?'

Nat did not answer, his eyes following the rest of the Maguires who were hurrying up George Street. Cold raindrops dappled her head and trickled down her brow. 'Why?' she demanded again.

'There's nobody at home to feed me,' he said, then looked down at his bare dirty feet.

Bright saw them too now, and tempered her approach. 'Where's your mother?'

'Hull.'

The rain was growing heavier. Bright pulled her shawl over her head. 'What's she doing there?'

Nat shrugged and kept walking, his head and shoulders glittering with droplets.

'When's she coming back?'

Nat didn't want to answer, but Bright kept repeating her question. 'I don't know! I don't think . . . I don't think she is coming back.'

'Bloomin' heck, you mean she's left you?'

'No! She wouldn't leave me, dummy. It's that Sep Kendrew who took her away.'

'But . . .'

'Just shut up being so bloody nosey!'

'What're ye getting mad at me for?' demanded Bright. 'I never made her go.' She flounced ahead and hurried after her family.

She was going to leave him. Everyone for whom he had ever held affection always left him – his mother, Bowman – but he made no attempt to stop her. *Come back*, his mind begged. Come back! As if by telepathy, Bright turned back and stopped, squinting against the needles of rain. 'Are you living on your own then?'

He drew level, nodding.

'Glory be to God, I'd never be able to do that. Come on!' She ran to catch up with her parents and, after a few chattered words, they stopped briefly, turned to look at Nat and signalled for him to follow before hurrying onwards across waste ground and up a narrow lane. He quickened his pace but did not run, unsure that he wanted any interference from them. They were at their doorstep before he caught up.

'Is it true what Bright says?' Mrs Maguire's gentle eyes looked with pity upon his bare feet, when they were all inside the house. 'Your mother left ye?'

'She didn't leave me.' Nat looked around so that he would not have to meet that gaze. The room was as he remembered it, warm and welcoming, with Granny Maguire looking as if she had been sitting in this position since last he had been here. Indeed Nat had never seen her on her feet. 'Sep took her away.'

'But you're on your own in the house?' pressed Mrs Maguire.

Nat admitted that he wasn't living in a house and briefly told them the facts. They were horrified. 'Why haven't ye come to us before now, child?' Mrs Maguire removed her shawl and shook the rain from it before hanging it on a hook and putting the kettle over the fire. Wet wool became the perfume of the hour.

'I wasn't sure whether you'd send me back to that school.'

'Would we do that?' demanded Mr Maguire. 'Didn't we take y'in to live with us before?'

Nat nodded, inventing an excuse. 'I don't want to be no trouble.'

'Trouble?' cried Bright's mother. 'Won't you be doing me a favour? I've a pair of Eugene's boots that he's outgrown. They're too small for Patrick an' not quite good enough to sell. I've been keeping them in case they'll fit somebody. You're just the ticket! Come on now and grab a piece o' the fire.'

7

So, Nat had a family at last. The trouble was, it was difficult to believe this was true. He lived in a house full of people, it vibrated with humanity, yet being amongst them sometimes he could feel incredibly lonely, and when he went to sleep at night he feared that he would wake up to find it had all been an illusion. One could not just wave a magic wand and be part of a clan; the others forgave each other's sins because they were flesh and blood, but would they forgive and defend him?

This fear was compounded when the school board official finally caught up with him. He had visited the Rawlinsons, Nat's supposed foster parents, and had been told that he had run away. The police were alerted and soon discovered Nat's whereabouts. To the boy's great relief Mr Maguire told them that he was prepared to act as Nat's guardian and make sure he finished his education. A place was found for him at a nearby school. 'And ye'll have to go, Nat,' Mrs Maguire told him in a gently persuasive tone – he had never seen her lose her temper. 'Cause if ye don't then Mr Maguire and me'll be in serious trouble, an' ye wouldn't do that to us, would ye?' Nat shook his head and went off to school with the best of intentions, which did not endure. In only a matter of days he regressed into truancy. Naturally the Maguires were informed by the school. Bright's mother was mortified that he had put them in this position. Her husband was less judicious. 'Look, the lad's almost twelve, ain't he?' demanded Mr Maguire. 'I can't see the sense in making him go to school for a couple more months if he'd rather work. Sure, he'd be more use to us paying board, wouldn't he?'

'But what if the authorities . . .'

'If they want to make an issue of it, let them! We've done our duty by sending him off to school. Tis not our fault if they can't keep him there, but if he won't go to school then he can work!' Mr Maguire fixed a dark warning eye on Nat. 'Tell ye what, get Pat and Gene to take ye down to the ironworks tomorrow morning.' His youngest sons had acquired employment there.

'Er, no, it's all right!' The Maguire boys, though not unkind, were a bit rough for Nat's liking. Besides, he had vowed that he would have no master but himself. 'I've already got plenty of work lined up.'

Maguire showed surprise. 'Doing what?'

'Odd jobs, selling scrap – you can make good money out of it.' Nat chose to omit that he also shovelled dogmuck, having to resort to this less frequently now.

'Well, I do admire a little enterprise. So long as you can put your cash on the table on a Saturday with the rest of us, and it's earned by honest means, then that's fine by me.' And Maguire's consent marked the end of Nat's schooldays.

Bright loved him being here, though his insistence on meeting Denzil and the gang every evening confused her. 'If I live to be a hundred I'll never understand the English.' Mr Maguire's quotations were a great influence on Bright, as was his example. 'What d'ye want with them when ye've all this company at home?' Mr Maguire only ever went out on a Saturday night to the pub and even then he took his sons with him. His family was everything to him, and all he wanted to do was relax in their midst.

Nat found it hard to explain that he was different from Bright's father, that sometimes he found the Maguire household claustrophobic, that quite often he found their dialogue incomprehensible when they talked of 'going home' some day when they already were at home, that he needed to be with different people. 'They're my pals,' he told her.

'So am I.'

'Well, I play with you an' all don't I?'

'Only between school and teatime.'

'I don't have to play with you *all* the time.' Nat turned to go.

Undeterred, Bright skipped after him. 'Can I come with ye?'

He wanted to say no but was too cowardly, so gave a half-hearted, 'If you want.'

When Nat turned up with a girl the others jeered. 'He's brought his sweetheart!' Nat warned them to shut up but they paid no heed, in fact Denzil took immediate action. 'We don't allow lasses in t'gang.'

Hurt, Bright retorted, 'I don't want to be in your stupid gang! I only came to be with Nat.'

'Well you're not allowed on our territory,' announced Denzil.

'And you've got muck under your chin,' accused Spud.

Bright was contemptuous. 'Tisn't muck, it's a mole.'

Denzil poked her in the chest. 'Just bugger off.'

Bright wheeled away, head down, hoping that Nat would follow. Feeling responsible for her, he turned an agonized face to the others. 'I'll have to take her home.'

'What for?' asked Denzil. 'She isn't your sister is she?'

'No, but I live with her mam and dad. I'll have to go . . .' Nat ran after Bright.

'You big lad-lass!' bawled Denzil, and threw stones at them.

Furious with all of them, Nat did not speak to Bright until she had spoken to him first, and even then was morose.

Happy that he had placed her friendship above all others, Bright overlooked his sulky features and tried to make him feel better with a denunciation of the gang.

'Stupid boys, you're too good for them – anyway you don't need anyone else, I'll be your friend forever.'

'Thanks,' muttered a dismal Nat, wondering how he was ever going to retrieve membership of the gang, the taunts of lad-lass still burning his ears.

The next day, when Bright left school, he wasn't there to meet her. When he failed to come in for tea Mrs Maguire said she would save him some, but her husband decreed that if he couldn't be at the table with everyone else he could go without. Of different mind, Bright filched a slice of bread to give to him later.

Jeers of 'Lad-lass!' were the only welcome Nat received when he approached the gang's meeting place in Patrick Pool. He tried to defend his action. 'I had to take her home! Her dad'd thump me if I didn't.' He couldn't imagine Mr Maguire ever thumping anyone and was glad that none of the boys could guess that he was lying.

Denzil parleyed with the others, asking if they should take him back into the gang.

'We don't want anybody who plays wi' lasses,' said Gunner.

Nat beheld him with scorn. 'You're a big daft lass yourself.'

Gunner advanced with menace. 'I'm gunner thump you.'

Denzil egged him on. 'Come on then, Gunner, thump him!'

'Aye, mug him one!' chorused Spud and Roger, and all began to prod Gunner into action.

Encouraged, he raised his fists like a prizefighter, towering over Nat. Nat held himself at the ready and tried to remember Clem Giblet's line of defence. He began by jabbing Gunner in the middle. The big body, soft as a slug, doubled over immediately. Nat's confidence grew.

'Hit him again, Nat!' Denzil had changed sides.

Nat smashed his fist into Gunner's mouth. It was the

most revolting thing he had encountered in his life, the feel of soft flesh splitting under hard knuckles, the sight of Gunner's teeth edged with blood, and yet . . .

'Go on, gob him, Nat!' Denzil exhorted him.

Gunner was on the floor, rolling about, hands over his face with the boys in a tight circle over him. Nat prayed for him to stay down while Spud shouted, 'Get up you big fat cissy!'

Gunner scrambled to his feet. Nat keyed for attack, poised to strike again, but there was no need. Gunner barged through the jeering circle and ran away.

The others gathered round Nat, dealing congratulatory thumps to his shoulder and welcoming him back to the gang. The lust for blood was up. A wild-eyed Denzil pronounced, 'Let's go kill some Irish bastards!' The excited search began for weapons. Staves were cut. Denzil pulled the gang's standard from his pocket – a dirty piece of linen with a skull and crossbones daubed on it – and tied it to the end of a pole. He pronounced Nat the standard bearer and gave orders to march for Walmgate. Then suddenly Nat remembered, 'Eh, I live near there.'

It was no obstacle. 'All right, we'll go down here instead,' announced Denzil. 'I know where there's an enemy hideout.'

The troop embarked down Church Street, pausing only to giggle at a display of corsets in a shop window. A lady held her dress aside so that it might not be soiled by the ruffians. Her gentleman companion raised his stick at them. They dodged him and went on to ambush the small group of Irish boys who were on their way home from altar service. The battle was brief. Encumbered with the standard Nat barely had time to throw a few flailing punches when Irish reinforcements appeared, forcing Denzil's squad to fall back. Denzil bawled for them to retreat and all fled back to the safety of their own territory, where Denzil waved his prize triumphantly – a prayer book, which later they burned as a symbol of contempt. The standard was used to mop each boy's blood – though Nat didn't actually have any – and was reverently folded back into the general's pocket until the next battle.

When he got near home Bright was waiting for him on Foss Bridge. 'It's time for bed! Me dada's sent me to look for you. Where've ye been?'

'I had things to do,' he told her.

'I bet you've been with them lads!'

'I can if I want to! Just 'cause I live in your house doesn't mean I have to be with you all the time.'

'Right then!' Infuriated, she dug into her pocket and flung the piece of bread at him. 'I was saving that for your supper 'cause you missed tea, but you can stick it up your bum, mean bugger!' She ran off towards home, tears in her eyes.

Ashamed and hungry, Nat picked up the bread, dusted it off and ate it before going home to meet the consequences of Mr Maguire's wrath. Would he be homeless once more? However, it appeared that Bright had made no complaint and after a mild rebuke about his non-appearance at the tea table Nat was treated to a cup of bedtime cocoa.

Grateful for his friend's lack of spite, Nat decided to reward her by donating more of his time and was there to meet her the next afternoon when she left school. 'There's a load of dead wasps in that trap I made.' He had filled an old jam jar with water and left it on the outside windowsill. 'Do you want to come and count 'em?'

Bright was quick to accept and skipped along with him to examine the jar which held a lot of dead wasps and a few live ones still trying to swim. Using a stick she raked them out onto the yard. The live ones made a bedraggled attempt to sting her. 'Let's cut their heads off!' proposed Nat.

'Ooh, aye! That's what they did to the French kings and queens. We've been learning about the Revolution. I'll get a knife.' Bright ran into the house.

'What d'ye want with a knife?' asked her mother and, when told, uttered, 'What have I given birth to? Disgusting child! Take that old thing there and don't cut yourself.'

Bright seized the knifeblade with no handle and ran outside to apply it with glee to the insect. But the ligature was amazingly tough and no amount of rigorous sawing could decapitate the wasp.

'Here, gimme a go!' Nat took over, but his efforts were no more successful. 'This knife's rubbish. Anyway, it's a bit boring. Away, let's do summat else.'

'You always want to do something else,' scolded Bright. 'Twas you who suggested the game.'

'I've just changed me mind, that's all,' replied Nat.

'I'll bet ye've even changed your mind about marrying me,' Bright tendered out of the blue.

Nat reddened. 'No I haven't.'

Bright turned all coy, examining her nails. 'How old d'you want to be when you get married?'

Nat thought upon it. 'About . . . seventeen.'

'I think I might like to wait till I'm twenty-five,' mused Bright.

'That's ancient!'

'Tisn't,' replied Bright. 'Our Michael was twenty-three when he got married. Gabriel is twenty-two an' hasn't even got a fiancée. Anyway, I wouldn't be able to be a teacher if I was married.'

'Teacher?' Nat was aghast. 'I'm not marrying a teacher.'

Bright sought to explain. 'I've just said I wouldn't be a teacher if I was married.'

Nat was adamant. 'Well, I'm getting married when I'm seventeen. I'm gonna buy my own house.'

'Oh, where?' Bright grew excited.

'Anywhere you fancy,' bragged Nat. 'I've already got quite a bit of money put by.' He faltered, wondering if he had made a mistake in telling her; she might find his cache under the loose floorboard upstairs.

'From collecting scrap?' Bright had not known it was so lucrative.

Nat turned dark. 'Well, not from robbing churches if that's what you mean!'

'I didn't! You don't have to do that sort of thing now, do ye?'

He shook his head. 'Scrap collecting's a good enough job for me.'

There was to be little scope for this occupation in the following weeks. October brought floods of such magnitude that the streets of York became as Venice. There had been constant rain for two days. On Thursday the fourteenth the level of the river was six inches above normal. Between Friday evening and Saturday noon it rose at a rate of six and a quarter inches per hour. On Sunday morning it had risen to sixteen feet at Lendal Bridge and on Esplanade, only the tops of trees were visible. Built at the top of an incline the Maguire's house just escaped, but those who were unfortunate enough to live where the road dipped into Walmgate found the Foss lapping around their parlour walls. Part of Bright's journey to school had to be undertaken by rowing boat. Looking out from her bedroom window her heart was filled with rapture at the sight. In Nat it produced the total opposite. Just as he had gazed upon the sea at Scarborough, the encroaching waters made him feel inexplicably desolate, raising thoughts of his mother, thoughts he had kept buried deep inside. After her abandonment of him, he had sworn never to think of her ever again, yet even in moments of fun, when he and the gang built a raft and paddled around the flooded streets pretending to be Indians, her memory lurked beneath the surface.

Maria's unbidden presence was also revived when Nat suffered his usual bout of bronchitis during the winter months. In contrast to her maternal tolerance, his incessant coughing was nothing but a source of irritation to his room mates.

'Every time I'm just falling asleep he starts!' complained Eugene at the breakfast table, his eyes ringed with dark hollows from the lack of sleep.

For once the brothers showed unity. 'Aye, he nearly blasts us out o' bed,' added Gabriel. 'Shouldn't he be sleeping by the fire to keep his chest warm?'

'Granny's bed's by the fire,' pointed out his mother. Old Mrs Maguire slept on the sofa.

'She won't mind, will ye, Gran?' called Thomas to the old lady, who responded with an abstracted nod.

'He'd have to sleep on the floor,' said Mrs Maguire.

'Who cares? Anyway,' Eugene jabbed his fork at the ceiling, 'doesn't he sleep on the floor up there? It'll be more comfy for him down here.'

A wan-looking Nat came downstairs.

'Oh Christ, do we have to listen to it over breakfast an' all?' muttered Gabriel. Shoving two rashers of bacon in between two slices of bread he rose. 'I'll eat mine on the way to work. Tis no good, I'll have to find meself a wife.'

'I can't help coughing,' objected Nat as others joined the exodus.

'We know that.' Even Mr Maguire was irritable. 'But, well, tis a dangerous bark . . . '

Nat endorsed this with an imitation of a Gatling gun.

Maguire closed his eyes. 'Jesus, Mary n' Joseph . . . Gabriel's right, you'd be better off by the fire.'

'He'd be better off *on* the fire,' muttered Eugene.

'You're all mean!' scolded Bright, when Nat had gone outside to the closet. 'Instead of complaining we should be looking after him and taking him to the doctor.'

'Sure we haven't got half a crown to spend on the doctor, darlin',' said Mr Maguire.

'Well, we could buy him some medicine at least!' exploded Bright. 'I'll buy it. I've got some money saved up.' She had been given a few pence on her First Communion and for errands she had done for people after school. It had been meant to pay for a birthday present for Nat, but medicine was much more practical.

'Suit yourself.' Her mother showed signs of weariness. 'Go down to Nurse's and she'll give ye the right jollop.'

As it was Saturday there was no school. Immediately after eating her porridge Bright departed to buy the medicine. On her return she made Nat sit by the fire, opposite Granny Maguire, wrapped up in a shawl, and pampered him all day long. During the following week she ran home from school in order to nurse him. The illness ran its course but Nat thoroughly enjoyed the rare coddling and when he was well enough to go out he felt rather guilty at abandoning Bright in favour of the gang. Thus he told her, as he wrapped up warm this February evening, 'You can come if you like.'

She looked surprised. 'I thought ye were going to meet your friends?'

'I am, but you can come.' Nat prayed she would refuse.

The brown eyes looked dubious. 'All right, but if they get clever I'm coming home.' She reached for her hat and shawl.

'Going out?' Mr Maguire was just on the way in from work as they left. 'Well, be in for eight o'clock, Bright — and take good care of her, Natty.'

The gang had not yet assembled when Nat and Bright arrived at the camp in St Sampson's churchyard. Nat half hoped the others would not turn up, but they did and as he had imagined they made vociferous objection to the female presence.

'She's cured my bronchitis!' Nat hoped his firm reply would work with Denzil. 'I owe her a favour.'

Denzil must have been in a good mood. 'Oh all right then, she might come in useful if we need wounds tending. Gunner, will you shut your gob!' During the exchange the other boy had been coughing and clearing his throat.

'You've got bronchitis,' said an experienced Nat.

174

'Nah!' The leader was dismissive. 'His balls haven't dropped yet and somebody's told him if he keeps coughing that'll do the trick. Have yours dropped yet?'

Nat blushed to the roots of his hair, wishing Denzil would not be so coarse in Bright's presence. He mumbled a yes.

'I don't believe you. Let's have a look.' Denzil made a laughing grab for Nat's clothes.

'Behave, Denz!' A scowling Nat fended him off.

'What're balls?' enquired Bright with interest.

All present laughed apart from Nat. 'Nowt! They're just being daft,' the embarrassed lad told her and rubbed his hands together. 'Eh, it's a bit cold, isn't it? Shall we make some winter-warmers?'

Finding the cans posed a difficulty but once these were scavenged from people's bins, the rest was no effort. Denzil had a ball of twine with which to make handles for the winter-warmers, and Roger had the matches. 'He's an expert wi' fire,' Nat informed Bright as he punched holes in his can and handed it to Roger who stuffed it with rags and set light to it. After a moment whizzing the can round and round by its string, the rags inside began to glow. When all were lit the boys sat with their hands to the warmth, Nat sharing his with Bright.

Denzil suggested they go out onto the streets to find amusement. Out here it was still too cold for there to be much entertainment and after a while the youngsters grew bored of making fun of passers-by and Denzil had another idea. 'Eh, Rodge, give us your matches a minute!'

'What you gonna do with 'em?'

Denzil snatched the matches and gave them to Bright. 'See that old bloke there?' He pointed to a man who was obviously wealthy for he was well-dressed and had a silver top to his cane. 'Go and sell him these.'

'They're mine!' Roger made to snatch them back.

'Shut up, Rodge!' Denzil turned back to Bright and urged, 'Go on.'

'Why would I want to do that?' asked the girl.

'It's a bit of fun.'

Bright was always ready for mischief but could not imagine how this could be gained from selling a box of matches. 'What shall I ask for them?'

'Oh, it doesn't matter – a penny!' Denzil gave her a shove.

The boys watched her approach the gentleman who turned and looked down at her in surprise. At first he didn't appear to take the bait, but then after compassionate appraisal of the waif-like face he delved into his pocket and exchanged a coin for the box of matches.

'Right, come on!' Denzil led the assault and the others followed, as yet unaware of his intentions.

'Caught you, you old lecher!' Denzil grabbed the man's arm and addressed one of the boys. 'Go fetch a policeman, Spud! We'll teach him to take advantage of a young girl.'

'What the deuce . . . ' The man tried to shake Denzil's hold.

'This girl is only thirteen! You must've known that when you paid her for immoral purposes.'

'How dare you!' The man swivelled round. A small crowd had gathered. 'I merely purchased a box of matches from her.'

'A likely story!' scoffed Denzil. 'Where are they?'

'Here!' The man brandished the box.

'They're not new – look, the box is all scuffed! You gave the girl money to let you have your way with her.'

'That is preposterous! I only felt pity for the child!' The man began to panic as the crowd tightened around him.

Bright was flustered too – what was going on?

Denzil turned to Spud. 'I told you to go for a policeman!' The bemused lad did as instructed.

'No, it's all a big mistake! Tell them!' The man entreated Bright, who felt sorry for him now.

'He did buy the matches, Denzil, like you wanted. It's true,' she told the curious onlookers who then began to move away.

Denzil, his plan exposed, blustered. 'All right, well, if you pay us ten shillings we won't fetch the police.'

'So that's your game!' The man raised his cane and lashed out with it. Everyone scattered, including Bright. As they fled they heard his threatening cry, 'Blackguards! I'll have the law on you!'

'You stupid bitch!' A breathless Denzil cursed her when they had reached the safety of a derelict building. 'We could've made a load o' money if you hadn't opened your gob!'

Bright was still terrified from the chase. 'Well, ye didn't say anything about that!' She looked to Nat for protection. He did not seem too frightened, nor did the others, for once they had caught their breath they started to giggle about their exploit. Denzil too was caught up in the laughter, and any danger was past.

'Is this what ye do all the time?' asked Bright.

Nat nodded. 'Mostly.'

She made no further comment on what she considered dangerous behaviour, but told herself to have a long talk with Nat when they were alone.

'I wonder where Spud's got to,' mused Nat, then smirked. 'Eh, you don't think he really went for a copper, d'you?'

This did not appear to perturb anyone except Bright. 'I'm cold,' she said. 'Can we go home?'

Nat wasn't ready. 'It's a bit early. Rodge, light us a fire.'

The rags from one of the winter-warmers were used to set fire to the pile of debris they had scraped into the middle of the floor. For a time they all encircled it, till Bright complained, 'I'm still cold.'

'Aye, it's not very big is it?' observed Gunner, whizzing his can around to keep it smouldering.

Roger grinned. 'So, you want a big fire, d'you?' Taking up a rag, he dipped it into the flames and when this had ignited he went to a pile of refuse in the corner and ignited this.

'Aw!' Bright covered her mouth as the flames took hold. The sight of this seemed to excite Roger. His eyes gleamed as he lit more and more rags and scattered them around igniting debris. The flames from the separate fires joined up to form one large blaze. The youngsters stood transfixed, watching it grow. Bright shattered the spell, dropping her can as she exclaimed, 'I'm off!' She ran outside. The others joined her but stopped to watch as the fire took hold of the walls.

'Isn't it great!' Roger's eyes were aflame with ecstasy. 'Look, oh look! Listen to it crackling!'

The fire expanded, the heat from it compelling the youngsters to move back and watch from a safe distance.

'I'm off home!' Bright took Nat's arm. 'Come on!'

'Just a minute, I want to watch!' Nat was infected with Roger's zeal.

She tugged at him frantically. 'Nat, we'll get caught!'

Her words were prophetic. The beacon could be heard and seen from streets away, drawing people out of their houses. 'You'd better go.' Nat nudged her into action. Bright did not argue but ran. Others came running too, amongst them a police officer.

'The stupid get, he was only meant to pretend!' Denzil cursed at Spud, before fleeing.

Nat and Gunner ran too, leaving Roger transfixed by the red glow of the inferno to be easily caught by the police officer.

'Stop those boys!' Holding the main culprit by the collar he shouted for assistance to the crowd, but Denzil and Gunner managed to evade capture and disappeared into the night. Spud had miraculously vanished too, each abandoning Nat and Roger to their fate.

Well ahead, Bright did not turn to see their capture and ran most of the way home.

Mr Maguire interrupted the family conversation as his breathless daughter joined their midst. 'My, look at the state of ye! Ye didn't have to run all the way home, tis only half past seven.'

Bright sank onto the fender and leaned on her grandmother's legs, trying to catch her breath. 'I thought it was later!'

'Where's himself?' asked her father. 'Didn't I ask him to look after ye?'

Bright hoped she did not look too guilty. 'He brought me home first, then went off somewhere with his friends.'

'Well, he needn't think he's staying out till midnight,' warned Mr Maguire. 'At ten o'clock this door is locked and he sleeps on the doorstep.'

It was as Mr Maguire went to undertake this duty later that there was a knock at the door. 'Just in time!' he called, expecting to see Nat when he opened the door. Instead he found a member of the constabulary. 'Oh . . . '

'Mr Maguire, I believe you are the guardian of a Nathaniel Smellie.'

'Jazers, what's he done?' Mr Maguire gave a heavy sigh, and was further exasperated to be informed that Nat, along with another boy, had been detained in relation to a case of arson.

'Arson! Jazers Christ!' Mr Maguire put his head in his hands as the officer left some time later. 'We've only been harbouring Beelzebub.'

Bright was already in bed, though she could hear the commotion below and knew what it was all about. She wondered whether to go down and tell them that it wasn't Nat who had started the fire, but then her daddy was far too angry to listen to reason tonight. Tomorrow would be soon enough.

Tomorrow came and she was no braver, but as it turned

out Nat had no need of her testimony; after vigorous questioning the police believed his story that he was not the one who had started the fire, but had merely been present when his friend played with the matches – 'But I warned him not to!' Neither he nor Roger disclosed the identity of their companions that night.

Nat had feared that the man they had accused of propositioning Bright might come forward, but he had not, obviously wishing to keep the delicate matter to himself. At the conclusion of the legal proceedings, Roger was found to be a danger to the public and was ordered to be detained at Her Majesty's Pleasure. Nat, found wanting in discipline was lucky enough to escape with another spell in Mary-gate. 'If lucky is the word!' quoted Mr Maguire, still unaware that his daughter had been involved. 'My God, the lad's been out barely six months!'

This time, number thirty-four as Nat was to be known, would remain at the Industrial School until the age of sixteen. In contrast with his last period of incarceration he decided to make use of his time here by attempting to learn a trade.

'Well, at least you're showing signs of owning a brain this time, twenty-seven.' No matter how many times he was corrected Mr Chipchase persisted in using Nat's old number. 'Let's hope we can make something of you, though I doubt very much if it'll be a carpenter judging by this effort.' The officer affected a pained grimace as he inspected Nat's third wasteful attempt at a mitre joint, then tossed the ill-fitting pieces of wood aside. 'At the rate you're going we'll end up with an awful lot of jigsaws. Why don't you try origami?' He patted Nat's shoulder and handed him a broom. 'Sorry to thwart your efforts, twenty-seven, but I think you'd be more use to me with this.'

Alas, this was not to be Nat's only failure. He had little

aptitude for any of the other trades either, and after a few months was relegated to labouring jobs. 'I'm not bothered!' came his hostile retort when mocked by his peers. 'I'll be going back to collecting scrap when I get out of here. Who needs a trade? You watch, I'll make more money than all of you put together!'

On all too infrequent occasions the monotony was broken by a visit from Mr Maguire and his youngest daughter, the first of these meetings at Easter and now, again, in June. He noticed a change in Bright straightaway. She had done her hair in a different fashion but it wasn't just that. She looked — older somehow — 'womany'. Yet, contrary to this hint of maturity, she kept blushing every time he looked at her. It made him redden too.

Bright squirmed in her white summer dress. 'We're off to the Grand Yorkshire Gala next week. I'm going up in a hot air balloon.'

'I said ye *might* be able to,' corrected Mr Maguire, fanning himself with a newspaper. It was Nat's double misfortune to be locked away during one of the hottest summers ever.

'I'm off an' all.' Nat, infected by Maguire's action, used his cuff to wipe sweat from his brow. 'Our band's playing there.'

'I didn't know you were in the band.' Bright showed delight.

'I'm not, I just meant the school band.'

Bright flushed. 'Oh . . . '

'Hey, d'ye still have that tin whistle we bought ye?' asked Mr Maguire.

Nat looked downcast, but more at the memory that the whistle provoked than the loss itself. 'No, it was locked up in the house when . . . you know.'

'What?' Maguire had forgotten.

'When his mam left,' whispered Bright. She returned to the former topic. 'There's going to be fireworks at the gala, too! It'll be great. I'm glad they're letting ye go – I might see ye there.'

Nat said he hoped she would, but on the day there were so many hundreds of people milling in the brilliant sunshine on Asylum Fields that he could not see his friend. He did however meet Mr Chipchase on his day off, an encounter which prompted surprise. He had not realized that any of the officers were married with families, but here was Chipchase with his wife on his arm and two adult-looking sons.

'Why, if it isn't our very own Grinling Gibbons!' Mr Chipchase paused to deliver a cynical smile from under his boater. 'Enjoying yourself, twenty-seven?' Receiving a mumbled affirmative, he nodded and moved on without introducing his wife.

Nat was not particularly keen to meet her, she looked a miserable bitch. However, he was interested enough to follow the Chipchase family through the crowd for a while, envying the sons who were allowed a hot-air balloon ride and wondering if Bright had succeeded in persuading her father to allow her up in one.

She had. 'Oh, it was really exciting!' she told him when next they met, clasping her hands to her breast. 'But scarey too, especially the bit where ye look down an' see all these faces getting smaller and smaller . . . ' She gushed on and on about it in her usual fashion until she saw Nat looking bored and asked, 'Did you get to go? I never saw ye.' He nodded. 'Did ye have a go on that Alpine Glassade? I did –I caught me dress at the top and put a big rip in it!' She turned to laugh at her father, then back at Nat. 'Hey, the Duke and Duchess of York are coming in October! Will ye be going to see them?'

Nat shrugged. Ever since Kendrew had rudely acquainted him with his true origins he was no longer interested in royalty, though he would keep his invented surname. 'I'm not bothered, but I suppose they'll drag us there.'

Bright frowned at his lack of enthusiasm. 'Oh, it'll be lovely! I can't wait to see her dress.'

With his obvious boredom in the subject, Bright's conversation petered out, leaving it to Mr Maguire to provide the chat with only the odd comment from her. Why was Nat behaving like this? Had Bright directed the question at Nat she would still be no wiser, for Nat did not know the reason himself why these strange moods came upon him. He wanted to dispell the confusion on her face, wanted her to know that he looked forward to these visits for weeks ahead, but the moods controlled his every action. He knew he must present an uncaring image, feared it would drive his friends away, yet he could do absolutely nothing about it.

One year ended and another began. Still the Maguires persevered with the otherwise friendless youth, though each visit became increasingly awkward. Neither Nat nor Bright could understand it — it was as if they were strangers, blushing with embarrassment for no apparent reason. However, on this particular occasion there was good reason for Nat's discomfiture as he sat listening with half an ear to Mr Maguire's monologue. It had finally happened as old Bramble Conk had warned: his acts of personal abuse had resulted in him damaging himself. Something had leaked from his insides and he did not know from whom to seek help. He must sit here as if everything were normal, unable to tell his friends that he was slowly dying.

'Are you listening to me?' demanded Maguire, causing Nat to jump.

'Yes!' Nat composed himself and tried to look interested, though he had no idea what Maguire had been saying.

As the man pressed on with topics that varied between the Grand National and Mr Gladstone's resignation, Nat's eyes strayed to Bright, performing a quick examination of her curves before looking away. It was sufficient to lure his mind onto a dangerous track and before he knew it something was happening – down there. Oh no! He pressed his thighs together. Please don't let it happen in front of Bright! Stop thinking about it! Stop!

Forcing himself to concentrate on something awful whilst trying to show interest in his visitors was a feat Nat was unable to manage convincingly. The Maguires left shortly afterwards, Bright questioning her father over Nat's odd behaviour when they were on the way home. 'I can't understand it. We're the only ones who go to see him, yet it was as if he wanted us to leave.'

Mr Maguire had forgotten the agonies of puberty and did not recognize them in Nat. 'Ah, well, I expect he's embarrassed at having us seeing him locked up in there,' was his explanation. 'Sure, ye don't have to go again if it upsets ye.'

Bright was hasty to disabuse him of this assumption. 'Oh no! I like going.' And she did, even though it was embarrassing – for her, not for Nat. Indeed, it was embarrassing to go anywhere at all with this feeling that people were staring at the lumps under her bodice that had sprouted virtually overnight. Half of her felt like a woman and the other half like a child. Nat had changed physically too. Whereas they had always been of similar build, he was now taller by two inches. His hands were those of a man, and she had noticed the beginnings of a moustache on his upper lip. Yes, they had both changed considerably and though one part of her character was excited by her womanhood, another side mourned the loss of their childhood bond. How would she ever be able to have the same intimacy with Nat when he came out?

Nat was fourteen when the authorities decided to release him on licence in the February of 1895, which meant that the remainder of his sentence would be carried out in the service of some upright citizen. It was almost a disappointment to think that he would miss the fortnight's holiday in Scarborough, especially after a winter as cold as this. How would he fare in these short trousers when out there the rivers were frozen solid? As ever, Mr Maguire saved the day. On being told of Nat's release date he arrived with an appropriate gift for the occasion: a pair of long trousers.

'Well, tis not decent for a man to be going about in short breeches now, is it?'

The beneficiary agreed. Since Maguire's last visit he had discovered from an older youth that what he thought to be some awful malady was in fact just part of growing up. Mr Maguire was right; he was a man. In both body and mind. He had much more confidence now and was able to hold a conversation with Mr Maguire on an equal footing – though as he held the trousers against his legs he half wished his visitor would leave so he could try them on.

'Sure, they're only a pair that has grown too short for Patrick, but there's plenty o' good wear in them.' Mr Maguire coughed. 'Jaze I think I'm getting a dose o' that there bronchitis o' yours. Bright sends her fondest wishes. She couldn't come today but twon't be long afore you're coming out so she'll see ye then. By the way, I'm going to speak to the superintendent before I go,' added Maguire, 'tell him we're willing to take ye back.'

Nat's pleasure at the trousers faded. 'I can't, they're only letting me out on licence. I'm off into service.'

'Ah, well now, won't herself be disappointed.' Maguire scratched his nose. 'I suppose they know what they're doing, but ye would have been quite welcome with us, Natty. Will ye come and visit us on your day off?'

Nat promised he would, but later discovered that there was to be little opportunity for this. The post was in Leeds. He was to be stablehand to a Mr Wood.

'And I trust you will not let us down again!' Mr Raskelf pinned Nat with a warning eye.

'No, sir, I'll do my best.' Nat stood before Raskelf in his long trousers – from child to man in one step – and meant what he said. Without being compelled to go to school the world out there was a different place. He had a job and a future.

Mr Chipchase took him down to the station and put him on a train to Leeds. 'Mr Wood will meet you at the other end. Well, goodbye and good luck, twenty-seven. Take care of yourself and try not to get into any more trouble.' He rubbed Nat's shorn scalp.

Far from appreciating the gesture Nat resented being treated like a schoolboy and did not wave as the train pulled out, though Mr Chipchase remained on the platform.

The journey took about half an hour. Not knowing who to look for when he alighted, Nat got off the train and dithered on the platform. In the event Mr Wood found him.

'You Smellie? Suppose you want summat to eat?' Thus was the limit of his greeting.

Nat was peckish but did not like the man's tone and so replied, 'Not hungry yet.'

'Oh, miracle of miracles!' Wood gave a cackle. 'You'll be the first lad I've known who didn't eat me out of house and home. Away then!'

Nat followed him. Wood was extremely short, could not have been more than five foot. Looking down on him Nat felt superior, or at least he did until he discovered the lowliness of his position.

His instruction began immediately on arrival. 'There's no time like the present. The stables haven't been done today, what with the other boy leaving me in the lurch, so you can do them.' Wood led Nat to the stables, of which there were ten. It transpired that he bought and sold horses

for a living. 'Right, I'll just introduce you to the others.'
These were having their lunchbreak. 'This is Tom, Simon,
Lewis, Ben and Michael, you answer to them.' He turned
to the others. 'This is – oh, we can't have everybody calling
you Smellie. What's your first name?' Nat told him. 'Right,
Nat, Simon'll show you what to do. I'm off for my dinner.'
On this abrupt note he left.

'Well, thank you very much for interrupting my break!'
The young man who was to instruct Nat muttered
sarcastically. 'This is just what I need while I'm eating me
sandwiches. See them gloves there? Put them on and follow
me. Right, you start at yon end.' He gestured at the end
stable. 'You pick all the horse tods out of the litter and put
them in that wheelbarrow.'

Nat felt this must be designed as humiliation. 'With me
hands? Why can't I use a shovel?'

'Because, stupid – '

'I'm not stupid!'

Simon cuffed him round the ear. 'You're all stupid at
that ragged arse school! You can't even move shit from one
place to t'other without being given instructions. We've
had to put up with five buggers from there and they've all
left. Now listen, stupid. You don't use a shovel because the
litter was only put down yesterday, it's still good. So, you
do as you're told and pick up the hoss tods one by one, and
that's to be done in every stable. Got it? And careful how
you treat them hosses.'

Nat considered that this last command should have been
given in reverse, for the horses did not treat him kindly at
all – and they were so big! Every time he bent down a hoof
would lash out from some direction, and if it wasn't a hoof
it would be teeth. 'Bastard!' he cursed the occupant of one
stable as it sank its teeth into his thigh. Looking round for
a fork or a broom with which to keep it at bay he found
nothing and so thumped it on the nose as it came at him
again. It whinnied and bucked. Luckily it was tied up,

allowing Nat to jump out of the way of its hooves and run outside where he bolted the door. This performance was repeated in half a dozen of the stables. By the time he had finished he was fuming. Wincing at the pain in his thigh he limped back to Simon. 'Done it. Do I get summat to eat now?'

'Let's see.' Simon took him by the ear and hung onto it during the inspection of the entire row of stables. 'All right, well done.' He let go of Nat's ear. 'You can have something to eat.'

Nat trailed after him into the tack room, where they had first been introduced. 'Mr Smellie's done a good job,' he shouted to the others who were busy polishing harnesses and carrying out various other chores. 'He's going to have some dinner.' He steered Nat towards an upturned box on which was a knife and fork and a plate. The plate bore two horse turds.

Nat felt the anger boil up inside him. An audience had gathered to watch. Simon was chortling good-naturedly. 'Don't get mad, it were only a joke!'

Nat aimed a kick at Simon's groin. The young man's legs crumpled and his eyes almost popped out of his head as he fell to his knees with a gasp. Nat was about to aim another kick, this time at his head, but Michael ran forth, caught the leg and tripped him. 'You little bastard!' The others grabbed him too and pulled him to his feet. One of them tried to clutch his hair, but finding it too short grabbed his ear instead.

'What did you do that for?'

'I'll kill you!' spluttered Nat, lashing out with his feet as Simon's agonized face only now came up off the floor. The victim remained on his knees, clutching his groin.

'It was a joke!' Michael repeated Simon's explanation. 'We do it to every new boy.'

'You don't fucking do it to me!' hissed Nat.

'You maungy little get!' The youths' defensive attitude

changed suddenly. One of them grabbed the horse droppings from the plate and shoved them into Nat's face, grinding them into his skin. 'You'd better find yourself a sense of humour if you want to work with us. Now get lost, before we tell Mr Wood what you've done to Simon.' Michael gave Nat a shove. 'That temper'll get you nowhere.'

Nat turned his back on them and strode away, wiping the horse manure from his cheeks. Much as he fumed over the parting words he knew they were right: temper would get him nowhere. He must be as calm and calculated as his tormentors. The swines! Just when he had the chance of a new life there was always someone ready to spoil it for him.

During the afternoon, which he spent lying low, he imagined ways in which he might get even. Simon's temper cooled before Nat's. When the latter emerged from his hiding place in order to cure his hunger, Simon called to him, 'Sorry, I didn't mean to make fun of you.'

'Fuck you,' said Nat under his breath.

Simon did not hear. 'Come and have something to eat, you must be famished – something proper this time.' When Nat ignored this he started coaxing, 'Come on! I didn't mean it, honest.'

'I'm not hungry.' Nat remained sullen.

'All right, don't believe me then, but I'm off for my tea, so you might as well come too 'cause there'll be nowt else till breakfast.' Simon disappeared round the side of the building.

Nat struggled with his hunger for the next few minutes then, hating his own weakness, wandered in the same direction. When he came around the corner Simon had already gone inside up the stairs to the lads' living quarters. Nat paused at the bottom of the steps, then ascended. His workmates were already at the wooden table helping themselves from the huge pan of stew that Mrs Wood had sent over, as she did most nights. 'Fetch that chair up.' Mouth full, Michael pointed with his fork.

Nat had taken in the situation very quickly. All appeared normal. Grabbing the chair he swung it over to the table and sat down. 'Help yourself.' One of the others, Nat couldn't remember his name, handed over the ladle. Nat wasted no time in filling his plate. Michael threw him a knife and fork.

'Ah!' As if remembering something he should have done, Simon took a mouthful of bread and left the table. Nat was already shovelling meat and carrots into his mouth as Simon returned. 'You'll want some dumplings with your stew, Nat.' He threw two round objects onto Nat's plate, showering the others with gravy and drawing forth howls of complaint. Nat stopped eating and fixed his eyes to the plate where two horse turds sat amongst the meat and vegetables.

'I told you he'd fall for it again! They're all bloody thick!' Simon led the communal laughter, then pointed at Nat. 'That'll teach you to kick me in the balls, you little arsewipe.'

Nat put his hands to the underside of the plate and hurled it upwards to roars of objection and much dodging of gravy. He charged from the room, clattered down the staircase and out into the freezing night.

Half an hour in that cold told him he would never see the morning if he stayed here, but he could not share a room with those swines, he just couldn't. Perhaps if he knocked at the door of Mr Wood's house . . . after a moment he made towards it, but when he arrived he could not lower himself to beg for mercy. Instead he leaned against the wall, clutching his arms around his shivering frame.

The door opened. A woman hurried out to the midden pile, looking startled when she saw him. Her booming voice drew attention that he would rather not have had. 'What're you doing out here, love?' It was Mrs Wood, whom he had met on his arrival, a countrified type with red cheeks and a mob-cap. She was taller than her husband, her bright blue eyes on a level with Nat's. He did not answer. 'Oh, them boys been pulling your leg, have they?' She gave a knowing smile. Her teeth were like those of a horse.

You soft old bitch, thought Nat. The contempt must have shown on his face, but Mrs Wood chose to ignore it. 'What did they do?'

'They put horseshit in my food.'

'Oy! Don't you use language like that in front o' my wife!' Mr Wood had been listening through the open door and now rushed out to deal Nat a hard blow.

Nat flushed. 'Sorry,' he mumbled to Mrs Wood, rubbing his ear. 'I forgot where I was.'

'Well, that'll be the last time or I'll give you something you won't forget!' The diminutive Wood was furious.

'Norman!' boomed Mrs Wood, and laid a restraining hand on her husband's arm. 'The boy's said he's sorry.' She turned to Nat. 'So you haven't had any tea?'

'I haven't had anything since breakfast,' complained Nat.

'Aw!' Mrs Wood turned to frown at her husband.

'I asked if he were hungry when he arrived! If he's too daft to say yes then what can he expect?' Mr Wood went back into the house.

'Well, you'll not get much work from him if you don't feed him!' Mrs Wood took Nat's hand. 'Come on, let's get you summat warm – eeh, these hands, they're frozen!' She rubbed them between her own rough palms. 'Good job we don't expect you to milk cows.'

Nat was too hungry and cold to feel any gratitude towards Mrs Wood, but later with a bowl of untainted stew inside him he tendered a half smile in recognition of her charity.

'Were it good?' asked his employer's wife.

'Aye. Thanks.' Contented, Nat remained in his chair.

'Well, don't just sit there!' For the past twenty minutes Mr Wood had kept throwing Nat black looks from his seat at the kitchen fireside. 'You've had summat to eat, now go back where you belong wi' t'others.'

Nat balked at the idea of spending the evening with his tormentors. 'I were going to wash t'pots.' He directed his offer at Mrs Wood, knowing she would be more receptive.

'Eh, you've found a good un here!' she cried to her husband, her great teeth flashing. 'What a nice lad! There's no need, though, I have Betty to help me.'

Nat was swift. 'I'll do 'em with Betty then. You sit yourself down.'

'Oh, I'll not argue!' Mrs Wood joined her husband at the fireside while Nat proceeded to clear the table and take the pots to the scullery.

The washing up delayed his return to the bunk room by only half an hour, but at least it gave him a chance to get warm before crossing the yard. Not to mention that whilst Betty wasn't looking he was able to take a sharp knife and a piece of cake from the larder. When he left the cake was in his stomach and the knife in his pocket.

There were many sarcastic taunts to endure before the other lads grew bored and undressed for bed. Nat forced himself to be calm. Retaliation would wait. Slowly the noise of coughing and farting from his room-mates ceased, until only the growl of Michael's snoring prevented Nat from making his move.

'For God's sake, shut up!' Tom threw a boot at Michael. The latter moaned, turned over, and silence was resumed. Nat lay tense and waiting. After what was probably half an hour he lifted his head and looked round the dormitory. All were still. Knife in one hand, blanket over the other arm, he rose from his straw pallet and crept towards the nearest bed – Simon's – where he halted and glared down at the occupant. You piece of shit – he gripped the handle of the knife and directed it at the unconscious youth — you think you're it, don't you? But one cut, just one and you're nowt. Anger made the blade jerk. Goodbye, horsefucker.

Nimble of step, Nat took to the stairs and was out into the night. Putting the knife between his teeth he took the two ends of the blanket and knotted it round his throat like a cape. Prompted by devilment, he headed for the stables. Remembering which of the horses were most compliant when he had cleaned their stables today he chose only these. The knife was well chosen too. In no time at all the deed was done. The last victim turned a bemused face to examine the remains of her tail. With the resulting pile of horsehair transferred to a sack, the marauder embarked on the road to York. Cloaked in his blanket, Nat laughed with delight as he pictured Simon's discovery of the mutilated nags and his consequent explanation to his employer.

8

'Well I never did, we've got a royal visitor!' Mrs Maguire responded to the knock on her door and pulled a shivering Nat along the passage. 'Away to the fire darlin'! Sure, what in God's name is this you're wearing?' She tweaked the blanket that Nat clutched around himself. 'Stinks to high heaven.'

Mr Maguire was there too, obviously preparing for work. 'An' what're ye doing here? Didn't ye say the fella at this school had found you a job?'

Nat's teeth were chattering. He hunched over the fire near Granny Maguire, whose spoon was precariously raised and lowered over the bowl of porridge on her lap. 'Changed his mind.'

'And have they just let y'out then?' Maguire looked at the clock. 'Jesus, couldn't they wait to get rid of ye? Tis only twenty to six. Have ye had breakfast?'

Nat shook his head.

'Downright inhuman – get him something to eat!' Mr Maguire ordered his wife, then pulled his dangling braces over his shoulders and shrugged himself into a jacket. 'I'll have to go or I'll be late for work. See you tonight, Nat.' Donning his hat, topcoat and scarf he grabbed his lunchcan and left.

'Ye can't keep doing this, Nat,' reproved Mrs Maguire, doling out some porridge, then wiping Granny's mouth and divesting her of the empty bowl.

'I'll pay for my keep.' Nat pushed aside the blanket to dig into his pocket.

'Sure I wasn't referring to money – God in Heaven,

where did ye get all that anyway?' Mrs Maguire's mouth had fallen open at the number of coins he laid on the table.

'I didn't steal it!'

'Now did I say ye did?'

'It's wages.'

'For what? I thought you told Mr Maguire ye didn't get the job.'

'I did, but it didn't last very long.' Nat omitted to say just how long and Mrs Maguire knew better than to ask.

'Ye've run away again, haven't ye?' Bright's mother couldn't look stern, although she tried. Nat hung his head. 'Oh, don't fret! Eat your porridge, I haven't time for explanations now, the rabble will be up shouting for their breakfast any second.' Already she could hear the creak of upstairs floorboards.

Nat shoved the money across the table, keeping only a few pence back for himself. 'Take it, then I won't feel so bad.'

'Get along with ye, I can't take all that! Keep some for yourself.'

'I don't need it.' Nat's refusal was made easier by the knowledge that he still had his cache hidden here from before his incarceration.

'Indeed you do, if only to buy yourself a razor. Look at the whiskers on ye. My word, you've changed since last you were here.'

Nat touched his upper lip self-consciously as, in dribs and drabs the rest of the family appeared for breakfast. Mary and Eileen first, then Martin who, at twenty-three, was the eldest son at home now. 'Mr Maguire would have told ye that Gabriel was married last year, did he not?' queried Mrs Maguire. 'Aye, and Thomas is gone for the priesthood.' She gave a proud nod. 'These two are doing well at the ironworks.' Eugene and Patrick seated themselves, giving only a cursory nod to Nat. None of them had seemed surprised that he was here. One by one they departed for work. Bright had still not risen. Curious, Nat finally enquired as to her whereabouts.

Mrs Maguire smiled. 'Ah, won't herself be delighted to see ye! I let her stop in bed till the others have gone. She hasn't so far to go as them an' ye know how cramped it is at this table – why, here she is now.'

Bright was stunned to see him and apparently embarrassed, for she turned crimson.

Nat was quite astounded too. Bright had altered even in the few months since she had last visited. She was much taller and . . . rounder. His eyes fell on her breasts. She pulled her navy-blue cardigan over them and came to the table, offering only a smile and, 'Hello!'

Nat mumbled a greeting and waded through his third dish of porridge.

'What d'ye think to this one?' Mrs Maguire put a bowl before her daughter. 'Hasn't he grown?'

Bright smiled and nodded, then began to eat. Far from injecting her with even more confidence than she already possessed, the change from girl to woman seemed to have had the opposite effect, at least in Nat's company. She yearned to examine those dark good looks more closely, but this idiotic shyness allowed her eyes to dart only as far as Nat's sinewed hands that cupped the porridge bowl. Instead of a little boy's presence there was now a man's. True, she had been gripped by this transformation on the last couple of occasions she had visited him, but here in her own home it unsettled her even more.

'First time I've known you lost for words,' said her mother. 'Oh, of course I'm forgetting you've seen a lot more of him these last two years than I have. Ye never told me how much he'd altered.'

How would I put it into words, thought Bright, her eyes fixed on the porridge.

'By the way, will ye be taking your dinner to school or coming home?'

'Coming home.' Bright had only just decided this on finding Nat here.

'You're still at school?' Nat was incredulous. His friend was the same age as him, fourteen years old.

'Why, didn't she tell ye?' cried Mrs Maguire. 'Our Bright has been accepted as a pupil teacher. Isn't that grand?'

Bright had deliberately withheld the news of her achievement at her last visit and warned her father not to say anything either. The gulf between herself and Nat was wide enough. Without looking up, she gave a diffident laugh. 'Nat never liked school. He won't reckon much to me being a teacher.'

He surprised her. 'It's good for you, though – I mean it's what you wanted, isn't it? To be a teacher.' Then, quickly, he lowered his head and worked his spoon around the bowl to catch every last bit of porridge.

Bright dared to lift her eyes and caught a glimpse of the boy within the man; Nat's hair still fell in that dark uncontrollable curtain over his eyes. 'Well, I'm not a proper teacher yet . . . '

'Ye teach a classful o' children don't ye?' contradicted her mother.

'Only the younger ones.'

'Even so! If that isn't being a proper teacher I don't know what is. Do you, Nat?'

Bright wished her mother would shut up. All this talk about education would surely add to the strain on her friendship with Nat – he had sworn that he would never marry a teacher. 'Well, yes but, I'm only an apprentice. I still have a lot of exams to pass, and years of training ahead of me.'

'Well, if it were me doing all that hard work,' answered Mrs Maguire, 'I'd be claiming a bit o' credit. Don't you take no notice, Nat. Sure, we're all very proud of her.'

Bright took a quick mouthful of porridge, then gave a

self-conscious little smile. 'Well, I don't know about that. Me father thinks I'm mad.'

'Ah well, and so he does,' confirmed Mrs Maguire to Nat with a smile to show she was joking. ''Tis a good thing she's the last of the brood. With the others all having proper jobs, as Mr Maguire puts it, then he can afford to indulge his favourite.'

Under constant scrutiny from Nat, Bright's tentative mannerisms persisted throughout breakfast and even more so when it was time to leave the table, feeling him watching her every move as she brushed her hair in the mirror over the fireplace. Unaware that his observation was so blatant, Nat continued to examine the girl. Bright was a lot tidier these days. Her hair was glossed back and held with a tartan ribbon. Instead of a grubby pinafore she wore a fitted dress that ended three inches below her black stockinged knees, and proper women's shoes replaced the ungainly boots of old. His eyes ran up and down her body again, stirring natural instincts. Embarrassed, he turned back to his empty dish and placed his hands over his lap, attempting to think of other things besides breasts. 'I think I might go for a wander round town this morning.'

'Going to meet up with those pals o' yours ye mean,' corrected Mrs Maguire.

Why does she have to see right through me, thought Nat, and shrugged as though this had not been his intention at all. 'Never heard anything of 'em for years.'

'Before ye go would ye fill that coal bucket for me?' asked Mrs Maguire.

'Aye, in a minute.' Nat was waiting for the bulge in his trousers to deflate. 'I'll just get warmed through.'

'Sorry, am I keeping the fire off ye?' Bright jumped away from the mirror.

'No, no, that's all right.' Nat hardly dared look at her now.

'I've finished anyway, I'm off to school. Will I see you at dinnertime?' She wrapped a shawl around herself.

'Er, might do . . . '

'Might's not good enough,' cut in Mrs Maguire. 'I'm not cooking a meal to be wasted.'

'All right, I'll see you at teatime,' answered Nat.

Bright showed a flicker of disappointment, then made for the door. 'Bye, then.'

After she had gone Nat brought in the coal, then put on his cap and tied the blanket round him.

'Hey!' Mrs Maguire counted out some of the coins he had given her. 'Take off that wretched thing and buy yourself a decent coat. I'm not having anybody in this house going round like John the Baptist. Sure, I can't think why ye have to be told when ye had all this money yourself.'

Nat pocketed the cash, around ten shillings in all. 'Thought I might need it for something more important.' Having a sudden idea, he folded up the blanket. 'Shall I put this upstairs?'

'Oh, you've decided to stop with us then?'

He looked humble. 'If you'll have me.'

Mrs Maguire winked. 'Go on! You know where you'll be sleeping.'

Bounding upstairs, Nat deposited the blanket on the floor and lifted a rug. The piece of floorboard was still without nails. Taking out his knife he prised at the wood. His cache was intact. Satisfied, he replaced board and rug, then went back downstairs, shouting, 'Bye!'

Visiting the first shop he came across in Walmgate he purchased a secondhand overcoat. It made him look older but his cap devalued the effect so he bought a hat too, then remembering his childhood ambition he asked if the man had a tie. Thus kitted out he went into town, with just about enough money left to purchase a cheap razor.

Gunner did not recognize him as their paths coincided at

the top of Fossgate. Nat had to repeat his salutation before the boy showed any recognition. They had both matured but Gunner was five inches taller and with his big frame seemed to tower over Nat, looking much older than fourteen. His responses, though, were still those of a child. 'Ooh, look at the toff!' He patted the other's hat. 'You must have a good job.'

Nat resented the patronizing attitude and adjusted his headgear. 'I had one, but it wasn't that good. I prefer to work for meself so I chucked it in. Is this what you do then?' He flicked a rather contemptuous hand at the broom with which Gunner had been sweeping the roads until Nat's arrival.

Gunner showed no embarrassment. 'Aye, this is it.' He gave a few half-hearted sweeps then went back to leaning on the broomhandle.

Cold was seeping through the soles of Nat's boots. He began to stamp his feet. 'Seen anything of the others?'

'I'm meeting them tonight as a matter o' fact. Apart from Rodge o' course . . .'

'Aye, poor old Rodge.'

'Come an' join us.'

'All right.' Nat hopped from one foot to the other. 'Look, I'll have to get moving, Gunner, this is freezing my balls off.'

'Oh, grown some, have you?'

'Same place, is it?'

'No, we're meeting at the river camp. Some buggers pinched our HQ while you were away.' Outnumbered by the enemy they had been unable to seek revenge for this audacity. 'But now you're here we'll have enough men to drive 'em out. I haven't had a good fight in ages.'

'See you tonight then.' Nat moved on.

It was too cold to wander the streets for long with no company. Nat went home, thereby incurring Mrs Maguire's displeasure.

'Didn't you say ye wouldn't be in till teatime?'

'It doesn't matter if there's no dinner for me.' He sat by the fire and rubbed his hands whilst the others finished their meal. 'I only came back for a warm.'

'He can have this, I can't eat it all.' Bright was delighted that she would have ten minutes with her friend before it was time to return to school.

'There's no need for you to starve,' answered her mother. 'I've made enough for everyone, but only 'cause I know what some people are like. I just wish they'd say what they mean! Sit ye down.' A grateful Nat joined the diners.

'Did ye see anything of your pals?' asked Mrs Maguire.

'One of 'em,' answered Nat. 'I'm seeing the others tonight.'

He tucked into his meal, unaware of the disappointment he had inflicted on Bright.

Nat spent the rest of the day by the fireside, only tearing himself away in order to shave the down from his upper lip. When he left the house again he took a winter-warmer with him, though it had little effect on the freezing cold riverbank. However, it was good to be with the gang again after such a long absence and there was plenty of laughter as Nat related his experiences in Marygate, concluding with the episode of the horses' tails. Afterwards it was time to hear their news. Denzil had a job in a slaughter-house. Spud worked in a chocolate factory and Gunner, as he already knew, swept the city's gutters. The time went too quickly. After such long confabulation, the general opinion was reached that it was too late to launch an attack on their former HQ tonight. 'I have to be in by half past nine.' Spud rose from his heels and spent a moment or two rubbing his cold knees. 'Anyroad, I still don't think there's enough of us to take 'em on.'

Even Denzil agreed. 'Aye, an' it's bloody freezing.'

'Aw, I were looking forward to a good scrap,' complained Gunner.

'Tell you what,' said Denzil, 'I'll bring you a rice pudding tomorrow, you can try and knock the skin off that.'

Gunner blushed at the laughter and made ready to depart.

'Thanks for not spragging on us, Nat,' offered Spud before moving away.

'I wondered when anybody was going to mention that.' Nat trailed after them.

'Well, you don't expect any medals d'you?' exclaimed Denzil. 'It's only right you don't give your partners away. If anybody ever spragged on me I'd rip their guts out.'

All went home and met again the following night to compare more tales, but once these dried up there was little to do. Hence it was suggested that they did not meet up again until the thaw, a piece of news that gladdened one particular maiden's heart. Despite the atrocious weather Nat managed to find employment of one kind or another and if there were no odd jobs then there was always scrap to be collected. However, his preferred occupation would always be romping with the gang and to Bright's dismay when summer came round again the old comradeship was resumed on a regular footing.

This balmy Friday evening found Nat, Gunner and Spud congregated on the riverbank, trying to light a fire on which to bake some potatoes, using two sticks and a piece of string.

'Wish Rodge was here,' Nat cursed, and blew at the puny wisp of smoke they had created.

'Aye, not just for the fire-lighting neither,' voiced Spud. 'We've still got to get our HQ back.' Aware of another's presence he glanced up from his labours expecting to see Denzil, but it was a well-dressed boy who seemed to be paying a lot of attention to the proceedings.

'What you gegging at?' demanded Spud.

The yellow-haired boy in the Norfolk jacket and knickerbockers murmured something.

Gunner looked up too and frowned. 'What did he say?'

Nat continued to rub his sticks together. 'It sounded like, "fack orf".' How elegantly the abusive phrase was delivered from well-spoken lips, thought Nat.

His large companion rose with a growl and strutted over to the boy on the balls of his feet. 'What did you say to us?'

Unflinchingly, the stranger repeated his offering.

'I'm gunner thump you,' came the response.

Polite insolence from the boy in the white collar: 'It's a free country.' He turned to the others, whose efforts had so far come to nothing. 'I can light your fire if you want me to.'

Gunner poked him in the chest. 'Don't think you can escape a bashin' as easy as that.'

The boy remained cool. 'Bash me if you can,' he challenged with the superior air of one who is used to dealing with menials.

Nat grew tired of Gunner's posturings. 'Oh shut up! Let him light the fire if he wants.'

The boy had some matches and soon had the fire going. Nat shoved a number of potatoes around the edges.

'What's your name?' asked Spud.

Brown eyes glanced up at him. 'Noel Scaum.'

'How old are you?'

'Fifteen — is this a gang?' When told it was he added, 'Can I be in it?'

'You can for me,' said Nat, who admired the newcomer's rich appearance and what he represented — though the self-assured attitude was irksome.

'It isn't your say-so,' warned Spud. 'You'll have to wait for Denzil.' Their leader was late tonight, probably been kept in by his mother, but no one would dare taunt him with this.

Noel asked, 'Who's Denzil?'

'He's our leader,' informed Gunner. 'Anyway, what does a toff like you want to join us for?'

Noel was about to explain that he had plenty of friends of his own kind but they never wanted to do anything more exciting than torment the servants. However, just then he saw a bandy-legged boy shambling down the riverpath. He laughed and pointed. 'I say, look at him!'

Spud growled a warning under his breath, 'That's Denzil,' but it didn't have much effect.

Noel was either very foolhardy or just plain crazy. As the bow-legged youth neared he sniggered, 'Pity he's only got two of those legs – two more and we could make a nice Queen Anne table out of him.'

Denzil proffered an evil scowl, but said nothing. Noel was not afraid; the others were. Allergic to violence, Nat made the hasty recommendation, 'He can light a good fire! Shall we let him be in our gang? What about his initiation?'

Denzil's pale eyes studied him for a moment, before their owner declared that the first part of the ceremony would be held in abeyance. 'I can't think of anything for him to do yet. We'll just carry out the second part for now.'

Nat could not bring himself to urinate on that beautiful suit. 'I've just been, I can't do owt.' The others had no such qualms, drenching Noel, then rolling him in the mud and eventually throwing him into the river. But whilst they stood back laughing, Denzil prevented Noel from getting out. The yellow-haired boy swam a little further along the bank, but Denzil went with him and nudged him back into the water. He kept shoving him back until the exhausted boy panted, 'Please let me get out, I'm going to drown.' Calmly, Denzil pushed him back again.

'Let him out now, Denz,' advised a worried Nat.

Without warning Denzil flew at him, punching and hitting uncontrollably whilst Nat could only curl up like a hedgehog and hope to come out without serious injury. Meanwhile the others were helping Noel from the water. Denzil's temper ran out as quickly as it started but he was left with that wild look that so frightened the other boys. 'Right, I've thought of something he can do!'

Noel was still trying to recover his breath. 'Can I do it another time? I'll have to go home and change.'

'What's up?' sneered his tormentor. 'Are you frightened your mama and papa'll be cross? You'll do it now or you can't be in the gang.'

Noel was uncertain whether he wanted to be in the gang now, but feared another bout of violence if he refused. 'All right . . . what do I have to do?'

Denzil gestured across the river. 'Pinch a boat from Hill's boatyard.'

Noel risked sarcasm. 'Where am I supposed to hide it, up my trouser leg?'

Denzil said nothing but his eyes glittered again, moving the other boys to action.

'Let's take our spuds with us!' Nat wiped the smear of blood from his lip, then used an iron rod to oust the potatoes from the fire. Tossing the red hot vegetables from hand to hand in an attempt to cool them, the boys escorted a dripping Noel up and over Lendal Bridge, then hung back to watch him approach the boatyard. For a time they couldn't see him as with bared teeth they made ginger attempts to consume the potatoes which, though black on the outside, were still almost raw. Then to their delight and surprise he appeared and beckoned them with a furtive wave. They threw aside their unpalatable tubers and pelted down the slope to find a rowing boat in the water complete with oars.

'Quick, get in!' Noel flicked back his wet hair and picked up an oar.

'I'm rowing!' Denzil barged past, grabbing the oar. The others clambered precariously about the craft, leaving Noel to heave the boat away. Denzil bent into the oars, alert for the owner of the boat to come running. 'How did you do it?'

'The man was attending to a customer,' explained Noel, not divulging that the customer had actually been himself. If Denzil found out that he had actually rented the boat there would be hell to pay.

After a time, Denzil concluded that rowing was too strenuous and said that Noel could have a go. He himself knelt on the seat, shading his eyes with a hand, like some intrepid explorer. They had just passed Blue Bridge when Spud said, 'Eh, look at that big rat in the water!'

The so-called rat was in fact an otter which was swimming ahead of the boat.

'Let's get it!' said Denzil. 'Come on, Noel, row faster!'

The otter veered towards the bank. The boat followed. Nat leaped out and hauled the boat in so that the others could alight. Denzil grabbed an oar from Noel and with a bloodcurdling yell charged along the riverbank in pursuit. Gunner beat Spud to the other oar, both following their leader. Nat and the yellow-haired boy looked round for weapons then, armed with rocks, they too pelted after their quarry.

The glistening otter ran into some undergrowth. Denzil thrashed amongst the nettles with his oar, sending bits of greenery flying. The otter broke cover. The boys streamed after it again. Nat threw half a brick that caught the animal on its rump. It squeaked and checked its flight. Yelling and brandishing their weapons the boys fell upon it. Denzil raised his oar and brought it down upon the otter's head. Shouting with glee, Spud contributed his own blow to the dead creature while all danced round in celebration of the successful hunt.

'God, that's the biggest rat I've ever seen!' Denzil picked up the otter by its tail and dangled it proudly.

'Actually, it's an otter,' provided Noel, then shrank beneath Denzil's glare. 'Well, it could be.'

'Biggest rat I've ever seen.' Spud copied his leader. 'What we going to do with it?' No one seemed to know.

Noel, shivering in his wet clothes, tried to be helpful. 'You could have it stuffed and use it as a sort of trophy.'

This time Denzil looked approving. 'How do we do it?'

Noel explained that it needed to be done by a specialist, so the boys were obliged to make their way back into town. Alas, the unmoored boat had drifted and was far out in the middle of the river. Denzil gave Nat a thump for his carelessness and said they would have to walk.

It was common practice for the shops to remain open until late and many still had their canvas canopies erected to protect their goods from the evening sun. The boys wandered beneath these canopies, looking into every window until, finally, they happened upon a taxidermist in Feasegate. Denzil read out the diploma in the window: '"References to the Nobility" – I wonder what that means?'

'It means they stuff royalty,' provided Noel. There was raucous laughter as they entered the shop.

The taxidermist beheld the saturated Noel and the others with reprehension; he had met such young wags before. Denzil laid the otter on the counter. 'Please, sir, can you stuff this rat?'

Nat marvelled at the way this brute could sound so unusually polite when in the company of adults.

The man looked down his nose. 'Young man, I do not stuff things. I preserve and fashion them into a life-like pose. It is within my capabilities to do so with a rat but this, my dear fellow, is an otter.' With a flourish, he produced a list of charges.

Denzil's mouth fell open. 'Oh, we have to pay for it?'

'Do I take it that you are bereft of cash?' The man leaned over the counter. 'Then in that case I suggest that you all vacate the premises before I find myself obliged to practise my art upon you.'

The boys left, Denzil having retrieved the otter. 'Doesn't matter, I can do it myself,' announced their leader. 'There can't be much to it.'

'I think you'll need sand,' suggested Noel.

'I know that! I'm not a dummy. Anyway, I'll do it at home. I'm off now.' As usual, when Denzil left so too did Spud and Gunner.

Nat and his new acquaintance stood there, looking after them. When Denzil was out of sight Noel murmured, 'He's bloody mad. I'll wager he'll be up for murder one of these days. Well, I'm not going to be his victim.' He turned to Nat. 'Come home with me whilst I change, then I'll show you a good hideout in my garden. We can form our own gang.'

'You can't have a gang with just two people.' Nat didn't particularly like the newcomer as a person but was curious as to his background. 'Still, I could come and keep you company for a while.'

Noel lived in a huge gabled house in Hull Road. Nat could not believe it when he was conducted to the front door of this mansion. Never had he felt so conspicuous in his poverty. Noel led him across the hall and ushered him into the drawing room. The door opened onto a jolly chorus, which ended abruptly as a soggy-looking Noel and his companion entered.

'Noel, whatever have you been up to?' His mother rose from the piano stool.

'I tripped and fell into the river. Nat helped me out.' Her son indicated the ragamuffin who lurked behind him and whose mouth gaped at the vision of loveliness. Festooned with jet, she wore a gown of Eau-de-Nil with leg o' mutton sleeves. Her brown hair was caught in a topknot with three rolls at the fore, under which blue eyes stared disapprovingly at Nat. He averted his gaze.

'Well, do go and change, dear, you really shouldn't have come in like this when you know that Father and I have company.'

An aloof and elegantly gloved arm waved dismissal and Mrs Scaum turned back to the guests, who were close friends. 'It's fortunate that you're acquainted with Noel's eccentricities, but I really must apologize for my son's behaviour. I don't know why it is but he gravitates towards the most appalling boys. One despairs whom he'll bring home next – probably gypsies.'

Noel's father, casual in a polka-dotted smoking jacket, black trousers and white spats, waited until the door had closed before scolding gently. 'I wish you hadn't seen the need to speak so candidly in front of the boy, Elizabeth. It could hardly be of his own choosing that he dresses so humbly, and he did come to Noel's aid.'

'Dear Steven, ever the philanthropist,' smiled one of his guests, a Mrs Powers.

Her husband agreed. 'You'd probably find a good word if old Nick were to come in here disguised in rags.'

'I've never been one to condemn a person for what they wear if that's what you mean,' answered Scaum reasonably.

'It's not simply the boy's clothing!' Mrs Scaum rapped him lightly with her feathered fan. 'Did you not see the shifty gleam to his eye? He looked quite a rogue.'

Her husband dissented. 'Embarrassment, my dear! How would you feel in his place surrounded by all these wealthy people?'

'Wealthy? I shall remind you of that when next I ask for a new dress and you refuse on the grounds of poverty!'

Noel was upstairs changing. He threw his wet clothes on the bedroom floor and slipped into dry ones. Nat, mesmerized by the contents of the room, said even less than usual. He went over to the window and gazed down upon the garden; its limits were not visible from here, appeared to stretch for acres.

When Noel was dressed the two went outside. The evening air magnified the scent of roses and honeysuckle, which hung around the walls like a heavy cape. There was a stream with a bridge over it, looking completely natural.

Excited, Nat took off, thudding across the wooden planks and racing down a leafy passageway where he happened upon a cage full of exotic-looking creatures. 'Look!' He turned a thrilled face on Noel, who wandered up casually and grinned. 'I know, they're Golden Pheasants, Father's pride and joy. Here, you can feed them if you like.' Reaching for a tin of grain, he passed it to his new friend, then unlatched the cage. 'Quick! Get in.'

Noel should be called Nosey instead, thought Nat; he fired a continual round of questions whilst all Nat wanted to do was enjoy the moment. Had it not been for his surroundings Nat would have been long gone, but he just could not leave all this. He couldn't. For the first time ever he was in touching distance of how the other half lived and he did not want to let go.

'Come on, they've had enough.' Noel led him from the cage to a weed-ridden hideout at the bottom of the garden. 'I sometimes come here for a toss.' The two lolled here for a while, though Nat would have preferred to be in the more ornamental surroundings. 'What does your father do?'

'I haven't got a father.' Nat snapped off a dandelion, examining the white milk that oozed from it. 'What does that look like to you?'

Noel grinned, but was not to be deterred from his probing. 'Is he dead?'

'Yes.'

'What about your mother?'

'She's dead too.' The dandelion was tossed aside.

'Sorry. Where do you live then?'

Noel's curiosity was becoming irritating. Nat parried with a query of his own. 'Anyway, why do you want to hang around with me and the others? Haven't you got any posh friends?'

Noel was amused at being thought of as posh. 'Of course I have, but they never want to do anything exciting. I want adventures.'

Nat thought how immature and naive this sounded. 'I'd swap my adventures, as you call them, for your life any day. Do you still want to be in the gang, then?'

'I suppose so . . . ' Noel scraped his boot along the floor. 'I don't like Denzil very much, do you?'

Unsure of how far he could trust his companion, Nat merely shrugged.

'You won't tell him I brought you here, will you?' The yellow-haired boy sounded anxious.

Nat shook his head. He didn't want to share this with anyone, would even eject Noel from the garden if he could.

'Mother would throw a fit if I were to bring him in here.' Noel looked awkwardly at his new friend. 'Sorry about what she said earlier. She thinks everyone who doesn't wear a suitable outfit is a criminal.'

'You'd better not tell her I've been in the lock-up then.'

Noel looked astonished. 'Have you really? What for?'

'Nowt. You don't have to have done anything for them to bang you up in there. I first went in when I was nearly ten for not going to school. I hadn't been out a few weeks when they nabbed me again.'

Noel felt a thrill of danger at associating with a tearaway. 'But surely you must have done something wrong?'

'What's wrong about not wanting to go to school?'

'Is that all?'

'Yes . . . ' Nat made a casual addition. 'Well, this lad who used to be in the gang accidentally set fire to a building, but we didn't have anything to do with it. I got nabbed and put away again. So if you hang around with us you know what to expect.'

Noel was thoughtful. 'If my parents should ask what your father does for a living, tell them he's an engine driver or something.'

'Why?'

'Well, you can't say he's a lawyer or a doctor can you? An engine driver is a more realistic occupation.'

Nat tilted his chin in defiance. 'Why should I have to tell them anything?'

The boy gave a pacific smile. 'You don't of course, but they'll want to know who I'm associating with and if you tell them you're an orphan they might be inclined to dig deeper and find out you've been inside. If you just give them a straight answer then they probably won't ask anything more.'

'I'll tell them me dad works on t'railway – that's what Mr Maguire does. I suppose he's like me dad in a way.' Nat rubbed his chin. 'By, I could do with a shave.'

Noel's brown eyes widened in admiration. 'Gosh, how long have you been shaving?'

'Ooh, a good while.'

Noel touched the imagined moustache on his upper lip. 'Father won't allow me to have a razor. He says I've enough years ahead of me to get bored with shaving.'

Nat was suddenly generous. 'You can have a go with mine if you like. I'll bring it next time we meet.'

'Thanks!' There was a call from the house and Noel got to his feet. 'Oh fack, I'll have to go.'

'Is that your mother?'

'No, it's the maid.' The yellow-haired boy tugged at his stockings. 'Shall I see you tomorrow?'

'If you like, but make it the afternoon, it's the lads' half day.' Nat stood reluctantly and looked for the exit.

'Master Noel!' The call came again.

'Coming, Starkey!' Noel showed his friend to a back gate. 'Where shall I meet you?'

'Same place by Lendal Bridge. I'll be there after dinner.'

Noel, understanding that by dinner Nat meant his midday meal, nodded, then grinned. 'I wonder where that rowing boat is by now?'

Nat managed a smile too. 'Probably floated down to the

sea.' He was disinclined to leave. 'I wonder if Denzil's stuffed that otter.'

Noel laughed aloud, brown eyes shining. 'The big rat! I can't wait to see it. Goodbye, Nat, I'll see you tomorrow!' He closed the gate.

Noel could barely hide his laughter when a proud Denzil held up the trophy, which did not actually resemble either otter or rat nor in fact anything that had once possessed life. The fur was completely matted with dried blood and the body was a shapeless lump with huge stitches in the belly. Noel glanced briefly at Nat who showed no amusement and so he, too, forced himself to keep an impassionate face and asked how Denzil had accomplished it.

'I took all the guts out and stuck some bits of wire into its head to keep it upright, then filled the gaps up with rags,' said a proud Denzil, placing the otter on the ground for all to admire. 'Good isn't it? But we need a proper place to keep it, so today we recapture our old camp. We have enough men now that Noel's joined us.' He took the standard from his pocket. 'Find a branch.' Gunner found one and the banner was affixed.

'May I carry it?' asked an eager Noel.

'Go on then, but you walk behind me.' Denzil led them through town to the derelict St Sampson's, where sheep were penned in the graveyard awaiting their transfer to the butchers' shops in Shambles. Here he called a halt and crouched by the railings of the churchyard, narrowing his eyes for signs of the enemy. A pretty young woman sashayed past. 'Good afternoon, miss!' Denzil called politely, then muttered with a leer, 'By, I could put my boots to that.'

Nat, unfamiliar with the term and knowing Denzil's propensity for violence, assumed it meant he wanted to kick the girl, but was mystified as to the reason. However, he had no time to have this explained for their leader was beckoning for them to advance with stealth upon the enemy. To the joy of all their numbers were about equal and with the advantage of surprise Denzil, Nat and the others emerged the victors, driving out the interlopers, stealing the beerbottles they had collected and once again taking up residence.

With an accompanying chant of triumph, the branch that Noel carried was rammed into the soft earth, its banner fluttering as a warning to others. Later, Denzil went to collect the stuffed otter which he exhibited on a tombstone. 'There! Doesn't it look good?'

Nat dared not even glance at Noel.

'Are you coming tomorrow?' Denzil asked the latest member of the gang.

'I can't,' responded Noel. 'I'm not allowed out on a Sunday.'

'Do you want to come cow-walloping next Thursday, then?' offered Denzil.

'I'd like to but I'll be at school.'

'You still go to school?' Spud was amazed. 'You ought to get yourself a job.'

'My father wants me to matriculate and be a doctor. Aren't any of you still at school?'

'Nah!' Spud was derisive. 'We've all got jobs. I work at Rowntrees, Gunner works for t'Council, Denzil kills cows . . .'

'Ugh, really?' Noel wrinkled his nose.

Denzil assumed a look of maturity and nodded. In truth he was only qualified to separate the offal from the slaughtered animals.

'And Nat . . .' Spud looked puzzled. 'What exactly do you do, Nat?'

'I collect scrap and sell it.'

'Do you make much money?' asked Noel.

The other was nonchalant. 'Enough to live on.'

'What school do you go to then?' enquired Spud.

'Archbishop Holgate's.' Noel felt childish beside these working men.

'Never heard of it.'

'It's down Lord Mayor's Walk.'

'Bet it's posh.'

'No it isn't,' replied Noel.

'Must be if you go there.'

'I'm not posh.'

'Yes you are! You've got a posh voice and a posh name.'

'No I haven't.'

'What do they call you Noel for, then?' demanded Spud.

'Because I was born at Easter.' Noel expected laughter but over-estimated Spud's intelligence.

'Are you coming cow-walloping then or not?' asked Denzil. 'We're all taking the morning off work, pretending we're sick.'

Noel bit his thumb. He had enjoyed himself more than yesterday; Denzil was not so bad after all. 'I suppose I could always play truant. It's nearly the end of term and we've done exams. All right, I'll see you then!'

Gaining an answer, Denzil grabbed his putrid-smelling trophy and turned for home. 'I'm taking this so nobody steals it. See you at Walmgate Bar first thing on Thursday morning!' Spud followed and shortly Gunner left too.

Noel turned to Nat and made fun of Denzil. 'I don't know who he thinks is going to steal that – it stinks like nothing on earth!'

Nat had to share his laughter.

'I didn't like to ask in front of the others, did you bring your razor?' Noel had been looking forward to using it all day.

'Sorry, I forgot.'

'Oh, well, I'd better make for home. Shall we walk together?'

With Nat's agreement they fell into step and Noel asked

him about the meeting on Thursday. 'What exactly is cow-walloping?'

Nat felt good at being able to impart his knowledge to the other boy, and did so good-naturedly. 'Sometimes you'll get a bloke what buys a herd at the Cattle Market and he needs a lad to help him drive them back to his farm.'

'Oh, I see. We'd better wear old clothes then.'

'I haven't got nowt else,' grumbled Nat.

Noel tried to make up for this faux pas. 'Would you like to come for tea on Monday afternoon? You could meet me from school and we'll walk home together – and bring your razor! Don't tell the others, though.'

Nat looked keen, as if he would share this with Denzil!

After a Monday's scavenging, he followed Noel's directions to Archbishop Holgate's School and was there when his friend came out. Noel looked at the grubby, ragged figure with the bag of scrap over his shoulder and wondered what his mother would say when he took Nat home again. Far from unnerving him the idea brought a grin to his lips. It was fun to annoy Mother.

Noel was correct in his assumption; his mother was displeased. However, in her husband's absence she was far too cowardly to expel Nat and politely instructed her son and his friend to take tea in the kitchen. Afterwards, Noel enjoyed his first shave and in return guided Nat around the entire house. Nat liked Mr Scaum's study the best, possibly because it contained an ivory chess set that he could not stop looking at. He picked up a knight. 'Why have these horses no bodies?'

'It's called a knight.' Noel made to leave. 'Don't let Father involve you in a game of chess, it'll bore you to death.'

Turning the knight in his fingers, Nat cast an eye after Noel, then quickly pocketing the ivory piece he followed. It was still in his possession when he got home.

Noel joined the boys for cow-walloping on Thursday and thoroughly enjoyed himself, promising to see the gang the following evening, though when Friday came he did not show. His parents had discovered his truancy and, blaming Nat's influence, had confined him to his room for the whole weekend However, the following Friday he did turn up. 'Sorry I couldn't come last week. Mother kept me in for jigging school last Thursday.'

Denzil was contemptuous. 'Goody-goody.'

Noel blushed and sought a topic to divert attention from him. 'Where's the trophy?'

It was Denzil's turn to look awkward. 'Forgot to bring it.' In reality his mother had traced the appalling stench to the bottom of his wardrobe and had thrown the deformed creature out. 'Anyway, I've had an idea to make some cash. Follow me.'

Denzil led a foray into the urinals on King's Staith where he and his cohorts set about trying to extract the pennies from the locks on the doors. After much probing Denzil said they would have to rip the locks off completely; this they did, carrying them back to their headquarters where they spent much of the evening withdrawing the coins through the slit by aid of a knife. Noel pronounced the evening, 'Pretty exciting.'

Denzil's expression turned crafty. 'I've something even more exciting for next Friday. How about doing a creeper?'

Noel leaned forward with interest. 'What's that?'

Denzil rolled his eyes at the other's naivety, then explained: 'We creep into people's houses when they're asleep.'

'What for?'

'For somebody who's supposed to be posh you're bloody stupid! To rob 'em, o' course.'

Noel covered his unease with an enthusiastic, 'Oh!'

Others were uneasy too. 'It'll mean stopping out late

until everybody's asleep,' observed Gunner. 'Me dad'd come looking for me.'

Denzil showed impatience. 'Look, dummy, you go home as usual, then when your mam and dad are asleep you climb out the window or summat and meet us here at, say, midnight. I'll need a week to plan things but by next Friday I should have summat worked out. What about you, Nat?'

'No trouble for me to get away.' Since his illness Nat had bedded permanently downstairs by the fire; there was only old Granny Maguire to see him go and she was in another world.

Spud too claimed he could manage it. Denzil turned back to Noel. 'Don't suppose you'll be allowed.'

'Of course not,' Noel grinned, 'but I'll be here anyway!'

Everyone turned up at the appointed time. The night-time streets were deserted save for the odd musical drunk and the beat policeman, whom they dodged quite easily. Their movements had been meticulously planned earlier that evening. It would be too ambitious to choose a large house for their first job, which might well be guarded with dogs and watchmen; better to select one more modest. Excitement surged as they crept down the moonlit alleyways.

In King's Court their leader stopped and looked over his shoulder to whisper, 'This one looks good. Nat, see if you can open the window.' Nat took out a penknife and inserted it under the top sash trying to manipulate the catch. Much grunting and heaving went on as first Nat, then Gunner and Spud, struggled with the jammed window. Defeated, Nat shook his head at Denzil who, with bad temper, ushered them on to the next house where the same performance ensued. Noel looked on, raising a hand to check that his distinctive yellow hair was concealed under the black woollen scarf and hat he was wearing. Whilst the others tried to shift the window, the onlooker performed what he assumed would be a futile attempt on the door, turning its handle. It was open! He hissed at the others, who were still red-faced and huffing over the window.

'Shush!' Denzil turned to warn him, then saw the open door and chivvied the others into action.

They were inside the house, their hearts really pumping now. Even Nat, who was used to coping with danger, felt the need to empty his bowels. Noel could not believe he was doing this, felt as if he were dreaming it all as he, like the others, felt his legs carry him involuntarily around the house. Pockets crammed with treasures, Denzil pointed at the ceiling. Noel almost defecated and clenched his buttocks to prevent this. The idiot wanted them to go upstairs into rooms where people slept! But isn't this what you wanted, he asked himself – excitement? The boys went to the stairs, taking each tread in the most gingerly fashion. Noel felt a desperate impulse to giggle and had to press a hand over his mouth to avoid doing so.

Using gestures, Denzil ordered Nat to open a door. Pulse thumping in his head, Nat turned the handle a millimetre at a time, awaiting a creak. The catch unloosened, he pushed the door open ever so carefully and inched into the small room. The double bed used up most of the space; in it were two sleeping mounds. One by one the boys edged into the room and with one eye on the bed started to pocket items from the dressing table. Nat reached for a watch on the bedside table – when a nightcapped figure sat bolt upright in the bed, automatically made a grab for the intruder and caught him by the arm!

At Nat's yell the others piled for the stairs, running for their lives, all except Noel who, seeing Nat's desperate fight to escape shouted after them, 'Cowards! Come and help him!' With his accomplices fled from the house Noel dithered frantically, his bowel uncontrollable now. The man's wife was awake and making a terrible din. In his struggle Nat had succeeded in half dragging the man out of bed, but was yet in his grasp. Noel made a dash, bit the man on the arm, thus releasing the captive, then beat a hasty retreat down the staircase, closely followed by Nat. Out into the night they ran, not knowing nor caring where their so-called friends had gone, not stopping until they were far away from the scene of the crime.

'Oh fack!' Noel ripped off his hat and scarf and fell against a wall, his breathing laboured. He felt dirty, not just because of the mess in his pants but for his behaviour towards the victims of his crime. Oh, yes it had been exciting! But the couple were elderly, their house – their home – much more modest than his own and above all hovered the terrible knowledge of what this would do to his parents if he were found out.

Nat took a deep breath and raised his head to look at his friend. 'Thanks.'

Noel merely nodded and continued to pant. 'I'll have to go home now.'

Nat could smell the reason for his friend's anxiety but did not mention it. 'Ay, me too.'

Noel was disorientated. 'Where are we?' He replaced his hat but left the scarf to trail from his hand.

Nat was similarly confused and forced his brain to concentrate on this place where he had been many times before. 'Oh, down here.' He motioned for Noel to accompany him down Fossgate, and when this merged with Walmgate they parted company; no cheery farewells this evening.

Noel, plagued by his conscience all night, did not sleep one wink. Saturday was not five hours old when he rose and went back into town. It was more difficult than he had anticipated – visiting the house he had burgled last night. The terror was fresh in his mind, but he forced himself to approach the door. The hour being early there were few people about but he looked around him many times before dropping the items he had stolen through the letterbox and running for his life. And still he felt dirty.

'Your turn, Noel!' Denzil, heading the collection of booty that Saturday evening, turned to the last member of the gang. Noel presented empty hands. 'I'm afraid I haven't got anything.'

'What!'

'I did, but I dropped it when I went to rescue Nat.' That should ward off any further condemnation, thought Noel. Accuse them before they accuse you.

His theory cut no ice with Denzil, who considered the episode to be Nat's own fault and suffered no guilt himself. 'Well, don't think you're getting a share of this!' He pointed to the bag of jewellery, cash and other valuables.

'I neither want nor need a share.' Noel was aloof. 'I only did it for the thrill.' And I certainly won't be doing it again, he added to himself, thinking of the poor old man and his wife as their belongings were split between the four young robbers.

After the division of spoils the boys left the camp and wandered around town. By now a feeling of anti-climax had set in. Out of the blue, Denzil turned and punched Spud in the face.

Spud yelped and held his cheek in dismay. 'What did you do that for?'

'Cause I felt like it,' replied Denzil, then walked on as if nothing had happened.

No one dared look at each other, but continued to mooch around town looking for entertainment. Hating the atmosphere but afraid to leave, Noel ransacked his brain for a jape to lighten the load. When the brassy tones of a Salvation Army band approached he was given a chance. The boys paused to watch and when the tubas and cornets marched past, Noel leaped into the road and began to follow them, doing the most ridiculous walk as if his limbs were made of rubber. The others enjoyed his antics, but even this grew boring after a while and finally to the relief of all Denzil announced that he was going home, allowing others to do the same.

As usual Nat walked part of the way with Noel who, when the former was about to take his leave, said, 'It's only early, would you like to come to my home for a while?'

Nat showed eagerness and the two were about to move on when a girl's voice shouted, 'Nat! Wait on!'

Nat groaned. 'Crack on you haven't heard.' But the cry came again and out of politeness Noel stopped to wait for the girl who hurried after them down Walmgate.

'Good evening!' He smiled at her. She returned both smile and greeting, then addressed Nat. 'Where're y'off?'

'I'm just going with Noel to his house.'

Where once Bright would have asked if she could come, all she uttered now was, 'Oh.'

Afraid that his visit to the boy's house was about to be curtailed, Nat turned desperate eyes to his friend. 'Would you mind if she came with us?'

'Of course not!' Noel moved across the pavement in order that Bright could walk between them.

Relieved, Nat smiled down at her. 'You won't believe your eyes when you get to his house.'

Bright discovered the truth in his statement even before she entered the gate. 'Is this all yours?' she gasped.

Noel laughed. 'My parents', yes. Come in.' He opened the gate for her.

Unused to such gentlemanly treatment, Bright stood back until he waved her through to enjoy an episode of sheer delight. The roses were her favourite. Nat watched her trip from bush to bush, inserting her nose deep into the cluster of petals, inhaling the wonderful scent. 'Come on!' he yelled. 'I'll show you the birds.'

A glee-filled Bright pelted over the wooden bridge to be shown the Golden Pheasants. 'Can we feed them?' She was asking Noel but Nat, carried away, exclaimed, 'Yes!' Grabbing the tin of corn he opened the cage and shoved her inside. Noel raised an eyebrow but made no comment. After a short dedication to feeding the birds, Nat led the way back to the lawned garden where the boys threw themselves down onto the grass and Bright entertained them with an abandoned dance.

Nat sneaked a peripheral glance at Noel, trying to divine if he too was watching the breasts jiggle under the thin summer frock. A dart of jealousy caused him to leap up and run to the dancing girl, grab her hand in a possessive manner and drag her laughing across the lawn to another secret pathway. Noel ran after them.

In the house Mrs Scaum was watching the trio. 'He's brought that wretched boy again, and a female. I hope she doesn't lead Noel astray. Just look at the way she disports herself.'

'She might be a thoroughly decent girl,' responded Mr Scaum. 'You shouldn't malign her so.'

'Forgive me if I'm wrong, but you showed similar charity towards the boy,' retorted his wife. 'And he repaid you by luring Noel into truancy and destroying your chess set.'

'It's not destroyed, there's only one piece missing.'

'One piece or five, it's still ruined if the set is incomplete.'

'It could have been knocked from the table by . . .'

'We've looked high and low, Steven! It seems too much of a coincidence that on the night Noel brought that boy home the piece went missing – and Noel admitted he took him into your study.' A misdemeanour for which Noel had been reprimanded.

'Even if he is the culprit I can't just go and bluntly accuse him.' Scaum lit his pipe and came to look out of the French window alongside his wife.

'At least question him,' urged Mrs Scaum. 'And when he's gone you'd better speak to Noel about consorting with girls like that one.'

The youngsters' get-together was interrupted by the appearance of Mr Scaum, who wandered calmly around the pergola and waved as if he had stumbled upon them by accident. 'Hello, there! Nat, isn't it?' He came over.

Nat nodded, feeling uncomfortable.

'And who is your young lady friend, Noel?' Mr Scaum waved across the flowerbed as Bright lifted her head from a rose and caught him looking at her. She waved back.

'That's Nat's friend, Bright,' explained Noel.

'Pretty name.' Mr Scaum drew on his pipe for a while, adding the scent of tobacco to that of rose and honeysuckle. 'Well, I won't interrupt your play.' He turned to go, then wheeled back. 'Oh! By the way, I appear to have mislaid one of my chessmen – the maid has probably knocked it off the board when she was dusting. If either of you see it lying around just pop it back on the board would you?'

'What was he looking at me for?' muttered Nat when Mr Scaum's back was turned.

Noel attempted to look surprised, though the topic of the chessman had been raised before in his presence.

'I'll bet he thinks I pinched it.'

'I'm sure he doesn't.'

'Anyway, I'm off now.' A sullen Nat turned on his heel, calling to Bright as he went. 'Away, we're off!'

Noel followed. 'Why do you imagine my father was accusing you of stealing it? Is it because you feel guilty?'

Nat was angry. 'I don't have owt to feel guilty about! And in case you'd forgotten, you steal too.' Satisfied at the other's look of dismay, he added less passionately, 'Anyroad, I'm not going because o' what he said, I'm just bored sat here doing nowt.'

A disappointed Bright caught up with her friend as he made for the gate. Noel traced their footsteps.

The girl looked over her shoulder. 'Was that your dad?' When Noel gave confirmation she flashed a smile. 'He's got a bum on his chin.'

Noel had to laugh, for he knew what she meant. 'It's called a cleft!'

'Looks like a little bum to me – you've got one too.'

Dismayed, Noel put a hand up to probe his chin.

'I like it.' Bright felt herself grabbed by the arm and pushed through the gate.

'See you next Friday?' enquired Noel and looked concerned when Nat offered a curt, 'Maybe,' and left without looking back. The girl waved though.

In the week that followed Bright spoke of little else but her visit to Noel's house. 'Will ye be going tonight?' she asked Nat this Friday morning at breakfast – as she had asked every single morning.

'I might do.' He had become exasperated by her fixation, not to mention that the interrogation over the chess piece still rankled. She asked if he would take her. 'I don't know if I'm going!'

'Oh, but if ye do . . .'

'By, I could put my boots to you!' exclaimed Nat, abandoning his breakfast.

Several jaws dropped open. Mrs Maguire projected horror. 'Nat!'

Before he had time to enquire about his crime Nat felt his collar grabbed by Martin, as he was frogmarched to the scullery and a bar of soap rammed at his mouth. He twisted his head this way and that to avoid it.

'Wash your filthy mouth out!' Martin grappled with him. 'An' think yourself lucky Dad's gone to work or he'd belt ye black an' blue!'

Nat managed to wriggle free and ran to a corner, back to the wall, eyes wild and confused. 'What have I done?'

'Don't you ever talk to my sister like that again!' Martin stabbed a warning finger into his chest.

'I wasn't really going to kick her!' Nat rubbed a cuff over

his mouth, trying desperately to remove the taste of soap. 'It's just a saying! It doesn't mean owt.'

'What?' Martin scowled. When it slowly dawned on him that Nat had not fully understood the sexual implication of his announcement, he relaxed somewhat and took a pace backwards, combing his hair with his fingers. 'Right . . . right, well just don't say that again to Bright — to any woman, understand? Go and apologize.' He turned his back on Nat to hide a smirk of amusement at the misunderstanding and breakfast was resumed in peace.

'Sorry.' Head down, Nat did not look at Bright.

She said it was all right. 'So will ye take me?'

Nat sighed. 'If I go, yes!' Though I doubt I'll be invited again, came the glum thought.

He was to be pleasantly surprised. Noel was as eager for his company as ever when they met up that Friday evening in St Sampson's churchyard. The chess piece was not mentioned. After an hour or so of mischief the two boys left their companions and walked home together.

'Summer hols soon,' announced Noel. 'I'll be able to come out every day, apart from the fortnight when we go to Whitby.'

'We'll all be at work,' replied Nat.

Noel lost his effusiveness. 'Oh . . . I'll have no one to keep me company. How boring.'

'You can come and help me find scrap,' offered Nat, restoring his friend's enthusiasm. 'Course, we don't need to do it every day. We could spend some time at your place.' Nat was dying to get there again.

'Anything you like.' Noel was happy to oblige. 'Anyway, I'd prefer it without the others. They're a bit thick aren't they? I mean they're all right, but . . . oh, I don't know.' Judging by Nat's face he had said too much. It was true, though, the others weren't very stimulating. There was paradox here, for Nat offered little in the way of conversation, but there was just something that appealed to him in the boy's face; something about his clean-cut features that demanded finer attire. Ragged and uneducated though he might be, there was nothing oafish or clod-like about him as was the nature of those he mixed with – Spud and Denzil and Gunner. 'What I meant was, I don't look upon them as friends as I do you.'

Nat was flattered. Yet much as he was amused by Noel's company he could not bring himself to commit his total friendship, because it was just not in him to give himself totally to anyone. Beneath the air of camaraderie was a resentment for all the things Noel had: a mother, a father, big house, money, brains . . . how could Noel even want to be his friend? What had Nat to offer? Uncomfortable as he might feel, he used Noel's sentiment to his own advantage. 'It's early yet, shall I come to your house for a while?'

Noel was affable. 'Certainly.'

'Oh, no!' Nat tucked his chin into his chest and muttered. 'Look who's waiting for us.' As they neared the end of Fossgate he could see Bright leaning against the wall of the drapery store.

Noel shaded his eyes. 'It's your friend, isn't it?'

'Sorry. She keeps pestering for me to take her to your house again. I said I'd ask you . . .'

'Well, I don't mind if she comes occasionally,' answered Noel.

Pressed against the wall, head down, Bright had not seen them yet. 'So is it all right if she comes with us now?' asked Nat.

Noel did not appear to be keen on the idea. 'I suppose so.' They had almost reached her and still she didn't come galloping over the bridge as was her usual course of action when she saw Nat.

He looked puzzled. 'Wonder what's up with her.'

She heard his voice now and lifted her face. Her cheeks were stained with tears. The boys paused beside her. 'Me Granny's died,' uttered Bright, then immediately turned away, weeping. Nat bit his lip and stared helplessly at the other boy. He could not abandon her.

Noel understood. 'Maybe we'll leave it for another night.' He backed away. 'And you'll both be welcome.'

Nat tossed him a look of gratitude then, without words, shepherded the sobbing Bright towards home.

Noel, too, proceeded homewards. When he removed his jacket later he found a chessman in one of its pockets.

9

The old lady's funeral took place on Sunday when all workers could attend. Unable to afford a hearse, the two eldest Maguire sons negotiated her coffin on a handcart, one at the front and one at the back, with the prodigious Maguire clan trailing behind. Nat was just glad to get the corpse out of the house. Since Friday it had been lying in the front parlour surrounded by candles and drunken weeping relatives. The atmosphere had been unbearable.

Despite feeling pity for Bright he could not imagine what all the fuss was about. 'I mean, it's not as if she ever talked to you, is it?' he said in a ham-fisted attempt to cheer her up. 'And you've got loads of family left. I've got nobody.' As far as he was concerned his mother was dead.

'I loved my granny!' Bright burst into tears of outrage.

'I'm not saying you didn't!' Nat looked awkward and bent to scratch his leg. After a long pause he added encouragement. 'You can come to Noel's with me on Friday if you want.' Bright's red-rimmed eyes emerged from behind her handkerchief and she nodded acceptance. Nat had an afterthought. 'You won't be crying all the time you're there, will you?'

'I won't come if you don't want me!' Her face collapsed again.

'Course I want you! You're my best friend.'

She blew her nose. 'What about Noel?'

'He's all right but he's too posh to be a real friend — don't tell him I said that though! Else he won't invite us any more.'

Bright managed a damp grin. 'He's nice though, isn't he?

much better than any of that gang of yours.' An alarming thought came to her. 'Do they go to Noel's house, too?'

There was a twinkle of conspiracy in Nat's eye. 'No, me and him pretend we're going home then we go to his house. You're not to mention it.'

'As if I would! Anyway, I'm not likely to see them am I?' Bright had kept well away from Nat's companions since the fire. She was cheering up now. 'Will ye be going every Friday evening?'

'Probably.' Nat did not mention that he would be seeing more of Noel in the school holidays. He was not so much of a martyr that he wanted Bright's company all the time.

'Can I come too?'

'What, every Friday?' He looked doubtful. 'Oh, I'd have to ask him . . .'

'We'll be able to spend more time together during the school holidays, maybe go for picnics in the country.'

Nat had forgotten that Bright would be off school too. 'I have a living to earn.'

'Oh, yes . . . well, I could help you collect scrap then.'

'It's no work for a girl.' Nat was pulled in two directions. Sometimes he was filled with all kinds of passion for Bright, wanted to hold her, kiss her . . . but then at other times he just had to be with his own sex. One was always inhibited in the company of females. 'Still, it's a good idea about the picnic. We could go on Saturday, just you and me.'

This and the promise of regular weekend jaunts appeared to mollify her, allowing him to spend most of the vacation with Noel, often hunting for scrap but more often being at Noel's house. He loved it here. The feeling was not reciprocated by Noel's parents, in particular Mrs Scaum who wanted her husband to forbid the boy's presence.

'On what grounds?' Scaum looked helpless.

'That he's a thief, for one,' countered his wife.

'Oh, now . . .'

'You know it's true!'

'The chess piece was returned.' It had mysteriously reappeared on the board.

'Only after you confronted him.'

'Well, I've said before that I'll give him the benefit of the doubt if only because Noel seems very attached to him.'

'That in itself is even more worrying!' argued Mrs Scaum. 'He'll lure Noel into bad ways.'

'Have you considered that the reverse could happen, that Noel could be a good influence on him and nip his criminal tendencies in the bud? It was only a chess piece for heaven's sake.'

'A chess piece which you insist he didn't steal!' persevered Mrs Scaum.

Scaum tired of the argument. 'When I receive firm evidence that the association is bad for our son, then I will terminate it at once. But my dear, Noel has few friends . . .'

'I'm sure the boy's only using him!' interrupted his wife. 'Mark my words, you'll see.'

'Then we'll see.' He bit on his pipe. The topic was closed.

However, it was Mr Scaum's philanthropy that was made to appear a little misplaced when he caught Nat using a brass letter opener to prise up the lid of the piano.

'What the devil do you think you're doing!' Foregoing his usual calm manner he lunged at Nat and grabbed the letter opener from his hand.

The boy already had his excuses. 'It was locked! I was only . . .'

'I know it was locked!' Scaum was angry. 'I locked it because I'm sick of people tinkling on it whilst I am trying to read on an evening. Look at the damage you've caused!' He probed the gouges on the mahogany lid. 'Where's my son – Noel!' Noel came running.

'Where have you been?' demanded his father.

'Just to the . . . you know.' Noel was flushed.

'Well, you might like to know that in your absence your friend here has ruined my piano!'

'Sorry, Father.' Noel hung his head, wondering how Nat could be such a barbarian.

'Sorry is not enough!' Mr Scaum wagged the letter opener. 'If Nat cannot pay for the damage it will come out of your hide!' He turned and marched from the room, afraid that if he remained he would throttle both boys.

'What's he so mad about?' The perpetrator dismissed the marks on the wood. 'It's only a few chips.'

Noel disagreed as to the severity of the damage. 'It could mean replacing the entire lid.'

'Well, what does that matter to him, he's got bags of money.'

Noel had been brought up to respect others' property. Even if he had stolen, he had never caused wilful damage and with this act Nat had fallen in his esteem. 'He hasn't as a matter of fact.'

'Who're you trying to kid!' sneered Nat, his contempt more for himself than for the other. What on earth had made him do it? He had surely spoilt his chances of coming here again.

Noel was cool. 'I know we have a splendid life compared to you, but honestly we're not that rich. Why do you think I have to go to grammar school? Because my father can't afford the fees for anywhere better. Yes, we have a nice house but that was left to my father in his uncle's will, it costs an awful lot to maintain. Father works very hard, but from what I can gather he's not very well paid – although he's never actually told me, I've only overheard Mother grumbling. It would take months of hard work to save up for another piano lid.'

'I work bloody hard too but I'll never be able to afford owt like this!' Nat lashed out at the piano leg with his boot. 'And you!' He shoved Noel in the chest. 'You only bring me here so you can show off your fancy things!'

'How dare you!' Mr Scaum, as if not believing it the first time, had returned to make further investigation of the damage. 'How dare you throw my son's friendship in his face! How dare you abuse our hospitality by vandalizing our precious belongings!' He shook with a fury that travelled down his pointed finger. 'Let me give you a piece of advice . . . '

Advice! They were all so free with advice. Nat clenched his teeth and glared at the carpet as Scaum waded into him.

'If you are to keep your friend then you must take that chip off your shoulder, and until you do you can stay away from my house. Do you hear?'

Nat merely turned on his heel and left without so much as a goodbye.

Mr Scaum addressed his son: 'Noel, I sympathize I really do, but I've given Nat every chance . . . '

'I know, I'm terribly sorry, Father.' Noel felt sick both at Nat's behaviour and the loss of his friendship.

'You have no need to apologize for his wrongdoings.'

'I won't bring him here again.'

At his son's crestfallen face, Scaum modified his anger. 'Oh look, I know how you two get on. If he takes the chip off his shoulder he'll be fine. Just as well we're going to Whitby on Saturday, it will give me a chance to cool down.'

Bright, preparing for her Friday night treat at Noel's house, was dismayed to learn that it had been cancelled. 'He's off on holiday,' mumbled Nat. 'I won't be seeing him for a while.'

Bright laid the hairbrush back on the mantelshelf. 'Suppose ye'll be with Denzil and the others all night then?'

Something in her face touched Nat. 'I don't have to see them at all, we could go brambling or summat, it's a nice night.'

She turned an eager smile on her mother. 'Oh can we, Mammy?'

'So long as ye don't expect me to make all these brambles into jam,' answered Mrs Maguire, repairing one of her sons' shirts.

'I'll bake you a nice pie with them!' Bright sprang into action, crossed a shawl over her chest and knotted it behind, then went to find a receptacle.

After she and Nat had gone Mrs Maguire nibbled her lip and said to her husband, 'I forget that child of ours is growing up. Should we ought to have sent one o' the lads with them?'

Maguire laughed at the notion, barely raising his eyes from his evening paper. 'And him as much a brother to her as the rest o' them? Away with ye, woman!'

In only fifteen minutes the youngsters had left the over-crowded city behind them and were combing the hedgerows for blackberries. The briars were laden and in next to no time the basket was half full. Pausing to rest, Bright popped one of the dark fruits into her mouth, grinning impishly at her partner. In response, Nat scooped up a handful of berries and crammed them into his own mouth, purple juice spurting with his laugh. Not to be outdone, Bright used both hands to scoop fruits into her mouth, abandoning all vestiges of newly attained woman-hood, laughing and spluttering as the juice was smeared all over her cheeks, then falling to the grass in hysterics as Nat pretended to eat the entire basket.

In the smiling calm that followed Nat reclined on the grass whilst Bright returned to filling the basket. He watched her dextrous fingers move over the briar, watched the way her shoulderblades jutted from the light material of her dress, the curve of her jaw dappled with juice, the fineness of her wrist bones, the glow of her hair in the evening sunlight. She turned to look at him and he was smitten with the urgent desire to kiss her.

Bright felt his concentrated gaze and offered a blushing riposte. 'Are ye going to let me do this all on my own?'

Leaping to his feet, Nat came to stand beside her, plucking haphazardly at the berries and wondering how to make his approach. His forearm accidentally brushed hers. Bright issued a self-conscious laugh and half turned to receive a clumsy impulsive kiss. Then, though both tingled with excitement, they continued with their task as if nothing had happened.

On the way home he took her hand. Bright prayed that he would kiss her again but, alas, this did not happen and before they reached the city he had released his grip in case anyone should see them. When they arrived home it was as if no intimacy had taken place. Indeed, in the barren weeks that followed Bright could almost have believed she had dreamed it.

It was October before Noel decided to meet up with the gang again. When, on that autumnal Friday evening, he arrived at St Sampson's churchyard he found Nat's response as cool as the weather. Only the two of them were here at present, which gave Noel the opportunity to broach the subject of their inglorious parting. 'Father's calmed down now, the piano was fixed while we were away. It didn't need a new lid, just some french polishing. It looks as good as new – mind you, it cost a few quid. Anyway, Father's agreed to let me bring you home again.'

Nat was airy, holding his palms to the fire he had lighted. 'Who says I want to come?'

The yellow-haired boy was obviously disappointed. 'Yes well, only if you want to.'

'First he accuses me of stealing his chess piece . . .'

'Which you did!'

'Then he goes mad cause of a few scratches on a piano!'

'They weren't just scratches!' Noel's cheeks were pink, not merely from the cold. 'I know from the amount of money that was confiscated from my allowance. I won't get anything for the rest of the year and all because of you!'

Nat's reply was nasty. 'You can always steal some! Huh! I wonder what dear Father would say if he knew you'd broken into folks' houses and pinched stuff.'

Panic rose to Noel's throat. 'I didn't pinch stuff I put it back!'

Nat was astounded. 'What?'

The other hesitated before repeating. 'I put it back — through the letterbox. I felt terrible, Nat. Those two old people hadn't done anything to me! Why should I want to steal from them when I have enough money of my own?'

'If you've got enough then what're you whining about the bloody piano for?'

'How would you feel if it were your piano, that you'd saved hard for and I was the one who attacked it?'

'Chance'd be a fine thing,' scoffed Nat.

'I thought you were my friend.' The tone of Noel's voice held no anger now, only betrayal. 'Friends don't do that to one another.'

Nat was peevish. 'Oh, take that!' He shoved his hand into his overcoat pocket and threw a handful of coins at the other youth. 'We can't have you forking out for something I've done, can we?'

Noel did not attempt to field the coins, some of which rolled along a gravestone. 'I don't want your money, Nat.'

'Hah! You've been chuntering about it enough!'

'You don't seem to understand!' Noel railed at the lack of intelligence. 'Yes, it was a lot of money but I'd willingly pay it if I thought our friendship meant anything to you.'

'It does mean summat!' Exasperated, Nat leaped up and gathered the fallen coins. 'Here! Look, take them. I'm sorry, all right? I didn't mean to bust your stinking piano, I'm sorry! I'm sorry.'

Noel wondered whether to hand back the coins, but

deciding this would exacerbate Nat's annoyance he put them into his pocket. 'Thank you. Are we still friends?'

'Yes!' snapped Nat.

'Do you want to come to my house next week?'

'Not if your dad expects me to tug my foreskin every time I see him.'

Noel could not help a laugh. 'I hardly think he'd appreciate that!'

Nat did not realize his gaffe. 'Well, I don't do that for nobody – eh, shush now, Denzil's here.' He repositioned his hat.

One by one the gang members assembled and passed half an hour around the fire relating each other's news. Spud confessed, 'I got the sack today.'

'What for?' asked Gunner.

'Nowt!' Spud was still confused as to what he had done to deserve this.

'You must've done summat wrong.' Denzil turned up the collar of his jacket.

'How can there be anything to get wrong?' demanded Nat. 'He's only a bloody chocolate basher.'

'Spud'd get owt wrong!' laughed Gunner.

Noel put his hand to his dimpled chin and looked thoughtful. 'I hear they're looking for a new village idiot at Tockwith if that's any help.' Made to look a fool, Spud lurched for him and a period of wrestling ensued.

'Makes no difference to me if I've got a job or not.' Gunner sighed when the tussle was over. 'Me mam and dad never let me keep anything out of me wages.'

'Oh, I thought you told us your father was always giving you backhanders,' queried Noel, more cheerful now that his friendship with Nat was on an even keel.

Spud felt this required explanation. 'No, when he says that he means his dad hits him.'

'Oh really, Spud? I would never have twigged.' Noel heaved a sigh.

Gunner heaved too, but with boredom. 'We haven't had a good scrap in ages. Are there any posh schools open today? We could go and look for somebody to punch.'

'There's the Blind School,' suggested Noel.

This was one reason for which Nat could be glad he had not thrown Noel aside; he always had some apt riposte that the others often failed to interpret, not realizing that he was making fun of them. Nat often wondered if he too was a victim of Noel's wit, and whether the boy was merely using him for amusement just as he himself was using Noel as a bridge to the material comforts of the Scaum household.

Nat was growing bored of the gang, and now in possession of intelligent male company he had no further need of the others. Noel was right, most of them were stupid. Gunner pilfered anything he could lay his hands on and like a magpie stole things for which he had no earthly use, simply for the hell of it. Nat could not see the point of this, knowing that you had to sell your gains in order to become rich. Spud was . . . well, just plain stupid, and Denzil . . . Denzil was another kettle of fish altogether, having the ability to invoke fear in all of them. They were afraid of meeting him but afraid of not meeting him. It was not simply that he would repay any misdemeanour with violence; Nat had lived with the threat of violence for much of his life and had learned to cope with it. No, it was some much greater fear . . . why, then, did he himself continue to associate with people he despised? Because all your kind are like this, came the answer. Only Bright shone out like a jewel.

With little to do that evening, Nat had much time to ponder on his strange bond with Noel and his own act of vandalism that had come close to jeopardizing it. When the gang broke up for the night he had decided to relinquish his membership.

He should have known there would be confrontation.

On Sunday when he did not turn up the gang members came looking for him. 'Bet you thought you were going to Noel's house instead, didn't you?' Denzil had that mad glint in his eye. Nat's heart sank and he tried to defend his secret, casually popping an aniseed ball into his mouth. 'Why would I want to go there?'

'Lying bastard! I've seen how pally you are, always going home in the same direction – '

'Yes, but his house is further down t'road than mine . . .'

'Well, we've got time for a walk haven't we lads? Nat can take us.'

'How do I know where he lives?' protested Nat.

Denzil wasted no further time arguing but dealt him a blow. Nat cried out, almost choking on the aniseed ball whilst holding his stinging nose. Denzil held his fist in readiness. 'If you know it's further down t'road you must know where it is! Tell us or I'll bray you again!'

'All right!' Nat cringed at the blood on his hand. 'I think he lives down Hull Road but I'm not sure what number. I'll try and find it.'

'You'd better.' Denzil gave him a push. The reluctant Judas led them to Hull Road, where for a time they hid behind a tree to spy upon Noel's house.

Then Denzil gave a jubilant hiss. 'They're off out!'

A miserable Nat watched the family climb into the carriage and drive away. Denzil gripped his elbow. 'You can take us inside now.'

'The maid'll be in!' protested Nat.

Denzil slapped his face. 'That's for lying to your leader! How would you know he had a maid if you haven't been here? All that bollocks about not knowing the number . . . right, we'll start in the garden and have a look through the windows. The maid can't be in every room at once. Have they got a dog?'

Nat shook his head and was then dragged along on the

expedition. The others were astounded by the size of Noel's garden. Denzil seemed to take exception at the neatly edged beds of perennials and began systematically to rip out every plant. Spud and Gunner followed his lead. Nat tried to distract them, saying he thought he had seen a face at the window. This postponed the wanton vandalism for a moment, but soon Denzil and his cronies were seeking more plants to destroy. Everything small enough to be uprooted by hand was hurled about the garden. The rest was trampled and split and wrenched and twisted. Then, 'Let's go down here,' said Denzil.

Nat, aware of what would happen if the gang took that path blurted, 'No, let's go down here! There's a stream.'

But Denzil was already on his way and inevitably came across the cage of Golden Pheasants.

Nat loved those birds – had tried to forget that he didn't actually own them and indeed regarded them as his own. 'I'll let you feed them if you like!' he panicked.

Denzil looked at him with those frightening eyes. Nat handed him the tin of corn. Denzil took it then stepped into the cage. The pheasants strutted nervously. Denzil threw a handful of corn at them. They croaked and flapped about. He squatted and held out his open palm, offering food. The creatures eyed him warily, then one by one came to eat. There was a yelp. Denzil sprang upwards clutching his hand. 'The bugger bit me!' He lashed out with a boot. The pheasants ran amok. Spud and Gunner laughed and began to race around the cage, stirring the birds into hysteria. Feathers flew. The carnage which Nat had feared began. Denzil snatched at a bird and ripped out the ornamental plumage from its tail. Other atrocities followed. When he had finished, not one bird was left alive.

Denzil stood, panting, to inspect the results of his bloodlust. His pale blue eyes glanced at the others who appeared dumbfounded at the havoc they had caused. Then he picked up a long drooping tailfeather, inserted it in his hat, put one hand on his hip, the other affecting a feminine gesture, and grinned. Spud and Gunner shared a guilty laugh. Nat was rigid with shock.

'Let's go see what there is to pinch in the house!' came Denzil's order, and Nat was left standing alone in the cage amongst the beautiful bodies. Anger rumbled and boiled within. In his mind he roared at Denzil, you crazy rotten bastard! But only in his mind, for it was beyond his courage to challenge that lunatic. Faced with the sudden image of Noel coming across the massacre, he returned to his senses, looked around to see if he was being observed, then made for the gate. He was very quiet when he got home. No one noticed; Nat was always quiet.

Later that afternoon, the Scaums returned to a ransacked house and an exhibition of butchery. The police were called, but it was not until some friends called round unexpectedly that evening that the identity of the culprit was mooted.

'This is what you get for letting that slum boy into your home,' said Mr Powers, the one who had been there at Nat's first visit.

'Nat?' Mr Scaum looked at his son, who had just come in to say goodnight before going to bed.

'If that was his name, yes. I really don't know what the world's coming to. These hooligans . . . there was no such thing when I was a boy.' He shook his head.

'Nonsense,' replied Scaum. 'Just because someone has invented a new word for it, it doesn't mean they've invented the condition. There have always been ruffians. I remember walking down the street with my mother when I was perhaps five years old and a gang of youths elbowed her into the gutter.'

'A little rough horseplay, yes, but there was never such gratuitous violence.'

'In 1854,' said Scaum as if reciting a history lesson,

'someone broke into my grandfather's home, tied him up and proceeded to torture him until he told them where his money was. On finding the money, one of the thieves then smashed my grandfather's fingers with a hammer just for the joy of it. He was sixty-two years old and consequently suffered an apoplexy from which he died. Say what you will, the savage has always been inherent to society. However,' his eyes became grave as he turned to his son, 'just because we accept their existence it does not mean we will allow them to go unpunished. Noel, Mr Powers is correct, I shall have to put forward your friend's name as a suspect.'

Noel spoke up with confidence. 'Nat would never do a thing like this.'

'Maybe not alone, but he did it all right. I saw it in his face when I rebuked him for his abuse of you. He resented my words. Your friend may be a lesser villain but he's still of that ilk; one of the spoilers and the ignorant, who have nothing themselves, see a person who has bettered himself and decide that he shall not have it. Well, I've given Nat every chance. Tomorrow we must contact the police.'

Noel's stomach lurched. He knew that Nat could not possibly be to blame, but if he revealed that Denzil was the real culprit then further crimes may come to light and Noel himself might be incriminated for the robbery.

His father noticed his concentration. 'I do hope you are not toying with the idea of shinning from your bedroom window to go and warn him. Don't look at me like that, I know you do such silly things. Believe me, he's no friend to you, Noel.'

Noel had no alternative but to go to bed, feeling guilty at letting his friend down. Before he reached the top stair however a thought occurred: how had Denzil known where he lived if someone had not informed him? Nat would have to take care of himself.

Bright had woken with pins and needles in her leg. With

the utmost delicacy, so as not to wake her sisters, she turned onto her back and tried to restore the circulation by wriggling her toes, but the agony persisted. Slipping from under the bedclothes she began to hobble around the bedroom floor, flexing her leg muscles. It was pitch black and cold. There was not a sound from outside.

Back and forth, back and forth. The pins and needles eventually subsided. Bright shivered and was about to return to bed when she heard a faint noise. Moving to the open door she cocked her ear. There it came again, the sound of weeping from downstairs. After the merest hesitation she began to descend. Halfway down she felt the warmth from the kitchen fire creep up her legs and over the rest of her body. A stair creaked. The weeping stopped.

Nat pretended to be asleep when the girl crept to his fireside bed and kneeled down, but she knew his breathing was too quiet for slumber and touched him gently. 'What's wrong?' When he did not respond she decided he must want her to go and made to rise.

Nat's arm shot out from under the blanket and caught her arm. 'Stay a bit.'

She sat back on her heels. 'Do you want to talk about it?'

He made no great display of outraged manhood; Bright had surely heard him crying. He shook his head.

Bright made a guess. 'Was it Denzil?' She was all too aware what a monster the youth could be.

When he nodded she sighed. 'Did he hurt ye badly?'

Nat's voice was gruff but the tears were under control now. He had forgotten the blow to his nose. 'Not me.'

Bright was glad about that. 'He hurt Noel?'

'It's to do with Noel, yes, but I don't want to talk about it.' Apart from the awful images of the afternoon and the nightmares that had woken him he did not want to ponder on the fact that it could lead to another spell of detention. He could not stand it. He just couldn't. It wasn't fair. He hadn't committed any crime but sure as anything they would blame it on him. 'Talk about summat else.'

Her brain was too fogged to conjure up a topic at this time of night. 'I should be in bed – what hour is it anyway?' She squinted at the clock but was unable to make out the time.

'Don't know.' Nat rolled onto his back and put his hands beneath his head. After a gap of silence he asked, 'What d'you see when you look at me, Bright?'

She squirmed and was glad the darkness hid her blush. 'Just . . . you.'

Nat did not appear to want anything deeper, appeared to be talking to himself more than to her. 'I often wonder what people see when they look at me. A villain? I know the blokes at Marygate do, even old Chippy, and specially Bramble Conk. What goes through his mind when he's laying a birch across me back? Does he enjoy it? Or does he try to think of summat else to take his mind off it, like I do? I couldn't do it to anybody, not unless I hated 'em. What's up wi' me? What have I done to make everybody hate me?'

Bright's heart ached. 'They don't! All of us here like ye.'

'Why?' he demanded. 'Come on, why d'you like me?'

Alarmed by his aggression she was lost for an answer. 'Well, we just do.'

He was sullen. 'I think you feel sorry for me.'

'That's not true! We like ye because . . . you're nice and quiet and kind and gentle.'

'If I'm that nice and kind why doesn't everyone else see it then?'

'Well,' Bright twisted her nightgown, 'ye have to show people what you're really like, just by saying thank you and little things like that.'

'Why should I have to suck up to them?' hissed Nat. 'What makes them better than me?'

'Nobody says they're better – and it's not sucking up, tis just good manners. If ye don't say what's in your heart

244

how will they know? They can't see through that tough expression.'

Nat gave a negative response. 'Huh! If they think you're soft they take even more advantage of you. What about when I was a little kid? Nobody even liked me then and I hadn't done anything apart from jigging school — and I only did that so's I wouldn't get belted every day!'

Bright sighed and hugged herself. She was beginning to feel cold. Though the fire glowed her nightgown was inadequate protection for an October's eve and there was an empty corner where Granny Maguire used to be. 'Can I come in with you?'

His frustration aired, Nat settled down. Quite naturally he lifted up the blanket and she snuggled up beside him as she had done a hundred times before when playing mothers and fathers. Often when this happened Nat would pretend she was his mother, making out as if she had never left him, cuddle up and transport himself back in time with the fervent wish that he could begin life all over again. Tonight, however, was different. Something scarey began to happen. Pressed against her, Nat felt an erection forming. Acutely embarrassed he did not know which way to move. The erection became more and more obvious. Had he been alone it would have been ecstatically simple to alleviate it, but how could he do that with Bright here . . . and then he realized the true significance.

Bright's heart was racing and she did not know why. Nothing but her own paralysis compelled her to stay here; it would be wiser by far to return to her own bed, but her limbs refused to move. Nat's arm came around her. He had never done that before, not in this way. She covered it with her hands, feeling his skin burn her trembling palms. He began to hold her more tightly. He kissed her cheek. Bright lay there pinioned both with happiness and fear.

Then . . . oh dear God what was he doing, touching her there? And why wasn't she stopping him and pushing him away? She lay like a stone whilst he ran exploratory hands over every part of her body, *every* part, and then he raised himself and straddled her, pushing her nightgown right up to her chest. Oh Mother of God, what if anyone should come down and see what he was doing! But she could not stop him. He wormed the lower half of his body between her legs, then lay on top of her, kissing her face. She kissed him back. His cheek was soft and furry, his breath tasted of aniseed and his hair smelled of woodsmoke. He pressed his lips over hers, harder this time. Something leaped in her breast. She became like jelly. Nat began to fumble urgently below. Bright was drowning in embarrassment – how would she ever face him in the morning after she had allowed him to do these things to her? But she just could not stop him, was too frightened even to try. Thank goodness the darkness hid her shame. There was a tapping at her inner thighs. He was shoving something into a cavity she did not even know she had. She didn't know what or where or why but knew from its warmth that it was human flesh. He started to thresh about on top of her, grinding her into the rug. She clutched his back. Pain came – dreadful pain. She wanted to cry out but people would come running. She strained her neck, trying to escape it, trying to push him off, but he was too heavy and it had all gone too far.

Nat knew that he was hurting her but he could not stop now. His thrusting gathered momentum. He hurled himself at the resistant flesh until he finally exploded with a violence that seemed to drain him of everything he had. He sagged in a heap on top of her, and lay there rising and falling in time to her own breathless panting.

Bright stared over his shoulder into the night. What had they done? The act was of such enormity it must change their lives, change everything about them. She wanted to cry but tears would not come.

Nat moved, then rolled off her, not looking into her face. 'Sorry, I couldn't help it.'

Bright lay in the same position. The part between her legs felt raw but she could not move, could not speak.

'I love you.' Nat dared to face her then. He put his hand on her and kissed her cheek. The action helped to ease her paralysis. She turned over to face him. It hurt to move. He pulled her closer, wrapping his arms round her. She wanted to ask all sorts of questions – what did you do to me? What will come of it? – but was too afraid. She lay in his arms, enjoying his kisses, his embrace and his smell.

Soon, though, he pressed her onto her back and tried to impale her again. This time she heard a voice, her own, whisper, 'Don't, please don't. It hurts.'

He fell back immediately. 'Sorry, I didn't mean to hurt you. I love you. It'll be better next time.'

She whispered through her pain and embarrassment that she loved him too. 'I'll have to be getting back to bed.'

'Don't go yet.' He kissed her pleadingly. 'I promise I won't do anything. Just let me cuddle you. I love you.' And he meant it.

It was almost three in the morning when, bruised but joyous, she crept back to her shared bed, unable to sleep through exhilaration and fear. Nat fell asleep immediately.

Bright's blushes were spared the next morning. When she came down to breakfast Nat had already gone out. Half of her was glad, the other half ached to see him. At the table she kept her head down, sure that everyone could see the difference in her. There had been some panic when on rising she had seen the smudge of blood on her nightgown and felt more of it trickle from her. She had put her coat over it and rushed down to the privy before her sisters were half awake, but when she had got there she had seen it wasn't blood, just a sticky wetness. Still, it was no comfort, for she must be damaged inside to remain so tender.

'Are you ailing for something?' asked her mother, startling her. 'Picking at your food like that.'

'She must have a sweetheart tucked away,' put forth Eilleen, drawing more blood to the young one's cheeks.

Mr Maguire said jokingly, 'If I find out who it was I'll cut the fellow's heart out. To be sure I'm her only sweetheart, aren't I, darlin'?' Bright gave a smiling nod and wondered how long it would be before her guilt was exposed.

She mooned over Nat all that day whilst ostensibly teaching her class, wishing school was over and she could be with him. But once home, she found it hard even to look at him, afraid that he had changed his mind. To her relief when their eyes met by chance she saw the light of affection in them and squirmed with happiness. After tea she volunteered to wash up on her own. Nat said he would help, but once in the scullery he started to kiss and touch her. Bright tried to fend him off and hissed, 'Don't be so indecent!' But she cherished his fumblings all the same.

'Are you coming down to see me tonight?' His arms linked her waist, preventing her escape.

'I daren't.' His kisses were lovely, but Bright didn't want to risk *that* happening again, whatever it was.

'Please,' he crooned in her ear. 'I love you.'

'Our Eilleen nearly woke up when I got back into bed last night.' Why did she have to lie to protect herself, why not just say no?

'Go on. Please, Bright.' He nuzzled her. 'Please.'

'You promise you won't . . . you won't do that again.' Surely it couldn't be healthy for her heart to keep thudding like this.

Nat mouthed her neck. 'I promise.' He felt himself inside her already. He had been thinking of it all day – walking down the street, eating his dinner, collecting his scrap iron, he had thought of nothing else. He had looked at youths his own age playing daft games and thought, what babies. He'd never be able to do without it now. He'd just die if she wouldn't let him. He wanted to do it this instant . . .

Someone touched the doorhandle. Both youngsters leaped apart, Nat to the far end of the scullery, Bright to the sink, as a grave Mr Maguire put his head into the kitchen. 'Nat, will ye come out here, please.'

Bright, deep in industry over the stack of pots, raised her head in terror, prepared to be exposed, then swallowing the vomit in her throat followed Nat and her father to meet her punishment. On encountering the policeman however, she knew it was something entirely different.

'Nathaniel Smellie, I'm arresting you for theft and wilful damage of property belonging to Mr Steven Scaum.'

Smellie! Bright had almost wiped it from her mind. She hated the name as much as he did and had never told him that she had discovered it.

The policeman was about to lead Nat away with little explanation. 'Won't you tell us the details at least?' begged Mrs Maguire.

The officer replied, 'Yesterday afternoon a house belonging to Mr Scaum was broken into. A number of items were stolen. What the intruders did not steal they destroyed, including the family's pets which were butchered quite mercilessly.'

'Oh Nat!' Mrs Maguire put her apron over her mouth. Bright felt sick – no wonder Nat had been unable to speak of it last night.

'Just a minute, just a minute!' her husband intervened. 'Who said Nat did this?'

'Mr Scaum gave us his name and address. As a matter of fact we've been wanting to question Master Smellie for some time about some missing horse tails, only we couldn't trace him.'

'What the devil have horse tails got to do with this?' demanded Maguire.

'This boy,' the officer wagged a finger, 'was taken in by a Mr Wood when he came out of Industrial School the last time. He repaid the gentleman's kindness by running away.

When he'd gone Mr Wood discovered that every one of his horses had had their tails docked.'

'Wasn't me,' lied Nat, with a plausible expression.

'Cut their own tails, did they?'

'It wasn't me, I tell you. Why do I always get the blame?'

'Maybe because you're always guilty,' replied the constable.

'Hey, now wait a minute!' Mr Maguire pointed a finger. 'A man's innocent till proved guilty.'

'Is that so?' The officer appeared to be enlightened. 'Well, whilst we're on the subject of guilt you could be in trouble for harbouring a runaway.'

'How would I know he's a runaway?' exclaimed Maguire. 'And sure you fellas didn't look for him very hard, he's been here a twelvemonth.' He shot a dark glance at his wife who cringed. 'Did you know anything about this?'

'Well, I did and I didn't.' Mrs Maguire looked nervous. 'Nat told me he left the job at Leeds 'cause they were too unfriendly like.'

'He said nothing to me!' Maguire frowned upon the boy.

'I think twas just that he was lonely, d'ye see,' explained his wife. 'He wanted to come back and live with his friends.'

'Well, I've just had a glimpse of how Master Smellie treats his friends,' said the officer, 'and I can tell you I've never seen anything like it. Those poor damned birds – excuse me, missus!' He apologized to Mrs Maguire, 'but he ought to be flogged!'

Bright thought the policeman took enjoyment from telling the Maguires about the carnage in the Scaums' garden. She herself fought tears and Mrs Maguire seemed close to them.

'Oh no, Nat wouldn't do a thing like that,' vouched the head of the house.

'Mr Scaum seems to think he did, so I've no option but

to take him in. You'll get prison for this,' the officer told Nat.

'Nat didn't do it!' Bright stepped forward and blushed when everyone turned to look at her. 'But . . . I know who did.'

'Don't tell!' warned Nat.

'I have to.'

'He'll get me!'

'Who'll get you?' demanded Mr Maguire. 'Point him out, I'll give him ten heads.'

'Denzil Kneebone,' said Bright.

Nat collapsed inwardly as the name was issued. Pushed into a corner, he admitted that Denzil and his friends had been the main culprits and that he himself had run home before the others broke into the house. 'They forced me to lead them there.'

'You're still an accomplice,' said the policeman in disgust. 'You stood there and watched him do that to those birds. You're as bad as he is. What about the horse tails? It's no good hanging your head, I know you did it!'

'Sold 'em,' mumbled Nat.

'Who to?'

'A marine dealer in Taddy – can't remember his name.'

'Well, it doesn't matter, you're the one who's going down for it. A fine way to repay kindness!' He led Nat away.

Bright appealed to her father. 'Daddy, don't let them put Nat in prison!'

Maguire performed a helpless gesture. 'What can I do, pet?'

'Ye could go to court with him!' responded Bright. 'Tell them it wasn't Nat!'

Tearing his smoky eyes away from her distressed face he followed the policeman and Nat to the door. 'When will the case come up?'

The officer shrugged. 'It's not for me to say, but it

shouldn't be long now we know all the parties involved. Call in at the station in a few days.'

'I will.' Mr Maguire struck his brow with the palm of his hand. 'Though God knows that boy is more trouble than the six o' mine put together.' He addressed himself directly to Nat, at the same time indicating his daughter. 'I hope you know that if it wasn't for this one here I wouldn't be putting meself to all this trouble. Haven't I enough children of me own without looking after other people's?'

Nat bowed to the greater force as the officer shoved him out into the street. Mr Maguire, feeling sorry for the boy, called after him, 'Oh, don't worry yourself! I'll be there when they take ye to court, saint that I am.'

One by one the culprits were rounded up and appeared together at the Police Court. Denzil, positive that Nat had been the one to inform on them, barely took his eyes off him all the time they waited in the corridor. It was the first time Nat had seen Denzil's parents. Both looked quite normal, law-abiding and very worried at the court appearance. It was hard to imagine from which of them the boy had inherited his mean streak. Spud was accompanied by his mother, who looked more like a grandmother, and Gunner was the image of his father; a great big brown-eyed softie. Nat himself was accompanied by Mr Maguire, the only one of the family present. Bright had not been allowed to come. Neither, obviously, had Noel. Mr Scaum was waiting in the corridor alone, hurling reproachful glances at his son's erstwhile friend. Nat tried to avoid his eye and wondered briefly what Noel's reaction had been to all this.

The court heard that Nathaniel Smellie was a perpetual offender. Nat cringed as Denzil smirked at the name. Besides this latest dreadful episode he was also charged with the theft of five horse tails and absconding whilst under licence to the owner of said horses. A catalogue of his faults was presented to the listeners. Once this was over, Nat assumed the case was drawing to a close, for who would speak in his defence? Amazingly, one person was prepared to offer mitigation, and even more incredibly it was Mr Scaum who rose to his feet – though it was only due to the urgent behest of his son at the breakfast table that morning.

'Your Worship, it may appear strange that I as the injured party am about to issue a word in defence of one of the culprits. Having only met Nathaniel Smellie quite recently I am not at all qualified to remark upon his past misdemeanours, but the boy has confided a great deal in my own son who has begged me to make his background known . . . '

'Thank you, sir,' replied the Lord Mayor, presiding, 'but we are in possession of the boy's record.'

Scaum persisted, 'Then you must feel as do I that to have lost both one's parents by the age of ten is significant reason to err from the path of righteousness. From the time of his mother's death he has had no parental guidance – '

'That's a lie!' Mr Maguire sprang up. 'I treated that boy like my own son!'

'Sit down! Sit down!' The Lord Mayor called for order and the case proceeded to a low grumbling from the Irishman in the gallery. 'Once again I thank you, Mr Scaum, for your most noble intervention on behalf of Smellie, though regretfully I must advise you that your plea is wasted on this ne'er do well. The court is well aware of his background and, I might also add, of the number of good people who have tried to help him, to no avail. So, let us waste no further time but proceed to the other miscreants.'

In turn the backgrounds of the other culprits were dissected, theirs being somewhat briefer than Nat's. Eventually, after much deliberation the Lord Mayor gave his verdict. 'It is the opinion of this bench that Denzil Kneebone, however he may try to present himself as an innocent, is the chief offender here.' Nat, who had resigned himself to being saddled with this dubious honour after the performance Denzil had put on, could not believe his luck. 'He instigated the most wilful acts of violence against Mr Scaum's property and livestock. We feel that his crime is far too heinous to warrant referral to anything less than reformatory and therefore we are sending him to such an institution for a period of three years.'

Denzil looked impassive. His parents were distraught.

'Nathaniel Smellie, you may not have been the main author of this crime but you were the one to lead the other boys to Mr Scaum's home and by your presence there you are just as guilty. Since the age of ten you have been in and out of Industrial School and have shown not the slightest hint of reformation. Every effort to help you has been thrown back with ingratitude. You were found a good steady job with Mr Wood who treated you with the utmost charity. You were in his house barely twenty-four hours when you decided to rebuff his help. It was not enough for you to abscond whilst under licence, no, you augmented this crime by severing the tails of his horses, thereby reducing their value by five pounds each. Since that time who is to say what other questionable activities have taken place? I see no merit in sending you back to Industrial School where you have learned absolutely nothing . . .' Nat almost wet himself; oh Christ, he was going to reformatory with Denzil! 'However, one or two people, including your victim Mr Scaum, have spoken in mitigation. It is only on behalf of their pleas that I am going to give you one last chance to cure your recidivism. I shall return you to the custody of the officers at Marygate Industrial School for two years in the hope that by the time you are released you will have mended your ways. Otherwise, the next time you stand before me you will be sent to prison. Do I make myself understood?'

Nat heaved a sigh in relief and delivered a simple, 'Yes, sir.' Relief brought a look of smugness to his lips as he glanced at Denzil, then waited to hear Spud and Gunner's sentences. Both received terms at industrial schools, one at Leeds, the other at Halifax, in order to prevent their activities from continuing inside.

'You are all obviously a bad influence on each other,' rebuked the Lord Mayor. 'Sergeant, take them down.'

As all the boys were led away, Denzil lunged towards Nat. 'I'll fix you when I come out, *Smellie*!'

10

Noel expressed a desire to visit Nat, but his parents forbade it. 'That boy has been a bad enough influence on you without teaching you the tricks he has undoubtedly learned in that place,' reproved Mr Scaum, 'though I hold myself partly to blame in assuming that at your age you could be trusted to behave in a responsible manner. Heaven knows what you've been up to, associating with those boys, coming home at all hours, giggling like an imbecile ... and you certainly haven't been doing your homework! Your last school report was atrocious. I'm sorry, but there has been enough indolence, Noel, and now you must buckle down to some hard work if you're to go into medicine.'

Noel's mother agreed. 'You have just seen what happens to those who don't have the benefit of a good education and parental guidance. Forget all about that character, my son.'

'But Nat's my friend,' pleaded Noel. 'He'll think I've let him down. I must go.'

'Out of the question!' warned Mrs Scaum. 'If you cannot find any decent chums then I shall find you some myself.'

And Noel had to resign himself to the fact that he would never see Nat again.

Bright was downhearted at the loss of Nat's company too, though it was a deeper loss she felt than mere friendship. However would she stand the long absence? Two months had passed and still the heartache was unbearable. She could see the ache in Nat's eyes too when she and her father had taken him Christmas gifts. Much as she desper-

256

ately wanted to see him it had been a mistake to go, for the parting afterwards had been just dreadful. The way Nat had followed her to the door with his eyes made her fear that he might try to escape.

This fear was always at the back of her mind when she went off to school each morning, gnawing away at her as she taught arithmetic and abetted by an even deeper threat. The thing that was meant to happen to her every month had not happened since the end of October. Bright would probably have overlooked the timespan had not her sisters' regular cycles alerted her. Eilleen and Mary's had always coincided with hers, but they had had theirs twice to her once. Of course the irregularity could merely be due to her youth. She recalled when it had first happened, and her mother had told her all pink-faced and coy that the Cardinal would visit her once a month: 'Or it could be less often with you being so young. It's so's you'll be able to have babies when ye grow up. Tis a nuisance, I know, but isn't that a woman's lot in life. An' once a month isn't much to pay for the joy of having children, is it now?'

But it hadn't happened since October and now it was almost New Year. There had to be something wrong. Did this absence mean that she wouldn't be able to have babies? The mere thought of that was terrible to Bright, who wanted lots of children when she and Nat were married. There was of course a more frightening possibility for the loss of menstruation. Bright had the grave suspicion that it might be because of what Nat had done to her, that he had somehow damaged her or simply because they had been wicked. Yet whom could she consult about this unconfessed sin? She had not even dared to mention it to another woman let alone the priest. Just put it to the back of your mind, she told herself firmly, and all will be well. Things never happen if you keep wishing for them.

In January she went down with a chest cold and sickness. The cold cleared up in a few weeks but the sickness lingered, leaving her feeling like a limp rag. Everyone was most sympathetic, bringing her lozenges and fruit to aid her recovery.

'Maybe we should have her to the doctor,' opined a worried Mr Maguire when his favourite child continued to vomit even after being dosed with all the well-tested home remedies.

Bright was reluctant to consult the doctor, fearing that he would find something seriously wrong — the Cardinal had still not paid his visit. 'I'm well enough,' she told them as she prepared for school. 'It'll go away when I've something to take my mind off it.'

'Well, isn't that one for the books!' laughed sister Mary. Bright had always been a terrible patient, having everyone run around after her. 'Ye normally crack on you're at death's door if ye have so much as a toothache. I've never known you to turn down a bit of attention.'

A strange expression had come into Mrs Maguire's insipid eyes. She chewed on the end of her thumb. Bright noticed her discomfiture and asked, 'What's the matter?'

'Nothing, nothing.' Mrs Maguire was her usual serene self. 'But if ye still feel bad at the end o' the week ye can go to the doctor like your father says.'

Bright's anxiety was somewhat allayed by Friday as the malady finally dispersed. 'I've never felt so good,' she announced to her family, her hair and eyes even more bright than usual.

'Ah, and don't you look it, pet!' smiled Mr Maguire, hugging her. 'Me and your mammy was getting awful worried about ye. Is she not a picture of health now, Mother? Her little face is as round and blooming as a peach.'

Bright frowned; there was that expression again on her mother's face, a mixture of puzzlement and sadness. As quickly as the last time it dispersed. 'She's looking wonderful,' agreed Mrs Maguire, and a relieved Bright was able to breathe again. Even if the Cardinal had not paid his visit there could be little amiss when she felt so good. She had put back all the weight she had lost and more besides; too much perhaps, for the buttons on her dress would not fasten and she had taken to wearing her childhood pinafore again to cover the gap until she got around to altering it. Her underwear too was becoming constrictive, especially over her bosom.

Thus Bright, in her ignorance, tried to dismiss all the signs of pregnancy, until one Saturday morning, in late February when she was on her way to confession, the child in her belly quickened. It was only a brief tickling sensation under her navel, but stopped her so effectively in her tracks that it might have been a sledgehammer. She gasped aloud, then hurried on. The child moved again, and Bright knew that it was a child; she didn't know how, she just knew. Her terrified mind tried to grapple with the equation. Her mother had said the Cardinal visited so's she could have children, but the Cardinal hadn't visited . . . yet still she was positive that the thing inside her was a child, and she also knew that it was a heinous sin to bear a child before wedlock. There was such a girl who lived nearby. Both she and her family were reviled by all. Bright hadn't really understood how the baby had got there – she still didn't – but it took little intelligence to deduce that it was all connected with the act that Nat had forced upon her.

All the pent up fear of recent months surged to a head. Bright began to run. She ran past the church. She ran and ran but could not escape the truth. Eventually coming to rest by the city walls she broke down sobbing, her prime thought being the shock this would be to her parents, especially her father who doted on his little girl. What can I do? Oh Blessed Virgin, tell me what to do! Twisting her handkerchief through her fingers, she had an idea: she must go and see Nat, tell him what had happened.

Without further care as to what she was going to say she ran most of the way to the Industrial School, where she set up an urgent knocking. An officer answered. Thank heavens it was the nice one, thought Bright, though he looked rather impatient just now.

'Please,' Bright gulped in her breath, 'it's very important I should see Nat.'

The officer was firm. 'My dear, I'm not permitted to let you in.'

'Oh, I beg you, please!' Bright's lower lip trembled and she started to cry.

An alarmed Mr Chipchase came outside to tend her tears, mopping at them inexpertly with his own handkerchief, like an elephant using its trunk. 'Oh, now now, what on earth is the matter?'

Bright tried to compose herself and once again begged that she might see Nat. 'Please, I wouldn't ask ye unless it was important!'

'Yes, yes, I realize it must be, Miss Maguire,' sympathized Chipchase, who knew her name for she and her father were Nat's only visitors. 'But you know there's another week to go before you're allowed to visit. I don't make the rules and I can't alter them to suit him. Even so, if you've some important message I could – '

Bright backed away. 'Oh no – no, it doesn't matter, it's not important!' She was beginning to calm down now, saw that she would gain nothing by panic. But panic fluttered around her breast, ready to take flight if given rein. 'It can wait a week.' Abruptly, she turned away.

Concern in his brown eyes, the man tried to be more helpful and called after her. 'If it's private . . . well, you know the boys aren't allowed private letters but if you'd like to scribble a note I'll respect the need for discretion.'

'No, no!' She forced a smile and continued to move away. 'I'm sure it can wait another week.' It had been madness to come – how would she have told him? Now she had a whole week in which to prepare herself. A week in which to pray that it was a mistake.

She reached Foss Bridge without even knowing how, her mind in constant turmoil and her limbs like rubber. Realizing with a start that she was almost home, she paused to gather her thoughts. How could she tell her family? What would she say? Don't be silly, you haven't even been to a doctor, how do you know it's true? Leaning against the bridge she stared at a group of mallards paddling through the oily water. I can't go to a doctor, I just can't.

An older girl approached. Bright noticed her but gave no sign of recognition. She had always been warned not to associate with Biddy Riley, who was deemed far too worldly. But as the slovenly figure loomed nearer so a thought came to the frightened girl: perhaps here was one who could offer a logical explanation. Dare I ask? Biddy had almost drawn level. Go on, go on, ask her now! Biddy was almost past. Take your chance before it goes! 'Hello, Biddy.'

The girl looked surprised. She knew the speaker only vaguely, but returned the greeting. Bright hovered. How could she begin? 'Er, have ye seen Louisa Costelow?'

Biddy looked set to walk on, peering over her shoulder with a quizzical eye – the other girl did not usually pass the time of day with her. 'I have not.'

'Oh!' Bright nipped her lower lip between her teeth. The thing inside her had just moved again. 'She said she'd meet me here but I've been waiting ages with no one to talk to . . .'

Always glad of company the other stopped to add her weight to the bridge. 'I ain't going nowhere.' It was obvious to anyone why mothers were reluctant for their daughters to associate with this young woman. Her whole demeanour was brazen as she looked Bright up and down. 'You still at school?'

'I'm a pupil teacher.'

Biddy nodded. 'Always guessed you'd be clever. Wish God'd given me brains instead o' these.' She clamped two oversized breasts.

The younger girl blushed, yet her partner had provided an excuse for the question she needed to ask. 'Well, I suppose you'll make a good mother.'

The listener's face blackened. 'And what's that supposed to mean? Somebody been saying I'm up the pole?'

Bright was confused but it was apparent she had upset Biddy. 'No! I'm sorry . . . I just meant . . . '

'Well, I'm not! People're always saying that about me.'

'Saying what?' Bright was afraid her source of information might leave.

'That I'm having a bairn! Well, I'm not.'

'Oh!' Bright showed repentance. 'I never meant – '

'Honestly, the cheek of it!' Biddy's face was still dark with offence.

'Sorry, I don't know anything about – that sort o' thing.'

Biddy cooled down and appraised the other. 'No, I shouldn't think ye do. I just thought somebody'd been spreading tales. Lads are allus going on about me, just cause I got big tits. That's all they want.' Seeing her partner was still mystified she shook her head. 'Doesn't matter.'

Bright looked forlorn, desperately hoping that the other girl would take pity. 'Nobody ever told me about babies, how they're born and that kind o' thing.'

Biddy gave a sly laugh. 'How they get in the woman's belly, ye mean! Simple – the man sticks his thing in ye and nine months later out pops a baby.'

Panic overtook Bright's whole body again. She pushed herself from the bridge.

'I'll bet ye want to know where he sticks it!' grinned Biddy.

'No!' Bright already knew. 'Sure, it doesn't look as if Louisa's coming, I'd better go home. Bye!' She ran.

'Charming,' muttered Biddy, and flounced off.

*　　　*　　　*

Nat knew nothing of Bright's visit. Mr Chipchase was well aware of how unsettling these little incidents could be. The boy would wonder what had made her so worried as to try and see him a week early, then this would cause him to worry about her and it would prey on his mind and before the week was out he would have made a bid to escape. No, decided Chipchase, it was wiser to let him remain in ignorance. Besides, Nat had another surprise visitor that day, although this one was allowed entry. In actuality he came not just to see Nat but everyone, the masters too. No one recognized Bowman at first, in his naval uniform and black beard, until Mr Chipchase squinted through the bits of sawdust dangling from his forelock and said, 'Why bless my soul, it's number eight!'

'Able Seaman Bowman presenting for duty, sir!' Bowman stood to attention, then whipped off his hat and marched forward to shake the officer's hand. Chipchase returned the shake vigorously and turned to Nat. 'Twenty-seven, look who's here!'

Bowman put his hands on his hips. 'Still number twenty-seven – have you been in here ever since I left?'

'No, it's that silly old bugger who can't remember my new number,' explained Nat when Chipchase's attention was diverted. 'I'm only back in here because of somebody else's crime. It was just my bad luck to be there when he did it.'

'Oh, course!' Bowman's eye was cynical as he looked the youth up and down. 'Well, well, grown a bit haven't we? Almost a man.'

Delighted as he was to see his old bodyguard, Nat felt patronized. 'I am a man.' From the gleam in his eye there was no doubting what he meant.

'Oh, dipped our wick have we.' The hirsute chin lifted in recognition. 'In here or out there?'

'With a girl, of course! I'm no bugger.'

'You said it, chum.' Bowman nodded and laid different

263

emphasis on Nat's proclamation. 'You're no bugger, no bugger at all. You're just a silly little prick who thinks he knows better than his betters. I don't know why I wasted my breath giving you that advice before I left. For God's sake get some sense into that thick crust!' After an impatient pause he demanded, 'Truthfully, how many times you been in here since I left?'

Nat averted his eyes. 'This is my third time altogether – but it wasn't my fault!'

'It never is,' said Bowman. 'That's why they build these places, to put all the good boys who never did a thing wrong in their lives. It's always the other chap's fault. What's your mother think of you?'

Unhappy at being reminded of her, Nat hesitated over his answer. 'She left me.'

'I'm not bloody surprised.'

'Not because I was bad!' The joy of being reunited with his old pal was beginning to wane. 'She went off with some bloke.'

'Well good for her. I dare say she deserves a bit of happiness after all the trouble you must've caused her.' Bowman looked stern. 'Listen to me, there's blokes in here had a much worse start in life than you. I'd expected to see plenty of 'em still here but I only see two. That's cause the others have learned their lesson while they've been in here.'

'Or else they're in gaol,' came the insolent mutter, which Bowman ignored.

'They don't just put you in for punishment but so's you'll learn something – and look at you, still pushing a broom like the kid of ten I left. Call yourself a man?' Bowman growled. 'Stop blaming everybody else, get off your arse and start learning something – anything – cause you're heading down a lonely road, boy.'

Bowman left Nat to mull over what he had said, little thinking that the words would have an impact – Nat would cut off his nose to spite his face before he took advice. Expecting to find himself spurned when he reapproached the boy later, he was encouraged when instead Nat asked questions about his naval career. 'Do you enjoy being in the Navy?'

'It's a great life,' he answered. 'Mindst, it's a bit like being in here at times, if you know what I mean. You have to provide your own enjoyment.' He gave Nat a dirty wink. Nat grinned. Bowman did not preach any more, concentrating instead on telling Nat about all the countries he had visited and all the different nationalities of women he had had. 'I've had clap in six different languages! And money? I've almost enough to retire on!'

'I've got money saved,' announced Nat.

'Well, I shouldn't brag too loudly else while you're in here somebody will have it sniffed out and spent before you get out.'

'Nobody'll find it. I'm gonna be rich.'

'Huh! Listen, plank skull, you might've saved in the short time you were out, but think of all the unproductive years stuck away in here when you could have been with me seeing the world and saving up at the same time. I wonder who'll've saved most, thee or me?'

Nat's face creased in thought. 'Is it hard in the Navy?'

'I won't kid you it's easy, 'cause it's not. There's some right bastards in charge. But if you keep your nose clean, your eyes front and your arse to the wall you'll get a lot of enjoyment out of it. If you put a bit more effort into this stretch I'll come and see how you're going on next year and if I think you're worth it I'll put in a good word for you with the Navy.'

Bowman remained for much of the evening, entertaining the boys with tales of the sea until evening assembly. Before they went off to bed, Mr Raskelf boasted to the assembled school that old boys such as this served as a fine example of the school's influence; 'I pray that all of you will follow in Bowman's footsteps, and also in those of our surprise guest, who I am about to introduce to you. But before any further ado let me inform you that the school inspector will be making an official visit very soon . . .'

Nat groaned. He always dreaded the inspector's visits for this meant tests in every subject. It also meant that the inmates would have to paint the building for his arrival. Bowman, now on the front row of the audience, grinned at the awful memory. This year, however, it transpired that there was going to be a reward at the end of it all, for fifty boys at least.

The superintendent explained: 'Now, as I was saying, we have a surprise guest come to see us, another old boy whose achievement is even greater than Bowman's. On release he emigrated to Canada and has over the decades worked so hard that he is now one of the most respected ranchers in the west. He is here to speak to you now – Mr Edward Carrington!'

Raskelf made way for the guest who took the podium, nodding in awkward appreciation of the tribute. 'I'm sure I'm not worthy of such high praise,' this was directed at the superintendent, 'but your words are much appreciated, sir.' He turned back and ran his eyes over the audience before launching into his speech, which was delivered in an odd mixture of Canadian jargon interspersed with flat vowels, a giveaway of his northern origins. There were youthful smirks and nudges between members of the audience. 'I can see you're tired, boys, so I won't take long in what I have to say and I hope you'll find it to your interest. Mr Raskelf was correct in part of what he said, I have worked hard, but that is only one of the reasons why I'm where I am today. I was once just a boy like you, and you, and you,' his eyes fixed on three youths who blinked under his direct gaze. 'I'm not about to go into the reasons for my being here, suffice it to say that until I came under the care of the officers of this establishment I was without any kind of direction. It is to this school that I owe a lifelong debt for the discipline and dedication to duty it instilled in me. The time has come for me to repay that debt, so, having spoken with my neighbours, together we have inaugurated a scheme for taking fifty underprivileged boys to a new and exciting life . . . '

His appetite whetted for adventure by Bowman's tales of abroad, Nat listened assiduously whilst Carrington went on to explain about life on the prairies, about the long sunny days and wide open spaces, the wildlife to be seen and the breathtaking scenery.

'Canada is a great country, a wonderful place to live,' proceeded the speaker. 'But it is a young country too, a great part of it without settlement, especially in the west where I come from. We need new blood to ensure its future growth. To those who are willing to work hard I can offer a fine life, the finest life a boy could wish for – but I cannot lay too much emphasis on the word *work*. After what I've just told you about the hot summers and the wonderful countryside some of you might be regarding this as an escape from the discipline of school; make no mistake, it is not. The winters are bitterly cold and the toil can be backbreaking. Most importantly, the Canadian government wishes to make it clear that this is not a dumping ground for those who wish to proceed with their criminal activities in a new world. Any misdemeanour will find you on a ship back to England. Understand that right now.' Again he fixed his eyes on individuals of the audience, before his tone became once again affable. 'But I'm sure that none of you would be stupid enough to throw away such a wonderful chance and to let down the good Canadian folk who'd be kind enough to take you into their homes.' He glanced at the superintendent. 'Now, as I said there are only places for fifty boys, so without throwing some kind o' lottery Mr Raskelf and myself had to work out who was going to qualify. Would you care to elaborate, sir?' Carrington indicated the podium.

Raskelf took the stage again. 'I would indeed, and if you have nothing further to add, Mr Carrington?' The visitor shook his head and backed away. 'Then I am sure the boys would like to show their great appreciation, not only for your most interesting speech but also for the fantastic opportunity you are about to extend to them.' He instigated a round of applause, then addressed the audience. 'It seems to me that the fairest way to do this is to wait until after the inspector's examinations and then to calculate which boys have made the most progress since their last assessment.'

Hearing this criterion for eligibility, Nat's interest palled. He would never be selected. Even if he had shown improvement he wouldn't be chosen because Raskelf didn't like him – so why waste the effort?

The superintendent beamed at the Canadian visitor. 'Well, Mr Carrington, may I once again extend the thanks of the entire school. I am certain everyone found your speech riveting – why, I almost wish that I could go and live in Canada myself!'

'You would be most welcome, sir.' Carrington donated a gracious nod and received a final burst of applause.

Still cheerful, Raskelf concluded the evening assembly. 'Now, boys, I hope that you are not too excited to sleep, for you will be expected to rise bright and early for your labours ahead. I bid you all good night!'

After Raskelf's dismissal, Nat did not join the crush of boys who wanted to shake Carrington's hand, preferring only to share a few words with his friend Bowman before retiring for the night. The dormitory buzzed with talk of the Canadian scheme, but Nat contributed nothing and was soon asleep.

Directly after breakfast every boy was given a paint brush and a strip of wall to redecorate. Before the week was out the entire building was painted and polished.

The school inspector arrived and was greatly impressed. As he toured the ranks of assembled boys he congratulated them and stopped periodically to ask a question. Nat hoped the man would not stop before him. He was coming nearer. Oh, no.

'And you are?'

'Number thirty-four, sir.'

'Tell me, what is your favourite occupation, thirty-four?'

The question was not as difficult as Nat had feared. He had the sudden urge to be reckless. 'Sleeping, sir.'

The inspector looked disconcerted; his mouth had a quizzical edge. 'How strange! And why is that?'

''Cause it's easier than being awake.'

The man exchanged a glare with the superintendent, shook his head at this insanity and moved on.

'See me later, thirty-four!' muttered Raskelf as he passed.

'Count yourself lucky I spoke up on your behalf!' reproved Chipchase, releasing Nat after he had spent the rest of the day and night locked in a cell without a proper meal. 'Mr Raskelf wanted to deny you visiting rights, though why you should have people forever bending over backwards to help you is a mystery.'

'Thanks,' said Nat.

'I did it more for your little pal than for you. She was most put out when I told her she couldn't come in last Saturday.'

'Bright called last week?' Nat frowned. 'You never said owt before.'

'What would be the point?' Chipchase conducted him towards the breakfast hall. 'Anyway, she's coming this afternoon so behave yourself. What an idiotic thing to say to the inspector – sleeping indeed!'

Nat laughingly told Bright about his impudence when she came to visit that Saturday afternoon. He seemed much more cheerful this time, and afterwards he went on to tell her about Bowman's visit. Usually it was she who did all the talking, but this week he was not so bereft of topics, proceeding to tell her about the Canadian trip. 'Lucky devils, whoever they are – certainly won't be me.' Noting that she looked preoccupied he said, 'You're looking a bit maungy. What's up?'

All week Bright had been rehearsing this, saying in her imagination, Nat I'm going to have a baby; Nat, I'm having your baby; Nat we have to get married . . . but here she was with the opportunity to blurt it out and what did she say? 'I'm all right.'

The opportunity was gone. Nat's expression changed and he groaned. 'It's the examinations on Monday. I don't expect to do any good in them. You don't fancy sneaking in here and taking them for me, do you?'

She looked vague. 'What?'

His eyebrows descended. 'I don't know why you bothered coming! You've hardly said a word and you're not listening to owt I say.'

'Yes I am!'

'Tell me what I said then.'

Bright lowered her head. It was a few seconds before he realized she was crying.

'Christ, what's up?' He stared at her in horror, then looked round in embarrassment to see if this was being observed.

She covered her face with a handkerchief and fought to compose herself. 'I came to see you last week but Mr Chipchase wouldn't let me in.'

'Aye, he just told me a bit ago – did you get the wrong day?'

She shook her head and breathed deeply. 'I had something to tell ye.'

He waited. Bright did not enlarge. 'Well, what is it?'

'Oh, God . . . I can't say it.' She sniffed. 'I didn't know it'd be this hard.' She balled her hanky, then sat plucking at it. 'You know . . . that night when . . .'

'Ssh!' Nat's arm shot out and touched hers. 'I know which night – Christ, I think of nowt else in here.'

'Do you?' She sounded hopeful. 'Do you miss me, Nat?'

'Course I do.' He looked uncomfortable and wished she would keep her voice down.

'You know – '

He cut her off with a testy, 'I *know*.'

'No, I'm not going to say anything about . . . that. I was just going to say, d'you remember when you said, well, you said you were going to marry me when we grew up?' He nodded. 'Well, did ye mean it?' Her eyes were red and anxious.

Nat studied her face for a while. Something warned him to be very careful. 'Ye-es,' he replied at last.

A big sigh of relief burst from her. 'Oh! That makes it a bit easier to tell you. Nat, I'm – ' She bit her lip, then summoned him to lean over and whispered in his ear.

'What!' Nat sat bolt upright. All heads turned to look. He laughed in embarrassment. The spectators laughed too and turned back to their conversations. Nat covered an oath of, 'Shit!' with his hand and looked devastated.

'You'll still marry me, won't ye? I'm not being forward in asking, after all it is Leap Year and a girl's prerogative to be the suitor.'

He stared at Bright – no longer bright. As if it wasn't bad enough being incarcerated in here she wanted to imprison him with a child. He was fifteen years old, for God's sake! Suddenly he wanted to see things, do things, travel the world. How could he travel with a millstone like her round his neck? Yet through his sheer heart-thumping terror he heard himself say, 'Yes, of course I will. Nothing's changed.'

She sought confirmation. 'Ye still love me?'

'Yes, yes . . . ' No, I bloody hate you! All love had vanished. How could you love someone who gave herself so easily? And then he stared at her freckled face and melted. Oh yes, he did love her! But how could she? How could she do this to him . . .

Visiting time was almost over. 'I'd better go now.' Bright rose. He glanced at her pinafore. There was nothing to see.

'Wait!' He urged her to sit down and whispered. 'You don't look fat enough. How do you know you're . . .?'

She blushed. 'I just know. I can feel something moving inside me.'

Nat drew back, a look of slight revulsion on his face. 'But you don't know it's a — it could be worms or something.'

She was eager to grasp any explanation. 'D'ye think so?'

'Could be. There was a lad in here who had this great big worm coming from his bum.' Nat remembered that the appalling boy had dangled it proudly in front of his face.

Bright shook her head and sighed. She was used to encountering pregnant women in the neighbourhood. Nat might not be able to detect her increased girth but it was there all right. Her sisters had noticed it too, but up to now thought it was only due to growing into a woman. How would they ever dream that such a thing had happened to her? 'I don't think it's worms, Nat. I remember me mam being sick not so long ago, and when I asked her what was wrong she said she wasn't ill it was just because she was having a baby . . . but she never had it, cause it was dead or something. Anyway, I felt sick just after Christmas. When it went away I thought I was all right but, well, there's other things too. I don't think there's much doubt, Nat, I'm sorry.'

'When will you have it, then?' His voice was dull.

'I don't know. I asked this girl how long it takes — '

'You've told people!?' He was aghast.

'No, I didn't say it was me! We were just talking in general. She said it takes nine months from the man — well, from when ye did what ye did to me. I guess that's the reason this has happened.'

Nat wrung his hands. 'Don't know, must be, I suppose.' He had never really associated the act with conception, only pleasure.

Bright nibbled some loose skin on the inside of her cheek. The news had obviously stunned him as she had expected it would. For herself, she felt over the worst, knowing that he would marry her. Oh, dear God! She had just remembered his real name. How awful to be called Mrs Smellie! Guilt drowned her shallow thought and she glanced around. The supervising officer was asking visitors to leave. Rising again, she told him, 'I'll have to find a way of breaking it to me mam. I'll tell her first. She'll tell me dad. Oh Nat, I don't know what he'll say! At least now I can tell them you'll stick by me. And maybe the guardians'll show mercy and let you out to marry me.' She hesitated, then bent and kissed him. 'Oh, I do love ye!'

He followed her exit with a wan smile, and remained hunched in his chair, steeped in utter despair.

Mr Chipchase was inquisitive to learn the reason for Bright Maguire's premature visit. Judging by Nat's face and the fact that he had not moved an inch it was of some import. 'Anything I can help with, twenty-seven?'

Nat emerged from his trance. 'No sir, I'm just thinking about the examinations on Monday.' With that excuse came a sudden answer. If he did well in the tests then he might just get chosen to go to Canada – and escape!

'Ah well,' Mr Chipchase was saying, 'I don't suppose you'll be straining your eyes over your text books tonight – eh, where are you leaping off to?'

'Sorry, sir!' Nat looked determined. 'I want to do a bit of reading before teatime.'

'Reading? Whatever next?' Chipchase shook his head.

Nat urged himself to concentrate on the text books. It's your one chance of a new life. You've got to be chosen. *Got to.* The words went in through his eyes but refused to imprint themselves on his memory. Try! *Try*! But all he kept hearing was a squalling brat, and he wanted to run.

With the great weight lifted from her shoulders, Bright's step was much lighter on her way home. Everything was going to be fine. She felt wonderful. However, when she arrived and her mother smiled a welcome she realized that breaking her secret was going to prove far more difficult than she had anticipated, and decided to postpone it until tomorrow. If it were true that it took nine months then there was plenty of time left.

But tomorrow turned into yesterday, and by the end of the week she had still not told them.

During that week a frantic Nat had worked harder at his lessons than he had ever done in his life. The results of the examinations were due to be announced at this evening's assembly. There had to be some improvement, just had to be. Awaiting the results Nat pictured the scene in the Maguire household, wondering when Bright's father would come to abuse him; there was no doubt that Mr Maguire would be very angry.

'Thirty-four!' Nat jerked at the mention of his number.

'Very good progress there,' stated Mr Raskelf from the podium. 'Well done, boy – thirty-seven!'

Nat drifted back into thought until the more important list of numbers was announced: those fifty boys who had made the most improvement during the year. After Raskelf's praise Nat began to feel more confident.

'Fourteen, eighteen . . . '

Get to it, get to it! urged Nat.

'Nineteen, twenty-five . . . '

Behind his back, Nat's fingernails dug into his skin.

'Twenty-seven, thirty . . . '

Yes, yes!

'Thirty-six . . . '

Nat's heart leaped – maybe Raskelf had jumbled the

numbers up! He clenched his fists, willing the next number to be his.

'Forty-nine, fifty-one . . . '

Nat's hopes caved in. The remainder of the list fell on deaf ears. Whilst the lucky candidates exchanged thrilled whispers, Nat just wanted to vomit.

The superintendent had completed the list and now folded it. 'Let us all applaud those who have shown such improvement and wish them well for their journey on Saturday.' There was a burst of clapping. Nat did not join in. 'And I think a special round of applause is warranted for two boys who tried extremely hard and were only a whisker's breadth from reaching the list of emigrants — numbers thirty-four and one-one-two.'

Nat gave terse acceptance to the applause. Already he was working out how to escape from here.

Officer Chipchase, unable to account for Nat when it was time for lights out, feared he might have absconded, but eventually found him brooding alone in the darkness of the boiler house. 'What're you doing here?' he called from the doorway. 'You should be in your dorm.'

'I can't hear meself think up there,' grumbled Nat, chin resting on the palms of his hands.

Chipchase plodded down the steps. 'You don't sound too happy about going to Canada.'

Hope sprang into Nat's breast. 'Did he miss my number out?'

Chipchase frowned. 'No, I heard twenty-seven called out as plain as day.'

So cruelly misled Nat could have punched the man, but restrained himself and said through gritted teeth, 'I'm not twenty-seven, I'm thirty-four.'

'Are you? I could have sworn . . . ' The elephantine features crumpled in bemusement. 'Oh well, surely you're delighted with your progress if nothing else?'

'Hasn't done me no good though, has it,' sulked Nat.

'Well, it certainly hasn't helped your grammar, but surely it's an improvement if only for your own self-esteem.' The officer took this opportunity to light his pipe, relaxing against a warm wall.

Nat watched the matchflame ignite the tobacco. 'I really wanted to go to Canada.'

'Can't say I blame you. It sounds like a fine country.' Chipchase sucked on the pipestem, observing Nat with one beady impassive eye through the gloom.

'Not just because o' that . . .' For the first time in his life Nat confided in someone other than Bright. 'I have to get away.'

Chipchase sensed that the urgency was real, and asked quietly, 'Why?'

Nat didn't look at him. 'She's having a baby.'

'Oh dear.' Chipchase closed his eyes and took a puff of tobacco. 'Your little friend who comes to visit?'

Nat nodded, watching the wisps of smoke writhe through the darkness.

'Why, she's not much older than y – ' He broke off as the true calamity hit him. 'You don't mean it's yours do you?'

Well, I don't mean yours, stupid, thought Nat, but again he merely nodded.

Chipchase almost dropped his pipe. 'You idiotic – how did it happ –' With testy exclamation he checked himself. 'I mean, it must've been during those few months you were out presumably?'

'We only did it the one night.' Nat looked cheated. 'Just before I got clapped up in here again. She told me when she came to visit.'

The officer puffed thoughtfully, filling the boiler room with the smell of golden shag tobacco. 'So that's what she wanted the other week.'

'If I'd found out sooner I would've had more time to swot for those exams.'

Chipchase jabbed at Nat with the pipestem. 'Don't you dare go blaming me for not letting her in!'

'I'm not, I'm just saying – '

'No! You're trying to shift the blame again! You'll never accept responsibility for what you've done, will you?' Chipchase felt like slapping the youth. 'You're like every other boy in here, blaming your parents, your teacher and every other Tom, Dick and Harry – oh, yes you do! And while I concede that some of you might have been badly let down there comes a time when you're old enough to be responsible for your own actions, and your time has just come!'

He watched Nat sag into despondency. 'Oh God, what a mess. Has she told her family yet? No, she can't have done or we'd have had them hammering at the door after your blood.'

'She wants me to marry her,' muttered Nat.

'How can you marry her, you're only fifteen! How old is she by the way? As if it makes a difference.'

'She'll be sixteen in September.' Nat picked at a scab on the back of his wrist. The area was covered in scars from past assaults.

The officer watched unmoved. Almost every youth in the school had self-inflicted disfigurements like this. 'And when does she have the baby?'

'She doesn't know.'

Chipchase's pipe belched out smoke like a demented steam engine. 'Of course, we're overlooking something here. I suppose you are sure you're the father? If she's that sort of girl she could have gone with anyone.'

Nat pondered on that night. He hadn't really forced himself on her had he? She could've stopped him if she'd wanted to. All she had to do was say no. There was nothing for him to feel guilty about. No, he could not do it. Much as he wanted to escape he could not blacken the character of his only friend. 'She's not like that, Mr Chipchase. It was my fault.'

'Hallelujah! The lad's admitted to something at last, not that it'll do you much good.' The officer heaved and shook his head. For a time he was silent, the low growl of the boiler matching his mood.

Having succeeded in making himself bleed, Nat stopped picking and watched the badness ooze out of his flesh. 'I was hoping to start a new life.' His voice was hollow.

Chipchase studied him. 'In Canada? Would you seriously? Or would you let everybody down as you've done time and time again?'

Nat sensed a weakening of the officer's anger, knew that Chipchase was his only avenue of escape. If it meant crawling, he would. 'I swear I was going to try if I'd been chosen, Mr Chipchase. Bowman got me to realize . . . '

'Who the devil's Bowman?' Chipchase was confused.

'You know, number eight! He got me to realize where I've gone wrong. I've been doing a lot of thinking since he came.' The youth bent his head but glanced at the officer from beneath a dark wave of hair. 'If I could just get on that list . . . '

Chipchase knew when he was being manipulated. 'And how do you propose I wangle that? I don't pick who goes! If they keep adding a name here and a name there we'll shortly find we're sending the entire school – and good riddance, some might say.'

'Some of 'em don't deserve to go as much as I do. Look at Pugh – fifty-five – he's always busting tools and things.'

'Clumsy he might be, but to my knowledge fifty-five hasn't yet put somebody up the stick! There's no way you can go to Canada, twenty-seven, especially if the superintendent were to find out about this.'

Disappointed, Nat fell back on Bowman. 'Maybe the Navy . . . '

'Or the Foreign Legion!' Chipchase sighed heavily again. 'What are we going to do with you?' He cupped one elbow and chewed on his pipestem, envisaging the scene when the girl's father discovered her condition. 'When are you six-teen?'

'January.'

'The baby would be more than six months old before you could marry her.' He saw Nat's face. 'Always assuming you want to, and you don't, do you?'

Nat had to play this carefully. 'I want to do what's right.'

'Well, you haven't made a very good start at it.' In the strained hiatus, Chipchase thought of his own marriage. There was no comparison with number twenty-seven's situation, both he and his wife had been virgins when they had wed in their late twenties and no one had forced them into it. It was never a grand passion but they had been loving companions and had two fine legitimate children. There was no parallel with this incident – except for one thing: Chipchase knew what it felt like to be trapped and unhappy. Two years into his marriage he had realized he had made a dreadful mistake, which was by then too late to rectify. If he, who had gone into it with open eyes, could feel trapped how would twenty-seven feel being bullied into a lifelong commitment? He himself could escape to his workshop and gain fulfilment in his craft, but twenty-seven had no skill, no escape. Not unless someone were to help him.

Chipchase took a last few puffs of tobacco, then moved up the steps towards the light. 'Leave it to me. I'll think on it and see if I can come up with anything.' He sighed, pocketed his pipe and ushered Nat from the boiler room. 'You'd better go to bed now – and try not to worry.'

What a daft thing to say to the boy, he thought later when lying sleepless beside the wife he no longer loved. Of course twenty-seven would worry; he himself was worried. How was he going to get twenty-seven included on that list? For there was no other answer, Nat must get completely away. But who says it has to be you who helps him?

Why should you care? You're only here to keep the lad on the straight and narrow and little thanks you've had for your pains from twenty-seven. Why should he inspire pity when thousands had not? What about the girl? You're not thinking much about her, are you? What must she be going through? Mrs Chipchase started an irritating snore. Her husband compressed his lips. It's her own fault, she shouldn't have let him. She'll have enough people to worry about her, just you concentrate on getting twenty-seven out of here. But why? I have absolutely no idea, Chipchase told himself.

He dallied with the idea of creeping into the superintendent's office and adding twenty-seven's number to the list, hoping no one would do a re-count, but if they did then twenty-seven would be even more cruelly disappointed and he himself would have to answer the charge of fraudulence. No, he would have to arrange it so that one of the numbers was deleted and twenty-seven entered in its stead. How? Chipchase sighed, turned over and after a violent nudge of his wife to curtail her snores, fell asleep.

The morning before the voyage the fifty successful boys were assembled to receive instructions apropos of their emigration. In the afternoon it was work as usual, though the buzz of excitement persisted in the labour rooms. A troubled Nat was labouring in the carpentry department, collecting stray nails off the floor to be used again, his mind on a more important assignment. It was obvious at this late hour that Chipchase had been unable to get him onto the list. Nothing of pertinence had occurred between them since the eve of Nat's confession. As ever, he was on his own. With the cache that lay hidden under the Maguires' floorboards he could have made his escape and got far away, but he could hardly ask Bright to fetch it for him. Without money escape was impossible. At least she had not told her parents, for there had been no trouble from that quarter, nor from the superintendent. Chipchase had obviously kept the matter to himself even if he had failed in his vow to help. But truth would out, and in the interim Nat was frantically racking his brains for an answer.

There came a loud rebuke. Officer Chipchase was holding up a fret-saw blade minus its handle. 'Who did this? You, boy! Fifty-five!' He glared at the assumed culprit, Pugh, his anger not solely for the crime but at his own inability to find a key to Nat's problem, which had been plaguing his mind all week.

'Sorry, Mr Chipchase.' Pugh looked dumbfounded at the outburst; the officer was usually very tolerant. 'I didn't mean to, it just came off in me hand.'

'Well, if that's your best excuse I should be most careful when applying hands to parts of your anatomy!'

Pugh chanced a sideways glance at another boy.

'Stop smirking!' commanded Chipchase. 'If you didn't go at your work like a native wielding a machete you might find your tools lasted a bit longer. Every week you manage to sabotage one thing or another. Why did you just leave it lying there? Did you expect it to mend itself?'

'No, sir. Sorry, sir.'

Pugh did not appear chastened enough for the officer who, disliking the youth at the best of times, prolonged his verbal assault. 'And what do you think you're doing with that band-saw?'

Pugh gawped at the machine in question. 'I were just going to cut —'

'And where's the guard?'

Pugh looked guilty. 'It's there, sir.'

'It's there, sir!' Chipchase mimicked the youth's drawl. 'I know it sounds like an innovatory idea, fifty-five, but don't you think it would be more effective as a guard if it was fixed over the blade?'

Nat proceeded to gather up nails, but now his mind was

working more efficiently. Chipchase had provided food for thought.

'I couldn't give a fig if your gross negligence results in your decapitation. It's simply that this happens to be the most expensive piece of equipment in the room and if you put it out of action the superintendent will be rather cross.'

Pugh apologized again.

'Delinquent! You'll be maiming someone with your carelessness.' Chipchase terminated his diatribe to prowl around the room. Heads bent, the boys continued with their work.

A period of industry followed, during which Nat shuffled through a bunch of possible solutions to remove number fifty-five from the list of emigrants. He envisaged throwing a handful of nails into the machinery on which Pugh laboured, hoping that at least one of them might ricochet, leap into Pugh's eye and blind him. Or when Pugh turned away Nat could surreptitiously remove the guard in the hope that the blade would amputate Pugh's arm. Nat mulled over many dark scenarios during the following hour, but found them all wanting. It was impossible to act without being caught. Towards the end of the afternoon, when tools were being packed away, he had grown resigned to the fact that Pugh was going to Canada and he himself was not.

'By, old Chippy was in a mood today, wasn't he?' said another inmate as much later a group of them went upstairs to carry down the emigrants' luggage to the hall — the final insult to Nat.

'I heard that, forty-nine!' Unseen, Mr Chipchase had ascended behind them. 'And you boys, stop playing around on the staircase! Fifty-five, haven't you been in enough trouble today? Any more and you're for it.'

'Ooh, I'm trembling,' smirked Pugh when the officer had shoved past and proceeded upstairs.

It was as the group neared the top of the staircase that

Nat was granted a last ditch attempt. Excitement started to churn his stomach. Whilst others hefted luggage back down to the hall he held back, his eye fixed on Pugh. There were others who could just as well be victim, but none so good a choice as the one disliked by both officer and inmate alike. Bit by bit the luggage was removed; there were now only a few boys left in the dormitory under Mr Chipchase's supervision.

'Come on, get your backs into it!' Mr Chipchase still wore his frown. 'What are you playing at, twenty-seven?'

'I can't lift this on my own, sir!' Nat grunted and heaved at the trunk. 'Pugh, come and help me!'

'Weakling!' The bigger youth swaggered over, toting a haversack on his shoulder and made a grab for one of the handles on the trunk.

Nat grasped the other and tried to lift it. 'Aagh, me back!' He dropped his end of the trunk.

Mr Chipchase looked round briefly, sighed, then left the dormitory. 'Come on, stop acting the goat!'

With himself and Pugh at the rear, Nat suddenly found the strength to lift the trunk and the pair carried it from the dormitory. 'I'll go first,' volunteered Pugh as they reached the top of the stairs. Nat could not have wished for a better invitation. As Pugh made his descent he himself affected to flounder and in doing so hooked a toe around Pugh's ankle. The youth tripped. With a yell, both he and the trunk clattered to the lower floor, leaving Nat hanging onto a banister. Whilst others rushed to the victim's aid an astonished Officer Chipchase stared up at Nat as if in disbelief.

Nat's flesh crawled at the realization that his act had been witnessed. Hardly daring to breathe, he waited to see how the officer would react.

'Sir, I think he's dead!'

Chipchase was roused from his shock and rushed to examine Pugh's lifeless form. 'No, no he's still breathing!'

There was relief in his tone. 'He's badly hurt, though – we need the doctor!' A boy was despatched to fetch medical aid. In the shocked interval, Mr Chipchase once again raised his eyes to look at Nat. But Nat was gone.

When the headmaster was informed by Matron as to the gravity of Pugh's injury – a fractured skull – he had no option but to delete him from the list. 'A great shame,' he told his wife, 'but we cannot delay the voyage for one boy. Would you be so kind as to unpack number fifty-five's belongings. And please send Mr Chipchase to see me.'

The matron replied that Mr Chipchase was already waiting outside his office. The superintendent asked her to send the officer in and was deleting number fifty-five from the list when Chipchase entered. 'Ah, Mr Chipchase! I was about to send for you. I believe you were present at the time of the incident in which fifty-five was injured?'

'Yes, Mr Raskelf, a very unfortunate accident, especially at such a time.'

'So it was an accident?' At the other officer's frown Raskelf hurried to add, 'I cast no aspersions on your supervision, Mr Chipchase, it is simply that a boy has been hurt and I have to answer to the powers that be.'

'As far as I am aware it was a complete accident,' replied Chipchase. 'Although I had previously had to warn fifty-five about acting the goat on the staircase.'

'Yes, he is rather an idiot.' The superintendent nodded and sighed. 'Ah well, fifty-five has paid dearly for his tomfoolery.'

'Yes, a great shame,' agreed Chipchase, 'but then his misfortune is another boy's luck – you will be finding a replacement, superintendent?'

'Oh . . . why yes, naturally.' The superintendent lowered his eyes back to the list. 'Let us see who narrowly missed being selected the first time. Ah,' a note of doubt entered his voice, 'I see it is our recalcitrant, thirty-four. Well, we cannot send him.'

'If I may say so, Mr Raskelf, this is just the sort of opportunity that boy needs to show him that hard work can be rewarded. He never had much cause to trust us in the past, did he?'

'Nor we him,' Raskelf looked sour. 'I hardly consider thirty-four to be a suitable ambassador of this establishment.'

'And Pugh was?' Chipchase raised a cynical eyebrow, then continued to press his argument. 'I know for a fact that twenty-seven – ' he sighed at his own error; these stupid blasted numbers! 'I meant to say that thirty-four has studied extremely hard and has made great strides . . . '

'It would take little effort to improve upon his results of last year.' Raskelf was half-amused. 'He could hardly have had poorer marks.'

'I don't wish to contradict, sir, but if I recall, when you announced the results at assembly you yourself commented on how well he had done.'

'I believe I said he had made some progress, Mr Chipchase.'

'Then should we not consolidate that progress by granting him this opportunity? I wish you could have witnessed the boy's face when he learned that he had just missed being selected. The disappointment . . .' Chipchase shook his head. 'I beg you to grant him this chance, superintendent. Let him see that effort can be rewarded. I am convinced that, if thirty-four is allowed to go it will be a turning point in his life.'

Raskelf sat back in his chair and laced his hands over his waistcoat. 'You seem to have become something of a champion for number thirty-four, Mr Chipchase.'

'No more than any other boy who deserves a chance.'

'I beg to differ that thirty-four deserves a chance, but that is by the by. Much more interesting is why you continue to show such faith in him.'

Chipchase made a gesture of helplessness. 'I'll be honest,

Mr Raskelf, if the boy were to remain here I'd have no faith in him at all. He would probably end up in prison and be a burden on society for the rest of his life. That's my main reason for wanting him to go to Canada. In such a big country there'll be so many more roads open to him than that of crime.'

'Much as I might be glad to be rid of him the authorities there would not thank me for inflicting such a liability. He has no trade to offer,' countered Raskelf.

'No, but a good labourer is always an asset – and fifty-five was hardly a skilled craftsman.'

The superintendent retained an air of reluctance, but by and by after long consideration he came to the decision that the school would do well to be rid of thirty-four, and he gave up the argument. 'Very well. Send him to me.'

Mr Chipchase had some difficulty in finding Nat, who had been lying low since the incident. Acting on past experience, the officer went to the boiler room and without seeing anyone, shouted into the darkness, 'Twenty – tut! Thirty-four! Mr Raskelf wants to see you immediately.'

Nat emerged like a worm from its hole and peered up at Mr Chipchase, trying to gauge his mood. With the officer's apparent qualm at meeting his eye, Nat feared the worst. Therefore, his relief and astonishment was all the greater when he slouched along to Raskelf's office and was ordered to pack his belongings immediately. He was going to Canada in the morning.

The weekend came and Bright had yet to reveal her condition to her parents. Each time she had come anywhere near to telling them the words had lodged in her throat. Maybe, she told herself, maybe if I made my confession before God it would help. With this in mind she went to church on Saturday and eventually broke her silence in the privacy of the confessional.

After she had spoken there was a shocked interlude. The

priest knew exactly to whom he was speaking, knew that the girl was little more than a child herself. 'Have you told your parents yet?'

Bright wrung her hands and whispered, 'No, Father.'

'Then you must go home and tell them immediately. Unless . . . unless your reason for sharing this with me is that I should inform them? In which case I have to refuse. This is your sin. It should come from your own lips.'

'Yes, Father.' Bright waited in torment.

The priest could hear the sound of her breathing. 'Is it that you're waiting for penance?'

'Yes, Father.'

He sighed and shook his head. 'My child, I'm thinking you've penance enough ahead of you, but if it makes you feel better, go and say three Hail Marys and throw yourself on the mercy of Our Lady.' He muttered absolution and Bright left the confessional.

She used the Hail Marys to prepare herself for the confrontation at home, squeezing every bead so hard that when she had finished the imprints remained on her fingertips. When she left the church the sun was shining. With every step she committed herself. 'I will tell them today . . . I will.'

But when she got home cowardice once again bound her tongue. As usual on a Saturday night her father and brothers had bathed and were now out enjoying themselves at the pub whilst the females wallowed. The bath in front of the fire was screened by a clothes horse draped in linen, just in case of unexpected visitors. Bright was never more glad of this privacy than now as she quickly rinsed and towelled her fruitful body and clothed it again before any of her family witnessed her shameful condition. But how much longer could she hide it?

In the end it was blurted out between two mundane sentences. Her mother was washing up the Sunday pots and Bright was drying. She screwed the teatowel into a cup, turning it round in her hands. 'I like these cups, they're a nice shape.' She put it on the table and in the same breath said, 'I'll be needing some cups myself shortly when me and Nat get married. Have ye washed this pan here?'

Mrs Maguire stopped washing and leaned heavily on the stone sink, head bent. 'So . . . tis true, then?'

Bright's lips parted. 'You know?'

Mrs Maguire's head drooped even lower. She didn't look at all well. 'For weeks I've feared the worst but daren't confront it – oh, Bright, how could ye do this to us? How am I ever going to tell your daddy?'

'What's herself been up to?' called Mr Maguire quite jovially from the parlour.

'Oh, God, I thought he was asleep!' Bright's mother clamped a hand over her mouth and stared at her daughter, who grasped her own hands to her bosom.

When no one answered him, Mr Maguire stretched, patted the chair arms and decided to go for a walk. He came into the scullery to get washed. 'Don't all answer at once. What's herself been up to, I asked.' He was quite jolly, until he saw the nervousness in his wife's eyes. Then he turned his confusion on Bright.

'I'm going to have a baby, Dada.' How easily it emerged now.

For a moment Maguire laughed, then he saw that this was no joke and the smile on his lips vanished. With a roar he picked up a stack of plates and hurled them at the wall where they shattered to smithereens. Astonished, the rest of the family crowded into the doorway. Bright and Mrs Maguire jumped out of the way, but Maguire grabbed his wife. 'How long have you known?'

'Dada! Please don't hurt Mam.' Bright wrestled with him. 'I've only just told her. Nat hasn't known that long and . . .'

'Nat!' roared Maguire. 'Why the scheming, cunning little shite!' That he rarely swore made this curse all the more potent to the listeners. 'I take him in and he takes advantage!'

Bright tried to calm him. ''Tis all right, we're going to get married!'

'You're bloody right you are! I'll make sure he goes down that aisle if it's on bloody crutches.' Maguire bullocked his way through the audience and down the passage.

'Where're ye going, Tommy?' His wife ran after him.

'To kick the shite out o' my future son-in-law!' The door slammed.

Maguire's re-entry a good hour later was just as violent, his face purple with fury. He said not one word but hauled on a drawer and started to toss clothes around. Mrs Maguire begged, 'What're ye doing, Tommy?' He didn't answer. When she repeated it he lashed out at her. She tumbled over, clutching her face. Bright ran to her. Martin advanced on his father.

'Keep out of it!' warned Maguire, so fiercely that his son backed off. Mary and Eilleen cowered behind their brothers as Maguire started to hurl clothes at Bright. 'There! Now, get out!'

She beseeched him with her hands. 'Daddy, what's . . .'

'What's wrong? What's wrong?' he bellowed at her like he had never done before in her whole life. 'You tell me you're having a bastard and ask what's wrong!'

Tears pricked Bright's eyes. 'But didn't Nat tell you we'd be married?'

'He didn't tell me anything cause he wasn't bloody there!'

Bright's lips parted in shock.

'He's gone!' Mr Maguire's tanned face was a picture of nastiness. 'To Canada, they tell me. Hah! He knows where he's best, that one.'

Bright gasped. 'But . . . he wouldn't have gone on purpose! They must've sent him. He wouldn't leave me!'

'I asked them – they said he didn't have to go if he didn't want to so I think you know where you stand, milady! But went or sent tis all the same, and now you can be on your way too!' Maguire stuffed what he thought to be her belongings into her arms.

'These aren't my clothes!' She threw them down and began to pluck at his sleeve, entreating him, 'Dada, where will I go?'

'To Canada – to Hell for all I care, you dirty little . . .' He raised his fist.

'Tommy!' Mrs Maguire risked taking the violence that seemed about to be inflicted on her daughter. 'There's no call to throw her out, there must be something we can do – I could pretend the child's mine!'

'Don't be such a bloody eejit, woman!' Spittle flew from Maguire's lips. 'They all know you've just aborted – and how are ye going to explain the fact that she's walking about with a belly out to here?'

'She doesn't show! We could send her away to have it. Nobody knows I've lost the baby, they didn't even know I was having another.'

'They'll know! The fussy old faggots around here know everything! They'll know it's a bastard – and I'm having no bastards in my house. Out!' He spun Bright around by the shoulders and shoved her at the door.

Unable to protest through shock, Bright found herself outside, with garments scattered round her and the door banged in her face. She stood there for a moment before crumpling in tears and sheer terror. Abandoning her sisters' clothes, she walked, sobbing, from the house, whilst neighbours twittered and scowled in reproof. Having witnessed the noisy exile they had no need to ask what was wrong. And now, as those whom she had called her friends turned away from her in the street, Bright knew for the first time how Nat had felt when his mother had left him – completely alone.

11

Throughout the long and exacting sea voyage he had tried to focus on the adventure that lay ahead, but the inner voice kept reminding him: this is just what someone did to your mother. Each time the voice accused, Nat would remonstrate with himself; there were all sorts of differences, why, he could list a dozen reasons to justify his actions. No one could accuse him of desertion, he would have done Bright no favours by marrying her in his present status, and it wasn't as if she had no one to look after her. Better by far to take this temporary leave until he had something to offer her. If what he had been told about Canada were true there would be all sorts of opportunities open to a young man who was willing to work hard, and whose name was not a preconceived synonym for trouble. If he did not take this chance he would never amount to anything. *I'm sorry, Bright, I'm so sorry.* But I'll come back, I swear it. In a few years he would be more able to look after a wife and child. Now, with thousands of miles of sea between him and his problem, he could look upon it more objectively, quite liked the idea of having another human being who was part of himself . . .

'Land ahoy!' The youthful cry pierced his introspection. Along with his fellow travellers he rushed excitedly on deck, everyone draping themselves over the rail as the Gulf of St Lawrence yawned before them, waiting for the ship to berth – only to be informed that this would not take place for a long while yet. Some groaned and returned to the warm inside. Nat and a few others remained hunched over the rail as, with agonizing slowness, the vessel nosed its way through the chilly waters of the great river and continued inch by inch through the province of Quebec. Nat was utterly exhausted after the gruelling sea voyage. Why had it taken so much out of him? Was he not accustomed to a similar dormitory at Industrial School? Yes, but at least at home the bed had remained still and there had been proper bedding; the shipping line had granted neither sheets nor dishes, the meals being served in metal pannikins. They might well have been transporting animals. And oh, the crippling boredom of all those days with nothing to look at but sea! He had lost track of what month it was, let alone what week or even what day.

After a time the river gradually narrowed, but by now only Nat and a few other stalwarts remained to brave the cold, hands tucked up under armpits for warmth. On the two shores between which they travelled they were able to see farm land running down to the water's edge, and occasionally a church spire towering amongst a group of small houses denoting a village, where metal roofs reflected a watery sunshine – picturesque, but not quite what Nat had expected. He glanced at the expressions of his fellow travellers, who appeared to be victims of the same anti-climax. Feeling hungry, Nat left the ship's rail and went below deck where he dwelled for a time until some fool shouted, 'We're here! We're here!' And again he emerged, only to have his anticipation doused once more as the ship continued to glide past the towering fortifications of Quebec City.

The river narrowed even further, though it was still very wide in comparison to waterways at home. Despondency and cold forced Nat to retreat again below deck, where he remained until at long last a mountain loomed out of the grey afternoon and official word informed the travellers that the craft was now on the final leg of its journey. Once again the deck teemed with excited youths as the contours of the St Lawrence eventually guided them into Montreal.

But where were the wide open spaces that Carrington had promised? Where was the blue sky, the golden wheatfields waving in the sun? This inland port was not a view to lift the heart after nurturing the spirit of adventure for days on end. The scenes being enacted on the quay were no different from those they had witnessed back in Liverpool: a man playing a fiddle, his upturned hat laid before him to receive the coins of the charitable, horses and carts, small barefooted urchins rolling an empty barrel, porters lugging trunks up and down gangplanks, scavenging dogs, women of dubious character parading for business, ragged loafers with clay pipes, and a Union Jack fluttering from the roof of a high building.

The immigrants exchanged glances, shivering in the chilly air and trying to hide the disappointment on their faces. One tried to convey optimism. 'Well, at least we'll be getting off this stinking old rustbucket.' There were murmurs of agreement. Nat said nothing.

After more painful delay the ship berthed. Nat tottered unsteadily down the gangplank to the quayside where he and his fellow travellers were herded together and checked to see that none had been inadvertently lost overboard. Mr Carrington, the man who had instigated the scheme, had travelled with them, but the officers of the Industrial School were left far behind him in their narrow little world. However, this seemed of no comfort to the youths who remained in a tight bunch, watching the activity around them with suspicious eyes, for now they had discovered that there was a difference after all. 'They're all talking foreign!' hissed Nat to his neighbour. 'He never mentioned that. How are we gonna understand 'em?'

Registration dealt with, Carrington looked up from his clipboard and, sensing their disillusionment and confusion, patted the nearest shoulder. 'Don't worry, boys. It gets better, much better. You step this way after me and you'll see some really fine old buildings.'

'If I'd wanted to see old buildings I could've stayed at home,' grumbled Nat, who had never appreciated architecture. To him there was no difference between these tall stone-faced edifices, some with verandas, and those of York. Of more import to the exhausted voyager was what their interiors had to offer. All Nat craved at this moment was to achieve sleep in a proper bed rather than a ship's bunk, and he hoped that the next stage would be an introduction to his new guardians so that he could enact his wish. Instead he and the others were taken for a meal. Apparently there was to be another journey in order to reach their final destination – the district of Alberta, a south-westerly section of the North West Territories. Carrington informed them that the train did not leave Montreal until eight in the evening.

Contrary to the man's promise things did not get better. It grew darker and colder and despite Nat's attempts to learn otherwise almost every voice he heard spoke a foreign language – even the train that had just pulled into the station looked and sounded like nothing he had heard in England. In the spray of light that shone from its headlamp he could make out a large shovel-like contraption on the front of the engine. It had an oddly turned funnel too; and when it released steam, the effect was more of a wail than a whistle.

Eventually they were loaded on board the Canadian Pacific Express that was to take them on the final stage of their journey. Nat voiced his heartfelt desire to Carrington, who had taken the seat beside him. 'I can't wait to sleep in a bed that doesn't go up and down.'

Carrington laughed and settled back. 'Me too, but it'll be a good while yet. We've another two thousand miles ahead.'

There rose a united groan of amazement. 'But that'll mean we have to sleep on the train!' exclaimed Nat.

Carrington gave an apologetic smile. 'It's not as bad as it

sounds. The seats can be made up into beds. In fact we could do that right now and let you boys get your heads down.'

With the aid of a railway official he went into action. Facing pairs of seats were drawn together to form beds, then from the roof above the tops of the windows more bunks were let down.

'Will we be there when we wake up?' yawned one optimist.

'Fraid not.' Carrington looked sympathetic and opened a book. 'We got another five days on board.'

Five days! Aching and depressed with exhaustion, Nat collapsed onto one of the lower bunks and not long after the transcontinental express had rumbled out of Montreal he was fast asleep.

Spirits were a little higher at breakfast the next morning, for they awoke to blue sky and sunshine. Now the train was travelling through open countryside the boys could see that Carrington had not lied and their expectations had not been in vain. Even if pockets of ice still dotted the landscape and the trees bore only the merest hint of green, the country was indeed as breathtaking as he had described with its thickly wooded hills, beautiful lakes and gushing streams. There was not as yet, however, any sign of the vast prairie that was to be their home – but then Carrington had warned them it was a long way off.

Nat turned his attention to his breakfast, pondering over all the exciting things that lay ahead. Yet amidst all these notions lapped the odd disturbing memory of Bright. He tried to convince himself that she would be all right, that she had a good family, which was more than he ever had. It was not as if she would be thrown out onto the street; they all adored her. Anyway, it was no good dwelling on it, he had to make a new life for himself here. Then, when he had saved lots of money he could go back and make an honest woman of her. Bright would be fine, he concluded, it's yourself you should be worrying about. What sort of people will you be going to? Will you be able to understand them? Even if they spoke English like Carrington it was not a version that was easy for a Yorkshireman to come to grips with. Without noticing it, he had nearly finished his breakfast. Mopping up the remaining bacon fat with a last morsel of bread he settled back, chewing, to gaze from the window.

By late morning the vista began to pall and his weariness and boredom returned, alleviated only by a meal break and desultory conversation with the other boys. The express must be travelling at over twenty miles per hour, but seemed incapable of escaping this wilderness of pine trees. How would he ever withstand another four days of this?

During the rest of the afternoon, whilst Carrington read a novel beside him, Nat catnapped, waking once to partake of another meal. He must have fallen asleep again for he awoke to see his own reflection in the darkened carriage window. Grinding his knuckles into his eyes, he stretched and yawned. The train was crawling. There were lights ahead. How long had he been asleep? What time was it? What day was it? He looked at Carrington who was asleep, his wide-brimmed hat over his face. Nat nudged him, then when the man awoke with a grunt pretended that it had not been him.

Face creased and puffy, Carrington laid aside his hat, ran his tongue around his dry mouth and pulled his watch from his waistcoat, yawning. There came an abrupt jolt, waking the boys who came round with startled expressions. 'It's okay, boys! We're just stopping to pick up some more folks.'

Nat asked, 'Where are we, sir?'

'Would you be any the wiser if I told you we were at Sudbury, Ontario? Relax, I told you we've a long way to go.' Carrington's face disappeared under his hat.

With a jaded groan, Nat wriggled his back into a less

tortured position and prepared for another long haul.

The following day was very much like the last, apart from the change in backdrop. Once this had registered Nat decided that the best way to cope with the tedium was to nap as often as he could in the somewhat futile hope that it would take him to his destination more quickly. There was no longer day and night, just sleeping, waking, feeding and sheer boredom. Did the others feel as bad as he did? Conversation had petered out a long time ago. I'm going mad, thought Nat. I can't stand it any longer. I wish I'd never come. I should have stayed and married Bright. Mr Maguire might have been furious but his anger would have been over a lot more quickly than this journey. Sleep, sleep, please let me go to sleep and not wake up.

Another cruel day dawned. How was he ever going to get through it? Between feeding and napping he had now taken to prowling up and down the train like a caged bear. Punishment, that's what it was, punishment for leaving her, for running away. But I haven't run away, I tell you, I'm going back! Even his sleeping moments were not restful, filled with images of an angry Bright who raked his face with her nails and spat obscenities at him. *I'm sorry! I'm sorry!*

Terrorized back to consciousness, Nat's eyelids shot open, then widened even further as the carriage left the track and launched into the air! There was nothing to be seen but water. With a petrified yell, Nat sat bolt upright and clung onto the arm of his seat, fully expecting to meet his death. There came a reassuring laugh close beside him. Carrington tapped the fear-stricken boy on the arm and directed his gaze to the opposite window to indicate rockface, so procuring the realization that the carriage was still on the track, albeit a narrow one. A ledge had been carved out of the vertical rock wall that rose sheer from the water's edge.

Nat exhaled his relief, then gave an embarrassed laugh at his unwarranted terror. 'It's the sea!'

'No, it's a lake,' the man corrected him. 'Lake Superior.'

'It's too big for a lake!' Nat pushed his dark hair from his brow and searched for a glimpse of land on the other side of the water, convinced that the man was mistaken. Only now, after all these excruciating hours aboard the train did he begin to appreciate the size of this country and the variation in its terrain – at times lush and green, at others parched and barren – and for a brief, marvellous moment the boredom was lifted, allowing him the thrill of wonder.

The next stop was at a place called Thunder Bay. Nat arched his back and without great interest enquired of Carrington, 'What're them big tall shed things?'

Carrington was adjusting his watch and replied without looking up. 'Grain elevators.'

Nat leaned back. Surely, surely it couldn't be much longer. Another day told him it could, and now there was added torture in that there was less to see from the window, for another stop at Winnipeg heralded the start of the prairies and from then on Nat really did think he was losing his mind. Each time he awoke the view was still of flat grassy plains and chestnut earth. The few trees to be seen in this vast nothingness were those acting as windbreaks to the occasional farmhouse. Other than this, there were only the variously coloured grain elevators at each small town station to break the mono-tony. Prairie . . . Regina . . . prairie . . . Moose Jaw . . . prairie . . .

Then at last some wooded hills! At last a change in the deadly routine! As the train approached its next stop Carrington alerted certain members of the group that their journey was almost at an end.

Nat came to life. 'Do I get off here, too?'

Carrington was by now as tired and short-tempered as any other traveller and did not appreciate this unnecessary question. 'Don't you listen, boy? I just called the names of those who have to get off. Just sit there till I tell you different.'

Nat had assumed that as all the boys were destined for the same district he would see them quite regularly. He was wrong. Between the first group of boys alighting and the next station another day ended. They would be hundreds of miles apart. He might never see them again. Not that he could summon an ounce of concern in his present state of fatigue.

On the fifth day of travel a distant line of mountains came into view and the flat prairie gave way to rolling foothills. When, after another long stretch, the train slowed down in its approach to the next station there were only a few boys left on board, Nat amongst them. Please, *please* make this my stop!

To his vast relief it was. Moving into the aisle he stretched, then peered from the window. As the Canadian Pacific rumbled into the station he caught a glimpse of its name. Calgary. Calgary? Wasn't that where Jesus was crucified? A fine omen that was. Too exhausted to display either excitement or despair, he shuffled and swayed along the moving carriage towards the door on lumpen tingling flesh. Wheels squeaking, the train lurched to a halt, causing Nat and the others to stagger. Then the door was flung open and he was standing on the wooden platform. At a guess it was early afternoon, but he did not know which day or what month, only that it was cold enough to make him shiver. They had left England at the end of March, so it took little intelligence to deduce that it must be April.

Waiting for his own and the boys' luggage to be un-loaded, Carrington rubbed a numb buttock, then used the same hand to wave at a host of people who were coming down the platform to meet him. 'Hey, John! Roy! How're ye doing, eh?' The two groups came together and a great deal of handshaking and back-slapping occurred, much to

Nat's impatience. 'Lucy! Jean! Good to see you. I'm fine – and you? Good! Great to be back!'

After the boisterous reunion Carrington offered an apology to both groups and set about matching boys up with their future guardians. Whether there had been any process of selection Nat neither knew nor cared. However, he liked the look of the middle-aged couple to whose charge he was rudely abandoned when Carrington departed with his own particular choice of boy, saying they must perform the introductions themselves for he just had to get home before he dropped.

Nat's guardian held out a callused hand as others did likewise to their own charges. 'Nice to meet you, son. I'm John Anderson and this is my wife.' When Nat merely offered a limp hello, Anderson added, 'Well're you gonna tell us who you are?'

Noting that those who might give his real name away were too occupied, the youth quietly announced his pseudonym. 'Nat Prince.'

'Well, that's a real nice name, isn't it, John?' With an approving nod from her husband, the homely Mrs Anderson extended plump digits. 'I'm pleased to make your acquaintance, Nat. How are you?'

'All right.'

Anderson's heavily jowled face turned strict. 'You always address a lady like that?'

Nat blushed. 'Sorry, I weren't thinking, ma'am.'

'That's better.' Anderson nodded and smiled to show he was not a pedant. 'Left any folks at home, Nat?' Nat shook his head. 'Guess we're your folks now.' Both looked as if they welcomed the prospect. 'Well, c'mon, Nat.' Anderson began to turn. 'Get your bag, we've a long road ahead before nightfall an' I need to stock up before we leave town. You can help me.' At this Nat's face drained. Anderson misinterpreted the expression. 'Oh, guess you want a few minutes to say goodbye to your pals. Well, Mrs

Anderson'n me'll just wander over there.' He pointed. 'You follow when you're ready – and don't worry that you're not gonna see them again. Even if we live far apart us folks get together quite regular at harvest and suchlike.' He and his wife said goodbye to their own friends, then made their way to the other side of the platform and stepped onto the dirt road.

Nat turned to the small group of boys and offered a dispassionate farewell before loping after his guardians, finding it hard to walk in a straight line after so much disuse of his legs.

'Any good at driving a buckboard?' enquired Anderson, unhitching the horse's reins from a post.

'Never tried, sir.' Nat tossed his case into the wagon.

'Well, now's your chance. Hop up!' The man handed the reins to Nat, then climbed up beside his wife and the boy. 'Just steer her down the street a-ways. I'll tell you when to stop.'

The mare would not even start until Anderson and Nat clicked encouragement. Even once the cart was moving, Nat, tired and disoriented, had no notion of how to steer it and with the street alive with various wagons and buggies there was danger of a collision. A laughing Anderson was eventually forced to bid Nat move over and drive to the general store himself. 'Let's hope you're more use when we get back home.' Though it was not said maliciously, the remark raised Nat's hackles. Anderson appeared not to notice the change in mood. 'You go with Mrs Anderson till I get the order together. She wants some women's doodads carryin'.'

A leaden Nat followed the blue bonnet and the iron-corseted rear up and down the verandas, in and out of haberdashers and dressmakers, cursing under his breath – especially when he noticed a sign advertising a vacancy for a stablehand with the instruction, *No English Need Apply*.

Mrs Anderson turned to wait for him to catch up,

noticed his eyes on the sign and patted his arm as they walked on together. 'Oh, don't you worry your head about that. Most folk round here aren't agin the English in general, it's just that one or two have had bad experiences. My family came from England you know. A long time ago, mind. Mr Anderson's kin're from Scotland, settled in Montreal then moved out to Manitoba. That's where we met as children.' She smiled at the memory. Nat decided that however warm Mrs Anderson's manner her face annoyed him with its piggy upturned nostrils. 'We grew up together, went to school together, then got married. Never been apart, except when John came out to the prairies to buy land. That was just after the railway was built. Thought we'd take our chance before we got too old. Mr Anderson had a decent enough job but, well, he knew it'd never get him anywhere and he'd always wanted to try his hand at farming, so we took advantage of the government land scheme and set up a homestead. That was nearly our undoing!' She laughed. 'We knew nothing about growing wheat; thought if you stuck the seed in the ground something had to grow. We sure learned different. The land we bought had barely any rainfall. First crop was ruined by drought, the next year it was frost. Oh, I can tell you it was heartbreaking. Mr Anderson decided he'd chosen the wrong sort of farming, so we cut our losses, came out here, met Mr Carrington and he talked us into setting up a cattle ranch. We started with a few Herefords and we've never looked back. No, sir.'

It seemed to a frustrated Nat that Mrs Anderson was very fond of the sound of her own voice. In each shop they visited she introduced Nat and then proceeded to ignore him whilst she spent an age gossiping until she concluded with a loud exclamation that Mr Anderson would have her hide if she spent any longer chatting. 'I guess you must be sick o' waiting on me too, Nat, thinking I'm an awful gasbag. I'm sorry, but when a woman doesn't get into town very often she tends to get carried away!'

Laden with parcels, Nat followed the woman back to the cart where Mr Anderson gave immediate orders for him to carry out some sacks from the store. 'What you two been doing? I've nigh on done the work myself!'

Mrs Anderson pulled a face at Nat, designed to make him laugh but not even producing a smile. Depositing her parcels in the cart he marched into the general store, anger raised to a dangerous level. Inside was an area of wooden flooring with a counter on three sides, each bearing glass showcases of fancy goods. There were shelves behind the counters filled with bottles, jars, boxes, packets, and another set of shelves above these bearing crockery. In every available space there were barrels and loops of rope, twine and wire. Hanging from the ceiling were pots, pans, buckets, kerosene lamps, an advertisement for seeds and two full rows of workman's gloves. In the middle of the floor was a cast iron stove, whose chimney pipe disappeared into the ceiling and whose warmth lured Nat away from his task. He held out his cold hands to it, trying to curb his frustration, knowing from experience that it would not get him to his destination any quicker and would only succeed in alienating his new guardian. Anderson was asking the storekeeper for a pair of gloves. Nat watched the two men. Both had moustaches; that was where the similarity ended. His living earned out of doors, Anderson's face was lined and weatherbeaten, his eyes like narrow slits due to his habit of screwing them up against the elements. His large moustache had once been black but there was now much grey in it, as well as at his temples; the rest of his hair was hidden beneath a wide-brimmed hat. Glancing down Nat noticed that the man's boots had high heels and his trousers were tucked into them. He had on a tan leather waistcoat. The rest of his attire and also his physique befitted a life working with cattle, whereas the storekeeper wore an apron over his suit, arm bands to keep his cuffs out of the way, had smooth hands and a rather prissy manner.

'Here!' Anderson threw the pair of gloves at Nat. 'Put those on, then take those sacks to the cart while I settle up with Mr Coughski.' He delivered this name with an actual cough appended by the word ski, then grinned at the storekeeper. 'That ain't his real name, I just call him Mr Coughski 'cause I can't get my tongue round his real one.'

Nat smiled at last, though this was more for his new gloves than Anderson's quip. He had never owned a pair in his life, and this gift helped a long way to easing his tension. There was relief too at the discovery that he could understand these westerners, even the man with the unpronounceable name spoke English, albeit with a strange accent. He stood for a moment admiring his gloved hands before moving into action. The sacks were heavier than they looked, and by the time he had finished his suit was white with flour, but with Anderson's praise, the donation of some candy and the news that they were going home, his heart was a lot lighter.

'Wait a minute!' Anderson stroked his chin and studied Nat. 'Lucy, there's something wrong about this boy . . .'

Whilst an apprehensive Nat exchanged looks with an equally bemused Mrs Anderson, the man wheeled and marched away, returning some moments later carrying a broad-brimmed hat which he promptly lowered onto Nat's head. 'That's better! Now you look more like a westerner.'

'Oh my, Nat, you really look the part!' laughed Mrs Anderson, at which her husband jumped into the buckboard and at last they were on their way.

The journey to his new home took nearly three hours, but Mrs Anderson's informative chatter made it seem less and there was also compensation in the scenery. If Nat had imagined that he had already witnessed everything that this country had to offer then he was mistaken, for this undulating pastureland with its mountainous backdrop and rushing rivers far surpassed anything that had gone before. Finally Nat began to take in the true vastness of Canada. To a boy who had never been further than York to Hull the thought inspired a sudden panic – how would he ever escape? He could run and run as much as he liked and not cover a quarter of this country in a year! But the soporific drone of Mrs Anderson and another look around him begged the question, why on earth would he want to escape from this? He had never known such beauty existed. Now, in the late afternoon, the sky was dark blue with not one cloud upon it. It was cold, very cold – there was snow atop the mountains – but even in the dying sun the colours were magnificent: deep purple and mauve and magenta, with shadows of black spruce and pine whose scent was carried on the breeze. At that point Nat reversed his former opinion of Canada. This country and its people with their funny way of talking had been worth the long journey. This was worth working for. He would work like he had never worked before, and save, and get rich, and then fetch Bright and the child to live in this glorious young land.

Nat was almost asleep when they reached the large, whitewashed house built of logs that was to be his home. There was another residence nearby, apparently the bunkhouse, from which could be heard uproarious laughter.

'Sounds like the boys've been making bootleg,' quipped Anderson. 'Never hear 'em laugh like that when it's time for work. We won't disturb them, you'll meet them soon enough.'

Remembering his brief awful time at Wood's stables, Nat hoped to postpone his introduction to the ranch hands for as long as possible, though not by the method that Anderson had in mind. 'Okay, Nat! Let's unload the cart.'

'Oh John, the boy's worn out!' objected Mrs Anderson

as he helped her down. 'Can't you get one of the others to do it?'

Her husband shrugged. 'Guess I could – you two go on, I'll join you in a minute.'

Thankful, Nat hefted his luggage and followed Mrs Anderson as far as the door, at which he paused to look inside. The glow of kerosene lamps gave an instant reminder of the Maguires' kitchen. Oh, this was a lot more grand, with richly coloured rugs on the polished wood floor, a dresser full of china, a massive table and various other pieces of well-turned furniture, lots of pictures in maple frames, and the biggest fireplace Nat had ever seen, but the air of welcome was one and the same. The similarity was endorsed even further by the Irish accent of the woman who came to greet her employer. 'Oh here you are at last, ma'am! I was just getting worried you'd had an accident.' She wiped her hands upon her apron and peered around Mrs Anderson to look upon the newcomer.

Mrs Anderson laughed. 'Well, I could lie and blame the train for being late but I'm afraid it's my fault for gossiping. I just can't help myself. Now, this here is . . . ' Arm extended, she turned to introduce Nat and upon finding that he was not behind her called to him, 'Well, come on in! Unless you're planning to eat on the porch.'

Relieved to hear that he was not expected to eat with the other workmen, Nat came out of the darkness.

'Nat, this is Mary. She helps me do the cooking and look after the men. I don't know what I'd do without her.'

Mary squirmed with pleasure and wrung her large hands whilst offering a greeting to Nat. Discerning in seconds that this bovine personality was nothing like Mrs Maguire, Nat immediately dismissed her as of no importance to himself and asked, 'What shall I do with me bag . . . ma'am?'

Mrs Anderson shared a fond laugh with Mary. 'Oh doesn't the boy talk so funny! Leave it there, Nat, till after you've eaten. It smells like Mary's got something good cooking for us.' Her eyes took in his grubbiness and she threw a towel at him. 'But first you'd better get yourself to the pump. I must confess you don't smell too good.'

Nat followed her pointing finger to a deep sink and, with Mary operating the pump, splashed water over his face and upper body.

Involved though she was in dishing out the meal, Mrs Anderson could not help but notice the scars of self-mutilation on his forearms. 'Why who's been doing that to you?' She put down the ladle and made as if to come and examine him.

He drew away, unable to admit that the wounds had been inflicted by himself, out of misery and boredom and an attempt to be rid of the badness inside him. 'It was just an accident.' Mrs Anderson did not appear to be convinced, but returned to her task. After drying himself he folded the towel as he had been taught at Industrial School and waited, feeling very strange.

The woman finished dishing out plates of stew and looked up. 'Well, come on son, sit yourself down!' She bustled to the door to call her husband but at that point he came in. 'Oh, John, you almost frightened kittens out o' me! Come on now, everyone eat.'

Nat was agog at the size of the meal and even though he was famished was unable to finish it. 'Sorry, I'm not used to getting as much as that — it was lovely though.' He directed his compliment at Mary.

'It surely was,' beamed Mrs Anderson. 'Don't you worry, it won't get wasted.' She scraped the remains onto her husband's plate.

'They musta fed you boys like sparrows!' opined Anderson, shovelling away at his meal in obvious enjoyment. 'Gonna do a man's work, gotta eat a man's rations. Few days here and we'll build some muscle on that skinny frame o' his, won't we, Lucy?'

Nat remained at the table while his guardians finished their meal, trying to keep his eyes open. Mrs Anderson noticed his drooping lids and, laughing, laid down her fork. 'You'd better show the boy his bed afore he drops asleep right there, John.'

Nat rose from his chair and went to pick up his luggage. 'S'all right, sir, I can find my own way. Is it that place over there?'

'Over where?' Anderson had risen too, mopping his moustache on a napkin.

'That . . . whatsit.' Nat's tired brain fought to remember what Anderson had called the other building.

'The bunkhouse? Why no, you'll be sleeping here.' The man frowned, stroking his moustache back to order, then noted the look of relief on Nat's face. 'Why, you didn't think you were just a hired hand, did you? Hell, if we'd wanted another cowpoke we wouldn't have sent all the way to England!' He and the women all laughed, then Anderson looked a little sad and glanced at his wife before the next hesitant offering. 'I don't know if you noticed all those little graves out there on the way in? No, well, it's too dark I suppose. Well, anyway, they were our children. None of 'em got beyond six months old.' Mrs Anderson had moved away to busy herself with the cooking pots, though the expression on her face told that she was still within earshot. 'After the fourth, well, we just couldn't seem to have any more and truth to tell we didn't want to go through it again. We'd kinda resigned ourselves to being without a family, till we heard of Mr Carrington's plan to bring you boys out here. All these years and we'd never even thought about adoption.' He looked into Nat's eyes. 'Guess what I'm trying to say is we don't want you as any hired hand, Nat. We want to give you a chance in a wonderful country, we want you for our son.' And Nat was amazed to see the man's eyes glistening.

Mrs Anderson came back then to deliver a spontaneous

hug – not to Nat but to her husband who turned aside to blow into his handkerchief whilst she addressed Nat, turning her wedding ring as she spoke. 'We want you to regard this as your home, Nat. We understand that you've only just met us and everything here is strange to you, but we'll do our best to make you feel welcome, and I hope one day that you could feel like we really are your folks. Maybe if you start by calling us Aunt Lucy and Uncle John?'

Nat felt as though he were caught up in a dream, but delivered a mechanical nod and smiled as best he could. Mrs Anderson stopped turning her ring and, reaching out, clasped him to her, whispering, 'Welcome home, Nat.'

Anderson cleared his throat and picked up Nat's case. 'Come on, son, time you were in bed! Let him go, Lucy, he'll still be there in the morning.'

Laughing – Nat had discovered that Mrs Anderson laughed a lot – she allowed her husband to show Nat up a ladder to the attic. 'Oh here! Take this lamp with you.' She passed one of the kerosene lamps to the boy. 'Hope you like your quilt, by the way!'

'He'd better,' grunted Anderson, shoving the case before him. 'After I had to put up with a houseful o' yacking women for it to be made.'

Mrs Anderson delayed Nat's bedtime further, grabbing his arm. 'When we heard you were coming I was so excited I wanted everything to be just right, and the spare quilt I have is so old, so I called a quilting bee and – oh, you don't know what that is! Well, I guess they call it that cause everyone buzzes around like a swarm of bees, helping each other with some task that's too much for them to do on their own and –'

'Lucy, let the boy go to bed.' Anderson, sounding tired himself, continued up the ladder.

'Oh, I'm sorry, Nat! Good night now!' A delighted Mrs Anderson clasped her hands and grinned at the Irish maid.

Holding the lamp before him, Nat dragged himself up

after Anderson into the loft wherein lay his room – his very own room! That his bed was only a straw mattress did not matter in the least. It was his and his alone.

'For heaven's sake say you like the quilt,' instructed Anderson.

'It's lovely,' inserted Nat.

Anderson chuckled and repeated the flat vowels: 'Luvely! Sorry, Nat, I wasn't making fun, I just like the sound o' your voice. Guess we must both sound odd to each other, eh?' He took a look around as if seeing the place for the first time himself, nodding in appraisal. 'I'll convey your thanks to your Aunt Lucy.' Then he pointed at the mattress with the abrupt command, 'You'll be shaking your own tick out in the morning, now. Just 'cause we said you're one o' the family doesn't mean Aunt Lucy's gonna run around after you. Well, good night, Nat. See you at breakfast. Wait till I get down the ladder before you turn that lamp out, now.' Rung by rung, he disappeared from the loft, closing the hatch door after him.

'Good night!' Nat remained there for a moment, still dazed by the Andersons' plans to adopt him. Flattering though it might be, he did not reciprocate their desire – though he was not about to throw all this away by telling them that. He turned down the lamp, plunging the loft into darkness save for the glow from the kitchen. Fatigue momentarily overturned by excitement, he threw open his window to be greeted by the throbbing whirr of crickets and gazed up at the twinkling constellations; he would have gazed forever had he not been once more overwhelmed by tiredness. Shutting out the chill of the night, he collapsed on his mattress, inhaling the sweet smell of his new life before he fell asleep.

Bright did not know where to turn, but instinct steered her feet towards the church. Father Cavanagh was sympathetic to a degree. 'Ah dear, I thought they'd take it badly, but sure you've only yourself to blame for your sinful ways. Come along with me. I'll hand you to the care of the Sisters, though what they'll say I don't know. You're a wicked girl, Bright Maguire.'

Throughout the duration of her pregnancy Bright was incessantly reminded of how wicked she was. The nuns were not maliciously cruel. On the contrary they gave her new clothes to accommodate her bulge and fed her and took care of her. They just would not let her forget her sin and the wretched boy who had deserted her. 'But don't you worry, my dear,' they soothed, 'we've found a good Catholic family who's willing to overlook the slur and take the child off your hands. Now aren't you fortunate?'

And Bright understood what the priest had meant when he had said she would spend the rest of her life making penance. The last two months dragged into eternity. The baby spun continually inside her, thrusting its heels under her ribs and performing acrobatics if she dared to roll onto her back. She urged the birth to happen, knowing that when it did her child would be taken from her. She would never see it again, as she would never see its father. Each time she thought about Nat the tears welled. How could he do this to her?

After nights of turmoil, Bright decided she could not let it happen. This was her child, hers and Nat's. He might have left her but that didn't stop her loving him and loving his baby. If they took the child she would be left with nothing. Yet how will you work with a baby in tow, she posed the question. Where will you live? Not here. They won't let you keep the baby. And you mustn't tell them your decision, for they'll try and talk you out of it: 'Everything has been arranged, my dear, you can't possibly back out now. Think of the welfare of the child.' She *was* thinking of it. Its fate consumed her every waking moment. If she chose to keep it she would brand herself a fallen woman and her child a bastard. Oh, but she just could not part with it.

A week or so before the anticipated delivery, details of the adoption became clearer. The baby would stay with her for a month to give it the best nourishment. Bright decided that it must be during this period she should make her escape, for it could not possibly be earlier. She was too bulky and where else could she give birth? But then she reflected that labour would weaken her, wear down her resistance, and how would she walk out of here carrying her newborn? They wouldn't let her out alone with it. Now. It had to be now, while she had the courage.

There was nothing to pack and no money. Bright waited until the nuns were at afternoon prayer and she herself was meant to be taking a nap. It was easy. She just walked out through the gates. No one stopped her. But the hard part started now. Placing a hand over her abdomen to calm the squirming child, she lumbered off down the street. There was only one place she could go – home. Her father would still be at work.

Mrs Maguire almost fainted when she looked from the scullery window and saw her daughter. With an anguished face she dragged her inside. 'Bright! Oh, Bright, what're ye doing? He'll kill ye if he finds ye here. Oh baby!' The distraught woman pulled Bright into an embrace, weeping and scolding.

Bright wept too. 'I couldn't stay there, Mammy. The sisters want to take the baby.'

'Oh but Bright, you're not intending to keep it?'

'Why not, tis mine! And Nat's.'

Mrs Maguire clicked her tongue. 'All the more reason I would've thought ye'd want to be rid of it.'

'No, Mam. Even though he left me I still love him. I'll always love him. And I know he loves me. I just know it. Don't blame him. He's just frightened cause he's too young to be a daddy . . . oh, Mam, I'm frightened too!' Bright fell against her mother's shoulder, sobbing her heart out.

'Oh, Bright Maguire.' Her mother stroked her head with frantic hand. 'You always see the good in folks. He doesn't deserve your love.'

'Help me, Mammy! Let me have the baby here.'

'I can't, I can't! Your daddy would kill me, and you too. You saw his temper when you told him about it.'

'But that was months ago. Surely he's calmed down?'

'Aye, he's calmed down.' Mrs Maguire's eyes looked distant. 'But it's as if he's dead. He's said some terrible things, Bright. He worshipped you. You know you were always his favourite. He'll never talk to you again, darlin'. He won't even see you. And take it from me, if he says it . . . ' She closed her eyes to shut out the pain. 'Please God, no one saw ye come in here, for my life won't be worth a candle if he finds out. I'm sorry Bright, I can't help ye darlin'.'

Bright's eyes were desperate. 'But . . . where will I go?' She clutched the child in her belly.

Whilst Mrs Maguire agonized, the front door sounded. She almost screamed and in a panic began to bundle Bright into the yard. 'Go!'

'But it might not be Dada.'

'Doesn't matter! Your brothers'll tell him. They won't have your name mentioned either.' Bright had been almost as precious to her siblings as to their father. None of them would lift a finger to aid her.

'But you have to help me! I've no one except you.' Bright started to cry again as she was ejected.

'All right, all right, but go now! Don't wait in the street. Go down to Castle Mills! I'll meet ye there when I can get away!' The door was slammed.

Heavy with pain and the child within, Bright lumbered through the maze of passageways that led onto Piccadilly, then on towards Castle Mills where she leaned on the stone bridge looking down into the lock. There was a film of oil on the water, amongst which floated bits of paper and rope. Bright stared into the scum. There came all at once an overpowering feeling to throw herself in. *Go*, urged the voice, *it's so easy*. She stepped back in alarm. The feeling came again. She hurried away towards town, walking round for a while before returning to see if her mother was there.

She wasn't. Afraid to stand near the water, Bright kept coming and going. Her back had started to ache from the weight it had to support. She found a bench and lowered herself onto it. The discomfort began to subside. She wondered what time it was and how long she had been wandering round. On this midsummer's eve it was hard to tell. The backache started to nag again. She shifted her body and, after a time, the ache went away. She decided to walk back to Castle Mills.

It was here on the bridge that her waters broke. She thought she was wetting herself, felt acutely embarrassed that passers-by might see the trickle that ran from the hem of her skirt and down the slope. As tightly as she tried to squeeze the muscles between her legs the trickle wouldn't stop. Her clothes were saturated. Oh where are you, Mammy? The backache was causing more discomfort. If her mother didn't come soon she would have to risk her father's anger by going home, for it was impossible for her to sleep on the street and she refused to go back to the nuns.

To her great relief, she saw a flustered Mrs Maguire hurrying under Fishergate Postern, and went to meet her, the wet skirts clinging to her limbs. 'Oh Mam, where've ye been? Twas awful. I just wet meself!' She blushed and covered her cheek.

Mrs Maguire groaned in despair. 'Oh, Bright . . . come on I've made arrangements for you – and not before time.' She crossed herself and steered Bright back under the postern.

Bright dug her heels in. 'Not with the Sisters?'

Mrs Maguire showed uncharacteristic irritation. 'No, no! Though I think you're ungrateful to throw their goodness away like ye have.'

'They're not taking my baby!'

'I've said not! For pity's sake, Bright, will ye come on. I have to get back, I've only dared slip out while your father's at the pub. I'm supposed to be in the bath.' Bright demanded to know where she was being taken. 'There's a woman the other end of Walmgate'll take y'in, but only for a few weeks while ye get right. Then I'm afraid ye'll have to fend for yourself.'

Bright started to flag. 'Will ye slow down? I've got a stitch.'

'That's not a stitch, Bright, it's the baby on its way.'

Bright lurched in fear. 'Will ye stay with me?'

'I can't, darlin'!'

'Oh, Mammy, please!'

'No! I have to get back or he'll kill me.'

Face contorted, Bright showed impatience at this melodrama. 'That's just daft! I don't know why you're so scared of Dada. It's me he's angry with. He blows his top but I've never seen him hit you.'

'Ah, my innocent child,' Mrs Maguire shook her head. 'There's more ways o' hurting . . . never mind, ye've got enough to concern ye.' And who would tell a daughter what happened in the privacy of a marital bed, when a man took out all his frustrations on his woman, twisted and bit her most sensitive flesh so that she had to cram her mouth with the sheet in order not to yell and frighten her children – and just because somebody had upset him at work or she hadn't done his meal on time. 'Ye probably won't have the baby till the morning. After your daddy's gone to work I'll run down and see ye.'

A fearful Bright was handed over to the woman in Walmgate who treated her kindly but was not her mother. In the following hour the pain grew so bad that Bright wanted to scream. If only she had known that in the next ten hours, on the longest day of the year, it would become so bad that she wanted to die.

Mrs Maguire arrived at eight-thirty in the morning, one hour too late to help her grandchild into the world. When she entered the sun-filled bedroom Bright was dozing, the child lying at the foot of the bed, wrapped like a mummy, a puffy-eyed, slightly oriental looking creature with the tiniest of noses. After shedding tears for the beauty of the tableau, Mrs Maguire sat quietly for a while with her daughter until someone kicked a bottle in the road, waking Bright. Confused for the moment she rubbed her hand over a belly that remained distended, looking at her mother without recognition. 'Aye, it looks as if there's still one in there,' quipped Mrs Maguire, then noting her daughter's alarm added quickly, 'sure, tis only joking I am! What d'ye think this is?' She scooped her hands under the bundle and laid it nearer to Bright, who smiled now.

Her eyes were tired but filled with love for the child. 'Isn't she gorgeous?'

'That she is.' Mrs Maguire touched one of the perfect little hands that curled over the edge of the blanket. 'Have ye thought of a name for her?'

'Oriel,' came the proud announcement.

'Oriel?' The grandmother looked weary at this new

outrage. 'What in Heaven's name possessed ye to name her after a window?'

Bright frowned. 'It's not a window.'

Her mother turned shirty. ''Tis a window, I tell ye! Sure, didn't I clean enough of them when I was a girl in service at Mrs Harper's. What sort of a heathen name is that for a good Catholic babe? The priest'll drop her in the font when he hears that.'

Fear shadowed Bright's face. 'I won't be having her baptized – and you're not to tell the priest she's been born.'

'But – '

'No, Mam! They'll try and take her away. They will, and I won't let them.'

Mrs Maguire's brow creased in sympathy. 'They won't, love. I'll explain to them that ye want to keep her.'

'No!'

One thing after another conspired to rob Mrs Maguire of her serenity. 'Bright, 'tis unheard of not to have a child baptized!'

'They won't have her!' Bright hoisted herself on arms that trembled like jelly, wincing in pain, and enveloped her newborn into a protective cuddle.

Mrs Maguire did not press the subject, resolving to persuade her daughter later. 'All right, all right, but where did ye get that dreadful name?'

'It's not dreadful.' Bright kissed the baby's head. 'When I was little, I once saw a picture in a book of this bird with lovely colours – '

'But she's no colour at all!' Mrs Maguire laughed softly and touched the infant's bald head. The translucent skin was marbled with blue veins.

'I know.' Bright laughed too. 'I just liked the sound of the word. Oriel.'

'Well, I still say 'tis a window!' But Mrs Maguire smiled now. 'Come to think of it, though, she is like a wee bird.

One o' those little baldy creatures that sometimes fall out o' the guttering.'

'Have ye heard what your granny is saying about ye?' Bright spoke to the child, who had woken and now gazed at her with dark blue eyes, scrunched up like a defensive hedgehog, a look of worry on her face, as if she was afraid of the world.

'Granny!' A scandalized Mrs Maguire covered her mouth.

Bright took one eye from the baby to venture, 'Are ye going to tell . . .'

'I am not! Don't you ever say or think it, Bright,' warned her mother. 'He won't ever want to see her. You'll only be hurting yourself and that wee thing.'

'Nobody can hurt me now.' Bright cuddled the newborn up to her freckled face. 'Now I've got her.'

Mrs Maguire sighed. 'I wonder if her eyes will turn brown later.'

'Could they do that?' This seemed to concern the young mother. She loved having Nat's blue eyes stare back at her.

'You surely don't want to keep having a reminder of himself?'

Bright did not answer, just feasted her eyes on the child. Mrs Maguire clicked her tongue. 'Will ye look at the state o' your hair! Here, let's see if we can find a brush to run through it.' On a chest of drawers lay a brush and hand mirror. Mrs Maguire offered them in exchange for the babe. Her daughter held the mirror to her face and gave an exclamation as a stranger looked back at her.

'And well ye might gasp,' observed Mrs Maguire. 'I doubt ye'll get a brush through that bird's nest.'

Her arm quivering and weak, Bright tried to bring her hair under control, still marvelling at the change in her visage. 'That'll have to do. I feel so weedy!' She put down the brush and mirror and studied her hands. 'These aren't mine. I think someone crept in during the night and swapped them for another pair.'

Her mother harumphed. 'Ye'll have to find a better excuse to explain *this* to everyone.' She handed Oriel back and paused for a while before announcing, 'I'll have to go now.'

Bright tore her eyes from her child. 'Will ye come again?'

'If I can get away.' Mrs Maguire kissed her daughter, then hurried home.

The woman had very generously given Bright a month in which to recover from the birth and find somewhere permanent to live. Then she must go. Bright had been here for two weeks. Tomorrow she must set about finding work. God knew this was the furthest thing from her mind. She felt so drained of energy – Oriel was the most demanding baby. At two weeks old she had such strength of character that Bright was forced to give in to her every whim. Hence she was totally exhausted. Yet happiness at having a daughter overcame all. When bathing her she would stare at the tiny body in wonderment. How could this have been inside her? She would sniff the child all over like an animal, push her nose into all the creases of that tiny body, growing drunk on the scent. And she would talk to her, tell her everything about how she had come to be born. Prior to the birth the thing Bright had feared most was the loneliness of being cast out from her family, but now with Oriel she would never feel lonely. The baby seemed to hang on her every word – indeed she almost appeared to be trying to reply with all the expressions she pulled.

There were, however, moments when Bright wondered what sort of world she had brought the child into, when she would cry and rage over all the cruelty and violence in the streets around her. And there were times when she would burst into tears over nothing. Sometimes she wished that there was an adult with whom to share her fears, but the woman whose house this was did not have time to sit and talk and her own mother had only managed to call in once since Oriel's birth.

Therefore it was a pleasure to see her this morning. Bright jabbered away, consulting her mother over her future. It was a happy half hour they spent together, but when Mrs Maguire got up to go there appeared to be something left unsaid, judging by her hesitancy. Bright asked what it was.

'I know you're going to be mad at me, but I couldn't sit and do nothing, so I've told Father Cavanagh. He's promised to come visit ye tonight and baptize herself here.'

Bright was horrified. 'He can't!'

'Now don't start worrying,' soothed her mother. 'I'll be coming with him. There'll be no trying to persuade ye to give her up.'

Bright moaned. 'Do the Sisters know I'm here?'

'Not unless the Father's told them. Stop worrying. Nobody wants to take her, they just want to do what's best. I'll have to go. I'll see ye tonight. I'll tell your father I'm going to church — well, it won't be a lie. Don't worry, it'll be all right.'

Bright sat there after her mother had gone, paralysed with fear. The nuns would come and whatever her mother said, they'd try to take Oriel away. You mustn't let them. Be strong. How can I fight them? I'm too tired. Oriel was sleeping peacefully. *You mustn't let them take her*, said a voice. *She'd be better off dead, and you're better dead without her. Go down to the kitchen, take a knife and cut her throat.* The voice was so real. She felt a prickling sensation all over her body. She could not breathe properly. No, I don't want to! *Do it*, said the voice, instilling its force into her, propelling her towards that knife drawer.

She ran, stumbling, and shut herself in a clothes cupboard. The panic took complete hold then, grasping her by the throat. She started to gasp. *Go get the knife.* No! It felt as though boiling water filled her ears and eye sockets. She took great gulps of fusty air, trying to squeeze herself into a corner of the cupboard, hiding behind the hanging coats. But the voice found her. *The knife. The knife.*

She burst from the cupboard and saw her beautiful baby sleeping. Get the knife and throw it away so you won't do it. No! I can't touch it! I don't dare! Sheer blind panic filled her body. She ran out of the house, not knowing where. Ran to escape the voice.

Exhaustion forced her to stop. She could feel little globs of puerperal blood seeping out onto the rag between her legs. *Blood, blood, blood.* The voice had followed her. She stood heaving by the roadside. The sun was shining. I'll have to die; if I go back I'll kill her, the thing in my head will make me kill her. Help me, Jesus, I'm going mad!

The river beckoned. Led by terror Bright went towards it, stood on the bank and looked down. She teetered for an age – then tipped her body in.

A man had been watching her from the bridge. Even before she had jumped he was pelting down the steps. When her body splashed into the river he was tearing off his jacket and boots, preparing to dive in.

She had swallowed much water and was already unconscious when he dragged her to the bank. Other people had witnessed the scene and helped him get her onto dry land, where he applied a clumsy life-saving technique.

She came round to find a panting man straddled across her retching body. 'Don't worry, someone's gone for an ambulance!'

Bright closed her eyes. She did not want an ambulance. She wanted to die. Make me die, she prayed, I can't stand it, please, please let me go. She felt the warm sun on her eyelids, smelled the newly mown grass, the earthy scent of the river, heard the chirrup of sparrows, the concerned murmur of onlookers . . . then her mind drifted off, to a place faraway.

Nat had lived amongst these lush foothills of the Rocky Mountains for almost three months now; he had watched the green grassy plains burgeon with a harmony of flowers, had been on a cattle drive, learned how to handle steers and how to cope with the everyday running of a ranch. The work was hard and his inner thighs had almost bled after his first full day in the saddle, but there was much to compensate; Nat had never eaten so much wholesome food in all his born days. Of the aspects he could have chosen that were better compared to his old life this was the one that sprang to mind above everything else. The wonderful scenery, the warm ranch-house, the affectionate guardians; each was a bonus, but to a youth who had always been hungry a full belly outshone all of them in terms of importance.

The initial qualm of being the outsider was beginning to fade. Everyone here seemed friendly and ready to help their neighbour. Nat supposed that it was a product of being so isolated; people couldn't fall out if they hardly saw each other. Yet it was no small triumph that adoptive Canadians from all over the globe – Germans, Ukrainians, Hungarians, English – could intermingle so amicably. Friendly, yes, but modest, no. From Mrs Anderson's description of their ranch prior to his arrival he might have assumed that they had hundreds of head of cattle, but in fact it was quite a small spread in relation to Carrington's, which he had visited. However, he would not change places with the boy whom Carrington had taken in, for that man had sons of his own and, unlike the Andersons, regarded the lad as nothing more than a hired hand.

Of the two Andersons he preferred the man. It was not that he disliked her, just that . . . well, one would have thought it impossible to feel suffocated out here in this land of eternal horizons, but Aunt Lucy could manage it with her swamping affection. She meant well, Nat knew it, and he tried to be grateful, but sometimes he grew angry with her for showering him with love, love that he could not return. He recognized that one day the title Aunt Lucy would not be enough and she would want him to call her Mother, and he just couldn't.

It had not taken long to discover that Anderson, or rather Uncle John, contrary to his gruff manner was an extremely sentimental man who almost shed a tear when any cattle had to go to market. Nat had used this to his advantage, coaxing Anderson into providing him with a horse, a dog and other more material benefits. Despite this mercenary streak Nat genuinely liked both the Andersons. He liked them enormously, but did not love them, could never feel for them the way he felt for Bright. Sometimes he felt guilty for not thinking about her as much as he should, but then he was so tired when he went to bed that he fell asleep the moment he closed his eyes.

Bright's absence was the one thing that detracted from his total contentment. He wondered if she had had the baby yet. Oh, she would certainly love it here! He could not wait to see her face as she underwent all the discoveries that he himself had made. There was just one drawback. How could he save for her fare when Anderson did not pay him for his work? It was not that the man was stingy, just that he regarded Nat as his son, which was obviously meant to be reward enough in itself. The only sign of hard cash was the few cents he gave Nat to spend on candy when they visited town, but these occasions were so rare that even if he saved the money up for five years it would not help to fetch Bright here. He had contemplated asking the Andersons for help, but feared that the news of an illegitimate child would soil his reputation in their eyes. He wondered briefly over the child's sex. No, he'd better not mention it to his foster parents until he had been here a little longer. The relationship was just too new. He could not let anything spoil it. Besides, it would be better to wait until the child was a little older and more able to travel before exposing it to such a gruelling journey.

He never once contemplated that such a life of isolation might be anathema to a gregarious person such as Bright. The nearest town was three hours away. True, there was a village within ten miles of here, where the Andersons went to church on a Sunday, but it was the tiniest settlement and nothing of import went on there. However, as one who did not need the company of many people this was of no concern to Nat, for there was no such thing as boredom here on the farm. Starting in the early hours whilst Aunt Lucy collected the eggs he would take the kitchen waste to the pigs, milk the few dairy cows, then take the milk to cool in the root cellar under the house – all before breakfast. Then there was the garden which had to be kept free of weeds, its potato hills to keep in shape and vegetables to attend to: pumpkins, cabbage, carrots, beans and onions. This Nat regarded as of lesser importance than the more masculine tasks of rounding up cattle, branding, and butchering pigs. He much preferred to be out in the saddle with Uncle John than in the vicinity of Aunt Lucy's cloying maternity, though neither of his foster parents was privy to his opinions.

Out of the blue, after Nat had gone to bed one summer's evening and the Irish maid was down in the root cellar collecting potatoes, Mrs Anderson laid her sewing on her lap and asked her husband, 'John, d'you think he likes us?'

'Your guess is as good as mine.' Anderson was perusing his Eaton's mail order catalogue and did not look up, his eyes totally hidden beneath a bushy brow. 'He sure doesn't give anything away, does he?'

'No. He seems happy enough, though.'

Anderson nodded and flicked over to the next page. 'Are you happy with him, Lucy?'

'Oh, yes! He's a lovely boy and no trouble. He's just so . . .' She could not think of the word and, hoisting her plump bosom, inserted her needle once more into the linen.

Her husband agreed, and raised thoughtful eyes from the catalogue, laying it on his knee. 'I guess life in that institution made him wary o' folks. He doesn't trust anyone, even folk who are trying to do right by him. He wonders why they're doing nice things for him, thinks there must be something in it for them. I'd like to convince him different, get close to him, but I'm not sure how. Each time I ask something he reckons is too personal he makes some excuse about having work to do.' He stretched and crossed his booted ankles. When the catalogue slithered onto the wooden floor he let it lie.

'I've done no better myself,' confessed Lucy, 'and if I as much as mention the word mother, why, he turns into a different person, gets this cold look in his eyes . . . ' Her needle lay inactive again as her eyes penetrated deep into her husband's face. 'That boy's been badly treated, John. It'll take a long time before he ever allows us to get close to him.' She toyed with an idea. 'Why don't you take him up into the mountains for a few days? Just the two of you. I can't imagine a better place for you to get to know each other, and there'd be nowhere he could escape to.'

John Anderson thought this a sound prescription, and the next day he discussed it with Nat. Hitherto, the mountains had provided only an awesome and alluring backdrop to everyday events. Nat was eager to grab the bait and asked, 'When can we go?'

'Well, all we have to do is load up a good supply o' food. We can go in the morning.'

'Can I take Roy?' The subject was a long-haired, cross-breed dog, large but docile. Nat fondled its ears, the only ears that had heard all his secrets. Roy was confessor and friend and scapegoat. Yet with all this, Nat was unable to think upon the animal as his own. There was always the fear that Uncle John could take him away.

Anderson twiddled his moustache, knowing that if he allowed Roy to come the boy would rely on the animal for diversion should any intimate query not be to his liking. He must have Nat's full attention if this trip were to succeed. 'Better not, there're grizzlies up there.'

Nat's dark hair had fallen over one eye. Gone was the institutional crop and the pallor. His face was tanned and healthy. 'He could look after us.'

'Not against no grizzly he wouldn't. Leave him here to look after Aunt Lucy. I've got my rifle to protect us.'

The following hot summer's day, with command of the ranch delegated to Anderson's top hand, he and Nat set off on horseback into the wild Rockies.

Even now there were new and glorious discoveries to be made about this land. Up, up they climbed, into lush mountain meadows, past teeming waterfalls, shadowy chasms, through fragrant forests and on and on towards mountains that were always one step beyond. Nat had always been aware of his own expendability, but now the sheer vastness of the wilderness reduced him to a grain of dust. In his youthful imagination those colossal summits had been mauled by some giant, their jagged faces raked and scarred by its enormous fingernails, then in some after-thought of mercy their wounds dressed in what from down here appeared to be moss but were in fact huge girdles of pine. Though fearful of the exacting climb, his imagination reeled upon those heights, how marvellous to look down upon the world . . . but alas, however high their horses climbed the mountain tops remained forever out of reach.

Even before dark Anderson was looking for a place to make camp and chose to do so by a huge mirror of emerald glass. Never an expressive boy, even Nat had to give way to a bout of exhilaration, jumping down from his horse and sprinting around the wooded perimeter of the lake, leaping into the air, making wild grasps at the sky. His antics made Anderson smile. 'I think this is just gonna work,' he told his mount as he unsaddled her.

With a campfire burning, the horses fed and hobbled, they settled down to their own meal, looking out across the lake. It was still not quite dark. Here on this sandy bank Nat could almost have imagined he was at the seaside, offering this to Anderson by way of intercourse.

The man thought this observation quaint in the face of such grandeur, but gave soft affirmation. 'It's certainly a beautiful place. You enjoying yourself, eh?'

Nat delivered an enthusiastic nod and continued to eat, occasionally wafting at the small cloud of mosquitoes that danced around his head.

'Don't say much, do you, Nat?'

Someone else had said that to him a long time ago. Here, with little occupation, Nat had time to think of her. 'I'm not one for talking, I'd rather listen.'

Anderson corrected him. 'I didn't say you don't talk much, I said you don't *say* much, there's a difference.' Breaking off from his meal, he used his fork to make patterns in the food. 'Take your Aunt Lucy, she can rackety-rack like a threshing machine but her talk don't amount to much, at least most times. Yet me, I don't talk as much as her but when I say something to somebody I'd like to think they're a bit more informed by what I've just told them. Understand?'

Nat understood very well but shied away with a non-committal shrug.

'What I mean is, Nat, I think we've told you a great deal about us, personal things, but well, we hardly know anything about you.'

Nat was swift in his reply. 'There's nowt much to know. I got sent to Industrial School for playing truant when I was ten and I've been there ever since, more or less.' He omitted to mention his crimes.

'Must be more to you than that,' Anderson pondered. 'You said you ain't got no folks . . .'

'Dead.'

'Both of 'em?'

'Yes.'

'I'm sorry.' Anderson stopped playing with his meal and put the tin plate on the sand, choosing his next words. 'Your Aunt Lucy thinks a great deal about you, Nat. So do I. We couldn't think any more of you if you were our own flesh and blood.' He waited for a response. The chirrup of crickets signalled that night was closing in.

Nat felt awkward, making silent apology. *You're asking me to love you and I can't. I'm sorry, you're nice people, I like living with you, but I just can't love you. I don't think I can love anybody except Bright.* In answer he gave what he hoped was a grateful nod, with which Anderson had to be content.

'Well, I hope in the next few days we'll both learn something, eh?' Anderson gave a disappointed smile and went back to his meal.

By the time they came down from the Rockies a few days later Nat had watched a mountain goat leap from crag to crag, woken each morning to blue jays, and had fallen asleep to the deep-throated howl of wolves. Once he had even seen a grizzly bear come down to the lake to drink. He had learned all kinds of things from Mr Anderson about survival in the wilderness, but Mr Anderson had learned only as much about his companion as Nat would allow.

They descended into the foothills. Along with the sweet smell of prairie grass Aunt Lucy was there to greet the two dusty riders when they came through the gates that balmy evening, their long shadows preceding them. Broom in hand, she gave one last whack at the pigs who had invaded her garden and came forth, her plump smiling face shaded by the frill of her sunbonnet. Anderson jumped down from the saddle to receive her delighted kiss. 'Good to see you, darlin'!'

'Good to see you, too, dear.' Her lips left his cheek to whisper into his ear, 'Was it worth it?'

Anderson glanced at his dishevelled companion. 'I think we had a good time, didn't we, Nat?'

'And are you any the wiser?' Aunt Lucy assumed her words to be too cryptic for Nat to interpret, but as the youth led both horses to the barn he caught the sad shake of head from the man and guessed that the trip had been the result of some conspiracy between them, an attempt to get closer to their adopted son. They must think he was stupid. Only one person could ever unmask his true feelings. He wondered as he unsaddled his horse what she was doing, and if she missed him as much as he missed her.

13

Bright was secured in an asylum for several weeks, during which time she was forbidden access to her child. Initially, she went about in a stupor: *am I in a dream? Do I really exist?* In this hazy condition she refused all food, to which the nurses responded with authority. After one example of force feeding Bright immediately conformed and hitherto life improved to a degree. The medical staff encouraged her to talk and listened to her fears. 'I'm terrified of all these mad people!' she wept to one nurse.

'Why?' came the level response. 'They're just like you.'

Reading the horrified expression on Bright's face she added more kindly, 'You're worried that we're going to keep you locked up in here, aren't you? Well, we're not. You've been through a great ordeal and your body and mind need to rest, that's all. And that's what's wrong with most of the others in here. So don't look down on them.'

With this sobering revelation, Bright learned to cope with life in the asylum, went along with the other inmates to make baskets, ate with them, cried with them, treating them not as mad people but as friends. The only friends she had.

Her mother had managed to visit once and tried to reassure her that Oriel was being well cared for by the Sisters, and had been baptized. This threw Bright into a frenzy and it was decided that the child be transferred to the asylum in order to show the patient that there was no conspiracy to rob her of motherhood; Oriel would be returned to her when she was able to care for her. Mrs Maguire was requested not to come again.

When she was deemed to be no longer a hazard to herself Bright was sent before the Bench for attempted suicide. Mercifully, the magistrates agreed that she had been suffering from temporary insanity due to parturition, and imprisonment was thought to be too harsh. Therefore she would not be sent for trial if she agreed to continue her treatment at the hospital, which she did. Still, there was no lessening of tension for Bright. She had met other women in the asylum who had been certified by their relatives for the crime of having a child out of wedlock. With no one to sign them out, they had become permanent residents. If no one signed for her . . .

Whilst she twisted her fingers in apprehension, the spokesman for the magistrates concluded with some heart-warming news: 'On your release, you are to be put into the care of a Miss Mary Bytheway. You will work for her as her servant and in exchange she will feed and house you. Miss Bytheway has also charitably consented to accept your child under her roof.'

Bright collapsed into tears.

The magistrate cleared his throat. 'I trust that you will show your gratitude by serving her well and will not try to dispose of yourself again.'

'Oh, no, sir! Thank you!' An earnest Bright clasped her hands to her breast. The magistrate gave an acknowledging nod and the ordeal was over.

I won't cry, Bright told herself as she was taken to be reunited with her baby. When I see her I won't cry, or they'll think I'm still mad; *I won't cry*.

She wept torrents. The moment a nurse appeared holding Oriel the tears just would not hold. She sobbed when the child was placed in her arms, dripping tears over Oriel's face. How she had grown! Four weeks' separation had made a huge difference to her appearance. She looked enormous. Still within the confines of the asylum Bright retained the fear that those who had witnessed her uncontrolled sobbing would keep her locked up. Not until she was out of the grounds did she begin to calm down, and even then she was not wholly relaxed.

'I'm sorry,' she told the middle-aged nurse who was to accompany her to Miss Bytheway's. 'I can't seem to stop crying.'

'It's understandable.' Her companion spoke kindly. 'You haven't seen your baby for a month. I'd be weeping buckets too if I was parted from my son – when he was a baby, I mean. He's grown up now.'

Bright donated a watery smile. 'Ye've all been very kind. I don't know what I'd have done without the clothes ye've given me.' She indicated the bundle in her left hand. Wrapped inside her shawl – the only reminder of her old life – were two nightgowns, a hairbrush, stockings and a change of underwear.

'Actually they were from Miss Bytheway,' explained the nurse. 'She'll probably have one or two more things for you when you arrive.'

'Who is she?' The young mother had not dared to ask before. 'I mean, why does she want to help me?'

The nurse frowned. Bright, who had noticed a large wart with a hair growing from it on the other's chin, was unable to tear her eyes away. 'I'm not sure why she took to you in particular. It's the first time to my knowledge that she's taken anybody in, but she's a regular visitor of ours, always bringing gifts for the patients. A very charitable lady.'

Bright managed to remove her fascinated gaze from the wart and looked down at the babe cradled in the hook of her right arm, as if including her in the conversation. 'She sounds nice. I was a bit nervous of meeting her.'

Even so, the apprehension did not entirely evaporate as she proceeded to the home of her benefactress, which was near the village of Fulford. The house was a tall, four-storey building in the middle of a terrace of ten, fronted by an iron gate and railings and miles of open countryside.

Bright could not believe she was going to live anywhere so grand. The nurse rang the doorbell and, when the occupant answered, transferred Bright to her charge and left immediately.

Miss Mary Bytheway looked about sixty years old. She was very prim and clean, and dressed in grey from neck to toe. Her skin was pale, her eyelids thin as tissue paper – Bright could see tiny mauve veins in them as the woman stared down at her; stared down because she was very tall. Her back was a ramrod with no sign of a dowager's hump. She had white eyebrows and hair, but this was very sparse, a fact which she had tried to conceal with a huge black bow. Her lips were full but, as if to deny any form of sensuality she kept them pressed together in an unremitting line of disapproval. There would be no joking with this one. Without a word, Miss Bytheway summoned the young girl inside. Bright took the two steps up to the front vestibule and moved past her employer, catching a whiff of buttermilk soap.

She lingered in the hall cradling Oriel, who was asleep. There was no sound. It was as quiet as the convent, an ambience which was enhanced by an expanse of stained glass in the vestibule door.

'I'll show you to your quarters.' Miss Bytheway conducted her to the stairs. Bright shadowed her up four flights to a landing, by which time both were short of breath, then through a doorway which obviously led up to the roof space. This flight had no carpet on the tread, neither was there any on the landing they had reached. Bright noticed a row of bells, then took three further paces into an attic room in which was a bed – nothing else, just a small iron bedstead covered in a patchwork quilt. Oh yes, there was something else, a chamberpot; but no mirrors, no chair. Bright looked around at the bare whitewashed walls, at the low sloping ceiling, empty cast-iron fireplace, then at the skylight. This was home.

'It's very nice,' she said politely, receiving a curt nod. Oriel was beginning to grumble. Bright went to put her down on the bed.

'Not there.' Miss Bytheway, clutching a lace handkerchief, indicated for Bright to follow her again and went into the other attic room. This much larger one had a fire burning merrily in the grate. There was a multi-coloured rug on the floor, a cupboard on which sat a row of dolls, a small enamel bath and a child's cot. Bright turned to the woman and grinned for the first time in weeks. 'This is wonderful! Thank you, thank you so much. It seems too generous to let us have a room each. Maybe I should move my bed in here?'

Miss Bytheway did not return her smile. 'No. This will be the child's room. Besides, if you move in here the warmth of the fire will induce you to oversleep and I will not tolerate that.' She looked at Oriel, who had started to grizzle again. 'You may attend to her, then come down and prepare tea.' She turned to go.

Bright spoke up in embarrassment. 'I . . .'

Miss Bytheway turned an enquiring blue eye upon her.

'I've nothing to feed her with. While I've been in hospital my milk dried up.'

There was a look of faint disgust. 'That is all attended to,' said the woman in a prim manner. 'You will find nursing bottles in that cupboard. The milk is downstairs in the pantry. Follow me.'

Bright laid Oriel in the cot and hurried after Miss Bytheway, returning in five minutes with a jug of warm milk and another of hot water. Oriel was by now red-faced and screaming to be nourished. Flustered, Bright opened the door of the cupboard to find the nursing bottle, paused briefly in wonderment as she saw the array of toys inside, then hurriedly removed the rubber teat from the end of the bottle and reached for the jug of warm milk. The child didn't appear to want it. Bright tried to insert the teat into the wailing maw but Oriel repelled it by craning her head in all directions. 'Come on now, don't be soft,' urged her mother, and let a drop of milk fall onto the baby's tongue. Oriel still shrieked. The milk trickled down her tongue and into her throat making her gag. Perhaps she needed changing, thought Bright. She put the infant down to search for a napkin.

Miss Bytheway appeared. 'I cannot have this noise! It can be heard in the drawing room. Why are you not attending to your child?'

'I am . . .'

'No you are not! Look at her, she is almost demented with hunger.'

'I've tried to feed her but she won't take it.'

'Stupid girl! Why do you think she's crying?' Miss Bytheway was still clutching a lace handkerchief in one hand.

'Perhaps she wants her nappy changing.'

'Tut! I can see you're not fit to cope alone. That child would be dead in two days. Give her to me.'

Bright held up the napkin she had just found. 'But – '

'Give her to me!' Miss Bytheway jerked her outstretched arms impatiently.

Bright had no option but to relinquish the screaming Oriel to the other woman.

'Now pass me the bottle.' Miss Bytheway took a chair by the fire and when handed the bottle put the teat to Oriel's lips. The child instantly began to suck. 'There! Didn't I say what was wrong. You have a lot to learn about children, Maguire.'

Bright hovered there lamely, watching the woman feed her child and feeling betrayed by Oriel. Looking around the room she noticed the amount of care that had gone into preparing it. Even the baby's name had been spelled out with letters on building bricks. Resentment goaded her to point out Miss Bytheway's mistake, though she did it in crafty fashion by altering the bricks herself.

The woman could not help but notice. 'May I ask why you have done that?'

Bright pulled the child's birth certificate from her pocket, her only valuable possession, and held it out for Miss Bytheway to see. 'Cause that's how her name is spelled.'

'Good heavens! What on earth possessed you to name your child after a window?' demanded Miss Bytheway.

'It's not a window, it's a bird.'

'That's O-r-i-o-l-e,' corrected Miss Bytheway.

Bright felt foolish. 'Well, I like Oriel.' She replaced the certificate in her pocket.

Miss Bytheway was annoyed at this truculence and snapped, 'Well, if you wish to retain your ignorance then let it be so – and there's no point in you wasting time watching! Go down and start preparing tea. There's some ham and some eggs in the larder.'

Without redress, Bright left the room and on her way downstairs investigated the rest of the house. Underneath her own bedroom were two more, one of which was obviously her employer's. It was like a palace. There was a brass bed with a canopy of rich material and tassels, pillowcases edged with thick lace, a bedspread which was the finest example of crochet work – it must have taken twenty years to make with thread as delicate as that – and there was a chest at the foot of the bed, a plump armchair, a bookcase, ornamental globes on the gaslamp that was suspended on a brass stalk from the ceiling, and – oh no, a bath. How many jugs of water would Bright have to carry up these four flights of stairs before it was filled?

The other room had a bed in it but looked unused. Bright descended a flight. On this floor was another bedroom and a huge drawing room with an elegant marble fireplace. There was far too much to take in at one glance. Bright merely gasped before continuing to the ground floor.

Shafts of light permeated the stained glass of the vestibule door, casting its colours onto the floor. At the foot of the stairs she was presented with four doors: one obviously led to the back garden, another under the staircase led to the cellar. She opened the one nearest to the front door and found a very pretty dining room-cum-parlour. The carpet was somewhat faded but it had been a grand one in its prime. The wallpaper was a pinky beige decorated with crimson roses and green sprigs. At the centre of the room was a small walnut table and four balloon backed chairs. Atop the cast iron fireplace sat an ebony display cabinet crammed full of pottery, china and glass. There were several gilt-framed portraits on the wall and dozens of prints and a few photographs of an elderly couple. There was a dark red velvet sofa, and a most ornate coal scuttle with what Bright considered to be a work of art painted on the lid — a galleon on wind-tossed seas. There were tapestries, lace runners and anti-macassars, macramé panels, exquisitely embroidered pictures, all done by Miss Bytheway she was later to discover, a beaded footstool, and stacks of cushions. The mantelpiece wore a red velvet skirt edged with bobbles. There was a lace curtain at the window, an arrangement of wax fruit under a glass dome, and a delft paraffin lamp with an opaque globe. On the sideboard there was an ornate ruby glass centrepiece from which hung ten little icicles. It was all very plush and forbidding, nothing like the family home Bright was used to. Feeling that she didn't belong here, she ducked back into the hall to enter through the last door which opened onto the kitchen. This was comparatively austere with only a pine table, a few chairs and all the necessary implements for cooking. Yet another door and two steps led to the scullery, where Bright set to work preparing tea.

In a while, the woman came down. Bright had set a place at the table in the dining room. Miss Bytheway nodded approvingly as Bright put the meal before her. 'I see you have a little more competence as a servant than as a mother.'

'Thank you, ma'am.' Bright wondered miserably why she had thanked her employer for the insult. 'Will that be all?'

'For the moment. You will return later for a list of instructions.' Even at the table Miss Bytheway still clutched the same handkerchief, toying with its lace edges.

'May I go and change Oriel?'

'There's no need, it's all done. She's asleep, so you have no need to disturb her. You must be hungry too, go and take your own meal in the kitchen. I shall ring for you if I require anything further.'

'Very good, ma'am. Thank you.' Bright dutifully left the room, but in a short while crept upstairs to check on Oriel. However, Miss Bytheway had not lied; the child was sleeping peacefully. 'You wee wretch!' Bright pressed her lips together, then went down to resume her tea in the kitchen, though the meal was soured by resentment. This woman seemed determined to take over her role as Oriel's mother.

This was confirmed later in the evening when Miss Bytheway once again gave Oriel her bottle, and afterwards it transpired that the elderly lady had an extra part to play – that of slave driver. The list of daily and weekly chores she had written out for Bright was two pages long. Whilst Bright had never been lazy, as the youngest child and the favourite daughter she had been somewhat cosseted at home and was not familiar with many of the tasks on Miss Bytheway's list. The old lady noticed the startled look in her eye and demanded, 'Well? Are you not up to the work? If not, then . . .'

'Oh yes, ma'am!' Bright was terrified of being relegated to the asylum. 'It's only that I've never done some o' these things before. I might need showing what to do.'

'Never washed clothes?' demanded Miss Bytheway. 'Never scrubbed floors?'

'Well yes, ma'am, but – '

'What is the point of hiring a servant and having to do the job oneself? With my engagement of you, Maguire, I had hoped that I would never have to ask myself that question again, as I have asked it countless times before. I had hoped that you, with a child to think of, would show more responsibility than your predecessors, that you would be grateful. But if you are unwilling to offer anything in return then I trust you will say so now.'

'I can do it, ma'am,' insisted Bright. 'It's just that this is such a big house. I mean, my family never had anything so grand, I've never had the practice . . .'

'Then you will get plenty of practice here. Use your common sense and you will have no argument with me.' Miss Bytheway sounded reasonable. 'Obviously I do not expect perfection in your first few days, I am not a tyrant.' To endorse this she indicated a pile of clothes on a chair. 'And one cannot expect you to be efficient without the proper accoutrements. Take those up to your room. You will find two print dresses, four white caps and four collars – which I expect to be freshly starched each day. You will be allowed two woollen dresses for winter.' She looked with disapproval on Bright's shabby footwear. 'I did not anticipate having to buy shoes. You will go out tomorrow for a new pair.' She interpreted Bright's expression and tutted. 'Don't worry! I shall give you the money. Little did I know that my act of charity might render me bankrupt.'

Bright thanked her and picked up the stack of clothes.

'You will find household cleaning items in the scullery cupboard. Before you go,' Miss Bytheway went to a shelf and removed a thick tome, handing it to Bright, 'I assume you can read?'

Bright was humiliated. 'I was a pupil teacher before . . .' She hung her head.

Miss Bytheway was unimpressed. 'Well now you are a servant, from whom I expect competence.' She placed the *Book of Good Housekeeping* on top of the pile of clothes in Bright's arms. 'This will be of great assistance. I suggest you refer to it this evening in preparation for tomorrow. You may go.'

Utterly downtrodden, Bright left the room. However hard she tried to concentrate on the book her mind kept straying to Oriel at the top of the house. What was the point in having a child one was not allowed to see? It wasn't fair. Nothing was bloody fair.

Later on at ten o'clock there came the opportunity to be with her baby at last. Miss Bytheway announced that she always retired at this hour and expected Maguire to do likewise. 'If you have to rise through the night to attend to the child do not make a noise. I shall expect a fire to be lighted in all downstairs rooms and breakfast on the table at seven-thirty. You will keep the nursery fire alight at all times. There is a receptacle in the yard in which to dispose of the hot ashes.' She came as close to a smile as was possible. 'Goodnight, Maguire.'

'Goodnight, ma'am.' Bright dimmed all the gaslights and ensured the grates were safe, then sneaked a jug of warm milk and a pail of boiled water to the nursery. She was determined not to miss the pleasure of giving Oriel her bath.

The child had not yet woken for her nightly feed so Bright had plenty of time to prepare this and the bath before rousing her. Oriel arched her back in brief protest as her mother lowered her into the water. 'Don't you dare cry, Oriel Maguire,' warned Bright. The infant relaxed and yawned, allowing her mother to scoop handfuls of warm water over her. Bright examined the tiny body for changes, setting up a one-sided conversation with the child. 'You really showed me up in front of Miss Bytheway, didn't ye?' Oriel beamed. 'There's no need to be so cheerful about it! Why did ye let her feed ye? Ye know how much I've missed ye. She's a weird old stick, isn't she? Never cracks a smile. Did ye see the gob on it when we arrived? Like this.' Bright contorted her mouth. The baby appeared to copy her, causing a giggle. 'I don't know how she manages to keep that bow in her hair, there's barely a wisp to pin it to – probably glued on.' Bright enjoyed another giggle with her baby, who smiled too. 'Ah, I'm glad we can laugh, baby. I've a feeling that life in this house is going to be very hard, for me at least. Still, I should be grateful that she seems to like you. Look at all the toys over there that she's bought for ye. Ye'd think if she loved babies so much she would have had children of her own. Who knows, she might have one somewhere – maybe she's a naughty woman like your mammy, but never had a chance to keep her baby. Oh, Oriel!' She wrapped the dripping babe in a towel and cuddled her intensely. 'I wonder what your dada's doing. He never meant to leave us, ye know. He'd love you if he saw ye.'

Bright opened the towel and smoothed her cheek against the infant's skin. Small hands flailed at her hair. 'Oh, baby, I could sit here all night and talk to you. I could, ye know. Yes, but I've to be up in the morning so we'd better get you dressed and fed.'

Wearing one of the fresh nightgowns that Bright had found in a cupboard, Oriel was given her bottle, linking her eyes with those of her young mother who talked softly to her all the while. When the bottle was drained Bright put Oriel over her shoulder and rubbed her back to bring up wind. The child began to doze. Bright succumbed to fatigue too. She tucked Oriel into her cot and, leaving the bath water to be emptied on the morrow, tiptoed to her cold little room.

Though exhausted, she lay awake for some time, missing Oriel, wondering how long she would be allowed with her child tomorrow and worrying over the list of chores. When she dropped off to sleep she had nightmares that Miss Bytheway wouldn't let her into the nursery, and woke up sweating to find Oriel crying for her two o'clock feed.

Dragging her body up she hurried on tiptoe to the nursery and picked Oriel out of the crib. 'Holy Mother, how can such a rotten stink come from a tiny angel? C'mon, let's get you changed.'

Afterwards, she carried both child and bottle back to her room. Pulling the covers up over them she fed her daughter, who was still beside her when she next awoke.

Bright had slept later than she intended. The clock in the nursery said six-fifteen. She had the baby to feed, four fires to light and breakfast to prepare in just over one hour. Frantic, she struggled into her new print dress, raging at all the buttons, then donned the headwear and apron. Streamers flying on her cap, she sped about her tasks, urging Oriel to hurry and finish her bottle so she could clean the grates and fill the coal buckets. Seven-thirty found her covered in stains – of milk, black lead and coal – which had her running up the five flights of stairs to change. 'And I've hardly had the blessed things on an hour!'

In the event, the mistress received her breakfast at seven-forty, for which Bright was reprimanded. After this Miss Bytheway took over the care of the child. With steps to scrub, brass to clean, clothes to wash, a rabbit to skin and cook for dinner and a succession of dusting and polishing, the only opportunity Bright had of holding her daughter was at bedtime and in the early morning. Life here was one constant round of work and as hard as she tried it was never good enough for her employer, who was forever picking faults. Bright would complain to her daughter – the only person she had to talk to – that this one old woman caused as much work as an entire army.

'Ye know, I find it very mysterious,' she told Oriel during one of their nightly 'conferences'. 'She doesn't appear to have any family, and no one else calls on her. Mindst, I'm not surprised she's no friends if the way she treats me is anything to go by. Apart from visiting folk in hospital the only place she goes is church.' Bright herself had not yet been to Mass, though she had lied when Miss Bytheway asked if she had for she still harboured the fear that the nuns would decide she wasn't caring for Oriel properly and take her away. This was irrational; she knew it was, the child was thriving here. But the fear remained with her. Indeed, fear of one thing or another was to dog Bright for the rest of her life. And there was not a day went by without her thinking of Nat. She thought of her family too. That was another reason for not going to Mass. Her father would be there and she wouldn't know what to say to him. She desperately wanted to see him — all of them — but by design rather than accident. Perhaps if she paid a secret visit to her mother first that would ease the way to a reunion.

One weekday morning, on impulse, Bright asked her employer, 'Er, might I be permitted to nip out and call on my mother, ma'am? Tis the only time she's alone, through the day.'

'But you have work to do here!' The elderly lady plucked at the sliver of lace that protruded from her other fist.

Initially, Bright had assumed that the ever-present handkerchief meant that her employer was suffering from a cold, but had come to discover that it was some kind of habit. 'I've done all there is to do before dinnertime. I wouldn't be long, an hour at most, and I haven't had any time off since I came here.'

Her mistress was astounded. 'You've been here barely a fortnight and you are asking for time off? Besides, I understood that your father had barred you from the house.'

'He has. That's why I have to go when my mother's alone. Please, Miss Bytheway, she hasn't seen her granddaughter in weeks.'

'I would have thought that would be a relief. I'm sure your mother does not wish to be reminded that she has an illegitimate grandchild.' She saw Bright's mouth open to argue, and flicked her wrist. 'Oh very well, you may go! I shall expect you back within the hour. But you cannot take Oriel. There may be a risk involved if your father returns unexpectedly. I shall take good care of her.'

So Bright was forced to go alone. Perhaps it was the right thing to do; it wouldn't be kind to march up to her parents' door holding an illegitimate baby. When she got to the Pig Market she found it difficult to go further, but eventually found the courage to do so. Unsure of whether to knock or go straight in, she hesitated before opening the door and listening for a moment. Her mother was humming in the scullery. Bright crept further in, then stopped dead in alarm. Her father was lying on a chairbed by the fire. She stood there frozen, then saw that he was asleep and quite obviously ill, for his face was like putty. Her mother was still humming. Bright deliberated. If she tiptoed past and into the scullery her mother would shriek, maybe drop a plate and wake Dada. If she retreated now, neither of them would be any the wiser, but she could not take her eyes off her father. She wanted to go and sit at his bedside and kiss his brow and beg his forgiveness. She heard an intake of breath; her mother had come out of the scullery, seen Bright and now stood transfixed. Mrs Maguire cast a terrified glance in the direction of her husband, who remained asleep. She did not know whether to summon Bright into the back or shove her out the front. After agonizing indecision she crooked her hand frantically and Bright tiptoed into the scullery, where Mrs Maguire closed the door. Still not saying a word she went out into the yard, beckoning furiously to her daughter. Only when the door was shut did she break her silence. 'For God's sake whatever are ye doing here? He'll kill the pair of us!'

'I had to come and see you! I miss you.'

The gentle eyes were tortured. 'Bright, the Sisters tell

me you've been found a good home with a lady who takes care of ye, be satisfied with that!'

'I can't! I hate it living with her! She doesn't talk to me. Mammy, you're looking at me as if I'm mad!'

Mrs Maguire looked uncomfortable. The memory of the asylum was all too fresh. 'No, I'm not!'

'You are! I'm not mad, I just want to be with my family!'

'The Bright Maguire I used to know wouldn't be so ungrateful.'

'I'm not, I swear it! I know how lucky I am to have a roof over my head and to keep my baby but I miss you, Mammy, I miss you!'

They both fell together crying.

'Your father's not well.' Mrs Maguire pulled away and sniffed into her handkerchief. 'We don't know what it is, neither does the doctor. It just seems like the light's gone out of him since you left.'

Bright's heart sank. Oh please God, not more guilt. 'Let me talk to him.'

'No! He'll never forgive ye, Bright, and you'll get me into bother.'

'Then I'll come to Mass and pretend to be surprised at seeing ye,' decided Bright. 'That way it won't implicate you.'

'It doesn't matter which way ye do it, you'll aggravate his illness, and you'll be hurting yourself too.'

'I'm hurting already, Mammy.'

Mrs Maguire saw that arguing was doing no good. 'Where's herself?'

'I had to leave her behind. Miss B wouldn't let me bring her. You'd think it was her child the way she goes on.'

Mrs Maguire was stern. 'Ye should be thankful she's not against her.'

'Oh, I am! But I hate the way she's taken over. The first chance I get I'm away to find another job.'

'Nobody'll take ye,' said Mrs Maguire with surety.

'Miss B did,' contradicted Bright. 'There must be others like-minded. Then I'll work and save and buy me and Oriel a place of our own.'

'Head in the clouds as ever.' An anguished Mrs Maguire reached for the sneck. 'Look, I'll have to go in, he may have woken.'

'Oh, must you? It's been lovely seeing you. Will you tell Dad I'll be at Mass on Sunday?'

'Sure I will not!' came the scandalized whisper. 'And I doubt you'll be welcome there ever again after the terrible sin you committed.' Mrs Maguire turned back to deliver an earnest plea. 'Won't you reconsider?'

Bright shook her head.

Her mother shook hers in despair, gave Bright a swift fierce kiss then left her alone in the yard.

Bright returned to Fulford well before the allotted hour, so pleasing her elderly employer who granted her request to visit church on the Sabbath.

Sunday came. Bright's pulse was racing even before she had left the house. By the time she reached George Street where the church was situated she was beginning to panic. Nevertheless, she went inside, crossed herself with holy water, genuflected to the altar and slipped into a pew. Her family was in the pew across the aisle. Her mother, having anticipated this, had already seen Bright and was looking nervous. The others had not noticed her yet, being immersed in silent devotion. One by one they raised their heads and sat back in the pew to await Mass. Bright continued to look at them. Martin happened to turn his head, saw her and froze for a second, then gave her the most despising look, which shook her to the core. He nudged those on either side of him, Patrick and Eilleen. Patrick shared his condemnation. Eilleen looked as if she wanted to smile but daren't. The others had all noticed Bright now. Only her father seemed unaware, as if he were in a trance. He looked extremely ill. Mass began. Bright slipped back into the familiar ritual. It helped to give her the strength she needed to face him.

When Mass was over she stepped into the aisle, genuflected, then turned to her father. He did not appear to recognize her. There was nothing in his eyes, neither love nor fury. He simply stepped past her and walked towards the exit.

'Shameless!' came the horrified murmur from an erstwhile neighbour. Yet another: 'How can she do this to her people?'

Bright ignored the accusing faces, the loud whispers, and took a step after him. 'Dada . . .'

She felt her arm caught and looked around to face her brother Martin. 'Keep away from him, bitch. Keep away from all of us. You've ruined this family.' It was the softest of murmurs, the cruellest of blows. Saying nothing more, the Maguires left.

Bright wandered in their wake, like a dog that has been abandoned but refuses to believe it. Then, outside the church anger replaced dejection. What had she done that was so wrong it could not be forgiven? None of this was her fault. 'How can you do this?' she screeched after them. 'You're my family! The ones who're meant to love me, to look after me! I didn't ask for any o' this! It's not my fault!' None of them, not even her mother turned to look at her. They continued to walk up the street in a tight bunch. She knew then that it was over.

14

The orange, amber and gold of fall gave way to the sparkle of frost and the cattle were driven down from the high plateaux to winter forage on the prairies. Now an accomplished hand, Nat joined in the drive, herding the steaming, bellowing mass across icy gushing rivers, down towards the log cabin where a hot bath and good food awaited, yelling and laughing to his companions and enjoying every minute, despite the cold.

Snow came, transforming the land. Indeed, Nat found his whole life transformed, for the hacking bronchitis that was his usual winter companion failed to arrive. Though there were deep drifts and the temperature plummeted to a level unheard of at home, the atmosphere was crisp and dry with brilliant blue skies, and occasionally the balmy chinooks would waft down from the Rockies to temporarily alleviate winter's grasp before the next onslaught. Nat did not mind the snow, even ventured out in it for enjoyment. Wrapped up in warm clothes, it was a joy to set out towards those mountains, even though he knew he would never reach them, content merely to look and to wish and to dream upon their summits as he trudged in the ghostly calm of that white wilderness, unimpeded by foggy alleyway and greasy cobblestone.

Sometimes, though, in certain lights the mountains turned to jade, bringing a deep inexplicable melancholy to his breast when for all this splendour, he would wish himself back in York with its narrow streets and narrow minds, just so that he could see Bright once again.

The thaw came. Frozen streams gushed new life into the

mountains and a million alpine flowers blazed across their meadows. That summer Aunt Lucy announced that she was planning a 'ho-down' in celebration of Queen Victoria's Diamond Jubilee. All their neighbours would be invited, however distant, which meant a reunion for Nat with other Industrial School boys, some of whom he had not seen since last Thanksgiving. Though not particularly close to any of them, they were nevertheless a link with his past and he showed pleasure at seeing those who turned up at the barn dance that summer afternoon, and to hear how all were getting on. Like his, their faces were tanned and healthy, their hair longer. However, apart from this it transpired that, for them, things had not improved much since their last meeting. They were still regarded as slave labour.

'You jammy bugger,' accused one of them, Rymer, on seeing all that Nat had on offer and envying the open displays of affection from the Andersons that Nat found so irksome. 'I'll bet you inherit the bloody place after they snuff it.'

Nat sought to correct the impression that he was rich. 'I don't get paid or owt, though! I mean they're good to me, but it's not as if I can do as I like. Where can you go with no money?' He shrugged.

'Why would you want to go anywhere else when you've got all this and your old bloke buys you everything you ask for?' objected Rymer, the others nodding. 'He'll be dead in a few years and you'll cop for the lot.'

A fiddler led the band into its opening number, and people took to the dance floor. The youths eyed a group of girls at the other end of the barn, who twittered and bridled and invited closer inspection. 'Go on, you go first!' Rymer elbowed Nat, who displayed non-interest.

'They're too young.'

'They've got tits, haven't they?' argued Rymer.

'You go, then,' suggested Nat.

Rymer laughed and turned to the other boys. 'Are you coming?'

Dickson turned up his nose. 'They're not my type.' When pressed for explanation he added, 'I only bet on certainties. You won't get anything out o' them.'

'That ginger-haired one goes like a rabbit,' leered Rymer.

'How would you know?' teased another boy, Simpson.

'I've had her,' came the reply.

'Go on!'

'I have!' And Rymer proceeded to go into lurid details. The others were not sure whether or not to believe him, and so invented exploits of their own.

'What sort o' woman d'you like then?' Simpson asked Nat who, to much laughter gave a coarse description of his fantasy, whilst in reality his vision was of Bright.

'Away, we're wasting time,' urged Rymer.

'I've told you, you go if you want to,' repeated Nat. 'I'm having something to eat before all them greedy buggers scoff it. The women'll still be there later on.'

In agreement, the youths broke from their talkative huddle to scrummage over the food tables, the contents of which had kept the womenfolk busy in the kitchen for days. Nat poured himself a glass of soda, piled his plate high and went to sit on a hay bale alongside Rymer and two others, where they continued their former theme until some other youth marched up to the girl of Rymer's dreams and whisked her onto the dancefloor. 'Oh well, she's a slut anyway,' he decided, and the conversation changed.

'D'you ever miss anything about England?' Nat asked above the music before cramming his mouth with food.

As always, Rymer was the most vociferous, spraying the listeners with flakes of cherry pie. 'You must be mad! I might not get paid much where I am but there's better places than England to go if I want to move on. I'm never

off back there again. Don't try and crack on you miss it?'
He took another bite, juice dribbling down his chin.

Nat tried to appear nonchalant and took a gulp of soda,
tapping his foot to the vigorous fiddle-playing. More
people were dancing now. 'I wouldn't mind going back for
a visit, just to show them bastards how well I've done – if I
had the fare.'

'You want to try your luck up north, then.' Rymer
finished his pie and sank his teeth into something else. Nat
asked what he meant. 'Haven't you heard?' Crumbs flew.
'There's been a massive goldstrike in the Yukon.' Nat
hadn't heard. Mr Anderson sometimes bought a newspaper when he went into Calgary but the last occasion had
been months ago. Rymer swallowed, wiped his mouth on
his cuff and lowered his voice. 'In fact I'm thinking of
striking out meself but I don't fancy going on me own. Any
of you lot want to come with me?'

The gastronomic offerings lost their appeal. A pastry slid
off Nat's plate and into the straw as his mind became
concentrated on fiscal matters. At the mention of gold, all
his good sense vanished. The early lesson of his childhood,
when the tramp had duped him with the fake coin, was
instantly obliterated in the heat of gold fever. 'When are
you going?'

'You interested?' Rymer looked excited. 'It'll take a bit
o' planning. Got to get enough provisions together, shovels
and things like that, and work out a route.'

Dickson voiced his reluctance. 'I've heard they get terrible winters up there, and it's a bloody long way.'

Simpson agreed, addressing himself to Nat. 'If I had a
good place to live like this I wouldn't be risking it to get
frozen to death.'

Nat pulled a face. 'We get winter here, don't we?'

'Aye, but not like they do up there. And we don't even
know if it's true about the gold.'

'You saying I'm lying?' demanded Rymer.

'No, but you have been known to get the wrong end of the stick and it's a long way to go to find it's a load of cock and bull.'

'So you two won't be coming then?' Having established this, Rymer reserved his conversation for Nat. 'Well, if you don't mind this is secret, so piss off and dance and let the men talk business.'

After the others had walked off, Nat said he was keen to press ahead so as to reach the Yukon before winter, but Rymer insisted that the trip needed careful preparation.

'You realize how far it is? I mean it's a bloody wilderness out there, you know.'

Nat taunted him. 'Why did you mention it, then, if you were going to go all chicken-hearted?' He drained his glass abruptly and set it down.

'I'm not backing out, I'm just saying . . .'

'Look, I've been up in the mountains plenty of times, spent days out there. I know how to survive.' Nat was recklessly boastful. 'I can get horses, tools, food . . .'

'All right!' Rymer fended him off. 'But I still can't go tomorr – ' He broke off as Mrs Anderson danced up, swinging her skirts and beckoning to Nat.

'I can't dance, Aunt Lucy!' Nat resisted her efforts to get him onto the floor.

'Oh, tush! I'll bet it's just an excuse so you can sit talking to your friend here.' Mrs Anderson dealt him a kiss then put an arm around both youths. 'I know it's a long time since you boys've been together but Mr McDonald's got a barn-raising bee coming up next month, so you'll have plenty of chance to chat then. Come on, now, be sociable and dance!' She whisked Nat away, but not before he had dealt Rymer a significant look that warned him to get his plan sorted out by the next time they met.

Nat was occupied in square dancing for the rest of the night and so missed any other opportunity to speak with Rymer, but that did not prevent the subject of gold from occupying his thoughts as he joined the final rendition of *God Save the Queen*. While the band packed away fiddles, guitar and concertina, Mary and Mrs Anderson cleared away the leftover food and the boy helped Mr Anderson to tidy up the barn.

'Did you have a good day, Nat? Enjoyed seeing your friends again? Bet you had plenty of interesting things to talk about.' Anderson unpinned the legs of a trestle and folded them under.

'Yeah,' Nat supported the other end of the table. 'Uncle John, have you heard anything about the gold strike up north?'

'Can't say as I have.' The man seemed more interested in his task.

'Rymer told me about it. He said he might go and try his hand at mining.'

'Fool's game,' came Anderson's denouncement as he folded his end of the table to meet Nat's.

'Why?' Nat flicked the catches that secured the trestle.

''Cause it is.' Anderson paused to rest. 'I never met a man yet who made a fortune out o' digging for gold.'

Nat showed a streak of his natural obstinacy. 'These men have been finding some wacking big nuggets.'

Anderson pinned him with a cynical eye. 'Seen 'em, have you?'

Annoyed at this belittlement, Nat blurted, 'I'm thinking of going meself.'

Anderson was about to move on to another task, but now wheeled round to deliver rebuttal. 'No you're not! I'm not having any son o' mine going on a damnfool goose-chase – why, I don't even know the country up there myself! You'll get yourself killed. Put it right out of your head, and don't you dare mention this in front of Aunt Lucy, she'll worry herself to death. Come on now, get this garbage picked up – and take that sullen look off your face, it's disrespectful to your Queen!'

* * *

At home in England, celebrations for the Queen's Diamond Jubilee had been less boisterous in the Fulford residence, though Bright's employer had allowed her to partake in a glass of sherry to mark the occasion. How different from the party that would be taking place at the Maguire household, and how Bright still missed her family.

The old woman imbibed the last drop of sherry and handed her glass to her servant. 'Most enjoyable!' She sat down.

Bright, who had been staring into her own empty glass, started, then came out of her trance. 'Oh, indeed it was, ma'am, and God bless Her Majesty.'

'Hear, hear. You can wash those now.' Miss Bytheway indicated the glasses.

Bright replied, 'Yes, ma'am,' and in her mind, added, Such a wonderful party. I don't think I'll ever get over the excitement.

'Oh, wait a moment! I have a little treat for Oriel.' Miss Bytheway reached down beside her chair and delved into a bag.

Bright thanked her for the chocolate drops and, putting them into her apron pocket, left the room.

She had just washed the glasses when the doorbell sounded and she hurried to answer it. 'Oh, hello, Sister.' At the sight of the nun a nervous hand came up to pluck at her collar. Her heart began to thud.

'Hello to you, Bright.' The nun's voice was a confidential whisper. 'I'm sorry to be taking you away from your duties but I came to tell you that your poor father died this morning.'

Too shocked to respond, Bright just stared. Being cooped up inside had made her freckles fade, but even so they now stood out in sharp relief against the pallor.

'Your mother thought it was only right that you should be told,' whispered the nun, touching Bright's arm, 'but she says you shouldn't ought to come to the funeral because it might upset people, you know. Anyway, I'm sorry to be the bearer of such horrid news.' She gave a last gentle pat of Bright's hand. 'Away back to your work now.' And with that she was gone.

Stunned, Bright shut the front door then wandered back into the hallway, closing the vestibule door too. Her face drained of any emotion she stood for a moment, then, feeling the little bag of chocolate drops rustle in her apron, she drew it out and stared at it before embarking in a leaden plod up the staircase. Reaching the top, she sat down in the nursery and gazed into space. Oriel was awake and playing in her cot. The child addressed her mother in gibberish. Bright took a chocolate drop from the paper bag and, mechanically, inserted it into Oriel's mouth, then ate one herself. Another for the baby, another for her. Then another, and another. The taste plunged her back into childhood, reminding her of the treats that her sister would bring home from the factory. How could they love her so much one moment and hate her the next? *They don't even want me at the funeral.* Oriel was yelling for another chocolate drop. Her mother did not move, but crumpled the bag in her fist. Her lip began to judder and her eyes bulged with tears. She let them tumble down her cheeks, crying and sobbing, drooling long strands of chocolate-flavoured misery upon her pristine apron front. *Dada. Nat.*

That Anderson assumed his command about the gold-mining would naturally be obeyed only went to prove how little he had learned about Nat during the last year. To him the matter was long forgotten when, several weeks after the Queen's Jubilee he, his wife and Nat arrived back from the McDonald homestead after spending a very enjoyable time helping to erect the new barn. Hence, a great shock was to come the following night when, awoken by a noise from outside, he peered from the window to investigate and sucked in his breath. There was Nat, trying not to make a noise, leading his horse from the barn, a horse that was packed with equipment.

Anderson blinked as if unable to believe such treason. Then overtaken by fury, he rushed downstairs in his night-shirt to surprise the eloper.

And surprise Nat it did. Having just donned his haversack, he gasped as the white-clad figure rushed at him out of the darkness.

'You were creeping off without saying one word of goodbye?' Anderson's whisper was loaded with incredulity.

'It isn't goodbye.' Nat looked shamefaced, one hand gripping the reins of his horse, the other rested on the head of the dog who pressed against his side, tail wagging. 'I'll be coming back when I've made my fortune.'

'No you won't, boy. If you go now you don't never come back.'

Nat sagged and tried to explain. 'Look, I . . .'

'Didn't I forbid you to go on this damn fool mission? Didn't I?'

'Yes.' Nat lifted his palm from the dog's head and ran a thumb between the strap of the haversack and his shoulder.

'Well, I guess you don't know me too well, Nat, cause when I say you don't go, you don't go. Get back to bed!' His yell was meant for one of the ranch hands, who had risen to investigate the disturbance. The bleary face ducked back indoors.

'I'm sorry, but I have to go,' responded Nat. His horse shifted from one leg to the other, creaking its harness.

'Why?' demanded Anderson. 'Give me one good reason, other than greed. You're prepared to risk all you have here – including the love of Mrs Anderson – for some stupid rumour about gold? God damn it, didn't you spare a thought for all the children she'd lost until she got you! Don't you know how your sneaking off like this will break

her heart? My God, you're even stealing her cooking pots!'
He had spotted a pan dangling from Nat's haversack.

Nat dropped his gaze, his blue eyes hidden under the
brim of his hat. 'I've said I'll come back.'

'When? In five years' time when you've exhausted your
claim or in a wooden box – which is far more likely. Why
did you think I forbade you to go? Because I knew you'd as
like get yourself killed as find gold. Why, you don't know
the first thing about life in those frozen wastes!'

Nat removed his hat in an obvious attempt to plead. 'I
have to try, Uncle John . . .'

'Don't you Uncle John me!'

'I'm grateful for all you've done for me.'

'Oh well, thank you, sir, I'm sure!'

'But I – I've a girl at home in England and I've sworn to
bring her out here when I've saved enough money, and you
don't pay me any wage!'

Anderson gasped. 'You expect me to pay for the
privilege of regarding you as my son?'

'I didn't ask to be your son! I would've been happy just
to work here as one of the hands. I'm sorry, I don't mean to
insult you.' Nat averted his eyes from the devastated
expression on Anderson's face. 'You're both really nice
people, but I can't behave the way you want me to behave.
I've got to have money, Mr Anderson.' He chose to dispense with secrecy. It didn't seem to matter now. 'This girl,
she's got my kid.'

The grizzled face twisted. 'You mean you ran out on her
just as you intend to run out on us! I see right through you
now, boy. No wonder you didn't give nothing away!
Coming here under false pretences . . . you never intended
to give your best to this country, all you wanted was an
escape from your problem. You're not doing this simply to
earn the fare to bring that girl here – why, if you'd cared
enough to confide in us we could've helped with that, but
it's sure as hell too late now. I don't want a son I can't

trust. You're motivated by self and nothing else. You don't give a damn about any of us, Mrs Anderson, me nor that girl. Why, you don't even care about that stupid dog! Look at him! How long d'you think he'd last in that frozen north?'

Nat ran the dog's tasselled ear through his fingers and made the reluctant decision. 'I'll leave him here then.' Roy had never really been his anyway.

'You won't leave him cause you're not going!'

'You just said you don't want a son you can't trust.'

Anderson blustered. 'I'm ready to give you one last chance if you do the right thing now.'

Nat felt he had nothing to lose. 'Will you pay me a wage for the work I do?'

'I will not – that's blackmail.'

The youth replaced his hat and inserted his foot in the stirrup, the loaded pack clanking as he moved.

'Dad-burn it, Nat, if you don't get off that horse we're finished! I don't want no son who puts money above his parents!'

You don't want a son at all, thought Nat, leaning forward in the saddle and clicking the horse into motion, you just want to prove how Christian you are, that you can mould a poor unfortunate wastrel into a fine upstanding citizen, so's you can say, look what I've done! Any boy would have sufficed.

But all he offered in reply was, 'I'm sorry,' as his horse carried him towards the road.

Anderson made a rush after him, setting the dog into a frenzy of barking. 'Just wait on a minute! Those're my tools you've got there! My supplies in that sack! I'm damned if I'll let you rob me of anything more!' He tried to grab Nat's leg.

Alarmed, for without supplies his expedition was doomed, Nat gave the buckskin a savage kick, narrowly missing Anderson's head. The horse grunted and lunged into a canter. Anderson still pursued him. Jolting up and down in the saddle, tools clanking in his back pack, Nat flung a hasty apology over his shoulder. 'I'll pay you back when I've struck lucky! I promise!' The gap widened between them.

Crimson with indignation, Anderson gave up his futile chase. The dog stopped too, but continued to bound around him, yelping. 'Don't you come back! Don't you dare come back!' Fists still clenched, he wheeled towards the house and saw his wife at the bedroom window. In the acute silence that followed Nat's departure he could hear her weeping.

Bright had been at the house in Fulford Road for almost a year when, faced with her inability to bear this loneliness, she began to look for another job. There was no physical search for she was hardly ever given time off unless she asked for it, and even then she was quizzed as to her destination and whom she was going to meet. Miss Bytheway seemed obsessed with the idea that Bright must be meeting a man and told her in no uncertain terms what would befall her. Consequently, Bright rarely asked for time off. Besides, where had she to go? She had no friends, nor family to visit. So the quest for a job with accommodation was confined to the front page of the *Yorkshire Evening Press* which she had to take up to bed with her at night, and over which she invariably fell asleep.

The search was unproductive for quite a few days until the post of general servant was advertised. It was a live-in position – ideal – but how was she to ask for time off? The advertisement did not state any particular time of application, so she decided to make it a Sunday when she could tell Miss Bytheway that she was going to Mass.

The house with the vacancy was rather too nearby for comfort, in Fulford itself, but she had to risk it. A maid answered the door. Bright's face fell. 'Oh, has the post already been taken?'

The other smiled. 'No, it's my job you've come for. I'm leaving at the end of the month to get married.' She told Bright to wait in the hall. 'I'm not sure it's a very good time to call. The mistress has just got back from church.'

Bright said it was the only opportunity she had. The other sympathized and said she'd probably get more time off here. After asking her name, the maid disappeared. She was gone for some moments, then came back to usher Bright into a very elegant drawing room which was much more modern than Miss Bytheway's. There was a woman present who said, 'Maguire – is that an Irish name?'

'Yes, ma'am. My parents came from Ireland. I was born in York.'

'Hm. Come and stand before me so that I may see you.' The woman looked her up and down. 'At whose residence are you employed at present?'

'Well, I'm not sure ye'd know the lady, ma'am. I work for Miss Bytheway, she lives in St Oswald's Terrace.'

The other looked thoughtful. 'Is that the eccentric woman?' Bright smiled and said she supposed Miss Bytheway could appear rather odd to others. 'Hmm, I'm not surprised you wish to leave. I've just seen her at church – a halfpenny she put in the collection plate! Show me your hands.' Bright displayed them, having no qualms for she had scrubbed them most vigorously before coming here. All her apparel was befitting a Sunday visit to church. 'Most presentable,' commended the woman. 'Very well, if Miss Bytheway will furnish you with references you may commence employment as soon as my present maid leaves. Speak to her to find out the exact date and ask her to show you your living quarters.'

'Oh, I'm very grateful, ma'am!' responded Bright, again admiring the room. 'It'll be lovely to work in such a house. There's just one thing . . .'

'Yes?'

'I,' *Go on, say it*! 'I have a child. I'd expect to bring her with me if I worked for you.'

'Out of the question! Why did you not tell me this before wasting my time?' The woman rang for the maid who, having been waiting outside, entered almost immediately. 'Green, show this person off the premises!'

'I swear she'd be no trouble, ma'am!' pleaded Bright. 'She's very quiet.'

'That is immaterial! I would never condone a girl such as you setting foot in this house with or without your child. Please leave.'

Bright gave up and left with the maid, who did not seem so friendly on the way out. This was to be her reception to every application she made. After ten similar rebuttals Bright resigned herself to spending the rest of her life at Miss Bytheway's. That life was made even more uncomfortable when someone let the cat out of the bag about her job applications. Bright did not know who it was, it could just have been a casual acquaintance or a neighbour of Miss Bytheway's, it didn't really matter. What was real was that Miss Bytheway was terribly upset and furious that her charity had been so rebuffed.

'No other person would have taken you in!' she railed at Bright. 'Indeed, you have had plenty of evidence of that lately, I'm sure, what with all your efforts to leave here thwarted. To think that I lowered myself! It's quite obvious that you are unwed yet I took you in, you and your illegitimate child whom I treated like a member of my own family – you know how fond I am of her. It's sheer jealousy that makes you want to rob me of her! You cannot stand the thought that I can give her more than you, that I care for her more than her own mother.'

'No, you could never do that,' whispered Bright.

'Don't be impertinent! You have not the faintest idea of how to be a mother, you are only a child yourself.'

But you didn't go through the pain – Bright confined her obstinacy to her thoughts – you have no idea what I'd go through for Oriel. She's the only reason I'm putting up with this, because if I left here we'd have nowhere to go.

'Pray tell me why you chose to be so churlish?' The old lady's hands plucked at her handkerchief. 'Have you not everything you need here?'

'Yes, ma'am, except that I earn no money.'

'Ah! So that is the nub. Not content with being clothed, housed and fed, you expect me to give you money too!'

I've upset her now, thought Bright, I might as well go the whole hog. 'I think I deserve a little wage, ma'am. I do a lot of work.'

'You also do a lot of eating! Why on earth do you need money when all your needs are catered for?'

'Oriel is only tiny now, but when she's grown she'll need clothes.'

'Which I will provide,' countered Miss Bytheway.

'With respect,' a trembling Bright stood up to her employer, 'Oriel is my daughter and I should be responsible for her needs. I – I'd also like to have more time to look after her, but you seem to think I don't care about that.'

'Of course you don't care! If you cared about her welfare you would never have had her in the first place! You had condemned that child to a life of misery until I stepped in and saved her – saved you both! I think you have forgotten that it was I who took you from the asylum, and could just as easily put you back there if I so choose.'

Terror prickled Bright's skin. 'I'm truly grateful that you gave me a home and food and work!' She wondered how she could manage to keep her voice level after such insults. 'All I'm asking is for a few shillings so I can be responsible for my own child, and to be allowed to see her more often.'

'And you imagined that another employer would grant you more time with her than I do?'

Bright hung her head. 'None of them seemed to even want her in the house, nor me.'

'You consider that surprising?' Miss Bytheway stood erect, her black bow quivering with indignation. 'Then consider this: if you had succeeded in finding another post you would have ruined that child's life completely and I shall tell you why. If by some chance Oriel was received into any other household she would be scorned, she would receive little education, when grown to adulthood she would be employed at the lowest grade of work. On the other hand, if she continues to live here I shall endeavour to teach her manners, how to speak correctly, I shall educate her myself – no school for her, where she would be reviled for her mother's sin! In short, I will protect her. She will never learn the slur of illegitimacy in this house. She will be cherished. That is what you were about to throw away, Maguire. That is what sort of a mother you are. Now, do you still wish to leave?' Bright had no option but to shake her head. 'Then we shall say no more about it.' Miss Bytheway lifted her head at the sound of a wail. 'That, I think, is Oriel telling us she is hungry. You have work to catch up with. I shall go and attend to her.'

The white-haired lady turned at the door, still looking annoyed. 'However, you are obviously under the impression that you have been mistreated here.'

'Oh, no!' Bright wondered why she had negated this when it was quite obvious that she was being exploited.

'I cannot have you harbouring feelings of bitterness against me, it will make your work suffer and we shall all be unhappy. Therefore, in addition to one florin per week, you will receive Sundays off. I may require you to light the fire and prepare breakfast but that will be all. The time will not be for frittering away, you may go to church in the morning and spend the afternoon in some useful pursuit such as reading or taking your daughter out for fresh air.' With this, the woman made a dignified exit, leaving a gawking Bright to marvel at her own powers of persuasion.

15

Nat waited several hours for Rymer at the appointed place before concluding that he was not coming. Having thought to his own safety, he built a campfire, then decided to bed down for the night, mulling over what to do. The plan had been to head north for Edmonton where they would re-equip with supplies before going on to the Yukon, but Nat had no money. Rymer had promised to bring what he had saved in return for Nat supplying tools and food. The other had also been in possession of a map and compass. It may be difficult to proceed without these but, daunted or not, Nat had little option. Maybe when he reached Edmonton he could sell the horse and buy what he needed in order to reach the Klondike goldfields. If Rymer turned up before morning, all well and good, but Nat was not going to let his absence ruin this chance of riches.

Having made his decision, he rolled nearer to the fire and tried to sleep, cursing Rymer and thinking of Uncle John's anger. Even for one who scorned company it was nerve-racking to be alone out here, with eyes peering at you out of the gloomy whispering forest and the bloodcurdling howl of wolves. With each rustle of leaf he imagined a grizzly exploding from the bushes to grab him by the throat. The image became all too real. He struggled to remove himself from the ripping jaws and moved nearer to the glow of his fire. *Keep calm.* Uncle John told you, if one comes you just stay still and play dead and he'll go away. His horse whickered and snorted. Nat sat upright to listen, flesh crawling. The constant whirr of crickets made it difficult to hear whether something was sneaking up on him. His ears strained. *Fool! Stop it, there's nothing there.* He lay down and closed his eyes, whereupon a manic figure came screaming at him out of the night: 'Waaaagh!'

Nat leaped up with a terrified yell and prepared to die as the whites of the madman's eyes loomed right up to his face.

'Rymer, you fucking bastard!' He fell upon his tormentor who was now doubled up braying and cackling, hardly able to find the strength to defend himself due to his uncontrollable laughter. 'I'll fucking kill you!'

Eventually, after a particularly effective blow from Nat, Rymer warded him off and clambered to his feet, still managing to uphold his amusement at the other's alarm. 'Oh, God, your face! You almost shit yourself!'

'Where've you bloody well been till now?' demanded a shirty Nat, and flopped back beside the fire.

'Didn't bloody wait for me did you, fart face?' Rymer sat opposite Nat upon his rolled up ground sheet and reached for the coffee pot that was balanced on some stones by the fire, wincing at the heat of the handle. 'Unless you hadn't noticed, I've only got two legs.'

The campfire illuminated Nat's frown. 'Well, that's gonna hold us back a bit.'

'Oh thanks! Make sure you're all right, won't you? I thought you said you could supply the nags?'

'There was nowt to stop you borrowing one,' parried Nat.

'Round here they call it stealing,' corrected Rymer, using Nat's tin mug as a receptacle for his coffee.

'It never bothered you before. What about the compass — I hope you got it?' Nat was aware of Rymer's plan to steal this from his guardian.

'As far as I know they don't hang you for pinching a compass. And, yes, I got it.'

'Would they hang you for stealing a horse?' Nat was curious.

Rymer took a sip of the coffee and shuddered at its bitter taste. 'Not sure, but I know a horse is worth more than a man around here.' He spoke from experience of his own treatment.

'Did you fetch your money?' asked Nat.

'I did better than that.' Rymer grinned. 'I talked two of the others into giving me all their savings in exchange for a cut of any gold I find.'

'And they believed you?' Nat looked disgusted.

'Eh, I don't steal off my pals!' objected Rymer. 'I meant it fair and square. I told 'em if they're too scared to do it on their own I'll do a bit o' prospecting on their behalf. They've been saving for a long time. Our boss never let us go into town so we never had a chance to spend it. Y'see, I been doing a bit o' thinking: wouldn't it be awful if the money ran out before we reached the Yukon? With their donations we needn't worry about that now.'

'No, but how much gold will they want in return?' scoffed Nat. 'Well, I can tell you now, this deal is nowt to do with me. I won't be giving them a cut of anything I find.'

Unable to palate either the coffee or the reply, Rymer tipped his cup at the ground. 'Don't worry, tight-arse, from what I've heard there'll be plenty to go round. Don't bother thanking me will you? How much money did you provide by the way?' The demand was sarcastic, Rymer knowing very well that Nat was penniless. 'A long way you would've got without me.'

Nat laid down as if to sleep. 'We won't get anywhere if you keep talking.'

Rymer jumped up. 'Right, I'll just have a piss.' He disappeared momentarily into the gloom, then came back to unroll his groundsheet. 'Where's that dog o' yours, by the way?'

'Left it behind,' mumbled Nat.

'You stupid sod! We could've done with it to pull our supplies.'

'He's not used to hard work, he would've just held us back.'

'Maybe, but we could've sold him to some mug – big buggers like him are worth a fortune up there.' Rymer threw himself down. 'Did you have any trouble getting away?'

Nat shuffled onto his side. 'Aye, t'old fella caught me.'

'What did he say?'

'He wished me luck and asked me to fetch him back a stick of rock with Klondike printed all the way through – what d'you think he bloody said?'

'Well, I don't know, do I?' objected Rymer. 'You're his blue-eyed boy.'

'Well, that wasn't what he called me when I left. Anyway, shut up and get some sleep.' Nat closed his eyes.

Rymer was silent for a while, then muttered, 'Do these bloody crickets get on your nerves?'

Nat had almost been drifting into oblivion. The intrusion brought a sigh. 'Not as much as you do.'

Unmoved, Rymer asked, 'D'you know what I'm gonna do with all this gold?'

'Buy yourself a new set of teeth,' growled Nat, 'cause if you don't shut up I'm gonna smash them out.' He tensed, waiting for Rymer to say more, but after a yawn and a few moments of rustling silence returned, and that was the last thing he heard until morning.

At first light, after breakfast, the two boys embarked into the wilderness on the first two hundred miles of their journey. The terrain was difficult to navigate, almost every step of their route imperilled by some natural obstacle: wide rivers over which they had no recourse but to swim, rocky outcrop that threatened to lame the horse, and deep chasms that yawned out of nowhere. Where there were roads these were primitive and often disappeared into bush. They shared the horse, one riding for so many miles whilst the other walked, then vice versa. In the weeks it took to reach Edmonton the trees had turned to scarlet and gold and the nights shimmered with frost. As if this were not hardship enough the food began to run out, necessitating meagre rations for the last leg of this arduous trek. Having no rifle, they were compelled to watch as a partridge broke cover and flew away. They laid snares without success, their only luck arriving in the shape of a solitary Blackfoot Indian who exchanged some dried meat for Rymer's knife. When they finally arrived at their destination in the fall they had not eaten for two days.

Edmonton was the main depot for fur traders and served the greater region of the north-west. Though the land around it was very flat the town itself was situated on a high table of ground overlooking the thickly wooded valley of the North Saskatchewan River, which at one point was a mile in width. The streets were wide, too, and never was an exhausted Nat more grateful to reach anywhere as he and Rymer led their jaded horse into town that sunny September day.

'Oh God,' puffed a weary and dust-covered Rymer, dragging his feet at the very thought of the thousands of miles that lay ahead. 'I don't think I can face going any further.'

Nat murmured reassurance, as much for himself as for the other youth. 'You'll be all right after a rest. Just keep your mind fixed on that gold.'

At that precise moment food took precedence over all else. Using Rymer's money they healed their starvation before taking a room in an hotel where they had a bath, a shave and luxuriated in clean cotton sheets for the next two nights whilst they and their horse recouped strength for the much longer excursion that lay ahead. By this time, the memory of that awful first leg was beginning to fade and Rymer's enthusiasm had returned. They bought clothes more fitted to the Arctic temperatures they would have to endure – padded coats, snow shoes, fur-lined boots and gloves – and as much food as they could carry, in the shape of dried meat, bacon, beans and biscuits. It transpired that they would have little need of the compass, having only to follow the hundreds of other prospective miners who had also stopped to restock in Edmonton.

'I've been talking to this bloke.' A smirking Rymer joined Nat, who was busy loading up the horse on the morning of their departure. 'He said if we'd taken the train to Vancouver we could've got a ship right up the coast to Alaska. We walked all that way for nowt!' He ended on a giggle.

'Oh, that's bloody hilarious, that is!' Nat shoved the other's elbow off the saddle and, with obvious bad temper, continued his task.

'Well, I weren't to know was I?' Rymer spread his palms. 'I've never done this sort o' thing before. Anyway, what we have to do now is to make our way over the Rockies.'

'Oh well, that shouldn't take us long.'

'Then through British Columbia to the coast. We must be able to go some of the way by river.'

'Hang on, I'll just stick a paddle up this horse's arse.'

Rymer dealt him a shove. 'No, dummy, we use it to carry the stuff most of the way and when we get to a river what'll take us to the coast we sell it.'

Nat performed a last check of the horse's cinch. 'Which way do we go then?'

Rymer consulted his map. 'I think . . . we need to head for the Yellowhead Pass, here.' He stabbed at the paper.

'Right, take your last look at civilization and let's be off then.' Without further preamble Nat bounced into the stirrups.

'I suppose that means I'm walking,' muttered Rymer to himself and, hefting his pack, followed Nat out of town.

The route to Edmonton which they had previously found

so exacting was as a Sunday School jaunt compared to the thousands of miles of wilderness that lay before them, with precipice, glacier and ravine all conspiring to hinder their fortunes. Hidden gorges awaited them like Venus flytraps waiting to catch any unfortunate insects, for indeed Nat and Rymer were as insignificant as flies upon this vast terrain. Nat enjoyed solitude, but even he was unnerved by such a degree of isolation and began to ponder on all the mishaps which could befall them. Why, if they should trip and fall victim to one of the numerous black caverns their skeletons would remain undiscovered for eternity! Prey to such thoughts, he was glad now that he had waited for Rymer, who at least was good for a joke to lighten the journey.

Contrary to all nightmares, disaster was to strike first in the shape of the tiniest chip of rock which became lodged in the horse's hoof. The lame animal brought quandary: they had counted on it to provide extra finance when they reached the nearest waterway, so did they leave it behind and throw away this source of cash, force it to walk on in the hope that a town was nigh, or remain here for a few days until it recovered? With the acceptance that they were going to lose money one way or another they decided to press on with the horse and by extreme good fortune happened upon a trapper's camp within a few miles. Here they managed to sell the nag, though at a far reduced price than it was worth. After spending the night amongst the first humans they had seen for weeks, they rose again to wend their lonesome way through canyon and creek.

Leaves fell, the temperature dropped. Their hair grew long, their clothes were filthy. Rations dwindled and their diet became monotonous, but with every hardship they kept reminding each other that there was gold at the end of this nightmarish trek. This and this alone kept Nat alive. There were many times during those weeks when Rymer would have gladly turned over and continued to sleep forever had his companion not kicked and bullied him into going on. Their morning greetings became less and less affable, new names were exchanged, none of them complimentary, but somehow the angry words and desperation served as fodder. Somehow, despite the months of hardship, they finally staggered upon the coast of British Columbia and, to much rejoicing that they would no longer have to rely on their aching feet, sought passage on a boat that would carry them north.

Their isolation at an end, Nat and Rymer found great pleasure in the company of other budding goldminers, for the vessel was crammed with men from every nationality and all walks of life; bank managers, butchers, tailors, gamblers, all infected by the same disease and each a source of information to be milked. The pair discovered from one who had investigated this more thoroughly than they had that there were rules and regulations to be followed. The North-West Mounted Police had stipulated that miners must have a year's supply of provisions in order to be allowed into the Yukon.

Rymer turned to glance at Nat. 'I didn't know that, did you?'

Nat was unconcerned. 'No, but we would've stocked up anyway once we're ashore.' He regarded the man's attire with a critical eye. 'You don't look like a miner.'

'That I am not,' conceded their informant, whose face had been wizened by the frustrations of his job rather than the outdoor life. 'But unlike you I had the nous to investigate every aspect of prospecting before I gave up my somewhat safer career. I was a bank clerk. Thirty years of counting other people's fortunes whilst I and my wife had to make do with a comparative pittance. Rather than rob the bank I decided to take my chance here. Oh, I have no illusions, it's going to be hard — I hope you realize that too.' He beheld his young companions with the falsely authoritative air of one who has always craved subordinates, and now seized upon these two as vessels into whom he could pour his accumulated wisdom.

Rymer assured him, 'We're not afraid of hard work, sir. Thanks for the advice, we'll stock up when we arrive.' Nat despised him for making them appear green, and looked away as if to disassociate himself.

'My pleasure, young man. Er, you hail from England if I'm not mistaken.'

Rymer grinned. 'Yeah, we – '

'What about you, sir?' Nat, unprepared to let Rymer tell everyone their business, turned to address an intellectual-looking man who stood eavesdropping nearby.

The man coughed and inclined his head. 'Oh, I am a schoolteacher, or was until a few days ago.' Nat balked and gave Rymer a nudge that suggested they depart. 'However, like this gentleman here I too have made vigorous investigation before embarking on my mission. It seemed only wise to do so.' Undeterred that the boys were edging away, he began to impart his own particular brand of knowledge which centred on the politics of the region. 'You see,' he tucked his thumbs behind his lapels, unable to eschew his previous role in life, 'the only effective route to the Klondike is by way of the Lynn Canal which cuts across the Alaskan panhandle, the boundary of which has never been clearly defined since the Americans purchased it from Russia. Our government is trying to claim jurisdiction over the head of the canal so that we miners can bring in supplies without paying American customs duties, and – '

Rymer cut him off. 'You mean we have to pay to get in?'

'As yet I fear the argument is unresolved.' The schoolmaster showed that he did not appreciate being interrupted. 'Now . . .'

Nat exchanged a look with Rymer, then abruptly dragged him away. 'What a tosser! I didn't go through all that just to be bored to death. Come on, those blokes look a bit more interesting.'

With such a diversity of passengers boredom proved easy to escape. What could not be evaded was the monotonous throb of the engine whilst one was attempting to sleep, the gut-churning swell of the waves, and the increasing discomfort of the weather. As before, Nat and Rymer kept despair at bay by repeating their creed: this would all be worth it in the end. Eventually, the ship reached the icy fiords of the Alaskan panhandle, and Nat and Rymer joined in the loud cheers that accompanied its berth, mercifully unaware that the worst part of their journey was still ahead of them.

Unsure of their next move, but nevertheless euphoric at being here, Nat and Rymer merely followed the example of all the other thousands of hopefuls as they tottered from the ship into the clutches of the Alaskan winter, breathing their disbelief at the savagery of the landscape.

On the beach hundreds of tents marked the starting point of the miners' journey, the breath of man and dog joining in one fetid pall on the icy air. Even in the brief moments that Nat and Rymer had been standing here the cold began to permeate the fur lining of their boots and Nat, banging his gloved palms together, suggested they should make a fire. After this, they pitched their tent alongside the others, melted some ice to provide water and warmed their innards with a meal of bacon and beans, the relief from which was all too temporary. As the afternoon dwindled so the risk of frostbite increased. Icy pincers tweaked at extremities, removing all feeling. In an effort to keep warm Nat and Rymer gathered wood with which to build a crude sled; this they dragged to the store in town and loaded it with the year's supplies they had been informed they would need. With the optimism of the young and foolhardy they struggled to drag the vehicle back to the camp; it would not budge. To much laughter from the more experienced onlookers, Nat gave the sled a furious kick and, after angry debate with Rymer, went off to buy a more serviceable one while Rymer guarded the provisions.

Night was cold beyond belief. Even tucked inside his sleeping bag and this enveloped by the tent Nat could not get warm, woken constantly by the agonizing ache in his kneejoints and the howling and fighting of sled dogs. Long before dawn came to these Godforsaken climes he was restless to be off.

He and Rymer breakfasted in darkness and by the time it did get light they were on their way to the Yukon along a trail of glaciers and snowdrifts. With many gone before them and no snowfall in the last few days the trail was hard packed, otherwise the load would have been impossible to pull without dogs. Nevertheless, it was not easy with one tugging from the front and the other pushing from the rear. The effort made them sweat, and moisture twinkled on the fur of their coats and immediately froze. That others had experienced similar hardships became all too evident from the abandoned canoes, worn out boots and broken bottles that littered the winding trail. Nat had hoped to make at least ten miles that first day, but after only half this distance their muscles and bones ached as if they had travelled for days and they were forced to stop and rest.

'It's no good,' rasped Nat when he had managed to catch his breath, the polar air scouring his throat and lungs each time he inhaled. 'We'll have to chuck some of this stuff off.'

An equally exhausted Rymer agreed. 'But what? We need all of it.'

Nat puffed, feeling the warmth of his own breath against his petrified cheek. 'Well, we can get rid o' one o' these tins o' meat right now.' He reached into a sack. 'I'm famished.'

'Oh yes, one tin is gonna make a big difference, I don't think.'

Nat was in no mood for sarcasm. Every tooth in his head ached with cold. 'Just make yourself useful and get a fire going!'

'You would have thought the shopkeeper would've warned us not to buy too many tins,' opined Rymer, hacking at branches of pine.

'He's hardly gonna chuck away custom, is he?' derided Nat. 'We should've known better.'

Wintriness forbade too long a delay. After the meal they performed a ruthless inventory, dispensing with the heaviest items on the sled, one of which was the tent. At Rymer's misgivings Nat exchanged logic. 'We're gonna be bloody cold whether we've got it or not! Let's get rid of some of these tins an' all.'

'But that bloke said we'd need . . .'

'I don't care what that tosser said!' Nat's jaws were even more painful with the reaction of hot food upon cold teeth. 'We won't be able to eat it if we're dead from the effort of dragging this bloody sledge. There has to be somewhere we can restock along the way. At the rate we've been going we'll average about two inches per day if we're lucky.' Tins were hurled over his shoulder, disappearing into the snow.

Thanks to the purge they made much greater headway in the afternoon. At twilight they laid their sleeping bags upon branches cut from snowladen pine, huddling up close together for warmth, and at dawn they set off again.

In this mode they travelled for mile after rugged mile, criss-crossing the tracks of bird and mammal, losing count of the days and weeks, being overtaken and left behind by dogsleds pulled by laughing huskies, until one day, with a unified cockcrow of triumph, they reached the Chilkoot Pass.

Here a stain of red serge against the dazzling backdrop marked the border post of the North-West Mounted Police, its purpose being to turn away undesirables and those who came with insufficient stores. Nat and Rymer struck out towards it. As they grew nearer, though, their hearty grins began to fade at the exhibition of maxim guns trained upon them and the uncompromising face of the

Law. Most of the men wore thick navy jackets over their tunics, fur hats, and mukluks on their feet. More unnerving, however, was the one who struck out to meet them in only a red tunic, tight pants and stetson — obviously to show that he was too tough to need a coat. That sort always had a lot to prove. Nat hung back and glanced at Rymer, having no need to voice a fear that was all too evident. What if, after all this effort, this torture, the police refused to let them through? What if the abandonment of a few tins had cost them a fortune in gold?

Rymer played with his wispy beard. 'Christ, look at them guns! Nobody mentioned them, did they? What if they say we haven't enough supplies?'

Nat attempted to be blasé. 'What's all this *we* business? I've got my supplies.' He pointed to the sled. 'Where are yours?' Rymer gawped at him.

'It's a joke.' Nat's sigh emerged as a frosty cloud.

'I never know with you,' grumbled the other, then stared back at the guns.

Nat lunged forward, commanding through gritted teeth, 'Away, we can't hang about here or they'll get suspicious. If they say we haven't got enough food just tell 'em we're on a diet, and stop looking so bloody nervous!' Attempting to appear confident, he and Rymer lugged the sled towards the border. At once their way was barred. Nat gave what he hoped was a manly greeting to the constable, who was circling their sled in the manner of a husky about to start a fight. The man barely looked at him, concentrating his eagle eye on the sled. Bitter cold had carved a meanness on his face. 'Unfasten those straps!'

Nat and Rymer tried to appear casual but efficient as they surrendered their goods to be weighed, each of them feeling bilious with fear. Nat prayed: *Oh God, please, don't let him stop us. If he does I think I'll go mad. I'll have to kill him. I will, I'll have to kill him.* Then the others would throw aside the pipes and cigarettes they were now smoking at leisure, open fire with their maxims, and blow great holes in Nat and his friend; already he could see his own body ripped by bullets, falling, falling, his blood staining the ice.

The pointer on the scales wavered, then was still, each eye fixed to it, waiting. The constable stepped back and flicked his hand in the direction of the border. Nat hardly dared to believe it. They were being granted right of entry! Helped by his partner, both of them trying not to rush, he began to reposition the goods on the sled, shoving them this way and that in a competent fashion before moving off, never once glancing at Rymer, still dogged by the certainty that a voice would ring out to call them back.

No voice came. *Thank you! Thank you!* Relief, however, was shortlived, for now another obstacle blocked their route to the goldfields: the great Chilkoot Pass. Nat and Rymer lingered to gaze in awe at the stairway cut into the ice, upon which dark figures laden by tools plodded upwards, ever upwards towards the bruised sky. The adventurers were to discover, from those others who gathered at the foot of the mountain range preparing to make the same trip, that the journey across the Chilkoot Pass went on for thirty-three miles! Horrified, Nat dropped to his knees and sank his face into gloved palms. How would they be able to carry goods weighing two thousand pounds on their backs, he demanded of Rymer? It was of course impossible. Short of turning back, there was no option: they must travel back and forth, back and forth across those thirty-three refrigerated miles until all their equipment was on the other side.

Had the weather been kind it would have been difficult enough, but as further hindrance to their passage came driving snow and ferocious gales. Through glaring slits of hatred they forged the way ahead, blinking ice-encrusted lashes neath the incessant torment of needles; arguing, fighting and swearing, cursing the weather and each other, snapping and snarling like wolves, driven to distraction by the clanking and rattling of shovel against pan. Even after they had conquered the Chilkoot Pass their torture went unabated, for still another five hundred miles lay ahead; but they could not travel it now, since the Klondike could only be reached by water. Seething with frustration and discomfort, they had to wait with the many thousands of people at the camp at the head of Lake Bennet, breaking ice to get drinking water, chopping down trees and building boats, until the thaw came. In those frost-bitten, vitriolic months only the shimmering vision of gold kept them alive.

Spring came late to this vicious northern land. Too slowly for those impatient to be rich, the sun began to rise a little earlier each day. The frantic drive to produce boats that would carry them to the goldfields was over. No longer was the peaceful air assaulted by the rabid growl of the sawmill, its jaws now tamed into a calmer beast. The craft were ready, lined up along the shore like frozen fish. Itchy feet paced the edges of the lake, their owners testing for a break in the ice, listening intently for that significant groan. Nat loafed beside the boat that he himself had helped to construct: oh that Chippy could see him now! The officer would be proud of him. With nothing much else to do he dwelled for a moment on the circumstances that had brought him here and thought kindly of Chipchase for the role he had played. When he had earned his fortune and returned to York for Bright he would pay a visit to this old acquaintance. When? Frustration came in waves. Melt! Melt, he urged the arctic land, squinting through the watery sunshine, desperately seeking a change in the ice, examining each barren branch for the drip of moisture that would tell him the final part of his journey was nigh.

Then, one morn to the echoing croak of ptarmigan, the landscape started to moult like the bird itself. Small holes began to mottle its wintry plumage, which were teased and widened by the sun, melting a little further each hour into a gown of lace revealing underskirts of brown. Leggy cranes made ponderous investigation of these grassy patches, snowgeese followed caribou on their northwards trek, and water began to ooze from the edges of the frozen river that groaned in the agony of its rebirth. How fast it happened now! Within an hour of those first cracks chunks of ice the size of wagons began to shift and jostle like huge lumps of uncut emerald, sapphire and zircon, with gulls riding on the teeming floe that roared towards the ocean. All at once the petrified water burst free of its winter prison, all at once came an excited rush to launch the boats, all at once the vast flotilla of ramshackle craft surged through the swollen torrent, down through the canyons of the Yukon river, their foolhardy crews oblivious to the danger of rapids, rocks and whirlpools, bouncing, tumbling, surging over the white water towards the goldfields of the Klondike.

Hair plastered to his brow, eyes wide, mouth agape in terror and exhilaration, Nat gripped the edges of his boat as it hit a wall of water, soared through the air and landed again, drenching the occupants. The bones of his knuckles shone white as he clung on for life, for to lose that hold was to die. No one would save him. All around him in the white water rapids craft broke apart, bodies were dashed onto the rocks and pulverized, swamped or drowned, all in the cause of gold. Another wall of water, another jarring blow and up, up into the air! He held his breath, felt every man do the same . . . then *down*! Crashing, bouncing, splashing into the raging morass. Gold, gold, gold! He chanted the magic word over and over again, urging his aching, freezing fingers to hold on. He could not come so far and die. Yet in his fear of death not once did Bright cross his mind; the only brightness that he feared to lose was that yellow precious metal.

After five hundred miles of rivers and lakes the reduced and battered fleet arrived in Dawson City. It was still intensely cold here, the road was frozen, but at least there was not that bitter wind to contend with for the town was sheltered by mountains. Even as they stood here, damp and exhausted, in a street whose telegraph posts were draped with banners that proclaimed such legendary names as Eldorado and Bonanza, Nat and Rymer could not quite believe that they had reached their journey's end, but gradually the very character of the place brought them down to earth. As Rymer, using Yorkshire parlance, had dubbed it, Dawson was a 'rive-arsing' city of about ten thousand inhabitants, whose dance-halls, saloons and gambling houses had sprung from nowhere out of a frozen peat-bog and now played host to people of every class, including those who were ready to divest the miners of their hard-earned gains: card sharps, prostitutes and confidence tricksters.

After such a journey, the youths decided they deserved a night of celebration and spent their last few dollars at the gaming tables of Diamond Tooth Gertie's saloon before going to try their luck in the creeks, not seeing it as waste, for there would be more, many more, to come.

The next morning, fighting a hangover, they set off into the wilderness to pan for gold. The sky was blue, the sun shone. Out of the brown scrub at the foot of tree-trunks peeped young green shoots. The deathly silence of winter was broken by the drilling of woodpeckers, and the whole atmosphere was one of hope. Thus, crapulence was soon displaced by an eagerness to begin work. And work they did. Though spring had come the ground remained hard and the young men were compelled to burn holes in the frozen dirt before they could begin sifting the gravel through their pans.

For hours they dug and sifted. No gold appeared. They moved on to another site and began the process again, and again, and again. Out of the spring sky came an unanticipated squall, dusting the land with icing sugar and so hampering their efforts. Nat was quick to sink into despondency, and Rymer tried to cheer him by saying there was always tomorrow, but tomorrow yielded nothing either, not the tiniest glimmering speck.

Forbidding this early adversity to halt them, they searched on, positive by the evidence of what they had witnessed in Dawson that gold was to be found if one was looking in the right place. At least the weather was becoming warmer and the days longer. The sun rose at three and did not set until eight or nine at night, and every hour of daylight was put to good use. Summer reached its spectacular zenith, all but the mighty resilient glaciers swooning to its persuasive caress. Loosed from their eiderdown the meadows exploded with fireweed. Petrified lakes burgeoned with trout that shimmered and leaped amongst emerald waters. Flies buzzed around dirt-stained faces whilst the young men toiled and struggled and panned. Throughout those all too short summer months when darkness did not come at all they laboured and roamed beneath the vast blue skies under the watchful gaze of eagles, their flesh one huge burning sore inflicted by voracious hordes of mosquitoes. They toiled and searched until the bushes were decked with ribbons of velvet from the antlers of caribou, a sign that fall was nigh, but despite all efforts the moosehide bags which they had hoped to fill with gold dust remained limp and empty.

Midas fingers touched the trees, and still the only gold they had encountered was in the whispering leaves of aspen. Soon these too were gone, lost beneath a pall of snow that would remain for months, muffling the trill of bird and cricket, plunging the land into deathly hush. The nights were long. Still their determination held. In the dark and silent winter they again lit fires to burn holes in the unresponsive earth, washed pans of barren shale by firelight, hoping, praying for the elusive glitter that would make this agonizing ache in bone and muscle all worth-while. Pain brought irritation, and in turn argument. Their faces became gaunt with both misery and hunger. Now they could not even look forward to a good meal to comfort them at the end of each arduous day, for supplies were running low and the fish were hiding deep below a crust of ice. In the summer an abundance of wild fruits had kept scurvy at bay, but now the corners of their mouths were cracked and scabbed, making argument physically painful, and thus they relapsed into a morose silence, dreaming not just of gold but of hot flapjacks and maple syrup, and a warm bed.

The New Year of 1899 howled across the flat open spaces of the valleys. The temperature dropped to fifty below. Driven by despair to the limits of his sanity, Nat made pacts with God and Satan . . . neither answered. Into each individual brain crept a maggot of suspicion, which nibbled and fed upon their unvoiced fear: what if the goldfields had been worked out by the thousands who had gone before? Neither dared to speak of this, the only certainty being that they could not proceed indefinitely. Nat, even in this pain-racked state too mulish to give up of his own accord, prayed for Rymer to voice the obvious. But his partner had been forged in the identical hardy mould and there followed several more of those long winter nights before relief was to come. Eventually, worn down by the elements and the futility of his labours, Rymer succumbed to the gnawing wind of failure and made the tentative suggestion that they return to Dawson's ice-packed streets.

Nat was never more glad than at this moment, but pride forced him to work on for a respectable period to illustrate that he was not the one to have weakened first. But he enjoyed no triumph, and the journey back to Dawson was undertaken with heavy heart. With their in-glorious return came the discovery that others had been more successful in their quest; gold still teemed into the city. At odds with the bitter jealousy there was also comfort to be had from this news, for at least now they were certain that the creeks were not worked out and they must simply choose a better location when they returned in the spring. For now they would have to drown their sorrows here on the few cents they had left, which both agreed miserably would not get them very drunk. There were, however, those more fortunate and generous souls who were willing to stand the luckless pair a drink. After their abstemious months in the wilderness it took very little to inebriate them.

To Nat and Rymer, who had not been in the city for long, it seemed from the rumbustious atmosphere that there were few laws to be observed in Dawson. Men raced their jingling dogsleds up and down the main street at will, the brothels ran their thriving businesses unchecked, and the boys themselves were allowed to drink and cavort as much as they liked that Saturday night without being judged a menace to anyone. Their luck appeared to have changed for the better too, for the bank clerk to whom they had spoken on the ship not only bought them a drink from his swollen purse but gave them each a coin to spend at the gaming tables. Rymer won, and with a drunken grin he immediately offered half to Nat.

Nat refused. 'I'll only lose it, knowing my luck. Keep betting and if you're still winning at the end of the night I'll take half of it then.'

Rymer cackled. 'That's what I like about you, you're not greedy!' He placed another bet. The wheel spun and his number came up again. In fact he was to win repeatedly for the next hour, at which point he announced that he would quit whilst he still had money to spend on something better. This something better turned out to be a brothel, where he and Nat enjoyed much debauched compensation until informed of the price this would cost them. Nat's slurred prescription that they make a run for it was not a good one. The snarling brawl that carried them onto the boardwalk in the early hours of the morning was to inflict graver injury than the cuts and bruises which distorted their cheeks. They had, it transpired, committed the one crime that Superintendent Steel, head of the North-West Mounted Police, refused to overlook: they had broken the strict observance of the Sabbath.

Apart from being customs collectors, land agents, magistrates, gaolers and law enforcers, the North-West Mounted Police were also mail carriers. It was amongst one of those mail bags that a wanted poster had arrived from Alberta and was consequently hung on a wall of the police barracks. During the hours that Nat and Rymer were in gaol, charged with being drunk and disorderly on a Sunday, the sharp-eyed police constable in charge of them received a jog to his memory, went over to peruse the notices that were strewn across the wall and discovered to his glee that one of the pair was a wanted man. Waking the prisoners by banging a metal cup on the bars of the cell he called, 'You there! You told us when we arrested you that your name is Nat Prince – is that true?'

Hungover, both youths groaned at the noise. Whilst Rymer ignored it as best he could Nat winced and tried to escape under his blanket, muttering, 'Course it's true.' God, his head hurt.

His answer delighted the constable. 'I knew it!'

'Christ, d'you have to make so much noise?' grumbled Nat into his pillow.

'Oh, I'm sorry I'm sure! I've just got one more little thing I want to say then I'll leave you in peace. Horse stealing.' The constable waited. There was no response. He became theatrical then. '"A horse, a horse, my kingdom for a horse!" That's what that old king said, didn't he? I know you're only a prince but I guess you must've thought you needed a horse yourself!'

It took Nat a little while to come round. Even when he did so the after effects of the alcohol prevented him from digesting the accusation. 'What the hell're you wittering on about?' He looked around the prison cell, trying to remember how he had got here. Rymer was lying next to him, shielding his eyes from the light that filtered through the barred window.

The scarlet-coated constable maintained his cheerful voice. 'I said, you're wanted for horse stealing!'

Nat winced and took his hands away from his creased and battered face to display incredulity. 'Horse stealing! Don't be daft.'

'You just confirmed your name is Nat Prince.' The man brandished the poster bearing a likeness of Nat, who gave a dumb nod. 'Well, this here poster informs me that you stole a horse and certain artefacts belonging to a Mr John Anderson.'

Nat began to sober up, dealing Rymer a thump and telling him to wake up. 'The horse was mine, he gave me it! Tell him, Rymer!'

The constable showed scepticism. 'Can you prove it?'

Rymer, at last come to consciousness, leaned on his elbow, made a face at the taste of his own tongue and offered in Nat's defence, 'How're you gonna prove he had a horse in the first place? I don't see it anywhere round here.' He indicated the gaolhouse. 'Unless you've got it hidden up your jacket.' The shiny buttons were rather strained across a portly gut.

'Don't get smart, boy! At the moment you're only here for being drunk and disorderly, but if you talk too much you might just talk yourself into being accessory to a major felony.'

Rymer shut up.

'Look!' pleaded Nat, hanging onto the bars of the cell. 'I didn't steal the bloody horse!'

'Mr Anderson says you did, and this here kinda proves

we got the right man.' Reaching into a corner the man produced a shovel. 'We found this in your pack.' On its shaft he pointed out the initials JA. 'I don't reckon that stands for Nat Prince.'

'How d'you know it's my pack?' demanded Nat.

'Because a kindly gentleman saw you being arrested and thought he'd better bring it here for safe-keeping until you sobered up. When are you gonna admit you're licked?'

'All right, I borrowed Mr Anderson's tools!' admitted Nat. 'But he knew about it. I told him I'd bring them back when I'd made a strike —but I didn't steal the horse! It was mine.'

'Well,' the Mountie laid aside the shovel. 'We'll find that out when you stand trial.' He turned his attention to Rymer. 'You gonna behave yourself now, boy? Good, cause I don't want to see no more drinking on a Sunday or it'll be more than a day in gaol, you'll be heading home with this fella.'

Nat almost vomited with the panic that rose to his throat. 'You can't send me back, I haven't made a strike yet!'

The constable merely raised an eyebrow before turning away.

'Please!' Nat gripped the bars and made frantic entreaties to the man's back. 'You've got to believe me! I didn't steal anything! I'm sorry about being drunk! Listen to me! It's not fair, I haven't done anything!' The door closed.

Heart thumping with panic, Nat continued to shout and bang and protest, but it did him no good. Whilst Rymer, after a bout of chopping firewood for the police log-pile, was allowed to return to the goldfields, he himself was taken in handcuffs on the long and painful route back to Edmonton to stand trial.

Anderson had been informed and had travelled north to attend. There was no sign of Mrs Anderson, to whom Nat could have appealed for mercy. Judging by his previous parting words there would be none from her spouse. Faced with Nat at the gaolhouse the rancher gave him a cool glare and then turned away. How easily he had shrugged off the affectionate mantle of Uncle John.

'This the boy that stole your horse, sir?' asked the police sergeant.

'It is,' replied Anderson without looking.

'Fraid we didn't get the animal back,' apologized the Mountie. 'He'd already sold it. Said you gave it to him.'

'He did give it to me!' Nat ranted at Anderson. 'Why're you lying?'

'Don't you call me a liar!' Anderson made a lunge at him. 'You think I'd let you keep that horse after what you did to my wife?'

'Just hold on there!' The policeman restrained Anderson. 'Are you saying that you did give him that horse?'

'I did, but what I give I can just as easy take back!'

The sergeant adopted a different tone. 'You mean you haul this officer all the way back from his duties in Dawson, then tell us you really did give his prisoner that horse?'

Anderson shrugged the restraining hand from his shoulder and hoisted his belt. 'I gave him it, yes, but that was when I looked upon him as a son and not a sneaking little thief! That horse was only his for as long as he lived in my house. Far as I was concerned, once he'd run off it belonged to me again.'

The sergeant was really annoyed now. 'So you figured you'd get the North-West Mounted Police to teach him a lesson! You think we're not short-handed enough with this darned goldrush that we have time to run after every wayward boy?'

'He committed a crime!' objected Anderson.

'The fact is, mister, that a fella can't be capable of stealing what's already his! You just admitted you gave the animal to him.'

'What about the other things?' demanded Anderson. 'The food, the tools, my wife's pans . . .'

'We didn't aim to bring him all this way just to stand trial for stealing pots and pans! Horse stealing's a serious offence and so is lying to an officer of the law.'

Anderson's moustache bristled. 'God darn it, I didn't lie! I still say that horse was mine!'

'You can say all you like! You've just admitted that you once gave that horse to him and that's sufficient to prove that the boy had every right to believe it was his. Now I suggest you leave my office before I get real angry and charge you for wasting my time!'

Anderson made no move to leave. 'What're you gonna do with him?'

The sergeant used his body to shepherd Anderson to the door. 'Don't you worry, he'll probably go to gaol for the theft of the tools et cetera, that was your aim weren't it?'

Anderson glanced over his shoulder at Nat, his face dark. 'News is that the British are asking for volunteers for this war they're fighting in South Africa. I don't see why good Canadian boys should risk their lives when dirt like you is ruining this country. When you come out o' gaol I suggest you join up, do something decent with your life for once. Whatever you do, don't come within a hundred miles o' my ranch.' He opened the door and left.

Nat only saw the man again briefly at his trial, at which he was to receive a prison sentence for the theft. However, there were others determined to speak their piece and to inflict additional punishment. The judge, having made it his business to uncover Nat's past, voiced disapproval that was not confined to the boy. 'It seems to me that the British authorities in sending you here hoped to rid themselves of an habitual criminal. Well, let them be in no doubt that we will not permit them to foist such characters upon us. As soon as you have served your term you will be escorted to Montreal and put on a ship back to England.'

Nat's only recourse was to defiance; 'I don't care, you can stick your bloody country!' But during the long lonely nights in gaol he had much time to ruminate. His one great chance, and he had ruined it. How could he face Bright? He was as penniless as when he had come here. Fool! Idiot! What was he going to do now? Who would employ him? He was nineteen years old, a man, but at that moment he felt like a small boy again. And it was all his mother's fault.

PART TWO

16

How precious were Sundays. Bright would rise early and take Oriel into her bed, where they would snooze until seven-thirty. Miss Bytheway did not require breakfast until late on the Sabbath. Afterwards they would go to Mass together, she and Oriel, though at a different church than the family who had abandoned her and one whose priest was unaware that she had tried to take her own life. If it was fine they would enjoy a walk along the city walls or the riverside before going home. It was rather a misnomer to call this Bright's day off, for she still had to eat dinner and therefore she was the one who had to cook it, but from then on her time was her own.

For the rest of the week life was as hard as ever and often without reward, for her employer had a poor memory when it came to wages and there was a limit to the number of times Bright could politely remind her. Nor could she object when given rotten jobs to do, for if she were dismissed it was not only a job she would be losing but her home – perhaps her daughter too, for as Oriel grew she was treated more and more as though she were Miss Bytheway's daughter, taking her meals in the dining room while Bright had to eat in the kitchen, except on Sundays which was obviously viewed as a great privilege by Miss Bytheway.

Things that once went unnoticed now began to tweak the three-year-old's intellect. 'Why doesn't Mother eat with us all the time?' she asked Miss Bytheway one particular lunchtime.

'Because your mother is a servant,' replied the elderly woman, as if this was sufficient explanation.

Oriel was an intuitive child; she had noticed the underlying animosity between the two women even though there were never any raised voices nor any hint of anger. 'Why don't you like Mother?'

Miss Bytheway was unmoved. 'One neither likes nor dislikes servants,' came the dignified reply. 'They are merely there to do one's bidding. Now stop tinkering with your knife and fork and eat your meal.'

If Bright had entertained worries over where her daughter's loyalties lay, she would have been heartwarmed to hear Oriel's current decision. It was hugs and cuddles made a parent, not rigid discipline. 'I don't want to eat with you any more, I want to have my meals with Mother.'

'Well, you can't. You are here not only to sate your hunger, but to learn manners also.'

'What's manners?' asked Oriel, swinging her white kid boots beneath the table and nibbling the prongs of her fork.

'Exactly my point! How can your mother be expected to teach you these things?'

'She's very clever,' parried the child.

'Not clever enough or she would be sitting in my chair and I should be the servant.' Miss Bytheway pursed downy lips around another morsel of spinach.

Oriel pondered on this. Maybe what Miss Bytheway said was correct. After all, her mother must be in awe of the old lady, for did she not do all her bidding?

After luncheon she went directly to Bright. 'Is Miss Byvway cleverer than you?'

Her mother was busy with the washing up, but had time

to look amused. 'I should think so. Doesn't she sit there while I do all the work?'

'Is that why you don't like her?'

'What a thing for a child to ask!' Bright clattered another bowl onto the draining board.

'Is it?'

'Who says I don't like her?' Cutlery rattled at the bottom of the sink as Bright's hand chased it.

'Me, I can tell.'

'You're too clever by half.'

'Miss Byvway says you're not clever at all.'

'The old . . . ' Bright compressed her lips and sloshed about in the water to show her disapproval. 'What's she been filling your mind with?'

Oriel's bottom teeth grasped her upper lip, like a bull-dog. 'I just asked her why she didn't like you.'

'Oh, ye didn't!' Bright had to laugh.

'She said . . . ' Oriel frowned to remember the exact words. '"One neither likes nor dislikes servants. They are merely here to do one's bidding."' The little girl looked proud of her achievement.

Bright gasped her outrage. 'And isn't that the truth! Here's me working from cockcrow till bedtime and do I ever get a word of praise? I do not. Not one compliment have I heard in this house.'

'What's a compliment?'

''Tis when a person says something nice about ye.'

'You make very nice gravy,' offered her daughter.

'Well, thank ye!' Bright tried to be good-humoured again. 'Look, Oriel, you're right in a way, I don't care for Miss B, but she was very kind in taking the pair of us in. I'd've been in the workhouse if it wasn't for her. Nobody would take an unmarried woman with a baby. I'll always be under obligation for that and so must you – though goodness knows she tests my gratitude sometimes. Oh, Mother o' God!' A black face at the window made her jump. Then she laughed, held up one hand with splayed fingers and mouthed, 'Five bags, please!'

Drying her hands she bustled outside to chat with the coalman. Even though he was middle-aged the opportunities to flirt were few and far between and seize them she must, at the same time thinking how pathetic she must seem. Oriel followed her. The blackened face was outside the gate now, hefting a sack from his cart. Bright smiled as he winked at her on his re-entry and travelled up the garden to the coal shute.

'Is the young lady here to check up on me?' he asked as he passed.

Bright grinned and laid a hand on Oriel's shoulder. 'No, we trust you, don't we, Oriel?' Though wary of all the tradesmen at first she had come to like this particular one. A couple of the others she still did not trust, they were a bit too familiar, but when this one winked at her it was as if her father were doing it. She felt safe with him, plus the fact that he did not treat her with disrespect just because she had an illegitimate child.

'Can you count to five?' he asked Oriel as he went for another sack.

The child wrinkled her nose and gave a half laugh. 'Of course!'

'Pity,' joked the man. Bright laughed, enjoying his all too brief company.

When the full quota had been deposited in the coal cellar the man puffed out his chest and came to the kitchen door to hand over his bill. Bright tried to keep him chatting as long as she could, for his tales of things that had occurred on his round could be very entertaining. Eventually though he glanced at the lane and exclaimed, 'Well! My horse is getting restless, I'd better be on my way. Good-day to you now.' And that was as near as Bright would ever come to having a man's attention. She and her daughter went back into the house.

'He's very dirty,' commented Oriel.

'You shouldn't say things like that about people, you'll hurt their feelings.' Bright returned to the sink. 'He's only dirty because his job is to carry coal. Someone has to do these jobs, not everyone can be their own master or mistress like Miss Bytheway.'

'I told her I want to eat with you.' Oriel swung on a corner of her mother's apron. 'She said I can't because I have to learn manners.'

'Manners?' Bright shook her head. The woman might know which knife and fork to use but made a sound like a pig when she ate. However, this was hardly the thing to say to Oriel, who would repeat it. 'Well, much as I miss your company I suppose she's right.' Another pot was washed and lifted from sink to draining board. Her hands were now crimson from the hot water. 'She can teach ye more than I ever could — mindst, I'm no dunce either,' she defended herself. 'Wasn't I a pupil teacher until I had you.'

Oriel looked pleased. 'I told her you were clever.'

'Well that's very loyal of ye, but ye'd better keep it to yourself in future.' Bright smiled down lovingly upon her child. 'So long as the two of us know it there's no one else matters, is there?'

And Bright convinced herself that this was true. As long as her child was happy no one else mattered, not even Bright herself. Her whole life was devoted to Oriel's well-being. At least this was one thing the two women had in common, though Miss Bytheway showed her concern in very different ways, ways that made Bright intensely jealous.

'We're going to the circus tomorrow afternoon,' announced Oriel to her mother during one of their Sunday walks home from church. It was August, and the sun bounced off the pavements making the city streets unbearably hot, but now as they reached New Walk there came relief. This bank of the Ouse was canopied by trees, making the last part of their journey more pleasant. The air was heavy with the scent of greenery and the path thronged with strollers: ladies in white dresses with parasols, boatered gents and children in their Sunday best. Oriel was wearing a huge sun bonnet and lace pinafore and trundling a little wicker perambulator. Her mother had to keep stopping to wait for her as the wheels encountered some obstacle.

'By we, I assume you mean Miss B and yourself.' Bright couldn't help the childish jealousy. In her nineteen years never once had anyone taken her to the circus.

Oriel was quick to reply, 'You can come too.'

'I don't think that was what Miss B had in mind,' answered her mother. 'Anyway, I'll have too much work to do.'

Oriel was thoughtful, steering her pram around a fallen branch. 'She said it was a birthday treat.'

'My God,' muttered Bright to herself. 'How many birthdays can one child have?' Oriel's birthday was nearly two months ago and Bright could still recall her own envy at all those gifts the old woman had given her − probably to overshadow Bright's own gift, came the malicious opinion. The amount of work I put into that rag doll, and all she has to do is open her purse.

Christmas had been the same − worse, in fact. Bright had been a loved and pampered child and though the gifts were never worth more than a few pence she had always been the centre of the family's attention at Christmas. Now that was gone and to watch Oriel be the recipient of similar attention from Miss Bytheway pricked childish envy in her breast. Inevitable guilt followed. What sort of mother resented her own child? I don't resent her, honestly I don't, it's just − oh, I just miss them, Mammy, Dada . . . the pain of loss seemed especially acute at Christmas and birthdays.

'Well, I hope you'll enjoy it,' she told her daughter in genuine enthusiasm. 'Barnum and Bailey's, is it?'

The infant peered up from beneath her frilly bonnet. 'I don't know.'

'Aye, I've seen it advertised. It's from America, I think.'

Thoughts of America led to thoughts of Canada and Nat. She wondered what he was doing there, and whether he would ever come back for her. What would she tell her daughter when the child eventually asked why he was not here with them?

Oriel interrupted her mother's dream. 'Where's that?'

'America? Across the sea. You'll have to ask Miss B to show you on her map when we get home.' Why do I do it? Bright chastised herself. Here we are, the only day of the week when we can escape the woman's clutches, and I have to raise her name.

'Do we have to go across the sea to get to the circus?' asked Oriel.

Bright chuckled and patted the child's shoulder. 'No! They've brought all the animals here in a big ship. I think it's on Knavesmire.' She pointed over the river, then laughed. 'Oh, ye will have to cross water to get to it, though only by ferry.'

It was this ferry that they were watching some months later when another child planted seeds of enquiry in Oriel's mind. Mother and daughter were seated on a bench, enjoying what was surely to be the last of the fine weather before winter arrived, when another little girl came skipping up to the bench and sat down beside Oriel, face a-brim with congeniality. Bright smiled up at the mother and offered a quiet hello as the other came to sit beside her. 'Isn't it beautiful for October — well, it's almost November!' exclaimed the newcomer. Bright agreed and a desultory conversation was interspersed with questions between the two little girls.

'Where do you live?' asked Oriel.

'Fulford Road,' replied the other.

'I live at number five St Odswald's Terrace.' Oriel could never get her tongue around Oswald's. 'I'm three years old.'

'I'm five,' came the important reply.

The two examined each other's attire. 'My father's at the war,' informed the blonde child. 'Where's your father?'

'Well, I can't sit here all day chatting!' Ignoring Oriel's enquiring face, Bright sprang to her feet. 'Come along, dear! Miss B will be cross if we don't have dinner ready on time. Goodbye!' she said to the woman with whom she had been chatting, and hurried away along the riverbank.

'Have I got a father?' Oriel's short legs tried to keep up with her mother.

Bright's stomach churned but she forced her voice to sound cheery. 'Of course! Everyone has a father.'

'Do you?'

'Yes, but he's dead.'

'What's dead?'

This was going to be more complicated than Bright had feared, but at least it lured Oriel's attention from the dreaded subject. 'Oh, tis when someone doesn't live on earth anymore but goes to live in heaven with Jesus.' Go on, ask who Jesus is, she silently urged.

Oriel complied. 'Who's Jesus?'

'I've told ye before. He's the Son o' God.'

'Who's God?'

'Don't you listen to anything in church?' scolded Bright. 'He made the world and everything in it.'

'Even me?' asked the little girl.

'Yes, me too.'

'Did He make my father?'

Bright gave an inward sigh. 'Yes.'

'Where is he then?'

'Up in heaven.'

'So . . . my father's dead.' Oriel began to flag at the pace.

'No, no!' Bright grew testy. 'I thought ye meant where is God. Your father, he's in Canada — that's across the sea,' she added before the child asked.

'Is he in a circus?'

'The questions you ask!' Bright was flustered.

Oriel cast her mind back to the conversation with the blonde child. 'Will he come to see us soon?'

'I don't know, maybe.' Bright was glad they were almost home.

'Is he a soldier like that other little girl's father?'

'No, I'm not sure what he does.'

Oriel's imagination was captured. 'Why haven't I seen him before?'

'Because . . . oh, look at the swans!' Why did I say that? Bright chastised herself. Didn't I always swear I would be honest with her, and what do I do when I get the opportunity? Oh, but it's a lot more painful than I could have imagined.

Oriel was temporarily distracted by the swans. When the pair of them resumed their journey home she seemed to have forgotten all about her father, but just as they reached the corner of St Oswald's Terrace the child piped up, 'Does Miss B know my father?'

'No!' Bright answered too quickly, too sharply. A look of woe clouded Oriel's face. 'Sorry, did I hurt your hand?' In her fear she had jerked the child's fingers. 'I didn't mean to.'

The little girl was composed again. 'It didn't hurt.'

'Oriel.' Bright paused on the footpath. 'Ye mustn't bother the old lady with talk of your father. She doesn't know him and . . . well, she doesn't like men. We don't want to upset her do we?'

Oriel had not noticed her benefactress's misanthropy but agreed that it would be unwise to upset her.

'And you're not to call her Miss B either,' warned her mother.

'You do.'

'Yes, but . . . oh why do I bother! Just don't, that's all.'

Oriel was not to be detoured from her previous topic. 'Will you tell me all about my father?'

'I can't, I have to cook dinner.' Bright stared down at her

child's enquiring face. The question would arise again and again if she avoided it now. 'Well, all right, I'll tell you later when I've done all my work and we can go upstairs on our own.' Feeling giddy, she moved on. 'Come on now, be a good girl and go get washed for dinner.'

'Luncheon,' corrected Oriel.

'Whatever,' sighed Bright.

During the Sunday meal Oriel announced to Miss Bytheway, 'My father's in Canada.'

Bright was in the process of inserting a forkful of lamb into her mouth. At Oriel's words she stalled, dribbling gravy down her chin.

White eyebrows were raised in disapproval of the peasant-like manner, then their owner turned back to Oriel. 'A good thing too.'

'Why?' demanded the child.

'Oriel!' Bright's eyes held a warning over the napkin with which she was mopping nervously at her chin. Only then did Oriel heed her mother's orders that she was not to mention her father to Miss Bytheway.

But the old lady had been provoked now. 'For the reason that he is shiftless, untrustworthy and a blackguard.'

Oriel was unfamiliar with any of these terms. 'Does that mean he's bad?'

'Yes – as are all men!'

At least it was not just her father who was maligned. However, Oriel was not a child to accept such blanket accusations. 'Mother said you don't know him.'

Miss Bytheway glanced sharply from child to mother. 'I do not need to have the misfortune to meet him! That he left your mother in the lurch is sufficient evidence of his character.'

Oriel turned to her mother, who was by now furious. 'Where's the lurch?'

'Oriel, be told!' Bright managed to contain her fury but her cheeks were as pink as the ruby glass piece on the sideboard. The expression on her mother's face was enough for the child. Oriel continued her meal in silence.

Later, in the privacy of the nursery, Bright returned to the misdemeanour. 'Why did you disobey me? I told you not to speak of your father to Miss B!'

'She doesn't like him.'

'She doesn't know him!' Bright was free to vent her anger now. 'D'ye think I gave ye that order for my own good? I knew what Miss B would say about your father, she hates men.' Her employer was invariably rude to the coalman and any other merchant who had the misfortune to encounter her when they came to deliver.

'Why?'

'I don't know and tis none o' my business! But it is my affair when she blackens your father's character and her not even acquainted with him. Didn't I say I'd tell you all about him later? But would you wait? No! Well, let me tell you I will not have you airing our private affairs in front of that woman! *I'm* your mother, not her!'

Oriel was too young to understand this argument. That she had deeply upset her mother was quite obvious, but she could not think how. Frowning, she replied to her mother's last statement as if Bright were stupid. 'I know that! I just – '

'Don't answer back!'

'But you – '

'Quiet!' Bright raised her hand. Oriel flinched. Bright's hand hung in mid-air, her mouth a hard line. Then she let the blow fall on her own thigh. 'For pity's sake, she's got us arguing now!' She bobbed to her knees and hugged Oriel. 'We must never let her come between us, baby. We're all each other has.'

'I don't understand.' Oriel was very close to tears.

'No, no.' Bright sat back on her heels, then kissed the forlorn brow. 'Don't worry, tis only your mammy thinking you're older than you are – sure, you act as if you're my mother sometimes, I forget you're only little. See, you're the only person I have to tell my troubles to, Oriel, the only one I can share my secrets with. If you . . . ' she bit her lip, tears springing to her eyes. 'I'm just so frightened that Miss B is going to turn you against me an' then I'll have no one.' Her voice cracked.

Oriel was an emotional child. At the sight of her mother's tears she started to emulate. They held each other, sobbing and wailing. Once her grief had been aired, Bright let out a wet laugh. ''Tis a wonder herself hasn't come dashing up here thinking I'm murdering ye! Come on, let's dry our eyes and make the most of our time before her ladyship rings that blasted bell. Come, sit by me on the bed and I'll tell you all about your father. Anything ye hear from your mother's lips will be true. Always remember that, Oriel. Miss B has reasons of her own for hating men, she'll tell you they're all worthless and it just isn't true.'

Eyes patted dry, Oriel sat close to her mother. 'What's my father's name?'

'Nat Prince.'

'That's nice.' Oriel rubbed her knees through the lace dress and jiggled her patent leather boots. 'What does he look like?'

Her mother's brown eyes misted over with nostalgia. 'He's got hair and eyes the same colour as yours. I'm not sure how big he is – tis more than three years since I've seen him. He would've grown by now. He was never much of a talker.' Here she smiled and hugged the child. 'Ye get that from your mother. He used to drive me mad sometimes, not saying anything, letting me do all the talking. Anyway, we were both very young . . . ' Embarrassment flooded over her as she remembered 'that' night, but she compelled her tongue to grant Oriel her birthright. 'Mothers and fathers are supposed to be married before they have children. If they're not tis a sin in the eyes of God and in the eyes of the people. Your father and me, as I said we were only young, too young to be married and something happened between us — don't ask me what Oriel, I didn't understand it myself and I'm not sure I fully understand it even now — but it resulted in you being born. Your father was at the Industrial School at the time.'

'Where's that?'

'Tis a place where they put naughty boys — he wasn't a bad boy at all, he'd never had much love nor guidance in his life and he just took the wrong road. His own mother left him all alone when he was eleven years old. Can you imagine how he must've felt, left to fend for himself at that age? He got in with a bad lot and found himself in trouble time and again. Anyway,' she hung her head and sighed, 'he was locked away in there and when I told him I was having a baby he was frightened, so very frightened, and somehow when he was given the chance to go to Canada he went. I didn't find out till it was too late. I was all alone then, my father threw me out . . .'

'Aw!' Oriel started to blubber. 'I hate him!'

'Oh no, no, ye mustn't hate your grandfather,' soothed Bright. 'He loved me really, he was just so angry that I'd let him down, let all the family down. It was all my fault, I should never have let things happen. The shame of it killed him — anyway, that's about all I can tell ye about your father. I never saw him nor any of my family again.'

Oriel's nose and eyes were streaming. There were dozens of questions she wanted to ask, but all she could see was her poor mother's maltreatment.

'Oh, there, there!' Bright hugged her. 'If I'd known it would cause such tears I'd never've told ye . . . but ye have a right to know. I'll always be honest with ye, darlin'. I'll always be here if ever you're in trouble. I'll never desert ye.' Not like they deserted me, came the private thought. Though outwardly excusing her dead father's actions to his granddaughter, Bright could not fully understand how her mother, now widowed and under no pressure, could remain so unforgiving. Mrs Maguire had not been to see her daughter, nor her granddaughter, once. It was obvious that she and the rest of the clan blamed Bright for her father's death. God knew, she had heaped enough blame on herself without having to suffer theirs too. Her attitude towards them had hardened now; she had no wish to see them either.

Oriel lifted her petticoat to wipe her eyes and nose, causing Bright to laugh. 'Miss B would be delighted that ye've picked up all her good manners.'

'I love you, Mother.' Oriel clung to her. 'I'll never leave you.'

'Oh you will.' Bright rocked her back and forth. 'One day you'll go out into the world and maybe meet a nice man and get married and I'll be the happiest woman alive. I'll not let you live your life for me. Just be happy, that's all I ask, and be whatever you want to be.'

They held each other thus for a while, then Oriel tilted her moonbeam face and sniffed. 'Will Father come back one day?'

Bright ached inside. 'I'm sure he will,' she replied softly. Oh, how she yearned at this moment more than any other for male affection. There had been so much of it from her father and brothers whilst she was growing up that its absence now left a yawning chasm in her life. Again, she reflected on what might have been had she not committed this great sin. Would she now have been embarking into matrimony with Nat, looking for a little house, preparing a nursery? Would she ever feel male arms around her again?

The first months of the new century were harsh. Milk froze in the jug and stalactites glittered along the roof-line. Miss Bytheway was normally a hardy soul, but even she succumbed to the foul weather.

'Will I get the doctor, Miss Bytheway?' enquired Bright

as her employer's hacking cough grated over the Sunday lunch table.

'It is very kind of you to think of me,' came the sedate if hoarse reply, 'but I have never needed a doctor in my life and I have no intention of changing my habits now.'

It wasn't you I was thinking about, thought Bright. Twas my aching head. Tis like a road drill when you start hacking and rattling. And not only that, what will I do if you die? I'll be out on the street. Obviously the old dragon would die some time, but Bright wanted to delay this as long as possible. 'I know it's none of my concern . . .'

'None at all.' Miss Bytheway suffered another fit of coughing. When Bright filled her glass with water she drank gratefully, allowing her employee to continue.

'But that could turn to pneumonia.'

The old lady took a tentative breath, then abandoned her unfinished meal, looking ghastly. 'Maguire, you are a servant not a physician! Kindly do your job and remove . . . ' Her voice trailed away in a weird moan as she fell face down into her mashed potatoes. Bright managed to leap up and catch her before she capsized to the floor, but not without knocking over several items as she collided with the table.

'Oh, Jesus, help me!' She struggled to hold the dead weight, her back almost breaking. Oriel tried first to push, then took an arm and helped tug the old lady's upper body back against the chair.

The little girl chuckled. 'Ooh, she's got potato all over her hair!'

'Never mind that!' scolded her mother. 'There's a doctor down the road . . . oh, no, you're too little! Oh, God, what will I do if she dies?' She squeezed her eyes shut, breast rising and falling. 'Think, *think*, woman! *Right*, go next door and ask if one of their servants will be so kind as to fetch a doctor for Miss B. Can ye remember that? Good! Hurry now, and don't slip on the ice!'

When Oriel returned Miss Bytheway was still unconscious and Bright was at her wits' end. 'Mother o' God,
what'll I do? What'll I do?' She had a brainwave. 'Smelling
salts! Have a look in the cupboard, Oriel. Hurry!'

The little child rifled every drawer and cupboard she
could reach, holding up several items for inspection. 'Is this
it, Mother?'

'No!'

'Is this it?'

'No! Oh, she's almost dead, I'm sure of it!' Bright was
creeping towards complete panic. 'Feathers! We'll have to
burn feathers!'

Oriel felt competent to help now. 'I know where there is
one!' She returned triumphantly in seconds.

'Shove it in the fire!' urged Bright.

'But you told me never to – '

'I know, I know, but tis all right just this once! Be very
careful and hold your dress away from the flame.'

Oriel stretched her arm to the fire, holding back her
dress with one hand and grimacing as the heat reached her
skin.

'That's enough!' cried Bright. 'We just need the smoke
from it.' Still struggling to keep the unconscious woman
upright she instructed Oriel, 'Put it under her nose – no,
not up her nose! Just there, yes, and waft it about.'

'It pongs,' observed Oriel.

The smoke tickled Miss Bytheway's nostrils and reached
her brain. She began to stir, then endured a dreadful
coughing fit that Bright felt would surely finish her off.
Please don't die, you old bugger, or I'll kill ye. However,
Miss Bytheway was made of sterner stuff.

'My best quill pen!' Her horrified bloodshot gaze rested
on the remains of the feather that Oriel had used to rouse
her. 'My mother's pen, ruined!'

'Sorry . . . ' Oriel tried to rearrange the blackened
strands of goosefeather, to no effect.

'Don't blame her!' Bright was exasperated. ''Twas a matter of life or death.'

'Tush! I only fainted.' Miss Bytheway grabbed the feather, moaned again and turned on her maid. 'Maguire, why did you allow this to happen?'

'We couldn't rouse ye!' Bright railed inwardly at the ingratitude of the woman. 'I had to do something till the doctor arrives.'

'I specifically forbade you to send for a doctor!'

'Well, he's coming!' Bright was firm. 'Sure, I thought you were dying.'

'Hoped,' sniped an ungracious Miss Bytheway.

'Now why would I want to see you dead?' In her anger Bright forgot her station. 'That's idiotic!'

Miss Bytheway's colour flooded back. She was about to censure her maid, who was now issuing profuse apologies, when the doorbell rang and Oriel scampered to admit the doctor who immediately confined Miss Bytheway to bed, 'For the next couple of weeks at the very least!'

'Quack!' spat the old lady at his departure, though she was too ill to disobey and allowed herself to be helped up to bed.

'Why don't ye move into this room?' Bright indicated the one on the first landing. 'It'll save your legs.' It'll save my legs too, came the private thought.

'That is my parents' room!' Miss Bytheway was shocked. 'I couldn't possibly move in there.'

'How long is it since they . . . passed away?' The maid hovered hopefully outside the door.

'Thirty years — at least that's when Mother died. Father outlived her by a few years.'

'Then I'm sure they wouldn't mind now.'

'But I would!' The old lady was determined to continue up the mountainous staircase.

It was this determination that kept her alive, Bright was

sure of it, though every night and morn she herself prayed to the Virgin and every saint she could think of for the health of her employer, just to make sure. By miracle or determination the invalid recovered, though she was ever-after prone to chest colds, even in the summer.

'What's wrong with me?' she raged at Bright, when another such illness kept her from taking Oriel to see the Prince of Wales, who was visiting York. 'No one gets a chill in the summer. Look at it out there!' She gestured with her handkerchief at the window. 'Brilliant sunshine and here I am confined to my bed like a weak, sickly pathetic old woman!' She thumped the mattress in frustration, then almost tore her handkerchief to shreds. 'Well, that's it, I'm finished! If this is the quality of life I can expect in my final years then I might as well die now.'

'Don't say that! Don't you ever say that.' In a trice Bright was plunged back four years and into that river, felt it close over her head, seep into her throat . . .

'Yes, you're quite right, Maguire!' The doughty Miss Bytheway rallied. 'I'm not one of those self-pitying weaklings, I won't let it beat me. I'm going to see the Prince of Wales, even if I have to die in the attempt.'

Heart still pounding, Bright was tardy in restraining the old woman. Miss Bytheway was already out of bed. 'Ye'll never be able to walk two steps, let alone two miles into town,' she warned, as a tremulous arm reached for her bodice.

'I don't intend to. You can hail a cab – don't just stand there, help me dress!'

'Miss Bytheway, there won't be room for a cab to move in town,' protested Bright. 'The streets'll be full of people. And you really are in no fit state to go.'

Suddenly feeling whoozy, the dame pressed a hand to her forehead and sank back onto the mattress. 'I hate to say it twice in one day, Maguire, but you are right. Rats!' Once more the handkerchief was subjected to a bout of frenzied tweaking. 'I detest letting Oriel down, she was so looking forward to it.'

Bright hung onto her temper. 'She doesn't have to be let down. I could take her if only you'd give me the afternoon off.'

Miss Bytheway's first response was to gawp, as if this were a preposterous suggestion, but after consideration she replied, 'Oh, very well! But you must catch up with your work when you return — and you are certainly not having the entire afternoon off! It takes half an hour to get there and half an hour to get back. A couple of hours will be sufficient.'

'Then I'd better go and get ready.'

'Oh, don't sound too grateful!' the invalid called after her. 'And you must leave me well provided with cordial et cetera. I refuse to suffer discomfort while my maid goes gallivanting off to enjoy herself.'

Bright tutted, but excitement was rising and it was with great anticipation that mother and daughter set off towards town for the royal event. They took a horse tram to Fishergate. In addition to the usual advertisements for Zebra Grate Polish and Grimbles Vinegar the vehicle was adorned with red, white and blue pennants and both decks were crammed with royalists. Bright had not been amongst so many people for a long time, their sweating bodies pressed in on her inviting a flutter of alarm. What had started as a delightful afternoon threatened to be ruined by an irrational panic which ebbed and flowed within her mind. But with the help of Oriel's distracting chatter, sanity triumphed. When the Prince of Wales appeared Bright cheered and waved with the daughter she loved, blissfully unaware that somewhere in the throng was another person who was close to her heart.

17

Nat had that very day arrived back in York, dulled of spirit and virtually penniless. Unwilling to rob, for the memory of prison was still raw in his mind, he had sought work in Liverpool to provide money for a train ticket home, but no one would take him. So, at the risk of being arrested for vagrancy he had set off to walk, relying on food from the Salvation Army. He could not explain why he had come back here. It was certainly not to marry Bright, for he still had nothing to offer her. However, the intense urge to see her and the child had lured his feet to his birthplace, and a city he knew well was as good a place as any to start earning his living.

The sight of those familiar narrow streets lined with bunting pulled him up sharp as he limped into town. How would he stand this cramped environment after the big skies of Canada? Well . . . it was too late now. The soles of his boots were almost worn through and his feet throbbed. He leaned against a wall to relieve the weight on them and also to get his bearings. A stray dog nosed him. He bent to deliver a pat. 'They've heard I'm coming and put the flags out,' he told it, then issued a bitter laugh and walked on.

Hungry and exhausted, he elbowed a bad-tempered passage through the crowds that lined the streets, jostling past vendors with their bundles of Union Jacks, strings of balloons and cheap souvenirs. All this was obviously in aid of a royal visit, but just which member of royalty this was he was in no mood to find out. Above the roof-line the Minster towered from every viewpoint, an overbearing symbol of Christianity. Eager to escape from all these people, he turned down Fossgate, heading for the doss-house. Nothing had changed here. The bridge on which he had played as a boy was just as he had left it, and he paused to look down upon the scum-laden water. Did Bright still live over there behind the Three Cups? The way he remembered her was as she had been as a young girl, but now she would be a woman of twenty. He could have passed her in that crowd back there and not even recognized her, nor she him. That was just as well. He had no wish to present himself in these dire straits. How tantalizing to know that under her floorboards lay an irretrievable cache. Walking on, he glanced through the archway that led to Bright's home – and almost collided with Martin Maguire.

For a second Bright's sibling did not know him and laughingly apologized. Then he peered more closely into the young weatherbeaten face and an expression of loathing flooded those Maguire features. Without a word he brought his knee up into Nat's groin. His surprised victim crumpled and fell like a stone to the ground, eyes bulging, feeling as if his genitals had been rammed right up into his throat. Expecting to be kicked, he rolled his agonized body into a foetal position, but Martin grabbed him by the jacket, half hauled him to his knees and beat a rapid tattoo on his face. Only when he was out of breath and enough blood had been drawn to his satisfaction did Martin speak.

'That's for my father!' he panted, shoving back his hair. 'And don't think that's the end of it cause my brothers'll want a go too!' He walked off, leaving Nat slumped on the pavement, still choking on his own genitals.

None of the passers-by cared enough to ask if he needed assistance, taking a wide detour around his filthy blood-stained body. Eventually, his testicles descended to their rightful place, enabling him to stagger to his feet and onwards to the dosshouse.

The next few days were spent draped over the line alongside tramps and other misfortunates, though his time here was far from unproductive. He set himself targets. By the end of the week he would be out of here and into respectable lodgings. By the end of the year he would be in a house of his own and married to Bright. The beating from Martin was understandable but it had only succeeded in making Nat more determined to see her when his finances improved. During the long voyage home he had had much time to ponder on his future. There were two roads from which to choose. Out of childish pique he could question the reason in trying to make an honest living when things always went wrong whatever he tried to do. Or he could choose the other road, do everything within the law, put not one foot out of place so that they had no excuse to imprison him again. That was easier said than done. For a start no one would employ him; anyway, he had no desire to be treated like a slave. He would do this on his own, start at the bottom and work his way up as he had tried to do before Denzil's madness had got them all locked away. He wondered briefly over the lunatic's whereabouts, then tried to put him out of his mind. That was one relationship which was definitely over. This time no one was going to spoil it for him, least of all Nat himself.

Once recovered from the assault, the young rag and bone merchant launched himself upon the city with a vigour that would have surprised his old masters at Industrial School. Beginning shortly after six he combed the riverbanks and gutters for any resaleable item. Then, when folk were up and about he would call out, 'Ra-bo! Hen ho Ra-bo!', knocking on doors all over the city and beyond its boundaries until seven or eight in the evening, or until his vocal cords gave out. At nightfall he would sort through his haul, picking out the best cotton and wool which he would sell to a man who took it to the mills at Bradford to be recycled into shoddy. In a matter of months he had saved enough to purchase a horse and cart, which allowed him to dispense with the man and take the stuff to Bradford himself. His call became well known in York. Children began to refer to him as Shoddy Nat, and would prance after his cart apeing his shout until, more out of fun than anger, he would leap down and cry, 'Gurt yer!' making them scream and run, much to their delight.

Such was his hard work and enterprise that by the following year Nat had the house he had promised himself and found that as well as storage space he could also afford to hire a boy who would collect rags for him on the day that he himself was in Bradford. Unfortunately, he was to discover that the boy was a crook. Returning earlier than expected one evening from the West Riding he disturbed his employee handing over a bundle of rags to another youth.

The one he did not know managed to flee, but Nat grabbed his employee and twisted his arm behind his back. 'What's this, one for you and one for me?'

'Aagh! They're only rags, Mr Prince!' Arm at dislocation point the boy stood on tiptoe in an attempt to escape the agony.

'Which I pay you to collect for me, not some other tow-rag!'

'It's a lot of hard work for sixpence!' The boy's face was contorted.

'It's even harder picking oakum for nowt! Ungrateful little . . . after I gave you a job an' all!' Nat released him with a shove. 'D'you want me to call the law? No? Well then, just get out of my sight, you're sacked.'

'Can't trust any bugger,' he told his horse as he locked his warehouse for the night. 'Now I'll have to waste time looking for another lad.'

He was still annoyed when he went to bed, fuming over the boy's ingratitude. *Stop it*, he told himself, or you'll never sleep. Think of something else. He turned over and thumped his pillow. It had been such a good day too. Why had that little runt had to spoil it? *I said*, think of something different! All right, what is there? By, this is a lovely bed. He wriggled into its comfortable mattress. All it needs to improve it is a female body lying on that side. But the type of female with whom Nat had been acquainted over the last few years would never be allowed in this bed. That place was reserved for another. So, when are you going to see her, then, he asked himself? Didn't you promise yourself that when your financial state improved you'd return to brave her family's wrath? He had a good business, a nice comfortable house and with people always ready to discard their old rubbish he had great prospects. Why delay? Because I don't fancy another thumping, that's why. But you don't have to go to the house, you could wait for her in the street. He sighed. No, I'll have to go and face Mr and Mrs Maguire, otherwise how am I going to spend the rest of my married life avoiding them? Get it over with. I will. Tomorrow . . . no, I can't, I have to see that bloke tomorrow about . . . and his train of thought moved away from Bright. When he fell asleep he had forgotten about her.

In the morning, though, after he had eaten breakfast and sat with his cup of tea planning the day ahead, a tap, tap tapping interrupted his thoughts. Curious, he stood and looked out of the window into the back yard. A thrush was endeavouring to produce its own breakfast from a snail shell, using a brick as its anvil. Nat watched the speckled bird and was immediately reminded of Bright. *You have to go and see her, face them. It's now or never*, he goaded himself. Gulping down the last of his tea he washed and dried his pots before making himself more presentable by means of a shave. Luckily he had just received his shirts back from the laundry. Grabbing a collar, he fixed it round his neck and then donned a tie. With his jacket on and his hair brushed he stood to attention before the mirror. Oh yes, very presentable. But the face that looked back at him was less confident, and his stomach had begun to churn. Blaming it on the bacon, he left the house and set out on foot for the Maguire residence.

On the way he purchased a bunch of narcissi from a barefooted flowergirl, rather by way of a peace offering than any show of thoughtfulness. There was yet a lot of black garb on the streets as a mark of respect for the old Queen who had died earlier in the year. Nat had barely noticed the passing of an era, so involved was he with his own life. The acid in his stomach bubbled and scalded as he stood before the Pig Market, urging himself to go in. *What's the matter with you? You're smart, you're quite well off, you've got a lot to offer her . . . but what if she's married to somebody else?* The idea hit him like a sledge-hammer. He hadn't really thought about that before. *Well, you're not going to find out by dawdling here.* Flowers held aloft and heart thumping, he strode to the Maguires' door and knocked.

It just had to be Martin who answered. Seeing Nat on his doorstep he went wild, but this time Nat was prepared for the blow and instead of resigning himself he dropped the flowers and grappled with Martin, each shouting and cursing at the other.

'I want to see her!' grunted Nat into the bigger man's shoulder as the other tried to crush him with a bearhug.

'Well, you can't!' Still clasping him, Martin lashed out with his boots whilst Nat hopped around to avoid them, the narcissi crushed underfoot. Other Maguires, hearing the uproar, rushed out to witness their crude choreography.

'Stop! Stop! Mind his lovely suit!' howled Mrs Maguire as her other sons joined in, grabbing Nat and pulling him away from their brother, but only in order to punch him themselves. It had been trial enough to stand up to a man who was ten years older, but now with three of them at him Nat didn't stand a chance.

'Go inside, Mam!' ordered Martin, his face dark with authority. 'We'll settle this.'

'Oh, don't hurt the lad!' Mrs Maguire was pulled inside by her daughter Mary, spared the sight of the viciousness that was inflicted upon Nat until he was forced to cry out, 'All right! All right, I'll go!' Dribbling blood, his clothes all ruined, he fended off his attackers with upraised palms.

'He's had enough, Martin,' Patrick warned his brother, who seemed bent on delivering more violence.

'I thought he'd had enough the last time!' spat Martin. 'I've a good mind to finish him altogether.'

'Whoa now!' The other two grabbed him. 'What d'you mean the last time? He's been here before?'

'He has! But I said nought cause I'd no wish to upset Mam – and if he comes here again I'll bloody well kill him!' His violent finger almost perforated Nat's chest.

Flinching, and cradling his ribcage, Nat backed out of the yard with the three brothers prowling after him. 'I know you're angry, and I can understand that!' he panted, words emerging on a bubble of blood. 'But I just wanted to say . . . I was sorry, and to see . . .'

'Sorry?' Martin's face twisted and he kicked at a broken flower. 'Jesus, you will be!'

'If you won't let me in will you just ask Bright to come out?' There was desperation in Nat's voice. 'I need to talk to her . . .'

'Get out o' here! Why d'you think she's hiding in the house? You think she wants to talk to you? Ye might as well be dead for all she cares. Get out, go on, get out! And don't come back or I swear we'll kill ye!'

'Why didn't ye just tell him she isn't here?' asked Patrick when Nat had limped away. 'He might try again.'

'Not him.' Martin thrust out his chest. 'He's not that brave.' He led the way back to the house.

'Oh, Christ, look at this!' He pointed to Nat's blood on

his shirt. 'I'll have to get changed and be late for bloody work – Mam! Mam! Have I got a clean shirt?'

Nat's recovery from his beating took longer this time, not simply because of the physical wounds but also the painful knowledge that Bright had severed their friendship. On reflection it was what he had expected in the first place. He had after all let her down. It was just so devastating to realize that he had not a friend in the world. Throughout everything he had always been able to depend on Bright, or at least on her memory, and now she was gone.

This rejection could have led him to ditch his ambition too – what had been the purpose of all this hard work if not for her? Don't kid yourself, his inner voice urged. You were doing it for your own self esteem as much as to win her; there's no reason why you should give it all up now. After all, ambition is the only thing you have left. Look at it another way, there're plenty of women out there who're much wealthier and more handsome than Bright – why, she could have changed an awful lot since you last saw her, could have become really ugly, you might run a mile if you saw her! True . . . but she's got my kid. This led to a bout of paranoia. Maybe she didn't want to see him because she regarded him as a bad influence on the child! Well, he'd see about that. She couldn't keep it hidden from him forever.

Again the voice censured: Don't waste your time! Get on with your life – and you can start by replacing that boy you sacked! Nat nodded to himself, knowing from experience how unhealthy it was to sit and brood. The rejection hurt deeply but he would get over it, and one day Bright would read in the newspapers how rich he had become and would be sorry she had not waited for him.

Britain's argument with South Africa dragged on into another year, but for Nat who had a vested interest they could continue blowing each other apart for as long as they liked. War meant guns; guns meant scrap metal. Although finding iron these days was as difficult as panning for gold, the rewards were just as lucrative and Nat was one of the few who did not join the street celebrations when the Boers were defeated.

During the summer of 1902 his business continued to grow, expanding from rags and scrap and shoddy into money-lending and other spheres. Remembering how in childhood he had exchanged crusts for favours, he now employed a similar tactic, showing willingness to do someone a good turn if the deed were reciprocated – and just in case it happened to slip any recipient's memory he entered the names of all who were beholden to him in a book, to be amassed like coins in a bank account until he himself required a favour and hauled in the debt.

It was as he went to retrieve one such debt on a grey June morning that he encountered the big lumbering frame of Spud Cato as both walked in opposite directions past the site of a razed church in Pavement. The man recognized him instantly. 'Nat! How're you doing?'

Nat, though reluctant to waste time, felt obliged to pass a few moments with his old pal. 'I'm all right now this bloody downpour's stopped.' An electrical storm through the night had brought teeming rain, making the gutters flow like miniature rivers and the air heavy with the smell of electricity and damp earth.

'Aye, we seem to have had nowt but rain lately, don't we? Eh! Have you heard t'King's badly? He's got lumbago. Me mam gets that, you know.'

'Aye? He mebbe caught it off her then.'

Spud never was one for irony. 'I don't think it's catching, is it?'

Nat could not think of anything to say, looking around whilst trying to conjure up a topic. Someone had forgotten to remove a Union Jack after the Boer War celebrations. It had obviously been outside the shop for weeks and was filthy with soot, the bedraggled linen flapping half-heartedly from its short pole. 'So how long've you been out, Spud?'

The lumpen face reproved. 'You're on dangerous ground there, seeing as it was you who put me in.'

Nat was quick to acquaint Spud with the truth. 'It wasn't me who ratted! Noel's father guessed it was us and sent them to arrest me. Bright – you know the lass I used to live with – she fingered Denzil thinking she was helping me. You know me, I'd never have dropped anybody in it.'

Spud nodded acceptance. 'Oh well, it's all water under t'bridge. Come and have a drink in t'Bird and Babby, just to show there's no hard feelings.' He jabbed his thumb at the nearest public house.

'Can't, I have to see a bloke who's gonna put a bit of work my way.'

Spud looked glum and rammed his hands into his pockets. 'Can he find a job for me while he's at it?'

'Haven't you worked since you came out?'

The big man shook his head and looked so despondent that Nat agreed to pass half an hour with him. 'How come you can afford to go for a drink, then?'

The dullard managed to produce a crafty grin. 'I can't –I were hoping you'd buy 'em, you're looking very prosperous in your top hat.' Nat laughed and went with him. Outside the Eagle and Child a crippled war veteran held up his mug. Nat might normally have walked past him, but as he wanted to parade his affluence before Spud he donated a coin, then retired into the public house.

Spud wrapped his large hand round the pint pot and took a grateful drink. 'Me laddo wasn't out long before he went back inside.'

'Who, Denzil?' Nat licked the froth from his upper lip, then dried it with the back of his hand.

'Aye.' Spud grimaced. 'In fact I'm surprised to see you looking so fit. He made no secret of wanting your balls.'

'Aye, they seem to be a very popular line. If I had more than two of 'em I could start a thriving business.' Nat took another drink, savouring the bitterness on the back of his tongue. 'I was in Canada when he was due out.'

'Canada?' Spud was impressed. 'How come?'

'Oh, it's a long story. It'll have to keep for another time.' Nat returned to the subject of Denzil. 'Why did he get sent back inside?'

'Stabbed a bloke and his dog,' replied Spud. 'He's fucking mad is that one. He'll have you if he sees you. You and that poncey Noel and that tart o' yours.'

Nat realized with a jolt that he did not like to hear Bright referred to in that manner. 'Haven't seen either of 'em for years.'

'No, me neither. I see old Gunner now and then.' He emptied his pot, then watched the last dregs of foam slide down to the bottom. 'Eh, I heard ol' Rodge got out a couple o' months back. I haven't seen him though. Think he lives in Sheffield now, married a lass from there.'

'It'll be warm in Sheffield then,' joked Nat. 'Hang on, I'll just have to disappear for a minute, Lady Smith wants relieving.' He rose. 'Here, go get yourself another pint while I'm gone. No, don't get me one, I'll have to be away soon.'

When he came back from answering the call of nature, Spud had only just been served. He sat down again to watch the big frame shamble from the bar with another foaming pot. For a time the ex-gang members swapped reminiscences, then Nat asked, 'Are you married, Spud?'

'No. I've got me mother to feed me and plenty of lasses to go with. Anyway, I can't afford it. You?'

Nat shook his head. 'No, I'm too young and beautiful to lumber meself with a wife. I'm happy enough on me own for the time being.' He turned the topic to one of employment. 'So, you were telling me you need a job . . . where are you thinking of looking?'

'Dunno,' Spud projected misery. 'Work's hard to get when you've been inside.'

Nat nodded in agreement and filed Spud away for future reference. 'If I hear of anything where will I find you?'

The other disclosed his address. 'I'm at home a lot these days – thanks, Nat.'

'Don't mention it. I'll have to rush now, Spud. Nice to see you. Bye!' When Nat left the public house he chastised himself for wasting time that could have been better used for earning money, when who should he bump into but a person who owed him some. 'I haven't forgotten, Nat!' blurted the man, even before a request had been made.

'Neither have I.' Nat took out his notebook. 'It's been . . . exactly two months and three days.' Though his tone was even, the look in his eye was enough to provoke nervousness.

The debtor hopped from foot to foot in an attempt to withdraw. 'I'm in a bit of a rush now, but I promise you'll have it by next Friday.'

Nat remained calm. 'If you think you can afford another week's interest, it's no skin off my nose.'

'Oh, hang on! I can't pay you until this bloke pays me! He owes me a tenner for some work I did and he's a bugger to catch . . .'

Nat cut him off with manufactured good humour. 'Oh, if that's the case I'll go get the tenner for you, but I take the lot.'

'I only owe you seven!'

'By the time you can manage to pay the interest will've boosted it up to a tenner.'

'Eh, that's not right, you're not having that much. I'll go round and get it tonight and fetch it straight to you.'

Nat patted him. 'You've just said this man is a bugger to catch. I know people like that meself. Don't worry, I've got ways of dealing with them.' He ducked back into the Eagle and Child, and shouted into the saloon.

There could be only one reason why the brute had been called upon. The man took one look at Spud and, fearing violence, mumbled to Nat, 'All right, you take the tenner and we're quits. Here's his name and address.'

'What did you want me for?' asked a bemused Spud when the man had hurried away.

Nat answered with a question. 'Want to earn yourself a quid? Go round to this address and collect the tenner that's owed me.' He handed over a bit of paper.

Spud's pendant lips mouthed the address. 'What if he won't pay?'

'Explain to him that I inherited the debt from Reg Sutcliffe. He's under no obligation to pay it today, but interest will be twenty per cent for every week he doesn't cough up. Speak to him politely, we don't want any nastiness. If all else fails then you can kick his head in.'

'What if I decide to keep the tenner once I've got it?' ventured Spud.

Nat lifted one of his black eyebrows. 'If you want to burn your boats, lad, I can't stop you.' Spud had always been physically stronger. 'But then again, if you want to make a regular job of it . . . ' The other was keen to insist that he had only been joking and asked to hear the deal. 'I might have a few more addresses for you to visit. I'll give you ten per cent of everything you collect. Deal?'

Spud gasped acceptance. Even if the ten per cent on offer only amounted to a pound this lackwit could never hope for a better opportunity. The two shook hands on it.

'Good! Well, you might as well start now and save me a job.' Nat tore a page from his notepad and handed it over. 'Each time you make a collection tick the name off the list. I don't want anybody accusing me of extortion.' With a grinning salute, his henchman departed.

The King's lumbago was to manifest itself as acute appendicitis, thereby postponing his coronation, but Nat's mind was far from such matters. The meeting with his old acquaintance that day had given him an idea for casting his nets into deeper waters. This required a visit to George Rex, the landlord from whom he had once rented accommodation, and the enquiry if Rex had any trouble from his tenants over payment of rent.

The other laughed at the lack of preamble – Nat was still on the doorstep. 'Aye, I do as a matter of fact. Why, thinking of going into property yourself and come for advice? I can tell you now, it's not worth it.'

Nat shook his head. 'No, on t'contrary I thought I might be able to help you. Can I come in?'

'Aye, you've got me intrigued.' Rex, a genial little man, let his visitor in, asked him to sit down and offered him a glass of port.

Nat accepted and after taking a sip wasted no time before proceeding. 'So, tell me about these bad tenants . . .'

'Scum,' came Rex's blunt response. 'It makes me laugh how people are always going on about landlords being ogres, I could tell them a thing or two about some of the tenants I've had . . .'

'Tell me then.' Nat crossed his legs, resting ankle on knee.

'Well, there were this one bloke . . . ' Rex narrated one tale after another about those who had cheated him. Nat listened in silence, allowing the man his head. 'You should see the state some of them leave the place in when they move on!' exclaimed Rex. 'That's if you're lucky enough to get rid of 'em. I've been stuck with one family for years. They only pay when they feels like it.'

'Why don't you just throw 'em out?' Nat assumed he was stating the obvious but the other man seemed to view this as a revelation.

'I couldn't do that!' Rex gulped his port and reached for the decanter.

'Why not?'

'Well,' the man was nonplussed, 'I'm not exactly built for it, am I? And the police aren't interested, I tried them once. Anyway, even if I could throw one lot out I might get another that's as bad.'

'So you're happy to fork out good money on repairing your own property for them to destroy again, whilst others decide whether or not they're going to pay you this week.'

'I'm not happy, no, but – '

'What puzzles me is, how could you afford to buy those houses and fill them with people who won't pay?'

Rex was quick to explain the anomaly. 'Oh, I didn't buy them! Nay, they were bequeathed to me by my father.'

Nat's response came out as an accusation: 'So everything that your father built up, you're prepared to fritter it through your fingers. You'd rather sit here knocking back that stuff,' he had noticed that Rex was fond of his port. 'Not much of a businessman are you, George?' Before the other could respond Nat shook his head. 'It's a crying shame and if I had the money myself I'd buy those houses of yours.' He meant it. How infuriating that a sop like George could be handed such riches on a plate and was too weak to keep them. 'But I haven't got the money and all I can do is to offer what help I can. How much are you owed in back rent?'

Rex looked awkward and bent his face to his glass. 'I'm not sure.'

Nat sighed and shook his head in rebuke, then put forward his deal. 'Let me take charge and I'll soon have your rents coming in regularly plus all the money you're owed.'

'I might not be good at making money,' smirked the other, 'but I'm not daft – how much?'

'Twenty-five per cent.'

'Nothing doing!' George Rex banged down his glass.

'Think about this carefully, George. Get yourself a bit of paper and calculate what you're getting every week at the moment, right? Then work out how much less you'd be getting if you accepted my offer. I can tell you the answer right now. You wouldn't be getting less, you'd be getting much more. Even after I've taken my cut you'll be a damned sight richer than you are now. Seventy-five per cent of something is a lot more than a hundred per cent of nowt, and you wouldn't have the worry over whether you were going to get paid next week. I'd be worrying about all that.'

Rex was thoughtful. 'How . . . ' He stopped.

'How do you know you can trust me?' provided Nat.

'No, I didn't mean – well, yes. You could collect all this money I'm owed and I might never see you again.'

Nat sighed. 'That's why I'm the businessman and you're not, George. It would be a bit silly of me to throw away a regular income for the sake of a quick haul, wouldn't it?'

'I suppose it would,' Rex agreed.

Nat had not finished. 'And if I wanted to throw money away it'd be a lot easier just to let you continue as you've been doing all along. You've had plenty of practice.'

Rex accepted that he was no entrepreneur. 'I still say it's a lot, though. What about, say, twenty per cent?'

It was difficult for Nat to prevent a look of amazement from crossing his face. He had only expected to end up with half this amount! Forcing himself to sound grudging, he heaved his chest. 'If that's all you think I'm worth then I have to accept. Give us a list of your debtors then, George. The sooner I start the sooner you'll have your brass.'

Pleased with himself, the slightly-built Rex went to a davenport and handed over a notebook.

Nat rippled through the pages. 'Not very good at book-work either, are you, George? Never mind, I'll go through it tonight and work out who owes you what.'

'How will you go about collecting it?' enquired Rex.

'Don't you worry about how and when, George, you're paying me to do that now.' Nat pocketed the book.

'Well, good luck, you'll need it,' offered Rex as his visitor left.

Nat was not so much relying on luck to persuade Rex's tenants to part with their cash as on the more tangible threat of Spud, to whom he delegated responsibility for collection of the debts, with the offer of a similar rate as before. He himself consolidated the success he had enjoyed with Rex by inviting other landlords to join the scheme. Some already had debt collectors of their own. Others showed a willingness to participate but offered a far lower cut than Rex had done. However, any percentage was welcome to Nat, whose only exertion was in counting the money when Spud had collected it. If he had any reservation at all it was in promising to pay his henchman a cut of the takings rather than a weekly wage, for when Rex's debts were eventually hauled in they provided a considerable sum. Even allowing for the fact that this had taken a couple of months to accumulate, it meant that Spud had averaged a weekly wage of ten pounds! Nat could have had his services for a quarter of this and his friend would have counted himself a rich man. But however much it irked him he had made a bargain and he must stick to it.

For a time the debts were recovered without violence, but this brought its setbacks. One or two of the debtors began to call Spud's bluff and were now proving obstreperous. The purse that arrived on Nat's desk this Friday evening was lighter than he had come to expect. 'I can get it,' Spud reassured him, 'but I'll need somebody with me.'

His employer did not particularly like having to resort to violence himself. 'Well, don't look at me. I'm not paying you and doing the job meself.'

Spud allowed his lower lip to droop, unsure of what to do.

Nat provided the answer. 'If you need help you'd better hire it.'

The other was dumbfounded — he had never envisaged himself as an employer. 'Can I do that?'

'Do what you like, you'll be paying him out of your cut.'

'Oh . . .'

'Well, you don't expect me to fork out when you're the one who can't handle it?'

'No, no, it's just . . . ' Spud grinned. 'If I pay this bloke would I be his boss?'

Nat marvelled at the stupidity of one who took delight in giving away money. 'As long as you can keep him in line. I won't be held responsible if he gets too rough, nor for anything you do, come to that.'

'How much do I pay him?'

'As little as he'll accept,' advised Nat.

So, Spud hired an assistant at a rate of two pounds per week, the debts continued to flow in, Nat took his percentage without having to lift a finger and everyone was happy with the arrangement.

Encouraged by the success of his new venture, Nat continued to purchase books of debts and collect rents until his improved finances allowed him to bring another of his many ideas to fruition, at which point he approached George Rex again. 'Rather than paying me a percentage to get your money every week, why don't you sell one of your houses to me? That one in Huntington Road. I'll give you a fair price for it.'

'How much?' was the abrupt demand.

'Two hundred.'

'Two-fifty.'

'Done.' Nat had been prepared to pay four hundred.

'You can buy the others for that price if you want,' offered the delighted vendor who owned three more properties.

'I can't afford them yet,' answered Nat, 'but if the offer holds good in a year's time I think we can strike a bargain.'

In his new capacity of landlord, Nat visited his property.

It was a big house, far too big for the two eccentric old bachelors who lived in it. With a little enterprise he could separate it into apartments and get four times as much rent. With no qualms he gave the old men notice to quit. When they ignored his request and barricaded themselves inside he dispatched Spud and his friend to visit. 'You can do what you like, within reason, but if you get too rough you're on your own, understand?'

News of the eviction spread. Though Nat could not be accused of using violence himself it was well known that he employed others to do it, and so he began to adopt an aura of menace. He was happy to perpetuate this notoriety, enjoying the flash of fear that his sudden appearance would invoke in others, for he knew from experience that, apart from wealth, there was no greater power than fear.

18

The same hand of providence that averted a collision between Nat and Bright on the afternoon of that Royal visit was also to spare her through the ensuing five years, mainly because she was kept far too occupied at the old lady's beck and call to venture into town.

During that five years Bright was also obliged to repeat the story of Oriel's paternity over and over again, for the child's tender years caused forgetfulness of the details.

'Tell me the story of when you had me,' she would beg when being tucked up at night.

'But it always makes you cry!' her mother would protest.

And the raven-haired child would snuggle under the covers and sigh, 'I know, but I like it.'

So Bright would lie beside her daughter on top of the covers, take her hand, and in her soft half-Yorkshire, half-Irish brogue would once more repeat the tale whilst Oriel boo-hooed into her shoulder.

When not weeping for her mother's tragic tale, nine-year-old Oriel was an extremely garrulous child who, despite Miss Bytheway's attempts to contain her spoke with the fervency of an auctioneer.

Bright often found it a strain too. 'Oriel darling, slow down,' she would urge as her daughter tried to convey some new idea. 'Finish your sentences — are ye thinking I'm a mind reader?'

But Oriel could not slow down, could not see why she should have to. Why couldn't people speed up? Miss Bytheway was so slow and her mother was almost as bad.

The elderly spinster had almost reached her seventies

and was of great concern to those who survived on her charity. With each day Miss Bytheway came nearer to death, and Bright to the threat of homelessness. She was ill yet again and the doctor had had to be called.

Bright awaited him now. She was always on edge when this happened, not simply out of fear that Miss Bytheway would die but because the old harridan would kick up such a fuss when the doctor came. It was so embarrassing, the things she said to poor old Dr Ingram, but at least he was well used to it. Bright noted with dismay the much younger face that met her when she opened the door this winter's morning. After receiving no invitation to enter, only a quizzical stare, he introduced himself with a smile. 'Dr Scaum.'

'Oh, I do beg your pardon!' Bright clutched her breast and gestured for him to enter. 'I was expecting Dr Ingram.'

'I'm afraid Dr Ingram collapsed in the surgery half an hour ago and had to be taken to hospital.' Noel removed his hat, the black overcoat with its astrakhan collar, and handed both to the maid, who looked familiar. 'I'd intended to take over from him on his retirement but it looks as though I'll be doing so a little earlier than expected now.'

Bright did not recognize the face behind the moustache. 'That's a pity – I mean, oh, I'm sorry, I didn't mean to offend ye!'

Noel laughed and, smoothing his wavy yellow hair followed her towards the staircase, bag in hand. 'That's quite all right. I seem to have induced a lot of disappointment in my patients, the elderly ladies especially were fond of Dr Ingram.'

'Miss Bytheway wasn't.' Bright laughed and deposited his hat and coat on a peg. 'I mean it doesn't matter which doctor it is, Miss B wouldn't like him.'

Noel smiled back, a genuine warm smile. 'Yes, I must confess I have been warned.'

'Oh good!' Bright led him up to Miss Bytheway's room

and entered. 'The doctor's here, Miss Bytheway. Tis a new gentleman, Dr – ' she turned to Noel with a question. 'Scaum?' He nodded.

'No matter. They're all quacks,' snapped Miss Bytheway.

Grimacing, Bright withdrew to let Noel in and closed the door after him before retreating downstairs.

When Noel descended ten minutes later an anxious Bright looked for signs of wear on his face. 'I hope it wasn't too much of an ordeal, doctor.'

Noel, who had been inwardly cursing Miss Bytheway as an old bitch, was generous in his opinion. 'I've had worse.'

'Not many, I'll warrant. Would ye care for a cup o' tea before ye leave?'

Noel was about to refuse but the familiarity of Bright's smile caused him to change his mind. An absent hand smoothed at his morning suit. 'Why, thank you.' He followed her into the dining room, which was also used as a front parlour, pausing to study a photograph of a military man and an elegant woman. 'Are these Miss Bytheway's parents?'

Bright had asked this same question of her employer. 'Yes, her father was a major in the York and Lancaster Regiment.'

'Ah! So that's where she gets it from.'

Bright shared his amusement. 'Please, take a seat. I won't be a moment.'

Instead of sitting, Noel played with his moustache and looked from the window at the modest front garden which held the skeletal remains of hydrangeas and little else.

'Would you like a biscuit?'

He turned to find Oriel offering a plate. 'No, thank you.' The pretty, black-haired child looked disappointed. 'But you go ahead.' He gestured for her to have one and weaved his way around the furniture to the sofa.

It was all the permission Oriel needed. Downing the

plate on the walnut table, she bit into one of the arrowroots and sat nearby. Her inelegant mastication grated the doctor's nerves. 'Perhaps I will have one.' He used the sound of his own crunching to drown the noise of hers.

'How is Miss Bytheway's health?'

Taken aback by the adult-sounding tone, Noel faltered. 'Er, she has a bronchial infection.'

Oriel nodded and used the same hand that was holding the biscuit to flick back her long hair. 'She's been prone to chest infections ever since she had pneumonia when I was little.'

Bright rushed in with a tray then. 'I hope Oriel hasn't been bending your ear too much, doctor.'

'Not at all.' Noel's brown eyes twinkled. 'We've had a very interesting exchange about Miss Bytheway's medical history.'

Oriel stopped crunching and eyed the doctor. Without a word she rose and left the room.

Nonplussed, the young man looked at Bright for explanation.

'I'm afraid my daughter thinks you're patronizing her.' Bright's face bore a hint of reprimand.

Noel looked suitably shamed. 'She could be right. I'm not very good with children.'

''Tis hardly your fault.' Bright smiled and poured him a cup of tea. 'Oriel doesn't realize she is a child. At Miss Bytheway's insistence she rarely mixes with those her own age and has to make do with adult conversation most of the time. I don't know whether it's good for her, but at least she's safe in here. There are some very cruel people out there.' She unconsciously covered her left hand to mask the absence of a wedding ring, a move which Noel detected.

'D'you think she'll forgive me?'

'I'm sure she will. Sugar, doctor?' She proffered the

bowl. After he had sweetened his tea, she began to withdraw. 'Well, if you'll excuse me.'

'Oh, please don't leave on my account! I can't bear to drink tea alone.'

Bright thought it must surely breach etiquette for a maid to take refreshment with a doctor and it showed on her face, yet at his insistence she agreed. Why shouldn't she? She was as good as he was any day.

'Excuse my impertinence,' Noel said after she had fetched herself a cup, 'but I have a feeling we've met before.'

Bright looked at him closely and for the first time during his visit noticed that she was not a bit nervous in his presence – at least she hadn't been until realizing it. Now she became deeply aware of his behaviour towards her. He spoke to her as an equal, not a servant. Excuse the impertinence he had said, as if she were a lady. For the past nine years Bright had been reviled by all, even her family – even by herself – and now here was this man treating her like a human being. So overcome was she that tears pricked her eyes, but she fought them. She had had great practice in controlling them since Oriel's birth and the doctor did not notice the gleam. If he did then he was courteous enough not to mention it. He took her mute gaze to mean that she thought him a fool and he blushed. Bright, only now aware that she had been staring, blushed too. The air of friendliness that had gone before now became momentarily strained until Noel punctured the membrane. 'Could I ask your name?'

She told him. 'Bright Maguire.'

The unusual name endorsed his recognition. 'I knew it! You're Nat's friend.'

Bright turned crimson as the memories swarmed over her like hounds on a fox. 'A long time ago. He lives in Canada now, I believe.'

'Really? Lucky chap.' Noel gave a wistful smile, then asked, 'I don't suppose you remember me?'

It had been the moustache that had thrown her, but she knew him now by the cleft on his chin. 'Your birds were killed!'

It sounded very much like an accusation. Noel's delight fizzled out. 'It really wasn't my fault that Nat was put away . . .'

'Oh, I know that!' Bright was acutely embarrassed. 'I wasn't . . .'

'I tried to protect him. I knew Nat would never do a thing like that.' He appeared to consider it very important that she believed him.

'I know, I know! I didn't mean to sound as if I was blaming you for him being put away. Twas all that horrible Denzil's fault.'

Noel nodded, suitably absolved. 'A nasty piece of work. I wonder where he is now?'

'Faraway, I hope,' issued Bright, then gave a shy smile. 'I see you've still got the little . . . on your chin.'

He touched the cleft, then laughed. The little bum, she had been going to say, but he wouldn't embarrass her by mentioning it. 'Afraid so.' Unaware that he was inflicting pain, he returned to the subject of their mutual friend, for he was eager to hear about Nat for himself. The boy's rude departure from his life had caused much pain and he had never found another about whom he felt the same way. 'How did Nat end up in Canada?'

She felt the knife turn in her gut. 'I'm not sure . . . I just heard.'

'Let's hope he made a go of it.' Noel nodded again and took a gulp of tea, which had started to form a layer of tannin. 'Well, it's awfully nice to meet you again.' He took another gulp from the cup and used his handkerchief to mop his moustache. 'I'd love to stay and chat but I'm afraid I've other patients to visit.'

'It's been lovely to see you too, doctor.' The air of affability had returned. Bright wondered how she could feel so completely at ease in his presence, but had no time to dwell on it for he was heading for the door.

'I'll call again in a few days.' Noel answered Bright's unspoken query. 'I'm not too worried about Miss B but it pays to keep an eye on an infection such as hers. In the meantime, call in at the surgery and I'll let you have some medication.'

'She won't take it,' warned Bright.

'So she said.' Noel was on the doorstep. 'I told her I'd take a funnel and administer it by force if she didn't do as she was told.'

Bright raised her eyebrows. 'You didn't!'

'Of course I didn't. You think I want to lose a regular source of income?' Noel laughed as the other covered her mouth. 'That's what I'd like to do though. She treated me like a witch doctor! The old . . .' He checked his tongue. 'Well, enough said or I shall get myself into trouble.'

'Say what you like, I wouldn't breathe a word!' Bright was laughing. 'I know exactly what you mean.'

'I'm sure you do. Well, goodbye Miss Maguire.'

So he had noticed the lack of a ring. Once again Bright self-consciously covered her wedding finger.

'Please apologize to your daughter for me.'

'I will. Goodbye, doctor.'

'Stupid man,' said Oriel, who came out of hiding once the door had closed.

'Don't be rude! He was nice, and he sent his apologies.'

Oriel turned up her nose. 'What if I choose not to accept?'

'I would guess he's the sort of person to say suit yourself,' laughed Bright. 'Ye want to think yourself lucky, I never had an adult apologize to me when I was a child.'

Intrigued by her mother's mood, Oriel forgot about the insult. 'You like him don't you, Mother?'

Bright cocked her head in assent. 'He has a way with him.'

'Will you marry him?'

'Oriel Maguire!' Bright raised her hand in mock outrage. 'Come here while I throttle ye.'

Oriel laughed and ran away.

When Noel called again he made it his business even before attending Miss Bytheway to atone to Oriel. 'I'm very sorry if it appeared I wasn't taking you seriously.'

Oriel studied him. He looked contrite enough. 'You're forgiven,' she told him.

'My humble thanks.' Little brat, thought Noel, how can such a pleasant woman give birth to that? 'Now, I'd better go and see if our patient will be as gracious.'

Later, he took tea with Bright again. Unlike the last time, Oriel remained. The young man wished she would go away but he pretended to take an interest in her. 'Oriel . . . ' His brow took on an inquisitive frown.

'Before you say it, I did not name her after a window!' The severity of Bright's tone was belied by the laughter in her eyes.

Noel looked askance but his voice was jocular. 'It was never my intention to show such ignorance, madam. I am well-acquainted with the ancient Kingdom of Oriel.'

It was Bright's turn to show ignorance over her daughter's name. 'Ye give me more credit than I deserve. Sure, I never heard of a kingdom called Oriel. Where is it?'

'Why, in Ireland! A very long time ago admittedly. That's why I assumed . . . with you being Irish yourself . . .'

'Oh no!' Bright laughed. 'I meant to name my daughter after a beautiful bird I once saw in a book but I spelled it wrongly, and hasn't every clever so-and-so pointed it out to me ever since.' It struck her how liberal the doctor must be; here they were discussing her daughter as if her illegitimacy counted for nothing. Obviously it didn't count with this man.

'Ah, I see.' Noel nodded. 'Well, you can now inform

436

those who poke fun that you gave your daughter such a regal name because of her queenly carriage.'

All laughed, even Oriel, who proceeded to glide up and down in most imperial manner. Noel watched and wondered but dared not ask, who was her father? Her visage led him to think of Nat. Was it him? Bright would have had to have been very young when she had given birth to her and the child did have the youth's dark straight hair and blue eyes. Admittedly, she was like her mother too, but the resemblance was more in the overall deportment than any particular feature. Still, he would not be so rude as to ask. The lack of a wedding ring was obviously of great humiliation to Bright who, whenever possible, tried to shield the offending finger from his gaze. Was it just his gaze or did she do it with any stranger? Why should it matter to him anyway? Aware of the lengthy silence, he shifted in his chair and asked, 'What do you intend to do with your life when you're old enough, Oriel?'

The child was glad that he treated her as an equal now and answered plainly. 'I'll be a nurse.'

Her mother was taken by surprise. 'When did you decide this?'

'When Miss B told me the story of Florence Nightingale.'

'Oh, and here's me thinking it must have been the profound influence I've had on your life,' complained Noel.

A bell interrupted them. 'Maguire!' commanded Oriel imperiously.

Flushing, Bright rose; so did a rather abashed Noel. 'Well, I shall be on my way. As Miss B has been so well cared for I won't need to see her again. Goodbye to you.'

When he had gone Bright turned on her daughter. 'Don't you ever say that to me again!'

Oriel's impish grin trembled. 'I was only making fun of Miss B, not you!'

'I don't care!' Bright wagged a finger. 'The doctor wasn't

to know and you won't speak to me again in that fashion, joking or no. I am your mother, remember that!'

Hurt that her humour had been misconstrued, as much for the fact that her mother could imagine she would be deliberately rude, Oriel lowered her head and began to cry.

This time Bright was not to forgive her so easily. 'And when the doctor comes again you will apologize to him for the embarrassment you caused. Go to your room!'

The incident faded into obscurity, for Noel was not to see Bright again for another year, when Miss Bytheway succumbed once more to her weak chest. Bright seemed pleased to see him, as did Oriel when he showed that he had not forgotten their previous conversation by asking, 'Tell me, do you still hold your ambition to be a nurse?'

'Oh yes, I've made up my mind,' came the firm reply.

'You wouldn't care to attend Miss Bytheway and save me the distress?' ventured Noel.

'I've got clothes to wash,' replied Oriel.

'Doll's clothes,' Bright hastened to inform the doctor.

'Ah well, I'd better get this over and done with,' sighed Noel. 'Onward Christian So-oldiers, marching as to war!'

Bright shared a giggle with Oriel as he marched up the staircase, whispering, 'The man's crazy!'

Whilst the doctor was upstairs, Bright put the kettle on. Oriel went back to her bowl of doll's clothes, squeezed out the water and began to peg them on a little line that Bright had fixed for her by the fire. 'Did you do this when you were a little girl?' Oriel loved to hear anything about her mother's childhood.

'Aye, but I never had more than one little dolly's outfit to wash,' said Bright. 'Heaven knows I've made up for it in this house.' She was distracted by a faint cry. Cocking her head she heard it again: '*Ra-bo!*' 'Oh good! I'll get a few pence for those old clothes of Miss B's.' They had been on a shelf in the cellar for weeks, had in fact been given to

Bright who had opined to her daughter, 'As if I'd wear any o' those! Stinking o' camphor and only fit for grannies. Still, I might get a few pence off the ragman.' And she had tossed them into the cellar. Now she rushed off to get them. 'Don't try and lift that kettle while my back's turned, Oriel Maguire!'

Grimacing at the smell of mothballs, she bundled up the offending articles and hurried outside. The ragman's cart was heading back towards town and was on Bright's side of the road, but had stopped two doors away to make a collection. Laden with clothes, the young woman stepped out of the gate when a blow hit her full force in the stomach. It couldn't be! Every pulse in her body hammering, she dropped the clothes on the footpath and fled back into the house before Nat had time to recognize her.

Inside, she slammed the door, whole body trembling, head and heart thumping and listening for the clatter of horse's hooves, the grinding of his wheels. It stopped outside her gate. Nat threw Miss Bytheway's clothes onto the cart, delighted at not having to part with any cash, and Bright heard the cart jingle off to the cry of '*Ra-bo*!' All the feelings of terror that she had managed to suppress for so long came ripping back. She was dragged into a dark tunnel, wanting to run but totally helpless to move, her brain unable to figure out how to work her legs.

'Mother, the kettle's been boiling for ages!' Oriel tugged at Bright's skirts. 'Mother!'

Getting no response, Oriel became alarmed and ran up the stairs, where she burst in upon doctor and patient. 'There's something wrong with Mother, she won't talk to me!'

'Oriel, you must not intrude in such a manner!' The old lady was most put out, hurriedly fastening her bedjacket and checking that her huge black bow was still in position.

'But she's acting very strangely!' Oriel directed her

anxiety towards the doctor. 'And she's going like this!' She began to pant loudly.

Noel was still holding his thermometer; as was his habit when in thought, he pressed it into the cleft of his chin where it nestled quite snugly. 'Perhaps I should go . . .' He looked to Miss Bytheway for permission.

'If you wish to reduce your fee for neglecting your own patient.'

He rose from the bedside, none too pleased. 'I had finished my examination, Miss Bytheway, but if you wish I can return after I've checked Miss Maguire's health.'

'Huh! There's nothing wrong with her other than being mentally unstable.' Having gained both child and doctor's attention, the wispy-haired invalid went on. 'You were unaware of it? Oh yes, she has always been subject to these bouts of hysteria. She was quite unable to look after Oriel when she was born, in fact she was so ill-equipped that she tried to do away with herself and they put her in the madhouse. That is when I came to the rescue.' Miss Bytheway donned a look of self-satisfaction. 'Not that I expect any gratitude. I did it for Oriel's sake, so that she would not be deprived of a proper upbringing.'

Noel was more annoyed than ever at such disclosures in front of the young girl, but he was curious too. 'I think I should go and see how she is.'

'Yes, perhaps you should,' agreed the old woman. 'She may need putting away.'

'I hardly think that will be necessary.' Noel left the room. Oriel preceded him, racing down the stairs.

Somehow, Bright had managed to regain composure in her daughter's absence. Still trembling, she had moved into the kitchen and forced herself to pick up the kettle, warm the pot, brew the tea, grasping at anything in order to regain normality.

Oriel dashed in. 'Mother, are you all right?'

Frowning, Bright struggled for speech. 'Yes, I'm quite all

right. Why wouldn't I be?' And slowly she was all right. When the doctor poked his face around the sitting room door there was little hint of the terrible shock she had received. Oriel was to inflict another. 'Miss Bytheway says you're mad. She says you tried to kill yourself.'

'What?' Nudged by panic, Bright's lips fell open.

Noel hurried to explain. 'It was very wrong of her to disclose such private matters. That woman! I wish someone would patent a medicine for cantankerousitis.' He studied Bright, who looked none too well, though she hardly presented the image of a madwoman that the old woman had painted. 'Sit down and let me take a look at you.'

'Oh no, please don't trouble yourself.' She filled her lungs with air, then began to pour the tea.

'Please, I insist.' Noel encroached further.

'No, no really!' She would not allow it, afraid of being forced to sit still, for then she would start thinking. 'Here, doctor, have a cup of tea.'

Noel accepted both the cup of tea and defeat. 'Oh well, tea's as good a remedy as anything. Thank you.' He tried to watch her without it appearing obvious.

'Mother,' Oriel chewed her lip, 'are you really mad?'

'I must be to work for herself.' Bright issued a nervous laugh and perched on the edge of her chair, taking erratic sips from her cup. Oh how dreadful for her secret to be revealed!

Noel looked disgusted. 'I don't know how you put up with the old witch.' Oriel giggled.

'I've no choice. No one else will employ me.' Bright urged her fingers to stop trembling. How long had Nat been back in York and why had he not contacted her?

'So she thinks she can do what she likes to you.' Noel sipped his tea.

'Oh well, I'd rather be the tortured than the torturer,' came Bright's ambiguous reply.

A bell rang. From instinct Bright was about to rise but Oriel put a hand on her shoulder. 'I'll go and see what she wants.' It was then that Noel decided he liked her. She was not so much of a brat after all and the smile that she reserved for her mother was quite enchanting. It was obvious they adored each other.

'Oh will ye? Good lass.' Bright sat down again and tried not to think of Nat, though her whole being still quivered.

'And inform Miss Bytheway that your mother is quite all right!' Noel called after her, then turned back to the girl's mother. 'A martyr in the making.'

'Pardon? Oh yes! She has far more patience with Miss B than I have. Tis all good practice, isn't it? For nursing, I mean. I must say she really surprised me with her ambition. She's utterly determined.' *Ra-bo! Ra-bo!* Nat was gone but his echo remained to haunt her.

'Let's hope she succeeds.' Noel looked approving. 'I'm sure that with her personality she will. Though heaven knows why she wants to do it. I can't stand sick people.'

Bright tried to cover a reproachful titter.

'Oh dear, now you think I'm awful.' Grinning, Noel toyed with the fob on his watch chain.

'No, I think you're funny!' sniggered Bright, forgetting all about her trauma for merciful seconds.

Noel was captivated by her laughter. 'Yes, I suppose people don't expect such things from a doctor. It's true I'm afraid. I'd never have gone into the profession of my own volition.' My God, why am I telling her all this, marvelled Noel, but could not prevent further divulgence. 'It was to please my father. He always wanted me to be a doctor, I couldn't bear to let him down. But sometimes . . . sometimes I hate it.' There was vehemence in his eye, then it was gone and he laughed again. 'I'm sure this can't instil much confidence in my medicinal skills.'

'You're a very good doctor,' soothed Bright.

'You're very kind. I suppose I'm not too bad at it,' admitted Noel. 'At least at treating ailments. Whether I'm any good with the owners of those ailments is another question. Still, what does it matter whether they like me or not if I cure them.'

'Oh, I'm sure they must like you.'

'I can think of one who doesn't.' Noel cocked his eye at the ceiling.

'Miss B doesn't like anyone,' revealed Bright. 'At least she doesn't like men.'

'Why?'

'I've never dared to ask.'

'Perhaps she was jilted,' ventured Noel.

Bright shivered. *Ra-bo! Ra-bo!* This was getting too close for comfort. 'I'm more interested in why ye don't like sick people, and you a doctor. I think ye must be pulling my leg.'

'What's so odd about it? Can you honestly say you like sick people, Bright?'

She flushed at the use of her Christian name. 'Well, I'd never really thought . . . I mean, I'm not a doctor.'

'They limp and hobble and shuffle into my surgery day after day, beffing and spitting and vomiting on me — oh, excuse me, that was uncouth!' Just because she was a servant didn't mean he could forget his manners. 'My mother's always taking me to task over it.'

'No, it's all right.' Bright gestured for him to proceed. 'I've had enough o' that meself from Miss B.'

'Yes, I'll bet you have. She's like hundreds of others. They come in and visit all these obscene practices upon your person then expect you to feel sorry for them. Well, I don't. Sometimes, I just wish they'd all disappear up their own . . . well, you know. Look, Bright, I'm being awfully familiar. I hope you don't take insult but I just feel that we've been friends for ages.'

Bright frowned in agreement. 'I know what you mean! I

don't quite understand it but I feel – well, I can talk to you.' Yet she blushed.

Noel found the display charming and was pleased that he had apparently taken her mind off whatever had upset her. 'Do you mind me rambling on like this?'

'Does it help to make ye feel better?' asked Bright, and when he made affirmation she added, 'Well then, complain all ye like. Sure, I'm used to it with her upstairs.'

Noel groaned. 'Oh, I don't want you to think I'm as bad as her.'

'Never! I still think you're odd though. Oh dear, now I'm the familiar one!' Bright touched her lips. 'Fancy saying a thing like that to a doctor.'

'A doctor, not God,' said Noel. 'Though some of my profession think they are akin to the Almighty.' His eyes quizzed the brown ones of his companion, wondering whether to dare ask the identity of Oriel's father. No, it was far too intimate a question for people who had met on only a couple of occasions, even if he did feel as if she was an old friend. He must curb this curiosity. She would tell him herself in time. 'Well!' He gave a final sigh. 'It's back to the grindstone for me. Oh, I almost forgot! I'm leaving the district.'

Bright was in the act of rising and now paused halfway. 'Does that mean you won't be Miss B's doctor any more?'

Noel detected a hint of concern in her eye. 'Of course not, who else would treat the old gorgon? No, I'm putting up my plate in town.'

'When will ye be moving?'

'In the next month or so. I've got my eye on a place in Low Ousegate. Once things are legalized I'll make sure you have the address.' He misread the look on her face. 'I know it's a lot further away and I'll understand if you don't want to traipse all that way to fetch me.'

'Oh no!' Bright had been thinking of Nat again and she shook him from her mind. 'It's not that much further – besides the tram probably goes right past the door.'

'You'll have to persuade her to install a telephone. I'm considering it myself.'

'Oh, I'd be far too nervous of using such a new-fangled thing!'

Noel laughed. 'Until the next time, then.' He retrieved his bag from the hall and took the hat which Bright held out to him.

'Goodbye, doctor.'

He turned. 'Call me Noel – after all, we've been through so much together.' In saying this he cocked his head in the direction of the old lady's room.

Bright grinned. 'To be sure. Goodbye, Dr Noel.'

Once the door was closed, it came back. *Ra-bo! Ra-bo!*

Nat, why didn't you come to find me? It can't have been that hard, surely? So why didn't you ask him when he was right there in front of you, her conscience asked. Why did you run away like a scalded cat? Because you're afraid of the truth. Nat doesn't want to know you either, just like all the rest. But he does, he *does*! I know he still loves me, he's just scared. Just scared.

19

Wealthy as Nat had become after ten years of running his business, he had as yet no wish to leave his rag-collecting entirely to an employee for, apart from not trusting anyone, he quite enjoyed rumbling around the city on his cart as well as the little bonuses it provided. It was surprising the things some people left in the pockets of their cast-offs; on a good day it could be as good as Christmas. Funnily enough, it wasn't the people from big houses who wouldn't miss a bob or two if they overlooked it, for their servants had had their pickings first. No, it was the folk who one would expect to be more careful with their hard-earned money. Nat always shook the garments as soon as he collected them, listening for that tell-tale jingle.

Today, though, under this drizzly grey sky, pickings had been lean. It was usually this way in the winter months; people waited until spring before having a clear-out. The few rags on his cart barely warranted the trip out of doors, especially as he was feeling so rotten, but a day of idleness was something he could not afford. He coughed, hunching into his overcoat with the discomfort in his chest. Ever since his return to York he had suffered bronchitis in the winter and this year was no exception. He was attempting to do as much business as possible before the inevitable occurred and he became too sick to carry on.

Sharing Miss Bytheway's aversion to doctors, he had so far borne this year's affliction with stoicism, relying on preparatory medicines and goose grease. Brow glistening, he rode through the streets on his cart stopping here and there to undergo a bout of coughing. Micklegate came to an end. He steered the horse across the junction and towards Ouse bridge. Traffic hemmed him in from all sides. Unable to move at his own pace he began to read signs and advertisements to pass the time: Reckitt's Blue for brilliant whites, Bovril . . . with agonizing slowness his cart moved over the bridge where the traffic came to a standstill. Nat saw the reason. A dray horse had bolted and charged straight through a plate glass window. The resulting carnage was a magnet for ghouls, and their vehicles were blocking the road. Nat coughed and expectorated as discreetly as possible into his handkerchief – he had always found spitting rather repulsive. Impatience rose. His eyes fell upon some gold lettering on a pane of glass – *Dr N. Scaum* – and he frowned. Could that be Noel? The image that sprang to mind was one of a fifteen-year-old boy, but after a quick calculation he realized that Noel must be almost thirty now, as he was himself. Well, well . . .

The traffic had begun to move again, but at a snail's pace. Out of curiosity more than anything Nat reached a quick decision and steered his horse into the gutter whence he got down from his cart, incurring the wrath of those who had to fight to get around the obstacle. Uncaring, he tethered his horse to a lamp-post and put on its nosebag before heading towards the building on whose window he had seen the gold lettering. Here it was again on a brass plaque: *Dr Noel Scaum*. Well, I never! He entered the dingy waiting room. Here were people like himself, coughing, wheezing, sneezing, grey-faced women and puking babes. He sat down near an inner door, shook the drizzle from his top hat and balanced it on his knee. There were a few dog-eared magazines on a table. Nat merely picked the skin from around his thumbnail.

When a patient emerged from Noel's consulting room another made to enter, but Nat was quicker and the look on his face forbade any argument.

Noel was scribbling on a card and didn't raise his eyes at

once. 'Good day, what can I do for you, Mr . . . ?' He looked up, then frowned in half recognition.

'Hello, Noel. I thought it must be you.' Nat placed his top hat on the desk.

'Nat!' After the merest flash of shock, the young doctor beamed and flung himself back in his chair. 'What a pleasure to see you. How are you?'

'I'm perfectly well, that's why I came to see you.'

'Oh, very droll.' Noel flexed his legs and swivelled the chair from side to side, eyeing his visitor intently. The dark hair fell the same way, but the snub-nosed innocence was gone. In maturity the lips were harder, the blue eyes cynical with just a hint of menace – until he smiled, then the hard edges melted away. The smile still held the air of inherent niceness that had attracted Noel to him in the first place. He portrayed genuine pleasure at seeing his old friend. 'Where did you spring from? I heard you were in Canada.'

'I was, ten years ago.' The visitor cleared his throat and smoothed his dark wave away from his brow.

Unconsciously, Noel mirrored the other's actions, then fingered his moustache. 'Didn't you take to it?'

'Oh aye, it just didn't take to me. They threw me out,' he added at the blond man's questioning look.

'Oh dear. I won't ask what for. So, what have you been doing with yourself since coming back here?'

'Breathing – just.' Once again he emitted a series of barks, grimacing with the effort.

'Yes, I must say you look ghastly.' Noel stood and leaned over to jab a thermometer into the other's mouth, then put his stethoscope to his ears. 'Open your shirt and let me have a listen. Good God!' After a moment he withdrew the instrument from Nat's chest. 'Sounds like a pack of wolves killing a pig, all that growling and squeaking. What do you take for it?'

'I thought you were the doctor.' Nat's reply was distorted by the thermometer.

'Bloody funny.' Noel removed the thermometer and studied it. 'I mean, are you taking anything at present?'

'Just some brown stuff.' He buttoned his shirt.

'Brown stuff? That description covers anything from sauce to shit.'

'It might as well be shit for all the good it does.' Nat fastened his overcoat.

Noel donned a more business-like air and wrote on a piece of paper. 'I'll give you something more efficacious. In the meantime,' he threw down his pen and took up a cigarette case, 'have one of these, it'll help you to cough up some of that rubbish off your chest.' He lit up himself.

Nat inhaled and immediately set to coughing.

'Oh bladdy hell.' Noel still retained his elegant delivery of an expletive. 'I don't think I can bear to listen to this.' He snatched Noel's cigarette and ground it out, but continued to smoke his own. 'Have a drink instead.' He poured Nat a small whisky from a hip flask, denying himself the same pleasure. 'If I start now I won't stop.' When Nat had finished coughing the doctor asked, 'So what have you really been doing since we last met?'

Nat downed the whisky, soothed by its warmth. It reminded him of his mother: *Drink this, it'll warm your cockles*, she used to say. He drove the memory from his mind and replied to the doctor's question. 'Sure you've got time to listen? There's a dozen patients out there.'

Noel was dismissive. 'If they're sick enough they'll wait.' He listened with obvious interest as his friend told him all about the business he had built up. Though heedful of the other's words his eyes strayed, noting the incongruity of the rag and bone merchant's smart outfit and his clean nails, neatly filed.

'I've left the horse and cart outside your door,' finished Nat. 'Hope it's not too much of an embarrassment for you.' He did not sound as if he cared.

'Not at all.' Noel retained his thoughtful air, rubbing a

digit up and down the cleft in his chin. Whatever the object, be it thermometer, pencil or finger, all things of this shape found their way to this groove. 'I'm glad to hear you're doing so well. Things could have turned out very differently.'

Nat tolerated the other man's scrutiny for a moment before grinning. 'I can hear your mind working, Noel. You're wondering why a rag and bone man dresses like this.'

Noel started and uttered an awkward laugh at being caught in such intimate examination. 'Oh no, I was just thinking if there's so much money in scrap why am I wasting my time being a doctor.' He gave another more relaxed laugh and tapped his cigarette at the floor to remove ash. 'What puzzles me is, if you've made all this money why do you still do the collecting yourself? It's a bit eccentric, isn't it?'

Nat shrugged, eyes on the tiny particle of ash that had settled upon the golden moustache. 'Other people wouldn't think there was anything odd in it. Rubbish and me tend to go together.'

'Oh, that's a bit hard!' Noel exhaled a cloud of smoke, so dislodging the fragment of ash which tumbled down onto his jacket.

'It's what a lot o' folk think of me.' There was the merest hint of bitterness in Nat's tone. 'Besides, I'm a bit superstitious. It's the only thing I've succeeded at, I'd be a mug to chuck it away. Anyroad, I enjoy it, love the surprises you get – you never know what you're going to find.' He went on to explain his appearance. 'But just because I do a job like this doesn't mean I don't want nice clothes. Oh, I'm no toff, nor never will be, but I spent enough years looking like a bag of rags. Anyway I need to attract meself a wife.' It was a glib remark. Nat was content to rely on the variety of sexual favours that his dark and soulful good looks had attracted to date.

'Don't we all?' agreed Noel. 'I never get enough time to socialize in this job. I'll probably end up having to marry someone my mother's chosen.'

'Still under home rule, then?'

'No, actually I have an apartment adjoining the surgery. Not that it makes any difference, I never have time to lure any women up there.' Something flashed in his eye. 'Speaking of women, have you seen anything of Bright since you've been back?'

Nat's whole demeanour changed. 'Why do you ask that?'

The doctor retained his innocent air but his suspicion about Oriel's paternity had just been confirmed. 'No reason, just that she used to be a close friend of yours didn't she? I mean, you lived with her family.'

'A long time ago.' Nat found himself unsettled by the way the doctor was staring directly into his eyes and pretended to busy himself over coat buttons that were already fastened. His chest felt ready to explode with cigarette smoke.

'Yes, that's what she said.'

'So you've seen her?' Nat's eyes came up to meet the direct gaze.

Noel looked into their blueness; they were watering from the man's efforts to control his coughing. He took a final drag of his cigarette before grinding the butt into the linoleum. 'Yes, I last saw her, oh, a few months ago. Her employer, Miss Bytheway, is a patient of mine, unfortunately. I've been visiting the old cow for the past five years.'

'How long has Bright been there?'

Noel shrugged. 'I'd guess about thirteen years.' It wasn't a guess. He knew that Bright had been at her present address since the birth of her child.

This made Nat think: he had never questioned that Martin might have been lying about his sister being in the Maguires' house on the day of Nat's beating.

451

'Are you her doctor as well?' He tried to sound casual, ending his query with a bronchitic wheeze.

'No. Bright appears to have an excellent constitution. It's just as well, she's worked very hard by the old maid.'

'Is she married?'

'No.' He's fishing for news of his daughter, thought Noel, and out of a sense of mischief did not offer any information whatsoever.

'So, whereabouts is she living then?' Nat took shallow breaths in order to avoid the pain of coughing.

His informant was unspecific. 'Fulford.'

Nat did not want to appear too concerned and merely nodded, but had the idea that his old friend was playing games with him.

'I visit the old girl once or twice a year. Shall I give Bright your regards the next time I see her?'

'I wouldn't mention it.' Nat brushed an imaginary speck from his lap. 'She won't want to be bothered with me. I caused her family a bit of upset being put away like that.'

Brown eyes quizzed him. 'If that was meant to be a dig at me . . .'

'Why should I take a dig at you?'

'Well, I just want to set the record straight, Nat. I tried my best to protect you but Father . . .'

'Yes, he would think it was me.' Nat looked sour.

The other reproved him. 'He was extremely fond of those birds.'

'So was I,' volleyed Nat.

'Yes, I know, and Father knew it too, but people have their limit for tolerance and I'm afraid you found Father's when you led Denzil to our home.'

'You think I had any choice once he found out I'd been there? I could've killed him for what he did.'

'Yes, we both know what he's like but I'm afraid others didn't. Have you bumped into him since you've been back?'

'D'you think if he was in York I'd be sitting here in one piece?'

Noel frowned. 'You don't mean he'd still take the opportunity to get even after all these years?'

'I wouldn't put it past him,' muttered Nat. 'You saw what he was capable of. I've always got me eye open for him.'

Noel winced. 'I'm sorry he got the idea that it was you who informed on him. As I said, I did my best to defend you but obviously not well enough. I truly didn't enjoy seeing you locked up, Nat. I would've come to visit if I'd been allowed to. I hope we can still be friends?' He meant it.

Were we ever really friends, thought Nat, but shrugged and said, 'Course. It all happened a long time ago.' He may need Noel some day and, besides, he had always enjoyed his company.

'An awful long time. Sometimes this job makes me feel very old.'

'You always said you wanted to be a doctor,' observed Nat.

'My father wanted me to be a doctor,' corrected Noel.

'Still bossing you about is he?'

'He's dead. He died some years ago of cancer.'

'Oh, sorry.' Nat tried to sound genuine. 'But if he was dead why couldn't you do what you wanted?'

'This may sound melodramatic to you, but I made a promise to him on his deathbed that I would do my utmost to fulfil his wish. Besides, I don't know what I want out of life so I may as well be doing this.' Noel shrugged, then after a moment took out his watch and sighed. 'Well, it's been wonderful to see you, Nat. I'm sorry if it appears I want to be rid of you but I'd better attend to those miserable fackers out there. Listen,' he added as Nat rose and picked up his hat, 'keep warm and come back if you start to feel worse. Don't lose touch again. Give me your address and we'll have an evening together some time soon. I mean it now.'

'Aye, I'd like that.' Nat scribbled down his address and telephone number on the pad that Noel shoved at him. 'And if you find you have nowt to wear I've got a little shop where I sell all the better stuff I collect. Some of it's real quality. I'll give you a discount.' He returned the pad to Noel, who looked at his writing.

'Thanks for the offer. Oh good, you have a telephone! I'll give you a ring – and don't forget the bloody medicine!' Noel called after Nat as he left, still coughing uncontrollably.

The rag and bone merchant climbed back into his cart, thinking about Bright. The name of her employer was very distinctive, he could look it up in a street directory and find out the address. *What would he do then?* He was not sure, and right now he felt too ill to act upon it. Stopping to buy a bottle of whisky he went home to bed.

Upon recuperating, Nat visited the library to look through the street directories, finding out that Bright, or at least her employer, lived at number five St Oswald's Terrace. After consulting a street map he jumped on one of the new electric trams and went there immediately. The vehicle dropped him very close to his target. Alighting, he paused there a while and looked across the road at the tall row of houses before starting to feel conspicuous. What an idiotic idea this was. He could be standing here all day and not catch a glimpse of her. Was not the beating from her brothers sufficient indication that she no longer wished to associate with him? But then if she had been living here for thirteen years as Noel had said then Martin must have been lying about her being in the house that day. She might be totally unaware of the episode. Go and knock, he urged himself. No, the fear of rejection was too strong.

Turning to look behind him he saw open fields. Another

turn of head to his left showed the village of Fulford. After standing here for a further three minutes he decided to wander towards the village for something to do, occasionally casting a backwards glance at the house in which Bright and his child were resident, hoping he would not miss their appearance. Even at this slow pace the journey into the village and back took little more than twenty minutes. He decided to adopt his former position as if waiting for a tram. He waited, and waited . . .

Bright was upstairs cleaning her employer's bedroom. The old lady had recovered from her winter bout of illness and was now in the dining room with Oriel. Bright finished polishing the mahogany and arched her back. Having taken down the lace curtains to wash, she had opened one of the windows to let in some air but it was starting to feel a bit chilly in here and she went to pull down the sash. Enjoying a moment's idleness, she gazed across the open countryside. The wintry brown had given birth to fat buds and snowdrops. On this clear spring day she could see right across to the Wolds. Wouldn't it be nice to go for a walk in the sunshine, to feel its warmth upon her face? How often in her youth she had been teased about her freckles, but so rarely was she allowed out of doors that these were hardly visible nowadays. Her dreamy gaze floated down into the street – and jolted her back to reality. Nat! She cringed against the wall for ten trembling seconds, then mustered the nerve to peep from behind the curtain. What was he doing here? He certainly wasn't waiting for a tram, he had just allowed one to go by. Why, he was watching the house! He did know where she lived after all, must have seen her that day when she fled from his call. *Ra-bo!* For one brief moment impulse urged her to run out and meet him – before cruel logic ate into her joy. If he truly loved her, why had it taken him years to return? Why did he not come right to the door? She continued to watch from behind the curtain, terrified at the sight of him, thrilled and saddened at the same time. Unobserved, she was able to take a good look at the face she had once loved . . . still loved. Her breast ached with the same intense longing that Nat had inspired all those years ago. The stark realization that he did not love her could make no difference to her own feelings. She had tried to make her heart see reason but the fact that it was beating like a drum at the sight of him now, even after all these years, belied her insistence that she was over him . . . and there was the added bond of the child.

Downstairs, Oriel, who was almost fourteen now, was insisting to Miss Bytheway that she intended to become a nurse.

Miss Bytheway had just finished writing a short letter which she now inserted into an envelope. 'I'm afraid that's impossible.' Her voice held conviction but was not unkind.

Oriel was tinkling the icicles on the ruby glass centre-piece. Her tone was lofty. 'Mother says I can be anything I want to be.'

'Oh does she?' A scrawling hand penned the address on the envelope. 'Well, your mother is quite wrong.' Miss Bytheway looked up. Her hair all but gone, the huge black bow had been dispensed with and in its place was a lace cap. 'Take the word of one who knows. I have you marked for a much better career – it's your welfare I have at heart.' She came as close to a smile as was in her repertoire. 'Here, be so kind as to post this letter for me, dear.'

The thud of the front door made Bright jump. Still employing the curtain as a veil she craned her head, but it was impossible to tell who had emerged because of the bay window on the storey below. The gate whined. Bright gasped at the sight of her daughter flouncing down the road. Nat had seen her too. He had come to attention. Bright guessed now that there could only be one reason that he did not come directly to the door and reintroduce himself, but skulked instead like a spy; it was not Bright he had come to see but his daughter. Who had told him of her existence? Was it Noel? Would he accost her? It was too late to stop Oriel now. Bright held her breath and watched.

Nat had been contemplating going home, but as the door of number five opened he became alert and turned slightly away in case it was Bright who should exit. Instead a figure, half-woman, half-child, skipped out into the road. His daughter. He knew it for a fact. He held his breath and watched her walk to the pillar box on the corner. Inserting the letter, she skipped back towards the house. Briefly she turned her face – *his mother's face* – sparking in him both longing and anguish. His eyes devoured every detail. The emotions he endured in those seconds were unbearable. The girl was going back into the house. He wanted to speak to her, tell her who he was – but she was gone.

Bright let out a relieved exhalation, but continued to watch him. Only when a tram rumbled along and Nat got on it did she allow herself to sag in relief and misery. He was gone, but his appearance had given rise to all sorts of problems. Should she warn Oriel that she might be approached by her father and so inflict a state of permanent apprehension? Nat might not come again and then how hurt and disappointed Oriel would be. She decided to do nothing for the moment, though the incident had made her jumpy. In future whenever she ventured out she began to take more notice of the people around her, imagining that Nat was watching.

Sometimes, Nat *was* watching. The sight of his daughter had lured him back again and again since that day. Once, he had even followed her when she and Miss Bytheway took a rare outing to town, had sat at a nearby table in a restaurant listening to their conversation, had heard her name – Oriel. It was obvious his child needed no financial help; the old woman was expensively dressed and well-spoken, and she would teach Oriel how to be a lady. But therein lay another problem. Was Oriel too much of a lady to accept him as her father? Many times he had come close to approaching her. Many times he had failed. One look at her told him she would not be too impressed to have a rag and bone merchant as her father. What choice had he but to love this young lady from a distance?

'You'll never be a lady,' reproved Bright as her daughter passed wind. 'I don't know why Miss Bytheway wastes her time.'

Oriel giggled. 'I didn't mean to, it just slipped out.' She had just brought a tray down from the old lady's bedroom. 'Good thing I didn't do it up there.'

'No, you thought you'd save it for your poor old mother,' accused Bright, wafting at the air, an expression of disgust on her face. 'My God, that would just about finish her off.' At the end of a year that had seen the death of their monarch her employer was once again bedridden.

Oriel removed the breakfast pots from the tray, the contents of which were hardly touched. 'I love it when Miss B gets ill.' She nibbled on a triangle of toast.

Bright laughed. 'A very sympathetic nurse you'll make.'

'No, it means that Dr Noel will be calling. I wish he came more often.' The doctor had been making annual visits for the past five years, had seen Oriel grow from a child to a young woman. 'It's so lovely to have someone to talk to.'

'Oh, thank ye!'

Oriel laughed. 'It's no slur on you, Mother. I just meant it's nice to chat with someone different from time to time, especially a man. The amount of men we get here you'd think the species was extinct.'

Bright was thoughtful. Was there too much interest in the doctor's maleness? Oriel was fourteen after all, a similar age to that which she herself had been when . . . no, no, she scolded herself! Fancy accusing Noel of a thing like that, and him a thorough gentleman. Can't you see it's a father she wants. And who could blame her thirst for male company, cooped up here all her life with two women, one a drudge and the other a tyrant. She forced herself to be charitable; that wasn't fair on Miss Bytheway, who despite her periods of illness had made a magnificent job of Oriel's education, even if she had not quite managed to elevate Bright's daughter to the heights of gentility she might have liked. It was just the unnaturalness of it all; a child needed two parents. And where was that other parent? She had not mentioned Nat's observation to Oriel for as far as she knew he had not come again, although part of her wished he would. Often she lay in bed and wondered what it would be like to be married, to have Nat lie beside her, to wake up every morning for the rest of her life and see his face. Many times she had dwelled on that night and the act that they had performed. Her thoughts towards it had altered. She found herself gripped by longings and desires that she could not explain, sometimes dwelled upon it so much that her lower abdomen became seared with intense heat, felt like she was ready to give birth to a lump of burning lead from between her legs . . .

The doorbell rang. Bright jumped. Oriel skipped to answer it.

'Ladies don't run!' accused her mother.

'Hello, Oriel!' Noel seemed as delighted to be here as the occupants were to see him, hanging up his own hat like a member of the household. 'See how quickly I respond to your command?' He patted the telephone that had recently been affixed to the wall near the coat hooks. Oriel had been the one to use it this morning.

Oriel treated him to her enchanting smile, then whispered, 'It's been there ages and Mother hasn't dared to use it!' She giggled. 'She jumps six feet into the air whenever it rings. Miss B thinks she's crackers. The old girl loves it herself. You ought to hear her bellowing into it. Not this morning, though, she's too croaky.'

'Oh dear, she won't be entertaining me with any Christmas carols then. And how are you? Still harbouring the ambition to be a nurse?' Every visit he asked this same question; it had become something of a joke between them.

'Of course.' Oriel adopted a prim and proper expression that was meant to represent her benefactress. 'Even though Miss B insists that I go to a school of commerce.'

'Ah well, that's not a bad idea. Take it from me, invalids can be very draining – hello, Bright!' He poked his head around the kitchen door.

'Hello, Dr Noel, come in out of the cold.' She was already setting cups on the table.

'Mm, what a delicious smell!'

'Mother o'God! I put some mince pies in the oven to warm for you coming and forgot all about them.' Seizing an ovencloth, she hurried to the range and rescued the pies. 'Oh they're all right – probably take the skin off your mouth, mind!' She laughed as she transferred them to a cooling tray, then came back to him. ''Tis nice to see you again. Are ye well?'

'How considerate of someone to ask the doctor instead of always the reverse. I'm very well indeed, Bright. Could I warm my hands before I venture upstairs?' He made directly for the fireplace, then indicated the swag of greenery that hung from the mantel. 'Oh, look at this! Somebody's ready for Christmas.' Bright told him it was Oriel's work. 'Very artistic.' He held his hands to the fire. 'Ah, that's grand! It must be nice to sit in front of a blaze like this all day instead of tramping round in the cold and subjecting oneself to all manner of infections.'

'Sit in front of the fire all day?' laughed Bright. 'Chance would be a fine thing.'

He grinned. 'I was only kidding. I don't envy you having to run up and down those stairs time after time. All I can say is it's a good thing you're never ill, or who would fetch and carry after her ladyship?'

'Well, yes, I don't ail much apart from the odd cold,' and the odd bout of madness, she added privately. 'Oriel must take after me too, though she hardly goes anywhere to catch anything.'

Noel had remembered. 'Hey, you'll never guess who's paid me a visit since the last time I saw you.' He spun from the fire. 'Our friend Nat!'

Bright almost fainted. 'Oh really – Oriel, go and inform Miss B that the doctor's here, will ye!'

But Oriel was watching the doctor. 'Did you say Nat?'

'Er . . . ' Noel had seen Bright's alarm and cursed his stupidity. 'Yes, he's just an old friend of mine.'

'Oriel, will you please do as you are told!'

With a huff, the girl complied, but went slowly in order to try and catch any snippet of information that might follow.

Noel realizing his error, did not speak until he was certain she had gone upstairs. 'I'm sorry, Bright, was I wrong to mention him?'

'No!' Bright gave a false laugh. 'Why ever should ye be? Er, did ye see him in a professional capacity or . . . ?' She wrung her hands as if trying to rid them of stubborn dirt.

Noel watched the tortured expression. 'Mm . . . I don't suppose I'd be breaking the Hippocratic Oath to tell you he had bronchitis.' Perhaps he had better not mention the night out he had enjoyed with their friend.

Bright nodded, trying to appear calm, smoothing a cloth on the table. 'Aye, he used to get it every year as a child. So, what's he doing back from Canada?' She gave no hint that she knew he had been back for some time.

'Apparently he was thrown out – been in York for ten years . . .'

Ten years! Oriel, straining to hear from the staircase, covered her mouth. My father has lived here for most of my life and has never been to see me. Bright had always spoken in such glowing terms of Nat that Oriel had remained confident that he would eventually come back. Now, she did not know what to believe.

'. . . has his own business trading in woollens and seems he's also a man of property.' All the while he spoke Noel watched her face and Bright knew what was in his mind.

'I'm glad he's done well for himself. D'you want to go up and see Miss B now, doctor?'

He had upset her. How stupid to throw Nat's name into the conversation like that when he was almost certain that their mutual friend was Oriel's father. It would wound like hell. What had possessed him? Nought but his own selfish desire to know. After visiting his patient, instead of tarrying as he usually did, Noel disappointed Oriel by refusing the offer of tea and mince pies, saying he had things to do at the surgery, thereby forcing her to turn to her mother in order to unravel the mystery. 'Why did you send me out when Dr Noel mentioned my father?' When Bright just stared she added, 'It was my father of whom he spoke, wasn't it?'

Bright lowered her face. 'It was.'

'Why doesn't he come to see us if he's been here all that time?' A strange and unpleasant mood had come over Oriel.

Bright nibbled her lip and shook her head, too upset to offer explanation to her confused child, for despite her airs and graces Oriel was only a child.

'Will you go and see him?' asked her daughter.

Bright lifted her chin. Her eyes were suffused with emotion. 'No. He's made it clear he doesn't want to see . . .' she cleared her throat, 'see us. So I think we'll leave him alone.'

For once, when her employer's bell rang the harassed maid voiced no complaint but hurried to answer it, eager to escape that bewildered look in Oriel's eye.

'Ah, Maguire!' Coughing and wheezing, Miss Bytheway tried to lever herself into a more comfortable position.

'Come and plump up my pillows.' Even though King Edward had been dead for over six months she retained her own token of mourning in the form of a black lace cap.

Bright rushed to her assistance, then asked, 'Would you like another drink, ma'am?'

'If you would be so kind.' Face drawn and even paler than normal, Miss Bytheway took the glass of lemon and honey from her servant and put it to her lips. 'Ah, that's better.' She relaxed against the mound of pillows and closed her eyes.

The maid replaced the glass on the table. 'Will that be all, ma'am?'

'No, that will not be all!' The translucent eyelids flew open and Miss Bytheway clasped her handkerchief in her fist. 'For some years Oriel has entertained the ridiculous notion of becoming a nurse.'

'What's so ridiculous about wanting to help people?'

The old lady scowled at the interruption. 'If it is charity which concerns you, Maguire, then there are other ways in which Oriel can be useful. You don't imagine I've imparted the benefits of my own education simply for her to waste it by emptying bedpans? She has a good brain, she is capable of much more.'

'Have you told her you don't want her to be a nurse?' asked Bright.

'I have tried to coax her in other directions,' the old lady inclined her lace-capped head, 'but she's far too busy chattering to take any notice of an old woman. No, it is your place as her mother to lay down the rules.'

Bright's temper flared. 'To be the one who disappoints her, ye mean! She's set her heart on being a nurse.'

'Maguire, I have spoken!' Miss Bytheway brought her handkerchief up to her mouth and coughed into it. 'I shall not say more. Suffice to say that if you value your own position you will persuade Oriel to see sense! That is all!'

Bright wheeled out of the room and downstairs. Not

even illness could subdue the old tyrant's need to control. 'The cheek of that woman!'

Oriel was still puzzled and upset over her father. 'Mother, why . . .'

'Do you know what she asked me up there for? I'm to order you not to become a nurse! How d'ye like that?'

Oriel was vague in her response. 'She's always trying to get me to change my mind, I take no notice.'

'Well, this time I think you have to take notice. She's adamant that you're not to become a nurse.'

Oriel sighed. 'Why?'

'Lord knows! Probably thinks it's not good enough for ye. She says,' Bright hesitated, 'if you continue with your plan, she'll throw us out – well, more or less. She said if I valued my position I'd do as I was told and persuade you to conform.' She gave a futile gesture. 'If I'm sacked we'll both be homeless. I don't think you've any choice.'

'Rubbish!' yelped Oriel. 'You're a good worker, anyone would employ you.'

'No, they wouldn't, not a single woman with a child.' Not to mention that that woman was regarded as mad, by her present employer and even by Bright herself.

'You've allowed that to rule you for far too long!' retorted her daughter. 'Letting her treat you like dirt because you're afraid that no other person'll have you. It's nonsense!'

Bright was angry at the lack of respect. 'It's not nonsense to those who have a child to feed and clothe! Tis all very well for you to be so high faluting, you've never been thrown out on the street!'

Oriel showed instant remorse and flew to hug the mother she adored. 'I'm sorry! I didn't mean to sound insulting, I know how much you've put up with for my sake! It's that silly old fool up there I'm angry with, not you. Please forgive me, I didn't mean it!' Apologies rattled from her lips like dried peas into a pot, whilst inside she felt as if all her dreams had been shattered.

Chest still heaving, Bright stroked her daughter's dark hair. 'I know, I know, it's all right. I didn't mean to get angry with you either. Ooh, that woman! Here, let me tie your ribbon.' She pushed Oriel to face the wall and refastened her blue bow.

Oriel sniffed. 'I won't be a nurse if you don't want me to.'

Bright was indignant and spun her around. 'It's not me who doesn't want it!'

'I know, but I mean I'll give up the idea if it's going to cause trouble.' Oriel drew away and looked into Bright's face, hoping her mother would not allow her to make this sacrifice.

She was to be disappointed. 'Oh, you're a good lass!' Bright hugged her. 'I know it's a lot to ask but it would be a load off my mind.'

Oriel nodded. 'I'm determined to do it one day, though – even if I have to wait until after she's dead.'

Bright crossed herself. 'Oh, don't say that. I dread to think what'll happen to me once she's gone.'

Oriel was scornful. 'Well, I should think that time is a long way off. The old despot's more likely to drive you to the grave before herself.'

Bright ended the conversation. 'You're probably right. Now, I'm off to the shop to get some more lemons for Her Highness. No wonder she's so sour, she goes through them by the hundredweight.'

'I'll go.' Oriel prevented her mother from leaving and, after donning coat and hat, went off to the village in the hope that some fresh air would dispel this hateful and confusing mood.

Unknown to Bright, Nat had been coming here quite regularly, it was just that she had been far too busy to notice him. As was his wont, he had been shivering outside for the last five minutes on the off-chance that he would catch sight of his daughter. The tram had arrived just in time for him to witness Noel leaving, and instead of alighting he had gone on to the next stop, having no wish to invoke questions from the doctor. He had just wandered back along the road when he saw Oriel coming out with a basket over her arm and, as she set off towards the village, he followed at a respectable distance on the other side of the road. Preoccupied, her eyes were cast down to the footpath and her expression grave. He knew that expression well, though he prayed that he was wrong; prayed to God that his child had not inherited his black moods. When she went into the village store, so did he, listening to every word she uttered. Upon the purchase of some lemons, she left. Nat bought a box of matches and followed her back to the house.

Through her wounded psyche, Oriel felt a presence behind her, frowned and turned to look over her shoulder. Fortunately, Nat was almost level with a tram stop. When his daughter turned he stopped and used the matches he had just bought to light a cigarette, pretending to be waiting for a tram, when, just at that moment one came and he was forced to get on it if he did not want to arouse more suspicion than he had already. As the tram whirred past her small figure she glanced up at it, thereby denying him one last look at her before the tram carried him into town.

This had got to stop. He was getting too close, was going to frighten her unless he came forward to explain who he was, and he just couldn't do that. With his anonymity gone he would no longer be able to get close to her if she herself did not wish it.

He alighted in Nessgate and was about to cross the road when he noticed a dog lying in the gutter. It had obviously been run over, one hind leg having been almost severed. Nat took a closer look. The dog lifted a large head to return his scrutiny, a look of tortured mistrust in its eye; it had apparently been suffering from neglect for a long time, its coat was matted and its attitude one of cowed dejection. Each time Nat made to stoop its lip curled up. However coaxing he made his voice, its growl forbade intimacy. 'Look, you soft mutt, you're going to have to take a chance 'cause none o' these buggers is going to help you.' Nat cocked his head at the indifference of passers-by. At his words the dog trembled and growled, but wagged its tail. 'Contrary bugger, aren't you?' Risking injury, he extended a tentative hand, laying it upon the dog's head. It quivered and growled and licked its pendulous jowls in fear, but did not bite. Nat ran his hand over the animal's back. Its eyes rolled in shifty manner.

Nat pondered on what to do with it, then with a flash of inspiration remembered that Noel's surgery was right around the corner. With ginger movements, he tucked his hands underneath its belly, scraping the backs of his leather gloves against the road as he inched them further under its weight. When he began to lift it gently it stopped growling, but drooled in terror. Its quivering ran through its whole body and into his own. 'You poor bloody sod.'

Trying not to jar the injured animal, he carried its not inconsiderable weight round to Noel's surgery where, with no one in attendance, he kicked on the door of what he hoped was the doctor's private apartment.

Noel almost choked on the brazil nut he had been chewing. 'What's this?'

'It's a Christmas present, what d'you think it is?'

'Nat, I'm a doctor not a fucking vet!' protested Noel, watching the blood drip all over his carpet.

'And I'm not a bloody detective! I don't know where to find a vet – just fix it for Christ's sake, my arms are breaking!'

Still protesting, Noel told him to bring the dog through to the surgery. 'Thank God there are no patients.' He lit a cigarette, looking flustered as Nat laid the animal on the couch. 'What a mess. Does it bite?'

'How should I know? He's not mine.' Nat straightened his back and attempted to brush the hairs from his coat.

The other tutted. 'I only allowed you to bring it in here because I thought it was yours!'

'I wouldn't treat a dog of mine like that.' Nat was looking for a place to lay his topper. 'He's a stray. Come on, stop arguing the toss and get it fixed.'

'All right, Saint Francis, hold it still!' Clamping the cigarette between exasperated lips, Noel reached for a bottle of chloroform and sprinkled some onto a pad. At the first whiff the hound struggled but Nat held him firm and soon he was too weak to object. Noel put a gauze cup over the animal's nose, then draped it with lint and peppered a little more chloroform onto it. 'Now, hold that there, Nat, and just add a few drops when I tell you to.'

Nat watched his friend gather his instruments, queasiness rising. When Noel produced a saw he balked. 'What do you need that for? His leg's only dangling by a thread.'

'Do you want me to fix it or don't you?' Noel drew on the cigarette and when Nat nodded he explained over a puff of smoke. 'The bone's shattered. I'll have to saw it cleanly further up. I'm not much of a surgeon but a dog can't complain. Christ, it bloody stinks.'

As Noel lowered the saw, Nat turned his face away. It did not help. The moment he heard metal teeth grate on bone he fainted.

The doctor kicked him into consciousness. 'Come on, Nat, you were the one who brought it in here!'

Groggily, Nat propped himself up on his elbow, then clambered to his feet, trying to keep his eyes averted.

'For God's sake keep it anaesthetized! Oh, facking hell, Nat . . . ' Noel blew ash from the dog's fur, then continued to saw, all the while cursing his assistant's inability.

At any other time Nat loved the way his friend swore. The most obscene words could sound like music from

Noel's lips, but right at this moment he could focus on nothing but that shambles on the couch. How he managed to remain conscious he did not know, but the dog underwent a successful amputation and now lay at peace with one bandaged stump.

'It's an ugly-looking bastard, isn't it?' Noel pulled up one of the animal's eyelids to reveal a bloodshot eye, then gathered his soiled instruments together. 'What do you intend doing with it now?'

Nat's thoughts had strayed to his daughter, seeing not the dog but her injured body upon the couch. He flinched, then took a deep breath and shrugged. 'Take it home, I suppose.'

'Well, it'll be in a lot of pain when it wakes up. Don't be surprised if it gives you a nip. If it does, come back for an injection, and I mean that! No messing about pretending you're tough, I know very well you're not.'

'Can you give me some pills?'

'No, it has to be given by injection.'

'I meant for the dog, to stop his pain.'

Noel gave a sour laugh and, taking out a container of tablets, poured a few into a small box. 'You can pay for them, mind. I don't think the National Insurance extends to dogs yet, though I wouldn't put it past the bloody government.'

Nat thanked him. 'Can I leave him here while I go home for the cart?'

'If you're quick. I don't want my rich patients coming here and thinking I'm a quack.'

'Thanks for fixing up the dog, Noel.'

'You're welcome.' The physician smiled. 'It wasn't half as bad a patient as some I have to deal with.'

'Maybe you ought to become a vet.' Nat was at the door.

'There's not enough money in it – hey, hang on! Oh no, it's nothing important.' He had been going to tell Nat of the effect his name had had upon Bright, but something prevented him. One day, though, he would ask to know the truth. 'I was just going to wish you Merry Christmas. Fack orf now and get that bloody cart.'

20

In the outside world King Edward's less ebullient heir, George, had come to the throne. Apart from a brief celebration this had had little effect on life at the house in Fulford Road. Miss Bytheway remained as domineering as ever, the long-suffering maid continued to lug pail after pail of hot water up four flights of stairs for her mistress's bath, ever in fear of the old lady's demise, and Oriel, unaware of being shadowed by her father, went dutifully to secretarial college, where she found that to be with girls of her own age made up for the denial of her primary ambition, at least for the moment. The earlier isolation from her peers did not cause any great difficulty, quite the opposite. Oriel thrived on all this new company and the invitations to other people's homes. The girls at college might seem immature, giggling at the silliest things, but Oriel accepted them for what they were and in joining their antics she found much freedom from the responsibilities she had taken upon herself at home. She had always felt as if she had to take care of her mother – and still did – but this daily separation, despite the mental effort it involved, allowed her the time to act like the young girl she was; to giggle with her friends at the sly winks from young admirers and to moon over some handsome teacher.

Bright had mixed feelings about her daughter's entry to the outside world. On the one hand she was proud of Oriel and was grateful that her selflessness had prevented further rows with the old lady. On the other hand, she did not like the feeling of inferiority that her fifteen-year-old daughter's achievement evoked in her, and worse still she was ever afraid that Oriel would come home crying after a fellow student had made a nasty remark about her lack of a father. Most frightening of all was the thought that now Oriel was prey to any man who might take a fancy to her.

Today, though, her child was safe. It was Saturday, there was no college and Oriel helped her mother with the household chores as had become her pattern, though Miss Bytheway was unaware of it. Bright herself made no complaint, for lately she had begun to think that what Oriel had said about Miss Bytheway driving her to an early grave might be true. She was not quite thirty-one, but the running of this big house took an awful lot out of her whilst Miss Bytheway, despite the more frequent bouts of invalidity, continued to mark time. This morning mother and daughter were chopping firewood in the back garden. A tree had blown down earlier in the year and though a man had sawn it into manageable logs it needed further reduction. Today was as good a day as any to replenish the kindling basket. Twixt comments, Bright swung the axe at the chopping block, her cheeks crimson and her brow glistening in the hot June sun.

Oriel, wearing an old dress and apron, elbowed her mother aside. 'Come on, give it to me, you're out of breath.'

Bright puffed, stood back and handed the axe to her daughter. 'I won't insult your kind offer by saying no.' There were damp patches on the underarms of her bodice. 'Oh, what I'd give to lie in bed all day like Miss B.'

Oriel indicated the chopping block and positioned the axe. 'Stick your leg on there and I'll try to oblige you.' Both laughed, then Oriel added, 'Did I tell you I've got a new one to annoy her? I keep saying "Oh, *by the way*, would you like so-and-so", or "*by the way*, have you heard this?" It really gets her goat!'

Bright pursed her lips. 'You'll never go to heaven.'

'Well, it's a small way of getting my own back for the

way she treats you.' Her daughter brought the axe down on a log.

'Yes, but she's given you a lot of things that I never could. You really oughtn't to tease her.' Bright glanced up as a gypsy came through the back gate.

'Would you be after buying some pegs off an old gypsy woman, lady? Tis a lovely face you have.'

Bright repossessed the axe. 'Go get my purse, dear.'

'Mother, you've got a drawer full of pegs in there! You fall for it every time.' Oriel both despised and admired her mother's kind nature. 'No wonder people treat you like dirt.'

'Shush! Go fetch it now.' Bright paid the gypsy for the pegs and received her blessing. 'The last thing I need is a curse putting on me.'

Oriel laughed as the gypsy shut the gate. 'You're cursed already and so am I, having to live with that one upstairs.'

With sufficient kindling having been chopped the two of them carried the basket of wood inside where Oriel, black hair all askew, put on the kettle for a cup of tea. 'Mother, I'm thinking of applying to be a nurse — just listen! I know what I promised but I don't see why I should have to kow-tow to her forever. I'm fifteen now, you don't have to look after me. Once I'm accepted I can live at the nurses' home.'

Bright was stunned by the unexpectedness of her daughter's remark. 'I don't have to look after you, but what about me?' she demanded. 'I'll still be out on the street when her ladyship finds out.'

'Mother, you're not thinking.' Oriel was patient. 'If you haven't got me to look after no one even has to know I exist, you can go and get a job anywhere.'

Bright looked mollified. 'Well, yes, I suppose I could . . . oh, but I couldn't leave her, what would she do without me?'

Oriel gave an outraged laugh. 'You've cursed the old

faggot for fifteen years and now you don't want to leave her!'

Bright laughed too as she made the tea. 'I know, it sounds daft, doesn't it? She's made my life a misery sometimes, but she's an old lady, I haven't the heart to walk out on her – and she was the only one who'd take me in when you were born. But you go ahead with your plan, dear.' She gave Oriel a resounding kiss. 'You'll make a good nurse, I know it.'

'Oh, thank you.' Oriel gripped her mother's wrist. 'I'm not quite sure to whom I should apply but I'm going down to the hospital this afternoon if you're agreeable? Don't tell her, she'll only take it out on you. I'll break the news when I come back.' She hoisted her shoulders in glee.

After lunch Oriel put on a frothy white summer dress, a hat bedecked with flowers, and went down to the hospital, asking to speak to the matron. She was asked if she had an appointment and when she replied in the negative was then asked the nature of her business. When she said that she wished to become a nurse, she was told to leave her name and to return on Monday with her birth certificate. Disappointed, she went home and told her mother, saying that this would mean she would have to take time off college. Bright showed understanding; if Oriel would soon be leaving college anyway, one day's absence was not going to matter.

On Monday, with maternal encouragement, Oriel once again donned her best outfit and returned to the hospital for her interview. There were other girls waiting in the tiled corridor. Oriel smiled at them, then stared straight ahead awaiting her turn and wondering if she would be able to bear the smell of her workplace. When her name was finally called she was shown into Matron's office.

'Sit down, Maguire.' The hefty bespectacled woman pointed at a chair. 'Now, why do you wish to be a nurse?'

Prepared for this question, Oriel gave her rehearsed

speech which appeared to be to the Matron's satisfaction. The interview lasted about twenty minutes and at the end of it Oriel felt that she had made a good impression. The matron actually smiled at her.

'Well, my dear, no more questions.' The matron's starched bosom crushed against the edge of her desk as she reached over to a pile of forms and took one. 'Let us just have a few details – have you brought your birth certificate with you, by the way?'

Whenever anyone issued the phrase *by the way* Oriel immediately thought of her benefactress and giggled mentally. What a row there would be when she confessed! 'Yes, I have it here.' She reached into her bag and handed over the document.

The woman gave a clipped, 'Thank you,' and unfolded it. 'Oh dear, you're very young!' She had assumed from the confident manner that Oriel was older. Something else had caught her eye too, and she looked up at Oriel. 'I'm afraid . . . we cannot take you.'

'Because I'm too young?' Oriel's smile became fixed.

'Because you are illegitimate, my dear. The profession cannot take you. I'm sorry.' The matron handed back the certificate. Lips apart, Oriel reached out to take it, but remained seated. 'I'm sorry,' repeated the woman, obviously waiting for her to leave.

Too dumbfounded to complain, Oriel stood, then went home. Somewhere along the way her shock turned to anger, whence she cursed her absent father. I hate you! All this is your fault. For years I've dreamed about making this my career and now I can't, all because you abandoned my mother! For a second Oriel railed at her mother's dumb loyalty – how could she have been so stupid as to believe he would come back? – but just as quickly she gave mental apologies. It wasn't that poor, lovely woman's fault that she had been betrayed. Oriel wished he were here now so that she could slap his face, punch and scratch him for ruining her life. The swine! But I'll get you back, she issued dark warning with each determined footstep. I'll teach you to hurt me and my mother.

'Have ye been accepted?' The moment her daughter entered the kitchen an eager Bright pounced – then saw the look on Oriel's face and moaned. 'Oh darlin', I'm sorry!' Expectant smile collapsed, she put her arms round the girl, who during the latter half of her journey had forced herself to regain composure.

'Turns out Miss Bytheway was right after all, doesn't it?' Oriel removed her flowered hat, hoping her disappointed expression was masking the true bitterness she felt.

Face creased in sympathy, Bright stroked her daughter's hair. 'Oh well, never mind, it's their loss. I'm sure there are many other people willing to employ an intelligent girl like you. What reason did they give for not taking ye?'

Oriel could never burden her dear mother with the true reason. 'I'm too young.' The straw hat hung at her side.

Bright rallied, holding her daughter at arms' length to exclaim, 'Oh well, ye can try again then!'

'I don't think so.' Oriel wrinkled her nose. 'I was very nervous at the interview. If I was nervous then I'd be no good in an emergency would I? Anyway, it's all over and done with.' The subjugation of her anger had exacted a price: repulsive black fingers of depression had begun to probe her mind. She had the urge to be alone. 'I'll just go up and get changed.'

Bright released her. 'I'll make you a cup of tea when you come down.' She bustled off into the scullery, allowing her false cheeriness to dissipate now that Oriel had gone. What a disappointment.

'Why is that girl not at college?' Miss Bytheway had heard the conversation in the kitchen but in her geriatric state it had taken her all this time to make her way from the front room. She was just in time to catch a glimpse of Oriel's devastated face before the girl went upstairs.

476

Bright turned from the hob, looking guilty. 'Oh well, ye might as well know. Oriel went for an interview to be a nurse today – but she was turned down, so there's no need for you to get excited! And I'd be grateful if you've anything to say you say it to me, she's been upset enough.'

'I can see she has.' Miss Bytheway clutched her balled up handkerchief in fury. 'And yes! I certainly do have something to say! Because if Oriel has been upset then you, Maguire, are responsible! Why do you think I wanted her to abandon the idea of becoming a nurse? Was it just to spite her? Of course not! I love that child! I have tried to protect her and I hope that in most aspects I have succeeded. I would have been wholly successful had it not been for her stupid idiot of a mother!'

Bright came out of the scullery, fearing that her employer was about to induce an apoplexy, for her face was crimson. 'Miss Bytheway . . .'

'Stupid!' The eyes might be veiled with cataracts but the obvious anger burned through. 'That girl has been upset needlessly. The reason she has been refused a nursing post is that she is illegitimate. Yes! And for that you are totally to blame, Maguire.'

Bright had taken the news like a slap in the face. 'But . . . Oriel said it was because she was too young.'

'Accept the word of one who is wiser than you, Maguire, if that girl was refused a post it was because she is illegitimate and for no other reason!'

Bright could not believe this cruelty. 'If you knew she'd get turned down why didn't you warn me?'

For a second the old lady adopted the ramrod stance of her youth. 'Don't try to put the blame on me! I had no wish to stigmatize the girl. Why do you think I turned to you for assistance? One would have expected a mother to have projected the outcome without having to have it smashed into her head with a lumphammer. I did everything I could to make you see reason but, no, in your pig-headed manner you thought you would do it your own way. Well, see how much heartbreak your stubbornness has caused. Heartbreak that could easily have been prevented if you had used your brain. I hope you're satisfied.' Having difficulty in maintaining her upright carriage, Miss Bytheway sufficed with a venomous look, before turning her back and retiring to the front parlour.

Unable to bear the fact that she was responsible for her daughter's pain, Bright never asked Oriel for the truth, and simply tried to make some sort of reparation by means of little treats and favours. Strangely, Miss Bytheway too was chary of confronting the issue and it was never mentioned in the house again. Only when Noel called to attend his patient the following spring did Bright resurrect the subject, in order to protect her daughter's feelings.

'I'd appreciate it if you didn't mention anything to do with nursing in front of Oriel,' she whispered as she took his coat that afternoon. 'She's had rather a disappointment.'

Noel tugged at his shirt cuffs, then picked up his bag. 'She's applied then?'

Bright nodded, still whispering. 'They turned her down.'

'Oh well, she's young, she can apply again.'

'No,' Bright curtailed him with a shake of head. 'They won't take her at all. It's . . .' She grimaced, then plucked up the courage to confide in Noel. 'Well, it's all my fault. Apparently the profession won't take anyone who's illegitimate.' There, she had made the admittance.

Noel responded with quiet outrage. 'I haven't heard of that before! If I had I can assure you I would have saved her the hurt. I'm sure it can't be right. Maybe if I have a word with someone.'

'No, doctor, I beg you not to say or do anything.' Bright guided him towards the staircase. 'I couldn't bear to see her hurt again. Oh, she was devastated.'

'I'll bet she was, but you're not to blame yourself, and I hope Oriel didn't blame you either.' Noel took to the stairs after the maid.

'Ah no!' Bright held up her skirts, looking over her shoulder at him. 'She never said a word. She's a lovely girl. Even in her own misery she thought to protect her mother. I'm sure I don't deserve such a daughter.' Her sorrowful smile adopted a twitch of cynicism. 'I'm certain Miss B would vouch for that too – twas she who told me the reason for Oriel being rejected. I was too much of a coward to have it confirmed.'

'You're not a coward.' Damning Nat for his abandonment of this lovely creature, Noel allowed his hand to touch hers as it slid up the balustrade, a gesture of comfort.

Bright thought this an accident and removed her own hand. 'Sorry, doctor. You're very kind to say so, but I am to blame.'

They had reached the first landing. Noel repeated his claim. 'No, you're not . . . Bright, I've never liked to ask before, but I feel we're good enough friends for you to regard what I am about to say not as interference but as a genuine wish to understand . . . is Nat Oriel's father?'

Bright's skin crawled. She felt the colour run up her throat into the roots of her hair. 'Yes,' she replied simply.

Despite this long-held supposition, Noel was assailed by a pang of jealousy at having it confirmed. However, he did not show his inner feelings to Bright, merely nodded. 'I thought so. She's very like him isn't she?'

Bright gave a sad smile and mirrored his nod.

'Have you seen him at all?' enquired Noel. She shook her head. They had both come to a halt on the staircase. For once the physician did not spring to Nat's defence. 'It's unforgivable that he's offered no help.'

She hesitated. 'I think it's because he's frightened. I wasn't being quite truthful, I have seen him – oh not to talk to, but I've seen him watching the house. Once he followed Oriel.'

'Did he speak to her?' Noel was alert.

'No.' Bright sighed. 'I was afraid he was going to, but he's been back several times and he's never spoken to her. He just watches.'

'Is she aware of who he is?'

'She's aware of her father's name, but obviously she doesn't realize just how close he is. I told her all about him when she was small, and she overheard you talking about him — no, it wasn't your fault!' She pre-empted his apology. 'You weren't to know and she shouldn't have been eavesdropping. But when she found out he was in York and hadn't been to see us, well, she was very upset.' As upset as I was, thought Bright, but could not imagine the true depths of Oriel's melancholy, for the girl had no wish to upset her mother by raising the subject. 'I'm afraid I may have painted too rosy a picture and she's always expected him to come back. I wasn't lying, I truly thought . . . well, I don't know what to do for the best now. If I tell her he's been watching her she might get her hopes up again. What if it's just idle curiosity on his part and he doesn't want any further contact?' When the doctor sympathized she began to move on.

Noel was angry with Nat. He had grown fond of Bright and did not wish to see her hurt. As the mention of his very name seemed to cause discomfort Noel did not refer to Oriel's father again but instead returned to the topic of Miss Bytheway's contribution. 'If Oriel herself didn't tell you of the real reason she was turned down for the nursing post how on earth can Miss B know? Maybe it was just conjecture designed to wound.'

'Then it certainly had the desired effect. Anyway, I think Oriel's over her disappointment now. She's doing very well at college and she intends to go into secretarial work when she leaves. So,' she turned her face to beseech him as they came nearer the door to Miss Bytheway's room, 'I'd be pleased if you didn't mention it at all — but thank you for being so understanding.'

His expression soothed her. 'Not at all. I'll keep well away from the subject when I see Oriel – where is she by the way?'

'She's in there,' Bright mouthed, jabbing a finger towards the invalid's room. 'Reading to Her Majesty. There's no college today.'

Noel issued a confidential nod then, donning his best professional smile, entered Miss Bytheway's room. Nat's face looked up at his entry – God she was like her father! The physician donated cheerful greeting to Oriel before noticing that there were tears streaming down her face. 'Good heavens! What . . . ?'

'The *Titanic*,' wheezed Miss Bytheway, 'a dreadful business. All those wretched people. Run along now, miss.' She patted Oriel's hand. 'You can read the rest of it to me later. She has a very soft heart.' This latter comment was for the doctor, who looked kindly upon Oriel and said he hoped to see her before he left. Echoing his desire, she folded the newspaper and left the room in order to allow him to treat his patient. True to his word, Noel made no mention of her disappointment, at least not to Oriel. He was, however, sufficiently annoyed and curious enough to ask Miss Bytheway whilst he was examining her how she had known that Oriel's illegitimacy was to blame for the girl's failure. The response he got was very enlightening, though ethics prevented him from disclosing this confidence to Bright. A shame, for she would have been extremely interested and much more would have been understood, but he had been sworn to silence by the old lady and he would not break his word.

There were, though, some hometruths to be shared with the man whom Noel judged to be responsible for most of Bright's suffering. All day it irked him, and immediately he had finished with his evening surgery he lighted the lamp on his carriage, put flame to his twentieth cigarette of the day and drove round to Nat's address.

Nat was relaxing by the fire in his back parlour with Talbot, his only company, laying across the hearth. It was a masculine room clothed in red wallpaper and leather upholstery, its decor gleaned from his memory of the Scaum residence but with the cosiness of the Maguire house too. The smell of burning wavered under his newspaper; he lowered it, sniffed and looked around. A tiny piece of coal had flown out and was singeing the dog's thick coat. 'You silly old sod, you're on fire! Get up.' The dog merely thumped its tail on the rug.

Nat gave a ruttly laugh; he had not long recovered from bronchitis. 'Can't you feel it? You must be daft.' He repositioned his paper as if to read, offering a hypothesis to Talbot. 'If I stood on your nose would you mind?' The dog continued to lay there, tail thumping on the carpet. Nat chuckled. 'If I shoved a red hot poker up your bum would you still love me?' Another series of thumps. Nat delivered his chesty laugh again, leaned forward and picked the cinder from Talbot's coat. In that same instant the doorbell rang and the hound ran off barking. 'Christ, you silly old . . . you nearly frightened the life out of me.' Nat followed the hound and held his collar as he opened the door to his friend. 'Now then, Noel, how are you? Take your hat off, I've told you before, Talbot doesn't like people in hats. Come in and have a drink with me.'

The doctor was swift to remove his Homburg and the dog lowered its hackles, though still nosed him with suspicion as he entered. 'Would you remind him I saved his life?' Noel attempted to take off his black coat, which was very tricky when one was pressed into a corner.

'He won't hurt you now.' Nat preceded his guest into the back room and poured two glasses of whisky. Noel hung up his overcoat and sat down without waiting to be asked. 'Is something burning in here?' He sniffed the air.

'Only the dog.' The doorbell sounded, drawing exclamation from Nat. 'I'm popular tonight.' He hurried after Talbot who had again sprung barking to the defensive.

'I doubt it,' muttered his guest.

Nat spared a glance for the tone, but continued to the door, returning with Spud whom Noel recognized at once.

'Hello, Spud, remember me?'

The visitor, being conversant with Talbot's idiosyncrasies, had removed his hat before entering, his big face creased in thought until Nat revealed the identity of the stranger. 'Oh aye! Now then, Noel, how're you doing?' Spud, his ears blue, edged over to the fire.

'I'm very well, thank you. How are you?'

'Oh, not so bad.' Spud played with the rim of his hat.

Nat did not ask his employee to have a drink. 'Got something for me?'

Drawing no offence from this abruptness, for he had come to accept Nat's unwillingness to socialize with him — he was after all the boss — Spud handed over the money he had collected and left shortly afterwards.

'He works for me,' explained Nat, reseating himself by the fire.

'Doing what?'

'Oh, nowt that'd interest you, just a dogsbody. He hasn't changed much, has he?'

'No,' agreed Noel. 'Some people never turn out like you expect them to, but Spud hasn't disappointed me.'

'Ah well, he can't be that daft 'cause he's got himself a wife and two bairns. It's more than we've got.' The host took up his glass. 'So, what have you been doing with yourself lately?'

The leather armchair creaked as Noel wriggled his back into it. He tasted his drink. 'As a matter of fact I've been speaking to Bright and your daughter.' As the colour drained from Nat's face he added, 'Punch me if I'm wrong.'

Nat took a drink to aid recovery. 'You're not wrong.'

'I don't know how you have the gall to admit it.' The visitor showed disgust.

The normally quiet man betrayed agitation. 'Why did you ask then – and what's it got to do with you anyway?'

The doctor put down his glass and leaned forward. 'Nothing in the least. I just came here to find out what sort of a shit could leave a young girl in that condition and run away. Have you any idea what she's had to suffer?'

Nat jumped from his chair. 'You don't think I'm proud of what I did? But for God's sake I was only fifteen . . .'

'So was she!'

'Yes, well . . . there's more responsibility thrust on the bloke, isn't there?' Nat began to circle the room, watched closely by a protective Talbot. 'We're meant to look after them. How could I look after her when I was locked up in there with no money? I didn't intend to go away for good.' He sat down again, snatched up his glass and emptied it. 'Once I'd made my fortune I was going to come back for her, only it didn't happen like that. When I came back to York I didn't have a meg, I didn't know if Bright still lived at home . . .'

'And you didn't bother to find out.'

'Oh, you'd bloody know! I did as a matter of fact, and all I got for my pains was the shit belted out of me by her brothers – twice!' Nat's blue eyes glistened with self pity and anger. 'They said she didn't want anything to do with me.'

'So you just gave up.'

'Oh stop being such a holy sod!' Nat jumped up again and clinked the decanter at his glass. 'You'd have done the same in my position and don't kid me you wouldn't.'

Noel was sure that his friend was correct, but wasn't about to agree. After gulping his whisky, he studied the face that he had come to know well, with all its little nuances, and watched intently as those dark good looks gradually relaxed from agitation to pathos.

The awaited explanation came. 'I fully intended to keep looking for her.' Nat was calmer now, his eyes beseeching the other to understand. 'But I didn't find out where she was until you gave me a clue, and then it was too late. I couldn't be a father to a fourteen-year-old girl who didn't know me from Adam – and she wouldn't have wanted a rag and bone man for a father. I doubt if Bright would have wanted me for a husband, either, after what I'd done to her.'

'And with that opinion you inflict yet another injustice on her,' accused Noel, sparking irritation in the other.

'Well, I don't know what she thought about it all do I? She might have hated me.' Nat spread his hands in despair, then looked into the other's eyes. 'Does she?'

It was such a pathetic request. Noel knew that with one kind word he could resolve the whole cruel saga, could write a fairy tale ending to Bright's unhappiness. But he did not, for if Bright was to be happy then he had suddenly decided that he would be the one to make her so. He did not know how, for his mother would never countenance his marriage to a servant. He did not know when. What he did know was that his own feelings would never allow him to play matchmaker between Bright and this man here. 'I have no idea,' he answered quietly, looking down into his glass. 'She never refers to you . . . except to express dismay that you've taken to spying upon Oriel.'

Nat snorted. 'Spying? I just wanted to make sure she was all right, that's all.'

'Well, she is all right, and her mother wants you to leave her alone. She doesn't want Oriel to be frightened by the persistent attentions of a stranger.' In retrospect that had been too harsh. 'I'm sorry to be so brutal, but that is what you are, what you've chosen to be.'

Nat hid his wounds under a mask of ice. 'If that's what she wants, I'll leave them both alone. And now you've got the information you came for, you've wrung this confession of guilt from me, I'd be obliged if you'd bugger off.'

Noel looked chastened and, with some reluctance, rose. 'I didn't come here to gloat, Nat. I came to speak frankly as somebody who cares about the pair of you, who recognizes the unfairness of it all. You'll do yourself no good by wishing for things that cannot be, believe me.'

Nat spoke through clenched teeth. 'I've said I won't bother her!'

The doctor felt unease that his straight-talking might have given birth to a worse problem. 'Yes, well, I sincerely hope this won't ruin our friendship?'

Nat dealt him a puff of derision, then at the look of genuine concern in the other's brown eyes, he relented. 'Oh, what the hell . . . I'll give you a ring next week.'

The other looked relieved and left in a more ebullient manner. 'Good! We'll have a night on the town and see if we can find you a wife — it's way past time you were hitched.'

'Oh aye, and what about you?' There was a sardonic twist to the lips that drained the whisky glass.

'I wouldn't inflict my mother on any poor girl.' Noel laughed. This was his pat answer when anyone enquired as to his lack of a wife. In truth it was just that he had never met a female he wanted to be with for the rest of his life. He knew that folk considered him odd. He thought it odd himself that he had never felt really attracted to a woman until he had met Bright, and even now it wasn't a sexual attraction but that of a dear friend. She would make a perfect wife, except for the handicap of her station, but this was not insurmountable. With this in mind, he went to the hall, making the error of donning his hat before he reached the exit. In a trice Talbot was up and barking. Nat enjoyed a touch of malice before restraining the dog, who finally allowed the doctor to leave.

Alone again, Nat pondered on what his friend had said. 'What d'you think, old lad?' he asked Talbot. 'Do you think I need a wife?'

The dog gazed at him adoringly and thumped its tail.

'No, neither do I,' agreed his owner. 'We're all right, on us own, aren't we?' He gave an empty sigh, then refilled his glass and sat back in his chair. Did he mind that Bright viewed him as a threat? His memory took him back to the evening he and Bright had lost their virginity, had conceived Oriel; he imagined her warmth around his flesh, her tenderness at his tears . . . yes, he minded, but what could he do? He supposed Noel was right, a man of his age should have a wife and children, maybe then he would be able to forget Oriel and her mother.

Knowing her concern, Noel was quick to inform Bright that Nat had promised to abandon his surveillance.

Her brown eyes widened. 'You've seen him?'

'Yes, I bumped into him by accident in town the other day,' lied Noel, forbidding any questions on the other's whereabouts, 'and took the opportunity of relaying your fears. I don't think you'll have any more trouble.'

'Oh . . .' An immense sadness came over Bright; it showed in her eyes.

'That was what you wanted, wasn't it?' Noel's face was perplexed, though deep inside he had guessed now that to remove Nat's physical presence had not been enough. Bright was entrapped by a memory.

Too late, she tried to hide her grief. 'Yes of course. Thank you, Noel, that was very thoughtful of you.' She smoothed her apron and led him up to Miss Bytheway's room, wanting to enquire, did Nat ask about me? But she was too afraid. 'Was he well?'

'Yes, quite well. As a matter of fact he's to be married.' Noel felt this comment was only slightly premature.

Bright flinched and said nothing more as they went to the old lady's room.

When he came down, Noel took tea with the mother and daughter as usual and, before leaving, posed the question, 'How long have I been coming here now? Six or seven years?' He laughed. 'It's odd, isn't it, all that time and yet I must have only spoken with you on a dozen occasions when I've come to tend Miss Bytheway. If you add up the actual days, we haven't really known each other more than a fortnight! Yet I feel as if we're lifelong friends.'

'We are in a way.' A nostalgic Bright was thinking of the times she and Nat had visited the other's house in Hull Road.

He nodded thoughtfully. 'Yes, I suppose we are.'

Oriel, sensing the different atmosphere, was watching them like a hawk, eyes darting from one to the other.

Noel leaned forward, impelled to ask if he could perhaps visit in a non-professional capacity, but was at the last moment inhibited by what others would say. There was no rush. It would wait a couple of years. Now that Nat was out of the way it wasn't as if anybody else would want her. You're waiting for your mother to die. No, I'm not! It's just . . . well, there'll hardly be others queueing up to marry her, will there. I can't see the need for haste. Feeling Oriel's intent gaze, he turned to catch her. She started, then smiled. He grinned back and rose abruptly. 'Well, I'd better say goodbye until the next time.'

'We look forward to seeing you then, Noel.' Though smiling, Bright was only half aware, the other half of her mind picturing Nat with his bride.

In fact, Nat's bachelorhood was to continue for another year and in the end it was not loneliness that propelled him towards matrimony but a much greater threat. A war that had been on the cards for months now exploded across Europe. The August sun, which only last week had beaten down upon a sea of boaters and white duck suits, now illuminated regimental badges upon a mass of khaki. York thronged with eager volunteers, hustled and bustled with housewives rushing to queue for supplies that would carry them up to Christmas. Troops were mobilized by car, cab and motor cycle, and every green sward became a training ground or airfield. At first it was predicted that the duration of hostilities would be short, but when blood continued to spill over into 1915 Nat decided to act, for if push came to shove it would be the single man who was called to arms.

Nat had never had difficulty in attracting women, who seemed to find a challenge in the combination of his dark looks and cool reserve. It was with this same icy detachment that he selected a pretty candidate whose father was in trade, showered her with artificial charm and proposed wedlock. Under such determined onslaught the girl was swept off her feet, though her parents were more reticent and decreed that the couple must get to know each other a little better before they granted their consent. They were also unhappy that a mature man of thirty-four showed no inclination to join up, but Nat assured them he was every bit as patriotic as the volunteers and would enjoy a much more important role here by supplying the Army with metal for its guns. Their decision swayed, Violet's parents finally gave their consent for Nat to marry their girl.

Whilst the war had spelled momentous change for some it had done little to alter Bright's world. After the initial excitement of waving Fulford's soldiers off to the battlefields and marvelling over the aeroplanes that took off within view of her rear window every day, she continued in her drab mode of life. On this cool but beautiful April morning she rose and dressed as normal, went down, waking Oriel on the way, ran outside with a jug to the milkman's cart, made breakfast and set a tray for her employer.

'I'll take it.' Oriel came in, suitably dressed for the weather in a blue knitted jacket over a white blouse and navy skirt. Arms above head, she tried to fasten her ribbon

489

into a bow. It was her final year at college, though she had no idea what she was going to do once her secretarial examinations were over. Her mother took charge of the ribbon, then gave her a tray which Oriel carried to the old lady's room.

Bright finished dishing up their own breakfasts and seated herself at the table, reaching for the teapot as Oriel reappeared.

The girl sat down, her face almost as white as her collar. Immediately Bright knew what had caused that pallor. 'Oh no, she isn't?'

Moisture welled in Oriel's eyes and she nodded. The joy of this lovely morning caved in. Bright banged down the teapot and clasped her head in her hands. 'Oh my God, what're we going to do?' For a while they sat there, stunned, then a tear rolled down Oriel's cheek and Bright came around the table to comfort her. 'Oh, there!' She cradled her daughter's head, stroking and petting.

Oriel, face still buried in her mother's bosom, made groping motions with her hand. Bright produced a handkerchief from her apron pocket and gave it to her. Oriel mopped her eyes, then blew into the square of linen. 'Sorry.'

'You don't have to apologize,' comforted her mother, returning to her chair, though sitting sideways on facing the fire rather than the table. 'It's natural to cry when someone you know dies.'

'Yes, but it isn't as if we were close.' Oriel had never received so much as a hug from Miss Bytheway. 'I liked her in a way, but she was so mean to you . . .' Feeling somewhat disloyal, the girl heaved a shaky breath.

'Well . . .' Bright tried to offer some snippet of Christianity, but failed, unable to forgive the old lady for her cruelty over the years. 'I feel sort o' funny that she's gone, but life goes on for us and there're more important things to worry about now.'

'About the house, you mean?' Oriel rubbed her eyes, then lowered the handkerchief.

'Yes. I know we haven't seen any signs of relatives, but they're sure to come creeping out of the woodwork now there's a house in the offing.' Bright crossed her arms over her threadbare dress, sighed, and examined the toe of her boot. 'I suppose she chose as good a time as any to leave us homeless. What with this war on there doesn't seem to be a shortage of jobs for women.' Yet the idea of working for someone else after all these years was rather daunting. 'I'll have to go out looking this afternoon. If I find a job straightaway then maybe I can rent a house. Even so, we'll be living on bare boards for a while.' She swivelled to face her daughter, pushing aside her unfinished breakfast. 'This is going to sound callous with her not yet cold, but I've got to think of our own survival. I'm not prepared to be thrown into the workhouse after all the hard toil I've done for her. So, I'm going to collect one or two things together and sell them. Just to give us enough money to last until we get on our feet.'

Determination in her eyes, she began to clear the table. 'And I'll have to get them now before her lawyer appears on the scene. Nothing of great value, just odds and ends that can be sold easily, or even things we can use ourselves.' She hesitated at the look on Oriel's face. 'D'ye think I'm wicked?' Old accusations and Catholic guilt returned to haunt her; *You're a wicked girl, Bright Maguire.*

The young woman's smile was one of surprise mixed with admiration. 'How could anyone call you wicked after all you've had to put up with? Take all you can, you deserve it. It's about time you stood your ground.' She too, rose, adjusting the elaborate belt buckle that was digging into her abdomen. 'Come on, I'll help you – and please don't worry about going into the workhouse.' She leaned over to return her mother's act of comfort. 'I'd never let it happen. Why, in a few weeks I'll be qualified, I'll have a good job and can help you with the rent – but that doesn't mean we shouldn't take what we can from here, so come on.' She went into action. 'I don't see why people who have never cared about her should benefit just because they're kin.'

Bright carried the pots to the scullery then came back. 'Well, we can soon find out if there are any relatives. You look through her bureau for any letters or documents. It's crammed with stuff. I'll just go and take a look at Miss Bytheway. It would be awful if she was just asleep and came down to find us!' Managing to laugh through her worry, she added, 'Better still, will you telephone Dr Noel and ask him to come? He'll have to issue a certificate.' Whilst Oriel obliged she herself went upstairs.

Sure enough, the old lady was dead, though she had not been so for long; a teardrop shone in the socket of her eye like a diamond twinkling from the shadows. Bright gazed upon her for a brief moment, wondering how such a tyrant could look so angelic. It was an odd experience. She shuddered, crossed herself and pulled the blankets over the lifeless head. Then, conquering feelings of guilt, she turned her attention to the dressing table and Miss Bytheway's jewellery box. There were many nice brooches. She examined one or two, wondering whether the diamonds were paste or real, this ignorance forcing her to replace them. If they were real there might be questions asked if she tried to sell them. Wiser to stick to more mundane items, like the linen sheets in the airing cupboard or the copper pans in the kitchen. Moving from room to room, she began to accumulate a bundle of linen, towels and other fine things, until her arms were full and she returned downstairs to see if Oriel had found anything.

The young woman spun guiltily at her mother's entry. 'Oh, I thought it was Miss Bytheway!' She laughed and clutched her throat in relief. 'Come and look at this. I think you'll be interested.'

Bright deposited her bundle on the table and came to take the slip of yellowed paper. 'Did you contact Dr Noel?'

'Yes, he said he'd come straight away. Go on, read it.'

It was a birth certificate. As she read the faded writing Bright's jaw dropped lower and lower. 'Why the old . . . am I reading this right?' she demanded of her daughter who nodded. 'She was illegitimate! I can't believe it. The things she said, the insults . . . and all the time . . . why would she make me suffer like that, knowing that her own mother had gone through the same?'

'I can only deduce that she blamed her mother for giving her away and was taking it out on you,' answered Oriel. 'There's lots more stuff here. I can't imagine why she kept it. Personally, I'd want to burn these letters if they were addressed to me.' She handed the pile of envelopes to her mother who was still dumbfounded. 'I've managed to piece the story together from these. Don't bother to read them all now, I can give you their gist. It appears that Miss Bytheway was at a foundlings' home until she was six, when she was fostered out to a wealthy couple who apparently had no children of their own. Those people on the wall.' She pointed to a photograph. 'Their relatives were not amused that they had taken in an illegitimate child and severed all contact with them. More fool them. Apparently Miss B inherited the lot when her foster parents died. That's it.' She formed a crescent with her mouth and shrugged, wondering if she would ever enjoy a similar fortune, but keeping this mercenary thought to herself.

'I still can't believe . . .' Bright looked angry, then forced herself to join her daughter's search through the desk, tossing aside papers that were irrelevant. 'Well then, it seems unlikely that she'll have named any relatives as her beneficiaries. Have you come across a will?'

'No, I was too engrossed in the letters.' Oriel began to flick through another compartment of the bureau. Just then the doorbell startled them. Bright went to admit Noel, jaw dropping at his form of transport.

'You've got yourself a motor car!' Her eyes ran along the glossy, red open-topped vehicle.

'Not from choice.' Noel had always found old-fashioned animal transport more reliable than machinery. 'The Army requisitioned my horse. If I can ever get the blessed thing to run properly I'll take you out for a ride one Sunday.' He made for the stairs. 'Usual place?'

'No, we stacked her in the coalshed.' Bright tore her eyes from the car, then clamped her mouth. 'What a thing to say! It must be the shock. You'll never guess what we've found out.' She went with him up the stairs. 'We were looking through her papers — just to find out if there were any relatives to contact,' she hastened to let him know that it was not from any criminal intent, 'and we found a birth certificate. It turns out that Miss B's mother gave birth to her out of wedlock!' Turning to give a scandalized laugh she saw that Noel was not at all perturbed.

'Yes, I'm afraid I'm already privy to that information.' He looked rueful as they turned the corner. 'Sorry, but she told it to me in confidence, otherwise I would have shared it with you. I knew you'd be interested.'

'Interested? I was furious! Treating me like a leper in some crazy attempt to punish her own mother.' Bright's feet proceeded to thud up another flight. 'How long have you known?'

'Remember when Oriel was turned down for the nursing post? I asked the old girl point blank how she knew it was because of Oriel's illegitimacy. She revealed that she herself had cherished the desire to become a nurse and had been rejected because of her own status. That's why she did her best to bully you into submission without having to reveal her true purpose. Obviously she wouldn't have volunteered the information, but when I was my usual pushy self she blurted it out in anger. I vouched to keep it a secret.'

Bright opened the door to the darkened room, whispering out of habit. 'Ah well, I don't suppose it matters now. I'm more worried about where my daughter and I are going to live.'

'Oh, yes . . . of course.' Noel paused to show concern.

'But that's not for you to worry about.' Bright ushered him to the bed. 'First things first.'

Noel made the necessary examination, then suggested they return downstairs where he wrote out a certificate. Oriel had stopped rummaging through the bureau in order to make a fresh pot of tea for the doctor.

'I'm afraid I can't stop,' Noel showed regret. 'I've got lots of calls to make.' He closed his bag and retreated towards the hall. 'Is there anything I can do before I go – will you be able to manage the laying out?' Bright did not relish this, but said they would be fine. 'Then I'll come back this evening if I may. In the meantime I'll try and think of a solution to your dilemma.' He left.

'What did he mean?' Oriel went back to her search of the bureau, calling to her mother, who had gone to draw the upstairs drawing room curtains out of respect.

'I told him we were worried about what would happen to us now Miss B has died.' Bright came back down, pulled a balloon-backed chair next to that of her daughter and joined the search. 'I can't see what he can do, but it's nice of him to be concerned.'

'Maybe he'll ask you to marry him,' teased Oriel. 'Carry you off on his white charger.'

'Soft article. Behave and look for the will.'

Oriel poked and pried through Miss Bytheway's documents, feeling none of the guilt suffered by her mother. 'What's this? No, it's an insurance policy on the house.' She tugged at another envelope.

'It's all right, I've got it here.' Bright unfolded the stiff parchment and cast her eyes over it.

Oriel saw at first astonishment and then indignance

flood her mother's face. 'What is it? Come on, don't keep me in suspense.'

Looking sour, Bright proffered the document. 'Here, read it.'

Oriel perused it for a while, then looked up with a little gasp.

'Yes, that's right, she's left it all to you! After all the years I slaved and curtsied and took her insults, let her treat me like a dog and not even . . . well, that's *it*!' Bright ripped off her apron. 'I'm not laying her out. I've got better things to do, like going to look for work!'

'Mother!' Oriel sprang up and chased Bright to the hall, trying to prevent her from putting on her hat and coat and leaving there and then. 'Come back inside, I'll make you a cup of tea.'

'Tea? I haven't time for tea, I have to find a job!'

'Stop it! You're getting hysterical.' Oriel tugged at her arm.

'I am not hysterical, I'm bloody furious!' Bright feared that her head was about to explode. 'Not even threepence! I'm not even worth that!'

'You are to me!' Oriel's eyes threatened more tears. 'Please, stop all this talk about getting a job. You're my mother and I love you, everything I've inherited is yours. You surely don't think I'd act the lady while my mother played the maid? How could you?'

Bright gritted her teeth. 'Oh, I don't think that at all. Tis her I'm angry with, not you!' Like many a placid soul, when Bright's temper was roused it was slow to deflate. 'That . . . witch!' Reluctantly, she allowed herself to accompany her daughter back into the kitchen where Oriel put the kettle on.

While the tea was brewing she wandered into the front parlour and picked up the will again, shaking her head in disbelief. 'Well, at least I don't have to go hawking those around town!' She referred to the items she had collected for selling. 'Unless you throw me out.'

'Mother!'

'Sorry.' Bright managed a weak smile as Oriel came through with the tea. 'I am glad for you, darling. It's just the shock.'

'I know.' Oriel was forgiving. 'If you really want to work, why don't you go into teaching like you intended to do before I came along and spoiled it all.'

Her mother was quick to reassure her. 'You didn't spoil it! You're the most important thing in my life. I'd never change the way things are. As for teaching . . . well, it wasn't really a vocation. Twas just that I was brainy at school and the nuns thought I'd be a good teacher. I enjoyed the bit I did, but a lot o' years have gone by and I don't think I could be bothered with a classful of children now.' Bright knew this sounded like an excuse, and in part it was. Any confidence that she might have had in her own abilities had been destroyed long ago. Not to mention the fact that she was liable to break out in a panic at the drop of a hat. It was not simply this, though, as she went on to tell her daughter. 'What I would dearly like is a chance to be myself, do things when I want to do them, spend time with my daughter.' She smiled at Oriel, then tried to explain how she felt about all of this. 'I can't forgive her for that you know. That's why I can't cry. Grateful as I am for the clothes she bought, the food, the toys, I can't bring myself to forget that she robbed me of precious moments. I know it's selfish . . .'

'You're not selfish!'

Bright shook her head. 'I know she spared me from something a lot worse, but I just can't help the way I feel.'

Oriel nodded her understanding, then picked up her cup and asked, 'What do we do next?'

Bright took a sip of her unsweetened tea. 'Never having received a fortune I wouldn't know. First I'll have to go and get someone to lay her out. If you'll lend me the halfcrown o' course – all right, I'm sorry, only joking. Then I'll go talk to the undertaker.'

'Which one? Do you want me to find out if they're on the telephone?' Oriel was more competent than her mother at making enquiries of the operator.

'You can't do something like this over the telephone,' replied Bright. 'Directly we've had this tea I'll go into town.'

'How much will it be?'

'Well, if it were me being buried twould be a fiver but I daresay she's left instructions for the full set o' horses with plumes and fancy what-nots.'

'I'll go with you,' offered her daughter.

'No, I'll be fine.'

Oriel looked sheepish and suddenly appeared very young. 'I don't want to be left on my own with her.'

'Oh, sorry, how thoughtless.' Bright had not paid regard to the fact that Oriel would view the old lady's death through different eyes. 'Of course you can. While I'm arranging the funeral you can nip along to her solicitor's and inform him that Miss Bytheway is dead.'

Oriel had a thought. 'Dr Noel's going to have a surprise when he comes back tonight, thinking to find us destitute!' She laughed into her cup, breast a-flutter with all manner of emotions.

'He surely is!' agreed Bright. 'What do you say we surprise him further with a nice roast meal – if we can manage to rustle up a joint?' She bit her lip. 'He was awfully concerned about us being thrown out of the house. I hope he isn't worrying about it all day.'

Noel had been too occupied to worry over his friend's plight during the first half of the morning, but towards noon as he was chugging back to his surgery he gave it his full attention and in doing so came up with what he hoped to be an answer. Nat had always been allowed to shirk his responsibilities; now he must be made to provide for his daughter's welfare. Instead of going to luncheon he drove to Nat's house, which he had not visited for some time. Contrary to the other's spoken intention to call on him after their previous exchange concerning his surveillance of Oriel, there had been no further meeting between them.

As it turned out his friend was not at home, nor was he at the nearby scrapyard. Thwarted, the doctor climbed back into his vehicle and drove back along the maze of city streets towards his surgery. He was juddering along Aldwark when, as if it had been arranged, he coincided with the rag and bone merchant travelling in the opposite direction. With little room to pass, he moved into the kerb, engine still throbbing, and waited for the other vehicle to draw alongside. Despite the seriousness of the occasion he found himself pleased to see Nat again; he could still derive much pleasure from his friend's good looks, even when he was mad at him. 'This is a happy coincidence, I've just called to see you.'

Still on the cart, Nat touched his top hat with a forefinger, then rested on his knees, reins in hands. 'Fancy car. I'm impressed.'

The doctor explained that the Army had taken his more reliable horse. 'I see you've managed to hang onto your nag.'

Nat laughed. 'They wouldn't take this old bugger, he's almost knacker meat. I'm just off for me dinner if you want to join me. Nowt fancy.'

Noel was wary of the three-legged dog who barked at him from a mountain of rags on the cart. 'Unfortunately, I can't stop. I just came to give you some news about a mutual friend of ours.'

'Behave yourself, Talbot!' Nat swiped at the dog which was doing its best to remove his hat with its teeth. 'He can't bear it you know,' he told Noel. 'Every time I stop he's always trying to pull me hat off.'

'Really?' The doctor was hungry and it showed in the impatient tone of his voice. 'Well, I won't delay you, I just thought you might like to know that Bright's in need of assistance. Her employer's just died and it looks as if she and Oriel will be thrown out of the house.'

'Stop it!' Nat barked at the dog, more intent on the conversation now. Immediately it obeyed but hobbled up and down the pile of rags whining. 'What can I do about it?'

The physician prepared to drive off. 'I've no idea, but you've got money, haven't you? Surely you could spare some of it for your daughter.'

Nat was deliberately obtuse. 'But you told me that Bright wanted me to keep away from her, that she wouldn't want my charity.'

'I would agree with that, but it wouldn't be charity, would it? You'd only be doing your duty, the duty you've neglected for so long.' Annoyed at the other's calm, Noel shifted the hand brake. 'I don't know why I thought you'd help. Move your cart out of the bloody way.'

'Keep your shirt on!' Nat did not budge, though his horse shied at the revving engine. 'If I send money she'll only send it back. I'll have to think of some other way to help . . . anyway, I appreciate you letting me know. What's the situation then? When are they likely to be thrown out?'

It was whilst Noel related what he knew that Oriel came out of the solicitor's office lower down the street and glimpsed the doctor leaning over the side of his car. Normally she would have hailed Noel, especially with such exciting news to impart, but as she approached she saw that he was deep in conversation with another and, not wishing to interrupt, she simply smiled to herself and made to continue past. The man to whom Noel was chatting looked familiar – ah yes, she had seen him a number of times on the tram to and from Fulford where he was obviously a resident. As she drew level he gave her a casual glance, then looked startled and quickly withdrew his eyes. Noel appeared to be startled too, but soon recovered and issued a cheery wave as she proceeded on her way.

Nat dared not turn. His wary eyes held Noel's. 'Has she gone?' When the other nodded he threw a furtive glance over his shoulder to watch his daughter retreat, his gaze never leaving her until she had turned the corner. He looked back at Noel and sighed. 'She's a bonny lass, isn't she?'

The other nodded. 'Are you going to help?'

'Course I am.' Nat arched his back. 'Though I don't know how. I'll have to think about it over dinner – are you sure you won't share it with me?'

Another vehicle turned into the road and would soon want to be past. Noel prepared to move off. 'No, really, I have to go. I'll call on you when I find out what's happening with Bright. I'm going round this evening.'

'What d'you need to go for when the old lass is dead?'

Noel was guarded. 'I promised to look in on Bright, she was very worried.'

This seemed to satisfy Nat, who allowed his friend to drive away, accompanied by Talbot's bark. As the other vehicle rumbled past, he sat for a moment, ruminating. Brooms in hand, two women stood gossiping nearby and Talbot's howls distracted them. 'Poor thing.' One of them performed a token sweep of the pavement, eyeing the three-legged animal who was staggering amongst the entanglement of rags. 'It shouldn't be allowed to suffer like that. You should have it put out of its misery!' The loud comment was for the dog's owner.

Jerked from his thoughts, Nat turned an arrogant face on the speaker. 'And should your husband have you put down just because you're ugly?'

The recipient was about to explode, when something in her detractor's face prevented it. 'Cheek of it!' Beckoning to her friend, she went inside and slammed the door.

'Fancy saying a thing like that about poor old Talbot.'
Nat reached behind him and tugged at the dog's pendulous
ear. The adoring hound appeared to laugh and shook
himself, his heavy jowls emitting a cascade of saliva. Nat
reeled to avoid it. 'You mucky bugger!' He clicked the
horse into motion. 'Away, let's go and have our dinner,
we've got a lot of thinking to do this afternoon.'

Wading through his corned beef sandwiches, watched
intently by his dog – Talbot had finished his own within
seconds – Nat racked his brain for an answer to Bright's
problem. As the owner of property he could put a roof over
her head almost immediately, but with Nat as her benefactor she would never accept. For the same reason he
could not offer money. He finished one sandwich and bit
into another, then formed a grimace at Talbot's drooling
gaze. 'You've had yours! Go and lie down.' Talbot hung
his head and crept off to a corner, burying his nose beneath
his tail. Nat took another bite, then stopped. 'I know
you're still watching, I can see your eyebrows moving!' At
the jocular tone Talbot lifted his head in expectation. 'Oh,
here y'are!' Nat threw the remaining sandwich at the dog,
who caught it from the air and gulped it down whole.
'Would you like to drink me tea an' all?' Nat proffered his
cup, then emptied it himself. 'I don't know why I bother to
feed you, you're not much use, are you? If you had
anything about you you'd offer to do those accounts for
me. No, I didn't think the appeal'd work,' he accused, as
Talbot curled up, stuck his nose under his tail and closed
his eyes. 'If you want owt doing, do it your –' A bolt of
inspiration stopped him in his tracks and he gasped. Talbot
showed the white of one eye, then closed it again. What an
idea! With one action he could provide Bright with a
regular source of income – far more than she could hope to
earn herself – but much more importantly he could bring
his daughter into his house!

Wasting no time he reached for his hat and coat. Talbot flew from his basket and within half an hour they were at the door of the college where Oriel was a student.

'Stay here,' he told the dog, who began to bark, 'and shut up! Shut up!' He cuffed Talbot's nose. 'This is important.' He left the subdued animal on the cart and went to find the person in charge.

'Oriel Maguire?' The headmaster of the college searched the air for a moment. 'Ah yes, I know the young lady to whom you refer. I'm afraid, though, she is not in attendance today, I received a telephone call –'

Nat interrupted. 'I know. It isn't her I want to see.'

The man stared at the visitor, whose blunt manner was in contrast to his gentlemanly dress. 'Then how may I help, Mr . . . ?' He remained gracious.

'Price,' Nat dropped a letter from his name. It would not do for Oriel to go home and tell her mother that she was working for him. 'I'd like to employ her as my secretary.'

'Well, that is quite simple, she is almost at the end of her course. Would it not be more appropriate to direct your request at her rather than myself?'

'I'd prefer the young lady to think that you've selected her for the job,' replied Nat. As the other frowned at the mystery, he continued, 'Let me explain and then you'll understand my reasons. The girl and her mother are in financial trouble . . .'

The man began to search his desk as if for explanation. 'I was unaware . . .'

'Just listen to what I have to say!' Nat was becoming annoyed. 'Oriel – Miss Maguire – and her mother have been living with an old lady who was responsible for their welfare. She's just died and so they'll soon find themselves homeless. By employing Miss Maguire I hope to provide them with an income, but I don't want the gesture to be regarded as charity.'

The headmaster was intrigued. 'Are you personally acquainted with Miss Maguire?'

'No, we've never met. The sad affair was brought to my
notice by a mutual friend. I promised to do what I could to
help. As I do genuinely need a secretary I thought this
would be the best way.'

The headmaster appeared to be satisfied. 'I'm sure the
young lady will fulfil your requirements. The moment she
returns to college I will put your request to her.'

Nat thanked him and bade him good day, hardly daring
to believe as he left the building that at last he was about to
achieve the closeness with his daughter that he had always
craved.

21

When Noel paid a visit to the house in Fulford Road that evening he was knocked sideways, not only by the excellent meal on offer but at the news of Miss Bytheway's legacy. It had yet to be granted legal confirmation, Bright told him, but on the surface it appeared as if all her troubles were over. Neither he nor Oriel mentioned seeing each other earlier in the day; Oriel had merely forgotten and Noel did not want to raise the subject for obvious reasons. Out of respect for the deceased, supper was a quiet affair, but those involved enjoyed a new intimacy. Oriel thought she was being very subtle when she yawned and went off to bed, leaving an embarrassed mother alone with the doctor.

Bright felt that this required explanation. 'I think my daughter realizes this'll be the last time we'll get to chat.'

'Does it have to be?' Noel relaxed at the opposite end of the red velvet sofa, enjoying a glass of Miss Bytheway's port. He had as yet made no mention about going to see Oriel's father and now that the danger of eviction was past he saw no need to call upon Nat again. 'My services may no longer be required, but I hope that a friend can still call upon another.'

Bright appeared to be delighted. 'You know that Oriel and I are always pleased to see you, Noel.'

'Good! Then I shall call much more frequently.' All sorts of plans were forming in his mind. However fond he was of Bright and wanted to put their relationship on a firmer footing, he had hitherto found it impossible to broach the subject with his mother. She would be too horrified. Now, the old lady's bequest had changed everything.

Oriel stayed at home for a week in order to help her mother with the funeral arrangements and also out of respect for Miss Bytheway, whose interment was a pathetic affair with only a handful of acquaintances at the graveside. During this period Oriel's financial situation was confirmed. Bright gasped when she found out just how much her daughter was worth, and almost cried when Oriel made the generous announcement that her mother could have anything in the world that she wished for.

'Aw, that's good of you – but I already have the thing I crave most. A little time for myself, time to relax in the bath . . .' Time for a man, came the private sentiment. Why aren't you out there doing something about it, then? You can't use Nat as an excuse after all these years. Oh, but she could. She reflected again on what life would have been like had she not surrendered herself to Nat – probably just like her own mother's, tired out just the same from looking after a large family.

Her daughter's interjection prevented her thoughts from becoming too melancholy. 'You must have some material need. Come on, indulge me, please.'

'Oh, I'd love a –' exclaimed Bright, then looked ashamed. 'No that'd be too greedy.'

'No it wouldn't! Come on, tell me,' urged Oriel.

Bright hesitated. If there was one thing she had always detested in this house it was the silence. 'Well, I'd love a gramophone – if ye don't think I'm taking too much advantage of your generosity.'

Oriel moaned. 'Mother, don't keep making it sound as if the money's all mine.'

'It was left to you.' Bright did not intend to be churlish, merely tendered what she saw as blunt fact.

'And I've chosen to share it with you! Once the bank account's sorted out you can draw money from it any time you want. And until then Miss B left enough cash in the house to cover our needs, so today – oh no, it's Sunday –

tomorrow you can go out and buy yourself a gramophone and plenty of music to play on it. Oh, don't!' Her mother was crying.

'You're lovely to me!' wept Bright.

How could Oriel prevent tears of her own? 'No, I'm not! It's you who's lovely. You deserve nice things after all the sacrifices you made when you were young – for my sake. I've never said . . .' She broke down, then managed to get her words out. 'Thank you for all you've done. Oh, God!' She laughed and cried at the same time. 'Aren't I just terrible?' She blew her nose. 'I could never be on the music hall performing all those mournful ballads, I wouldn't be able to get the words out without blubbering.'

Deeply touched, Bright embraced her.

Oriel continued in her generous theme. 'And we'll get you some new clothes. You must've had that dress since you came to work for Miss B.'

'I have!' Her mother laughed and patted herself. 'It's getting a bit tight but I doubt any other woman of thirty-five could still get into a dress she wore when she was sixteen, even if I do say it myself. Oh listen to us! We shouldn't be talking so frivolously with herself only gone a week.' Bright dabbed at her eyes. 'What's even worse though . . . it feels as if she was never here. D'ye know what I mean?'

Oriel agreed that the atmosphere of the house was definitely a lot lighter.

'I feel younger somehow,' concluded Bright. 'As if I've been in some sort of hibernation and now I'm being allowed to enjoy the youth I never had.'

'Yes, you look far too slim and youthful for my liking.' Oriel withdrew a bag of liquorice comfits from her pocket. 'Here, have a bullet, that'll put the weight on. Oh damn!' In offering the bag she had dropped it and the brightly coloured sweets rolled all over the carpet.

'Scrumps!' In a fit of glee Bright dived onto the floor to

make a grab for the comfits, laughing and giggling as her daughter joined the game, the two of them fighting and groping for who could get most.

Someone gave an exaggerated cough. In their peals of laughter they did not hear and Noel was forced to cough louder. This time, they looked up from their hands and knees into the amused face of the doctor.

'Oh, Noel!' Bright laughed, feeling stupid, and clambered to her feet. 'You must think we're barmy.'

'I was beginning to wonder if I'd come to the right place,' smiled Noel. 'I did ring but you were obviously having too much fun to hear me – saw you through the window.'

Oriel rose too and poured a handful of comfits into the bag. 'Most undignified. I can just hear Miss B turning in her grave.'

Bright offered reproof. 'That's not very respectful! What must Noel think?'

'Noel thinks what a lot of fun he's going to have in the company of two delightful young ladies this afternoon.' The doctor beamed. 'If, of course, they consent to putting themselves at risk in my rickety contraption.'

'You've come to take us out?' Bright clasped her hands in exuberance.

'Indeed I have. So put on your hats and coats and be so kind as to fill these bottles with hot water from your kettle, then I shall transport you to fields green and pastures new.'

What a wonderful time they had that Sunday afternoon in Noel's motor car. Protected from the cool April wind by foot muffs, hot water bottles, and rugs and hats tied on with scarves, they drove right out into the countryside, where one would hardly have believed there was a war on. The daffodils were in bloom just as any other year, the birds sang, lambs gambolled and Bright's heart soared above the rolling hilltops. How anomalous that in this time of austerity she was enjoying more treats, more pleasures, than in her entire adulthood.

'I can honestly say this is one of the happiest days of my life,' she declared to Noel when he returned them home that evening, after treating them to a cream tea at a farmhouse. 'Thank you, so much, Noel.'

'It was an honour.' Noel felt a tinge of pity. Poor Bright, to be so easily delighted. What she must have gone through all these years. 'I'll have to go now, I promised I'd do a voluntary stint at the Military Hospital. Must be going soft in my old age. I hope to take you out again when my patients allow it.'

'We'd love that, wouldn't we?' Bright consulted her daughter who responded with enthusiasm. Then, thanking him once again they waved him off and went inside where Bright gave a youthful laugh and said, 'Well, that was a lovely surprise!'

She was to express even more surprise when her daughter announced the next morning that she intended to return to college. 'Oh, I didn't think you'd be going any more.' A ripple of panic made the hair on her body stand on end: she was to be alone in the house.

Oriel herself did not seem to regard her decision as strange. 'I've worked hard for this certificate, I can't see any merit in throwing it away at the final hour just because I've been left some money.'

'Well, it'll be nice to be able to hang it on the wall,' agreed Bright, fixing her eyes on the painted galleon on the coal scuttle. Oh, please don't leave me.

'It's not for the wall! It's to get me a job,' Oriel tugged on her gloves. 'I'm not one to sit at home all day.'

'Tut! You don't have to. You can do anything you want now – why, we could open a nursing home so you could have your wish.' As soon as she had said it Bright wished she hadn't, for Oriel's lighthearted expression vanished.

'Be a nurse? No thank you, I gave up that childish idea

long ago. I haven't come this far just to empty bedpans.' She hoped that her mother would not comment on what was obviously Miss Bytheway's doctrine. 'No, I'd like to do something useful with my qualifications.' Attempting to hide her bitterness under a smile she asked, 'What will you be doing today?'

Bright did not voice her fear of being left alone. It would be a cruel burden to inflict upon her daughter. 'The same as ever, I suppose.' She put her hands on her hips and looked around. 'There's always housework to be done.' Don't be so silly, she chided herself, you've been alone before. *But not all day long.* Please God the occupation would stop her thoughts from running wild.

Oriel laughed. 'We can afford to hire someone to do that now!'

'I'm not the type to boss folk around.' Bright knew too well what that felt like. 'Besides, no one wants to work in service any more with all the money they get in the munitions factories. I'll manage.'

'Well, there's no need to overdo it,' warned Oriel. 'You've no slavedriver on your back now. Get yourself into town and buy that gramophone. I expect to see you dancing when I come home.' She looked in the mirror to stab a pin through her hat. 'Right, I'd better go. Don't have anything ready for lunch, I'll stay in town.'

'Oh, hang on!' Bright took sixpence from her purse. 'Could you bring home a sheep's head without eyes? It'll save me going out.'

With a sigh, Oriel took the money and left for college. Within minutes of arriving, however, she had received, by proxy, Nat's offer of employment and was so excited that she decided to go home at lunchtime after all.

'I've got a job!' She burst upon her mother who was dusting ornaments from the ebony display cabinet over the mantelpiece and almost knocked one of them to the hearth in her fright.

'You nearly gave me a fit! What are you doing home? I've no meal prepared. I'm just getting the room ready for my new gramophone.' Bright's forehead creased. 'What d'you mean you've got a job?'

As usual when caught up in excitement, Oriel delivered her words like machine gun bullets. 'Whilst I was away last week someone came in asking for a secretary and the headmaster proposed me!'

Bright allowed her duster to rest. 'But you haven't even passed your exams.'

'Oh pooh, that's just a formality!' Oriel took off her hat and threw it across the room like a flying saucer. 'Isn't it wonderful?'

Bright pursed her lips and retrieved the hat. 'Just because you own the place doesn't mean you can throw things all over for me to pick up.'

'Sorry.' Oriel showed contrition, accepted the hat, then urged, 'But aren't you glad?'

'Maybe I would be if I knew what it involved.' Bright straightened the pom-poms on the red velvet mantel cover. 'I mean, who is this person who wants you to work for him – I assume it is a man?'

'A Mr Price. The headmaster's going to make an appointment with him on my behalf!'

'Where does he live? Is he married? What line of business is he in?'

Oriel beat off the questions with a laugh. 'I don't know!'

'Well you should! Perhaps I should go with you . . .'

'Oh yes, and make it look as if I'm not fit to be out on my own!'

'I'm only trying to point out the dangers . . .' Even when Oriel was small, Bright had never quite felt that she had full control over her daughter as enjoyed by other parents, so repressed had she felt by Miss Bytheway's dictate.

'Mother, I'm quite old enough to judge this man for myself. If I don't like him I shall turn down his offer of work – even if it is an important position. Apparently I'm to be entrusted with all his business accounts.'

'And he's to be entrusted with my daughter.' At Oriel's protest, Bright held up her hands. 'Well, you surely don't expect me to let you go into a man's house without asking questions, do you? You're all I've got.'

Oriel understood then and came forward to touch her mother's arm. 'I promise I won't set foot in his house until I'm provided with more information about him. Now, can I get you some lunch?'

'No, I'll get it for you.' Bright moved into action. 'You have to be back at college – oh, and have you got a sheep's head, by the way?'

Oriel looked in the mirror. 'No, it looks pretty normal.'

'I'll clout you!'

'Sorry, but you didn't expect it until tonight anyway, did you?'

'No, but I thought I'd better remind you, what with your head being so full of this business.' Perhaps that had made it sound as if she wasn't interested in her daughter's future. Bright paused on her way to the scullery. 'I am glad for you, dear, I really am, it's just . . .'

'I know.' Oriel patted her tenderly. 'I know.'

After lunch Oriel returned to college. With time to ponder on the interview ahead her excitement had begun to dwindle. What was the point in going? She would only be turned down, as she had been rejected for the nursing post. Why, when she had no need of money, was she about to put herself through the humiliation of having to announce her illegitimacy? Oriel decided she would tell the headmaster she would not take the post. This she duly did, giving the excuse that her mother was rather worried for her safety.

The headmaster understood. 'Well, yes, I can see your mother's point of view. In fact I myself was rather uneasy at first, until Mr Price assured me of his charitable motives.'

Oriel frowned. 'I beg your pardon, sir, but I am not in need of charity.'

'No, no of course not, Miss Maguire, I did not mean to insinuate that you were.' He sighed. 'Oh look, subterfuge is not my forte. At the risk of breaking a confidence let me be frank. Mr Price specifically asked for you. He informed me that, although he had never made your acquaintance he had heard that the death of Miss, er Miss . . .'

'Miss Bytheway,' provided Oriel.

'Yes. That her death had left you and your mother in a desperate situation, and without wishing to insult you by charity he asked if I could enlist your qualifications as his secretary. As you would no doubt be seeking employment in the near future, I agreed to help. I hope I have done you no disservice.'

Oriel was completely bamboozled and stood there frowning. 'No, of course not. Though I can assure you that neither my mother nor I have any need of charity. We are quite able to support ourselves. Nevertheless,' she was burning to discover the identity of her prospective employer and even more importantly his reasons, 'I would like to speak to this gentleman. Can you give me his address?'

'Of course – in fact after I had spoken to you this morning I took the liberty of asking my secretary to make an appointment with him.' The man went into the outer office and returned with a piece of paper. 'This is his address. You are to call on Thursday afternoon at two o'clock.'

How would her curiosity ever wait that long? With her friends eager to hear the details, Oriel did little work that afternoon, too busy puzzling over the charitable stranger. Ego prevented her from divulging the full details of the conversation to them or to her mother, preferring to have everyone think that she had been selected for her qualifications rather than out of kindness. Yet who on earth would be so kind? She could not possibly imagine, and continued to rack her brain until finally Thursday afternoon came and the mystery was revealed – at least half of it.

Oriel's lips parted as the houseowner opened the door. It was the man to whom Noel had been talking only the other day! Well, that explained who had been his informant about Miss Bytheway's death, but it still did not tell her why he wished to help. Remembering her manners she introduced herself. 'Good afternoon, I'm Oriel Maguire. Mr Price, I believe?'

Nat felt as though a hole were being burned through his stomach. Oh God, why had he done this? How would he prevent her from discovering his real name if she was handling his letters? Could he bear to look at his mother every day? 'Yes, yes . . . come in.'

Her entry prohibited by a barking hound, Oriel remained on the footpath. The Georgian house, though large, had no front garden.

The man looked embarrassed. 'I'm sorry, I'm going to have to ask you to remove your hat.'

'I beg your pardon?' Oriel cupped her ear, his words obliterated by the din.

'Shut up, Talbot! Your hat! He's frightened of people in hats!'

Perplexed but amused, Oriel removed her hat and within seconds the barking had ceased. At the man's summons she followed him across the threshold.

The interior, though more spacious, was of a similar layout to her own home: a long hallway with two rooms downstairs to her right hand side and a staircase directly ahead. It had an extra doorway that apparently led to the kitchen. After depositing her beribboned hat on a peg, the man led her into the room that overlooked the front street. It was crammed with expensive furniture and had a white marble fireplace with columns topped by ram's heads. The decor was very elegant. Oriel wondered who had devised it. She finished her inspection and looked at him. When she had been standing there for some moments and nothing more had passed his lips, she began to feel awkward. 'I believe you need a secretary?'

Nat was jolted into the present. Her voice was nothing like his mother's. 'Yes . . .' Not knowing what to say he looked around and seized a pile of books, thrusting them at her. 'Do you want to look them over?' Worried that his face might hold the same menace for her as it seemed to do for others, he offered a smile.

Oriel smiled too, seemingly unafraid, and putting the books upon a table she began to peruse them. 'Your last secretary was a bit untidy.'

Nat, who had been following the line of her jaw, started. 'Oh, I've never had a secretary. I do the books meself.'

Oriel blushed. 'I'm sorry, I didn't mean to be –'

'No, you're right, they are a mess! That's why I decided to . . . what with . . .' You're bumbling, he told himself. Calm down! 'Well, it's become a bit of a chore so I thought . . .' He spread his palms, hoping she would understand.

She seemed to, and nodded. 'I may need a little assistance in learning your method but I think I'll be able to pick it up quite quickly.' Closing the ledger, she turned towards him, a question on her lips: had he recently moved his residence from Fulford, as she had seen so much of him there? Just at that point the telephone rang and Nat went into the hallway, though she could still see him as he spoke into the contraption on the wall.

In his absence Oriel wandered around the room, glancing briefly at the ebony-framed prints which were similar to the ones at home, then peering at the ornaments on the mantel: Staffordshire greyhounds, a benign looking tiger, a porcelain terrier, not one of them depicting human life. She wandered on, noting the heavy tomes on the bookcase which were far too demanding for her tastes. Talbot hopped after her, sniffing at her skirts. She flicked at his nose. 'Go away!' To her amazement he did as he was told, leaving her to ponder on the man in the hall. When he returned she would ask him outright why he had chosen her by name. Turning from the picture of a stag at bay she gave a covert glance through the doorway, catching his profile as he spoke into the telephone. There was about him a familiarity. Yes, she had seen him several times in Fulford, but the aura of familiarity was much greater than one would normally expect from a passing stranger. She wandered over to a mirror and primped her hair, still puzzling. She thought of Noel. She thought of her mother. Perhaps he was a friend of – and then she knew! The revelation was so violent that it almost caused her to run from the house. What had made her guess she could not say, maybe it was the reflection of her own eyes that had sparked the truth, but when she span away from the mirror as though burned she knew that the man in the hall was her father.

He was still talking, but from the tone of his voice was attempting to get rid of the caller. Could Oriel sneak past him and escape into the street before he noticed? Shoulders tensed, she began to edge towards the door. The dog, sensing danger, rose with a growl. Oriel stopped dead. The man, her father, had looked over his shoulder and seen the panic on her face.

'I'll speak to you tonight, Violet!' With this Nat put down the receiver and marched back into the room. 'Talbot, behave yourself! Sorry if he frightened you,' he said to a trembling Oriel. 'He's not usually this grumpy. I'll shut him out.' The dog was ejected and the door closed, so preventing her escape.

Oriel cleared her throat, hoping that he would remain convinced that it was only the dog who had scared her. 'It's quite all right. I think I made him jump.' She hoped her words were not slurred; her tongue felt like a huge wad of cottonwool. 'How did he lose his leg by the way?' *By-the-way, by-the-way*, this is my father.

'I don't know , he was in a terrible state when I found him. He's the only family I have – but I'll get rid of him if he frightens you,' Nat added hastily.

'No, no, don't do that! I'm sure he'll get used to me.' Oriel had no intention of ever coming back here but would say anything in order to escape. Why on earth did he continue this subterfuge? He knew that she was his daughter, he had asked for her by name. Why had he lured her here when he must guess how unpopular he was for deserting her? She felt a pang of disgust – the only family I have, he had said! How could he lavish attention on a dog and neglect his own daughter?

'So you'll come to work for me?' At her nod he beamed. 'Oh good! That's good.' You're too gushing, he warned himself. Start behaving like an employer. He brought his hands together. 'Er, well, Miss Maguire, we'd better discuss wages. Would two pounds a week suit?' Receiving Oriel's hasty reply that this was most generous, he ended with, 'Can you start on Monday morning?'

Much relieved to be shown the door Oriel said she could, and moved as casually as her nerves would permit into the hall. The front door was opened and she tripped outside into safety.

'Just a minute!'

Oriel almost wet herself. Forcing herself not to run, she turned.

'You're forgetting your hat.' Nat handed it to her.

From somewhere she conjured a laugh and, thanking him, took her leave. Immediately she was out of his view, though, she ran full pelt down the Georgian street as if the devil himself were after her, until she was out of his grasp. Coming to a halt, she held her aching stomach and panted, recalling every expression, every movement of his face, his eyes, his nose, his mouth, his hair, comparing him to the image of the frightened, maltreated youth her mother had always painted. Mother – what was Oriel going to tell her? She certainly couldn't tell her the truth, Bright would be much too upset. And what part had Noel played in this? She would have words for him when next they met. The sound of a barrel organ pierced her introspection. She lifted her eyes and, breath coming a fraction easier, she set off in the direction of home. The organ grinder's monkey held up his hand for a coin as she passed. Oriel spared only a glance for the pathetic animal, too busy concocting an excuse for her mother as to why she had decided not to go and work for Mr Price. Mr Price – hah, the swine! The one who, by his abandonment had destroyed her hopes of becoming a nurse, the one she had sworn to destroy . . . her step faltered. Yes, she had, hadn't she? Remember how angry and hurt you were at being rejected like some leper just because you had no father? Remember how your mother endured years of servitude at the hands of a bully because she knew that no one else would employ an unmarried mother? All those years when Bright would have loved to play with her child but had no time because she had no husband to support her. And now here was Oriel's chance of retribution, delivered by the culprit himself.

When she arrived home the shock she had received was nowhere in evidence. She smiled gaily when her mother enquired as to the character of the man who had interviewed her.

'He's very nice indeed! An elderly gentleman, very frail, very kind. You have absolutely nothing to worry about, Mother. Yes, he has a wife! I start work on Monday morning.' And God help him, came the grim thought.

Urged on by a combination of mischief and curiosity, Oriel

set off for work on Monday morning. Over the weekend she had managed to unravel some of the mystery: Noel had informed the man, her father, that she and her mother were about to be thrown out onto the street. She hadn't asked the doctor for confirmation and neither would she, for that would give the game away before she had the chance to play her part, but Oriel knew it to be true. Out of belated feelings of guilt for his abandonment of them her father had sought to offer charity in the form of employment. Just why he had chosen to do it anonymously escaped her at present, but she guessed that he was probably too ashamed to introduce himself.

The tram that carried her past the army barracks and into town was crammed with munitions girls and women in uniform. Placards greeted her disembarkation, announcing the latest horrors of the war: *Diabolical New Weapon: Allies Hit by Poison Gas.* Oriel cringed, but there was too much on her mind this morning to worry over unknown victims. During the journey between the tram stop and her father's house, she pondered on how she might ruin his life as he had ruined hers. With access to all his accounts she might discover some crooked deal or income tax evasion. For the present, though, she must gain his trust, must allow him to believe that she had no idea who he was.

Nat's face lit up as he opened the door to her. How pathetic, thought Oriel as she preceded him to the front drawing room. She, who was normally quick to tears over another's pain or injustice, spared not one iota of compassion for this man, the cause of all her ills. 'And how are you this morning, Mr Price?'

Nat had been doing a lot of thinking too over the weekend, and had reached a decision to come clean about his name. For one thing it would be impossible to keep up the pretence with Oriel handling his affairs, and for another he was not even sure that she knew the identity of her father. Noel had never mentioned that fact. There was always the risk that she would reveal his name to her mother, but it was one he had decided to take. 'Actually,' you sound like Noel, he mocked himself, 'my name is Prince, not Price.' He looked into her blue eyes for a flash of recognition. There was nothing.

'Oh really?' Oriel showed mild surprise. 'I was told . . .'

'Yes, I'm afraid that was my fault,' cut in Nat. 'The headmaster kept getting my name wrong so in the end I decided to let him call me Price.' He laughed.

So too did Oriel. He must think I'm stupid! Does he imagine that by revealing his name I'll fling my arms around his neck and call him Father? Or is this just a test to see if I know who he is, so that he can continue to cheat and lie? 'Oh well, shall we get on, Mr Prince? What would you like me to do first?'

Nat felt both relief and disappointment: relief that he would continue to have his daughter in his house, disappointment that she had no idea that he was her father. Don't be greedy, he told himself, you've got her here, just be satisfied. 'Well, there's those books that I showed you last week.' He indicated the ledgers. 'It's just a case of daily, weekly and monthly accounts, both for the scrap-yard and the shop.'

'You have a shop too?'

'Just a little place that sells second-hand clothes. I used to run it –' he had been going to say meself but felt that she, with her own nicely formed accent, might look down on him, '– myself, but I found I was overstretched so I pay a woman to do it now. That's something else I'd like you to attend to, the wages.'

'How many staff do you employ?'

'Just her and a couple of men at the yard. That's just down the street.' He pointed. 'You might find the accounts for that are a bit complicated at first, what with there being all different commodities — scrap iron, wool, glass and so forth — but if you get into difficulties just ask. I'll get somebody to bring the invoices here every day so's you won't have to go there, it's a bit mucky.' The carefully chosen words were difficult to keep up. 'But I might require you to go and collect the shop takings and receipts and things from the shop some evenings when I'm not here. I don't know if I mentioned it, but I also run a finance company.'

'You do have a lot of enterprise!'

For some reason she made him feel silly. He felt himself redden. 'Well, I might have a lot of irons in the fire but they're all pretty modest, so you won't be overloaded with work. Shall we go through t'ledger now?' Damn, he had done it again!

Pulling out a chair he asked her to be seated at the table, hovered for a moment examining the texture and length of her black hair, then sat down beside her, much nearer than was proper for an employer and his secretary. She moved her chair to create a gap between them, unwitting of the wound she had inflicted. Still, her presence was acute. He could smell her light perfume, and the faintest hint of mustiness as if her dress had been hanging in the wardrobe all winter and this was its first airing.

Even with this gap between her and the man she hated, Oriel felt his assault, wanted to leap up and confront him, ask him how he could desert a wonderful woman like her mother. Oh, but he was cool! He could sit here quite calmly when she herself was almost driven to distraction by his presence. Her nostrils twitched. The only other man she had smelled was Noel, whose body odour was masked by ether and besides he had never been quite as close to her as this. Together, they went through Nat's business accounts. Oriel commanded herself to attend his instructions, but failed, dwelling instead on the timbre of his voice, the light covering of hair on the back of his hand, the dark wave that fell over his brow, his surprisingly manicured nail as it traced each page.

'Would you like a cup of tea?' Nat's query was unexpected. Oriel replied that that would be nice. He rose and was gone for a considerable time. His return was heralded by a series of dull thuds on the outside of the door. Perplexed, Oriel opened it.

'Sorry, I had my hands full.' Nat entered, bearing a cup and saucer in each hand. 'I hope you like it strong? That's the way I make it.'

Oriel looked uncomfortable. 'Oh, I didn't realize . . . otherwise I would have offered. Don't you have a maid?'

'A maid?' The blue eyes looked askance. 'No, I couldn't be doing with anyone living in.' He handed one of the cups to Oriel. 'I have a woman who comes to clean for me, though, and a fella who does the garden. No, I prefer to live alone.' He put his cup to his lips. 'Ah, that's nice isn't it?'

'Very nice.' Oriel took a few sips, then indicated the books. 'But you're not paying me to drink tea. I really should get on.'

'Oh, yes.' Nat felt as if he were being dismissed and backed away. 'Well, I'll leave you to it, Miss Maguire. I shan't be going out today, not that I doubt your capabilities you understand, but it is your first day so . . . I'll be in the back if you need me.'

Need you, thought Oriel? Where were you when my mother needed help? But she smiled and managed to continue the pretence, turning up for work each day, each week with no hint of the bitterness that raged inside her, as bitter as the war that raged upon the mangled fields of Europe.

Nat made all manner of excuses not to leave the house when Oriel was present. Just to be under the same roof, to be able to pop his head into the front parlour under the guise of offering refreshment, was enough to lighten his heart. When she went home he felt a sense of loss, and if he was not meeting Violet he went to bed early in order to hasten the morning and Oriel's return.

His eagerness for matrimony appeared to have deserted him, for he did not press the matter with Violet's parents so much as he had done initially. In fact his preoccupation with Oriel seemed to have made him forget that there was a war on. Only when the question of a compulsory call-up was bandied in the newspapers did he set a definite date for the wedding. With this only a short time away, Violet was permitted for the first time in their courtship to visit Nat's house unchaperoned – though only when it was light, her mother had decreed.

Oriel's fingers were beavering away on the typewriter which she had persuaded Nat to buy when a tattoo was performed on the doorknocker that morning. She paused, then hearing Nat's footsteps in the hall continued with her work. The sound of the metal keys prevented her from hearing the caller's voice; in fact she did not realize he had invited his visitor in until, in the act of folding her completed document, she heard the tinkling girlish laughter. Inquisitiveness led her to the wall against which she held her ear, but the voices were distorted. There was nothing else for it but to go and find out what was happening.

Nat looked startled as, with a peremptory knock, Oriel came into the room where he and Violet were cuddling on the sofa. He jumped up; so did Talbot.

'Mr Prince, I'm so sorry, I had no idea that you had a visitor!' Most apologetic, Oriel was staring at a flustered Violet, who gave a little cry and pulled at her bodice.

Nat cleared his throat. 'Oh, Miss Maguire, this is my fiancée, Miss Violet Ward!'

Now it was Oriel's turn to be shocked. Fiancée! 'I'm terribly sorry for bursting in like this, Mr Prince,' she burbled, 'I just needed some advice on this invoice, but it's not important, I'll come back later.' She closed the door hurriedly and retreated to the front parlour to nibble her lip. Fiancée!

There was no sound coming from the back room now; at least Oriel could hear none of Violet's whispered entreaties. 'Come back to the sofa, Nat!'

Nat, looking troubled, took no notice. What must Oriel think of him?

'Nat! Are you listening to me?' Violet patted the leather sofa. Talbot wagged his tail and attempted to climb up beside her until she shoved him away.

Nat glanced at her now, voiced regret and came to take his place at her side. 'Sorry for that intrusion, Violet. She never comes in here normally.'

'You didn't tell me your secretary was so pretty.' Violet looked petulant.

Nat stared into thin air. 'I hadn't noticed.' Then he looked at the woman beside him and turned on his rare charm. 'Why would I bother looking at other women when I've such a beautiful fiancée?'

Violet giggled and fell into his embrace. When they drew breath, Nat rested his chin upon her shoulder and stared at the wall. What explanation would he give his daughter?

His fiancée drew back and caught his preoccupation. 'I hope you're not thinking about her?'

'Who?' He tried to appear cool.

'You know who! I must say, she seems very assured to be a servant.'

'Well, a secretary's not really a servant – behave, Talbot!' The dog was nibbling the base of his tail.

'Of course it is! She works for you, doesn't she?' Violet decided to impose her authority. 'She needs taking down a peg or two.'

'What are you going to do?' Nat's alarmed eyes followed her to the door.

'Sit there!' She pushed him back, laughed, closed the

door and went along the hall. Nat exchanged glances with the dog.

However, on her return she was not in the least amused. 'Nat, you must speak to her!' Her eyes burned with tears of outrage, her cheeks pink.

'Why, what . . . ?' Nat rose in concern.

'She used the most profane language!'

'What, did she –?'

'Don't ask me to repeat it! I couldn't possibly.' Violet pulled out her handkerchief. The dog sighed and buried his nose under his tail.

Nat scowled, then reached for a paper and pencil. 'Here, write it down.'

'I can't!'

'Violet, I must get to the bottom of this.' He brandished the pencil.

Hesitantly, she stooped over the paper and wrote, *I'm damned if I'll make your tea.*

Nat felt the urge to explode with laughter, but managed to keep his expression serious. 'Oh, you poor thing. I'll go and have words with Miss Maguire!' He marched from the room, shadowed by Talbot, but on closing the door he went not to the front of the house but to the kitchen where he put on the kettle himself. Before re-entering with the tea he said loudly enough for Violet's benefit, 'And let that be a lesson to you, Miss Maguire!'

'Did you dismiss her?' Violet looked satisfied that her order for tea had been carried out.

'Oh, I couldn't do that, dear.' Nat looked softly reproachful as he handed over a cup. 'Otherwise I'd have all that bookwork to do on my own. But she's been told her wages'll be docked for her rudeness.' You needn't think I'm going to risk losing my daughter over you, you silly little bitch. 'Don't worry, when we're married you'll have all the servants you want.'

An hour or so later Oriel heard Violet leave. After a

short gap, Nat's head appeared round the door. She assumed that he had come to issue reprimand for her show of disrespect to his affianced, but oddly he did not even mention it. 'Are you busy, Oriel?'

Oriel gaped at him.

Realizing his gaffe, Nat was quick to apologize. 'I'm sorry, I was forgetting myself, Miss Maguire!'

'But . . . how did you know my Christian name?' His secretary enjoyed a malicious tease.

'Er . . .' Nat shook his head, perplexed, 'you must have told me. I'm sorry if I caused offence.'

'I'm not offended in the least. You can call me Oriel if you wish.' She smiled at him. 'I'm surprised you haven't asked more about me. You haven't even asked where I live. I could be a criminal, you know.'

Nat smiled too. 'I can tell you're not.'

'How?' In girlish fashion, she tossed her head. 'You don't know anything about me, do you?'

'No, but I'm a good judge of character.'

'Really?' She watched his hands move up to grip the edges of his morning suit. His appearance had been given some attention since Violet's departure. He was exceptionally clean-cut, not a hair out of place, his shirt collar starched and gleaming. 'I must admit I was surprised that you didn't ask me more questions at my initial interview. Aren't you interested in my background?' Did this sound too familiar for an employee? Oriel decided she didn't care. He was obviously more afraid of her than she was of him.

'Of course I am,' replied Nat. 'I just didn't want to pry.' He had made it his business to learn all he needed to know from his doctor friend. Noel had informed him that his help would be no longer required, for Bright had been allowed by the new owner of the house to remain at her present address in exchange for rent; this was being provided by Oriel who had got herself a job. Nat had smiled to himself but had not, of course, revealed the identity of her employer. For some reason Oriel had not mentioned his name to the doctor either, or Noel would have twigged immediately. He wondered if her mother knew. He looked at his daughter. As she was obviously inviting him to enquire further, he tried to think of something that an employer might ask. 'Well now, how are you enjoying your job?' Oriel said that she was enjoying it very much. 'I must say you're coping very well. I was worried I might be expecting you to do too much.'

'On the contrary, I sometimes feel as though I'm not earning the very generous amount you pay me.'

Nat stilled her tongue. 'Let me assure you, you're worth every penny.'

'That's very kind of you to say so, though I still feel a bit of a shirker, as if I ought to register for war work, what with all the men gone to the Front.'

Nat did not like the inference that he was not doing his bit. His smile became fixed. 'You're not one o' them there suffragettes are you?'

Oriel remained pleasant. 'I'm not about to follow the example of some who make an exhibition of themselves, but I do believe women should have the vote.'

'And what does your father think to your views?' He knew it was rash the minute he had said it.

'He's dead.' How blithely did the hurtful lie trip off her tongue.

Nat was in the act of lighting a cigarette but now turned his full attention on her.

'You seem surprised.' She looked him straight in the eye, feeling triumphant as he withdrew his gaze first.

'No, I'm just sorry, I didn't realize.' Nat proceeded to light his cigarette.

'Why, should you have done? Anyway, there's nothing to be sorry about, I never knew him. He died a long time ago and he wasn't a very nice man by all accounts. Apparently he deserted my mother when I was just a baby.'

'She told you that?' Nat drew so hard on the cigarette that its lighted tip glowed like a volcano, presenting a rather diabolical figure with his black hair, black suit, black tie.

His daughter was unflustered and sighed. 'Yes, though I'd already witnessed her suffering for myself. He left her penniless, so I shouldn't imagine he would care in the least whether or not women get the vote. I'm glad he's dead and so is Mother.'

Nat tried to fathom those innocent eyes. There was something not quite right here . . .

But Oriel had left the subject. 'I must apologize again for bursting in so rudely before. I hope your fiancée wasn't too upset?'

The quiet dark man shook his head. 'No harm done.'

Why doesn't he mention my rudeness to her, thought Oriel, but asked instead, 'May I enquire if you have set a date for the happy day?'

'It's . . .' Still shaken, Nat underwent a period of thought. 'About seven or eight weeks, I think.'

Oriel laughed. 'You don't seem too sure! I trust you'll arrive at the church on the correct day.'

Nat assured her he had the date encircled on the calendar. 'May I ask if there's anyone in your life, Miss Maguire?'

'Oh no, I'm far too young!'

'Good, I'd hate to lose you — lose your very efficient services.'

Oriel thanked him and Nat left the room. She wondered whether to do it now, or wait until after he was married. To act now would mean that her quest for revenge was over and she could tell this wretched man exactly what she thought of him. But would this punishment be sufficient? Didn't he deserve more for all the years of hurt he had inflicted? Oriel realized with a start that she had come to enjoy this game. In the hope of prolonging her own climax of revenge whilst causing maximum damage to her victim she decided to wait until after Nat's wedding to drop her bombshell. Today or tomorrow, it would hardly matter. Either way, Miss Violet Ward's reaction to the news that her beloved had an illegitimate daughter would be the same.

The war raged on, one atrocity followed by another. This week it was the sinking of an American passenger ship by a German torpedo. Oriel, greatly upset by this morning's newspaper report, burst in upon her employer who was in the middle of a late breakfast. 'What d'you think about the Lusitania?' In the weeks that she had worked for him she had become increasingly familiar in her attitude.

'Dreadful,' replied Nat, with not exactly heartfelt emotion. He was more concerned with the drastic change in her appearance. The glossy black hair normally worn in a chignon had been mutilated into the kind of bob recently adopted by land and factory workers.

'I'm sure you'd be more concerned if it were your fiancée on board! All those little children . . .' Forgetting that she was in the presence of her enemy, Oriel allowed a tear to spring to her eye. Then, remembering where she was, she turned abruptly. 'Well, I'd better get on with my work. So sorry to have interrupted your breakfast!'

Nat had witnessed the tear and became pensive as he chewed his bacon, ruminating on Oriel's words. What would he feel if Violet had been on that ship? Nothing. Nil. Zero. Where others might have found shame in this admittance he himself had long since dispensed with notions of honour – if he had ever possessed any at all. Violet was a nice girl but he would not cry if he lost her. Yet, if Oriel and her mother had been on that fated liner . . . it did not bear thinking about.

Nat finished his breakfast, washed his pots, then made to leave. Since she had come to work for him, he had made constant excuses in order to stay in the house with his daughter, but eventually he had been forced to acknowledge that the business would not run itself and, reassured that she was here for keeps, he had gradually moved back into his routine. However, before he left he always popped in to share a few words with Oriel and today's offering was no different, save for its content. 'I'm sorry if I upset you before. I didn't mean to. It is a rotten shame about . . . you know.'

Oriel came to attention and looked around from her typewriter. 'Yes, well, all the war's a rotten shame, isn't it?' Whereas some would read of the tragedy and instantly forget, the image of those drowning people would mean days of depression for Oriel.

'Your hair looks very nice by the way.' He didn't really like it.

Oriel gave a tight smile, and he consequently left the room.

There was much demolition work going on around the city, and the hoardings that bordered the sites were papered with recruitment posters. Nat ignored all requests that his country needed him as he moved around York on his wagon, thinking more of his early beginnings at the Industrial School which, to his grim satisfaction, was amongst those buildings to be razed.

His thoughts had moved on to his impending nuptials, when the honk of a car's horn drew his attention and he looked around to see a grinning Noel about to overtake him. 'By the heck, I was just thinking of you!'

Eyes shielded by goggles – he had a slight infection in one of them – Noel continued to drive his vehicle alongside the cart. 'That's why you look so miserable, is it?'

The solemn face allowed itself to laugh. 'No, I was actually thinking of my wedding.'

'A happy event that must have been then!'

'I haven't had it yet.'

'What! No wonder you're looking miserable. How long have you been married?'

'Soft bugger, I mean I haven't had the wedding. It takes place at the beginning of July. I was going to call and ask you to be my best man.' Nat clicked his tongue at the horse and steered it out of the path of an army convoy. 'I hope you'll oblige. You're the only friend I have — except for Talbot o' course, and I don't think they make morning suits with three legs in 'em.'

'Best man?' Noel wondered why on earth he should feel any reservation. He wanted Nat to be married, didn't he? Then he and Bright could get on with their own lives. It was just something in the pit of his stomach . . .

Nat became uncomfortable at the odd way his friend was looking at him. 'What's the matter? Can't you do it?'

The goggled face came to his senses. 'I'd be delighted!' To endorse this Noel honked his horn in approval. 'Well, come on, tell me all about her. Is she rich? Is she pretty?'

'So so.' Nat shrugged.

'You don't seem very excited,' observed the doctor, alternating his glance between Nat and the road ahead.

'I'm getting married, not riding in the Grand National. Look out, you're going to flatten that bloody thing! You silly bugger, get it on the pavement!' His shout was for a man whose dancing bear had been performing a monotonous twirl in the road. 'Still going on in this day and age! You want locking up, you do, cruel bugger!' Many uncomplimentary remarks were exchanged between Nat and the owner of the dancing bear. 'Fade away!' Once past, the conversation reverted to Nat's wedding. He decided to show a little more consideration for his bride to be. 'Oh, she's all right is Violet. A very pretty lass as a matter o' fact. The war's made me realize I need a wife and she'll make as good a wife as any.'

Frowning, Noel sought confirmation. 'But you are happy with this arrangement?'

'As happy as I'll ever be.' Nat had everything he had always coveted; a big house and a garden like the one Mr and Mrs Scaum used to have, people under his command . . . but viewed from the angle of one who had achieved them the objects of his desire had become almost boring. What indeed was happiness? 'Sometimes, I hate this bloody place.' He looked around at the grim streets with their gloomy placards of war. How he still missed the wide open spaces of Canada and the sun beating down on his shoulders. They'd never have him back there, though.

The doctor had insufficient time to ask for enlightenment, but had a shrewd guess that Nat saw marriage in the same way that he did, as a convenience, but for very different reasons. 'Well, just let me know what day, what time and I'll be there. Congratulations, old pal. Have to go now, I'll see you anon!' Bashing several more honks from his horn, Noel sped off, though in some confusion over his feelings. If not wholly delighted with Nat's information, it did at least mean that now the path to Bright's heart was well and truly clear.

When he arrived at Fulford, which had been his intended terminus even before meeting Nat, he found her laughing. He threw his goggles down on the table and sat down by the open window in the kitchen, enjoying the breeze. 'What's tickled you?'

'The chimney sweep.' Bright gave another chuckle. 'I don't mean that literally. Twas just that he called me madam!'

'What's so funny about that?' Noel rubbed at the marks on his face caused by the goggles and smiled upon her with fondness.

'Well, look at me!' She opened her arms.

His reply was warm. 'I am, and you look wonderful.' Her bosom was draped in a soft, coffee-coloured material that fell in gentle pleats from her waist. At her daughter's behest she had had her tawny hair bobbed to match Oriel's. 'Every inch the lady you are.'

She was moved. 'Oh, Noel, you're lovely to me.'

'No, you're the lovely one. I'm sure my mother would think so too.' He picked at the grey cloth of his trousers. 'I wonder, could I take you to meet her some afternoon?'

This was most unexpected. Bright touched her hair, still not used to its shortness. 'Why, yes . . .' She came to sit nearby.

'There is a reason.' Noel sat forward on the hard kitchen chair, lacing his hands over his knees and taking a moment to phrase his words. 'And it might be better if you heard it now before you speak to my mother. She's . . . well, she can often be a little rude, and I don't want her to put you off. This is idiotic!' He jerked himself upright. 'Let me get to the point. Bright, you know how fond I've become of you and Oriel don't you?' She nodded and permitted him to take her hand. 'Will you marry me?'

It was no sensation. Once over the hurdle of their difference in station, Bright had been awaiting his proposal for some time. Keeping hold of his hand, she bent her head. 'Thank you for asking, but – I can't, Noel. I'm sorry, I can't.'

'But . . . why?' He seemed devastated.

'I can't explain.' She stroked the blond hair on the back of his hand with her thumb. 'I think it's just that I've got used to being on my own.' Her chocolate-coloured eyes portrayed earnestness. 'But if I were to marry anyone it would be you. You're a lovely man, a great friend, and I'm very fond of you, you know that.'

Noel frowned. He had never considered rejection. 'Is it because we're of a different religion?' He had been some-what concerned himself over her Catholicism. 'I'm willing to get married in your church.' Though what his mother would say . . .

'I hate to offend but I don't think they'd have ye, Noel.

They wouldn't recognize the marriage. Anyway, it's not that.' How could she say I just don't love you? Besides, she did love him, but not in the way that he wanted.

'Is it the war? Perhaps when it's over?'

'I can't make any promises, Noel.'

He withdrew his hand from hers, picked up his goggles and toyed with the strap. 'But I don't understand your reasons! Surely you can't enjoy being alone, I know I don't.'

Bright folded her hands in her lap. 'Then, can I be rude and ask why you've never thought of marrying before, Noel? Surely you've met ladies who are more suited to be a doctor's wife than I am.'

'I'd never really thought about it until I met you.' That was a lie. He had thought about it a great deal. He thought about how unnatural it was that he couldn't find a woman he desired. He didn't really fancy Bright in that way, but it wasn't just to stop people nagging that he wanted to marry her. He wasn't like Nat, using her for his own selfish purpose, he did genuinely care about her and want to look after her. Before she came along he had foreseen himself ending his days as a bachelor.

Bright frowned into his face. 'Your eye looks red, is it sore?'

'I've got conjunctivitis and don't change the subject! You're avoiding my question: do you like being alone?'

'I'm not alone, I have Oriel.'

'But that's a different thing altogether! One day she'll be married herself . . .' A look of recognition came over his face. 'It's Nat, isn't it? It's because of what he did to you that you're afraid to give yourself to anyone. Bright, I swear it wouldn't be like that with me. I would never make you do anything you didn't want to.'

'Noel, it isn't what you think!' Bright squeezed his hands in earnest. 'At least, it is partly true. I can't give myself to you because I still feel deeply for Nat.'

He gave a cough of total disbelief. 'How can you say that when he treated you as he did?'

'I know, I know, I'm sure anyone would think I'm mad, I don't understand it myself, but I can't stop the way I feel about him.'

'But you haven't seen him for years! You're living with a memory. That young boy doesn't exist any more, he's a man, and if I may say so a man with not too good a reputation – besides, he's spoken for.'

'I know, you've told me!' Bright covered her ears. 'But I can't help it, and I can't marry you, Noel, I'm sorry but I can't.' She fled upstairs and locked herself in her room, not coming out until she heard the front door slam.

A more composed Noel returned that evening to offer profuse apologies. Oriel passed a quizzical glance at her mother, who had issued acceptance and invited him to eat with them. Noticing a veil of strange reserve over the normally friendly atmosphere, Oriel waited until after Noel had gone to ask her mother, 'Have you two been having words?'

'What makes you ask that?' Bright made sure that the blackout curtain was properly drawn before turning on the gaslamps, their added illumination not required until now due to the light summer evening.

'Noel said he'd come to apologize – what for?' Oriel had changed into a pansy-coloured dressing gown.

Her mother continued to potter. 'He asked me to marry him.'

'What? But that's wonderful!'

'I turned him down.' Bright smoothed the chenille table cloth, then sat down by the hearth.

'Oh, why?' The face inside the dark bob crumpled in disappointment. 'He's lovely.'

'I know.' Bright's eyes were cast down to the rug. 'But it wouldn't be fair of me to marry him. I could never feel the same way about anyone the way I did about your father.'

'You're still waiting for him to come back,' breathed Oriel. Then incredulity rose to outrage. 'But he abandoned you!' Bright looked up at the vehemence of her daughter's exclamation but did not get time to speak. Oriel tugged the edges of her dressing gown more tightly across her bosom in a gesture of defence. 'And he abandoned me! I hate him! And if you want to know why, it's because he's the reason I could never be a nurse, because I'm illegitimate. So there, now you know!'

An anguished Bright leaned forward and reached for her daughter. 'That's my fault as much as his, darling!'

'Stop making excuses for him!' screamed Oriel, recoiling from her mother's hand. 'He doesn't want you and he doesn't want me! All the time you thought he was in Canada he was here in York and never came to see us! And all you could do was make excuses for him, saying he was frightened. The coward! He doesn't give one fig about us! And even if by some miracle he did wriggle out from under his stone and ask you to marry him, then you could say goodbye to me!' Eyes red with tears, she fled from the room and pounded upstairs.

Bright remained in her chair and wept.

In time, her angry sobs abated, Oriel moved from the bed to her dressing table. Seizing a fountain pen, she used it as a weapon, the nib almost tearing the paper as it scratched out its venom: *Dear Miss* – Wait a moment! She paused to instruct herself; if he were married that would remove him from the scene as far as Mother was concerned. No, I don't want him to be happy, I want to make him as miserable as I possibly can. Lowering pen to paper, she continued: *Dear Miss Ward* . . .

In the morning, before breakfast, she repented to her mother for her tone though not for her words. 'I didn't mean to hurt you but I meant what I said, Mother. I find it inconceivable that you could still love a man who treated you like that.'

A puffy-eyed Bright set the table as normal, but she refused to look at her daughter and her hurt was tangible. 'Then we must agree to differ.'

Oriel waited to be forgiven.

'Sit down and eat,' came the quiet order.

'Mother —'

'I don't want to hear it mentioned again.' Still refusing to look at her daughter, Bright picked up her spoon.

Oriel obeyed, but the meal was a painful affair and after gulping down only a few mouthfuls she excused herself, saying she had a letter to post on the way to work. The cheek she stooped to kiss was frigid, and throughout the day the memory of this kept driving her to the edge of tears. Her employer seemed unable to handle the change in her attitude and thus made himself scarce. This suited Oriel who, whilst she pounded on her typewriter, heaped mental blame upon him for her miserable state. Was he not satisfied with his desertion of her mother? Did he have to destroy everything? Well, she wouldn't let him.

22

Dear Mr Prince, read Nat that morning over his breakfast, *This is to inform you that our daughter is compelled to break off the intended matrimony with yourself . . .* He frowned and stopped eating. *You can, I am sure, appreciate the shock and humiliation that Violet has suffered at being duped, not to mention the outrage that we ourselves felt upon receiving the information that the young lady who is employed by you under the guise of secretary is in fact your illegitimate daughter.* Oh shit! *You will therefore understand our request that you are never to contact Violet again.* Though the letter was finished, Nat had difficulty in believing what he had just read and stared down at the piece of paper. His first instinct was to visit the Wards and protest, but then did he really feel such loss? The liaison with Violet had been manufactured after all. He could always find someone else. Of more import was how she had found out about Oriel. Yet again he pored over the letter, which failed to mention in what form or by whose hand the information had been received. It was all very mysterious.

Each morning, when Oriel had arrived for work she had examined her father's face for signs that her bombshell had landed. Today she thought she detected a slightly subdued air, but not an expression that told her he had been jilted. Surely her damning letter to Violet Ward must have arrived by now? Unless she had misread the address in her father's notebook, for he was an atrocious writer. Maybe it was simply that Violet was wondering what to do about it. After a week Oriel could bear the suspense no longer and when the opportunity arose she grabbed it.

Nat had come into the room where she worked to inform her that he was going out. She glanced through the window. 'It's a beautiful day. Let's hope the weather stays like this for your wedding – it can't be far off now.'

Nat stroked his cleanly shaven lip in embarrassment. 'I'm afraid there isn't going to be a wedding. Miss Ward's called off our engagement.'

'Oh, I do beg your pardon! I had no wish to intrude on a personal matter!' Oriel played with the ebony brooch at her throat. 'Please accept my condolences.'

'Thank you.' Nat studied her face for a moment, still toying with his lip. There was something affected about her commiserations. The glint in her eye did not match the uttered sentiment. Still, why should she care? As far as Oriel was concerned she was only his employee. Saying goodbye he turned and left the room.

But his uneasiness remained. What if . . . what if Oriel had somehow found out she was his daughter but remained silent? His heartrate increased. What if the thought of her father marrying someone other than her mother made her angry and jealous? Would she not do anything to stop that marriage? What if, what if? I've never heard owt so daft, he told himself. If she'd found out surely she would have confronted you? Why, you haven't dared to confront her, have you? No, but that's the way I am. Other people are different, speak to each other of their fears and emotions. But she isn't other people, she's your daughter, maybe she's just like you in that respect, maybe she can't voice her feelings, she could have known you're her father for ages. She must be a damned good actor then, he told himself, for she fooled you. Maybe he was just being fanciful, but oh at that moment he wanted desperately for it to be true! He wanted it to have been Oriel who had told Violet that she was his daughter, wanted to know that she felt strongly enough about him to reveal her shameful beginnings. From that day on he resolved to watch her more closely, though still he mentioned nothing of their natural bond, too afraid of losing her.

Oriel's triumph over the sabotage of her father's matrimonial plans did not bring as great a pleasure as she had anticipated. Yes, he was miserable, but then this quiet dark man was never exactly bursting with vigour. If she had hoped with this one act to compel him to blow out his brains then she had failed. To bring about his total downfall would take a lot more planning.

The books had turned up a few interesting details. Acquainted with many of his transactions, for he had mentioned them in passing, she had been intrigued to learn that not all of these were to be entered in her ledgers. There was no record of them anywhere. Her investigations had also unearthed a hidden safe, the contents of which she guessed to be thousands of pounds. She could only assume that his purpose was to avoid supertax, for which he must surely be eligible, though she was unable as yet to substantiate this. She had also found other discrepancies in his accounts. Insignificant though each of these might be, she hoarded each particle of information to be employed as grist in the process of her enemy's destruction.

Destruction on the Western Front prevailed upon another Christmas, though Oriel and those around her remained relatively untouched. It had once been a novelty for her and Bright to watch the aeroplanes take off from Knavesmire – her mother had even voiced a desire to go up in one – but now it had become an ordinary, everyday occurrence, as had all the other military movements in the city.

Christmas was a more expensive affair for everyone this year; the cost of all essentials had rocketed: coal, milk, bread, potatoes.

'I really don't know how the poor people are going to cope,' quoth Oriel to her employer in response to his query about what she would be doing over Christmas.

'Things are expensive enough normally. I don't know how they manage. I feel really sorry for them.'

Nat watched her putting on her gloves, using any tactic to delay her, for he would not see her again for two whole days. 'Aye, people're having a rough time of it aren't they?' He had given up trying to match her polished accent. 'I trust you and your mother won't go short of anything?'

'We'll get by.' Oriel smoothed the wrinkles from her gloves.

Nat stood in the doorway, preventing her from leaving. He had wanted to buy her a gift but had decided against it, and now made another offer. 'I'd like to make sure of that by giving you this Christmas bonus.' He held out an envelope. 'I'm really pleased with the work you've done.'

'I'm sure you pay me enough already.' Oriel was slow to take up the offer.

'Please.' He shoved the envelope at her. 'Surely your mother would find it handy, what with all the extra stuff she'll have to buy.'

Oriel accepted. 'Thank you, I'm sure she will.' The rift between herself and Bright had healed, though only because neither of them had mentioned his name since the argument. She asked, 'Will you be entertaining at all?'

'I doubt it.' Since Violet, there had been one or two brief flings but no one he would marry even in an emergency. 'There'll be just me and Talbot.' At the mention of his name the hound wagged his tail.

Oriel took a dangerous chance. 'Would you care to take your Christmas dinner with us? I'm certain Mother . . .'

'Oh, no, no!' As his daughter had so cleverly anticipated, Nat issued hasty refusal. 'I couldn't impose.'

No, or you'd soon be found out for the charlatan you are, wouldn't you?

'Besides, I don't like to leave Talbot on his own for too long, but thank you for the offer, it's very kind.' Nat breathed a sigh of relief as she accepted his refusal. 'Don't you worry about me, I'll find plenty to occupy me.'

'I trust that doesn't mean work?' censured Oriel. 'Don't you ever take time off to relax, read or something?'

'Perhaps I will.' Nat did not reveal that the books on his shelves had been chosen merely for their size and colour. He had not read one of them.

'Well, I'll bid you goodnight and wish you a merry Christmas, Mr Prince.' Oriel moved towards him.

Nat stepped reluctantly out of her way. 'And the same to you, Oriel –and to your mother.'

Alone in the house, he poured himself a whisky, fell into a leather chair and pictured himself at Bright's table. If only he could . . .

As prophesied, Nat spent the festive season alone, except for a visit from Spud which did not really count as he only came to deliver his collection. Noel called on the day after Boxing Day. However angry the other might make him, however hard he might try to stay away, he had always found himself wanting in self-discipline where Nat was concerned. He knew he would always keep on coming back. 'I was going to come yesterday but I thought you might be entertaining.'

Nat scoffed. 'Me, entertaining?'

'No one new yet, then?' The doctor had projected sorrow earlier in the year when his friend had announced that the intended nuptials had been cancelled, though he had not relayed this to Bright while there was still hope for himself.

'No one I'd want to spend Christmas with.'

'Cutting it a bit fine, aren't you?' Noel was asked what he meant by this. 'Oh, come on, you only want a wife to save you from going to war.'

Nat feigned affront, then delivered a secretive grin.

'As I said, you're cutting it fine.' Conscription loomed ever nearer. 'There must be a lot of desperate women who could oblige.'

'I don't doubt it, but pride prevents me from marrying any old trout and the decent ones all want to wait for this that and the other. If it's a choice of being shot or marry an ugly woman I think I'd choose being shot. How about you? Is your mother still pestering you for grandchildren?'

Noel twiddled his moustache. 'Yes, but I'm not about to marry for the sake of it – not like some.' He made no mention of his proposal to Bright, nor of her consequent refusal.

'It's all right for you!' laughed Nat. 'Safe in your doctor's job. Just spare a thought for those of us who aren't so lucky.' He hoisted his glass. 'Anyway, a belated Merry Christmas!'

New Year's Day brought the proclamation Nat had been dreading: conscription for single men. Thus he hastened his search for a bride, whom he finally cornered in March. There had been a thick layer of snow overnight but the afternoon's brilliant sunshine had transformed it to slush, which Nat's horse had flicked up onto the clothes of passers-by, Olive amongst them. There had been angry words at first, but when Nat had apologized the young lady had shown a generosity of spirit that had attracted more of his attentions and, wasting no time, he had asked her out. Unlike Violet's parents, Olive's widowed mother thought that chaperoning was old-fashioned, allowing Nat to press his suit unhindered. Apart from being pretty, Olive had a lovely disposition too and Nat, feeling instantly at ease in her presence, knew that he could live with this one.

Easter came. In the old days this would have meant one long round of churchgoing for Bright but, though she and her daughter still attended Mass, she had not sat through the Vigil on Good Friday for many a year. Oriel herself showed indifference to her religion, stating that she only went to church to keep her mother company. 'I can't see why you still go. From what you've told me the church wasn't much help when you needed it.'

Bright regarded this as sacrilege. 'I never meant to give the impression that it was no help at all! The nuns were very good to me, gave me clothes and food and looked after me when my own kin didn't . . . tis just that they thought you'd be better off with a married couple. I suppose they were doing it for the best, but I wouldn't have any of that. I was determined to keep you.'

Oriel felt privileged. 'If it had been left to the church I would never have known who my dear mother is. I view it rather differently than you do.'

'Well, you don't have to go to Mass.' Bright struggled with a hatpin. 'But I was raised a Catholic and I couldn't stop now after all these years. Anyway, tis a comfort.' And always in her prayers she mentioned Nat.

They went off to early Mass, returning for breakfast. Oriel had the day off work and later in the morning expressed a wish to visit the cemetery to put flowers on Miss Bytheway's grave. 'I feel I should after she left me all this. Are you coming with me?'

Bright wrinkled her nose. 'I won't if you don't mind, dear. I've had enough walking for one day. How long will you be? I was going to do lunch for twelve o'clock.' Oriel said she would be back by then. 'Don't be late, this fish cost the earth. I don't want it to boil away to nothing.'

As soon as Oriel closed the door Bright felt a prickle of anxiety and as usual in this situation rushed around the house seeking work to keep her mind occupied. At eleven-thirty she took the fish out of the pantry and slapped it onto a board in order to prepare it for lunch. Dead eyes stared back at her as she took up a knife. *Cut yourself*, said the voice. Oh, go away! Bugger off! She stared at the fish, imagining that those thick lips were gasping for breath. She knew what that felt like and began to gasp for air too. After all these years thinking she was all right the madness had returned. Do something! Anything to take your mind off it! Throw the knife away! I won't, tis stupid, I won't give in! With trembling hands she cut the head and tail off the fish, filleted it and put it in a pan. What would Noel say if he could see you now? Would he still want to marry you? No! How could you honestly marry anyone knowing you're mad?

The outer door opened. Oh thank God you're back! At the sound of her daughter's foot in the hall, Bright's panic began to subside. A smiling face came round the door, then looked worried. 'Mother, you're as white as a ghost! Are you ill?' However rare, she found these turns of her mother's very disturbing after what Miss Bytheway had said all those years ago. Perhaps her mother was going mad again.

Bright sighed and laughed. 'No, I'm just passing out from hunger. Now you're here I can get the fish on.'

'Sit down, I'll do the lunch.' Somewhat reassured by her mother's normal behaviour, Oriel pulled a chair away from the table.

'No, I've only to put the pan on the hob.' Bright dared not sit down. Only now did she begin to realize what a Godsend Miss Bytheway had been. How much more she would have suffered if granted the time to ponder on her madness; the work had given it less opportunity to manifest itself. Turning from the hob, she looked at her daughter who was now gazing out of the window to check on the progress of the spring vegetables. *Pick up the knife and stick it in her.* I won't! Get away! Her daughter turned and smiled. The madness receded. But it was always there in the background: Bright's own personal cross.

Over the weekend they painted hardboiled eggs, something Bright had not done since she was a child, and on Easter Monday Noel took them for a motor car ride to Acomb Green where, along with dozens of schoolchildren, they rolled their painted eggs. Noel, wounded by Bright's rejection but not totally overthrown, had continued to call at the house in Fulford Road, often taking her out for dinner or to the theatre. In view of the fact that she had turned down his proposal he had decided not to parade her before his mother, seeing this as an unnecessary ordeal. This innocent creature wouldn't last two minutes with Mrs Scaum. He smiled at the shouts of glee as Bright and Oriel followed their eggs down the incline, holding up their skirts in order not to trip, faces laughing beneath the extravagant Easter bonnets with their ribbons and flowers.

'Mine won't crack!' Bright called to Noel, holding the undamaged egg to show him, then throwing it down time after time, laughing and giggling almost hysterically.

Eventually the egg did fracture and she and Oriel came to sit by Noel on the tartan rug. 'This is dreadful!' Bright wore a guilty smile as she said it. 'All those poor men at the Front and here I am having the time of my life.' She began to pick the shell from the egg.

'The war's not exactly any of your doing, is it?' Noel was more thoughtful than usual, distant even. Bright glanced at him, still picking at her egg. Oriel did the same.

'I know, but I feel as if I ought to be doing more for the war effort. It's just that, well, I'll be honest, Noel, I'm sick of work and it isn't as if there's a shortage of volunteers. But people make ye feel guilty, ye know? Like, I was in the shop the other day and these women were going on about the Rebellion in Dublin and looking at me — cause they know I'm Irish — as if it's my fault! I mean I didn't do the shooting did I? I've never even been to Dublin. Doesn't stop ye feeling guilty though, does it?' She looked at Noel again. 'You're very pensive today.'

'Am I? Sorry.' Buttock numb from the hard ground, Noel changed the position of his white trousered legs, his eyes gazing at the crowds of squealing children upon the Green but not actually seeing them. 'I was thinking about the poor devils who were ferried in by ambulance last night.' He now helped out regularly at the Military Hospital which was just down the road from where Bright lived.

'Yes, I saw there were quite a few ambulances when I came back from Mass.' Bright had finished peeling the egg and examined it. The white surface had taken up a hint of dye from the paint.

He nodded. 'We've almost run out of beds, not to mention that we're run off our feet. We could do with more volunteers.'

'Well, don't look at me,' exclaimed Oriel. 'I'm not volunteering just to have it flung back in my face.' She bit into her hardboiled egg. Bright and Noel exchanged glances, and nothing more was said.

Noel was kept so busy by the casualties of war that he did not find the time to call on Bright again for another two weeks. By way of apology, and also as decoration for her gown, he brought a posy of violets which she wore when they went out dancing, though the evening's enjoyment was curtailed when Bright saw how tired the doctor was and insisted that he take her home.

Oriel had gone to bed early and so Noel took up Bright's invitation of cocoa. The act of making it reminded her of something she had read in the evening paper. 'Did you see in the *Press* that one of the Rowntree boys has refused to fight?' She sounded indignant. 'Well, this is the last tin of their cocoa I'm buying.'

Tired as he was, Noel showed amusement at her innocence. Then his expression changed and he looked at her in a strange way.

'What is it?' She touched her breast self-consciously.

'I didn't really want to tell you yet . . . oh well, I've joined up myself.'

'Oh, no! And here's me ranting on about conscientious

objectors. But surely you don't have to go — what made you do it?'

'Some idiotic notion of patriotism.' Fighting back a yawn, Noel accepted the mug of cocoa. 'I got carried away seeing all those poor devils arriving at the hospital without arms and legs and like the mad impulsive fool that I am I went and signed my name on the dotted line. I rather wish I hadn't now. Still, it won't be so bad as for some. I can tell you I sympathize with that Rowntree chap. I wouldn't relish shooting people.'

Bright had not looked upon it quite like this. She remained quietly thoughtful.

'Luckily my skills prevent that,' added Noel, tasting the cocoa then putting it aside to cool. 'I've joined the Medical Corps. I know I'm always grumbling about sick people but I'd rather deal with them than blast holes in some poor German, not to mention being unwilling to have my own posterior riddled with shrapnel.'

'Oh don't, I can't bear it!' Bright squashed her cheeks with her hands. The war had suddenly become personal.

Noel looked pained. 'I don't want to leave you, Bright.'

'I don't want you to go either,' she answered earnestly.

'I don't suppose . . .'

'Please.' Bright knew what he was about to ask and reached out to cover his lips with her fingers. 'You're my dearest friend, Noel, be happy with that.'

Noel could always summon humour. 'I'd hoped to make you feel sorry for me by telling you I was going to war.' When she looked alert he hastened to dissuade her from the wrong assumption. 'Oh no, it wasn't an invention, I really am going.'

'When?'

'Next week.'

'So soon? I expect your mother's upset.'

'I haven't told her yet. She's distraught enough at the inflated price of bread.' Unable to prevent a yawn, Noel sat upright and apologized, leaving his unfinished mug of cocoa on the table. 'I'd better go or we'll have folk gossiping about us and that won't do.' He ground his knuckles into his eye sockets. 'There's a show on Tuesday evening, will you accompany me?'

'You're sure you won't be too tired?'

'Don't rub it in!' He forced a laugh. 'I promise I won't fall asleep.'

'Then I'd love to.' Bright went with him, turning down the gaslamp before she opened the door to the street where traffic to and from the barracks was in constant flow. 'Noel, have ye seen anything of Nat lately?' When the doctor said he hadn't she looked distant. 'I was just wondering if he's been called up.'

'Shouldn't think so if he's married.' You cruel sod, why don't you put her out of her misery, he asked himself? You still won't face it will you? You just can't bear to see them together.

Oriel came home from work on Tuesday evening rather subdued. She had just met her father's new ladyfriend whom he was taking out this evening. Quite why it should bother her she wasn't sure. Maybe it was the fact that Olive was barely older than herself, or then again it might be just that she hated seeing Nat enjoying himself. Either way, she must wipe this expression off her face or Mother would be curious. She leaned her bicycle against the back wall before giving her divided skirt a brisk shake. The modest form of transport was not her first choice; Oriel would have liked to buy a motor car, but it would have looked very odd if she had rolled up to work in one of those, and besides, people were being urged to save fuel.

She entered through the scullery door. Bright had the sleeves of her best dress rolled up and an apron protecting the rest as she mashed the potatoes. 'You're looking tired, dear. Had a busy day?'

Oriel took off her gloves and unpinned her straw hat. 'Same as usual. Is Noel coming to dinner?' Her mother was preparing far too much food just for two.

'Yes, he's just down the road doing his bit.' Noel was at the Military Hospital. 'I hope he's here soon or this'll go cold. Then we're going to the theatre.'

'Ah yes, I forgot about that.' Oriel fell into a chair. 'Leaving your child alone again for the third time in a week.'

'Don't say that!' Bright looked guilty.

'I'm pulling your leg! You don't think I want to play gooseberry, d'you? Make the most of it, that's what I say.' Oriel was aware that Noel was leaving in a matter of days. 'Don't worry about me, I'll just stay home and rake out the cinders.'

'Will ye give over!' Bright swiped at her daughter.

The doctor arrived then and all sat down to dinner. Afterwards, leaving Oriel to do the washing up, her mother and Noel left for the theatre.

Acting in all innocence, Nat was at that moment on his way to the same venue. Living within the city walls meant that he was in easy range of any amenity and so this evening in early May he went to the theatre on foot, wearing Olive on his arm. There was no longer ulterior motive in Nat's attentions towards her. His only aim tonight was to enjoy himself. Last week had heralded conscription for all men whether married or single, so removing the shield of matrimony. It was now only a case of *when* rather than *if* he would be called up. Initially, he had contemplated breaking the news to Olive that there would be no wedding, but it was her birthday soon and even he was not callous enough to inflict disappointment at such a time. Besides, he might even marry her after all. She was a good sort. He turned his neck to look at her now, receiving a smile.

At every turn there was stark reminder that he could

soon be off to war: men in uniform, military vehicles thundering up and down, newspaper placards bearing words of doom, young boys who had 'dug in' amongst a pile of rubble on a demolition site to mimic trench warfare, their noisy imitation of machine guns following Nat along the street. As if this were not enough, Olive had to bring it up too.

'Every time we go out,' she told him, 'I always feel this might be our last night together.'

'Can't you wait to get rid of me?' he joked.

'Aw, you know I'd miss you!' She tapped the arm that linked with hers. 'But I must admit you'd look lovely in uniform. Wouldn't you like to see yourself in an outfit like that?' She cocked her head at an officer and his lady.

'I can't see me in a velvet hat and high-heeled boots somehow.'

'Dozey! I mean the officer – wouldn't you like to look like him?'

Not if I can help it, thought Nat, but answered laughingly, 'I don't think you can go straight in as a Major but I'll do me best for you, Olive.'

They sauntered on down the street, chatting quite amiably in the evening sunshine. Indeed, at that moment, even under threat of conscription, Nat felt happier than he had done for a long time: he had his daughter under his roof, a nice fiancée . . . of course, everything could look black in the morning, he never knew what mood he was going to wake up in, but for now he enjoyed his brief moment of contentment. He lifted his smiling eyes from Olive's and directed them ahead. A couple were walking down the narrow street towards them, an old woman and a bandy-legged man. It took only a moment for their identity to register. It had been twenty years since he had seen Denzil Kneebone but that did not lessen the shock of electricity that ran through his body and pulled him up in his tracks.

Olive felt the jolt, and glanced up enquiringly. Nat proceeded forward at a slower pace; there was no way to avoid Denzil, no turning to right nor left, they were on collision course. What would he say? The gap between them narrowed. In middle age Denzil's legs had become more bowed than ever. He cut a comic figure as he waddled along from side to side towards Nat, but Nat was not laughing. Olive was still looking up at him for explanation but he did not respond, eyes fixed on the pale blue ones which were staring right back at him. Denzil was almost level. Nat gripped the arm that was hooked through his. Not for a long time had he experienced fear like this . . . and then it was gone! Denzil walked past him without so much as a hint of recognition in those pale blue eyes, and waddled on down the street arm in arm with his mother.

The sweat of relief sprang to Nat's armpits. For twenty years he had lived with the threat of the lunatic's retribution, all for nothing. Denzil had not even recognized him! He wanted to burst out laughing.

'Nat, you're holding my arm a little too tightly!'

He looked down at the hand upon Olive's arm. His knuckles were white. 'Oh, sorry!' Releasing his grip, he rubbed her arm in a gesture of comfort. 'I'm just frightened you're going to get away from me.' Wearing a broad smile, he continued on to the theatre.

Olive was a giggler. She giggled all the way through the comedian's act; though Nat did not find it particularly funny her laughter was infectious and at the end of the turn his jaw was aching. She giggled all the way through the magician's act too, and the singer's – well, it was a rude song. She was still giggling when they came out, until a siren began to wail. 'Oh, good heavens, it's an air raid!' She clung to her partner and squinted first at the sky, then up and down the darkened street; only on busy corners was there electric lighting. 'Which way do we go?' Vehicles were shooting in all directions.

'This way!' As if in answer, a special constable appeared out of the night piloting the anxious crowd of theatre-goers towards a sign that invited them to *Shelter Here*. Taking Olive's arm, Nat escorted her across the road, dodging the traffic and hurrying in the direction of the constable's pointing arm.

'Oh, God, what an end to a lovely evening!' Holding onto her hat, Bright hurried alongside Noel to the air raid shelter where they squeezed in amongst the rest of the crowd. 'I hope Oriel's all right.'

'She'll be fine,' Noel reassured her. 'She's a sensible girl. It may just be another false alarm.'

Bright was not to be pacified. 'No, I think it's our turn this time.' She pressed herself against Noel's side, clutching his arm, hemmed in by all kinds of people, sweet perfume mixed with body odour, tobacco, spirits and cooking smells; all as one in their fear of the bomb. Please, please, God don't take her.

Oriel had been mixing her bedtime cocoa when the gas pressure lowered, causing her to freeze. Spoon hovering over mug, she waited, listening. All at once she felt very young and alone. Leaving the mug on the table, she hurried around the room, turning off gastaps as she had been warned to do in the event of a raid. Then, feeling her way through the darkness she made for the cellar. It was just too cold and dark; she could not sit down there alone, and so knowing that to do so was foolish, she went upstairs to bury her head under the sheets. As she reached the first landing she paused and drew aside the curtain to look across the back gardens in the direction of the river. There came the distant rumble of thunder, yet there was no rain, the sky was clear and full of stars. For a moment she thought she heard a low growl, but then it seemed to disappear and though she listened for a while all she heard was ringing silence. She stood there, ear cocked for a moment longer, then hurried on up the staircase. It was as she reached the second landing that she heard the growl again, louder this time. Peering out through the tall arched window she examined the sky. There was nothing to be seen except twinkling stars. She waited, craning her neck for the source of the growl that grew louder by the minute, the hair on her scalp bristling. Imagination rife, she was about to rush on up the stairs when she saw it, a huge cigar-shaped craft over Knavesmire. Fascinated, she stood pinned to the spot, watching as the zeppelin, like a prehistoric monster, sniffed out its target. There came a flash of blue light; Oriel squeaked and ducked into her dressing gown. Then there was an enormous impact and she began to pelt back down the stairs, a second explosion lighting up the whole staircase even through the blackout curtains. Oriel gasped and fled to the cellar where she cowered, shivering, on the icy stone steps, hands over her ears as a number of explosions shook the house in quick succession. Then silence. Trembling, arms pressed into her sides out of fear and cold, Oriel removed her hands from her ears and listened. There was no sound. After a few moments of peace she was about to open the cellar door when the zeppelin dropped the rest of its load. She cried out and once again cowered in a ball at the foot of the steps, hands over ears, for interminable minutes until all was quiet again. This time she was not so quick to emerge. Even when the growl died away she remained wary until a muffled all clear signal reached the cellar, allowing her to escape its cold depths and hurry back to the kitchen fire.

Once warmed through, though still shuddering from fright, she summoned enough courage to peep from behind the curtain again. Against a ruby sky, the zeppelin's trail of black smoke was just beginning to melt away, leaving behind the reek of explosives to tease her nostrils. Only now did Oriel register: her mother was out there!

In the darkened shelter, eyes pressed shut, Bright was

clutching Noel's arm when the all clear wailed, allowing her shoulders to sag in relief. A combined sigh went up from the theatre-goers, then shoulder to shoulder they began to drift towards the exit, chattering and laughing, yet apprehensive also at what damage they might find outside. Bright chattered too, though her loquaciousness was more from worry. 'I wish they'd hurry up,' she muttered to Noel, 'I have to get home to see if Oriel's safe.'

'Come on, we'll try and squeeze round this way.' Leading her by the hand, Noel edged around the mass of human flesh and managed to reach the exit, but there found his way blocked again. 'Sorry, after you.' He stepped back to allow another couple to go through the exit first, then his lower jaw fell open.

Bright gaped too, and for that second managed to forget all about her daughter. There stood Nat, his wife on his arm, staring her right in the eye. Heart in mouth, she could not tear her gaze from him. If there had ever been any doubt in her mind over how she would feel if they met, then it was dispelled now. The pain was unbearable.

Nat's blue eyes stared back at her, then slowly with a glint of enlightenment they rolled to her partner. For twenty years he had thought that Denzil was the one to watch out for, when all the time it was Noel who was the real enemy. How long had he been taking Nat for a fool?

No words were spoken between the two couples. Nat was first to turn away, shepherding a bemused Olive through the door.

'Bright, I'm truly sorry about that.' Noel tried to comfort her. 'I had no idea . . . what a thing to happen.'

'It doesn't matter.' Bright was trembling. 'Come on, we'll have to go. I'm very worried about Oriel.'

On the latter account there was much relief when they arrived home to find Bright's daughter frightened but unharmed. Voicing his gladness, Noel bade them both good night and nothing was mentioned about the disastrous meeting with Nat, though this did not prevent Bright from going to bed in tears.

At the next morning's surgery the doctor had a visit from his erstwhile friend. 'I thought you'd be here.'

'You thought right then, didn't you.' In a sombre mood, Nat took the proffered chair and looked Noel in the eye. 'Did you just forget to mention, when you told me to leave Bright alone, that it was because you had a vested interest?'

The doctor groaned. 'It wasn't like that! She was genuinely worried about the effect that your spying would have on Oriel. I've only recently started taking her out.'

The wounds of betrayal that Nat had experienced last night were still sore. 'Why her, when you could have anyone you want?'

'You talk about Bright as if she's not worthy of attention! She deserves some happiness after all the years of misery.'

Nat took this to mean that it was he who had inflicted that misery, and his words reflected the insult. 'So you're just taking her out because you feel sorry for her?'

The physician replied with dignity. 'No, because I'm very fond of her. I've known Bright a long time. Granted we'd seen each other only periodically before her employer died, but since then I've been calling on her as a friend and we get along very well.'

'Aye, I could see that from the looks on your faces last night.' Nat lit up a cigarette, not offering one to Noel. 'Didn't expect to see me there, did you?' He forced a vicious plume of smoke at the ceiling.

'Nat, when I acted as go-between I had no ulterior motive, it was only when I was certain that you weren't going to reappear on her doorstep that I made my feelings known.'

'You didn't make them known to me though, did you?'

Nat donned a crafty and unpleasant smile. Had they been strangers to each other the doctor might well have felt rather menaced, but he had known Nat a long time and he had no reason to expect violence.

'Well, no, but I've nothing to hide so you might as well know this too: I asked Bright to marry me.'

Nat took the blow well, not questioning the fact that Bright had accepted. 'I'd wish you good luck but you obviously don't need it. I can't see a servant turning down the opportunity of being a doctor's wife. Somehow, though, I don't think the pleasure'll be reciprocated by your mother.'

'I'm well accustomed to my mother's snobbery,' Noel assured him. 'It has no bearing on my decision. Besides, Bright isn't a servant any more.'

'She's not exactly a woman of means though, is she?'

Noel looked hesitant, then sighed. He had nothing really to lose by hiding it now. 'You might as well know the rest. Bright's daughter inherited all the old lady's money, the house, everything.'

Nat frowned. If this were true, then why did Oriel need to work for him? But he put this out of his mind for the moment and sneered at Noel. 'I suppose that had no bearing on your decision either? It's all falling into place now. You won't be badly off yourself then, and dear Mother can be pleased she's got a wealthy woman as a daughter-in-law. Is that why you've waited so long? Cause you knew the old lady was going to leave her summat?'

'Don't be so bloody insulting!' Noel decided not to reveal now that Bright had turned him down. Let the bugger stew. 'I told you, I held back because I knew you were Oriel's father and there might be a chance that you would do the decent thing but –'

'All right, all right, you've made your point. I didn't want her so she was fair game for anyone else. Enough said.'

'No, no, I want you to understand that I wasn't being devious . . . oh, very well I was.' Noel flashed a mischievous smile. 'I should have told you, I'm sorry, but I genuinely didn't think you were interested any more.'

Nat straightened. 'I'm not. You go ahead and marry her, I'm sure she'd rather wed a doctor than a rag and bone man. Anyway, I didn't come here for any of that. What I really want is for you to give me something that'll make me fail a medical.' He nodded as the other raised an eyebrow. 'That's right, I've finally got my marching orders. I presume there are things you can give me?'

'There are, but why should I risk my good name for you after you've accused me of all manner of dirty deeds?'

'Good name? Your name's not very good in my book, Noel. I think you owe me this much at least after the lies you've told me. Anyway, why this sudden show of integrity? I don't see you rushing to join up. Admit it, you're as frightened as I am.'

'I doubt it's for the same reason,' retorted Noel. 'I just don't want to kill people.' He tutted. 'You've heard most of my confession, so you might as well hear the rest. I've enlisted – yes, even though I didn't have to. Aren't I noble!' There was more than a touch of sarcasm to the latter announcement. Then his voice became even once more. 'I'm going to join the Medical Corps in a few days. I was rather hoping you'd come for a drink with me and a few pals before I go. All fair in love and war and all that.'

The dark-haired man gasped. 'By heck, Noel, I've never known anybody who could match you for cheek!'

'Wouldn't you feel awful if we parted with such bad blood between us and I got killed?' The tone was ironic.

Nat could not be bothered to argue. 'Oh, what the hell. Yes, I'll come. Now, will you gimme summat to fool this army doctor?'

Noel leaned back in his swivel chair and linked his hands behind his head, his tone affectionate. 'You silly sod, you don't need it! Your lungs are wrecked with all the bronchitic attacks over the years. It's a miracle they haven't packed up altogether. I could give you something that'd make interesting listening for the stethoscope but it'd probably kill you into the bargain. Take my word for it, you won't get through.'

Nat was wary, finding it hard to equate this look of fondness with the act of treachery that had gone before – but then he had never understood Noel. 'You're not fobbing me off with kiddums just to get me out of t'way?'

'Ooh, nasty! If I'm wrong you can come back and shoot me.'

Nat fired one last question concerning Bright. 'Will you get wed before you go?'

Even now Noel did not confess that she had turned him down. 'Probably.' He did not want Nat sniffing around whilst he was away. 'Now, about this night out . . .'

As soon as Nat entered the public house in which he and Noel had arranged to meet he knew that he was not going to enjoy this evening. It had nothing to do with their previous exchange, nor with the tap room which was cosy with its dark oak panels and the glow of copper in the yellow gaslight, but more to do with Noel's companions. Nat had always felt uncomfortable walking into a roomful of people, especially if those people were of a higher class than himself. He could buy as many fancy clothes as he liked but the moment he encountered anyone with an upper crust accent he was plunged back into his old rags.

'Nat!' The young doctor's face lit up and he waved. 'Come and join us. I've just got here myself.'

'You'd better grab yourself a drink first,' advised one of the others. 'Some party, when the host refuses to get his hand down.'

Noel feigned disability. 'Don't you know I suffer from spondulicksitis? Parting with money causes acute inflammation.' The others groaned at his pun, which Nat did not understand. 'Anyway, there's no treating – have you forgotten there's a war on? It's every man for himself, I'm afraid.'

When Nat returned from the bar with a pint glass, introductions were made. Most of the half-dozen men present were colleagues from the hospital, and hence a lot of the banter centred on medical jokes. To his credit, Noel did try to steer the conversation round to topics in which Nat could join, but after only ten minutes he had the feeling that it had been a mistake to try and mix his friends.

Nat had this feeling too, wishing he had turned down the invitation. He had never really been good in a crowd of people, even six was too many for comfort.

'Come on, Nat, drink up!' urged one of the group, Arthur. 'The idea is to see who can get the most down his neck before nine o'clock.' Due to wartime regulations, drinking hours had been pruned. Tie and hair askew, Arthur looked a possible winner in the race, although the others were not far behind.

Nat went to refill his glass and stood at the bar watching them, feeling rather embarrassed at the growing display of inebriation. They might be well-educated but watching them slopping back the liquor and bandying lewd jokes, Nat reckoned they were no different to the low life he had encountered in his past. Still, this was Noel's last night at home and he didn't want to ruin it by playing dog in the manger. Fresh glass in hand, he returned to the table to catch the tail end of an anecdote, which everyone found hilarious and rolled about with laughter. Nat smiled out of politeness but it was obvious that he had not understood.

'Come on, crack your face!' Arthur was very drunk now. 'Don't you appreciate my jokes?'

Nat raised and lowered his glass. 'Maybe I would if I knew what priapus meant.' The punchline had hinged on this word.

Noel laid an arm across the other's shoulders. 'Er, I think it's best to say that it's something which relates to a cult.'

Arthur spluttered into his drink; the others cackled too. This was enough for Nat, who assumed they were laughing at his lack of education and did not say another word for the rest of the evening. By eight-thirty the bunch was extremely drunk, the jokes got sillier and the conversation more unintelligible. Nat had had enough. Downing the last of his beer he rose and muttered to Noel, 'I'm off for a pee.'

'Has to keep you informed of his movements, does he?' All inhibitions removed by the liquor, Arthur did not even wait for Nat to be out of earshot before insulting him. 'It's a good job you invited us, old pal.' He draped his beery frame over Noel, who wafted the air and laughed. 'A fine last night you would have had if it was left to that boring little fart —he's hardly said anything all night, apart from "I'm going for a pee!" You should take him with you to the Front, he'd soon bore the Hun to death.'

Nat did not veer from his passage to the exit, but his mind seethed. If only you knew what I was thinking, the things I'm doing to you right now in my mind, the last word you'd have for me is boring. After relieving himself outside he returned to the table, but only to inform Noel, 'I'm off now.'

Tipsy and dishevelled though he was, Noel sensed his friend's controlled anger and felt guilty at inflicting his other acquaintances on this reserved man. 'I'll come with you.' He drained his glass and rose.

'Hey, there's another half an hour yet!' slurred one of the others.

'You stay with your friends.' Nat was already on his way out.

Out of desperation, Noel threw a pound note on the table. 'Here! Don't tell anyone or it'll ruin my reputation. Enjoy the rest of the night, I'll have to go, it's an early rise in the morning!' To cries of good luck and bon voyage, he hurried from the public house into the street. It was not yet completely dark but the alcohol had fuddled Noel's brain and he squinted up and down the road for a glimpse of his friend. Catching sight of Nat, he ran after him. 'Hang on! Come and have a drink with me at home.'

Eyes directed ahead, Nat walked on. 'I thought you had an early start?'

'It isn't even nine yet, for Christ's sake!'

'Go back and drink with your friends then, if you're quick you might catch last orders.'

'Oh come on, don't sulk!'

'I'm not sulking, I'm just going home so I don't ruin your party. Your friends just aren't my type and if I stayed there I'd say something.'

'I seem to remember that was the whole trouble! You hardly said anything.' Hands in pockets, Noel swayed from side to side.

'What's the point? They have their views, I have mine.'

'Then if you have views wouldn't it be better to air them instead of keeping them to yourself? That's what the art of conversation is all about, surely?'

'And have your friends get their fun at my expense? No thanks.'

Noel looked confused. 'I didn't hear them do that.'

'Oh, missed all the laughter, did you? I must've been hearing things.'

Noel removed his hands from his pockets and spread them in an effort to explain. 'They weren't laughing at you! They were just having a good time, that's all.' He was about to say more when he tripped over a paving flag and fell to his knees. 'Oh, fack! Nat will you bloody well slow down!'

The other swore too, then grasped Noel's elbow and hauled him to his feet. 'I don't know about you having another drink, you wouldn't be able to cram it in.'

Noel rubbed his skinned knees. 'I'm not drunk! It was

562

the frigging pavement, that's all. What did you mean, they were laughing at your expense?'

'Look, it doesn't matter.' Nat began to walk on. 'I'll never meet 'em again.'

There was concern in the other's reply. 'It matters to me if you think I set you up as a stooge.'

Nat showed more exasperation. 'I'm not blaming you, it was just . . . well, they seemed to think that I didn't understand all their big words. Truth, be known, I didn't,' came the added mutter.

'Big words?' Noel frowned. 'Do you mean priapus? Well, that's not very big, at least not in their case. Mine's quite huge.' He laughed, then sighed at Nat's lack of appreciation. 'God, I hate explaining jokes, it shows how bad they are.' He leaned on Nat. 'In essence, priapus is a prick, that's all.'

'So are your friends.'

'Well, they're not really friends, more acquaintances. I just wanted to make a big do of it. I might not have the chance again.' Even the liquor could not totally quell his nerves.

'Aye, well, that's why I didn't cause any trouble, though I could've kicked that bloody Arthur's teeth in.'

'So, you're not mad with me?' beseeched Noel. The other shook his head. 'Then come home and have a drink with me, Nat.'

The other's face laughed at him out of the dinge. 'We're almost to my door now. You might as well come in.'

Noel agreed, until he remembered Talbot. 'Oh, Christ, that bloody hound of yours.' A frantic series of barks accompanied the turn of Nat's key.

'I've told you, as long as you take your hat off he's a baa-lamb — aren't you, me old pal!' Nat bent to pat the three-legged dog who wriggled and snorted with pleasure and after a brief sniff at the inebriated Noel allowed him into the pitch-black interior.

When the gaslamps were lighted and the two men were ensconced in the rosy glow of the parlour, one on either side of the fireplace, glasses of whisky in hand, Noel exclaimed, 'I knew I had something to ask you! Did you get through the medical?'

'No, I'm chuffed to announce I'm a complete physical wreck.' Nat did indeed appear delighted.

'Good!' Noel raised his glass. 'Here's to your continued bad health! I say, how are things in the marriage stakes? Now that you've foiled all attempts to get you into the Army I don't suppose you'll have to marry that young lady who accompanied you to the theatre on Tuesday night?'

Nat swilled the whisky around his glass. 'I don't have to, no, but she's a nice lass is Olive and I could do worse, much worse.'

'You won't marry her!' scoffed Noel, dribbling whisky down his chin and making a ham-fisted attempt to wipe it off.

Nat gasped, pretending outrage. 'How the hell d'you know, clever bugger?'

'I just know.' It was uttered with supreme confidence.

'Want to put money on it, d'you?'

Noel's face remained drunkenly brazen. 'A fiver!'

'You're on!' Nat made a firm gesture with his glass. 'By the time you come back from the Front I'll be wed.'

'Oh, Christ, don't mention the Front.' Noel clapped a hand to his blond, wavy head. 'I'd almost managed to forget.' He slumped lower in the chair, extending his legs so that his boots almost touched those of the other man, almost but not quite.

'Shouldn't've joined up then, should you?' teased Nat, who was almost equally as drunk now.

'Thanks for the sympathy.'

'I'm not offering sympathy to the bloke who stole Bright from under me nose!'

'Oh, we're not going to keep harking back to that, are

we? You had your chance, you wasted it. She's going to marry me.' And Noel was positive that she would eventually accept.

23

Whilst Noel went to war, waved off by Bright and Oriel, Nat remained at home. It did not concern him in the least that people thought he was a malingerer nor that he had received two white feathers in the post, but to the much younger Olive his rejection of duty was a different matter.

'I would've expected you to be pleased about me not going away,' he told her. 'You're always saying how terrible it is for sweethearts to be parted.'

'It is,' she insisted, 'but – well, there doesn't look to be anything wrong with you and people think you're shirking.'

'I couldn't care less what folk think,' replied Nat. 'It might not look as though anything's wrong with me, but I tell you, if any of them had to suffer bronchitis every year like I do they'd soon eat their words, and I'm sure I'm doing a darned sight more for the war effort than some o' those who are at the Front. Anyway, less o' that. When are we going to name the day?' They had celebrated her coming-of-age last week. It had been Nat's intention to make the announcement at her birthday party, but Olive seemed shy all of a sudden.

'There's no rush, is there?' Olive studied the diamond and sapphire ring he had given her on their engagement.

'Blimey! That's a nice to-do. I thought you wanted to marry me?'

'Well, I'm still only young.'

'You weren't too young when we discussed it before – said you'd marry me when you were twenty-one.'

Olive twiddled the ring to catch the light, moving it back

and forth. 'I said I wanted to wait until *after* I was twenty-one. I didn't say the minute the clock struck twelve on my birthday I'd rush down the aisle.'

Nat's attitude became more serious. 'Do I detect an attack of cold feet here, Olive?'

She dared not look at him, but nodded and, after a long pause admitted, 'I've . . . well, I – I met this soldier . . .'

He had to laugh. 'How did I guess it'd be somebody in uniform!'

'I didn't mean it to happen!' She looked at him now, her earnest face seeking forgiveness. 'We just bumped into one another . . . I didn't mean to hurt you, Nat, honestly.'

'I'm not hurt.' He wasn't even offended; after all, he had been using Olive. 'Well, maybe a little bit.' He said this for her benefit rather than his own.

Able to look him in the eye now that she had confessed, she pulled the ring over her knuckle. 'You'd better have this back.'

He refused. 'No, you keep it. Sell it and buy yourself a nice wedding present.'

Olive studied him for a moment, seeking mockery, but the offer was genuine. 'Oh, you're so nice! It's taken me ages to pluck up the courage to tell you. It was nothing to do with you, it was just . . . well, it's difficult for a girl if her chap's not in uniform, you know.'

He nodded sympathetically, whilst bursting with ironic laughter inside; there he was only the other week hoping to spare her feelings by not cancelling the wedding and here he was now being jilted! Well, this marked the end of his marriage plans. The only woman in his life was his daughter.

To Nat's dismay he was to be robbed of much prized time with Oriel, for she announced a desire to cut down her hours in order to concentrate on the war effort. 'I don't want you to think that my work will suffer, I'll do exactly the same amount but in a shorter time. We all have to do our bit, don't we?'

'Yes, of course.' Nat was even more introspective than normal. 'Will it be voluntary work you're doing?' She said it would. 'Can I enquire what kind?'

'I expect it'll just be rolling bandages or selling flags,' admitted Oriel. 'Though every little helps. First though, I have to help Mother dig up the back garden.' With Noel's departure the war had become more personal for both of them and Bright had decided that she would make her own small donation by creating a vegetable patch.

Nat was not impressed. 'That's a man's job!'

Oriel arched a black eyebrow. 'Hadn't you noticed? All the men are at war – at least most of them.'

Nat always felt that his daughter was having a go at him when she raised this matter, as indeed she was. 'I'd be there if I could, y'know. I can't help it if I failed the medical.'

'Oh, I wasn't insinuating that you were a coward, Mr Prince!' How dare you say it, Oriel asked herself. He's going to slap you one of these days. 'I'm sure you're doing very useful work of your own, and I know your young lady friend must be grateful to have you safe at home.'

The emphasis on *young* had not gone unnoticed and helped to inject a terseness into his reply. 'Actually no, I think Olive would have preferred a partner with a few wounds to his credit. So if this is your roundabout way of asking why you haven't seen her for a couple of days . . .'

'I'm sure I wasn't trying to pry!'

'. . . then I can tell you I've been jilted again.'

Oriel enjoyed a private laugh of satisfaction but kept her face straight. 'You don't have much luck with women, do you, Mr Prince?'

He looked at her pointedly. 'Oh, I don't know, Miss Maguire, there are those who I find most trustworthy.'

Oriel inclined her head in gratitude – if only you knew! But there was disconcertment too. It was something of an anomaly that she could delight in his praise, could actually enjoy being in the same room and having these exchanges with him, whilst at the same time she was seeking revenge amongst the pages of his accounts. As yet unable to pinpoint anything fraudulent, she convinced herself that she only stayed under his roof in order to find something she could use against him, but was this true? Was it possible to hate somebody and love them at the same time? Yet there was no way that Oriel would admit to fondness of him. She reverted to her business-like manner. 'So, would it be all right if I cut down my hours, then?'

And Nat could think of no good reason to refuse.

With the clocks gone forward an hour the mornings were lighter and work on the garden began very early. Bright perspired and toiled with her daughter throughout the early summer, digging and raking, weeding and planting. Towards the end of June seedling cabbages had begun to show through the brown earth. Between weeding and watering Bright sold flags for the Voluntary Aid Detachment, organized jumble sales and collected newspapers for recycling. At night she would pore over the ever-growing casualty lists in the *Evening Press*, not really expecting to see Noel's name there for he was well back behind the lines, but one never quite knew . . .

One evening after tea whilst she mused over the lists of fatalities produced by the Great Offensive, Bright muttered out of the blue, 'I wonder if your father's been called up.' It was such a shock to Oriel that she almost regurgitated her meal.

Her mother was quick to note the expression. 'Aren't I even allowed to mention his name?' she asked quietly.

'You can mention whom you like!' Not knowing what to say, Oriel was shirty and looked for something to do, but there were only two teacups left to wash. 'It's none of my business.'

'Don't you ever wonder — I mean, I know what your feelings are about him — but don't you wonder where he is, if he's been killed or injured?'

'No.'

'I do.'

Her mother sounded so sad that Oriel felt incredibly guilty and would have liked to put her mind at rest, but to do so would spoil her own plans, not to mention the difficulty she would have explaining how she had come to be working for her father for so long without mentioning it before. She said nothing.

Bright's eyes continued to peruse the seemingly endless lists, then she gave a sharp intake of breath.

Oriel stopped focusing on the hearth and looked afraid. 'Is it Noel?'

'No, tis my brothers . . . the two youngest.' Bright glanced up at her daughter. There were no tears but her face was stark with sorrow. She lowered her eyes and read their names out loud. 'Patrick and Eugene, both killed in action.' Her hand came up to wind a strand of hair around her finger. 'I wonder if they were married.' She bit her lip and read on to the foot of the list. Her daughter came to look over her shoulder at the newspaper, resting her chin on Bright's tawny head. 'I should go and see Mother.'

Oriel did not reply, sad only for her own mother's sake; the rest of the Maguire clan could all be dead as far as she was concerned, after the way it had treated its youngest member.

Bright slept very little that night, mulling over whether to go and comfort her mother. Morning brought decision. Travelling on foot and still numb, she went along to find the house she had left twenty years ago and had not visited since.

More shock awaited. The Pig Market, the Three Cups and the squalid little houses had gone. A brand new road and a tramline ran through the place where her old home had been. Bright gazed along the new stretch of Piccadilly, as if hoping for her family to appear suddenly. When had all this taken place? Whenever in town she had always avoided this area for the memory was too painful, and now there was nought tangible to remind her. She turned and looked back towards Walmgate; little had altered there. Maybe the people who owned the fish and chip shop would know of the Maguire family's whereabouts.

No one had any idea. They were only able to tell Bright that the demolition had taken place about four or five years ago. Maybe it was as well, thought Bright as she wandered into town, unsure of her movements now; they wouldn't thank her for opening old wounds when the new ones were raw and weeping.

By the time the clocks went back in October Bright had received six letters from Noel, all cheerful and written in his entertaining style. She carried them in her apron pocket so that in the event of an air raid she and Oriel had something to laugh about whilst they hid in the cellar. There were two more zeppelin raids on York that year and countless false alarms. However, there was no deception in the never-ending procession of ambulances that came day and night to the Military Hospital. Bright thought of the terrible wounds that Noel must have to deal with; wondered too if Nat was amongst those injured.

Christmas came and with it a visitor, though it was not the one they had hoped to see; Noel was stuck in Europe. For a moment Bright did not recognize her elder sister, frowning at the grey-haired Irish woman in the threadbare shawl who stood shivering on her doorstep. 'Eileen!' She hesitated before throwing wide the door. 'Come in.'

'Thanks – terrible cold, isn't it?' Eileen followed her down the hallway into the kitchen, appraising her surroundings. 'Will your employer mind me calling like this?'

Bright was still frowning. 'No, no, she's passed away. Only Oriel and I live here now.'

'Ye mean . . . tis yours?' Eilleen was agog.

'Twas left to Oriel.' Slowly, Bright took up the kettle. 'Ye'll have a cup o' tea?'

'I wouldn't say no.' Looking self-conscious, Eilleen went to the fire to warm her blue hands. 'I expect you're surprised to see me.'

Bright remained placid. 'Just a bit.'

Eilleen gave a nod, then blurted, 'Tis time this whole business was over! There's been enough pain in our family. The others can do what they like but if I want to forgive my sister then I will.' Forgive *me*, marvelled Bright.

Now that the ice had been broken Eilleen was calmer, watching the other woman prepare the tea. 'We've both changed, haven't we? I wanted to come ages ago when I had my first son, but it was difficult ye know.' Don't you think it was difficult for me? reflected Bright. But she allowed her sister to talk. 'I shouldn't have let it go this long, wasn't sure if ye'd still be living in the same place — the Sisters told me where ye lived years ago, but well, people move on don't they? Thank you, that's lovely.' With grateful hands she took the cup of tea from her sister, then both sat down at the pine table. 'Mary'd like to see ye too.'

Bright smiled and said it would be nice to see her again, knowing that she never would.

'Did ye see about Pat and Eugene?' asked Eilleen. Her sister delivered a tragic nod. 'Terrible, terrible — they have five children a-piece ye know. Hey, I'm a grandmother now! You'd think it too, wouldn't ye?' Eilleen tapped her grey head and sighed. Bright thought how much like their mother she looked, emaciated and world-weary. 'My daughter Mary had twin boys last year.'

Bright said, 'It must be nice for you, for Mother too.'

'Aye, they're lovely babies.' Eilleen looked fond.

'Does she ever talk about me?'

'Who, Mother? No . . . no.' The older woman sipped at her tea. 'She's taken the boys' death very hard.'

'I tried to visit her when it happened,' ventured Bright. 'I didn't know the house had gone.'

'Best not,' whispered Eilleen. 'She's only funny.' She looked up as a young woman entered.

'This is my daughter, Oriel. Oriel, this is your Aunt Eilleen.'

Eilleen appeared to be embarrassed. 'Oh, hello.' She rushed the cup to her mouth, burying her face.

Oriel, who had just woken from an after dinner nap, was abrupt. 'Hello.' She turned to her mother. 'I'm going for a walk to freshen up. I'll see you later.' With a cool goodbye to the visitor, she left.

Eilleen issued an uncomfortable cough and was about to take another sip of tea but noticed that she had drunk it all.

'More tea?' Bright smiled at her, though her heart was a well of sadness.

The visitor accepted and remained for another hour, during which she supplied Bright with all the births, deaths and marriages within the Maguire clan, and in turn listened to Bright's news. Only when she heard Oriel's return did she make to leave. 'Well now, I'd better be off or my family will wonder where I am, tis almost time for blackout.' She wrapped her shawl around herself in preparation to meet the keen wind.

'Hang on,' said Bright and visited the dining room, returning with a paper bag. 'Tis not much, but . . .' Her voice trailed away. How could she say that her sister looked as if she needed them more than Bright did.

Eilleen took a peep inside the wrapping. 'Oranges – oh, God bless ye!' Her face wrinkled with pleasure, and she kissed Bright. 'It's been lovely to see y'again, darlin', and to meet your daughter.' She flung a quick smile at Oriel before hurrying to the door. 'Keep in touch now, won't ye?'

'I will.' Bright gave a last wave to her sister, then closed the door.

'Will you?' enquired her daughter gravely.

Her mother gave a brisk shake of the head as she cleared away the cups. They had deserted Bright when she had needed them most, and anyway, she had her own family now in Oriel.

It was getting too dark to see the other's face. Moving to the window she pulled the blackout curtains together making sure there was no chink of light, then turned on the gaslamps. 'I wonder what sort of Christmas Noel's having?' she said, then buried her face in her hands. 'God, I wish this blessed war was over!'

A few days later, in early January 1917, Bright received a sign that her wish might soon be granted, though it came without any official seal. At first, when Oriel rushed in from a night-time visit to the closet and issued the excited summons – 'Mother, come and look! Something's happening in the sky!' – Bright was impaled by fear.

'Oh my God, another zeppelin!' She was in her dressing gown, ready for bed. 'I didn't hear any sirens – and shut that door, you'll have us arrested!' Light was streaming into the garden.

'It's not a zepp!' Oriel snatched the cocoa cups from her mother and dragged her into the night. Bright objected that it was freezing, setting up an exaggerated clatter with her teeth. 'Just stand there and watch!' commanded Oriel and, grasping her mother's shoulders, turned her forcibly to the northern sky. 'I'll fetch your coat. It's the Aurora Borealis!' She dashed inside but was soon out again, unwilling to miss a second of the glorious display.

'Oh my!' Bright was an instant captive, eyes glued to the heavens while Oriel helped her into her coat. Then words were lost. Cuddled together for warmth, they watched, entrancement on their faces, as slowly but perceptibly an evening rainbow was born into an azure sky. At first it was the glow from a distant fire, but then the mass of colour shimmered and gyrated with the breeze, now a heavenly halo, now a vast luminous arc that stretched from horizon to horizon, and from this mass of cloud exploded rays of the most delightful hue and delicacy, violet and indigo and dazzling white, some with the transience of lightning, others constant like the beam of a searchlight that moved across the heavens.

Neither spoke until the magnificent entertainment was over, even then unable to tear their eyes away from the sky.

'Glory be to God,' whispered Bright, squeezing her daughter's hand. 'He surely must be telling us that the war will soon be over.'

Sadly, Bright's words of faith were granted no credence. The war bled on for another year. Whilst food became scarcer, queues grew longer, as did the lists of casualties, their numbers increased by this month's especial German atrocity, the torpedoing of a British hospital ship. The only piece of good news was that the Americans had joined the war.

People were dying on the homefront too, not only by German hand but from a deadly outbreak of influenza. 'As if there isn't enough to worry about!' moaned Bright as she draped countless religious tokens and medals around her daughter's neck in order to fight the dreaded scourge. 'If it's Spanish influenza why can't it stay in bloody Spain?'

'Mother, I'll never be able to walk with all this on,' objected Oriel, jingling the collection of chains and medals. 'I'll sound like Marley's Ghost.'

'Shut up and do as you're told! There's thirty have died in Yorkshire, I'm taking no chances.'

'Could there possibly be some saint you might have forgotten?'

Bright delivered a light slap. 'Behave, or you won't get a birthday party.' Oriel had today come of age.

'Some party it'll be! What are we having, cardboard food?' It was not of course a real party, just the two of them as usual, but Oriel and her mother knew how to have fun.

'Be off to work! While I slave away trying to make a feast out of powdered egg, rice and saccharin.'

Her daughter laughed and pedalled off into the hot June sunshine.

'You look very fresh and summery today, Oriel!' exclaimed Nat, when she arrived for work. His examination of her was more than was correct for an employer, blue eyes flitting from bosom to waist to hip to ankle. She had on a white pin-tucked blouse – under which was the collection of religious tokens – and a white button-through skirt.

Oriel peeled off her white gossamer gloves, dropped them into the crown of her hat and laid this on the hallstand. 'It's very gracious of you to say that to someone who feels a year older than yesterday.'

'Ah, your birthday, is it?'

'My coming-of-age.'

Nat looked askance. My God, was it that long? But he soon recovered enough to offer congratulations. 'Then may I wish you many happy returns – I would've given you the day off if I'd known beforehand.'

Typical! Oriel's frothiness evaporated. He doesn't even know my date of birth! But she remained civil. 'There's no need. It's just a day like any other.' She went to her desk and opened a ledger.

You stupid bugger! Nat cursed himself for his thoughtless remark, for by now he had come to believe that his hunch about Oriel was correct: she *did* know who he was. That was obviously why she had not mentioned anything to him about her inheritance nor revealed the identity of her employer to Noel; she knew he was her father and

576

wanted to be close to him without her mother knowing, for Bright would surely be angry. Quite why Oriel had still not confronted him about her paternity he had no idea. Perhaps she was just too much like him. Nat had lived too long with the habit of stifling his emotions; he would only speak about their relationship if she broached the matter first. He had suffered enough hurt and rejection in his life to risk exposing himself to more at his daughter's hands. Thus, they continued to play out their roles.

He left her with some mundane utterance and made as if to go about his work, but towards the end of the day he approached the subject of her birthday again. 'I'd like you to accept this.' He was holding out a black velvet box.

Taken aback, Oriel was slow to accept and when she eventually opened the box she gave immediate protest. 'I couldn't possibly!' A bright, golden locket shone out against the black velvet.

'I understand it's not the sort of thing a man usually gives to his employee . . .' Maybe now she would speak out. 'But you've done so much for me, so much good work, please take it.'

'You're most kind.' Oriel admired the locket for a moment before closing the lid. 'Thank you.'

'Aren't you going to try it on?' Nat frowned as she seemed about to put the box into the pocket of her skirt. He had expected more fuss than this; it was after all an expensive gift. 'Here, let me.' Forestalling all protest he removed the locket from its case and with trembling fingers attempted to fasten it around her neck. 'Sorry, I'm all fingers and thumbs! I don't think I can . . .' He nipped his tongue between his teeth, fiddling a while with the clasp, then announced, 'Got it! There, go and look in the mirror.'

'It's very nice.' Oriel straightened the chain, poised this way and that before the mirror, then unhooked the clasp herself and replaced the locket in its box.

Plunged into disappointment, Nat replied, 'Well, I won't

delay you any longer, I know you must want to get home. Having a party, are you?'

'Just myself and Mother.' Oriel went to fetch her flower-strewn hat from the hall and stood before the mirror to put this on and then her gloves.

Nat felt sorry for her. 'Haven't you got any friends to invite?'

'Oh yes, I've plenty.' Though this was an exaggeration Oriel did still occasionally meet the girls from her old college. 'I'll be having a separate celebration with them on Saturday. We're all so busy through the week. Good night, Mr Prince. Thank you again. I'll see you tomorrow.'

Collecting her bicycle from the garden she left by the rear exit and emerged into a lane. Once alone, she propped the cycle against the wall and took out the gold locket for closer inspection, torn between throwing the wretched item as far away as possible or wearing it around her neck. It was the first, the only gift her father had ever given her. She felt an intense urge to sport it against her blouse and say to everyone, to anyone, look what my father bought for me! But how could she? How could she feel this way about a man she had sworn to hate? Troubled, she re-placed the locket in its velvet box and cycled home, wondering how she could possibly hide it from her mother. In the end the only place she could think of was the cellar, where it lay in a dark corner untouched, but often in her thoughts.

By mid-July conditions were getting worse on the Front. The enemy had forced the Allies back over recently won ground and was now threatening Paris. The Army was growing desperate in its recruitment; men old enough to be grandfathers were being called up to reinforce the decimated ranks.

Throughout the year things went steadily downhill. Out on the chilly October streets, selling flags to boost VAD coffers, Bright made a comment to her fellow helper. 'I never realized what a lot of old people we have in York, did you?' Almost everyone she had approached was over sixty.

'It's not that we've got any more than any other town,' replied her colleague. 'Just that they look more plentiful because all the youngsters have gone to the Front. There's only the old folk left, and the children – and us. I wish I could do more, don't you?' They wandered along Parliament Street to where a screen gave the latest war news. 'Is your husband out there?'

Bright gave a wistful smile. 'I don't have a husband – my brothers were killed last year though and I've a friend who's out there. I haven't heard anything from him for a few months and he usually writes quite regularly. I hope he's all right.'

The woman was not very reassuring. 'Maybe he's been taken prisoner, like my husband.'

'Sorry, I didn't know.' Bright shivered and tugged her fur collar under her chin. 'I don't think my friend would've been captured though, he's not in the thick of it. He's a doctor.'

'That wouldn't stop the Hun,' came the bitter retort. 'If they'll torpedo innocent women and children they'll shoot anyone. Come on, let's walk, my feet are absolutely freezing.'

Due to the rationing of coal it was not much warmer at home. With only one fire lighted, the house with its spacious rooms and high ceilings became like an ice-box and Bright and her daughter spent a good half an hour pressed close to the kitchen hearth before rushing up to bed with hot water bottles. Driven from the top floor by the bitter winds that shook the house, they now shared the lower bedroom, cuddling up together for warmth.

'If I'd known the war was going to last this long I would've stocked up the coal cellar and the pantry, hoarding or not,' grumbled Bright, head tucked under the covers.

'My God, I thought we had it bad enough last Christmas. What sort of time are we going to have this year with no coal, no meat, no blasted bananas, bacon, buggering cheese . . .'

Oriel's silent giggles shook the mattress.

'And I'm sick to death of that blasted rice – it's like eating cotton wool! I know tis awful to say, but I almost don't care who wins, so long as it stops.'

'Don't let the neighbours hear you say that,' Oriel managed to laugh despite the cramp that was attacking her feet, 'or you can add broken windows to your list of complaints. I wonder if Noel will be home this Christmas?'

'Oh, don't have me worrying about him on top of everything else – I'll have nothing to feed him on! Not to mention that he'll probably think we're trying to get rid of him by not lighting the fires.'

It was just as cold when they woke. As usual, Bright was first out of bed and rushed down to lay a fire, the coal mixed with yesterday's cinders, which it had become an offence to waste.

'Have ye got your medals on?' she demanded as Oriel went off to work.

'Yes, all thirty-three of them.' The girl picked up her lunchbox.

'Don't be cheeky or tis bread and water for tea – oh sorry, bread's a luxury now isn't it?'

'Sarcasm!' Oriel, wrapped up like a mummy, went to collect her bicycle from the shed, dropped her lunchbox into the basket and pedalled off to work.

'Good morning, Mr Prince!' Receiving no answer, Oriel poked her head into the back room where she usually found Nat eating his breakfast at this hour.

'What? Oh sorry . . . good morning, Oriel.' Nat turned his eyes on her just long enough to see that her nose and cheeks were pink from her exhilarating ride, then folded the letter over which he had just been pondering and carried his breakfast pots to the kitchen. Oriel moved out of his way, noting that a rasher of bacon was untouched. In these frugal times such wastefulness was reprehensible. There had to be something pretty important in the letter to put him off his favourite meal. Interest whetted – this might just be the time to get her own back on him – she waited for Nat to leave, watched him through the window until he reached the scrapyard, then rushed into the back parlour and read the letter, which was from the Military: Mr Prince was required to present himself for re-examination. No wonder he looked worried! No one in their right mind was queueing up to volunteer so readily now that mutilated veterans had brought the reality of the war home. Replacing the letter, Oriel went back to her desk, but remained pensive for a while. Maybe the Army was about to save her the trouble of revenge. If he was called up for duty there was a more than likely chance he would be killed. The dark-haired girl nibbled her cheek. No, she would not like to see him dead – just hurt enough to make him see what it felt like.

The day of the appointment arrived. There was no way that Nat could avoid the medical, but he hoped that his lungs would once again preclude him from battle. As, however, with growing unease he watched decrepit men with flaccid breasts and huge beer guts being pronounced fit, he guessed what the result of his own medical examination would be. Apparently this time he was the epitome of British manhood; the lungs so scarred by disease had miraculously healed. His file was stamped A1 and he was told to present himself at a local school on Monday where he would be supplied with kit – *Next!*

'What am I going to bloody do?' he demanded of himself that morning on his return, hunched over the fire with a cup of tea. 'I'll be buggered if I'm going.' But what was the alternative – prison? He had had enough of that and he knew that conscientious objectors had it particularly rough in gaol. Anyway, how could someone who'd only ever been into a church with intent to rob now claim that he was a conchie? His nose had begun to stream from the change in temperature. He blew into his handkerchief, then stared into the red coals, racking his brains and muttering to himself. Talbot hopped up to shove his dry nose under his master's elbow, demanding to be stroked.

'Oh, bugger off outside!' Nat scowled at the interference and chased the dog along the hall and out into the street. 'I can't think with you hanging around like a bad smell.' Yet, in the precise moment that he ejected the dog he was provided with a solution and became instantly excited – old Talbot had inspired him once again! He couldn't amputate his leg, but he could chop a finger off – they couldn't make him shoot a rifle then, could they?

Revived by this last-ditch ray of hope, Nat rushed to the kitchen and took a carving knife from the drawer. Left or right? Which hand did one use to pull a trigger? Being left handed, he took a gamble and positioned his left hand on a chopping board. The long blade trembled, partly because he was holding it in his weaker hand, but mainly because to disfigure himself was the hardest thing he had ever had to do. He stared down upon his manicured finger, the nail pink and clean, urging himself to act, mouth and eye determined – but hand still trembling. He lowered the blade against the skin.

'Ooh shit!' He had nicked himself and shook his hand to relieve the sting. It was the wrong kind of blade; a cleaver would have been more efficient, but if he put the knife away now he knew that he would never do it. He would just have to employ the knife like a cleaver. Positioning his hand for a second attempt, he prepared his mind, set his jaw, raised the knife, *come on, come on* . . .

'Don't!' Oriel, hearing the dog whining outside, had

come to investigate and almost screamed when she witnessed Nat's attempt at self-mutilation.

He dropped the knife and span round on her.

'What are you doing?' The horrified words emerged through the gaps between her fingers.

'I . . .' Nat clutched his nicked digit.

'No, don't bother!' Oriel's hand fell to her side as she stalked up to accuse him. 'It doesn't need the mind of a genius to guess. You were trying to get out of conscription weren't you? Don't gawk at me like that! I saw the letter asking you to go for re-examination. They said you were fit, didn't they?'

Nat was plunged back into childhood, felt as though he were being chastised by his mother, but managed to reply, 'I'm not fit! Neither were all the other blokes I saw. They're sending us to block up the gaps and I'm damned if I'm going to be used as target practice for a country that never gave me anything.'

'You coward!' screeched Oriel. 'Given you nothing? What's all this?' Her hand whisked the air, pointing out the luxuries. 'I've a good mind to inform the authorities what you tried to do, and if you persist in trying to dodge your duty then I will!'

Outside in the frosty morning, his whines unanswered, Talbot hopped away from the door and looked for company: two eleven-year-old truants seemed likely fun, giggling and happy as they attempted to tie each other up with scarves. Enjoying the fuss they made of him, the three-legged dog went along with all that was asked of him, even sitting still whilst one of the boys rubbed a bar of soap around his mouth — until he licked his chops and tasted it. Then he backed away, slavering and clacking his tongue in acute distaste, his drooling jowls becoming a mass of bubbles, which the boys had intended and thought a huge joke, for they fell about laughing whilst poor Talbot shook his head and sprayed foam everywhere.

The mother of one of the boys came out to shake her doormat, saw the frothing jaws and immediately set up a warning screech. 'Rodney, get away from that dog – now!' In a panic, she turned this way and that, looking for assistance. 'Somebody get the police! There's a rabid dog! Rodney, get in this house now!'

The young perpetrator, feeling quite safe, laughed and giggled to the point of hysteria, his eyes streaming. His cheeky companion yelled, 'I'll go and fetch a policeman, Mrs Wheeton!' And he raced off.

Inside Nat's house, an argument raged. 'Oriel, you don't understand!' How mistaken he had been to think that she had known his identity; she could not know at all. 'I'm . . . your father.'

In return there was only disdain. 'I know that!'

Nat was shocked. 'And you'd still inform on me?'

'With pleasure! Why should you be allowed to dodge when others are dying to keep their country free?'

Nat's face showed that he could not fathom her. 'But . . .'

The pretty little face inside the black bob was spiteful. 'Let me save you the bother of asking! I've known all along who you were. The only reason I came here was to ruin you like you ruined my mother!'

The noise that came from Nat was one of a small animal. 'All the time . . . I thought you were working for me just so's you could be close to your father.'

'Huh!' The arrogance of the man, raged Oriel.

'I thought the reason you never said anything was because you were too shy.' His pained blue eyes accused her now. 'You little monster.'

'*Me?*' Oriel endorsed his image of her by baring her teeth. 'You hypocrite! You, who ran off and left my poor mother to her fate. She almost died because of you! No one would help her, not even her family! She was thrown out into the street . . .'

In the street outside, the boy had returned with uniformed assistance — the mention of a hydrophobic dog required immediate action. The police sergeant came armed with a revolver. Unfortunately he was also wearing a hat. Talbot, slavering and foaming, took one bloodshot look at the policeman's helmet and sprang to attack.

'Stand back!' the officer warned those who had come to watch, including the giggling perpetrators. 'If you get one drop o' that foam on you you're done for! Get back!' Talbot advanced, barking and drooling; the sergeant levelled his revolver . . .

Nat was trying to ward off his daughter's attack. 'Oriel, I was only a child myself!'

'I know all about it! Mother gave me the whole story. You might have been young but you weren't innocent — you were in a school for ruffians at the time — yes, she told me everything! Not to mention the things I've discovered for myself!' Her eyes were slits of malice. 'Ever since I was a little child I wanted to be a nurse, but I couldn't, and do you know why? Because of you! You ruined everything for me, because you didn't marry my mother! You can't imagine how long I've waited to tell you that I hate you. I hate you! You . . .'

'At least you've got somebody to hate!' Nat flung back at her, showing fury now. 'At least you know who your father is. I'll never know who mine was, never know where to direct the hatred.'

Oriel was suddenly afraid. The tables were turned. In his rage he looked demonic, his black hair falling over his brow, eyes suffused with emotions that had been restrained for twenty-five years, since his mother had abandoned him.

'Get out! Go on, you little bitch, get out!' He advanced on her.

Oriel, fearing that he might be going to kill her, ran out into the hall, tugging frantically at the brass doorhandle in order to escape into the street. He was charging down the hall after her. She tugged and twisted, then the handle came free, the door opened and Oriel leaped out onto the pavement with Nat close behind her. They both saw the levelled revolver.

'*No!*' Her father's cry was a horrible sound, the howl of a tortured spirit. Oriel covered her eyes as the gun went off, killing Talbot instantly.

For a matter of moments time was suspended. Nat, his face a mask of disbelief, could not take his eyes from the hole in Talbot's skull, the lolling tongue, the eye that dulled even as he watched. Oriel half emerged from behind her hands, fingers dragging at her cheeks. The police officer lowered his smoking revolver. There was the smell of gunpowder on the air. More people had come out of their houses to watch. Nat stumbled into the road and bent over his dog.

'Careful!' warned the sergeant. 'He's got hydrophobia.' For a second Nat withdrew on impulse, but then he frowned and bent to sniff at the foam. 'It's soap,' he murmured, and lifted confused eyes to the police officer, who in turn glared at the two boys whose faces, though white, still bore the ghost of former mischief.

They backed away. 'It were only a joke, mister.'

Before the sergeant could apprehend them there came a roar and a flash of movement. With maniacal strength, Nat seized both culprits, a hand round each throat, lifted them clean off their feet and charged with them to the other side of the road where he thudded each head against the wall. Rodney's mother screamed. There were horrified complaints from the onlookers. The sergeant plunged his revolver into its holster and rushed over, calling as he went, 'Stop or you'll be arrested!' But Nat was too deafened by fury, his fingers kneading deep into the adolescent throats, squeezing, cutting off life as they had cut off the life of his only friend, bashing their skulls against the wall, adding their blood to the red of the brick . . .

Oriel, the only one to understand how much her father had loved that dog, buried her fingernails into her cheeks as she watched in horror.

A final warning from the sergeant brought no end to the attack. With a grimace of resignation, he drew his truncheon and with one deft movement sent Nat toppling to the footpath, his young victims sliding down beside him.

'Anybody got a telephone?' demanded the policeman.

Oriel allowed her hands to drop away from her cheeks, leaving a series of red crescents where her nails had dug into the skin. She wanted to answer, yes, I'll get an ambulance, but her lips refused to move. It didn't matter, someone else had taken charge, leaving the sergeant and other onlookers to administer first aid.

'Who is he?' demanded the police officer when the boys had been made as comfortable as possible. 'Anyone know his name?'

He's my father. Oriel was still rooted to the spot, trembling. A woman turned to point at her, and she saw the policeman approach. 'Excuse me, miss, that lady over there says you work for Mr Prince, is that right?'

She could not turn her white face away from Nat's handcuffed body. He was just beginning to come round, his groggy head raising itself from the pavement for another look at his dog. She nodded and finally spoke, 'I'm his secretary.'

The sergeant showed understanding. 'Nasty business, isn't it – and it could all have been avoided. These young lads with their pranks . . .'

'Will he go to prison?' Oriel's voice was that of a frightened little girl. Hands behind his back, Nat had managed to shuffle into a sitting position.

'Well, they won't be handing out any medals to him.' The sergeant heaved. 'Question is, whether it'll be for assault or attempted murder – I've never seen a man so crazed.'

'He loved that dog.' Oriel could barely speak. Her father was now leaned against the wall, his face a picture of misery.

'Aye, I suppose someone loves those two little imps as well.' Rather stern now, the sergeant indicated Nat's victims. 'I know they did a rotten thing but he can't just go trying to throttle people willy nilly. Anyway, here's the cavalry.' A black maria had turned into the road. He left her standing there alone and went to drag Nat to his feet, bundling him into the back of the van. Never once did Oriel's father look at her. Shortly after the police vehicle had gone an ambulance came to pick up the victims and most of the onlookers dispersed, though some remained to gossip even though there was nothing to see but a three-legged carcass.

Oriel was still in a daze. The sergeant approached her again, accompanied by a woman. 'This lady says she'll make you a cup of tea.'

Oriel allowed the neighbour to take her arm and together they went into Nat's house. At the last minute she looked back over her shoulder to ask the policeman, 'What should I do about . . . ?' She gestured at Talbot.

'Council'll probably come and take him to the tip.'

Faint as Oriel was, she couldn't allow this to happen and extricated her arm from the woman's grip. 'Mr Prince wouldn't want that, I'll have to bury him.' She tried to pick up the dog but its dead weight was too much. The sergeant took pity on her and with the help of another man carried it through the house to the back garden. Oriel followed the droplets of blood.

Talbot's carcass was dumped without ceremony onto the lawn and the men made to leave. 'By the way,' the sergeant told her, 'your evidence will probably be required in court.'

Oriel was not too stupefied to realize what effect this would have on her mother. 'Aren't there enough witnesses?'

'To the assault, yes, but I was just thinking you might be called in mitigation by the defence, what with you knowing how he felt about the dog.'

Fighting down the bile that rose to her throat, she thanked him for his help, then allowed herself to be taken in hand by the neighbour and drank the offered tea. If there was one iota of fortune it was that the terrible scene had been enacted in the morning, giving Oriel the rest of the day in which to recover, a day that saw her bury the dog then go back to her work as if nothing had happened. When she reached home, she was sufficiently composed as to avoid exciting suspicion from her mother.

There was one dreadful moment when Bright saw the report in the newspaper, read Nat's name and gasped. Oriel knew what the other had seen and was forced to ask tentatively, 'What's the matter?' But her mother recovered and shook her head. ''Tis nothing more than we normally read, these casualty lists are dreadful.'

Oriel had her own excuses. When, in the middle of the night, unexpected tears flowed, she managed to forestall her concerned mother without resorting to lies. 'Oh God, I wish this war would end!' And Bright shushed and cuddled and comforted as she had done since Oriel was a child, and was none the wiser about her involvement in the cataclysmic event that had occurred that day.

During the weeks after her father's arrest, Oriel was in a state of apprehension that his legal adviser would require her presence in the witness box. This was exactly what the defence had in mind, but when the proposal was put to Nat it received negative response. 'I won't have her in court. If you force her I'll find another lawyer.' Yet his sentiment was not because he hoped to spare Oriel's feelings – though in part he did – but more that he feared her testimony. 'It would be useless to put her on the stand. She wouldn't say a good word about me.'

Thus, Bright knew nothing of her daughter's part in the tragic affair, and when the case appeared in print after a few months of Nat being in custody, neither mother nor daughter commented on his twelve-month sentence, though each was well aware that the other must have seen it.

With her quest for revenge well and truly fulfilled, Oriel should have felt triumphant; but she felt quite the opposite. The image of her father grieving for his dog had had a dramatic effect on her. He was not hard and callous after all, and to add to the pain of his loss she had mortally wounded him by her condemnation. He might have deserted her, but he was truly paying for it now.

She fantasized about going to see him in gaol, knowing that in reality it would not be possible. In a token of amendment she continued her secretarial duties, adding many more to her list; banking the money which a big, stupid-looking man brought round every Friday, dealing with any bills so that her father would not be in any more trouble than he already was, and keeping a general eye on the scrapyard dealings, though she left the practical side of that to the men who worked there.

Locked in his cell day after day, Nat fell into depression, for added to this incarceration was the awful knowledge that his daughter had wanted to ruin him. The little bitch! After all he had done to try and make things up to her. How could Bright have poisoned her mind so? To heap misfortune upon this tragedy he had learned that when his prison sentence was served he would be conscripted. Well, there were not many certainties at the moment but there was one thing of which he was sure; if, at the end of the war he was still alive, he was going to move away from York. What was there left for him now in that hateful and unforgiving place? Where his journey would take him he was not sure — maybe towards death, for at that moment he did not care if he lived or died. The only criterion of his new abode was that it must be as far away from England as he could make it.

24

'Noel!' Oriel blinked, then started up an excited dance. 'What are you doing here?'

'I can go back if I'm not welcome.' The greatcoated doctor affected to turn on his heel.

'Don't be daft!' Oriel seized his arm and pulled him out of the cold damp evening. 'Mother, it's Noel!' She danced ahead of him as he came down the hall and into the kitchen. It was Christmas Eve, and the room was suitably adorned with boughs of holly as it always had been at this time of year, though the poorly stocked fruitbowl was a sign of the times.

'Merry Christmas, Bright!'

She flung her arms around his neck and hugged him, then gave an embarrassed laugh, for she had never been so impulsive before. It was just the relief of seeing him alive. 'Oh, you look . . .'

'I know, half dead,' joked Noel, and laid his hat plus a couple of parcels on the kitchen table. 'I feel it.'

'I was going to say wonderful!' But she had to agree privately that Noel looked haggard. She took his greatcoat and hung it up. 'Sit down by the fire. Oriel, get the kett – oh, you've got it on. Well, what a lovely Christmas present!' She folded her arms across her fitted navy blue jacket and sat down on the edge of a chair to appraise him.

'There's another one there.' Noel indicated the small brown paper parcels on the table. 'One for each of you.'

Oriel moaned. 'We haven't got you one! We didn't know you were coming.'

'I've got half a sock knitted,' laughed Bright, 'if that's any use to you.'

'Thanks, I'll wait for the full set.' The moustachioed face grinned and joked as it had always done, but there was a change in Noel, something that neither woman could interpret. 'You can open them if you like.'

Excited fingers scrabbled over the wrapping. They were just like two children, thought Noel to himself, and smiled, though the effort was great. He felt so weary.

'Oh, how wonderful!' Bright put the sachets of perfumed bath powder to her nose and inhaled. 'Mmm! I'd love to rush upstairs and use them now, but maybe it's a better idea to save them until the war's over, when they allow us to put more than a teaspoon of water into the bath!'

Oriel too went into ecstasies, then asked Noel, 'What's it like at the Front?'

'Oriel, Noel's just got home, he doesn't want to talk about the war!'

Noel gave a light reply, though there was a lump of lead in his heart that he would carry forever. 'Did you hear I got a medal – the DCM?'

The two listeners were enraptured by his bravery.

'Yes, a Decent Covering of Muck.' He laughed at their cries of, 'Fraud!' 'I can tell you, you wouldn't have hugged me a few days ago, Bright! I was absolutely filthy, and riddled with lice – jumped off my patients and onto me. Two days ago this uniform could have wriggled here on its own.'

'Ugh!' Oriel squirmed. 'Don't they ever get washed?'

Noel was patient; how could she know? 'There's no time for that when you're under constant fire in the trenches.'

'Yes, we read in the papers that it was getting very bad,' murmured Bright.

Noel gave a weary nod. 'You have no idea how bad.' And I'm not about to tell you, came the private thought, or you'd never sleep again. He did, though, give them part of the picture; it wasn't right that they should remain in total ignorance. 'I'm one of the lucky ones, you know. I've only waited eighteen months for home leave; some of the others have been in the trenches for years – can you imagine what it must be like to stand, up to your knees in freezing cold water, for days on end, unable to change your boots – their feet look like lumps of dough – unable to sleep for constant bombardment and sniping? Yes, I'm lucky, I just have to deal with the German bullets second hand when they hit some poor young lad.' That wasn't quite true, there had been some hairy moments, but he did not want to concern his friends. 'Oh, enough, enough!' Adopting a manufactured grin he slapped his knee, sorry for the horror he had created on their faces, yet in one regard not sorry at all. 'I'm here to be cheered up, not to infect you with my misery. I hope I haven't called at an inconvenient moment. You both look as though you're set to go out.'

Oriel, with her glossy black bob, figure-hugging gown and high-heeled shoes, looked like she belonged on the pages of a high society magazine. 'Oh, you don't think I've overdone it, too?' Oriel sought reassurance. 'Mother said we wouldn't need a Christmas tree, she'd just get me to stand in the corner.'

'It was only a joke!' Bright had not meant to inflict hurt and now tried to make amends. 'I'm just jealous because she puts me in the shade.'

'Nonsense,' came the quick response. 'You're both delectable, I see you've let your hair grow again.' This was for Bright.

'Yes, I like Oriel's but I couldn't get used to wearing mine short.' She laughed. 'I suppose that sounds daft when I pin it up like this.' It was just long enough to wear in a bun again.

'I think it looks nice either way,' answered Noel.

'Thanks. Ye'll have supper with us?'

'Try and stop me, if you've no other plans of course.' His

hostess replied that they hadn't. 'What are you doing over Christmas – fancy going to a pantomime?'

'Ooh, yes!' Bright hoisted her shoulders, then gave a thoughtful murmur. 'But don't you want to spend time with your mother?'

Noel's face clouded. 'Ah, no . . . Mother passed away last year. Didn't I mention it in one of my letters?'

'No, I don't think so.' Bright racked her brain, wondering if she had overlooked it and feeling awful that she had not read his letters properly. Maybe he had told her and she had forgotten – but no, Oriel had read the letters too and she seemed just as taken aback by the news. Why did you instantly assume that Noel was right and you were at fault, she asked herself? You should trust in your own sanity.

'Noel, I'm so sorry.' She reached over and touched his arm. 'Didn't they give you . . . what d'ye call it, sentimental leave?'

Noel gave a fond laugh. 'Compassionate leave. I expect if I'd kicked up a fuss I could've come home, but I wouldn't have been able to do anything for Mother and I'm needed more out there. A family friend very kindly saw to everything. It's strange, though, going to visit that big empty house . . .' He hadn't expected to feel such a sense of loss; Noel and his mother had never been close.

'Will you live there yourself, after the war?' asked Bright.

'Not on my own, no.' Noel made no attempt to press his suit, though he examined Bright's face for a sign that his absence might have changed her view on marriage.

Obviously it had not. Her only response was to offer more commiseration for his loss. 'Well, you're welcome to spend your Christmas with us,' she told him warmly. 'And I'd love to come to the pantomime.'

'Actually, I meant both of you.' Noel looked at Oriel who nodded acceptance. His eyes tarried on her face for a moment. There was something different about her, he sensed. Yes, she was a grown woman now but it was more than that, something to do with her eyes. 'Does the offer include Christmas lunch?'

'For what it's worth,' chuckled his hostess.

'Then I heartily accept!'

After Noel went home Bright and her daughter attended Midnight Mass and did not see him again until noon the following day. They provided the best dinner they could with the poor list of ingredients in their possession.

'Remember how we used to give up stuff for Lent?' Bright made this light remark as she served up the meal. 'We don't have to do that now, Lent comes every day with all these shortages. It'll be a good job when they bring in rationing, like they've been threatening to do. All this queueing . . . well now, no more grumbling, tuck in, Noel, and enjoy yourself – and Merry Christmas!'

Noel promised to return on Boxing Day, though said he would not be there until evening as he had someone to visit. In the event he turned up earlier than expected; the person he had hoped to see was out.

'When are you going back?' asked Oriel. Noel tutted. 'I didn't mean it like that! It's just that I have to go to work tomorrow and wondered if you'll still be here when I get home, but if you're only on short leave I'll ask for time off.' So accustomed had she become to keeping up the pretence to her mother that it came as second nature now.

Noel said he had a whole fortnight, and so Oriel went to work the following morning, as she had done for the past two-and-a-half years.

During the afternoon she was busy with her ledgers when there was a knock at the door. The shock she received on answering it was nothing compared to Noel's. When each had finished staring at the other he said, 'I came to visit my friend.'

'You'd better come in.' Oriel showed the khaki-clad

doctor into the front room where she worked and, nervously wringing her hands asked, 'Would you like a cup of tea?'

'Thank you – is Nat at home?'

Oriel postponed her trip to the kitchen. 'No . . . he's in prison.'

'Christ!' Noel clasped his brow. 'I do apologize, Oriel, but you've completely floored me.' She was about to leave the room. 'Forget the tea! I need something stronger.'

'Whisky?' At his nod she went into the back room and returned with a glass. In her absence he had removed his greatcoat and hung it in the hall. 'I owe you an apology too. You must have had a surprise finding me here.'

'You can say that again!' Noel tossed half of the liquor down his throat and looked for somewhere to sit. Oriel indicated her own chair by the desk and took a footstool by the hearth, hugging her shins and resting her chin on her knees like a little girl.

'To save you asking, Noel, I do know he's my father.' When the other did not reply she added, 'Let me give you the story. I got this job in 1915 . . .'

'Let's dispense with the bits I can guess!' Noel dragged the chair closer to the fire. 'When did you become aware that you were working for your father?'

'From the first day.' Oriel returned his direct gaze.

'And you've obviously kept it from your mother – never even mentioned it to me.'

'If I had you might have let the cat out of the bag.'

Noel looked slightly hurt that she had felt unable to take him into her confidence. 'You know I wouldn't have told your mother if you'd asked me not to. I appreciate how difficult the situation must be for you; you must have been curious, yet didn't want to hurt her . . .'

'I don't simply mean that you'd tell Mother, but him too.'

Noel frowned. His lips snatched at the remainder of the

597

whisky. 'I can't take all this in. If your father told you who he was then –'

'He didn't tell me.' Oriel sighed and changed position on the stool. 'I saw him talking to you once and put two and two together – I already knew his name so it wasn't that difficult. It didn't hit me immediately, but once I was sure – well, it seemed the perfect opportunity to get back at him.' She held Noel's eye. 'A shameful admittance, isn't it? I tricked my own father so I could get revenge on him for the damage he did to us.'

Noel had seen too much on the Western Front for anything much to shock him. 'What I don't understand is how the two of you could be under the same roof for, what, two-and-a-half years and not mention the fact that you were father and daughter! It seems preposterous. Nat didn't even mention your working here to me – even lied about it.' *But you lied to him about Bright, didn't you?* 'I mean, I know he doesn't like to talk about personal matters but he could have told me in one of his letters.' That reminded the doctor of the probable reason he had not heard from Nat in so long. 'I wrote to him in October and he never replied. Was that when he went to prison?'

Oriel nodded and donned a mixture of guilt and regret. 'Your letter's on the mantelpiece. I'm afraid I opened it – I thought it might concern something important.'

'And if it had would you have posted it on to your father?' The brown eyes were accusing.

She hung her head and stared at the boots that peeped out from under her heliotrope skirt. It had been a pathetic excuse. She had just wanted to read Noel's letter herself. 'Sorry, I don't know which prison he's in.' Embarrassed at being caught out she rushed on, 'It was awful, Noel! I'd better start at the beginning. My father was called in for re-examination and was passed as fit . . .'

Noel made the wrong assumption. 'He tried to avoid conscription and they put him in gaol?'

'I wish that were the only reason.' Oriel sighed. This made painful telling. 'We were having an argument about it. I said some awful things, I thought he was going to kill me – anyway, Talbot was in the street and these boys, these cruel little – they lathered foam round his mouth to make it appear he had rabies, then someone brought the police, and they shot him.'

'Oh, dear God.' Noel clutched his brow in frustration at not being able to emit a stronger oath.

'My father was in the act of chasing me from the house – oh, he was so angry, Noel – and we opened the door and saw poor Talbot. My father went crazy, literally crazy. He picked up a boy in either hand,' she clenched her fists to illustrate, 'then he bashed their – oh, I can't, it's too dreadful!' She would never forget the sickening thuds of those skulls hitting the wall. 'The policeman had to hit him with a truncheon to make him release them. It's lucky he wasn't charged with attempted murder.' She had no idea why Nat hadn't been; it certainly wasn't because she had helped him. Oriel suffered guilt at that.

'Were you in court?'

She shook her head. The manner in which Noel was looking at her made her feel ashamed and she cried out in defence, 'How could I possibly testify on his behalf? All right, it was a monstrous trick I played on him, I've admitted that, but I would've expected a little understanding from you, I mean he is a rival for Mother's affections, you can't be all that happy about the hold he seems to have over her.'

An odd expression crossed Noel's face. He finished the whisky and put the glass aside. 'She must have had a tremendous shock when all this came out.'

Oriel's eyes were downcast. 'She still doesn't know anything – except what she read in the paper and of course neither of us mentioned that. She thinks I go out to work every day for a Mr Price.'

'She must know! I have an excuse for being ignorant but you two live in the same house for heaven's sake.'

'She doesn't, honestly. I could tell if she did.'

'That's one good thing I suppose.' Noel unbuttoned the top pocket of his khaki tunic, withdrew his silver case and lit a cigarette. 'So, you're only coming here to keep up the pretence?'

'Not just that. You'll laugh at this.' A glance at Noel's face told her he wouldn't. 'I felt so sorry for him that I decided I'd keep his business in order whilst he's in there.' The doctor asked for how long this would be. 'He received twelve months.' She studied his haggard features. 'Are you going to tell Mother?'

Noel was censorious. 'Why would I want to hurt her like that? You've managed to cover it up for this long, I don't think another twelve months will make any difference.'

'Don't think too badly of me, Noel,' begged the young woman. 'You've no idea what it's like to be in my position, to be told that you can't be a nurse because you have no father – that you do have a father somewhere, but he was too much of a coward to stay and do the right thing. That's another reason we were arguing that day: I caught him trying to cut off his finger so that he wouldn't be sent to war! I told him it was unfair of him to dodge his duty when you were out there patching up all those wounded soldiers. I told him what a coward he was.'

Noel was immensely sad. 'Oriel, if only you knew what it's like out there, you wouldn't send your worst enemy. I don't just patch up our boys, you know, but the odd German too.'

'I thought he was my worst enemy,' murmured Oriel, 'but I think perhaps that I'm my own.' The fire was getting low. She stared into its red embers, which suddenly shifted, making her jump back as a coal fell onto the hearth. Using brass tongs she replaced the cinder in the grate. 'I wish I'd never started this. I've felt so wretched since it happened, I can't sleep, I lie awake at night frightened to turn over for fear of waking Mother — we began sleeping in the same bed to keep warm,' she explained to Noel. 'If there was anything I could do to turn back the clock . . . we were just becoming friends, you know. He bought me a locket for my twenty-first.'

Looking distant, the doctor murmured apology for not remembering, his pity more for Nat at this moment.

'Oh, you've enough on your plate out there, I'm sure. Yes, he bought me that locket but I can't wear it. I've hidden it in the cellar. My life has become one long round of subterfuge — I should enlist in the Secret Service, I'd make a good spy.'

'I must go and see him,' decided Noel, nervously flicking ash at the hearth.

Oriel looked anxious. 'Will you tell him I'm sorry?'

'That's something you should tell him yourself.' Noel took one last long drag at the half inch that was left of his cigarette and threw it onto the fire. 'I'll go now and make enquiries as to which prison he's in.' He went to collect his greatcoat.

'Maybe I could write him a letter.'

Noel stood in the doorway, buttoning his coat. 'It wouldn't hurt. I'll see you later.' He was about to walk down the passage, then glanced back at her lonely figure, offering a small kindness. 'Don't feel too bad. He's probably a lot safer in there.'

Noel discovered that his friend was in Armley Gaol and managed to wangle a visit before he had to return to foreign shores — a favour granted more for his sake than for the prisoner's, even though the latter was in the sick bay. Nat was extremely unwell, both physically and mentally. Exhausted from coughing he provided little in the way of conversation, but that was not unusual even when he was in good health and Noel did not mind being the one to entertain.

The first few minutes were given to jocular comment about Noel's exploits in the Medical Corps. There was a point, though, when the talk must come around to the serious business of Nat's being in here. 'Oriel told me what happened. I'm really sorry – so is she.' Grey blanket up to his chin, the prisoner responded with a snort of derision that blew mucus from his nose, compelling him to wipe it. 'She is, Nat! I think she feels rather guilty too.'

'So she bloody should!' Nat was unforgiving. His face drawn by illness.

'Well, maybe, but she's trying to make amends by keeping your books in order and –'

'No!' The objection resounded off the stark forbidding walls of the prison. Nat raised himself on an elbow and removed an arm from under the blanket to wag a vicious finger. 'You tell her to leave my books alone. I don't want her prying through my business affairs seeing if there's any dirt she can get on me!' He started to cough, eyes bulging.

Noel jumped from his chair, grabbed another pillow from a spare bed, raised Nat and inserted it behind his head, then laid him back gently and pulled the covers up over him. When he sat down again it was to offer words in Oriel's defence. 'There might have been vengeful reason behind her interest before, but she's genuinely repentant now. She's trying to look after your business for you until you –'

'I don't need her help!' spluttered Nat. 'Tell her to get out.'

'All right, all right, calm down! I'll tell her.'

'Just tell me this, Noel – did you know her intentions?'

'No! I swear I didn't know she even worked for you until the other day when I went to visit you. I had a hell of a shock!' Noel tried to smooth the rift between father and daughter. 'She buried Talbot in the garden for you.'

'He'll make good fertilizer, I suppose.' The callous reply was to cover his pain and the doctor recognized this.

'She's done a good job for one so young, and she's your daughter, Nat, you might as well trust her to carry on.'

'I trust nobody!'

'Not even me?' Noel affected a look of hurt.

'Least of all you, you bugger.' But there was a glint in Nat's eye that was due to old friendship rather than just fever. He was calmer now, though his breathing was obviously painful. 'How is Bright?'

'She's fine.' Noel should at this point have told his friend that he and Bright were not married, but he did not want to incite more anger. Nat would never forgive him and he could not bear that.

Preferring not to think of the two of them together, Nat changed the subject. 'Anyway, even if I did trust you, you couldn't run my business from wherever you're at. Where is it, by the way?'

'Can't tell you I'm afraid, old chap. Military secret. The Hun might be listening.'

'Bad, is it?'

'As bad as it can be.' Noel leaned on his knees and stared at the prison wall. 'The way things are going, we could all soon be prisoners.'

Noel's words held great portent, for the situation continued to deteriorate into the coming months both at home and abroad. Whilst in Blighty there was some alleviation of the suffering by the introduction of rationing, so ending the huge queues, there was no such mercy on the Front. The Germans had broken through Allied lines at Ypres, almost half a million men had been lost in three weeks, and as General Haig stated, everyone now had their backs to the wall.

'Maybe the Americans will make a difference.' Bright tried to cheer up her daughter as they discussed the matter after that Sunday's lunch. Noel had informed her in his last letter that their new ally had arrived in the British sector.

Receiving no answer from Oriel, she remarked, 'You're very quiet today.'

Oriel raised one corner of her mouth but kept her eyes on the table, her fingers absently tweaking the cloth. She had been visited by depression since Nat's imprisonment; some days were good, some bad. Today was bad. However, as always she gave a different excuse to her mother. 'This war's just getting me down, that's all.'

'You're not the only one, darling.' It was a gentle reprimand. 'Other people have had it a lot worse than us.' Oriel did not answer. 'It must be horrible at the Front,' continued Bright, not really guessing how horrible. 'I wish there was something more I could do for those poor lads instead of all these piddling little things like knitting socks and balaclavas. I've been thinking, I might go down to the Military Hospital and see if I can be of any help there.' Oriel nodded, still playing with the tablecloth. With this hint Bright had hoped to nudge some sort of life into her daughter, but was now forced to be more direct. 'I'm worried about you.' She grasped the fretful hand, preventing it from harassing the cloth. 'You need more to do to take your mind off things.'

Oriel laughed but it wasn't a merry sound. 'Aren't three jobs enough?' Defying her father's wishes, she continued to run his business, as much for her own ego as out of responsibility. Apart from the secretarial work, she had two voluntary posts.

'Maybe they're not important enough jobs,' replied her mother. 'Why don't you change your mind about trying for a nursing post again? I'm sure things have changed in the last five years.'

'You mean they're so desperate they'll have anyone?' Oriel was not to be roused.

'I wouldn't have put it like that. I just mean they'll be glad of your help.'

'They can go sing for it.' Oriel rose from the table. 'I'm going for a walk.'

'It's not the nursing profession you're punishing, it's the soldiers who need you!' Bright called after her.

Oriel re-entered the room with her coat and a floppy plum velvet hat, but only to say, 'I'll see you later.'

'Well, I'm going to work with the wounded!' retorted Bright as the door closed.

True to her word, she did volunteer at the hospital, though her duties only involved mopping floors and making cups of tea. However, amongst those limbless, mutilated men she got an inkling of what the real war was like, and thanked God that Nat was in prison instead of out there in the muddy, bloody struggle. She wondered how he was coping with his gaol term – badly if her memory served her well. Every month of this war now seemed like a year to Bright, and that's what it must feel like to him being locked up in there.

One day Bright felt her mother die. No one had told her, nor was there any mention of it in the press, she just knew, felt something go out of her. It was the saddest feeling.

Well into the summer more people continued to die at home from the dreaded Spanish influenza that swept the world; every time her daughter so much as sneezed Bright performed an anxious examination of Oriel's brow to check whether she had a fever. The epidemic created havoc on the Western Front too, and there had been a month long lull in the fighting due to its crippling effects. Now, in July, there was renewed offensive and with the brilliant sunshine came hope that the tide was about to turn.

When Oriel came home one summer evening her mother was scraping new potatoes; something in their skins made her throat tickle and she would periodically stop to cough. Oriel threw her ration book on the workbench, then felt her mother's brow. 'No, no fever.' Partly due to the glad tidings from the Front and partly from the sunshine, her mood was lighter today, she could attempt a joke.

'That's not funny!' Bright flicked water at the culprit. 'I only do it because I'm worried about you.'

'I know.' With one arm Oriel gave her mother a hug and went to read the *Evening Press* before supper; it was the only newspaper they took nowadays. After cheering at the war reports which gave word of a victorious counter-attack that had the enemy on the run, she browsed through the other items, then gave a moan. 'The demons! Oh, those beautiful girls and that poor little boy – have you seen this?' Bright asked what it was. 'Those Bolsheviks have killed the Czar and his family.' Oriel had seen photographs of the Russian Grand Duchesses and thought they were exquisite.

'Oh well, tis sad, but haven't we enough to worry about here, darlin'?' Bright knew how these things could prey on Oriel's mind for days, and now tried a joke to lighten the impact. 'The way things are going there'll be another massacre at the bakery.' There were no fancy pastries or muffins, even fresh bread was a thing of the past. 'I'd kill for a teacake.'

Oriel managed a laugh, then put herself in the murdered Romanovs' place, screaming with them as they fell under a hail of bullets.

'Just concentrate on the good news,' urged her mother. 'It's surely almost over now.'

'You're always saying that,' replied Oriel. Every week her mother went to Mass and prayed for an end to the war.

'Well, I'll be right in the end won't I?' retorted Bright.

And so she was. Throughout the late summer the news-paper headlines continued to announce great victories. In September the Allies broke through German lines and with one victory after another, the end was finally in sight.

To add to both women's euphoria, Noel came home at the end of October on extended leave, though his appearance deeply shocked them. However he might clown about, parading his souvenirs for their amusement – donning the German helmet and twiddling his moustache to mimic the Kaiser – he could not hide the gaunt cheekbones and dark circles beneath his eyes . . . those painfilled eyes.

In the days before peace was officially announced the newspapers carried reports of its coming, whipping up a tide of patriotism that exploded into the streets on the morning that Armistice finally arrived. Churchbells that had been silent since the beginning of the war now pealed and clamoured and rang throughout the city, aeroplanes performed acrobatic stunts above the jubilant streets, Union Jacks fluttered at every turn and the parade ground at Fulford Barracks was a dancing, singing mass of rejoicing. By midday, crowds were flocking along the narrow streets to St Helen's Square and the Mansion House in the hope of witnessing an historic proclamation from the Lord Mayor. Oriel was amongst those who seethed into town. She had gone to work as normal in the morning, voicing her intention to bring home a souvenir edition of the *Evening Press*. 'It'll have sold out before the paperboys can deliver it to us!'

Bright would have loved to join the revelry too, but her fear of crowds prevented it and anyway Noel turned up, so they enjoyed their own celebration at home. They sat quietly together in the back room, with glasses of sherry, talking over old times, which inevitably drew someone else's name into the conversation. She had not spoken of Nat to the doctor for a long time, guessing how it must hurt to hear his rival's name from her lips. Yet now it was he who spoke of their mutual friend.

'Poor Nat, I don't suppose he has much to celebrate where he is.'

Brown eyes and a freckled nose peeped at him over the edge of the crystal as Bright took a sip of sherry. 'You know about that, then? I never liked to mention it.'

Noel admitted that he had heard, but did not reveal his source. 'I went to visit him the last time I was here. I thought he might refuse to see me, but he seemed quite glad. I suppose he's desperate for visitors. I didn't tell you, because I didn't want to upset you either.' He smiled. 'You know, the way we both try to spare each other's feelings it's a crying shame we're not married.'

She saw that he was teasing, laughed and rested the glass in her lap. 'You're very determined, Noel.' Then she returned to the subject of Nat's imprisonment. 'How did he look?'

'Not too bad, considering. Not as bad as I do, I suspect.' Noel had felt physically ill for some days, completely exhausted. He supposed it was as a result of all those months trying to alleviate the most terrible wounds under constant bombardment. Obviously that degree of stress would leave its own kind of wound. However, he did not mention to Bright just how bad he felt, but continued on the subject of Nat. 'He's still got his looks – mind you, I never had any in the first place.' Bright cut in here to say how handsome Noel was. 'Oh, it's no use trying to get on my good side now, you've had your chance.' They shared a fond laugh, then Noel added, 'I've written to him once or twice, but he doesn't reply. I suppose he doesn't have much news stuck in there.'

Bright thought the reason was more likely to be that Nat was not very good at spelling and did not want to look a fool. 'Ah well, I would guess he's only another week or so before he's out.'

Bright was wrong. In an act of mercy Nat, and several other prisoners who were due to be let out soon, had been granted early release. At that moment, Nat was on a train to York with the intention of ploughing through the mound of business that would have accumulated in his absence – if indeed he had a business left at all.

The year in prison told in his looks. Unable to maintain

his normally scrupulous hygiene under the barbaric conditions he felt filthy and very strange as he arrived back to such jubilation, recalling the last time he had arrived back here in 1900 to similar flag-waving – though not on such a huge scale. Every citizen of York must be out on those streets. Desperate to escape the crowds the pale, dark-haired man fought his way home on foot, for there were no cabs available, and collapsed in relief as he slammed his front door upon the world.

As he had anticipated, the house was like a mortuary. But how odd, as he opened the door of the front room the glint of coals provided warmer welcome, and the house was spotless. His cleaning woman had obviously continued her chores – but why, when she would have received no pay? An idle flick through the pages of one of the neatly stacked ledgers provided immediate answer to his question: Oriel had been paying the woman's wages. Whether Noel had not passed on his instructions or she had simply defied them, Nat neither knew nor cared. Compressing his lips he rippled the pages of one ledger after another, discovering that not only had she paid all his staff but also had taken on his entire business operation. She had dealt with banking, invoicing, rents, mortgages – everything. This young girl had worked a miracle . . . but Nat was furious. If he could have got his hands on her now then he would have strangled her.

Banging the ledger shut, he spun away from the desk and went to lean on the white marble mantelpiece, the anger on his face accentuated by the glow of the embers. The fire . . . she must have been here today. Would she come back? That was doubtful, with all the celebrating going on out there; she was probably enjoying her own festivities.

There was a gnawing in his gut. To still the flow of acid Nat sought food, but the pantry was bare except for a few condiments and a caddy of tea which was useless without milk. Oriel's efficiency had not extended to buying food for her father's return – but then she would not know he was out of prison. That was good, meant he held the winning hand. Taken by storm, that uppity little madam would not have time to summon the eloquence with which to condemn him.

He did not go into the back parlour for there he would find only reminders of his dead friend; even here in the hall was the odd stray white hair embedded in the patterned runner. The house that had been such a refuge ten minutes ago now seemed like a prison. Braving the crowds, he fought his way back into town with the purpose of going to Fulford and confronting her. However, the smell of food detoured his feet to a restaurant where he remained for half an hour, forming a plan of attack.

After a tasteless but filling concoction and a well-rehearsed speech he felt somewhat more equipped to cope with his task. Still, the crowds annoyed him as he barged his way through, waving Union Jacks under his nose. A woman grabbed his arm and tried to pull him into an embrace, but he held her at bay. He escaped . . . only to bump into someone who had an old score to settle.

Violet's face remained joyful, but her words were laced with malice. 'Oh, still not in uniform, I see!' She swayed with the crowd as it moved and eddied around her like a wave, but managed to stand her ground, determined to repay Nat for the hurt he had caused her. They had not met since the break-up.

Nat had had enough of vengeful women and cupped his hand to her arm. 'Excuse me, Violet.'

The well-dressed young woman with the Marcel Wave would not budge. 'Aren't you even going to ask how I am?'

He stopped trying to get past her and played along. 'How are you?' It lacked sincerity but Violet seemed intent only on her own response.

'I'm very well, thank you!' Indeed, she looked blooming, even if at this moment her radiance was marred by spite.

'In fact I've just got married – to a hero – he got a medal at Buckingham Palace. Yes, so you see what a favour you did me! He's an Australian. I'm setting off to join him over there next week, and it'll be goodbye to all this cold weather. It's always summer there, they say.'

'Well, that's nice for you.' Nat gave a tight smile and now began to ease himself past her. Their bodies squashed together, yet neither found anything erotic in the movement. 'I wish you good luck.'

'And I wish you good riddance!' Violet hoisted her Union Jack aloft and fluttered it tauntingly as he departed.

Not bothering to reply to her spiteful riposte, Nat pressed on towards Fulford, but not until he reached Fishergate did he manage to escape the crowds. Given time to think now, he pondered on what Violet had said: Australia – what better direction could one choose than the other side of the world, the farthest place from here? He laughed to himself; if Violet only knew that she had done him a favour. Yes, he would take her example and head for the sunshine . . . but first there was to be a showdown.

Bright almost fainted when she opened the door, clutching the jamb for support.

'I've come to see Oriel,' announced Nat.

'She – isn't here.' Her mind was swimming. Oh, look at his face, his eyes . . .

Nat brushed past her and marched along the hall, looking first in the front room, then going on to the kitchen. He did not show surprise at seeing Noel. 'Where is she?'

Bright had come after him, hands clasped over breast. 'I told you, she isn't here. She's at work.'

'Huh! No, she bloody isn't, otherwise I would've seen her. It doesn't matter, you'll just have to do!' Nat turned on her. The keen breeze had put more colour into the prison pallor. 'You're probably the one I should be blaming anyway.' The expression in his blue eyes was a mixture of anger and incomprehension. The first words he had uttered to her in twenty-two years emerged as accusation. 'I can understand you being mad at me – even though I was young it was wrong of me to run off like that – but how, how in God's name, if there is a bloody God, could you bring her up to hate her own father?'

'Nat . . .' Bright's mind was in turmoil. She pressed a hand to her thumping brow. 'I don't know what . . .'

'How could you let her try to ruin me?' he flung at her.

'Now, just a minute.' Noel, who had until now remained dumb, sprang from his chair.

'You keep out of it! I know she's your wife but this is between her and me, about our daughter!'

'*Wife*?' Bright felt the madness rushing through the arteries of her brain, her brow furrowed with confusion. 'I'm nobody's wife.'

Both she and Nat flung an enquiring look at the uniformed doctor, who held up his hands in a weary gesture of pacification and guilt. 'Just wishful thinking on my part. I'm sorry, I should have told you, Bright turned me down.'

On impulse Nat lashed out and felled the doctor.

Bright screamed and ran to tend Noel, who raised the top half of his body to lean against one of the fireside chairs, dabbing a handkerchief to his bloody lip. 'Nat, you'd better go!' Her command emerged on a sob.

'No!' A black-clad arm speared more accusation at her. 'First, I want to know why you made her hate me!'

'I don't know what you're talking about!' she screamed up at him.

'She doesn't, Nat!' Noel lengthened the odds against another blow by remaining on the carpet, though he could not have risen had he wanted to. 'Bright knows none of it.'

Bright turned to cry at the doctor, demanding, 'Do you? If so then would you tell me?'

Nat had whipped himself up in preparation of the attack and was not to be deterred. 'You knew she'd come to ruin me all along, didn't you?' he growled at Noel.

The answer was desperate. 'No, no! I swear I didn't.'

'I wish someone would tell me!' yelled Bright, and jumped to her feet, standing toe to toe with Nat.

'Don't give me any o' that rubbish!' Nat's dark hair fell over his brow, the whites of his eyes suffused with red. 'You must've known she was working for me.'

Her breast rose and fell like overworked bellows. 'Working for . . . ? I never!'

The contortion of his lips showed that he thought she was lying. 'You're asking me to believe that she came to work for me every day for three years and you had no idea where she was going?'

'I didn't!' Her brown eyes were wide and filled with tears. Oh, this was not the way their reunion was meant to be.

'Nat!' With the aid of furniture Noel managed to scramble up and grabbed his friend by the arms, though his whole demeanour lacked strength. 'Listen, Bright knows nothing about it and neither did I until I came to see you in prison. Oriel planned it of her own accord.'

'Planned what?' raged Bright. 'I demand to be told.'

'She pretended not to know who I was!' Nat shouted at her. 'Came to work for me in the hope that she could make some mischief, to get her own back on me for deserting the pair of you!' He had finally admitted it after all these years: he had deserted her. 'She even said . . .' He forced his voice not to crack. 'She even said she'd see me in prison, and by God if she didn't get her wish!'

'But I didn't send her!' Bright was pleading now.

His intended speech gone awry, Nat did not know what to believe. On one side there was Noel claiming it had all been a misunderstanding, when he himself had said that he and Bright were married, Nat *knew* he had. And on the other side was Bright, claiming total ignorance of everything and looking as wide-eyed and innocent as she had two decades ago when he had taken her purity. In complete turmoil, he reeled towards the exit. 'Oh, save your lies for each other! You're both a couple of frauds. I just wanted you to know what I thought about you – and you can tell that little bitch that I haven't finished with her yet!'

'Nat, don't run away!' Bright hurried after him down the hall, but he charged outside and headed back towards town.

'Leave him,' advised Noel, coming to slouch beside her on the doorstep, a thread of blood trickling down his chin. 'It's no good while he's in this mood.'

'I'm afraid for Oriel.' Bright spoke through her fingers, her wide eyes peering over them. 'What if he bumps into her in town?' For that was where Oriel must surely be; she obviously wasn't out working for her Mr Price.

'In all that mafficking?' Noel forced a comforting laugh. 'Not a chance. Come in, come and sit down, this must've been a terrible shock.' He closed the door on the outside world and shepherded a trembling Bright into the kitchen where he put the kettle on. 'I'm really sorry.'

She sat rigid in the chair. 'For what? For pretending that we were married, or not informing me that I have a monster for a daughter?'

Noel felt drained. It wasn't just the current unpleasantness; the malaise that had been with him all day had grown progressively worse, his chest felt tight and his head throbbed. With a sigh, he abandoned his efforts with the teapot and slumped in the chair at the other side of the fireplace. 'I didn't tell him we were married, I told him that I'd asked you to marry me. He just assumed that you'd accepted.'

'And you allowed him to.' This was the first time Bright had shown anger towards him; it may have been controlled but that did not lessen its impact.

'Yes . . . as I said to Nat a moment ago, it was wishful thinking I suppose, and pride.' And other reasons that he could not say. He picked a strand of white cotton from his khaki trousers and dropped it on the floor.

'Wishful thinking that I'd marry you?' she demanded. 'And why exactly do you want to marry me, Noel? It certainly isn't because you're in love with me. I can't recall you ever mentioning that emotion. Fondness, yes. Love, no. And for you to even say you're fond of me is a lie. Ye don't play a rotten trick like that on someone you're fond of.'

'Oh if life were only that clear!' Noel's head was spinning and he gripped his temples in an attempt to ease the torment. How could he explain the complexity of his actions when he did not fully understand them himself? How could he make excuses when he was his own worst accuser? How could he argue that he did love Bright in his own way, but that he loved Nat too? He imagined the look of horror and incomprehension that this would engender if he were able to admit just what kind of love he felt for Nat – it had taken Noel years even to admit it to himself. There was no answer he could possibly give that would not inflict more hurt upon her.

'You also mentioned pride,' inserted Bright when Noel appeared to have difficulty providing an excuse. 'Do I take it to mean that you felt so humiliated when a lowly housemaid turned down your proposal you felt you had to save face by lying to your friend?'

'No! I was bitterly disappointed it's true, but I never ever regarded my proposal as an act of charity. My feelings for you are quite genuine, Bright.' And in a way they were. Yes, he had been using her, but not in a malicious way, and the marriage would have been beneficial to both of them.

'Then I can only think it was done out of sheer jealousy,' responded Bright. 'You've always known how I felt about Nat and you were jealous that I couldn't show you the same love.'

Noel opened his mouth to deny this, but closed it again.

615

Kinder for her to believe this than the truth: the truth being that he had always envied the love that Bright and Nat had for each other, that he too yearned for Nat almost to the point of madness, whilst being enough of a realist to know that such a fantasy was doomed. For the sake of convention, the threat of ridicule, and the greater fear of rejection he could never and would never admit to his passion, but this did not deprive him of intense jealousy. So utterly consumed was he by this emotion that he had long ago decided that if he could not have Nat then neither would Bright. It had not concerned him when Nat had announced he was to be married, the doctor had known it had only been done from expediency, but this link between Bright and the man who had fathered her child was indestructible. And to complicate matters further Noel had to care for Bright too! Despite all the contradiction and the inextricable tangle of emotions there was no reason why this lovely and lovable woman could not find happiness and contentment in a marriage of convenience. Noel could have been a good husband in every other way . . .

But it was too late now. He finally confessed to her accusation of jealousy in a shamed tone. 'You're probably right.'

Bright fixed him with her eyes for a second, then turned her face away in disgust. Noel was about to admit that he had lied about Nat being married too, that their mutual friend regarded anyone else as second best to this woman. But Bright changed the subject in terse manner. 'So! Now that we've got that out of the way are ye going to tell me about Oriel before she comes in? What were her reasons for all this?'

'Don't be too hard on –'

'Just tell me! Then I'll be the one to decide how hard I'm going to be on her.'

Noel sighed again. On the hob the kettle boiled merrily away but neither of them went to remove it. In the following moments the doctor told Bright what he knew about Oriel's reasons for keeping her secret, ending with another attempt at mediation. 'She didn't mean to deceive you, Bright, she was only trying to protect your feelings, as I was.'

'I wish everyone would stop trying to protect my feelings!' Bright's fists came down on the arms of the chair. 'I'm a grown woman, I don't need my daughter to look after me — and I don't need you!'

Noel's brown eyes lost their glimmer of entreaty and became quite dead. 'Would you like me to leave?'

'Yes! I've things to say to my daughter and I don't want an audience.'

'Goodbye, then.' Noel wanted to touch her, but thought better of it, and collecting his hat from the table he left.

Bright let him go, seething with outrage at being patronized like this. Look after me indeed! Why had she always put Oriel's feelings before her own? Why hadn't she done as instinct had urged her to do and gone to see Nat years ago? The more she sat here the angrier she became about how life could have been so different, and when Oriel finally came home later that afternoon, waving a copy of the *Evening Press*, Bright struck it from her hand. 'Where have you been all day?'

Dumbfounded, Oriel looked at the paper that now lay unrolled on the carpet, then back at her mother. 'I was at work this morning, and then I went —'

'Working for Mr Price?'

Oriel hesitated — had her mother found the locket? 'Yes.'

'Liar!' Bright's placid temperament was overcome by fury. 'You've been working for your father for three years! You've lied, you've cheated and —'

'I can explain!' Oriel's hands came out to beseech her mother. 'It wasn't that I wanted to be with him, but that I wanted to ruin him like he ruined you.'

'I know!' Bright slapped down the entreating hands. 'Noel told me everything.'

How could he? Oriel raged at the doctor, tucking her hands under her armpits in an attitude of defence. 'But I did it for you!'

'Don't say it was for *me*, it was for *you*! You, who never had one hardship in your life, never had to go short. Apart from that one disappointment over the nursing business you had everything easy. I wish I'd had life so easy! I'll bet your father does too!'

Oriel was crying. How could her mother have forgotten that she had shared Miss Bytheway's fortune with her? Nevertheless she blurted, 'I'm sorry!'

'How could you be so vindictive?'

'And how could you be such a doormat!' sobbed Oriel. 'Letting everyone treat you with contempt!'

'And do you include yourself in everyone? Because as far as I'm concerned you've been the most contemptuous of the lot! How could you go out of this house every morning, lie and cheat . . .'

'I was doing it to protect you!'

'Ye were doing it to protect yourself! Ye knew if I'd been aware of your plans I would've stopped ye.'

Oriel turned her anger on the doctor. 'Noel should never have opened his mouth!'

'It wasn't Noel who did this to your father! Your own father . . . how could ye do it to him, Oriel?'

'How could he do it to *me*?' came the hot reply. 'How could he abandon me?'

'Well, ye'll have the chance to ask him 'cause he's coming back.'

Oriel's teary eyes looked suddenly afraid. 'He's been here? But I . . .'

'I know! Twas a surprise to me too – so ye see it wasn't Noel who gave the game away. Aye, it was a big surprise, and not a very pleasant one either. He came here with all manner of accusations, blaming me for the things you've done.'

'He had no right to do that! I've looked after that business on my own for a year just so he wouldn't lose everything.'

'Yes, Noel told me that after your father had stormed off thinking we were all in it together.' Exhausted, Bright fell into a chair and buried her face in her hands, rubbing them over her cheeks in desperation. 'God knows what he's going to do now.'

Oriel's heart was still pounding. She moved slowly to her mother's chair and in hesitant manner put a hand to Bright's shoulder. 'I'm really sorry. I'll go and explain to him. I never intended you to be hurt like this.' She bobbed to her knees and laid her head in Bright's lap, but when there was no comforting hand she lifted her face again. 'I'm not just sorry I've hurt you, but him too.'

Bright's mind hopped from one vague memory to another. 'I suppose you were there on the day he was arrested?'

'Yes.' Oriel's blue eyes misted over. 'It was awful. The poor dog hadn't done any harm, it was these two boys . . . oh, you should have seen . . . I felt so sorry for him.' She began to cry and bent her head to her mother's lap again.

Bright felt the warmth of her daughter's sobbing breath through her skirts. Tears rolled down her own cheeks.

Oriel felt the consoling hand upon her head and broke into racking sobs. 'I'm sorry! I'm sorry!'

'I'm sorry!' laughed the woman to Nat after dancing back onto his toe as the crowd carried her against her wishes.

He gave unsmiling pardon and tried to manoeuvre a passage through the shouting, singing, yelling mob. It was dark now, though not late. Since the afternoon's encounter with Bright he had been drowning his confusion in self-pity and beer in a public house that was as crowded as the streets. He was now quite drunk and not so tolerant of the crowd as he had been this morning, shoving and pushing its members out of his way, to which they showed no objection. Everyone was everyone's friend tonight, it seemed. Everyone's except Nat's. He staggered drunkenly on. Faces loomed out of the pack, leering at him, bodies draped in Union Jacks, grabbing, kissing, poking, prodding.

'Sorry!' Another apology, from another woman. She pressed her buxom chest against his, eyes gleaming with intoxication. Reading the signs, Nat grabbed hold of her hand, moved with her through the crush and escaped into a narrow lane that had no shadows. There were other couples here; he could hear their grunts and moans. The woman hoisted her skirt around her waist, then he unbuttoned his trousers and thrust himself up into her warm, moist flesh, hands digging into her buttocks, ramming her at the wall, again, again, again, again – fuck you, fuck you, bastards all! You've got your way. I'm going!

The woman gave a little shriek. With a last trembling, vicious lunge he exploded into her, then pushed her from him and hurried away, buttoning his pants as he went, back into the crowd, shoving, pushing, elbowing his way home.

Someone barged into him, thumped him in the chest; he did not stop to see whom, for the man was swallowed up into the throng. Nat weaved his way along High Ousegate, in and out, shoving . . . he did not realize he had been stabbed until he stepped into the light of a lamp-post and a woman screamed and pointed at the handle that protruded from his left breast. He felt pain now and groped at the iron post for support.

Satisfied at having achieved his belated revenge, Denzil melted into the crowd.

The woman entreated someone to help him but her cries were lost amongst the drunken singing and she was carried off on a wave of patriotism. No one else noticed his plight. Nat's eyes were wide in shock. Collecting his thoughts, he turned and tried to fight his way back along High Ousegate, instinct directing him towards Noel's surgery. People got in his way. Get out! Get out! He lashed at the air, one hand clutching his chest. Assuming he was merely drunk, no one took pity. Lungs fighting for breath, he continued to stagger through the milling throng, until finally he collapsed into the doorway of Noel's surgery, whereupon he set up a constant kicking with his boot.

Upstairs, Noel groaned. 'Oh, fack off will you?' The drunks had been a constant irritation all evening. Up until now he had ignored them, only because he was too tired to go and remonstrate. Never had he felt so tired, yet unable to sleep. Not even the half bottle of whisky had had any effect. Exhaustion seeped into his very bones, his head throbbed, his chest was as tight as a drum; he felt on the verge of nervous collapse.

The thudding at his door went on and on, and finally exhaustion was overcome by rage: how dare these bastards behave like this? They hadn't been at the Front, they didn't know what it was like, to try and put soldiers back together when there weren't enough pieces to go round, how dare they disturb the peace of those who had? Pushing himself from the chair, he kicked over the empty bottle and half charged, half stumbled down the stairs, turned the key and hauled on the door-knob. 'Look, you . . . !'

Nat collapsed at his feet. 'Help me! I need a doctor.'

Noel cackled and fell against the jamb. 'He needs a doctor and he comes to me!'

A desperate hand grabbed at his trouser leg. 'I've been stabbed.'

'Oh . . . shit.' Fighting off his debilitating exhaustion, Noel fell to his knees beside his friend.

Nat was holding the knife handle, eyes terrified. 'Pull it out!'

'No! Leave it there.' Noel tried to calm him.

'You bastard!'

'If I pull it out I might do more damage! Oh, Christ, how do we get you to hospital through all this?' After a moment's indecision, Noel launched his aching body at the stairs.

'Don't leave me!' Nat's hand came up to plead.

'I'm just going to telephone for an ambulance. Lie still, I won't be long!'

Nat fell back against the hard ground, the cold air swilling around his head. Someone had pissed in Noel's porch, he could not escape the stench. Through the open door the crowd was singing, '*Keep the home fires burning!*'

Noel's dark silhouette reappeared on the stairs, carrying pillows and blankets which he used to make his friend more comfortable.

'It hurts!' Nat wailed like a little boy.

Noel was examining the wound, trying desperately to concentrate on something other than the pain of his own body. 'I know, but I don't think it's hit anything vital. The thickness of your coat stopped it penetrating too far.' He was slightly concerned that it might have pierced a lung but there seemed to be no handicap to Nat's breathing other than his panic, and if he had managed to stagger here then he was probably going to be all right. Like a mother comforting her child he tucked the blankets around his friend's body, keeping out the cold that had suddenly attacked him too. Annoyed by the crowd he told Nat, 'Just shift your feet a bit, then I can shut that bloody lot out.' With much effort he managed to close the door, but this had plunged them into darkness and so he lighted a wall lamp before returning to bend over his patient. 'Hold on, the ambulance won't be long.'

Nat reached out for the other's hand. 'It feels like it's gone through me heart!'

The doctor stared at that supplicating hand, hesitated for the briefest moment, then clasped it. 'Well unless your heart is in a different place to everyone else's I don't think that's likely.' He returned Nat's grip, stroking the taut knuckles, the clenched fingers.

Nat was calmer but still frightened. 'A doctor wouldn't lie, would he?'

'Even a village idiot like Spud could diagnose that that knife is nowhere near your heart.' After a moment, Noel started to shake with silent laughter.

'What's up?' Panic lifted Nat's head from the pillow.

'It's all right! I'm not laughing at you.' Noel slumped onto the floor beside Nat, leaned against the wall and pressed close to the other's flank, oblivious to the cold now for the proximity of his friend was all he knew. Rubbing Nat's icy hand between his own as if to warm it, he felt the cold skin against his palms. It had a gently soothing effect upon the patient; upon the doctor also. 'Who did this to you?'

'I didn't see.'

'I'm not surprised in that lot,' muttered Noel, and closed his eyes, head swimming.

'I was just on me way home to pack up.' Nat sounded cheated.

'Oh, where were you going?'

'Australia.'

This had the effect of opening Noel's eyes, though he continued to massage the other's skin. 'You're serious?'

'I find it very difficult to be funny with a knife sticking out of me chest.'

Noel gave a low chuckle and closed his eyelids again. 'Don't worry, you'll still make it – I'd love to go with you.' Oh how he would love to.

'Oh aye?' Nat was cynical, tried to move and winced in discomfort. 'Bright wouldn't take kindly to that. I suppose you're still hopeful in that quarter – that's why you kidded me you were already married, so I wouldn't spoil it for you?'

The other gave a harsh laugh that started him coughing. Tasting blood in his mouth, he spat into his handkerchief which he quickly replaced in his pocket. 'The mood she's in she'd be glad to see the back of me.'

'Sorry if I spoiled it for you,' muttered Nat, not sorry at all.

Having brought his cough under control, Noel stared up at the flickering yellow gaslamp that did nothing to improve the dingy brown paint of the vestibule. 'Oh Nat . . .' he shook his head. 'Shall I tell you something?'

'I'd rather you got me to hospital,' groaned Nat, yet comforted by the stroking hand.

'I won't get you there any quicker than the ambulance. Don't worry, it'll be along in a minute. Whilst you're waiting you might as well listen, it'll make the time pass more quickly. You know this afternoon when you called Bright and me a pair of frauds? Well, you were right. No, listen!' His hands caressed Nat's skin, soothing any outburst. 'We are frauds, the pair of us, but I'm the best, a real dyed in the wool fake. That's why I found it so bloody funny when you said you needed a doctor.' He saw that Nat did not understand. 'I'm a quack, man! A charlatan. I failed the bloody test!'

'But . . . I've seen your diplomas. They're hanging on the waiting room wall.'

'I might be a quack, but I'm a bloody good forger.' Noel gazed down upon Nat's face, which looked jaundiced in this light. Confessions spilled from his lips. 'Managed to get hold of a bona fide certificate and filled in the rest myself!' His tired body shook with laughter. 'I've been carving up those poor buggers in the trenches for the past two years and not one of them had a clue; had my hand up a thousand twats, delivered babies . . .' He shook his head from side to side, eyes pressed shut in mirth.

Nat almost forgot his stinging wound. 'But how have you got away with it for so long?'

'Because I'm good! Oh, I was being flippant before, I did get through most of it, I mean I've been through hospital procedure and everything, there were just one or two hiccups that prevented me from getting the diploma. I didn't think it was fair! Just because someone's got a bit of paper doesn't necessarily mean he's a better doctor than I am! Some of them are bloody awful, I'd be ashamed to admit some of the things I've seen them get away with. So there!' He dealt a gentle series of pats to Nat's hand, at the same time lifting one freezing cold buttock from the stone floor. 'You've got something on me. You can hand me over if you want.' And at this moment I couldn't care bloody less, he thought.

'Why are you telling me this now?' asked Nat, who found what Noel had done outrageous. 'And why did you do it in the first place?'

The bogus doctor gave an exaggerated shrug, catching the weave of his jacket against the rough wall. 'I couldn't let my father down. It was as simple as that.'

'He wouldn't have been very pleased to see you in gaol alongside the likes of me.'

Noel's voice was sombre. 'There wasn't much chance of that, he was already dying.'

'What about your mother?'

'Mm . . . well, I rather tended to disregard her, it was my father whom I was desperate to please.' Noel was starting to perspire again and his head was throbbing. He winced. Loath to relinquish his hold on Nat's fingers he used his free hand to knead the pain. It did no good. 'I would have done anything for him. Anyway, when you're young you tend to think you're invincible.'

Nat did not possess such self-confidence. 'There must've been times when you thought you were gonna be found out?'

'Oh at first, yes, but I doubt I was any more nervous than any young doctor – and you know me, I can lie my way out of anything.' He sighed. 'The things our parents do to us, eh?'

There came the faint sound of a bell above the hum of the crowd. Noel cocked his ear. 'Here's the ambulance.' He sounded almost sad.

Nat felt relieved enough to hark back to the initial part of the doctor's conversation. 'When you said about Bright being a fraud too, did you mean she *did* know about Oriel's dirty trick after all?'

'No, clot! I mean she still carries a torch for you.'

Nat's lips opened to speak, but the ambulance had finally arrived. Noel was compelled to release the other's hand. He hauled his leaden body to his feet, opened the door and leaned against the wall as his friend was transferred to a stretcher. 'I won't come if you don't mind. I don't feel too good – might end up in the bed next to yours.' With one last reassuring grip of Nat's fingers, he let go of his friend. 'But I'll come and see you tomorrow, I promise.' He levelled a warning finger. 'Hey, and you owe me a fiver! You said you'd be married when I got back from the war. I'll collect it tomorrow.' His grin faded as the doors of the ambulance closed on Nat.

Now that he was no longer in charge of the crisis the exhaustion flooded back with a vengeance. He picked up the pillow and blankets, hardly able to drag himself up the stairs. You should see a bloody doctor, he taunted himself. After what seemed like a hundred miles he finally reached the top and capsized into a chair, still embracing the pillow that had bolstered Nat's head. He pressed it to his nostrils and inhaled the other's scent for long moments. Then, in groaning afterthought, he threw it aside and went to the telephone to inform Bright of what had happened.

'No, he's fine! I think it's probably just cut through muscle. He's . . . yes, yes, I promise.' There was impatience in Noel's voice. 'He's in the County. I'm going to see him tomorrow. I'll let you know how he is.' If I can drag myself there, came his thought. He caught sight of his face in a mirror; it looked almost blue.

At the other end of the line Bright felt that she could take no more, that she was about to drop. 'Thank you, Noel . . . and I'm sorry about what I said this afternoon, I didn't mean . . .'

'It's all right!' He was far too ill and tired to stand at the telephone listening to her apologies. 'I know, really, it was just the shock. Listen, there's something else I must tell you – no, honestly the wound's not life-threatening!' Stupid bloody woman, just listen. 'I was going to tell you this afternoon . . . you'll be angry . . . Nat isn't married – I know, I'm sorry, it was cruel! I know you'll never forgive me. Are you still there?'

Bright muttered a yes.

'Can we talk about it more fully tomorrow? Right, thanks . . . then I'll have to go. Oh! Listen to this: Nat says he's going to Australia! No, no, don't worry he won't be going in the next couple of days . . . no, really he's all right! Bright, dear, I'll have to go, my head's thumping – no, no, it's just the whisky. Good night – and don't worry.'

There were a lot of sore heads the next morning, not the least of these belonging to the sister who ruled over the ward in which Nat awoke to find himself. She was most put out when the ungrateful man expressed a wish to leave.

'You come in here, kicking up a fuss about a paltry little cut on the chest, telling us we're not doing our job properly, spoil our celebration . . .' The nurses had been enjoying a drink like everyone else. 'And now you say you want to leave? Stay where you are until the doctor says you can leave!'

Nat fumed, but rather than tangle with the harridan he did as he was told. Besides, his wound still hurt – how could she call it a paltry little cut with all those stitches, he'd nearly died! The doctor had told him, a fraction either way and the blade would have punctured a lung or a main artery. It just went to show what a quack Noel really was. He thought about Noel, remembering the devastating confession. How had he got away with it for so long? Well you didn't know he was a fake, did you, so why should anyone else? All day he waited for Noel to come. Maybe they would not let him in until the appropriate hour. By the time visiting was half over he knew that Noel was not going to turn up. He had been right about him all along. Noel could not be trusted.

He lay back against his pillows and cast a miserable eye over the jolly scenes at every other bed. Tomorrow morning, doctor's permission or no, he would escape this smell of disinfectant and cabbage that reminded him too much of the Industrial School.

Visiting time was into its final ten minutes when he felt a presence, and looked around to see Oriel. He immediately turned away.

In hesitant manner, she came closer to his bedside, hands toying with the clasp on her handbag. 'Can we speak to each other without arguing?'

'Who's arguing?' Still Nat did not look at her, instead pretending to concentrate on other people's visitors. 'I wasn't exactly expecting you.'

'I know, you were expecting Noel.'

'Oh, he told you, did he?' The remark was sour. 'I've been waiting for him all day.'

'I'm afraid Noel died this morning.'

He spun to face her now, saw that her eyes were red and puffy from weeping; even as he watched in horror fresh tears began to run down her cheeks. Oriel excused herself and blew her nose. Shocked to the core, Nat waited for her to emerge from behind the handkerchief. He was the one who had been stabbed, how come Noel had died?

She took a deep breath, still tearful, tasting the salt at the back of her throat. 'Yes . . . I can hardly believe it myself. They think it was the flu, but they're not sure. It took hold so quickly . . . he rang Mother last night to tell her about you. That's how I knew where to come.'

His pale face nodded automatically, stunned at Noel's impromptu demise. You bloody quack, you couldn't even diagnose yourself!

'That's partly why I came to see you.' Oriel dabbed at her eyes. 'To let you know about him . . . and to say I'm sorry I was such a bitch, and . . .'

'Oh, please, not now.' Her father looked weary, unable to take one more upset. 'Sorry will do.' He beheld his daughter miserably. Added to the tears, a wayward sprig of black hair had escaped the sleek bob and floated about in the draughty ward, lending a comic touch of humanity to the one he had always perceived as being superior to himself.

Oriel sensed that it would take a lot more than this meeting to remove the barrier that was between them; perhaps it would always be there, for as genuinely sorry as she was there remained a part of her that failed to understand how a man who had been deserted himself in childhood could then desert his own infant.

But this was not the time to ask why. 'I mustn't take up any more time, there's someone else to see you.' She turned and lifted her hand. The swing door opened and through it came her mother.

The sight of that little figure with the stick thin ankles, bright hair and wide brown eyes approaching down the aisle was more than Nat could bear. He had not cried since the night that his daughter had been conceived — tried desperately not to cry now, gulping back the lump that threatened to choke him, trying to avoid a display in front of all these people — but when he saw the tears mixed with the freckles down the side of Bright's nose he could not hold back. He covered his face, trying to hide his grief from prying eyes, whilst his body shook.

A bell rang, sounding an end to visiting time. Bright looked frantic and rushed to hold onto his hand, sobbing with him; Oriel sobbed too.

A nurse caught sight of them, hurried over and without a word pulled a screen around the bed, as she began to call for the visitors to leave. A hush came upon the ward in respect for those who cried – the patient must be very ill – and the visitors left in a combined whisper.

From behind the screen the racking sobs continued, until an indignant Sister appeared out of nowhere to scold, 'Stop that now! Goodness me, I can't have this, you're upsetting all the other patients – two more minutes!' And she vanished.

They laughed then, wet, sobbing, crimson-eyed laughs, then cried again, but more quietly this time. When tearducts were completely drained, Nat gave a shuddering sigh and sniffed. 'I don't know where they've put me clothes – I need a hanky.'

'It's no good giving you mine, tis pretty sodden.' Bright sighed too. How mundane were these words for two lovers who had not seen each other in twenty years. Yet how could one start to say the things that needed to be said?

'Here.' Oriel had a spare handkerchief in her bag, a pretty little scrap of embroidered lace which Nat filled with one blow, then clutched in his fist, reminding both women of Miss Bytheway. 'Don't suppose you want it back?'

She managed a smile, her lips puffy with all the crying. 'No thanks.'

Bright leaned on the bed, still holding his hand. 'Did Oriel tell you about Noel?' She knew that Oriel would have, but it was something to say.

He nodded, his eyes resting on the mole beneath her chin. 'I can't believe it.'

'Me neither.' She looked so sad. 'I spoke to him last

night on the telephone. I knew he hadn't been very well, but I thought it was just a cold. He never complained, not like me when I'm ill. If only I'd known. I was too full of myself . . .'

Nat cut her off, he didn't want to be reminded of yesterday. 'Oriel said it was the flu.'

Bright nodded, wondering if the same thought was going through his mind: they had all three been in contact with Noel, could all be dead themselves tomorrow. 'They say that doctors become immune to the illnesses they treat.'

But Noel wasn't a doctor, came Nat's illogical thought. He would never say anything to Bright about that, ever.

She tried to look cheerful, though her heart was gripped by a physical pain. 'He said you were intending to go to Australia. That's a long way.'

'I was, yes.'

'Have ye changed your mind?'

He shrugged somewhat half-heartedly.

'I think ye should go – make a new life for yourself. Ye've had a lot of sadness here.' Tears sprang to her eyes again.

'Will you come with me?' Who was saying these words? Nat could not believe they had come from his lips, couldn't believe he was exposing himself to more rejection. If she said no . . .

'Yes,' replied Bright without hesitation, without even looking at her daughter for approval.

'You will?' He seemed unable to believe it.

She nodded and squeezed his hand, more tears welling, spilling, trickling. People would never understand her decision – she could hear them asking, how could she hope to find happiness with someone who had hurt her so much – and how could she even explain? If you loved someone you loved them, no matter how much they had hurt you. And throughout everything Bright had never stopped loving Nat.

'Time's up!' In one brisk movement Sister folded the screen away from the bed, exposing Nat to ridicule from the other men; but he didn't care. She had said yes. He clung to her hand, beaming through his tears.

'What a lot of nonsense! Anyone would think you were terminally ill – the doctor will probably throw you out tomorrow. Come along now!' The Sister clapped her hands at Bright, forcing her to rise from the bed and pulling the covers to order.

'God help us, I'm glad you didn't go into nursing,' a muttered laugh passed from mother to daughter. 'This is what we would've had to put up with – all right, Sister, we're going!'

Oriel smiled at her mother's joke, but hung back as Bright said her goodbyes, feeling left out of it all, abandoned. At the drop of a hat her mother, her beloved mother, had agreed to leave her, to go and live the other side of the world.

Confident that her wishes were about to be obeyed, the sister temporarily left them to bustle around her other patients. Even in his heart-thumping, light-headed turmoil, Nat was quick to note the despondency on Oriel's face. 'You can come an' all if you like,' came his gruff offer.

She smiled, but the fact remained that her mother had not considered her feelings. She felt very hurt. 'I'll have to think about it. I'm not so impulsive as Mother. It's an awfully big step.' Maybe Bright would change her mind when she had time to reconsider the enormity of her action.

He nodded, then directed all his attention on the mother who remained in his warm grip.

'I'll have to go now.' Bright uttered a little laugh at his refusal to let go of her hand.

'But you'll come back?' His blue eyes searched hers for the merest hint of duplicity.

She gripped his fingers and kissed the tips of them, then